CODEX BLACK

A FIRE AMONG CLOUDS

WRITTEN AND ILLUSTRATED BY
CAMILO MONCADA LOZANO

INKING ASSISTANCE BY
ONIRIA HERNÁNDEZ VARGAS

COLORED BY
ANGEL DE SANTIAGO

FLATS BY
CHRIS EUBANK

@IDWpublishing
IDWpublishing.com

COVER ARTIST:
Camilo Moncada Lozano

ORIGINALS YA & MG EDITOR:
Megan Brown

ORIGINALS EDITORIAL ASSISTANT:
Jake Williams

LETTERING & DESIGN:
Nathan Widick

978-1-68405-959-1   26 25 24 23   1 2 3 4

CODEX BLACK (BOOK ONE): A FIRE AMONG CLOUDS. APRIL 2023. FIRST PRINTING. © Camilo Moncada Lozano. All Rights Reserved. IDW Publishing, a division of Idea and Design Works, LLC. Editorial offices: 2355 Northside Drive, Suite 140, San Diego, CA 92108. The IDW logo is registered in the U.S. Patent and Trademark Office. Any similarities to persons living or dead are purely coincidental. With the exception of artwork used for review purposes, none of the contents of this publication may be reprinted without the permission of Idea and Design Works, LLC. IDW Publishing does not read or accept unsolicited submissions of ideas, stories, or artwork. Printed in China.

For international rights, contact licensing@idwpublishing.com.

Special thanks to acquiring editor Erika Turner.

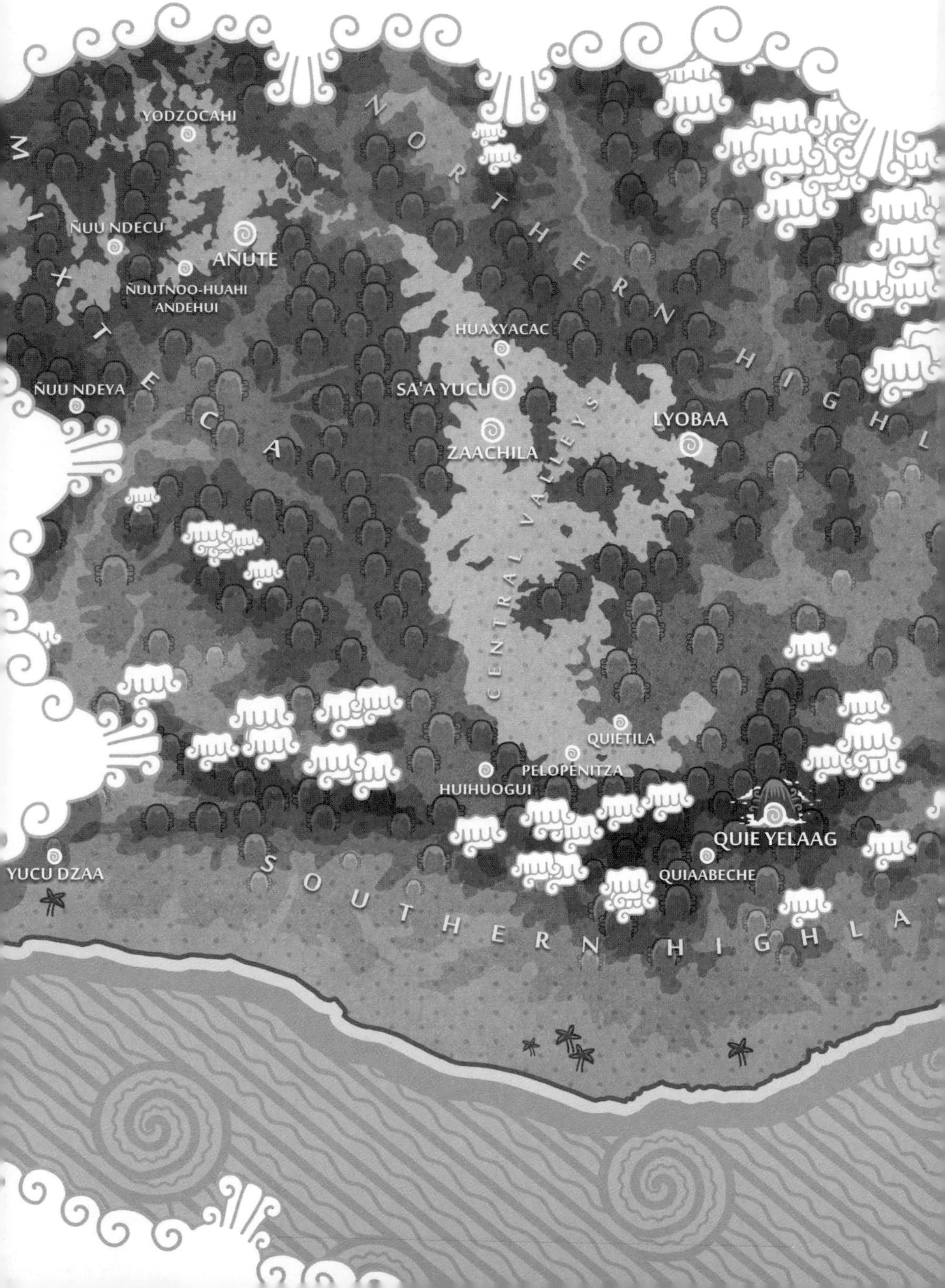

MIXTECA
NORTHERN HIGHL
YODZOCAHI
ÑUU NDECU
AÑUTE
ÑUUTNOO-HUAHI
ANDEHUI
ÑUU NDEYA
HUAXYACAC
SA'A YUCU
ZAACHILA
LYOBAA
CENTRAL VALLEYS
QUIETILA
PELOPENITZA
HUIHUOGUI
QUIE YELAAG
QUIAABECHE
YUCU DZAA
SOUTHERN HIGHLA

CEMANAHUAC - SOUTHLANDS
1493 CE

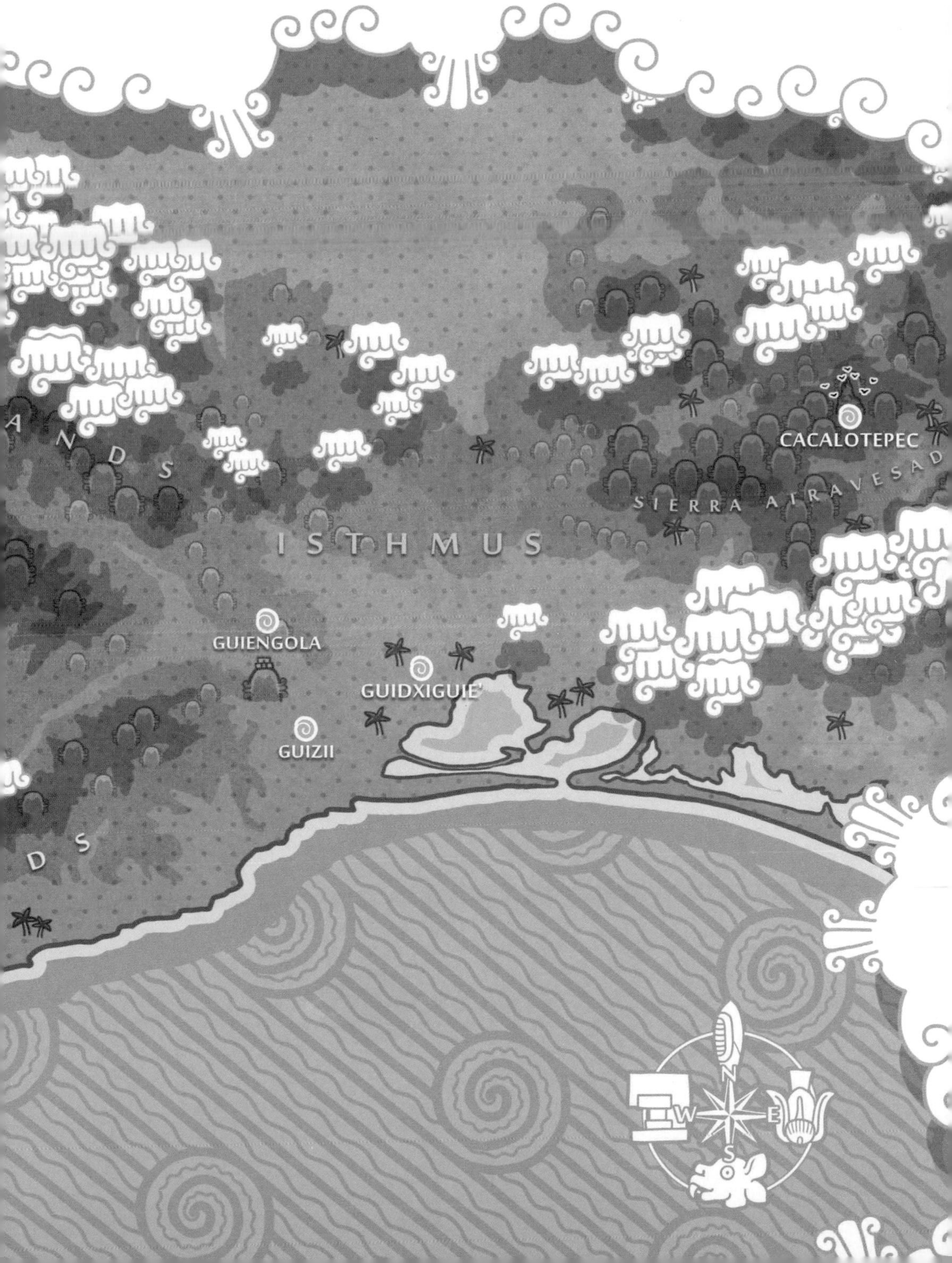
ISTHMUS
SIERRA ATRAVESAD
CACALOTEPEC
GUIENGOLA
GUIDXIGUIE'
GUIZII
N
W
E
S

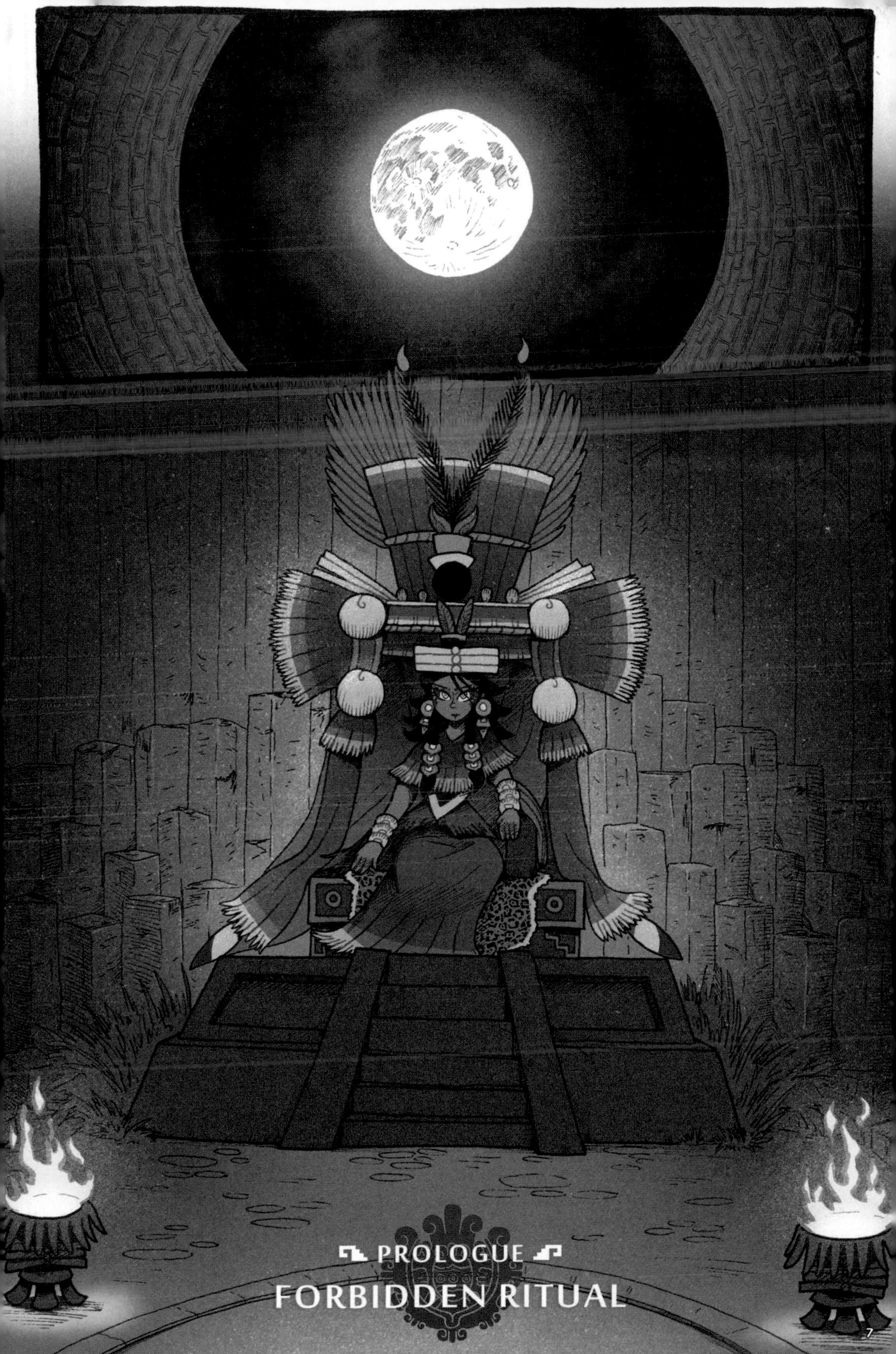
PROLOGUE
FORBIDDEN RITUAL

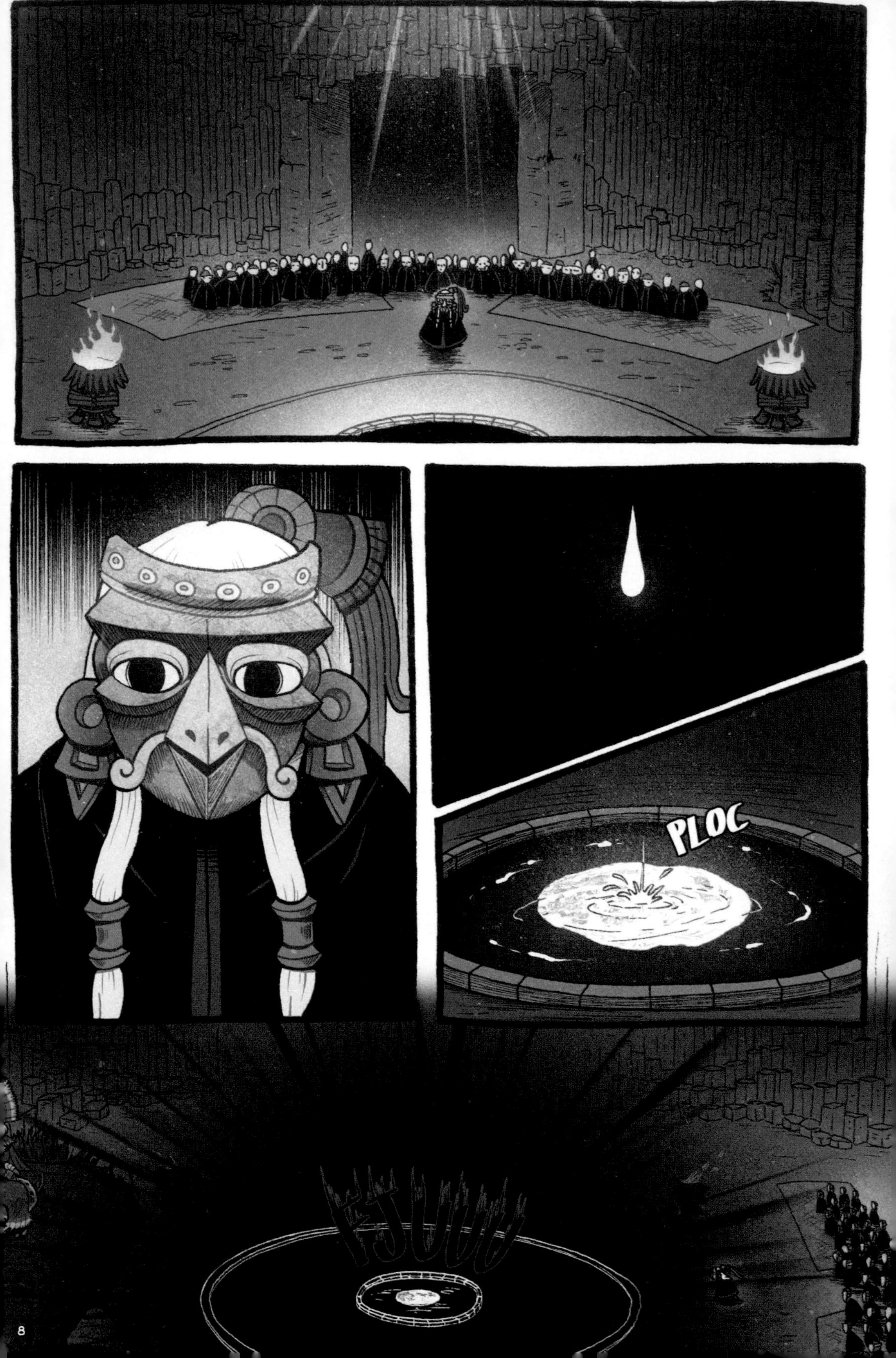
PLOC
FSUUUU

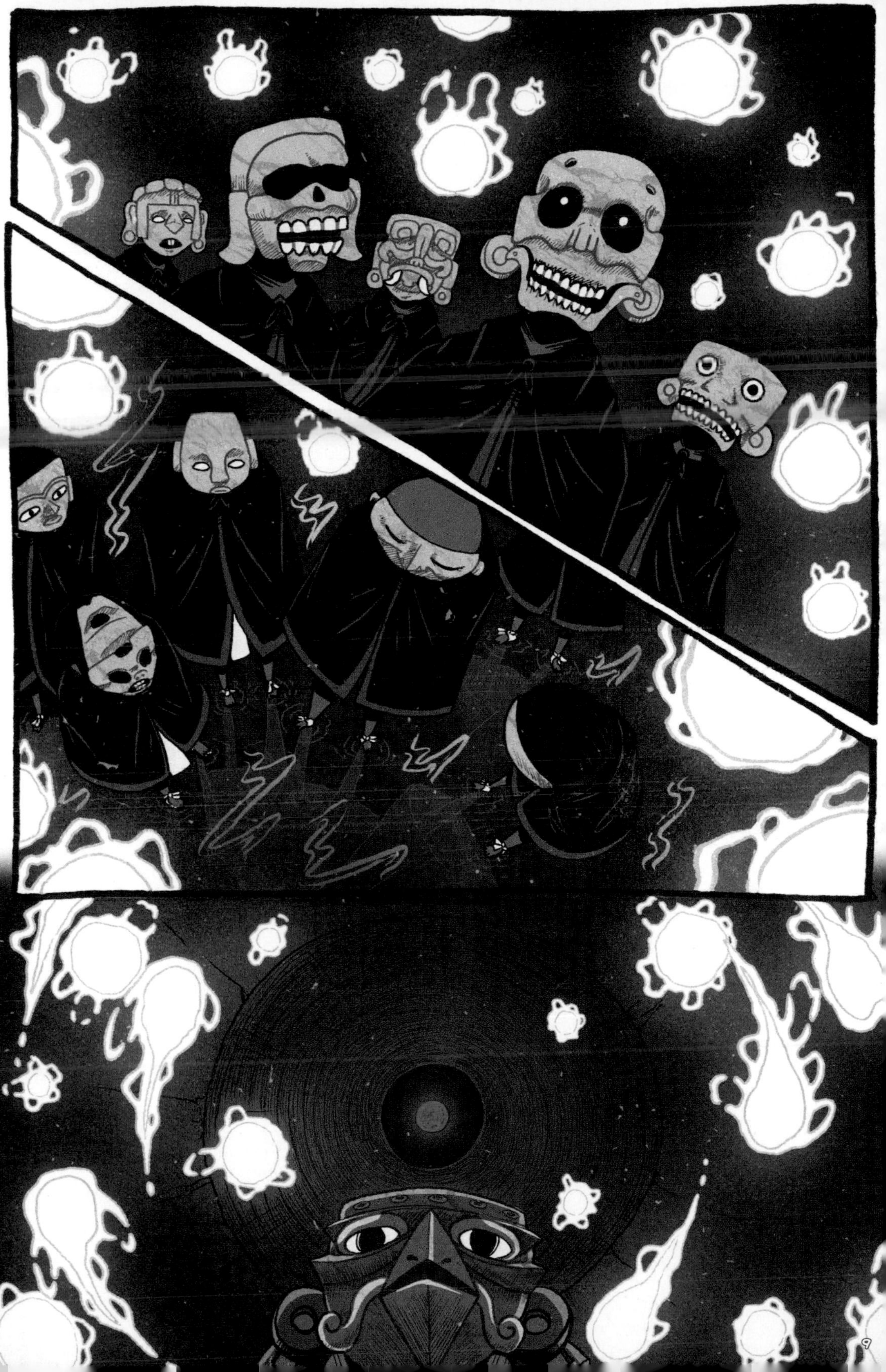

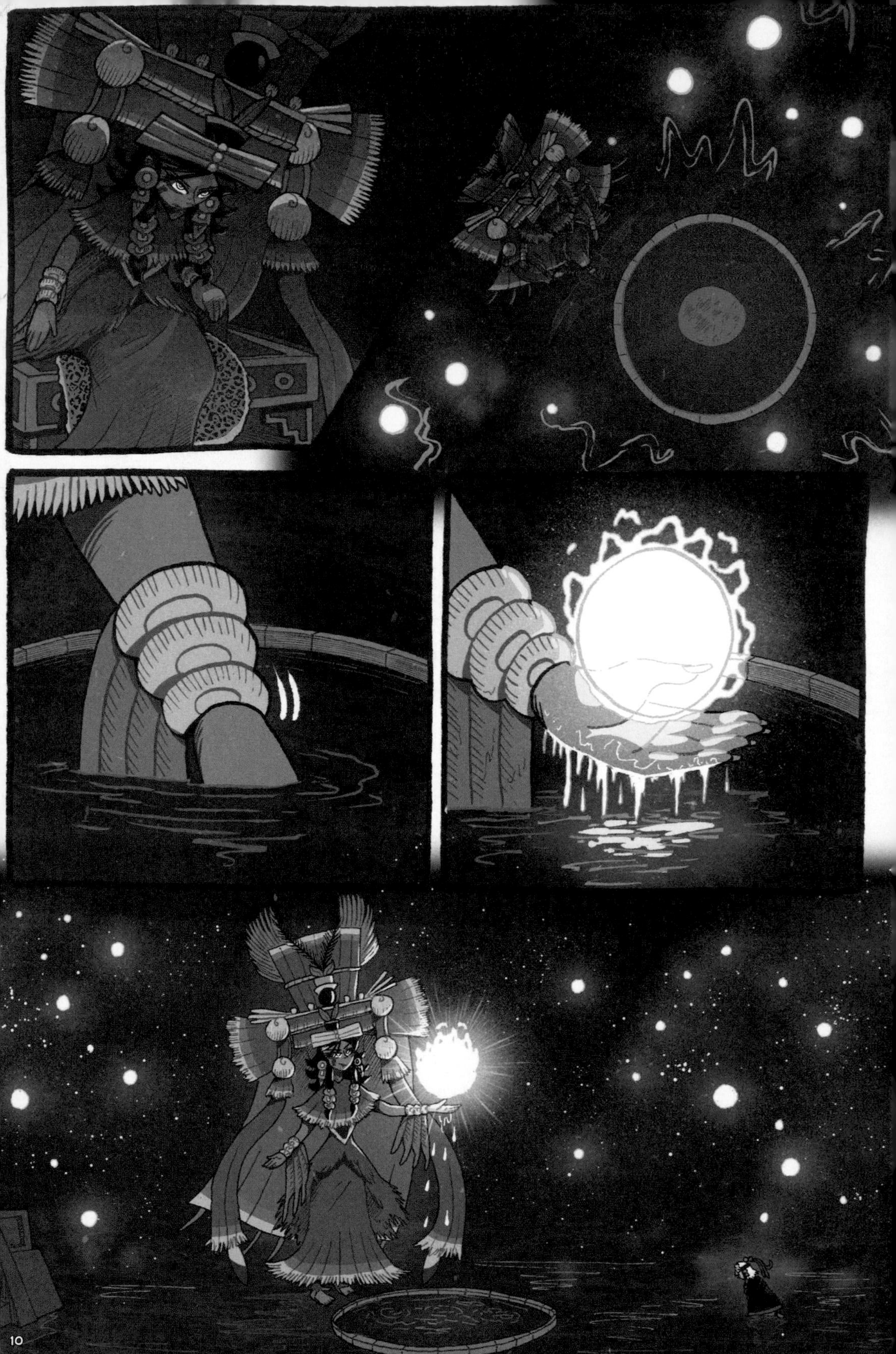

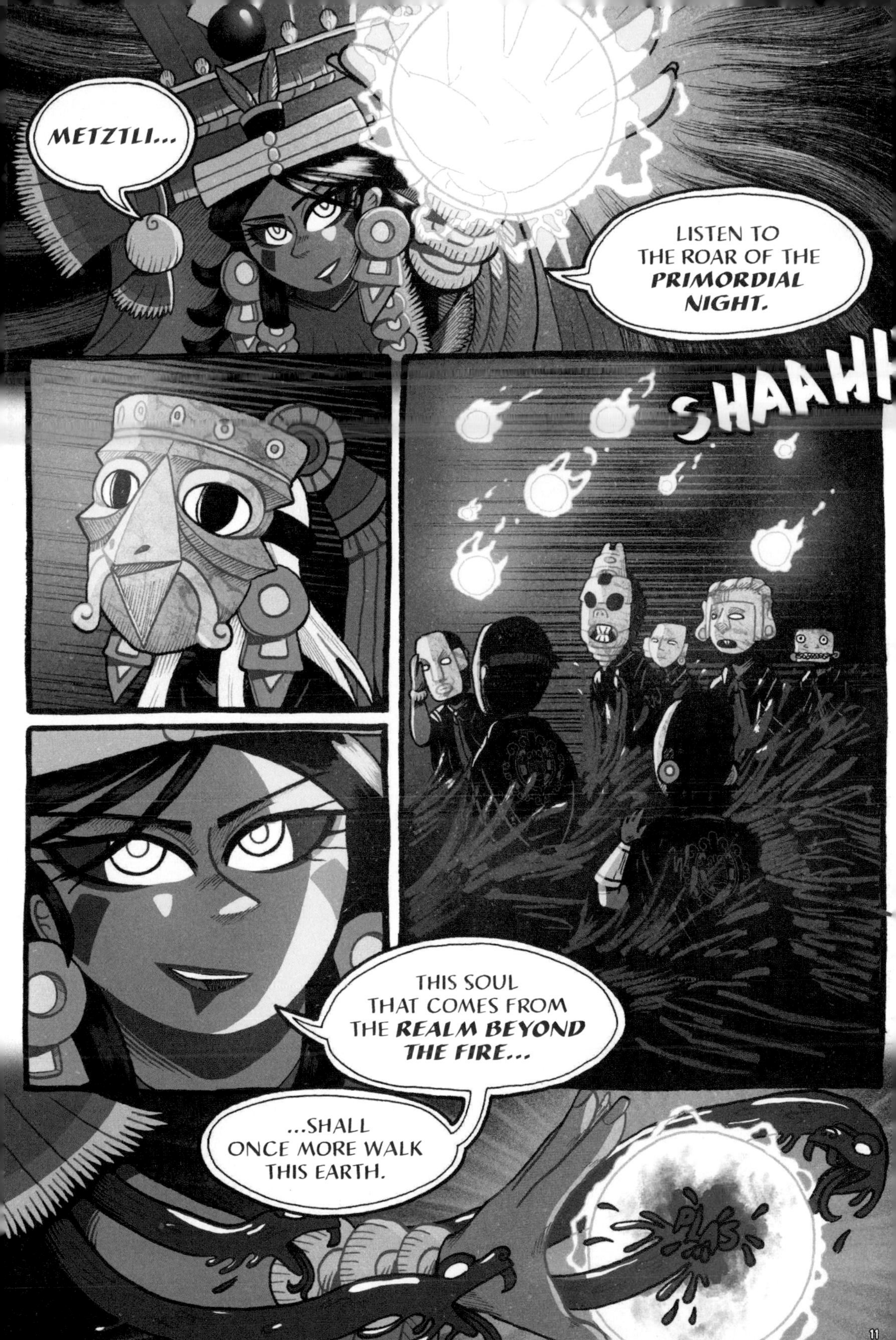

METZTLI...
LISTEN TO THE ROAR OF THE PRIMORDIAL NIGHT.
SHAAH
THIS SOUL THAT COMES FROM THE REALM BEYOND THE FIRE...
...SHALL ONCE MORE WALK THIS EARTH.
PLAS

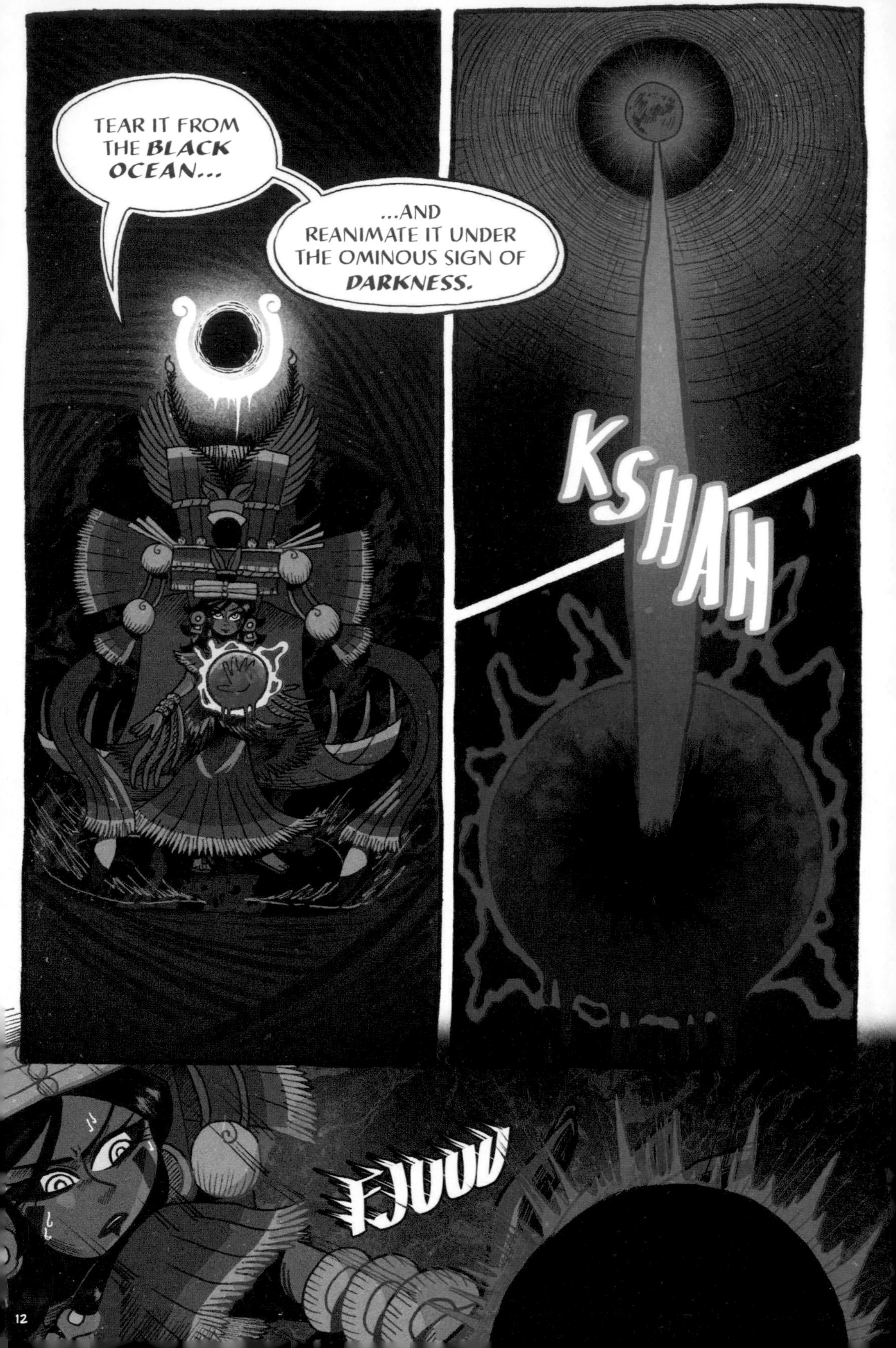
TEAR IT FROM THE BLACK OCEAN...
...AND REANIMATE IT UNDER THE OMINOUS SIGN OF DARKNESS.
KSHAH
FJUUU

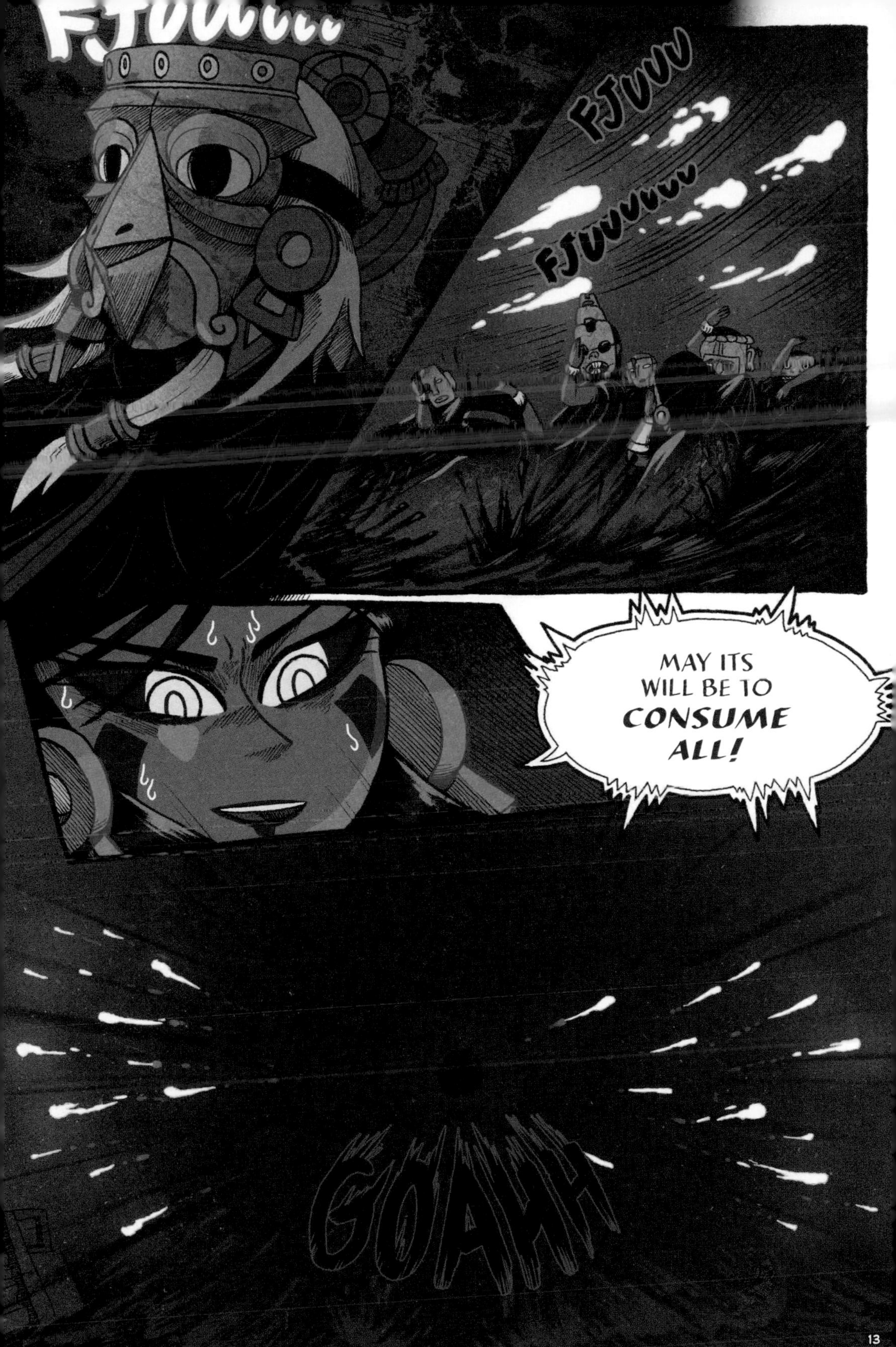
FJUUUUU...
FJUUU
FJUUUUUU
MAY ITS WILL BE TO CONSUME ALL!
GOAAH

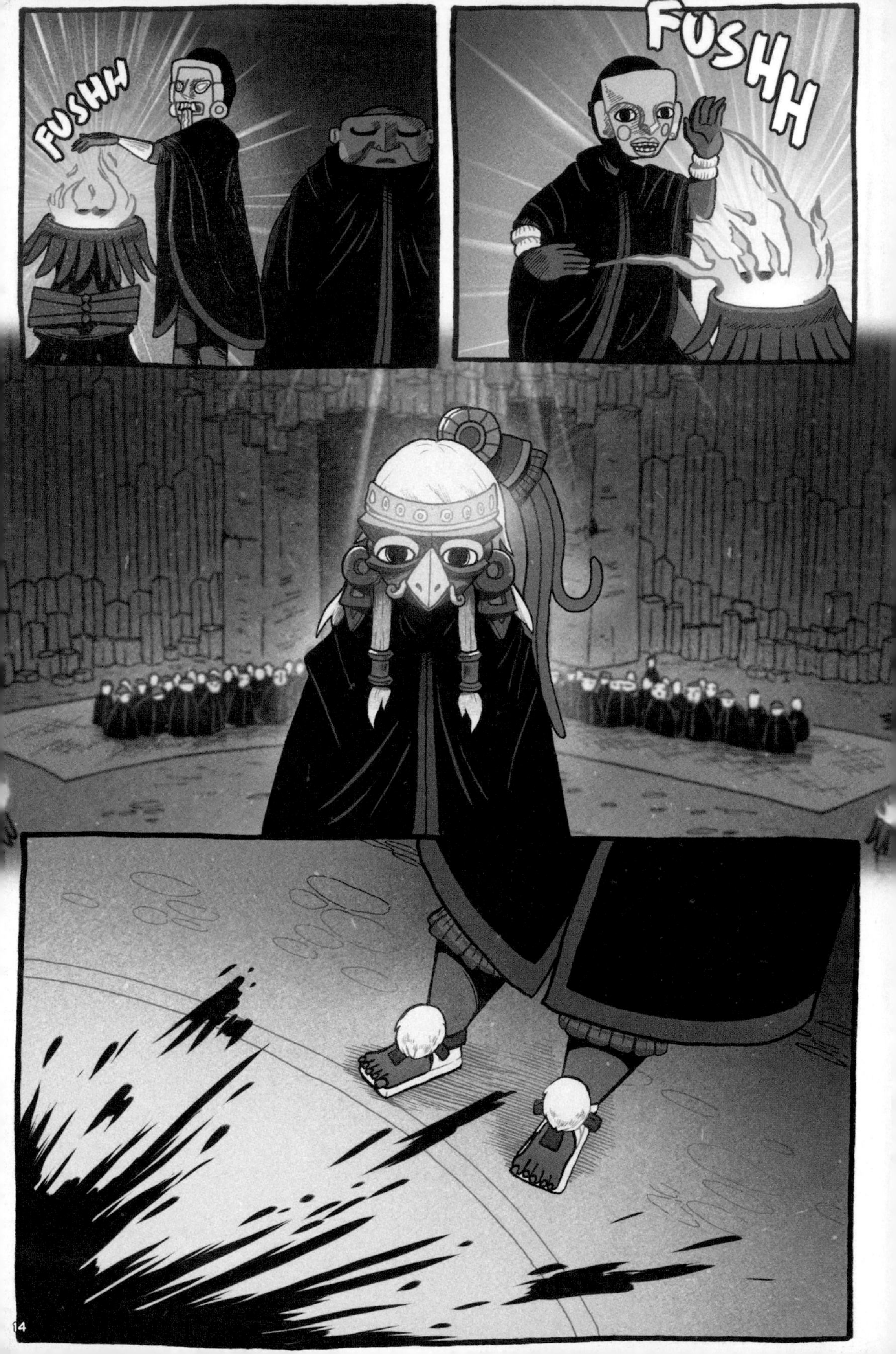
FUSHH
FUSHH

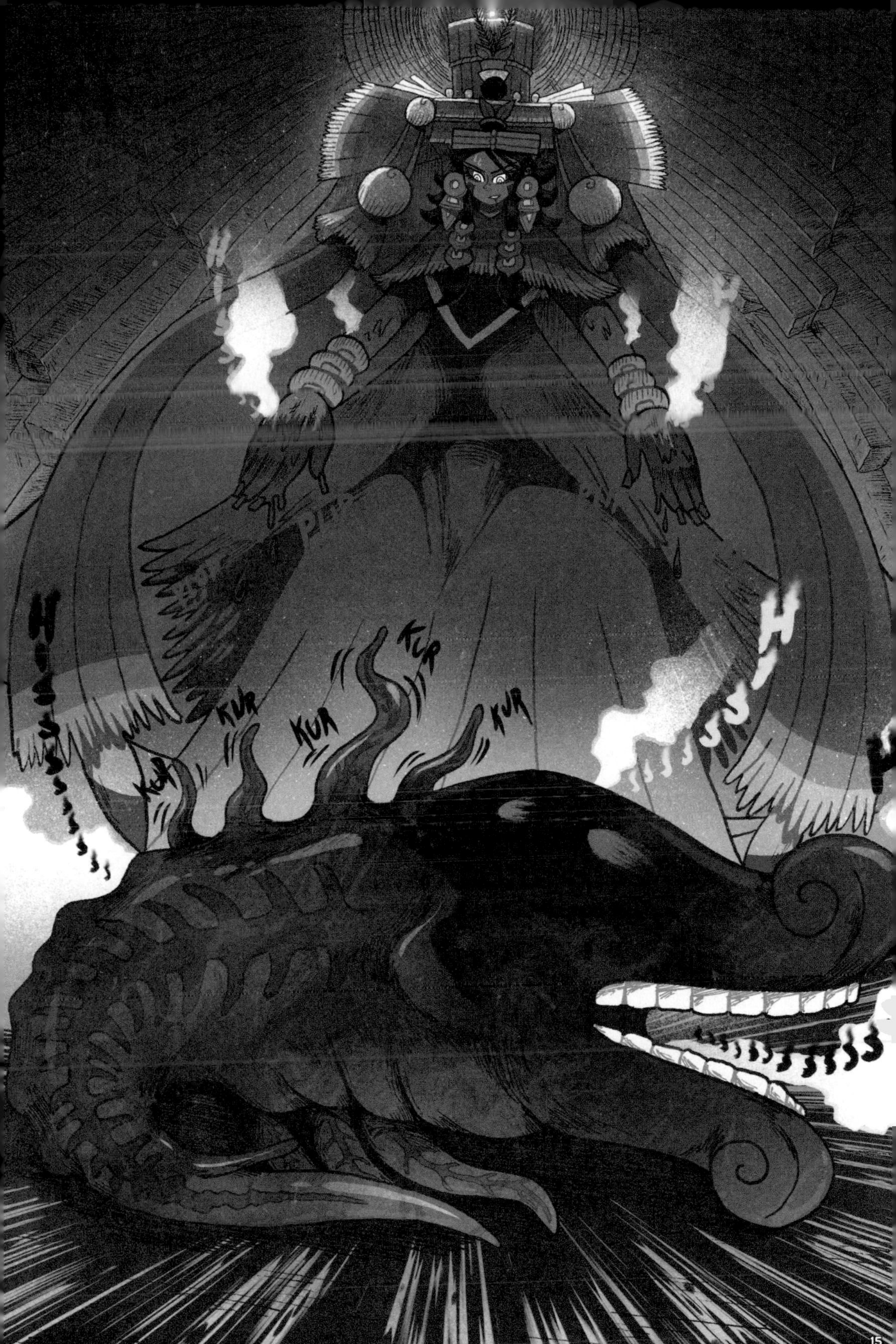
HISSSSSSSS
KUR
KUR
KUR
KUR
KUR
HISSSSSSS
SSSSSSSSS

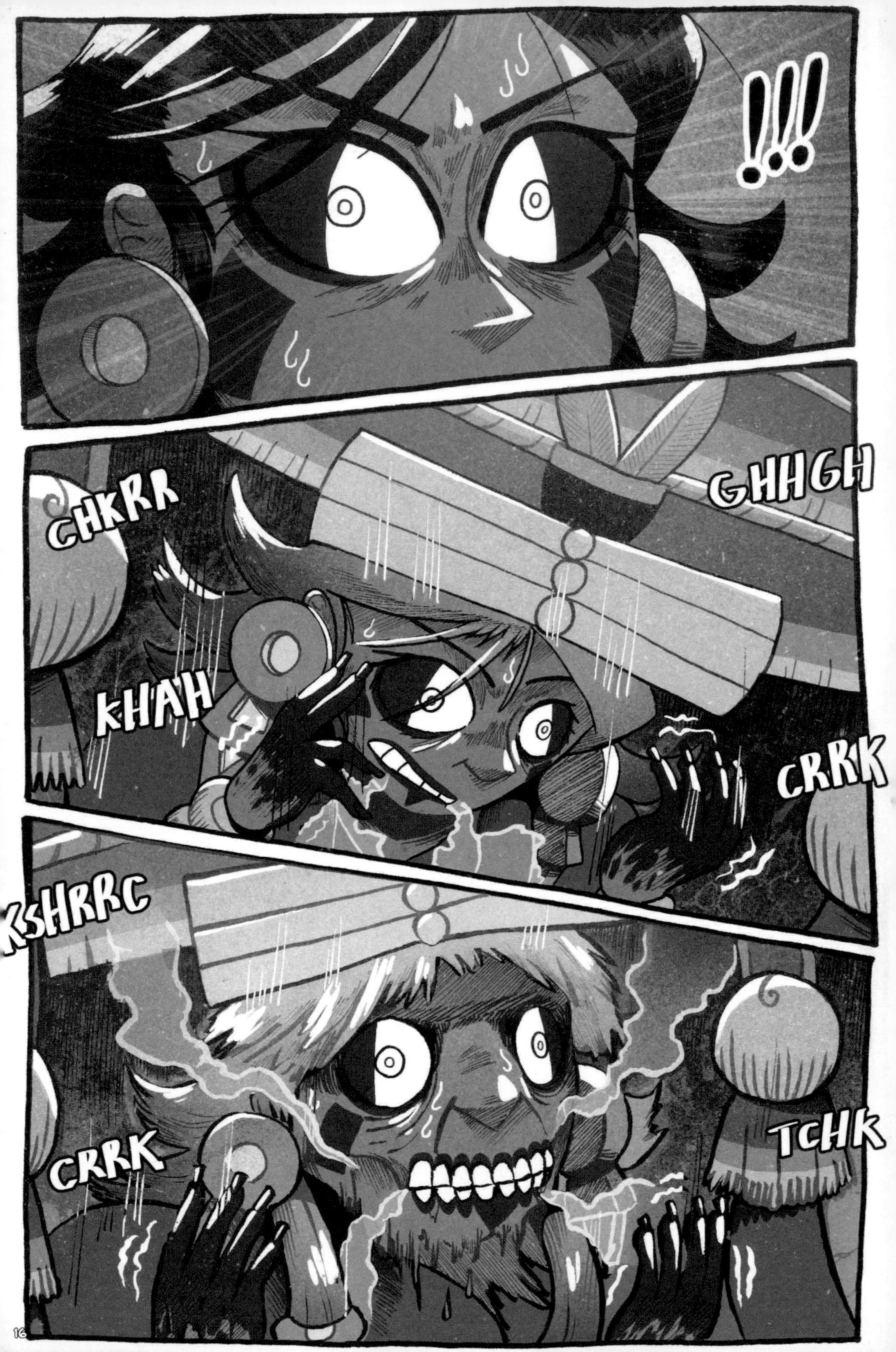
!!!
CHKRR
GHHGH
KHAH
CRRK
KSHRRC
CRRK
TCHK

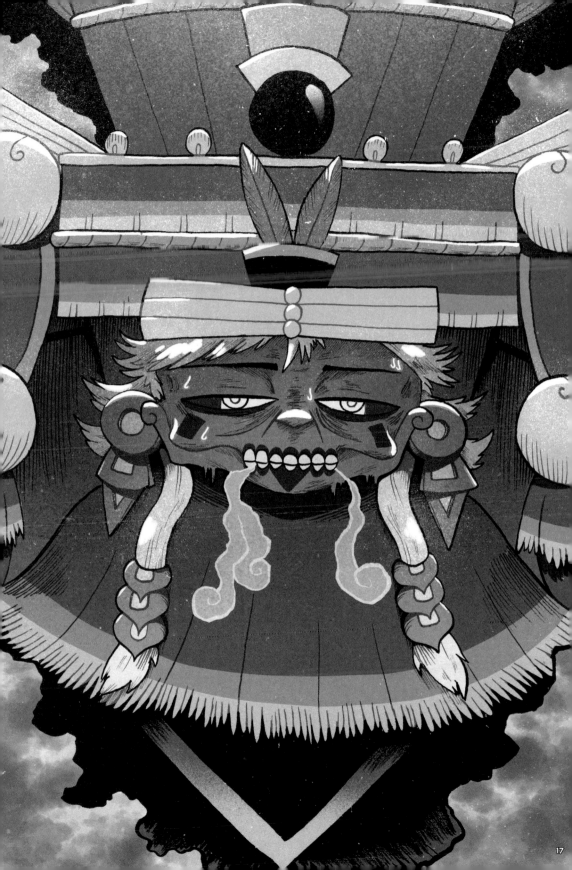

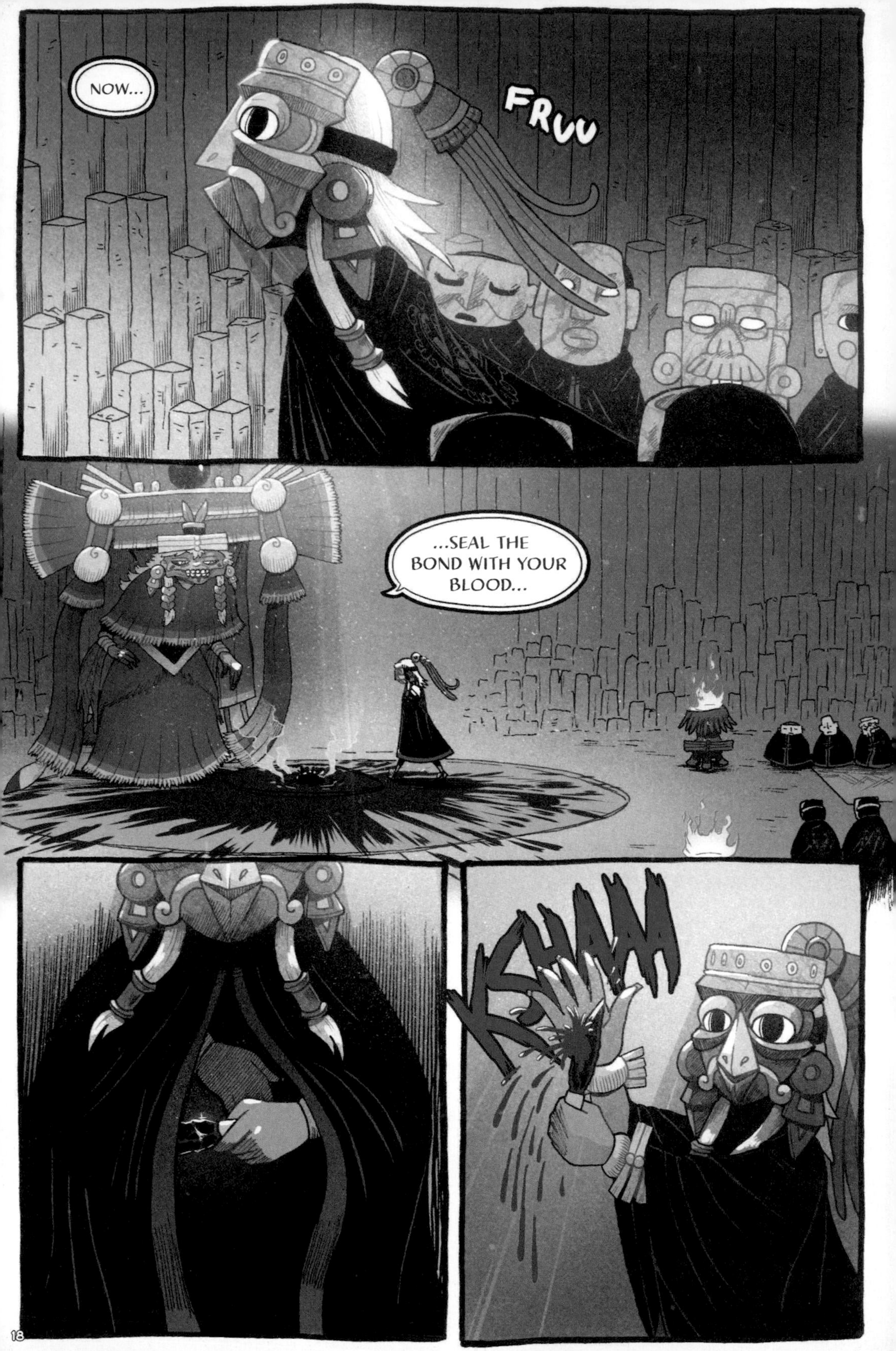
NOW...
FRUU
...SEAL THE BOND WITH YOUR BLOOD...
KSHAAA

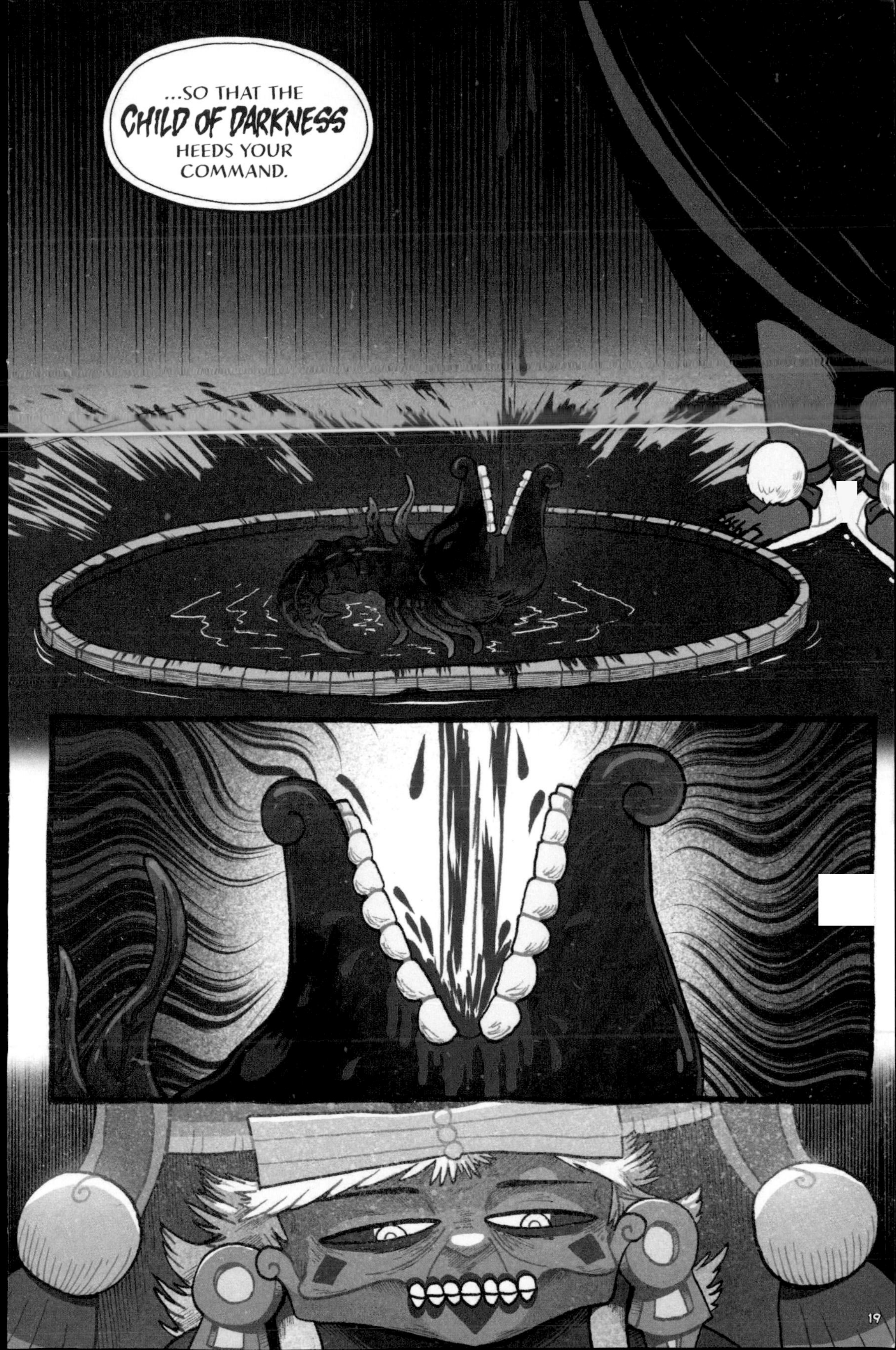
...SO THAT THE CHILD OF DARKNESS HEEDS YOUR COMMAND.

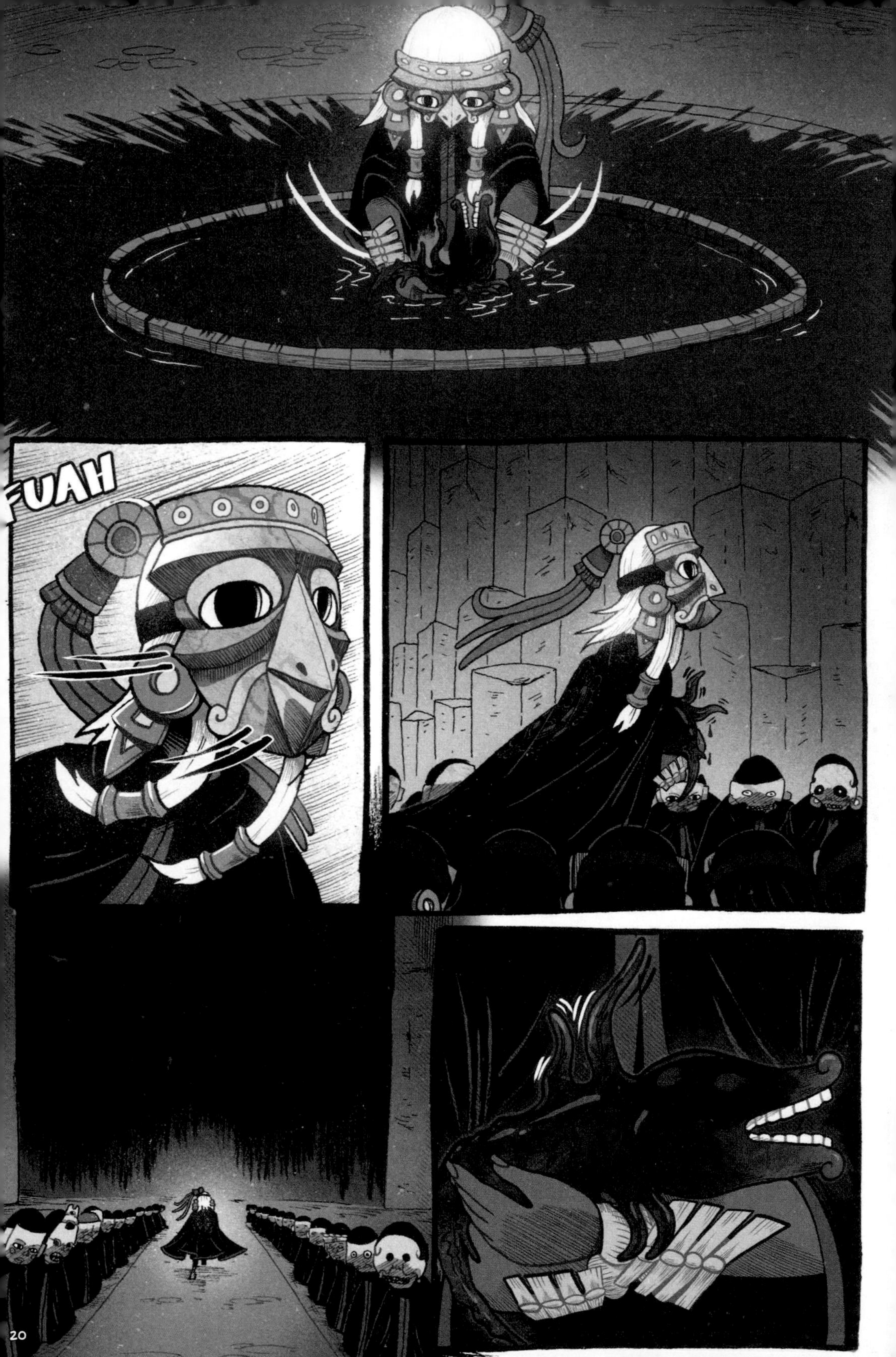
FUAH

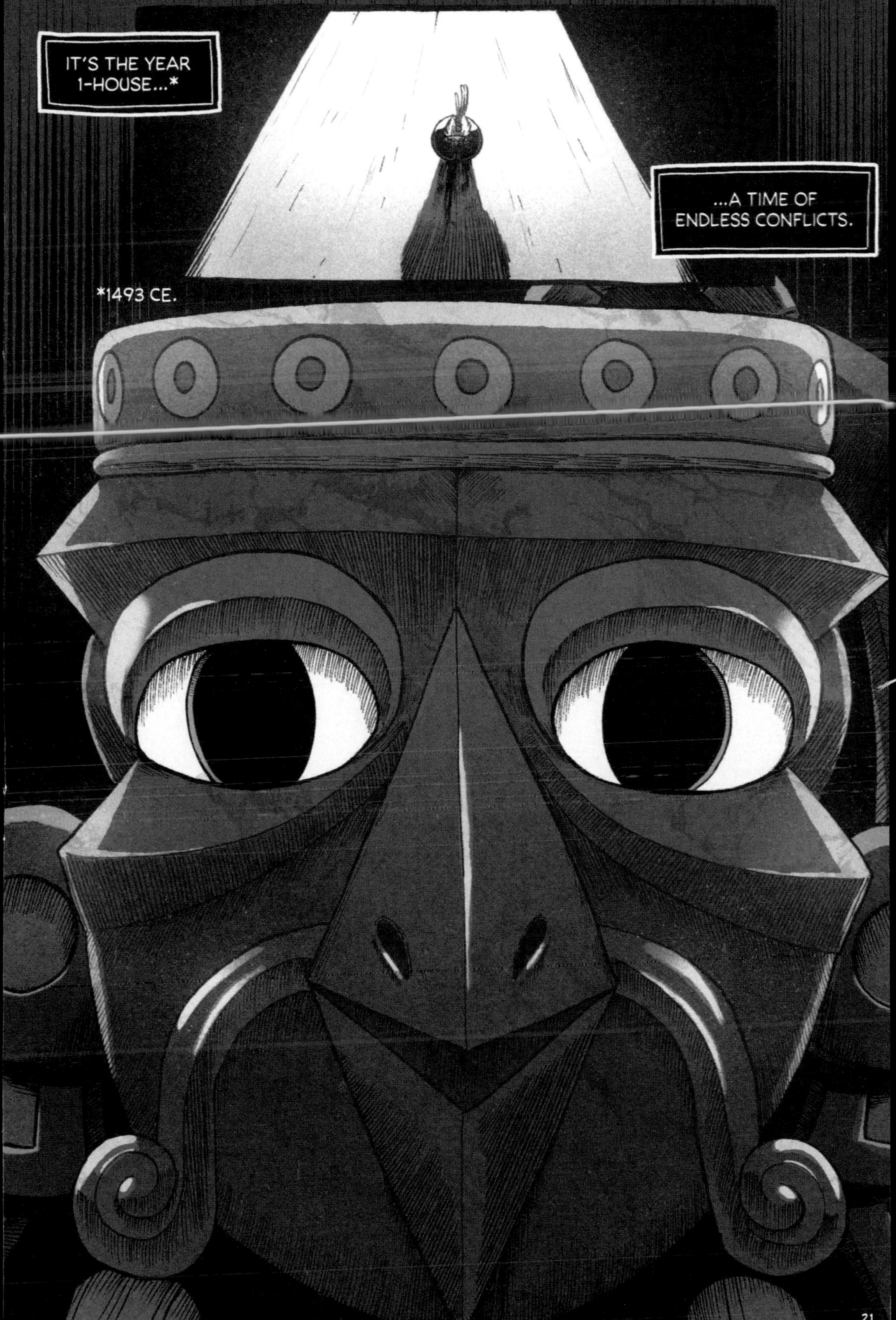
IT'S THE YEAR 1-HOUSE...*
...A TIME OF ENDLESS CONFLICTS.
*1493 CE.

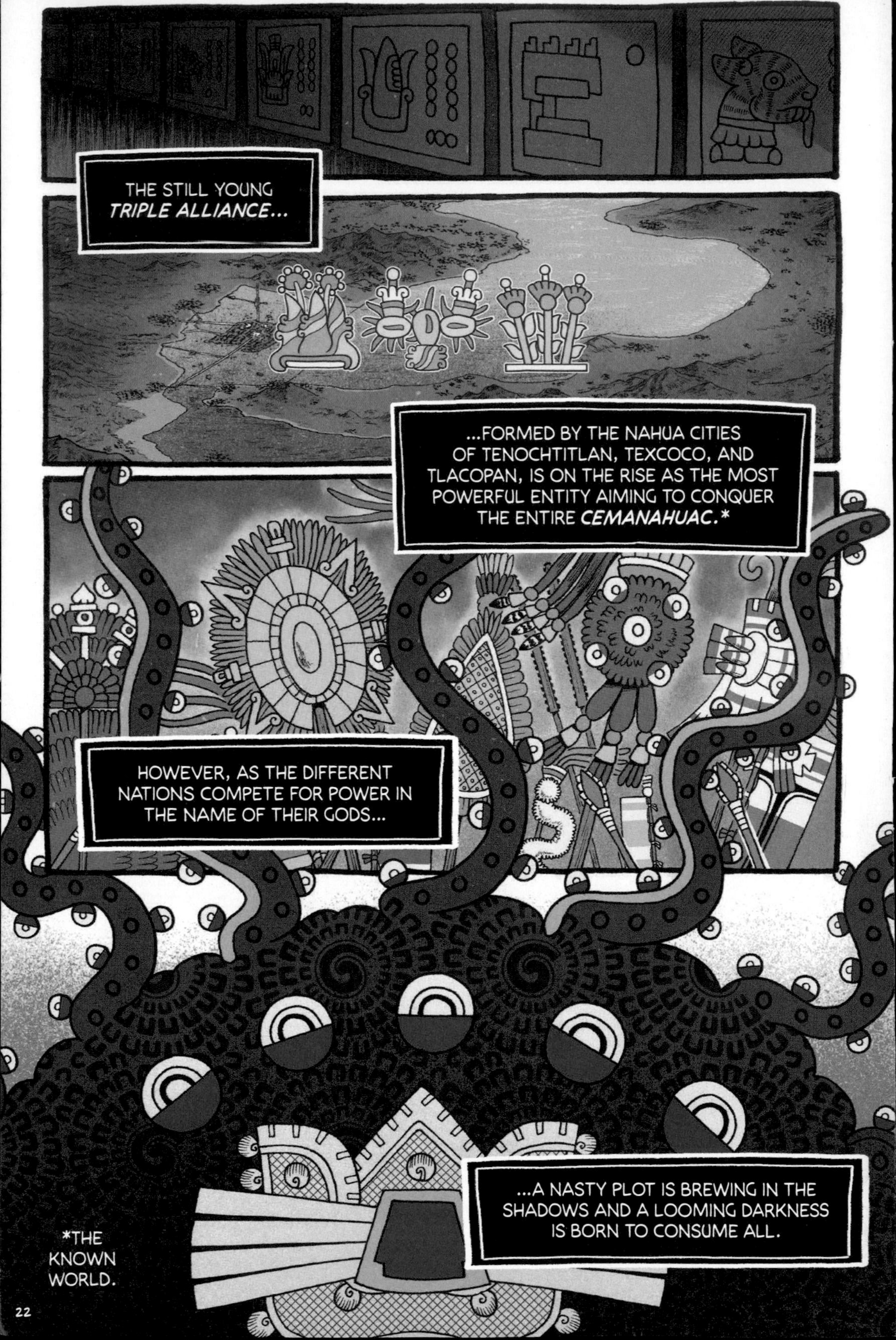

THE STILL YOUNG TRIPLE ALLIANCE...
...FORMED BY THE NAHUA CITIES OF TENOCHTITLAN, TEXCOCO, AND TLACOPAN, IS ON THE RISE AS THE MOST POWERFUL ENTITY AIMING TO CONQUER THE ENTIRE CEMANAHUAC.*
HOWEVER, AS THE DIFFERENT NATIONS COMPETE FOR POWER IN THE NAME OF THEIR GODS...
...A NASTY PLOT IS BREWING IN THE SHADOWS AND A LOOMING DARKNESS IS BORN TO CONSUME ALL.
*THE KNOWN WORLD.

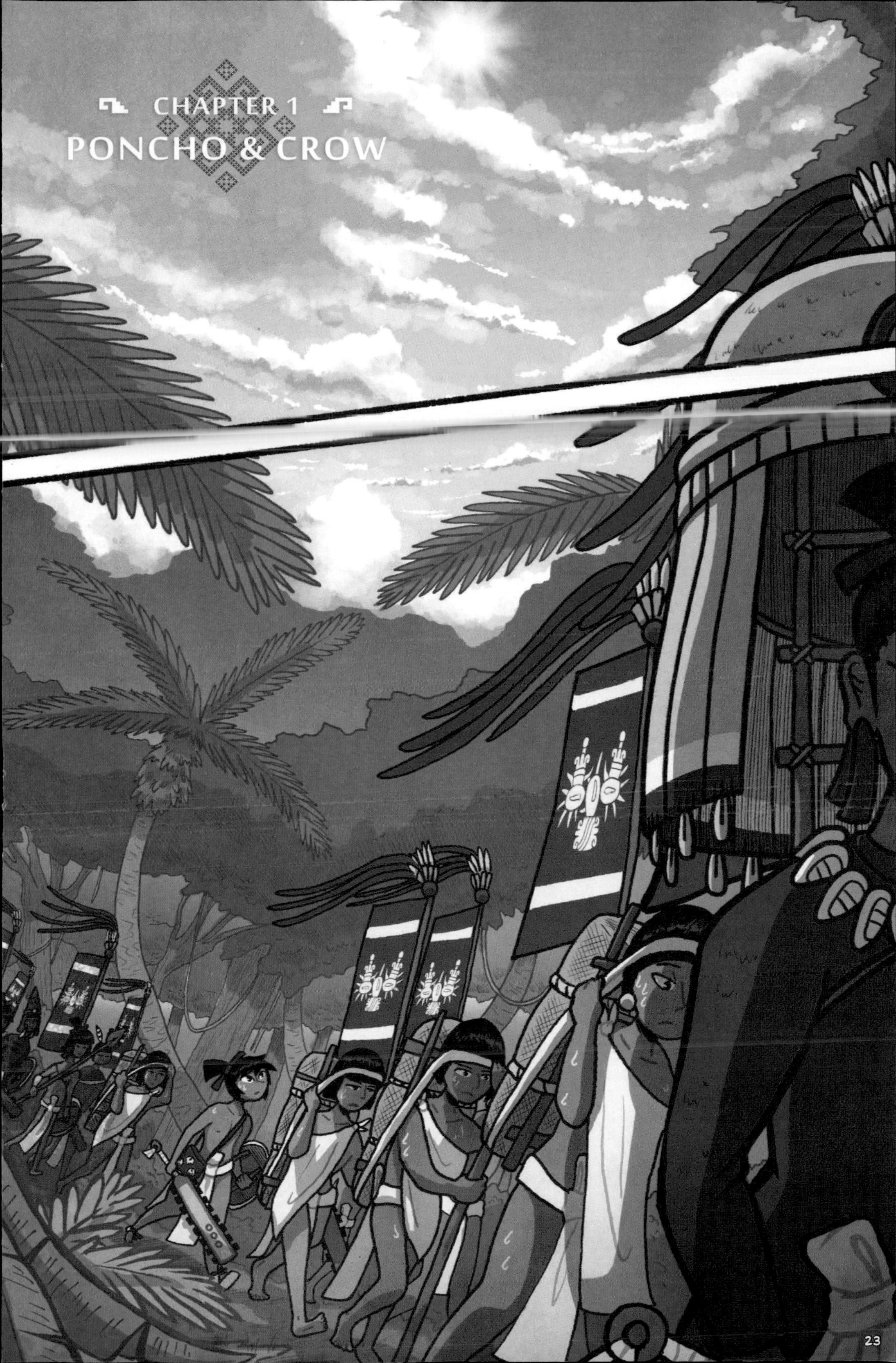
CHAPTER 1
PONCHO & CROW

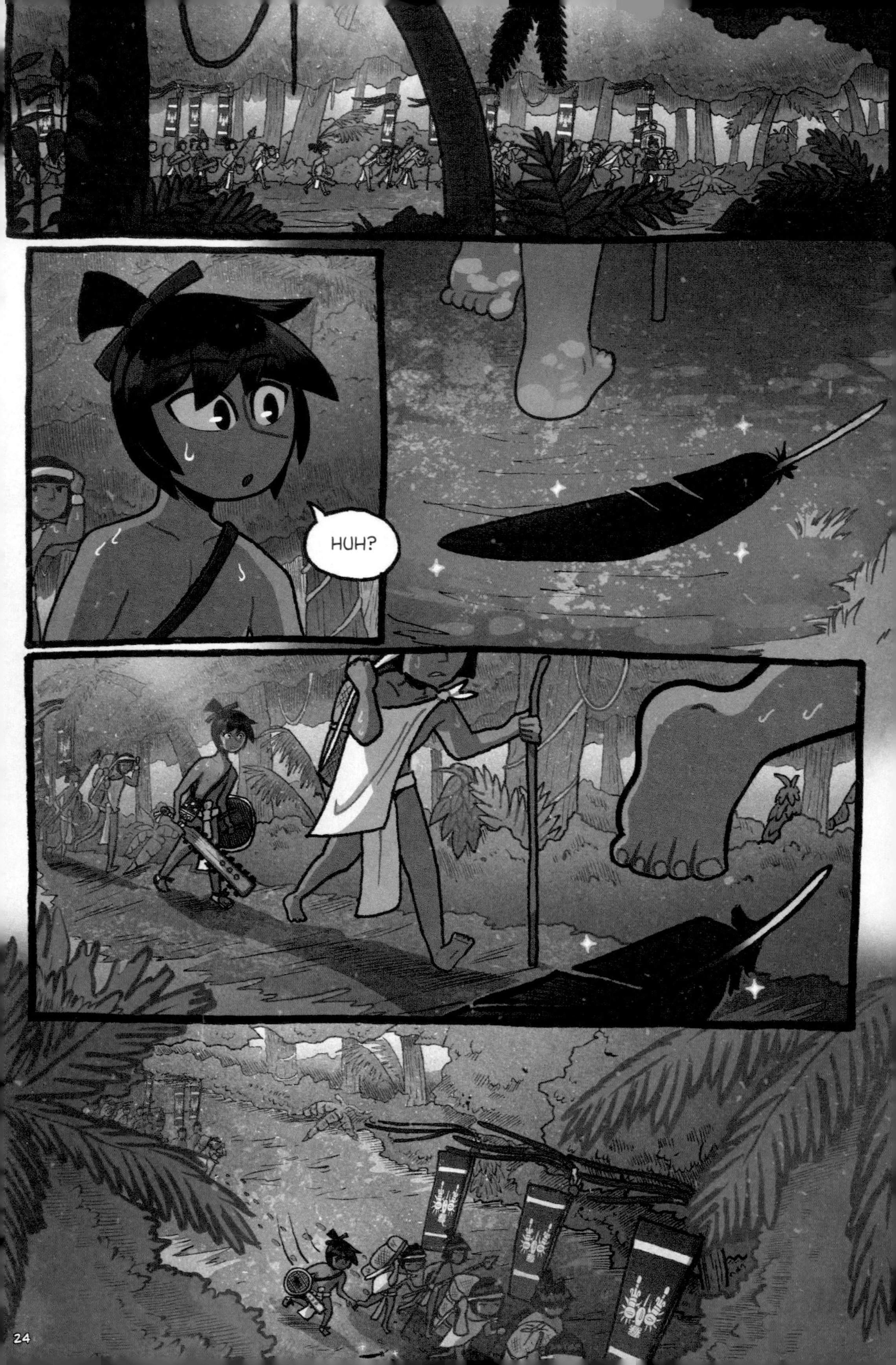
HUH?

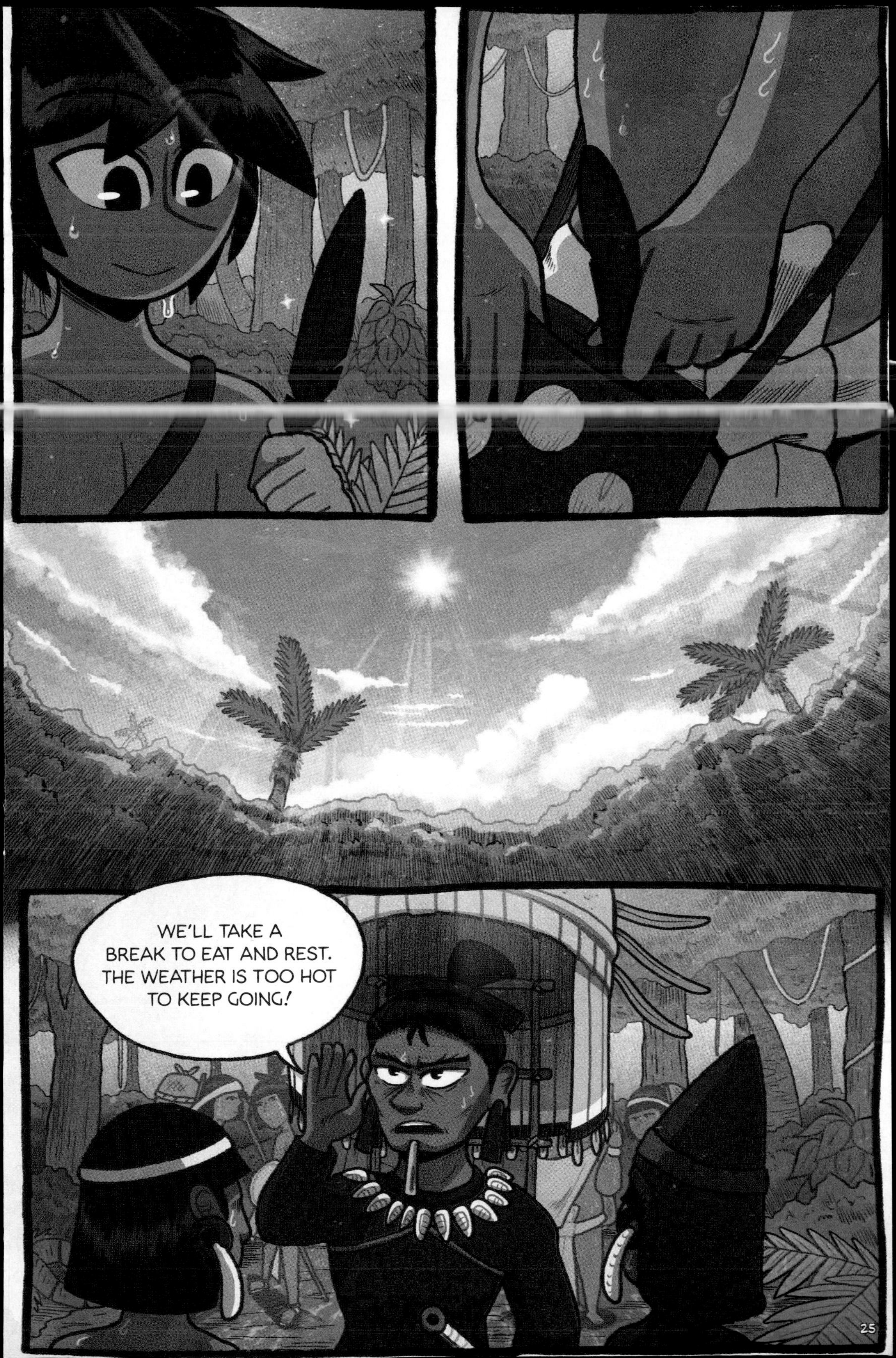
WE'LL TAKE A BREAK TO EAT AND REST. THE WEATHER IS TOO HOT TO KEEP GOING!

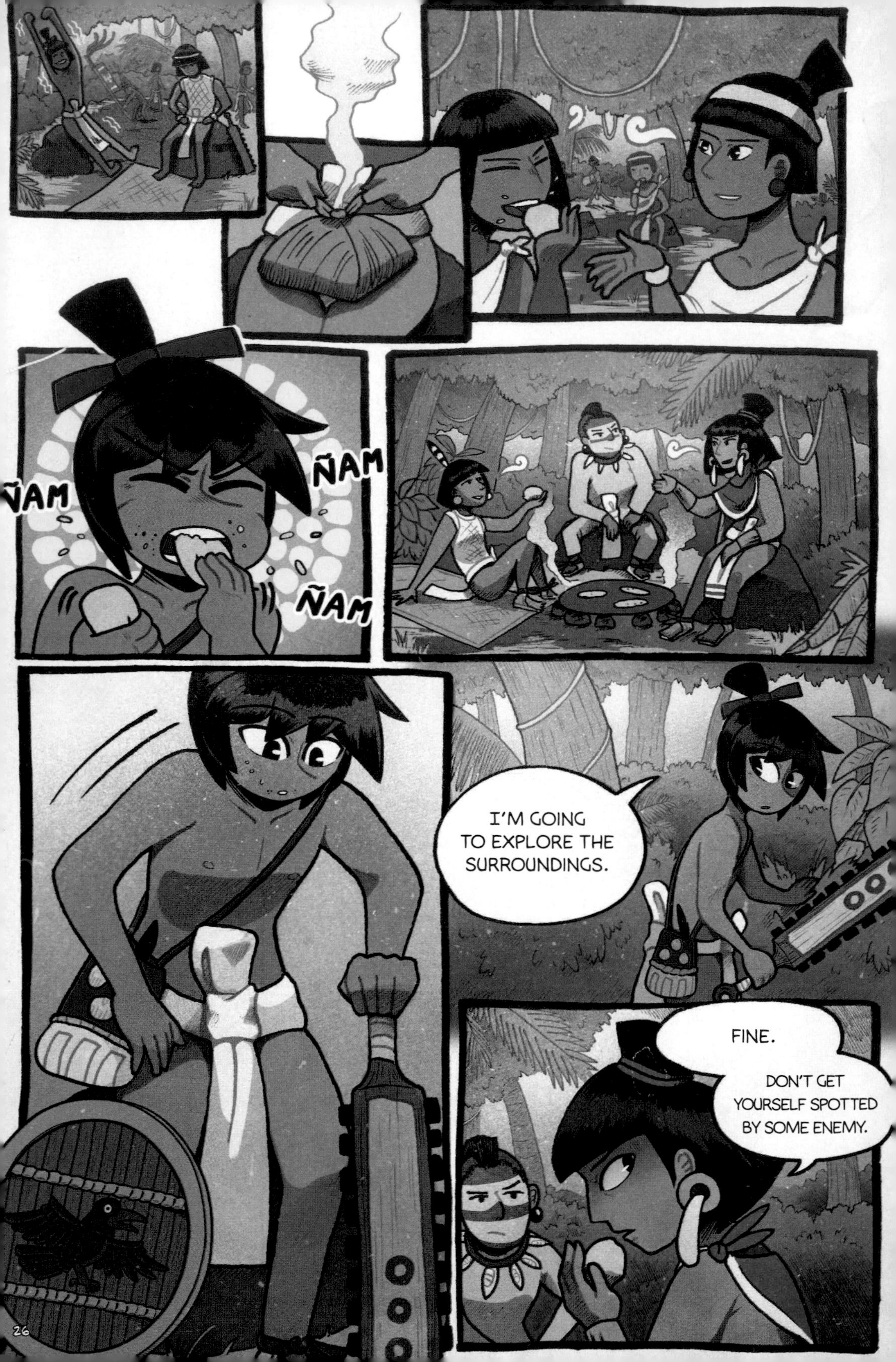

ÑAM
ÑAM
ÑAM
I'M GOING TO EXPLORE THE SURROUNDINGS.
FINE.
DON'T GET YOURSELF SPOTTED BY SOME ENEMY.

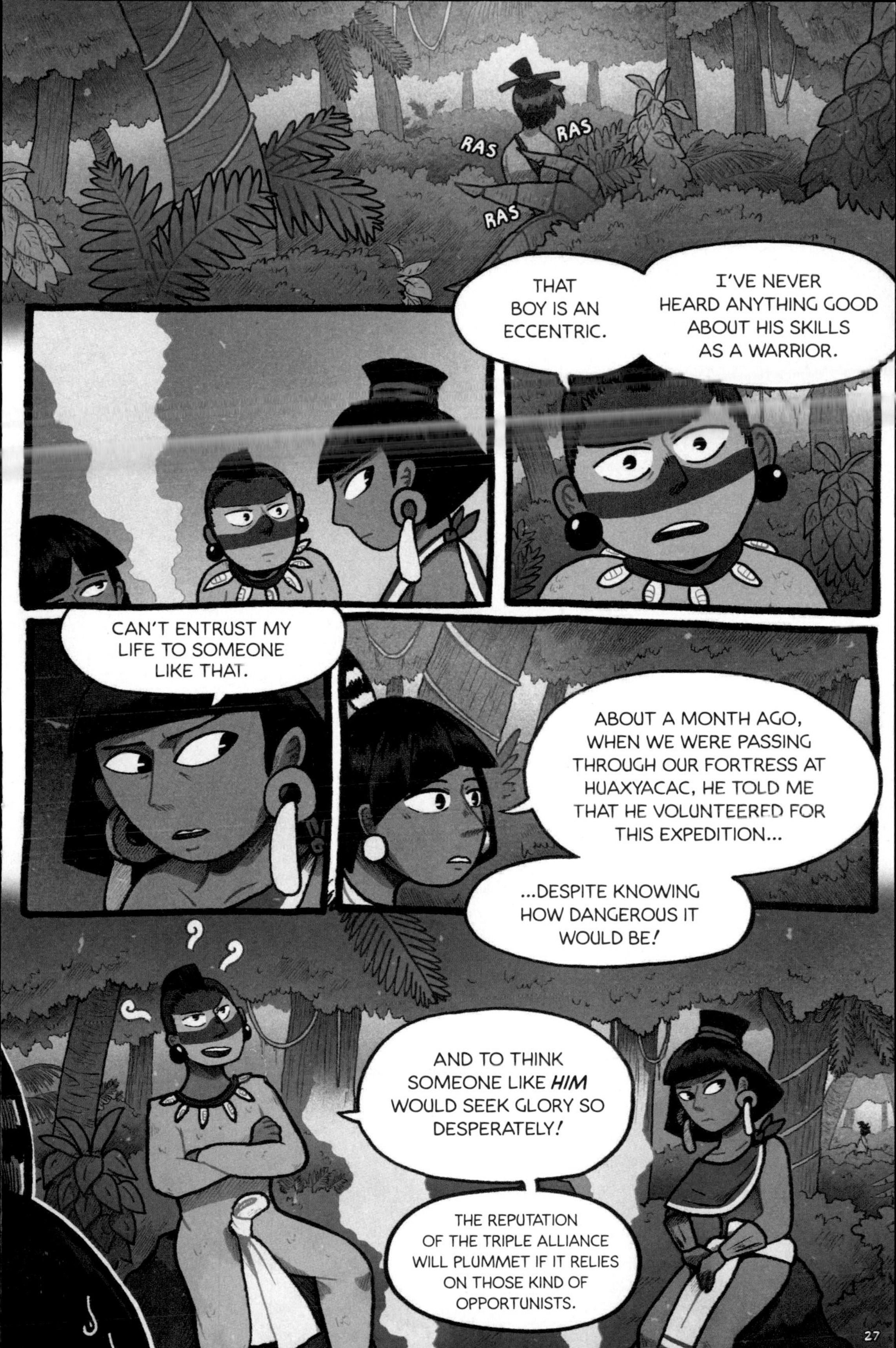
RAS
RAS
RAS
THAT BOY IS AN ECCENTRIC.
I'VE NEVER HEARD ANYTHING GOOD ABOUT HIS SKILLS AS A WARRIOR.
CAN'T ENTRUST MY LIFE TO SOMEONE LIKE THAT.
ABOUT A MONTH AGO, WHEN WE WERE PASSING THROUGH OUR FORTRESS AT HUAXYACAC, HE TOLD ME THAT HE VOLUNTEERED FOR THIS EXPEDITION...
...DESPITE KNOWING HOW DANGEROUS IT WOULD BE!
? ?
AND TO THINK SOMEONE LIKE *HIM* WOULD SEEK GLORY SO DESPERATELY!
THE REPUTATION OF THE TRIPLE ALLIANCE WILL PLUMMET IF IT RELIES ON THOSE KIND OF OPPORTUNISTS.

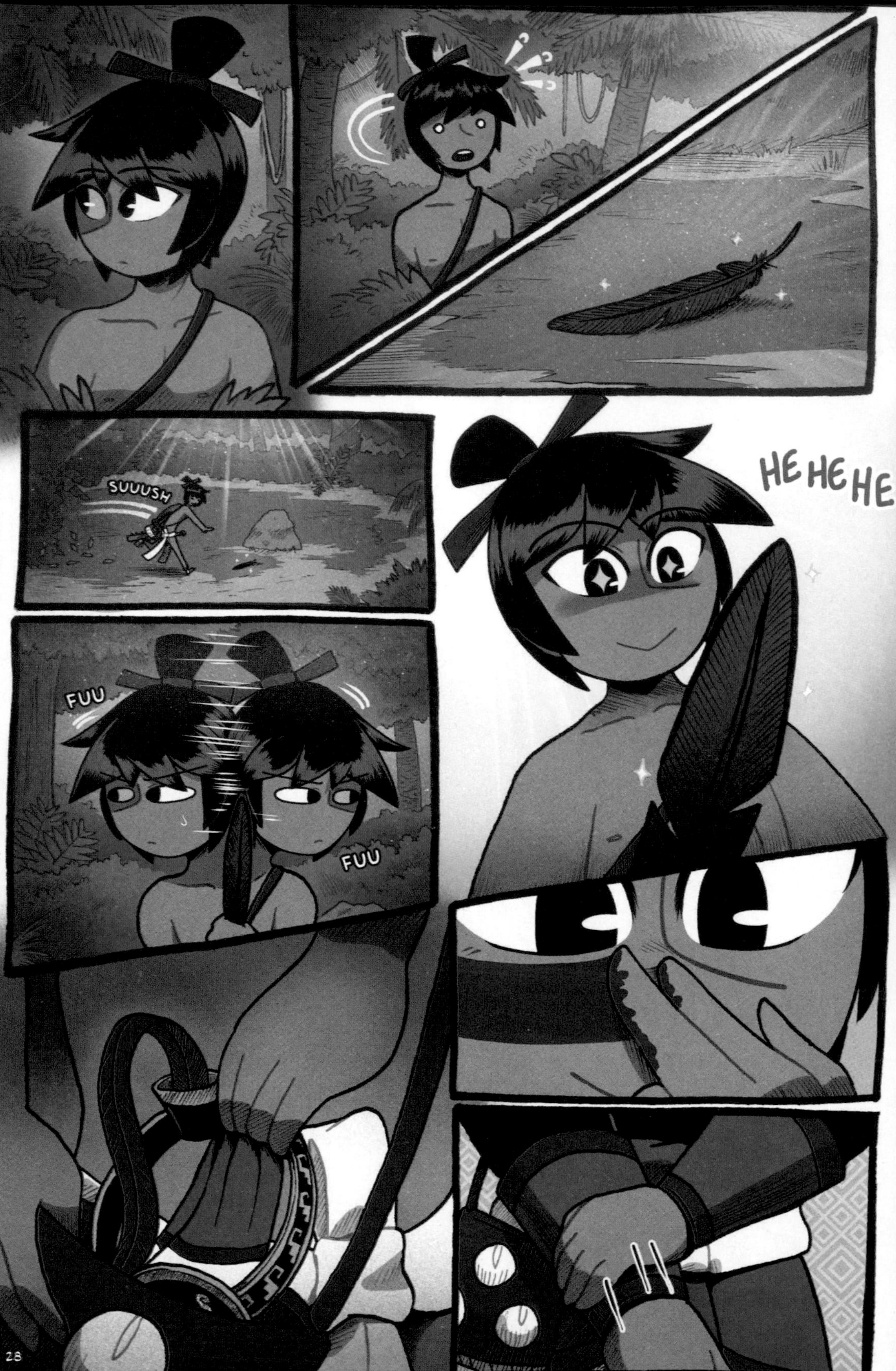
SUUUSH
HE HE HE
FUU
FUU

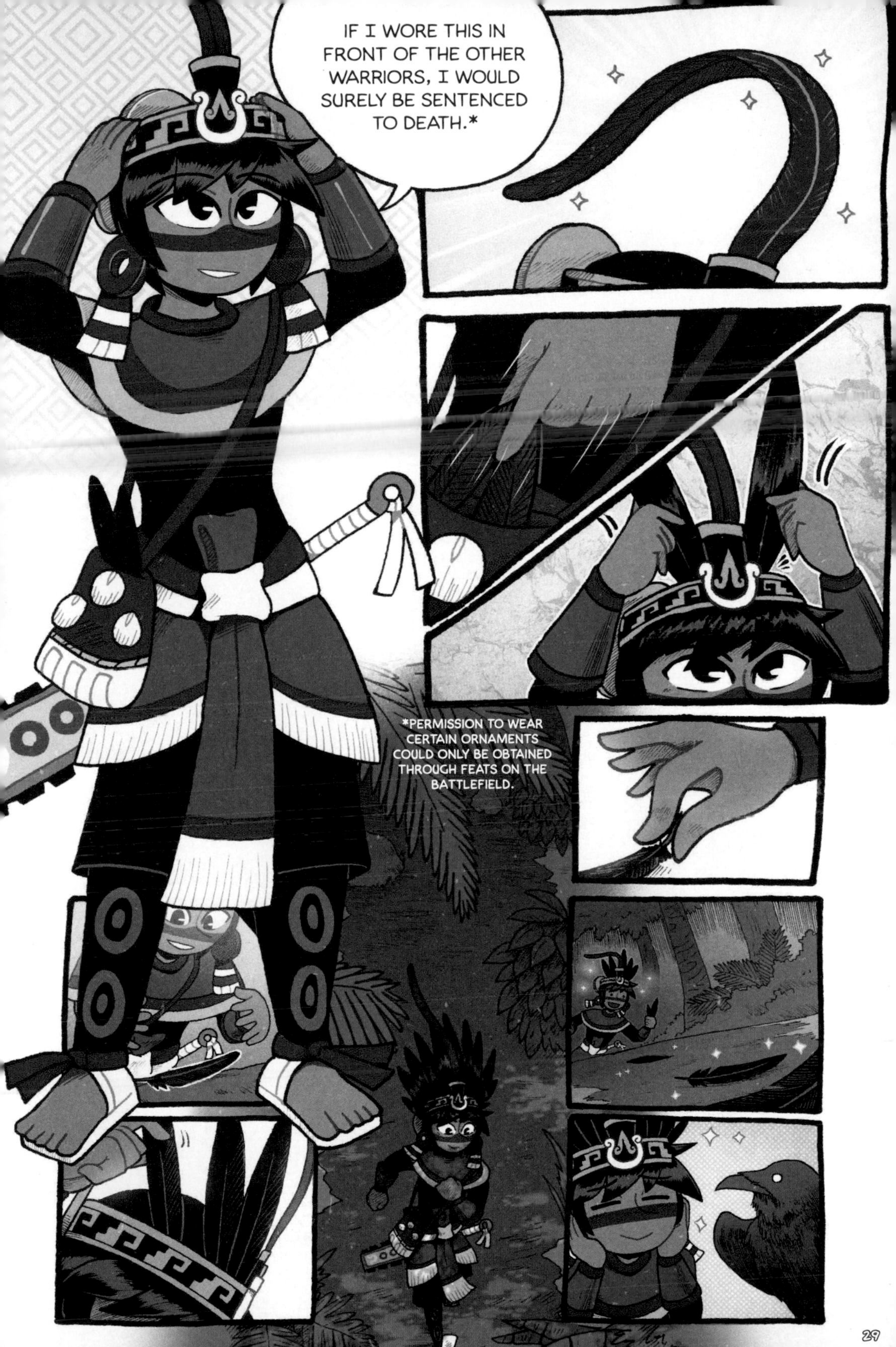
IF I WORE THIS IN FRONT OF THE OTHER WARRIORS, I WOULD SURELY BE SENTENCED TO DEATH.*
*PERMISSION TO WEAR CERTAIN ORNAMENTS COULD ONLY BE OBTAINED THROUGH FEATS ON THE BATTLEFIELD.

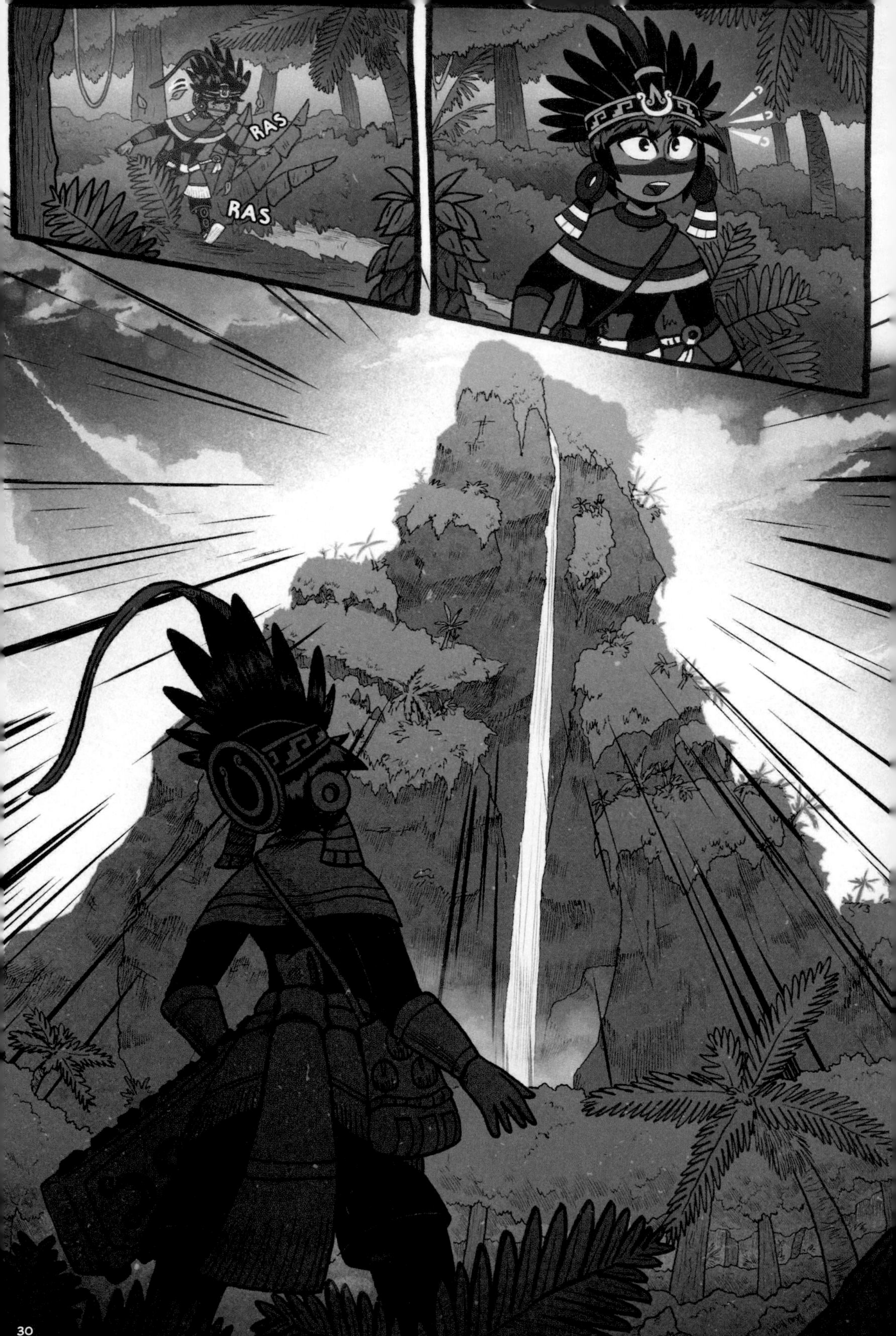
RAS
RAS

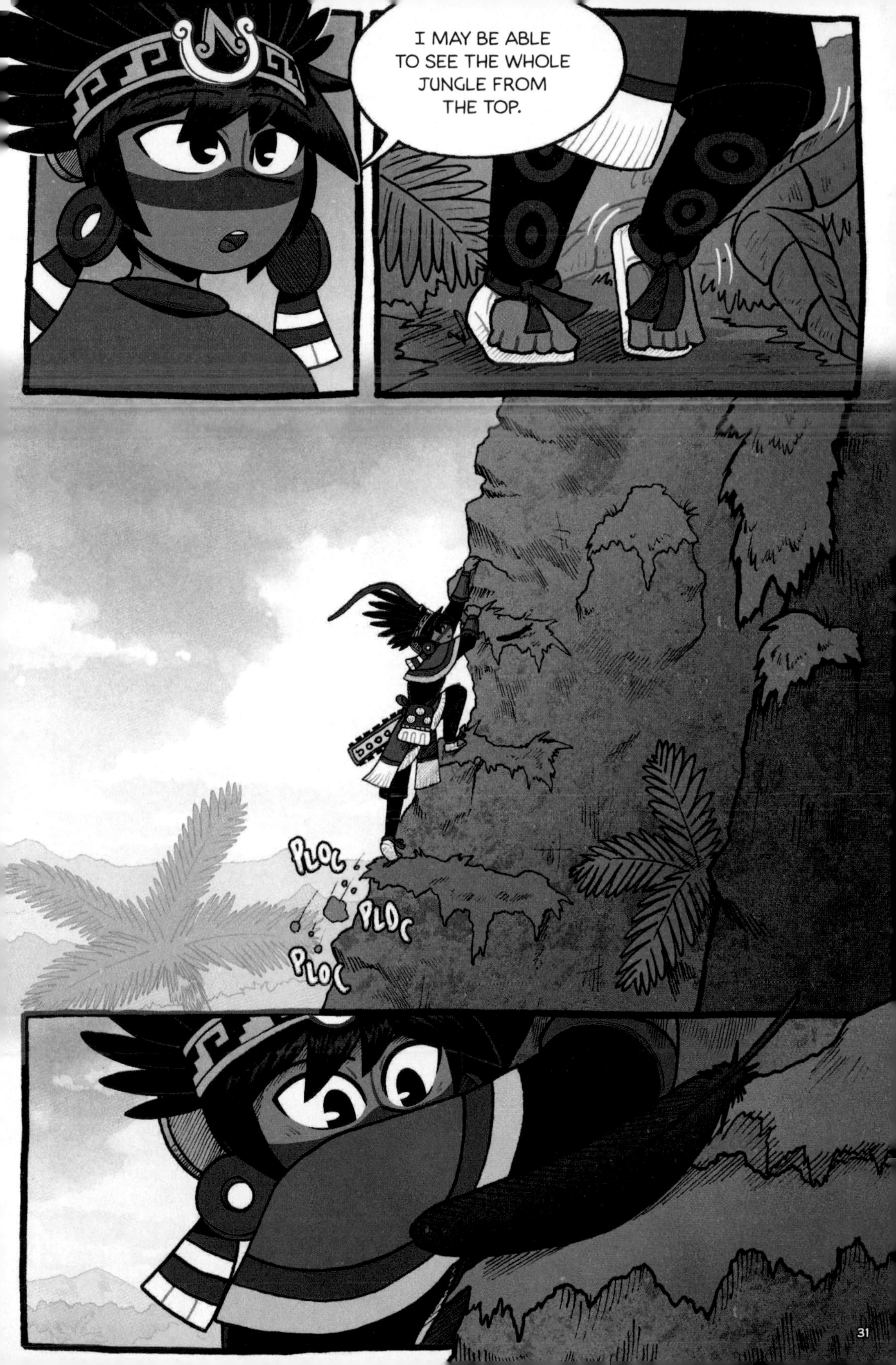
I MAY BE ABLE TO SEE THE WHOLE JUNGLE FROM THE TOP.
PLOC
PLOC
PLOC

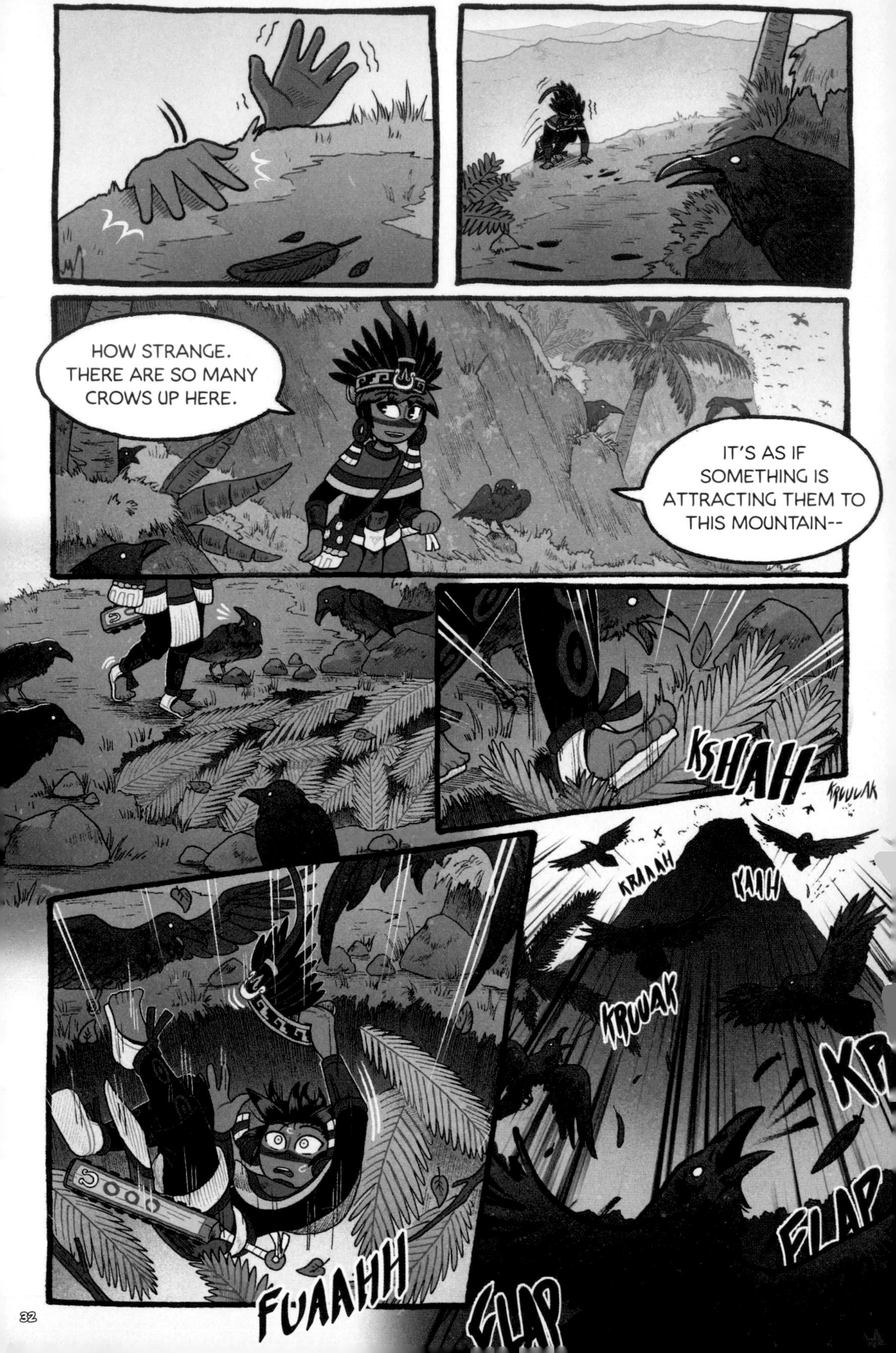
HOW STRANGE. THERE ARE SO MANY CROWS UP HERE.
IT'S AS IF SOMETHING IS ATTRACTING THEM TO THIS MOUNTAIN--
KSHAH
KRUUAK
KRAAAH
KAAH
KRUUAK
KR
FLAP
FUAAHH
FLAP

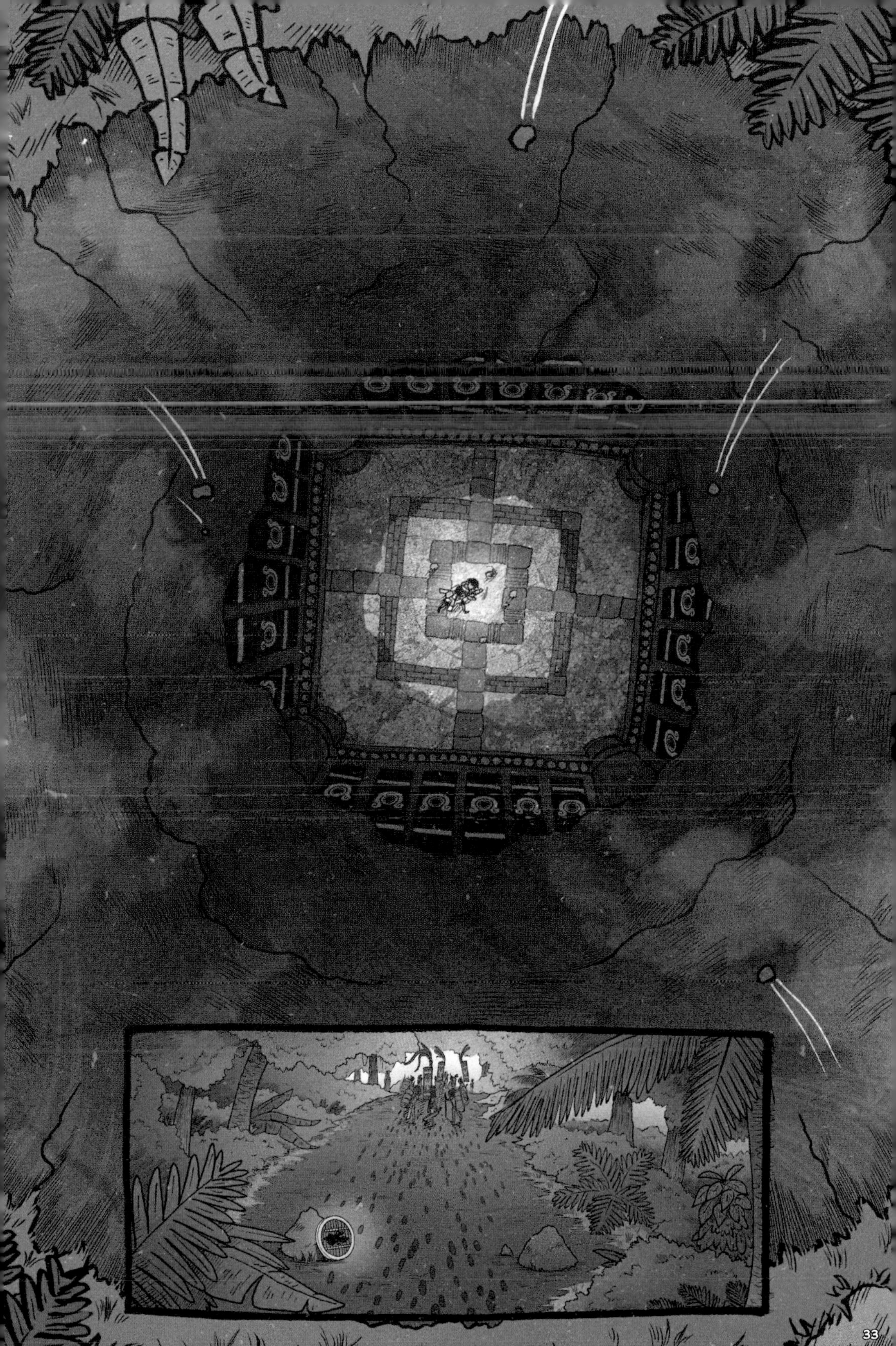

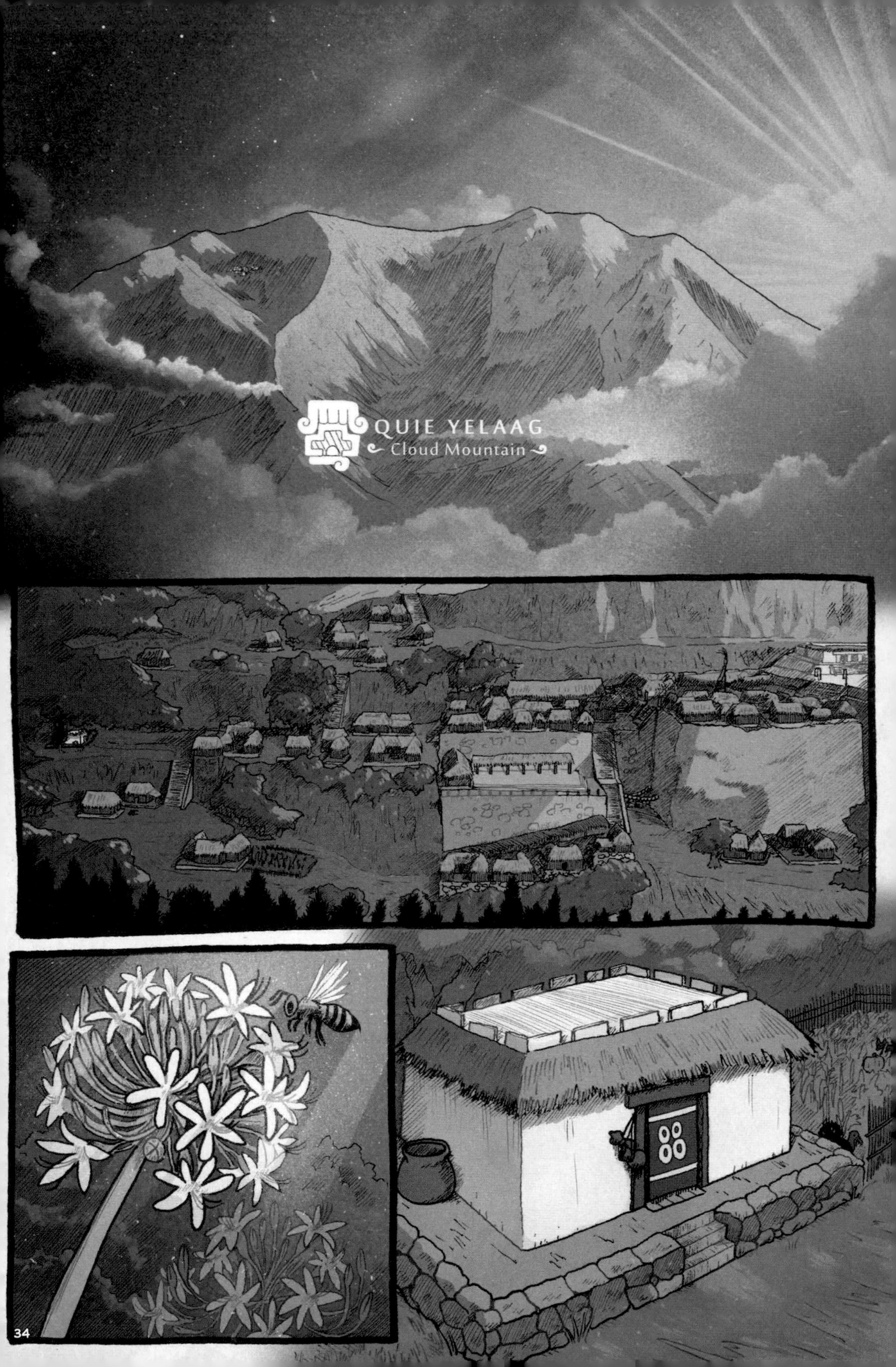
QUIE YELAAG
~ Cloud Mountain ~

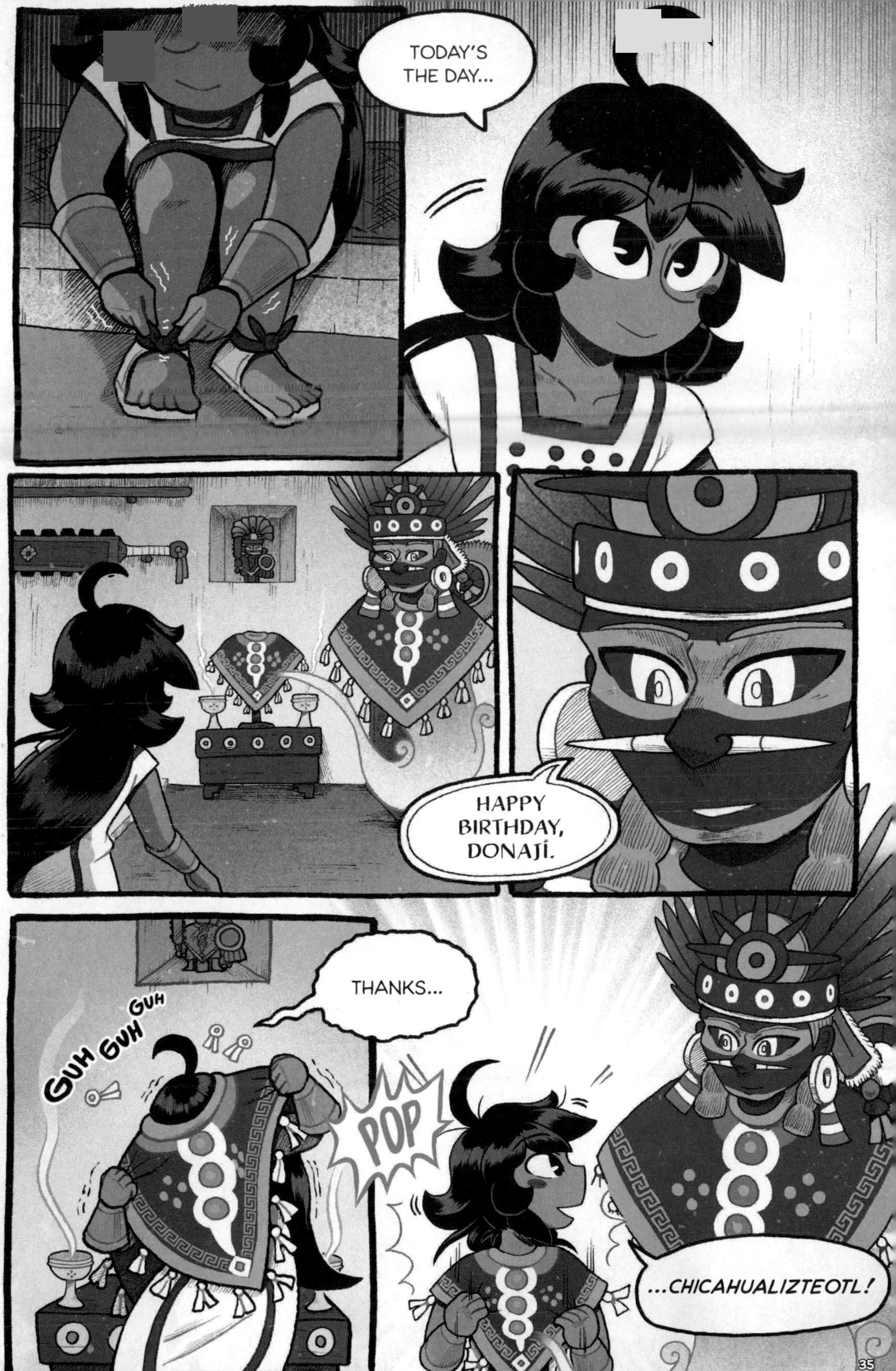
TODAY'S THE DAY...
HAPPY BIRTHDAY, DONAJÍ.
THANKS...
GUH GUH GUH
POP
...CHICAHUALIZTEOTL!

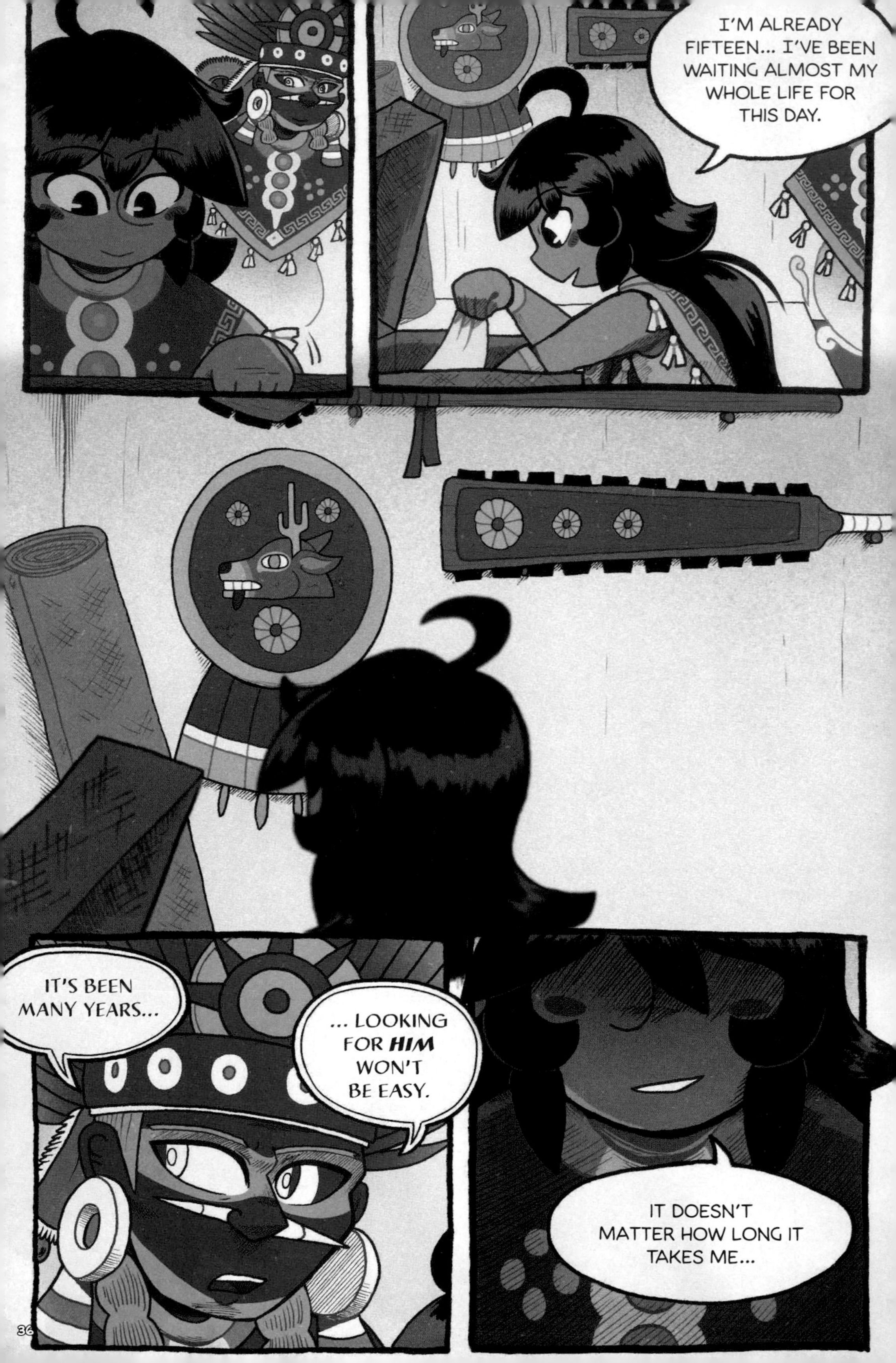
I'M ALREADY FIFTEEN... I'VE BEEN WAITING ALMOST MY WHOLE LIFE FOR THIS DAY.
IT'S BEEN MANY YEARS...
... LOOKING FOR ***HIM*** WON'T BE EASY.
IT DOESN'T MATTER HOW LONG IT TAKES ME...

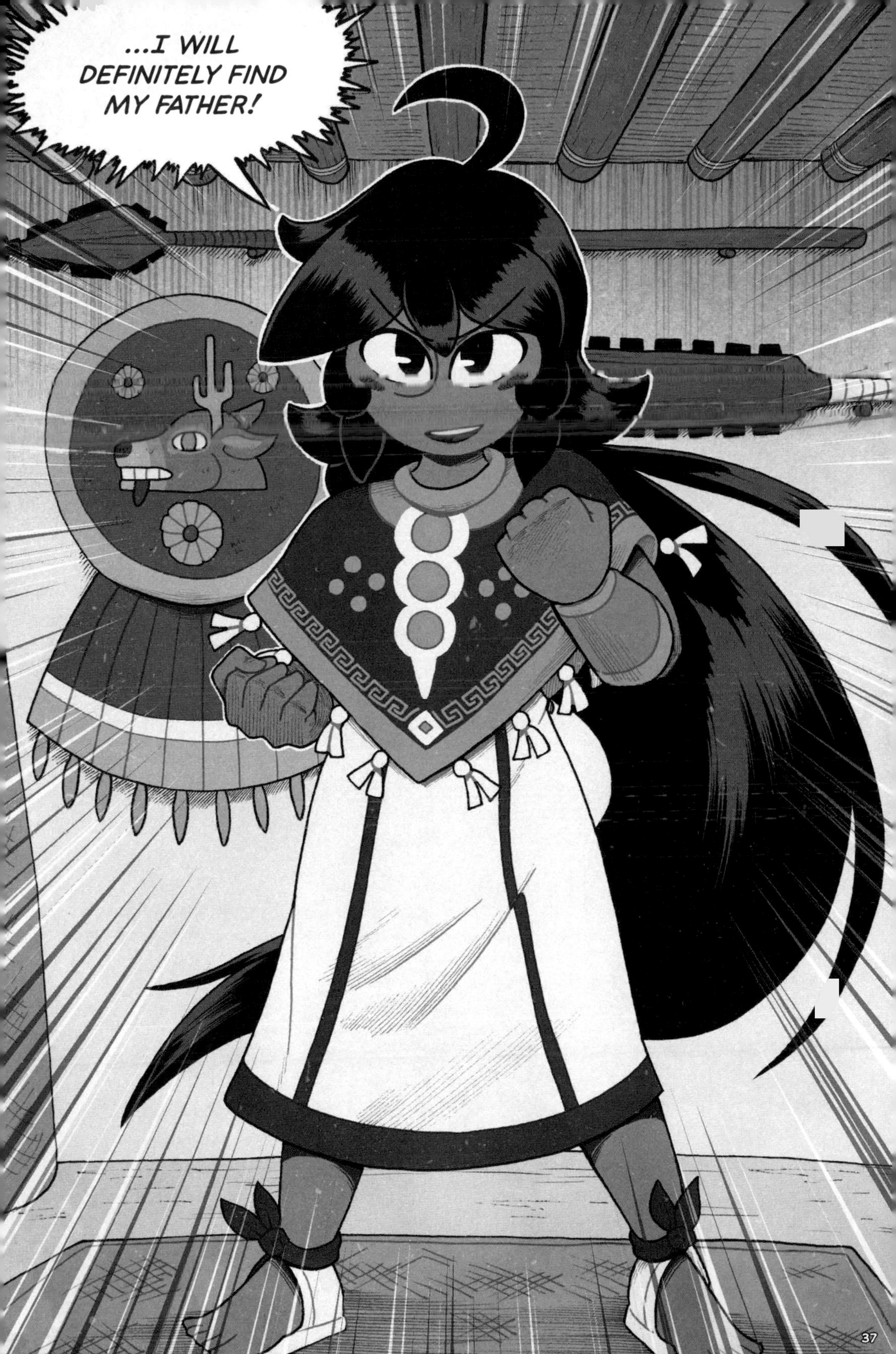
...I WILL DEFINITELY FIND MY FATHER!

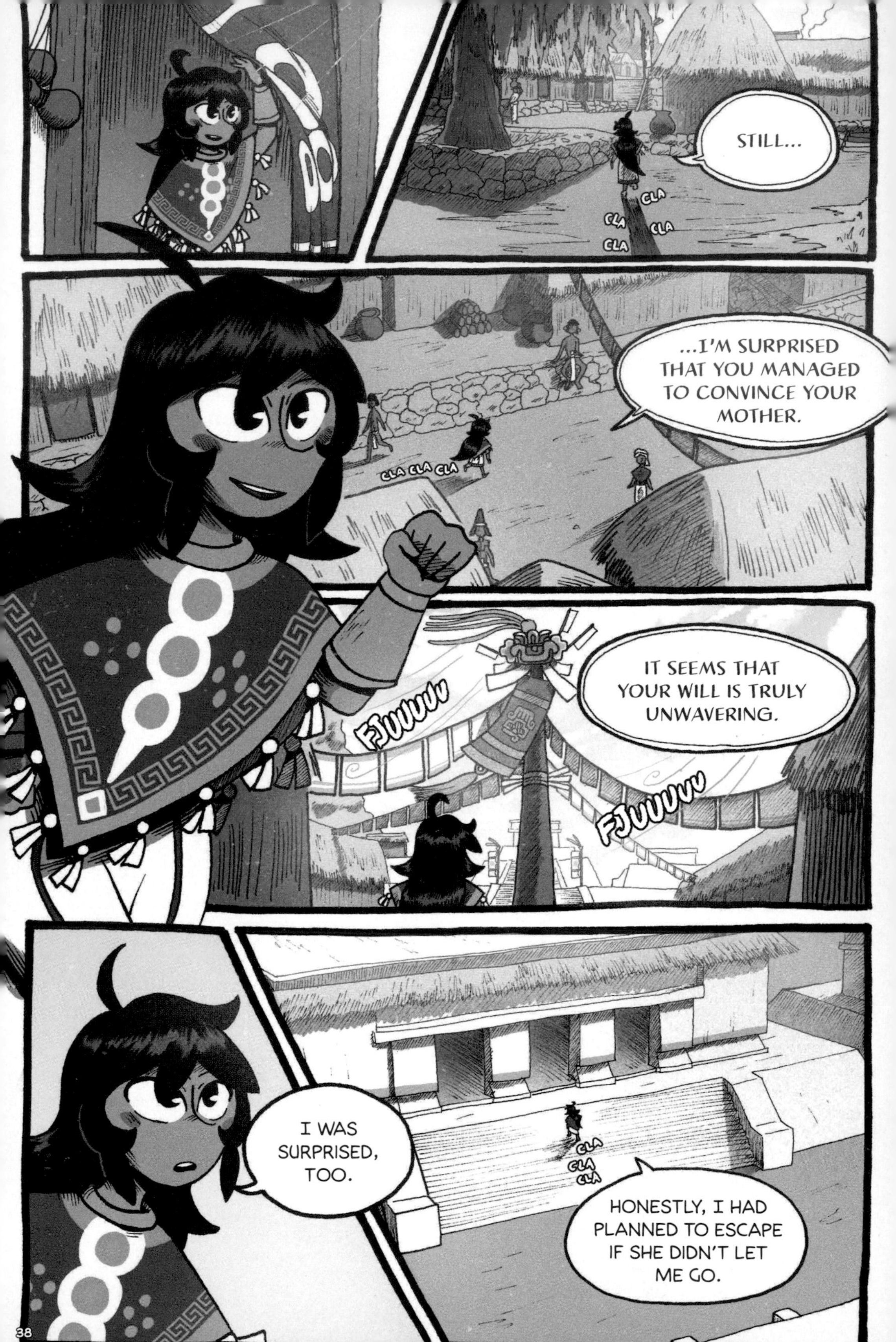
STILL...
CLA
CLA
CLA
CLA
...I'M SURPRISED THAT YOU MANAGED TO CONVINCE YOUR MOTHER.
CLA CLA CLA
IT SEEMS THAT YOUR WILL IS TRULY UNWAVERING.
FJUUUUU
FJUUUUU
I WAS SURPRISED, TOO.
CLA
CLA
CLA
HONESTLY, I HAD PLANNED TO ESCAPE IF SHE DIDN'T LET ME GO.

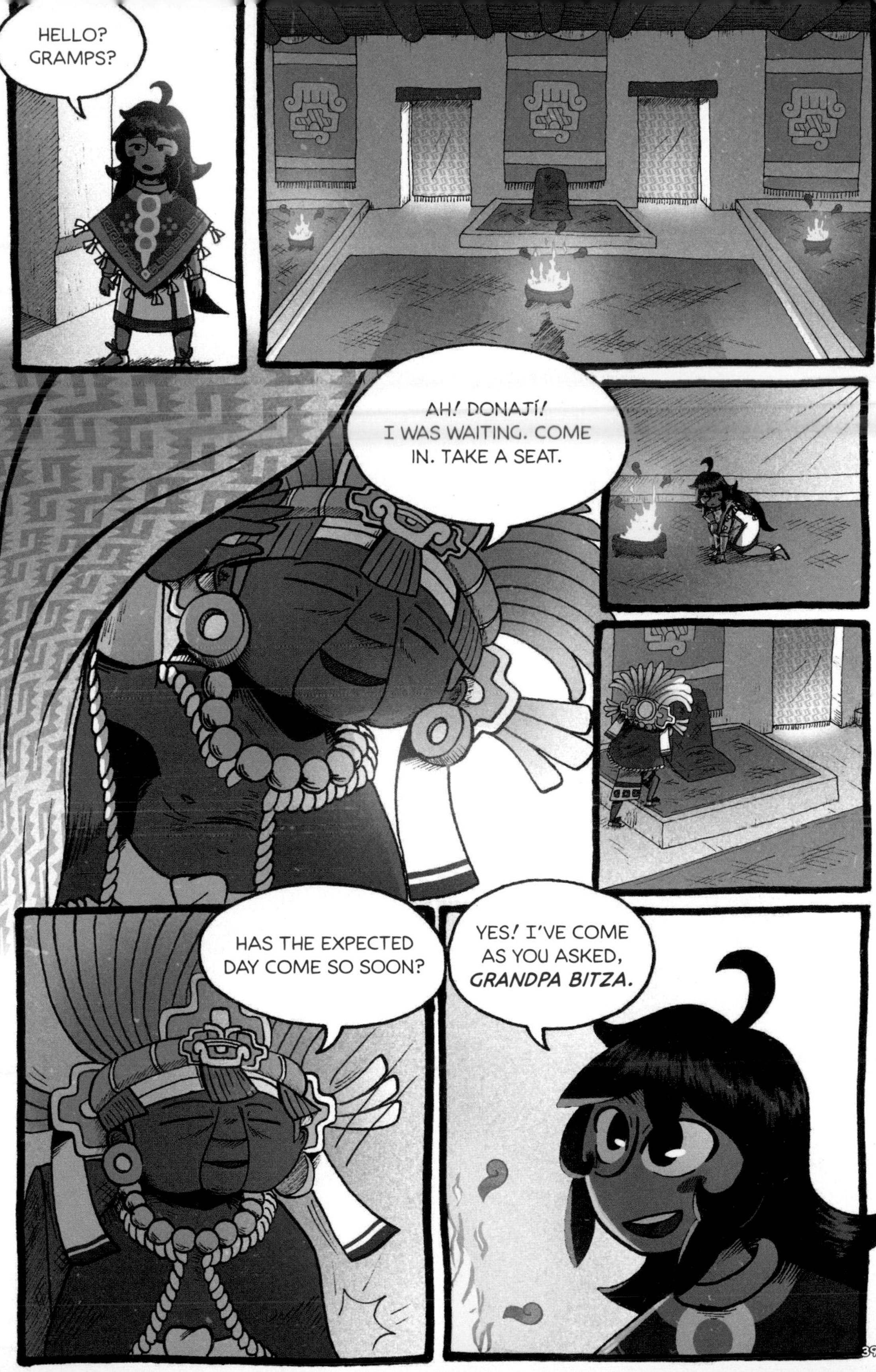
HELLO? GRAMPS?
AH! DONAJÍ! I WAS WAITING. COME IN. TAKE A SEAT.
HAS THE EXPECTED DAY COME SO SOON?
YES! I'VE COME AS YOU ASKED, *GRANDPA BITZA.*

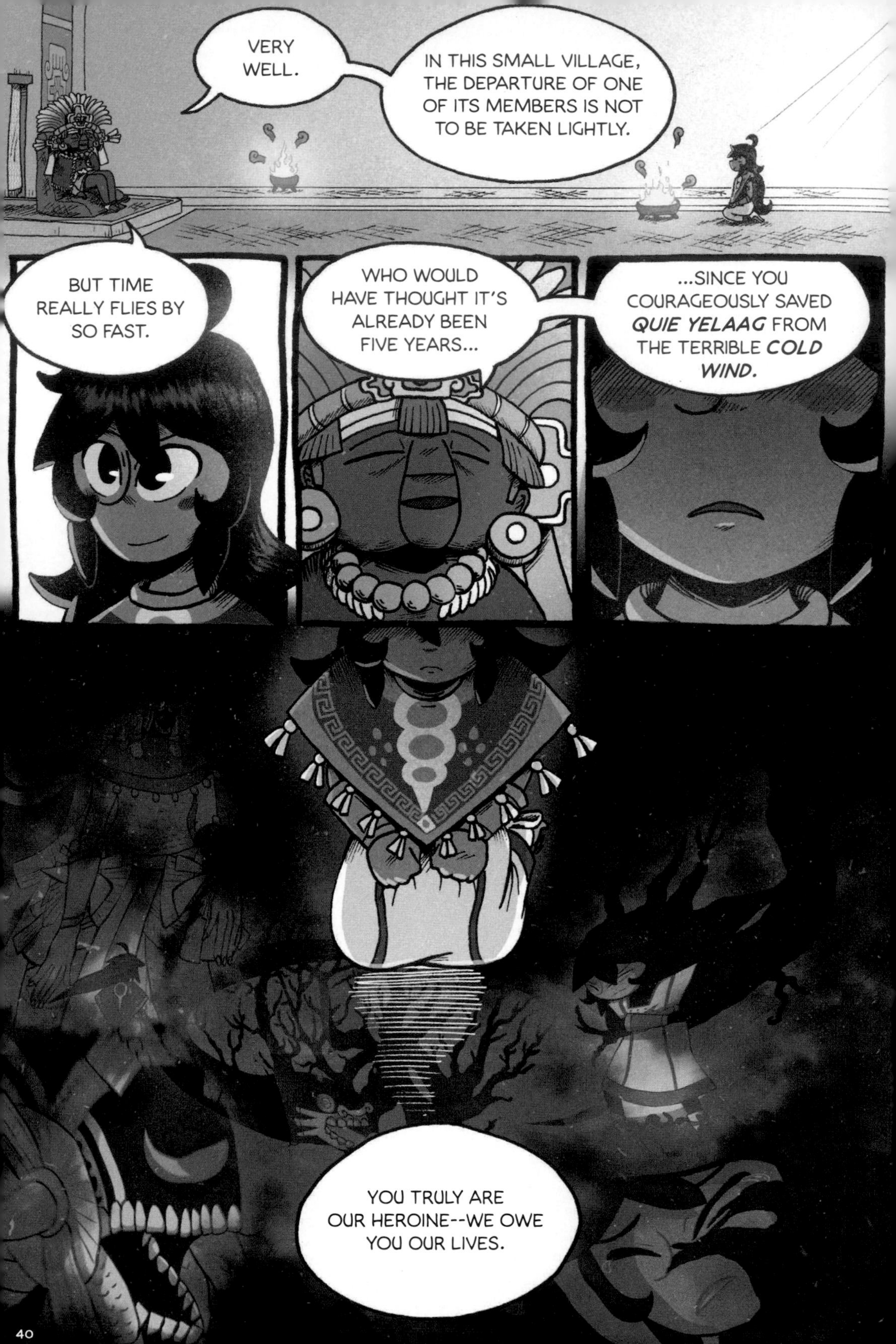
VERY WELL.
IN THIS SMALL VILLAGE, THE DEPARTURE OF ONE OF ITS MEMBERS IS NOT TO BE TAKEN LIGHTLY.
BUT TIME REALLY FLIES BY SO FAST.
WHO WOULD HAVE THOUGHT IT'S ALREADY BEEN FIVE YEARS...
...SINCE YOU COURAGEOUSLY SAVED QUIE YELAAG FROM THE TERRIBLE COLD WIND.
YOU TRULY ARE OUR HEROINE--WE OWE YOU OUR LIVES.

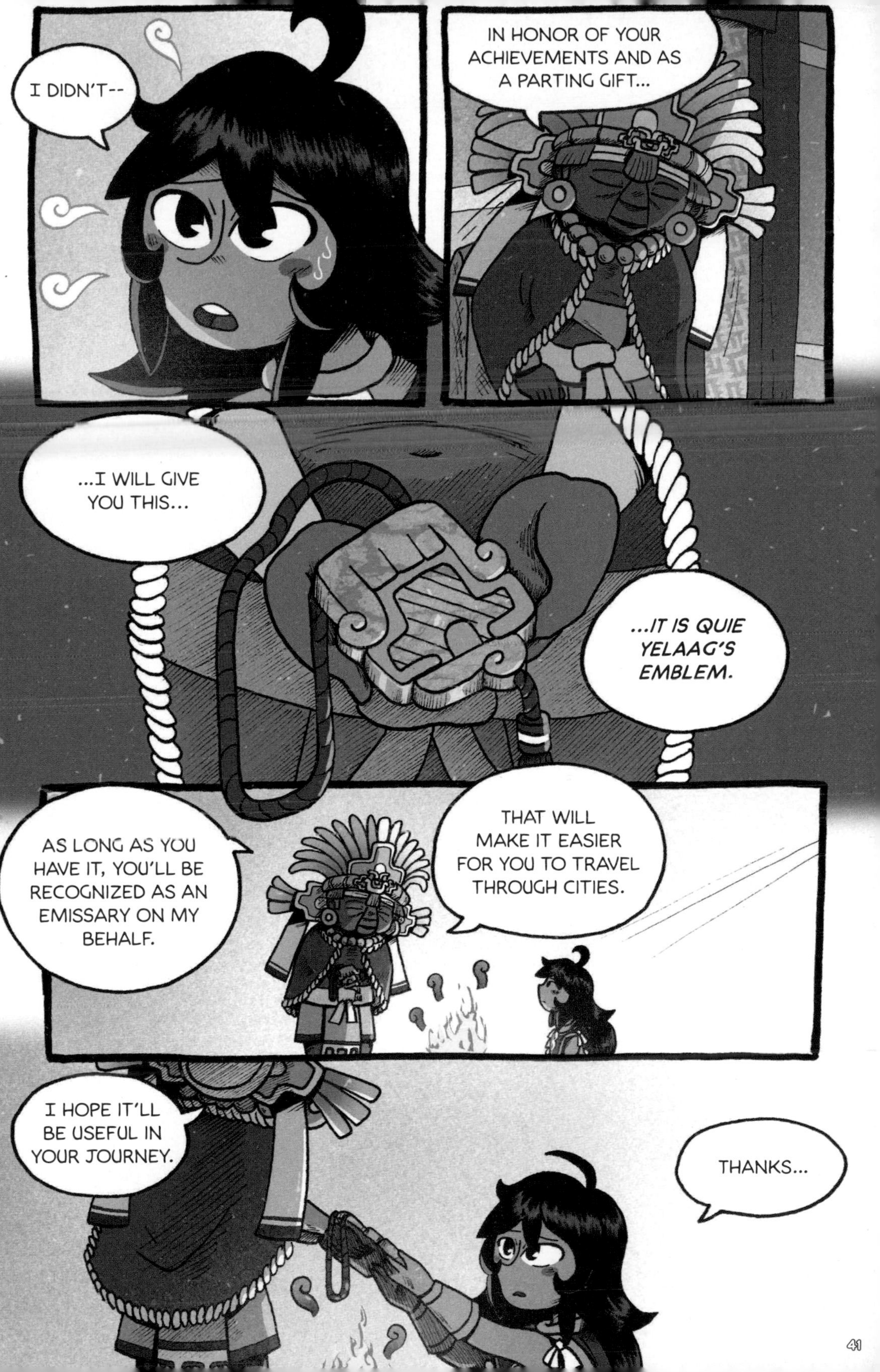

I DIDN'T--
IN HONOR OF YOUR ACHIEVEMENTS AND AS A PARTING GIFT...
...I WILL GIVE YOU THIS...
...IT IS QUIE YELAAG'S EMBLEM.
AS LONG AS YOU HAVE IT, YOU'LL BE RECOGNIZED AS AN EMISSARY ON MY BEHALF.
THAT WILL MAKE IT EASIER FOR YOU TO TRAVEL THROUGH CITIES.
I HOPE IT'LL BE USEFUL IN YOUR JOURNEY.
THANKS...

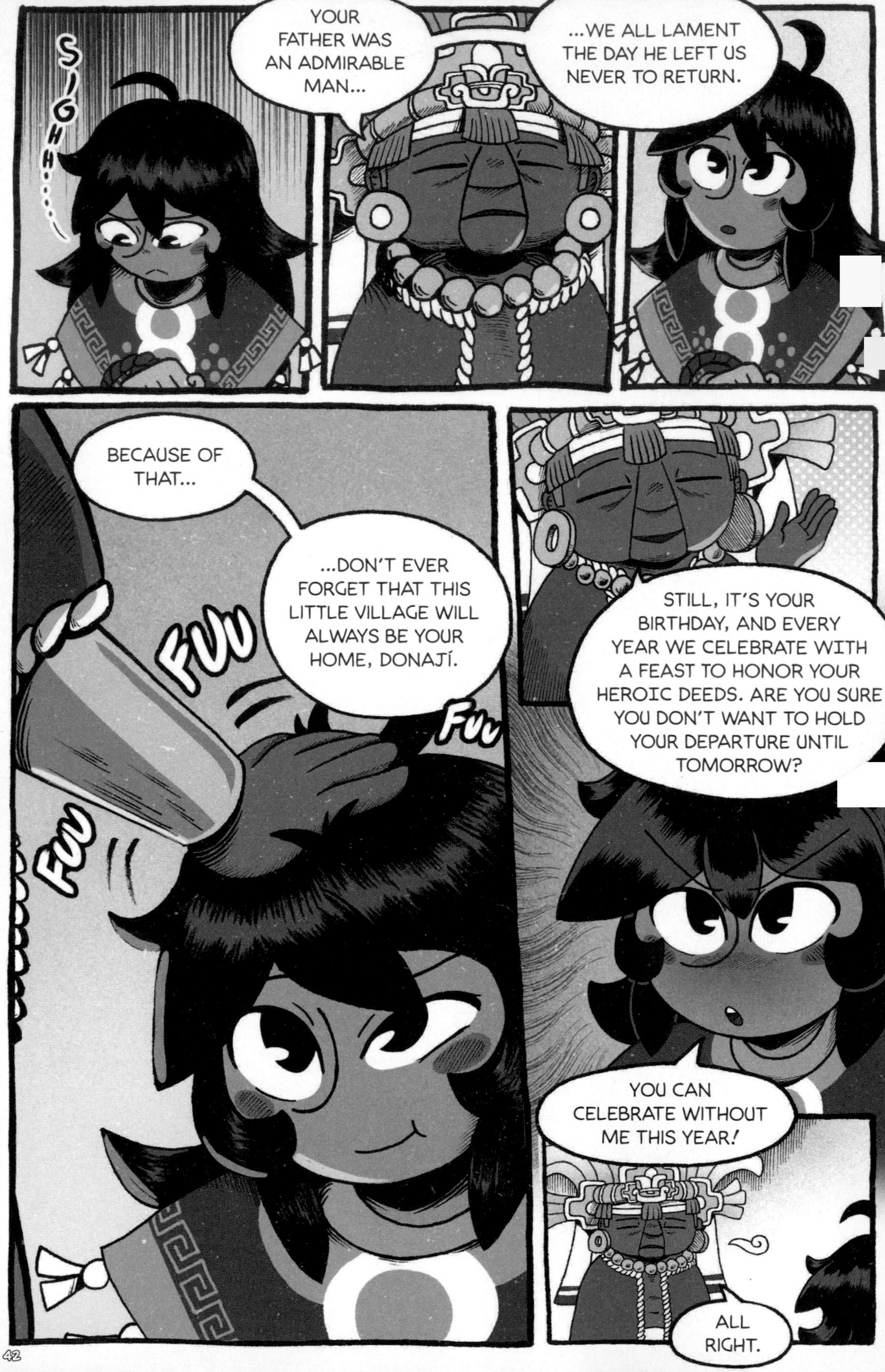
SIGHH...
YOUR FATHER WAS AN ADMIRABLE MAN...
...WE ALL LAMENT THE DAY HE LEFT US NEVER TO RETURN.
BECAUSE OF THAT...
...DON'T EVER FORGET THAT THIS LITTLE VILLAGE WILL ALWAYS BE YOUR HOME, DONAJÍ.
FUU
FUU
FUU
STILL, IT'S YOUR BIRTHDAY, AND EVERY YEAR WE CELEBRATE WITH A FEAST TO HONOR YOUR HEROIC DEEDS. ARE YOU SURE YOU DON'T WANT TO HOLD YOUR DEPARTURE UNTIL TOMORROW?
YOU CAN CELEBRATE WITHOUT ME THIS YEAR!
ALL RIGHT.

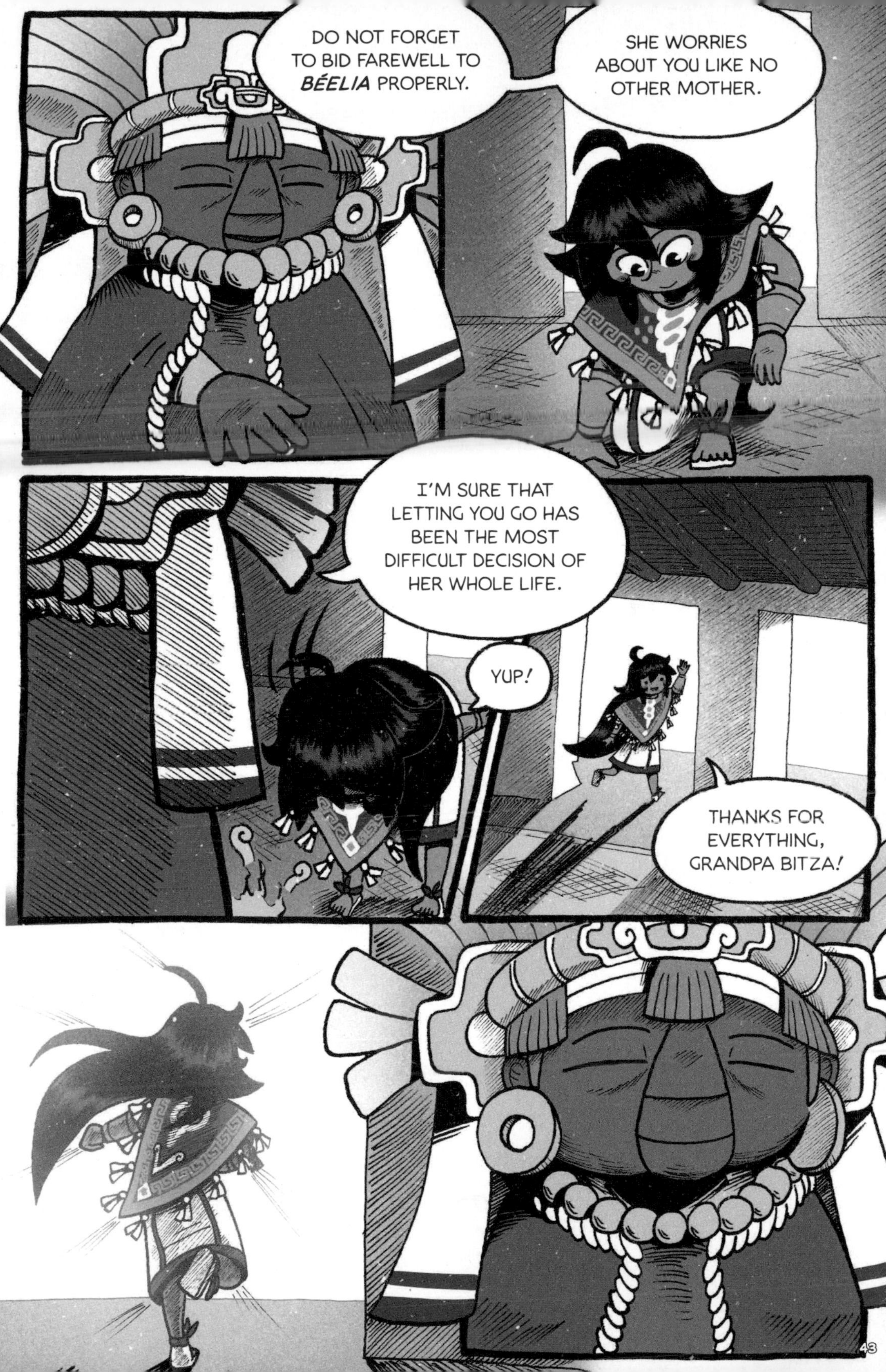
DO NOT FORGET TO BID FAREWELL TO *BÉELIA* PROPERLY.
SHE WORRIES ABOUT YOU LIKE NO OTHER MOTHER.
I'M SURE THAT LETTING YOU GO HAS BEEN THE MOST DIFFICULT DECISION OF HER WHOLE LIFE.
YUP!
THANKS FOR EVERYTHING, GRANDPA BITZA!

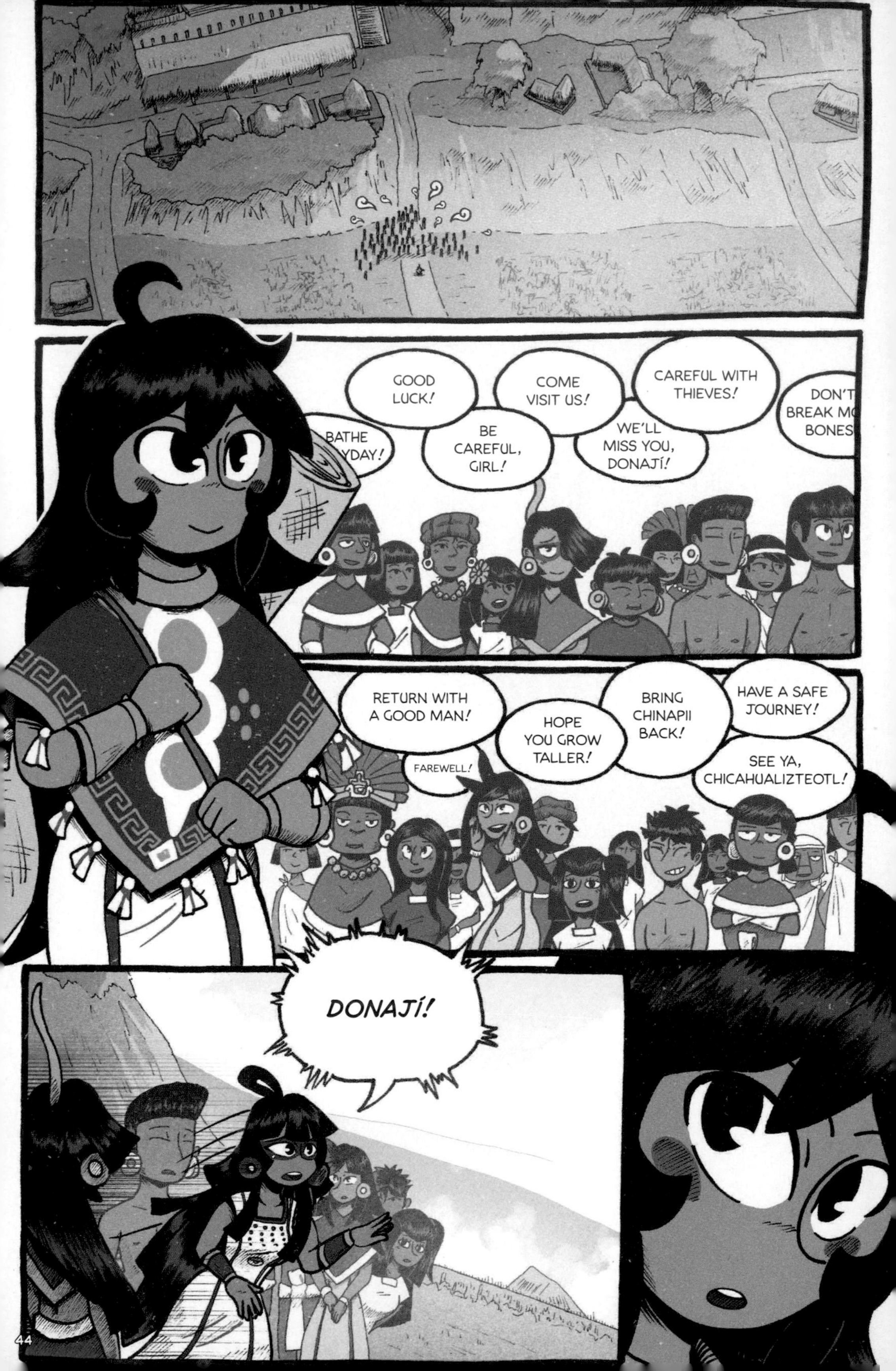
GOOD LUCK!
BATHE
YDAY!
BE CAREFUL, GIRL!
COME VISIT US!
WE'LL MISS YOU, DONAJÍ!
CAREFUL WITH THIEVES!
DON'T
BREAK MO
BONES
RETURN WITH A GOOD MAN!
FAREWELL!
HOPE YOU GROW TALLER!
BRING CHINAPII BACK!
HAVE A SAFE JOURNEY!
SEE YA, CHICAHUALIZTEOTL!
DONAJÍ!

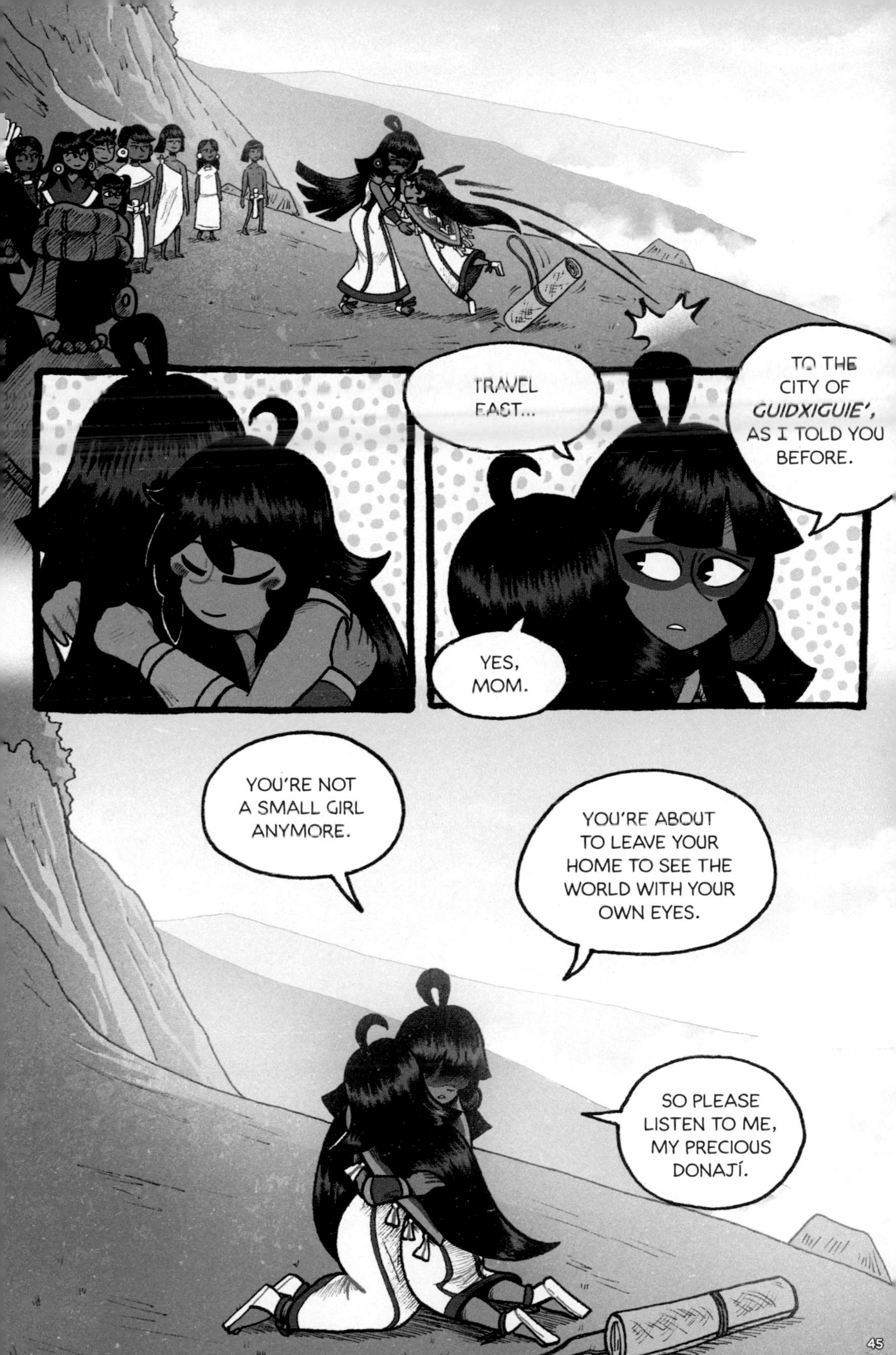
TRAVEL EAST...
TO THE CITY OF GUIDXIGUIE', AS I TOLD YOU BEFORE.
YES, MOM.
YOU'RE NOT A SMALL GIRL ANYMORE.
YOU'RE ABOUT TO LEAVE YOUR HOME TO SEE THE WORLD WITH YOUR OWN EYES.
SO PLEASE LISTEN TO ME, MY PRECIOUS DONAJÍ.

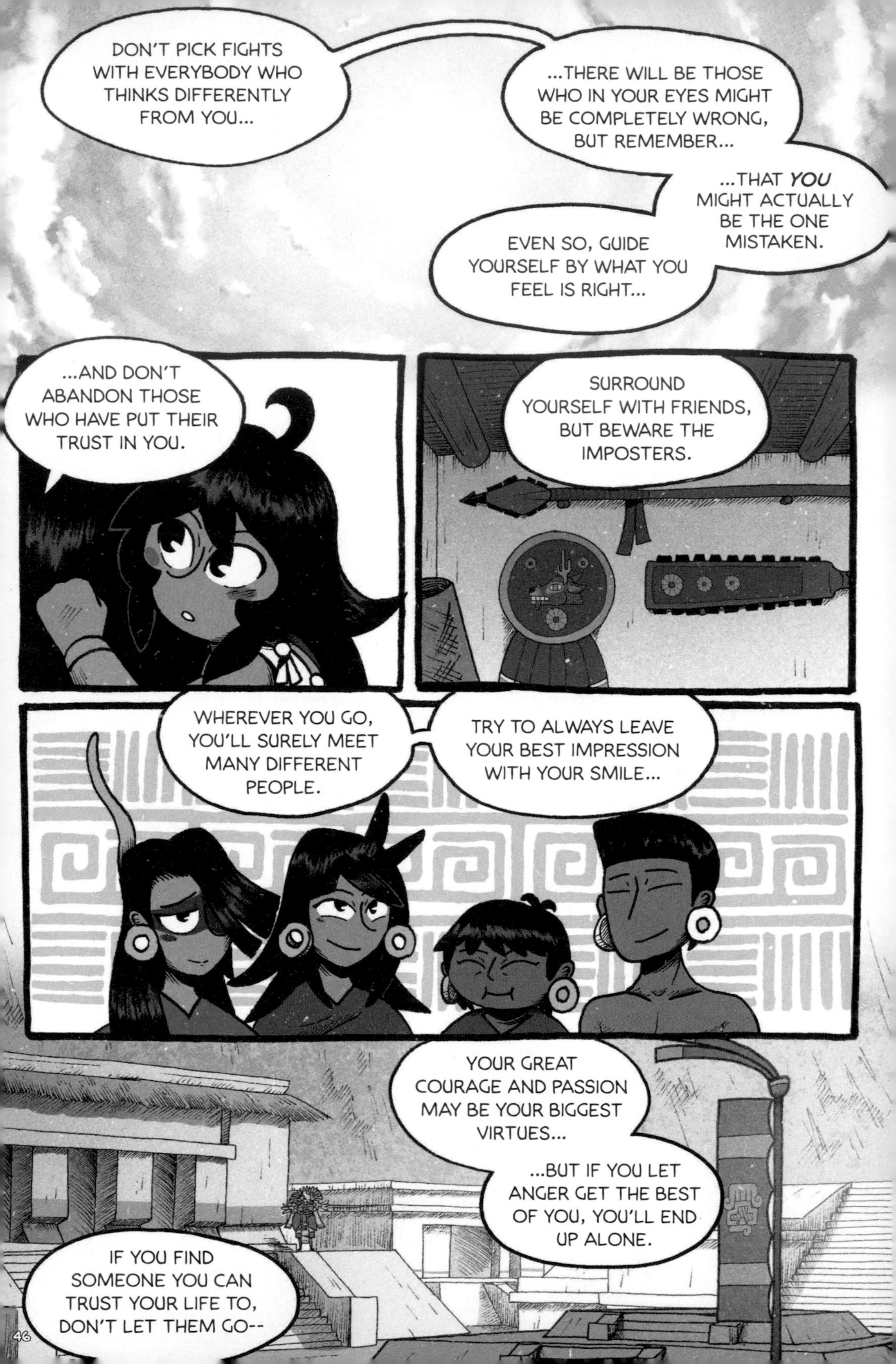
DON'T PICK FIGHTS WITH EVERYBODY WHO THINKS DIFFERENTLY FROM YOU...
...THERE WILL BE THOSE WHO IN YOUR EYES MIGHT BE COMPLETELY WRONG, BUT REMEMBER...
...THAT *YOU* MIGHT ACTUALLY BE THE ONE MISTAKEN.
EVEN SO, GUIDE YOURSELF BY WHAT YOU FEEL IS RIGHT...
...AND DON'T ABANDON THOSE WHO HAVE PUT THEIR TRUST IN YOU.
SURROUND YOURSELF WITH FRIENDS, BUT BEWARE THE IMPOSTERS.
WHEREVER YOU GO, YOU'LL SURELY MEET MANY DIFFERENT PEOPLE.
TRY TO ALWAYS LEAVE YOUR BEST IMPRESSION WITH YOUR SMILE...
YOUR GREAT COURAGE AND PASSION MAY BE YOUR BIGGEST VIRTUES...
...BUT IF YOU LET ANGER GET THE BEST OF YOU, YOU'LL END UP ALONE.
IF YOU FIND SOMEONE YOU CAN TRUST YOUR LIFE TO, DON'T LET THEM GO--

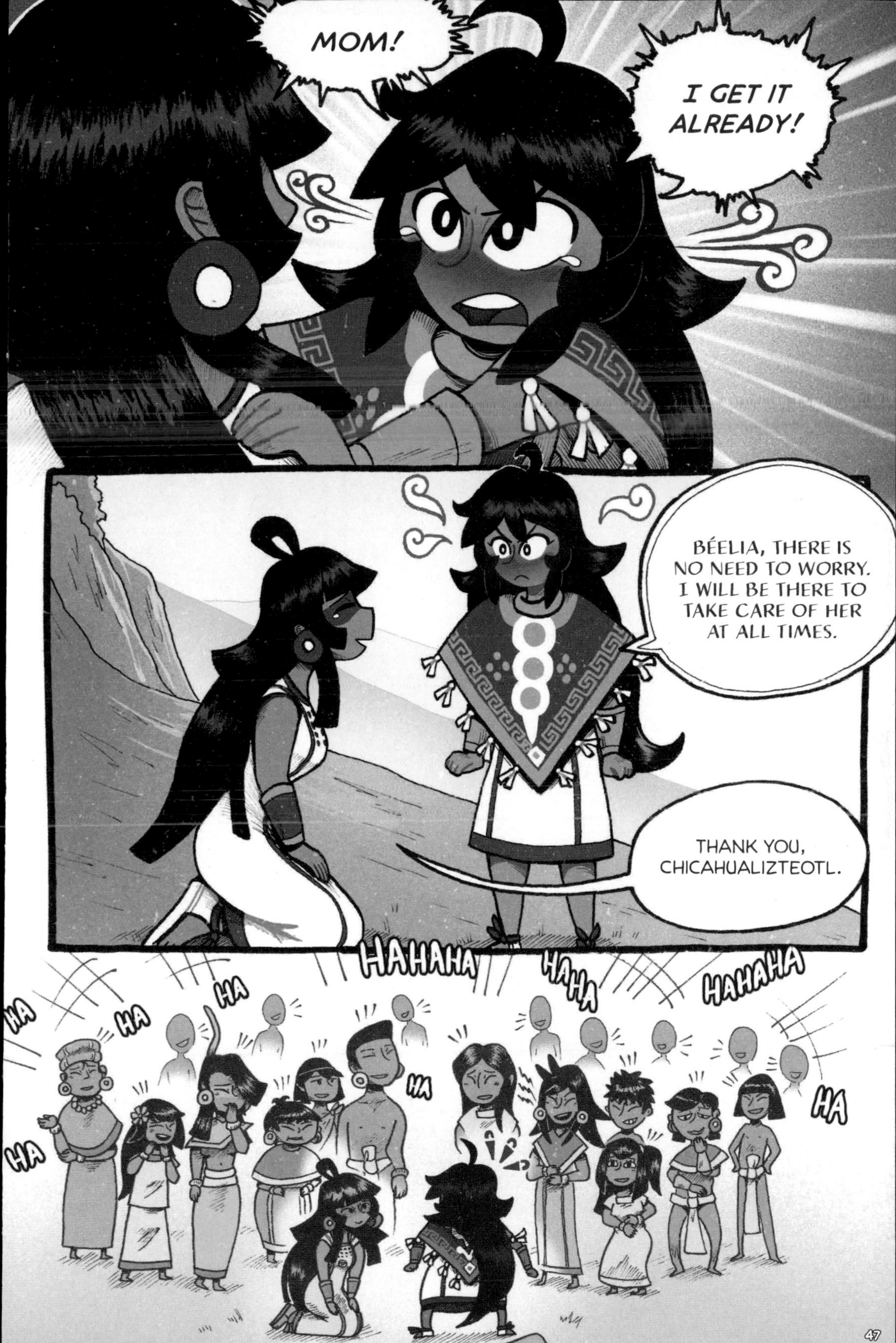
MOM!
I GET IT ALREADY!
BÉELIA, THERE IS NO NEED TO WORRY. I WILL BE THERE TO TAKE CARE OF HER AT ALL TIMES.
THANK YOU, CHICAHUALIZTEOTL.
HAHAHA
HAHA
HAHAHA
HA
HA
HA
HA
HA
HA

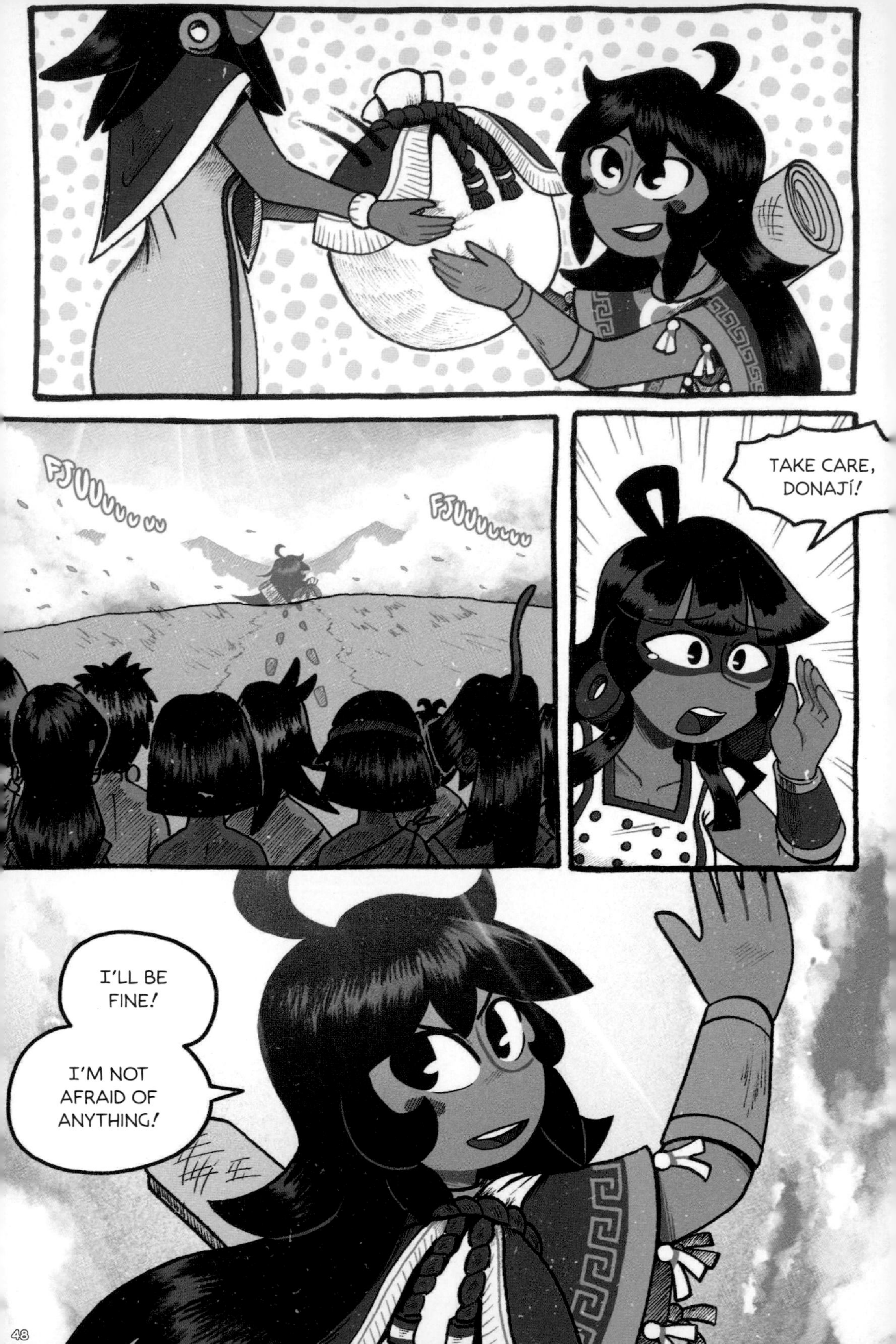
FJUUuuuuu
FJUUuuuuu
TAKE CARE, DONAJÍ!
I'LL BE FINE!
I'M NOT AFRAID OF ANYTHING!

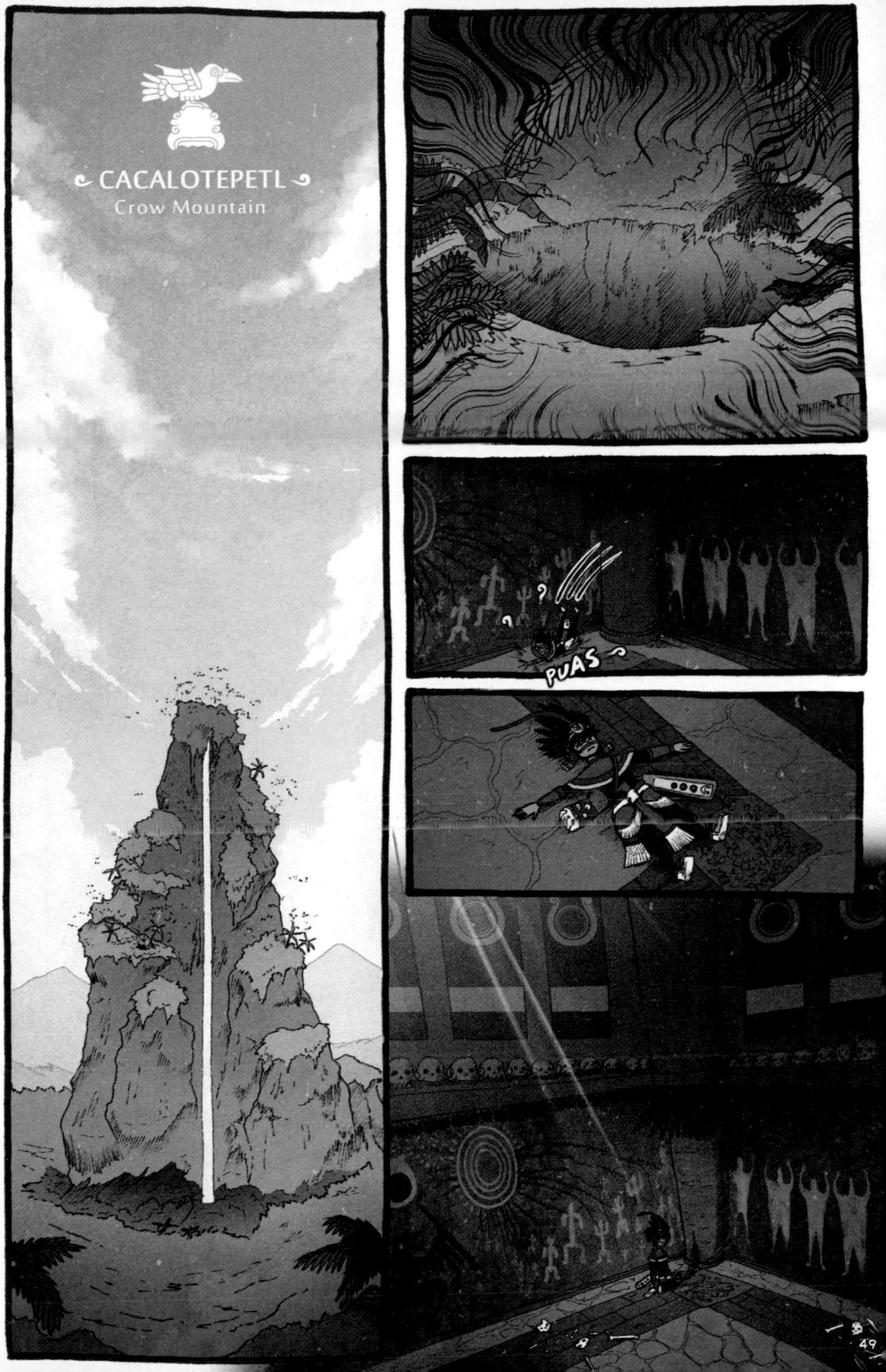
CACALOTEPETL
Crow Mountain
PUAS

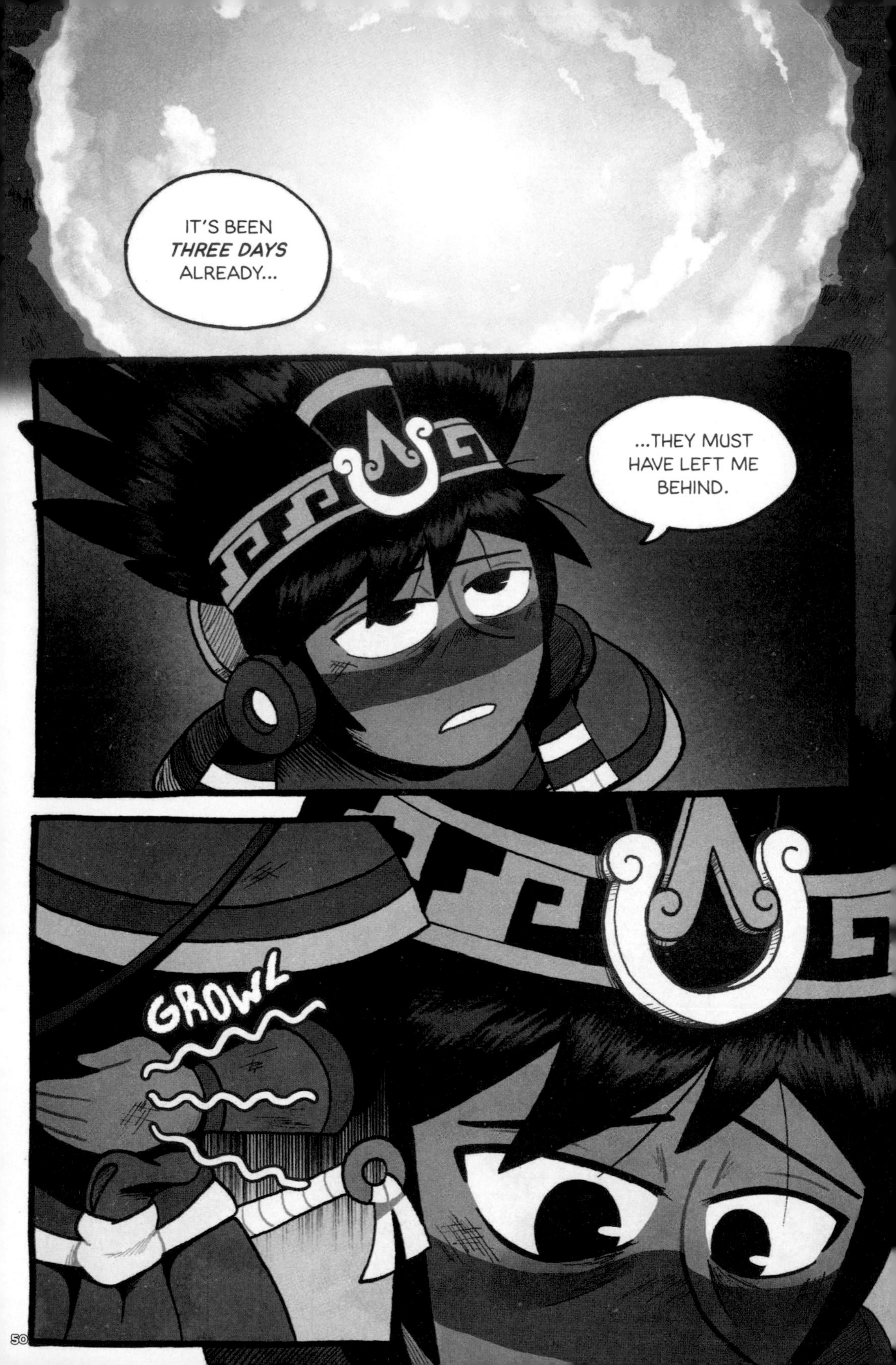
IT'S BEEN *THREE DAYS* ALREADY...
...THEY MUST HAVE LEFT ME BEHIND.
GROWL

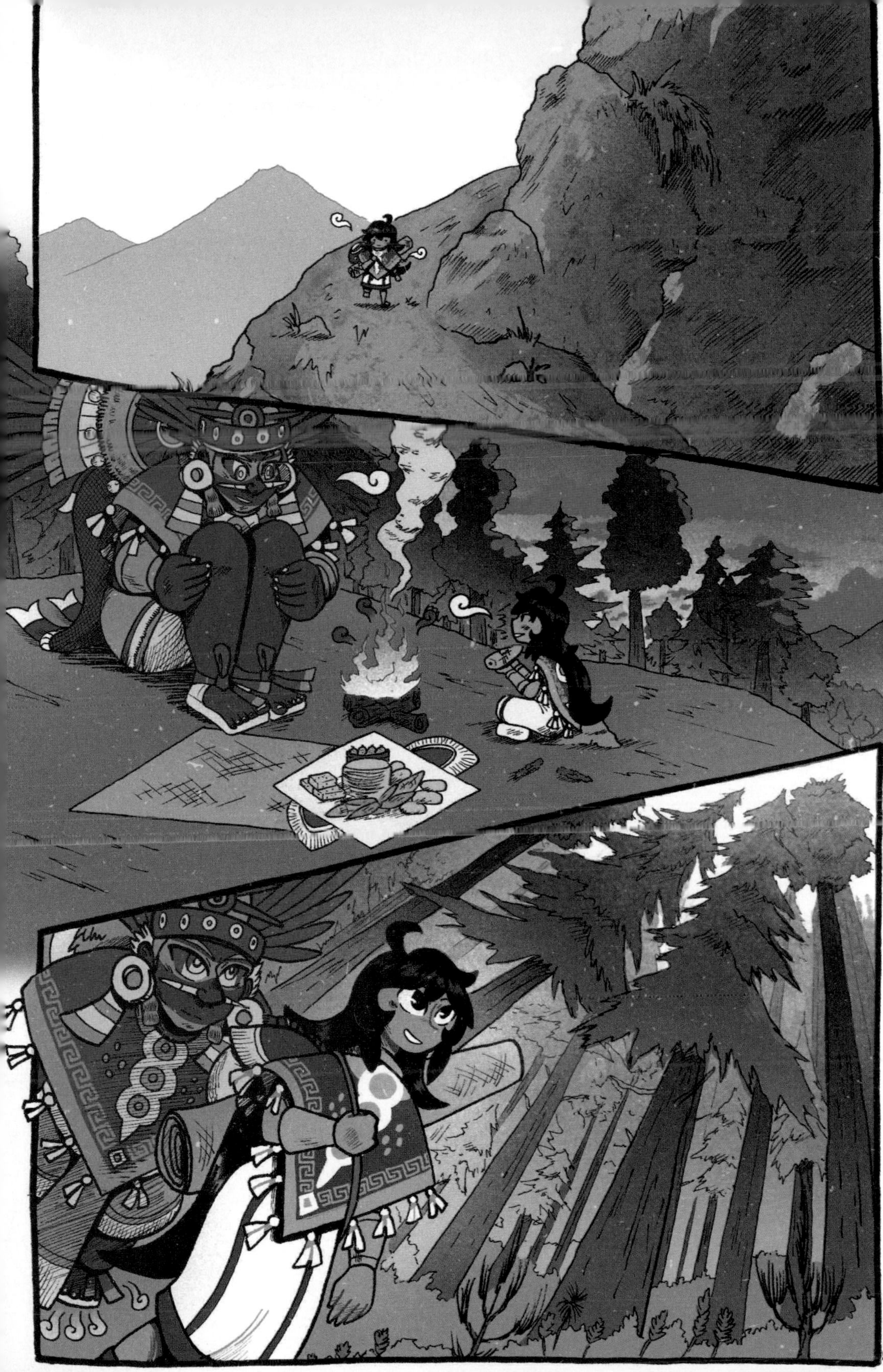

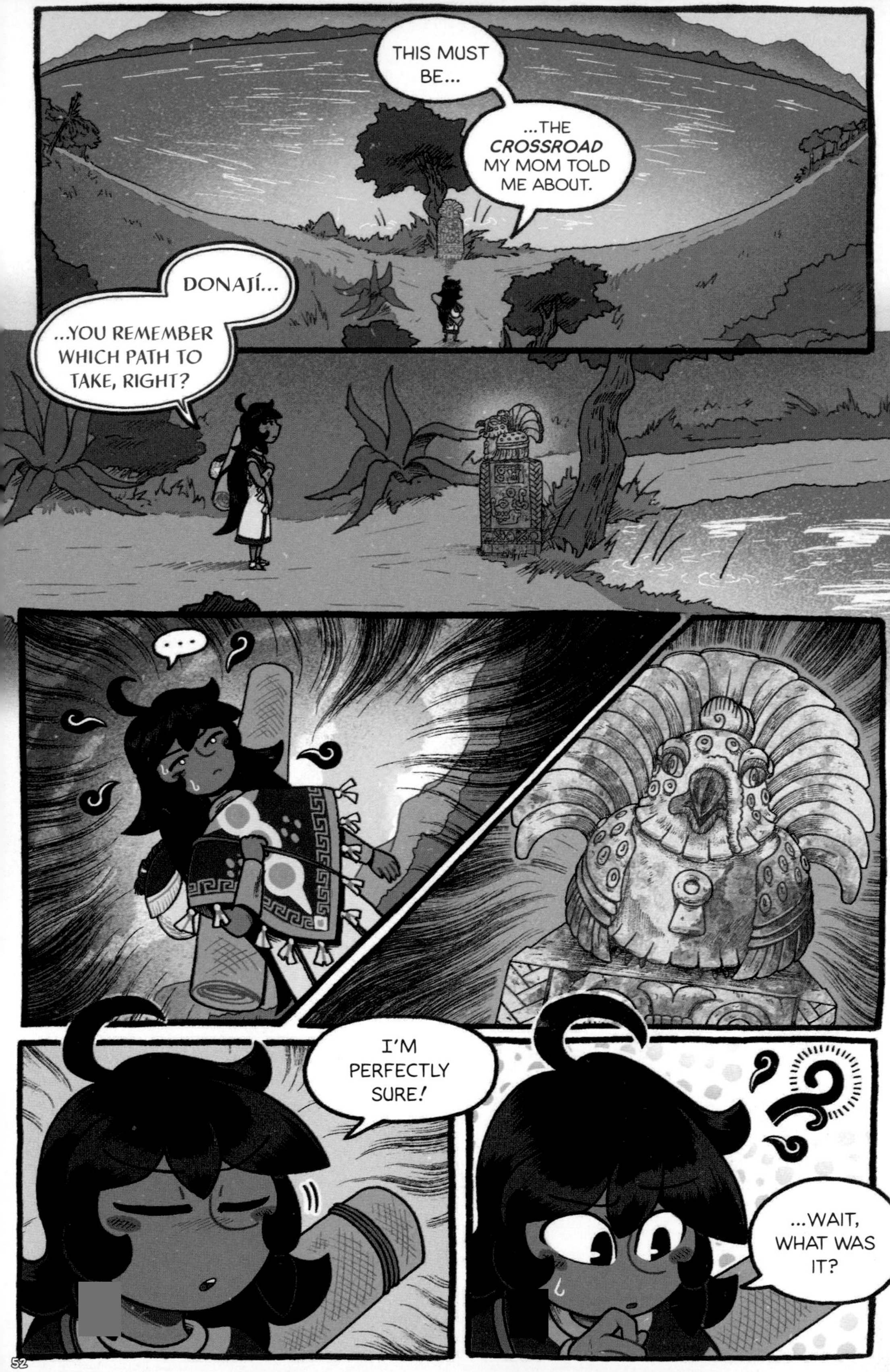
THIS MUST BE...
...THE *CROSSROAD* MY MOM TOLD ME ABOUT.
DONAJÍ...
...YOU REMEMBER WHICH PATH TO TAKE, RIGHT?
...
I'M PERFECTLY SURE!
...WAIT, WHAT WAS IT?

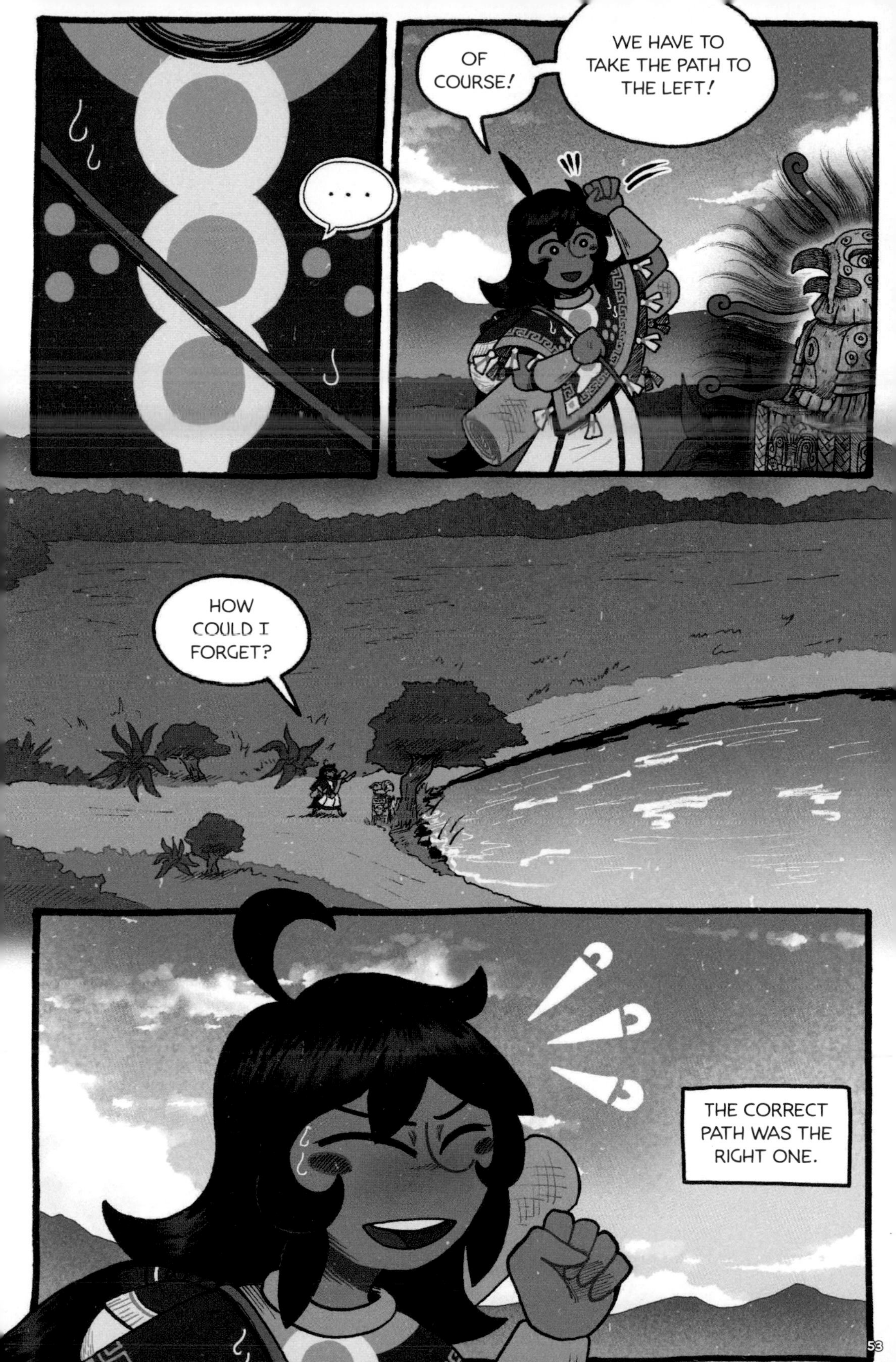
. . .
OF COURSE!
WE HAVE TO TAKE THE PATH TO THE LEFT!
HOW COULD I FORGET?
THE CORRECT PATH WAS THE RIGHT ONE.

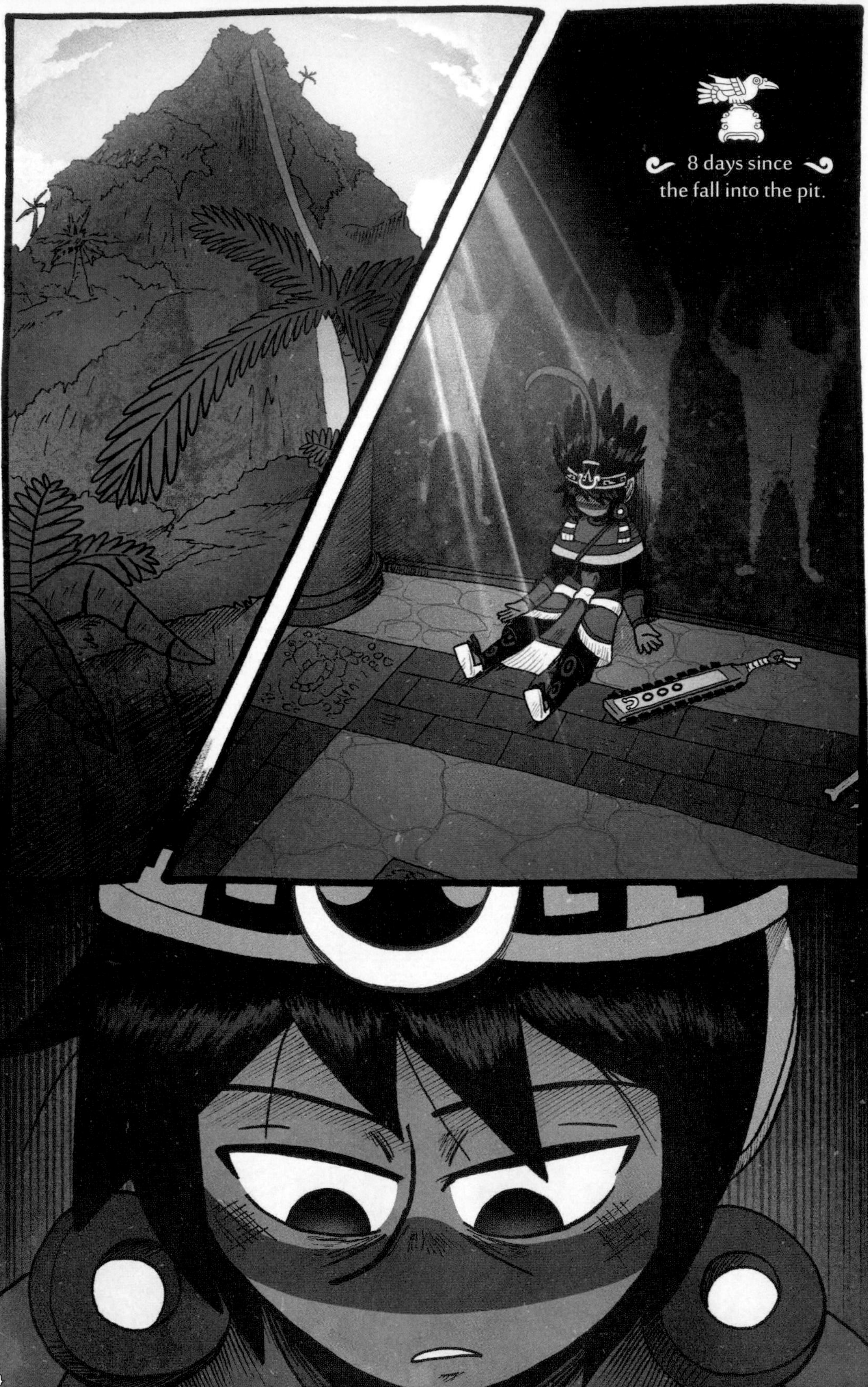
8 days since
the fall into the pit.

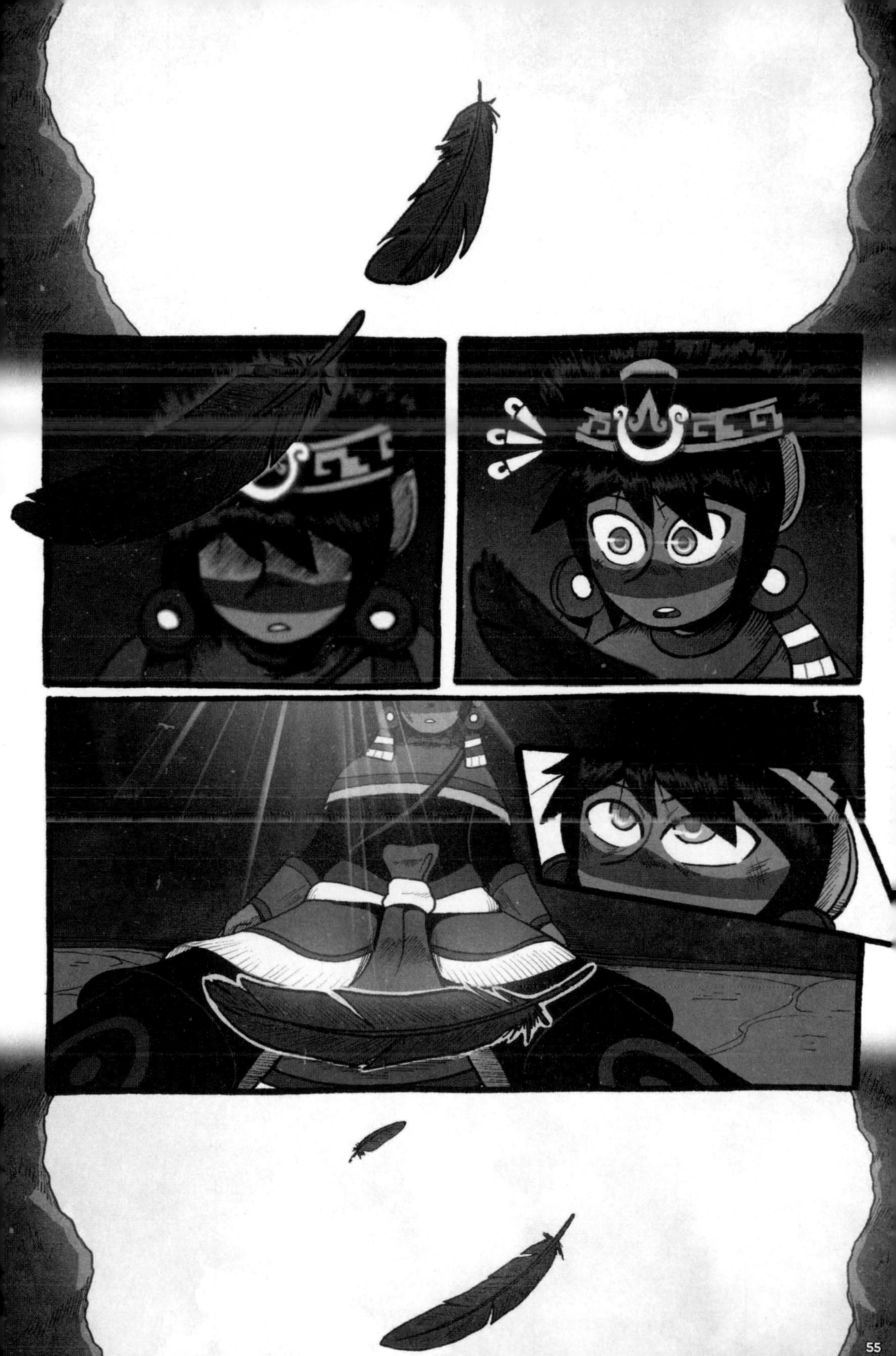

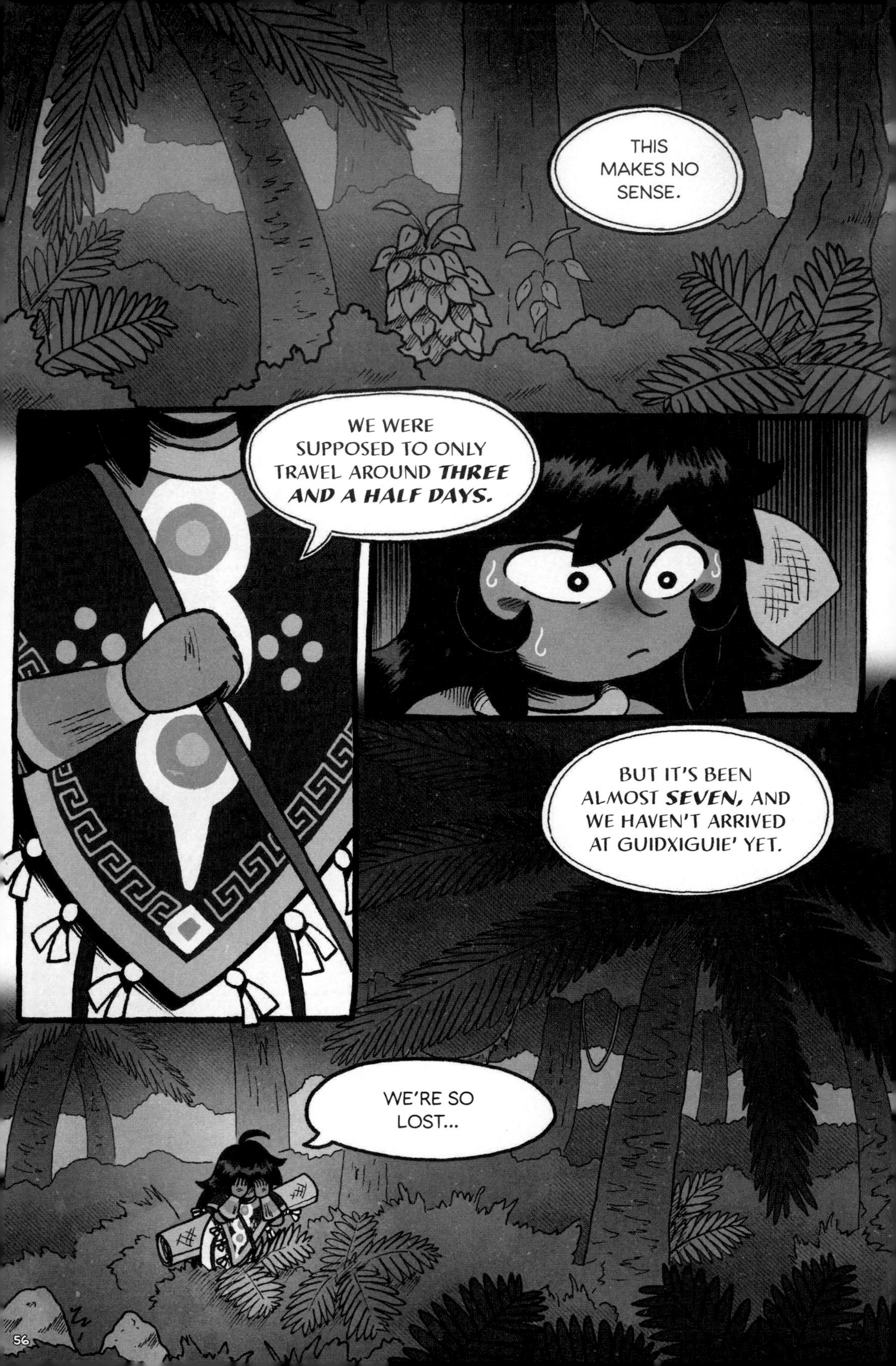
THIS MAKES NO SENSE.
WE WERE SUPPOSED TO ONLY TRAVEL AROUND THREE AND A HALF DAYS.
BUT IT'S BEEN ALMOST SEVEN, AND WE HAVEN'T ARRIVED AT GUIDXIGUIE' YET.
WE'RE SO LOST...

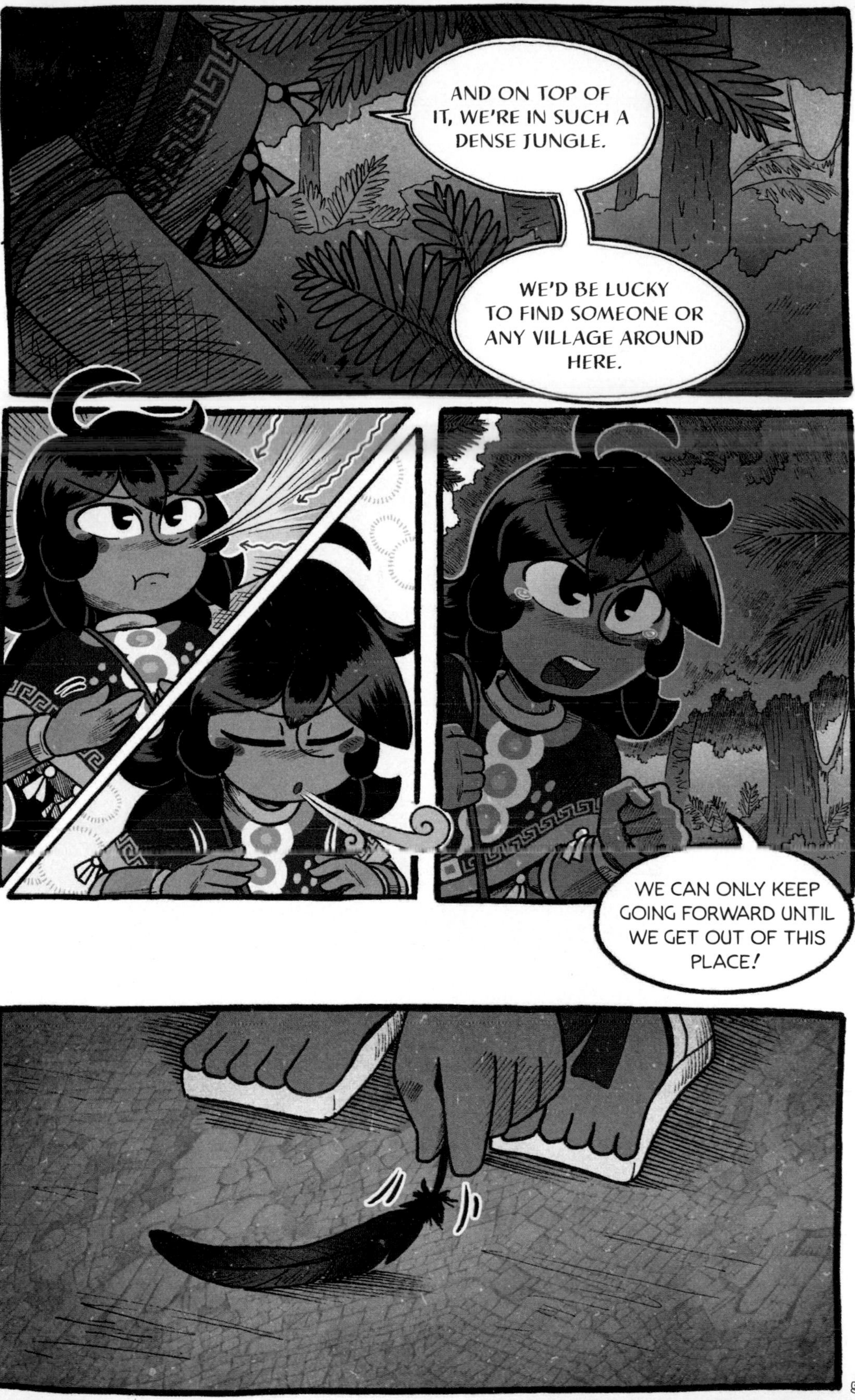
AND ON TOP OF IT, WE'RE IN SUCH A DENSE JUNGLE.
WE'D BE LUCKY TO FIND SOMEONE OR ANY VILLAGE AROUND HERE.
WE CAN ONLY KEEP GOING FORWARD UNTIL WE GET OUT OF THIS PLACE!

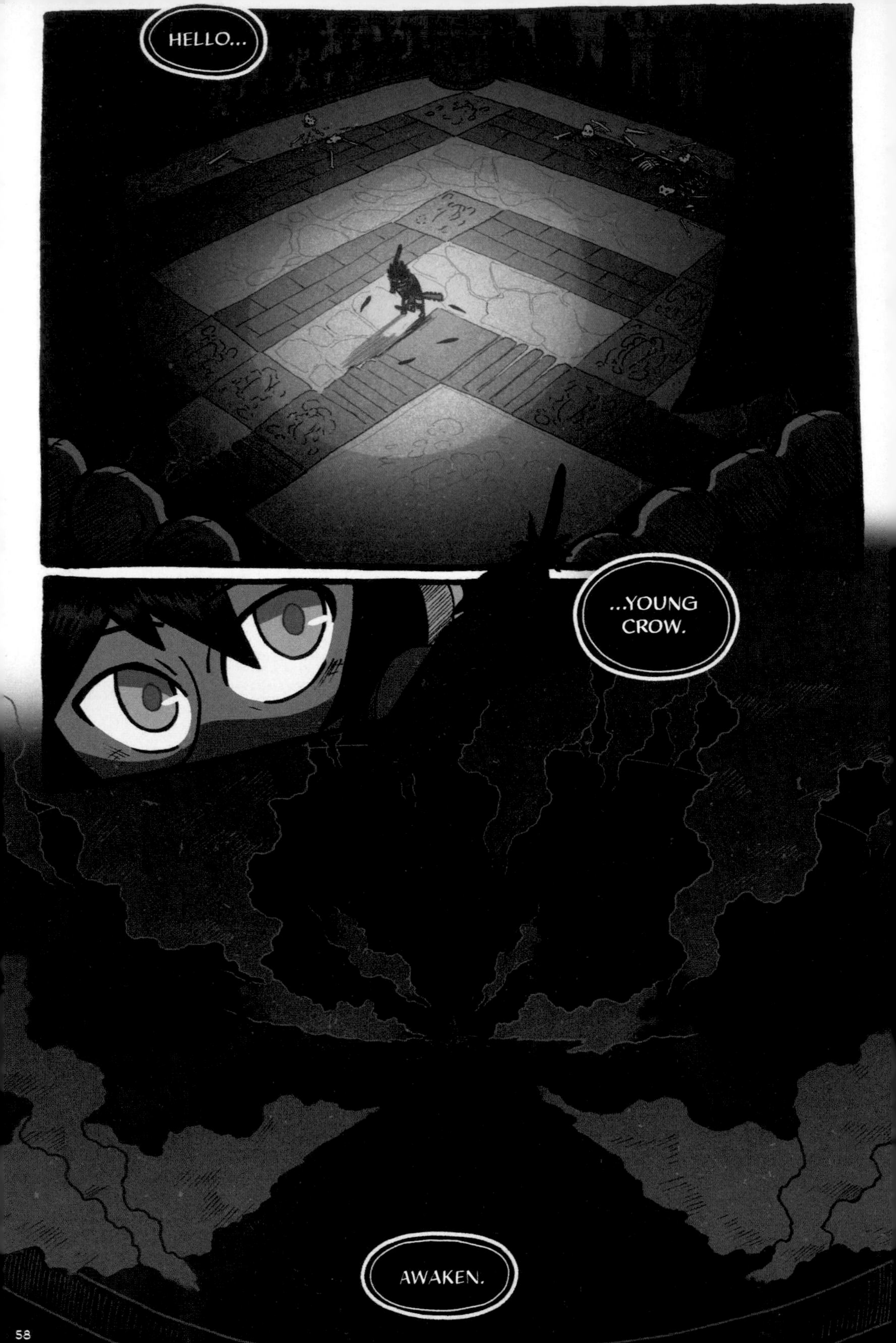
HELLO...
...YOUNG CROW.
AWAKEN.

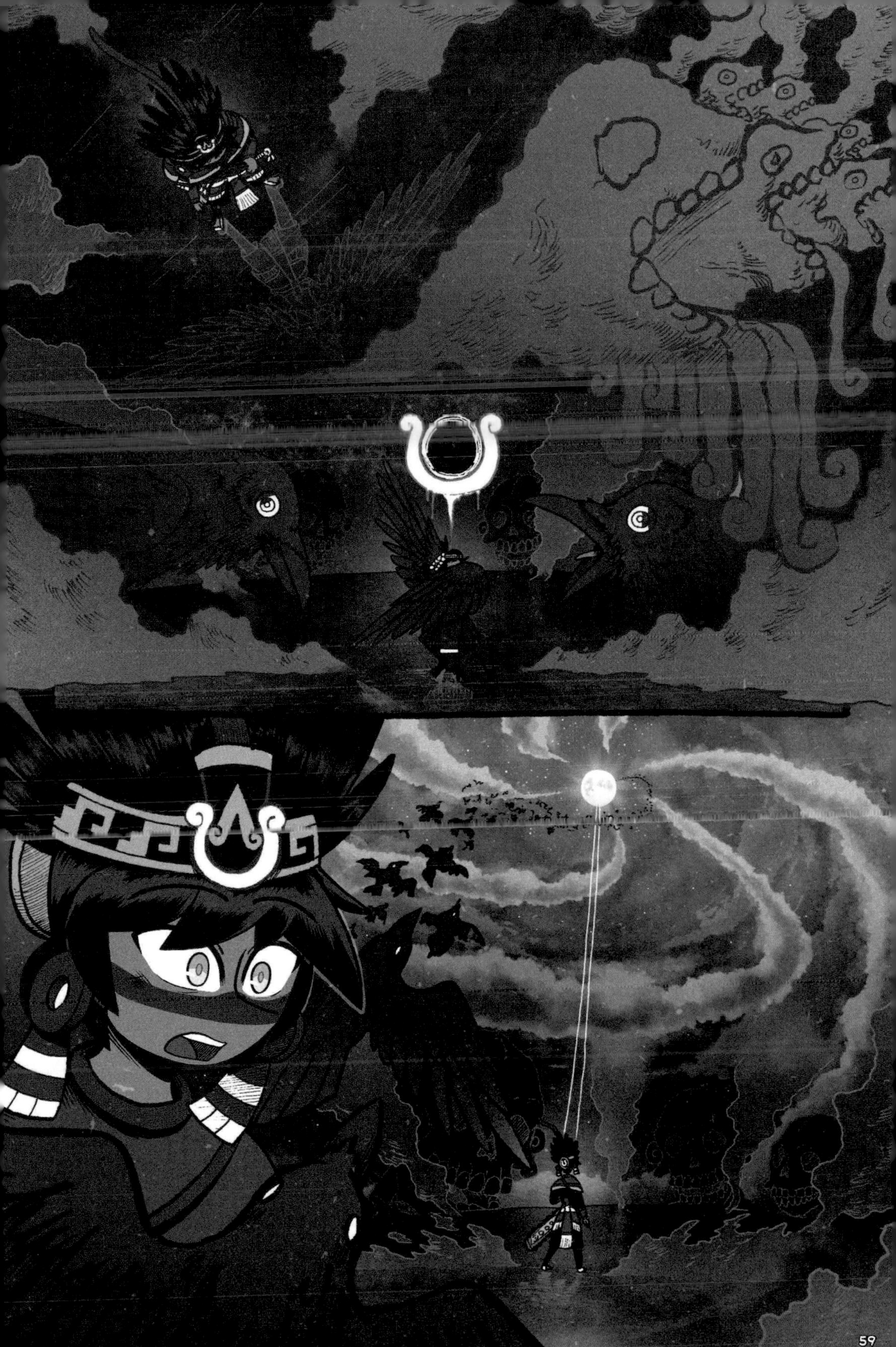

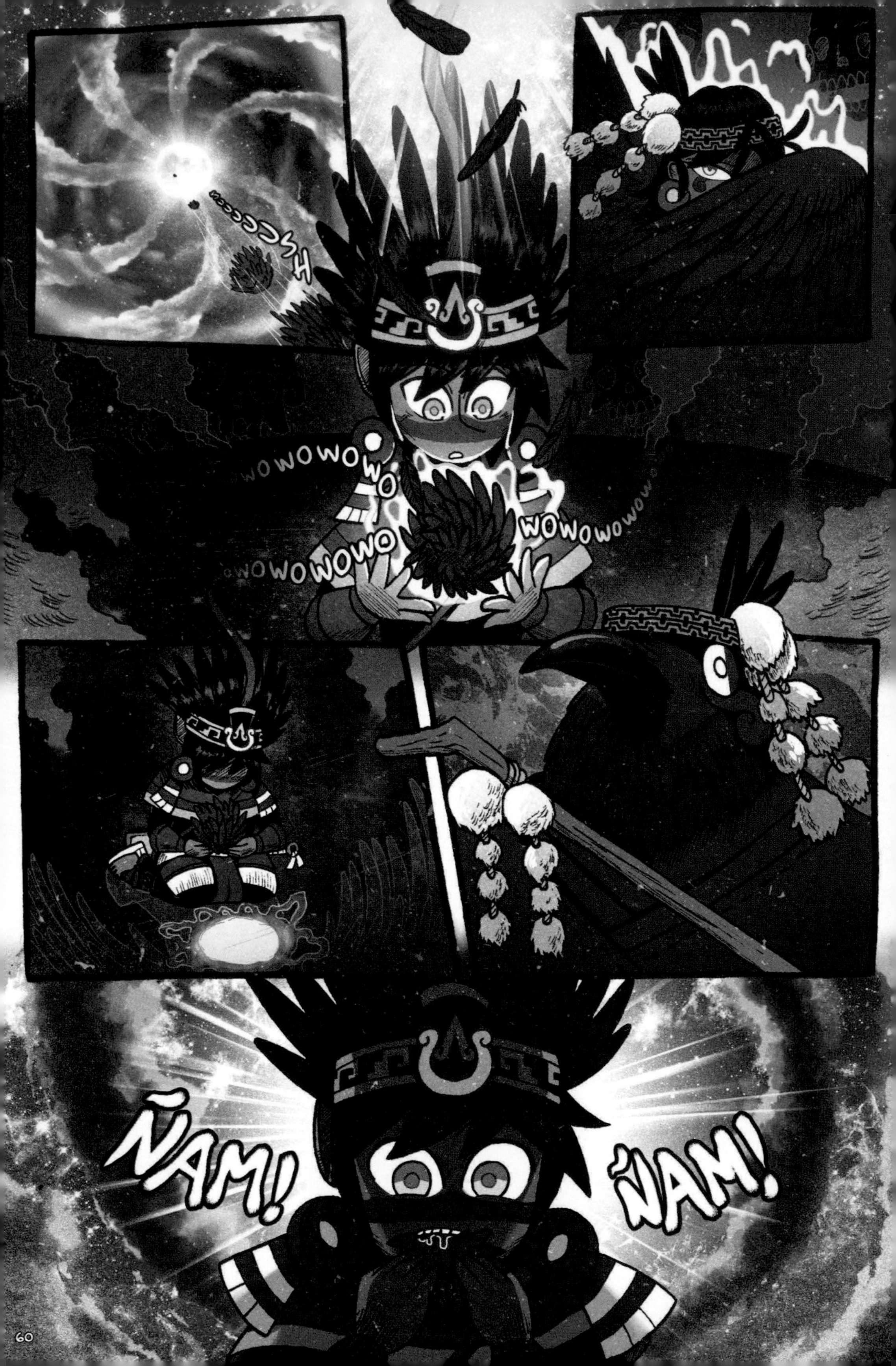
HSCCCCCCCC
WOWOWOWOWO
WOWOWOWOWO
WOWOWOWOWO
WOWOWOWO
ÑAM!
ÑAM!

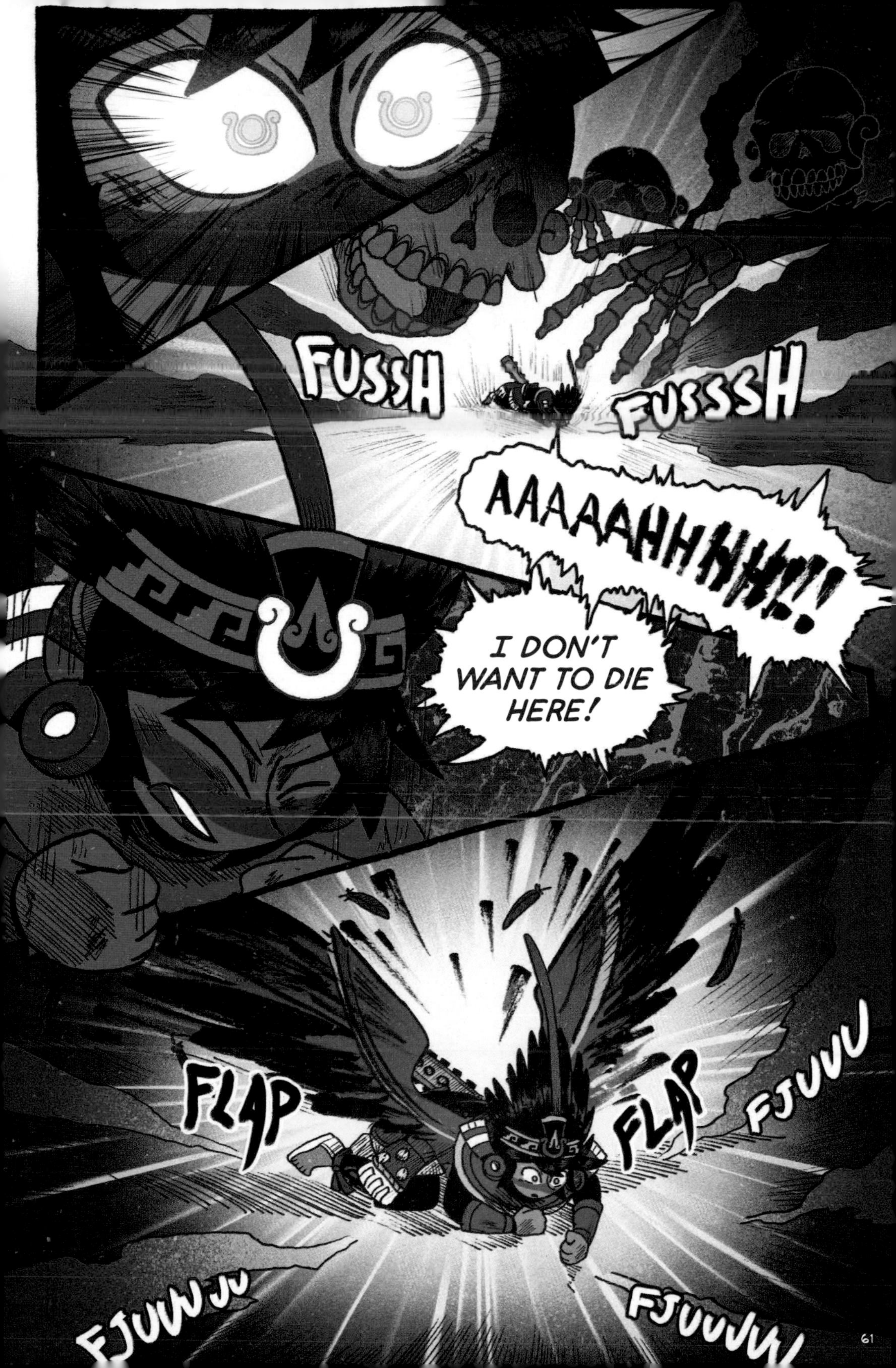
FUSSH
FUSSSH
AAAAAHHHHH!!!
I DON'T WANT TO DIE HERE!
FLAP
FLAP
FJUUU
FJUUUUU
FJUUUJU

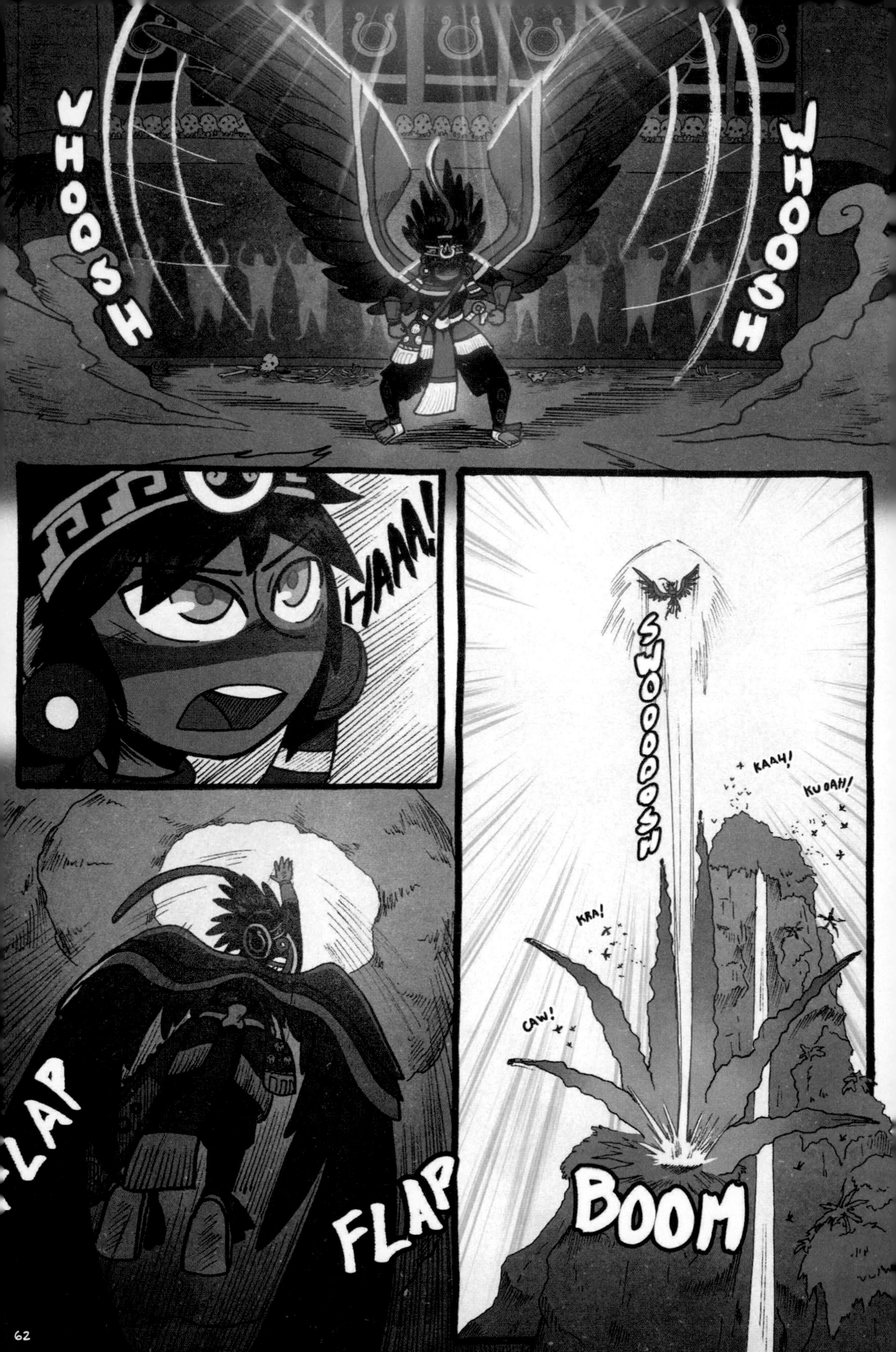
WHOOSH
WHOOSH
HAAA!
SWOOOOOOSH
KAAH!
KUOAH!
KRA!
CAW!
FLAP
FLAP
BOOM

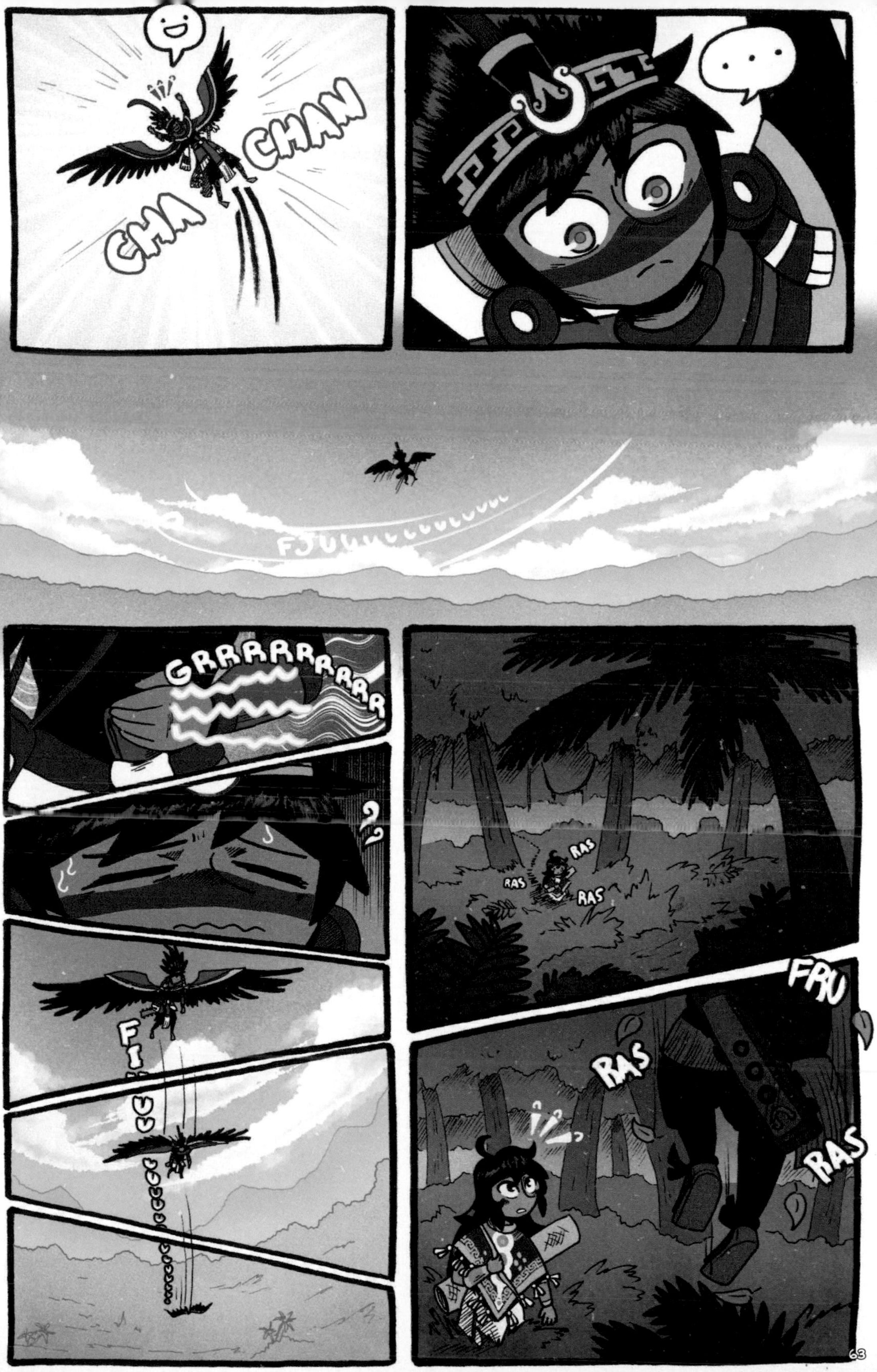
CHA
CHAN
...
FJUUUUUUUUUUUU
GRRRRRRRRRR
FIUUUUUUUUUUU
RAS
RAS
RAS
FRU
RAS
RAS

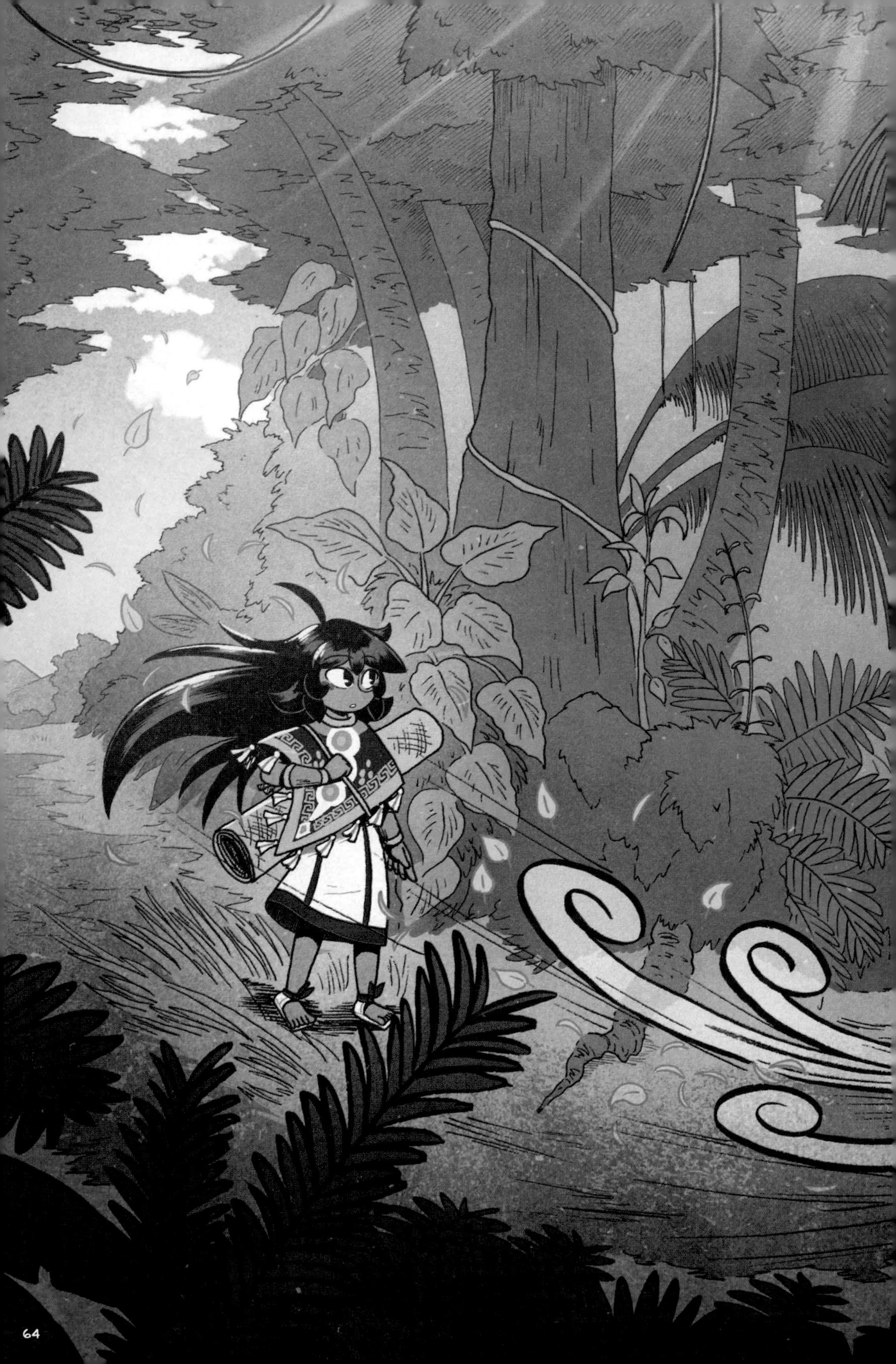

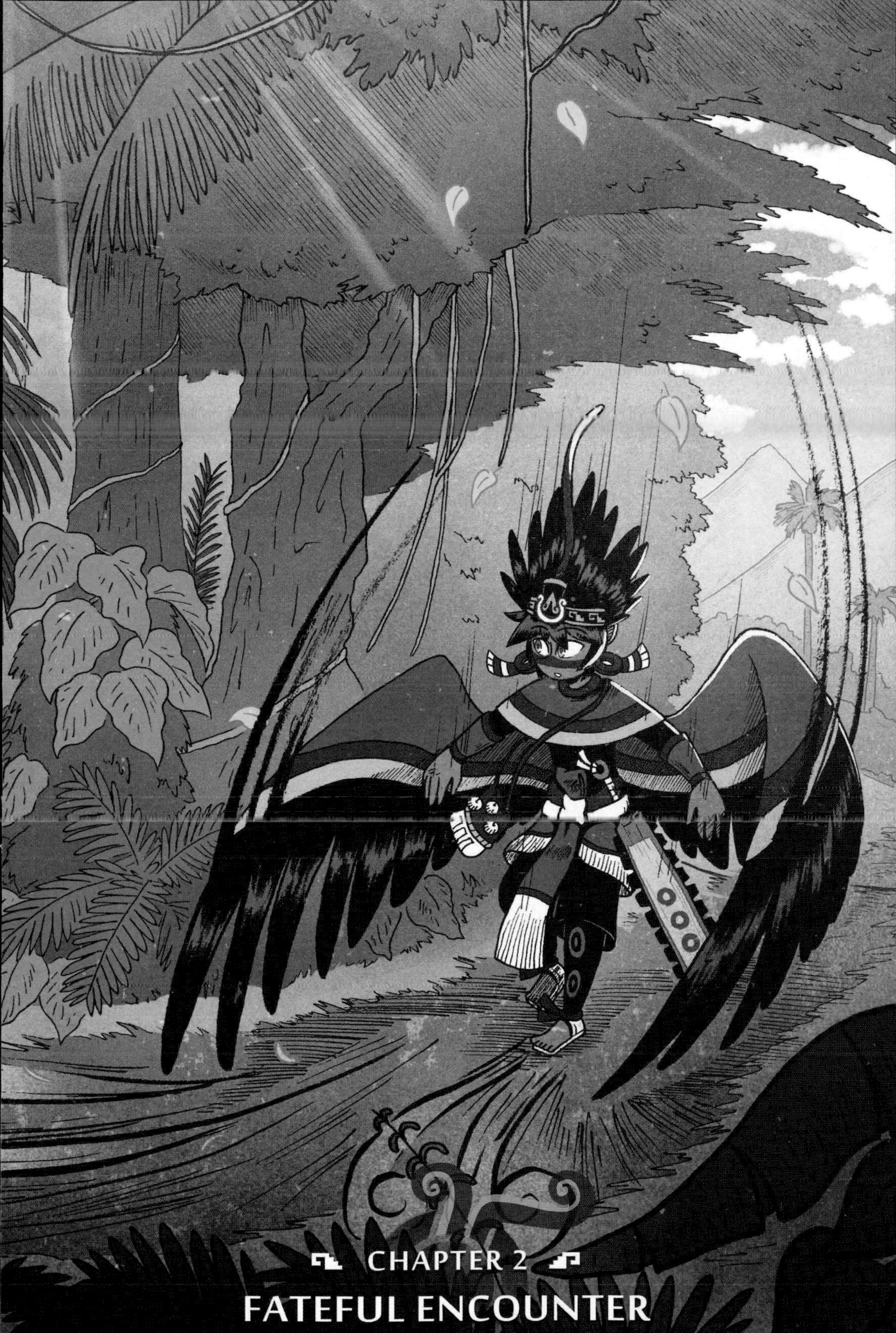

CHAPTER 2

FATEFUL ENCOUNTER

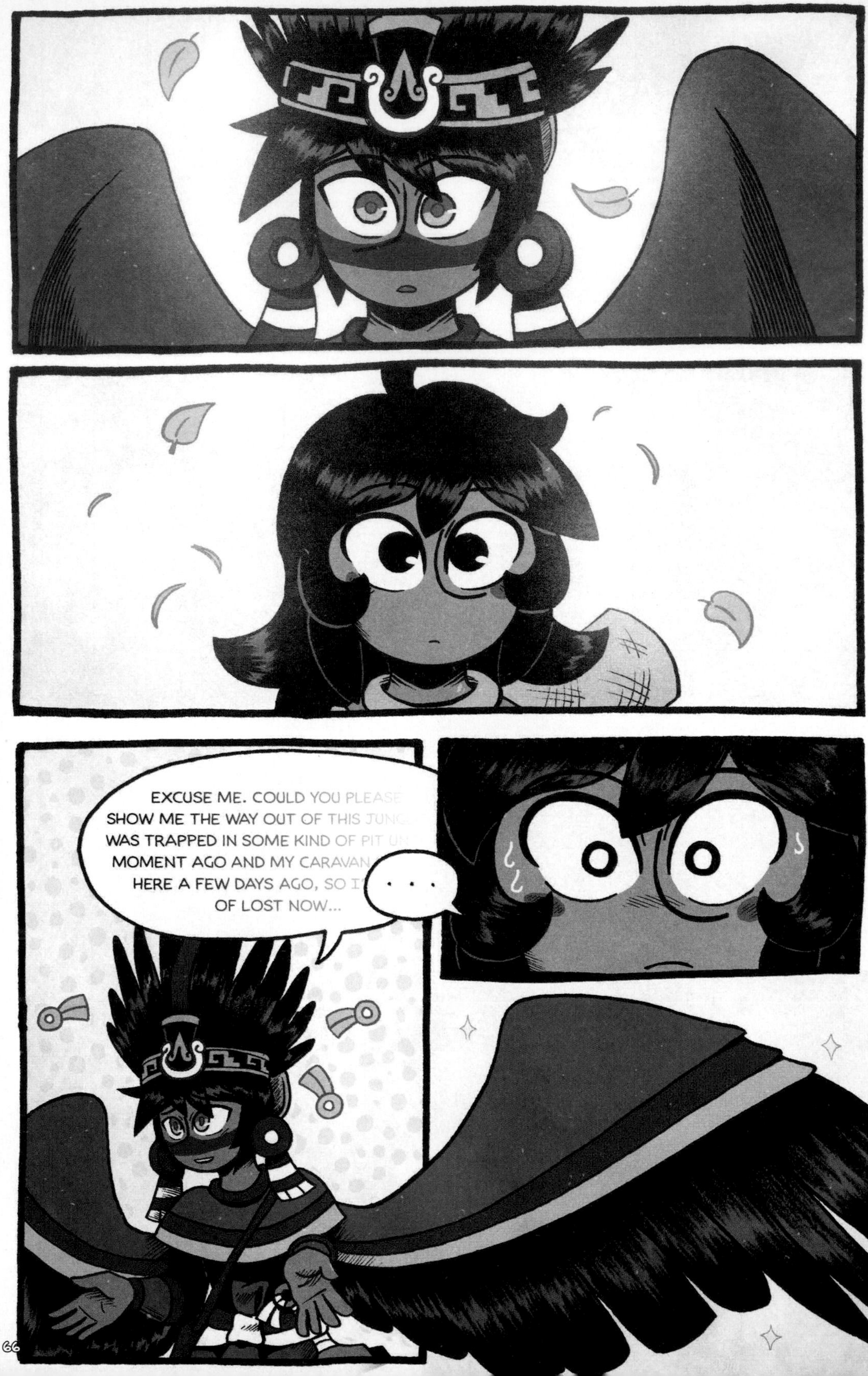
EXCUSE ME. COULD YOU PLEASE SHOW ME THE WAY OUT OF THIS JUNG WAS TRAPPED IN SOME KIND OF PIT UN MOMENT AGO AND MY CARAVAN HERE A FEW DAYS AGO, SO IT OF LOST NOW...
. . .

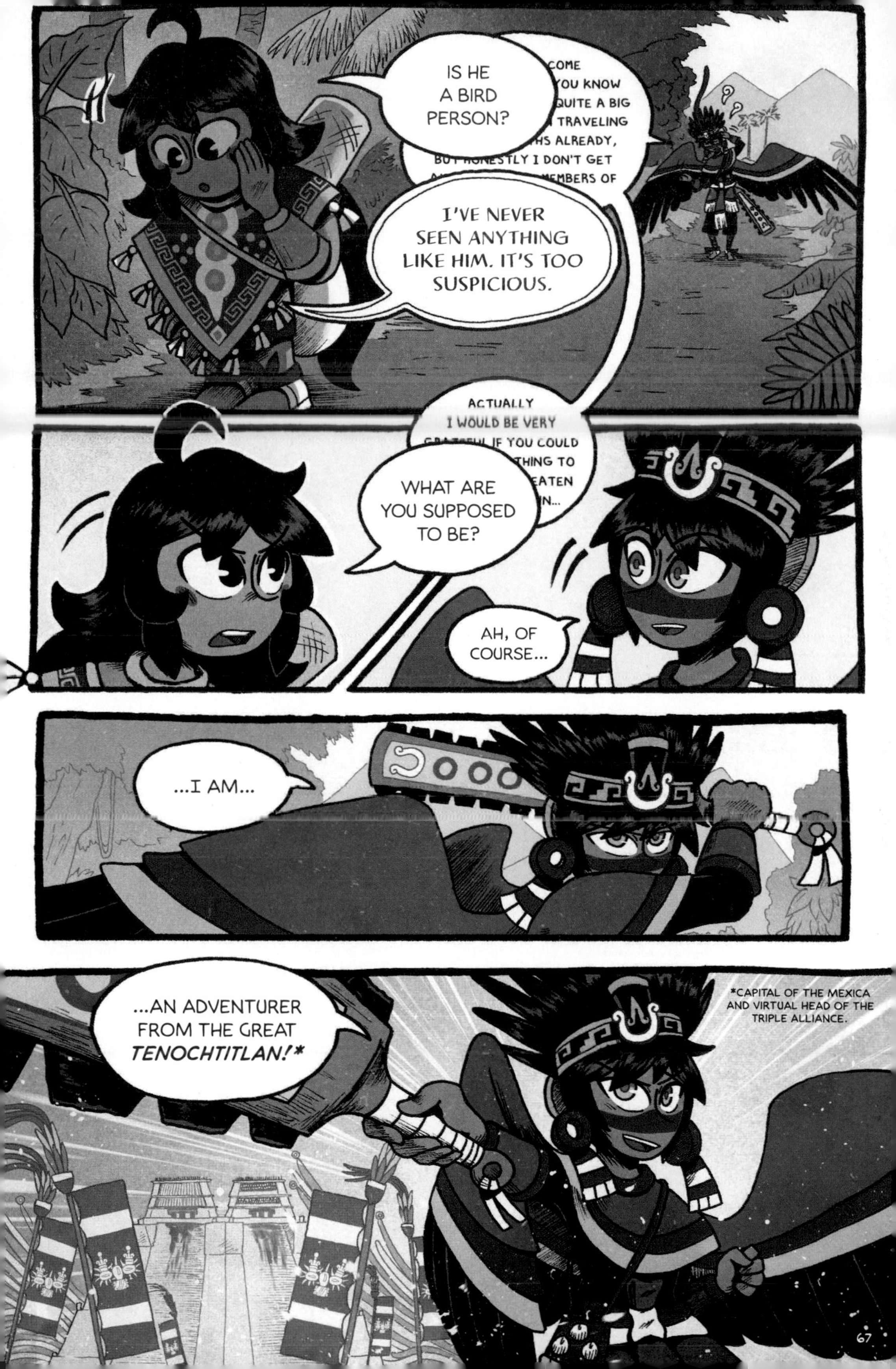
IS HE A BIRD PERSON?
I'VE NEVER SEEN ANYTHING LIKE HIM. IT'S TOO SUSPICIOUS.
ACTUALLY I WOULD BE VERY
WHAT ARE YOU SUPPOSED TO BE?
AH, OF COURSE...
...I AM...
...AN ADVENTURER FROM THE GREAT *TENOCHTITLAN!**
*CAPITAL OF THE MEXICA AND VIRTUAL HEAD OF THE TRIPLE ALLIANCE.

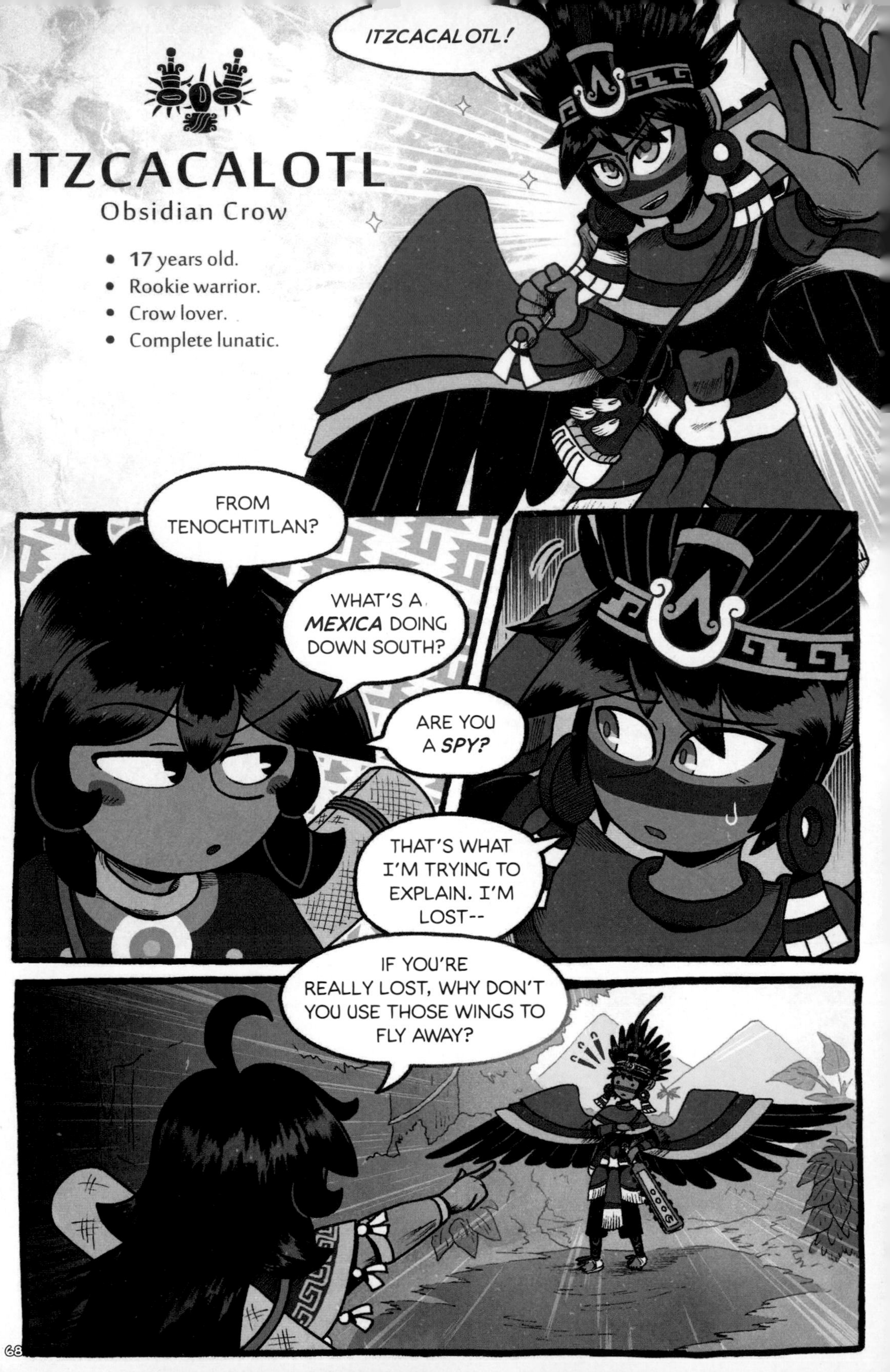
ITZCACALOTL
Obsidian Crow
• 17 years old.
• Rookie warrior.
• Crow lover.
• Complete lunatic.
ITZCACALOTL!
FROM TENOCHTITLAN?
WHAT'S A MEXICA DOING DOWN SOUTH?
ARE YOU A SPY?
THAT'S WHAT I'M TRYING TO EXPLAIN. I'M LOST--
IF YOU'RE REALLY LOST, WHY DON'T YOU USE THOSE WINGS TO FLY AWAY?

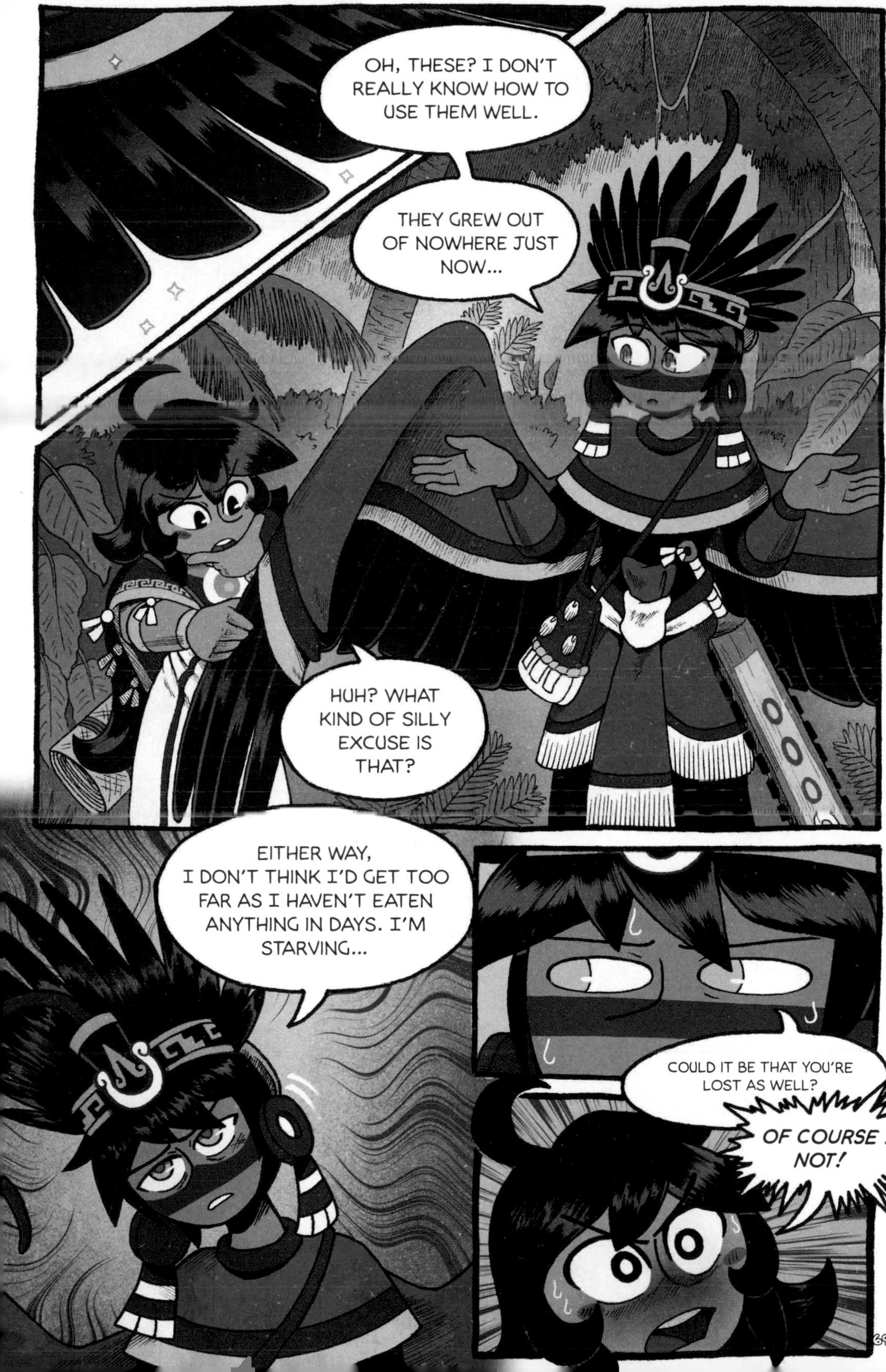
OH, THESE? I DON'T REALLY KNOW HOW TO USE THEM WELL.
THEY GREW OUT OF NOWHERE JUST NOW...
HUH? WHAT KIND OF SILLY EXCUSE IS THAT?
EITHER WAY, I DON'T THINK I'D GET TOO FAR AS I HAVEN'T EATEN ANYTHING IN DAYS. I'M STARVING...
COULD IT BE THAT YOU'RE LOST AS WELL?
OF COURSE NOT!

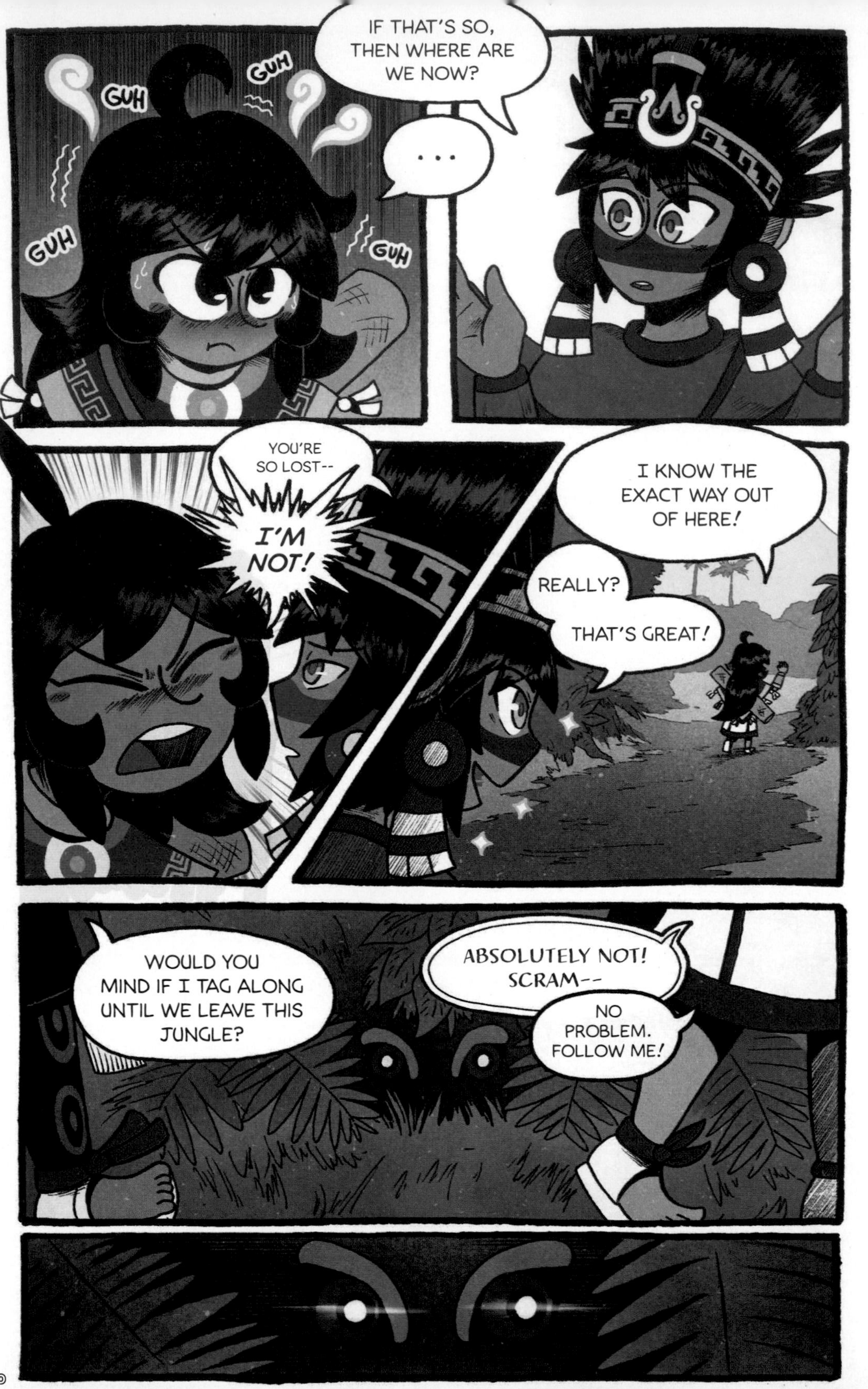
GUH
GUH
GUH
GUH
IF THAT'S SO, THEN WHERE ARE WE NOW?
. . .
YOU'RE SO LOST--
I'M NOT!
I KNOW THE EXACT WAY OUT OF HERE!
REALLY?
THAT'S GREAT!
WOULD YOU MIND IF I TAG ALONG UNTIL WE LEAVE THIS JUNGLE?
ABSOLUTELY NOT! SCRAM--
NO PROBLEM. FOLLOW ME!

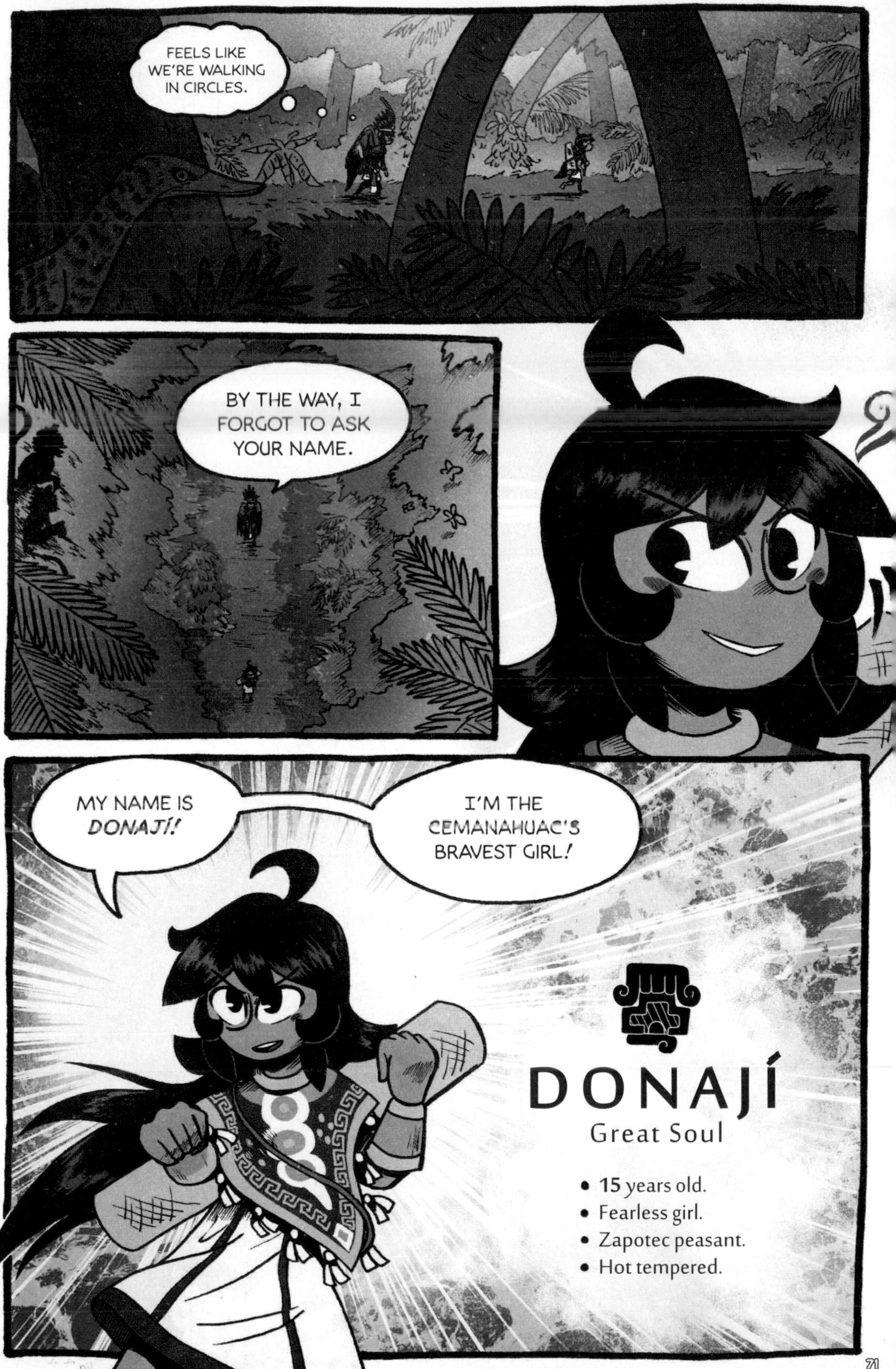
FEELS LIKE WE'RE WALKING IN CIRCLES.
BY THE WAY, I FORGOT TO ASK YOUR NAME.
MY NAME IS DONAJÍ!
I'M THE CEMANAHUAC'S BRAVEST GIRL!
DONAJÍ
Great Soul
• 15 years old.
• Fearless girl.
• Zapotec peasant.
• Hot tempered.

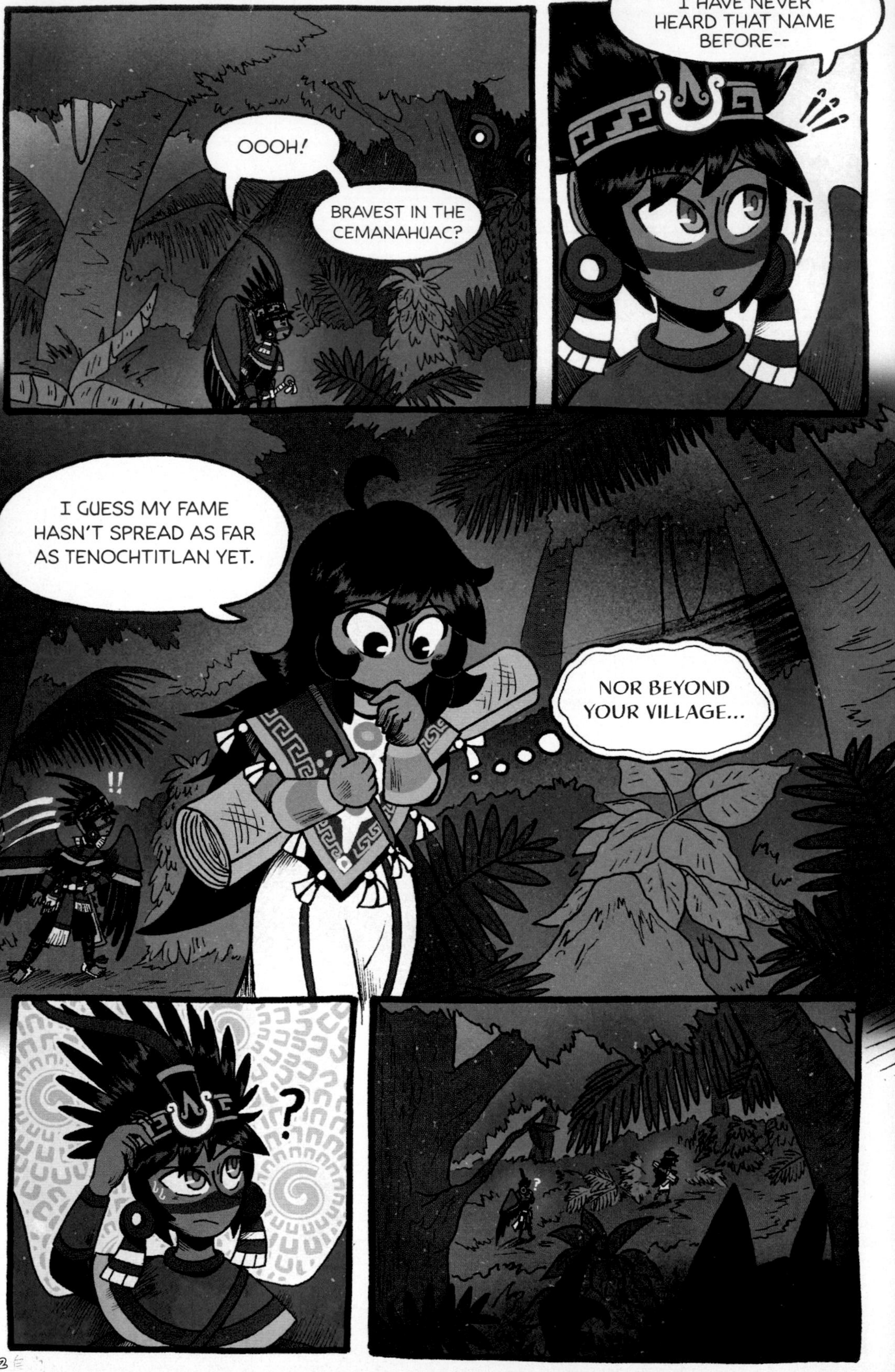
OOOH!
BRAVEST IN THE CEMANAHUAC?
I HAVE NEVER HEARD THAT NAME BEFORE--
I GUESS MY FAME HASN'T SPREAD AS FAR AS TENOCHTITLAN YET.
NOR BEYOND YOUR VILLAGE...
!!
?

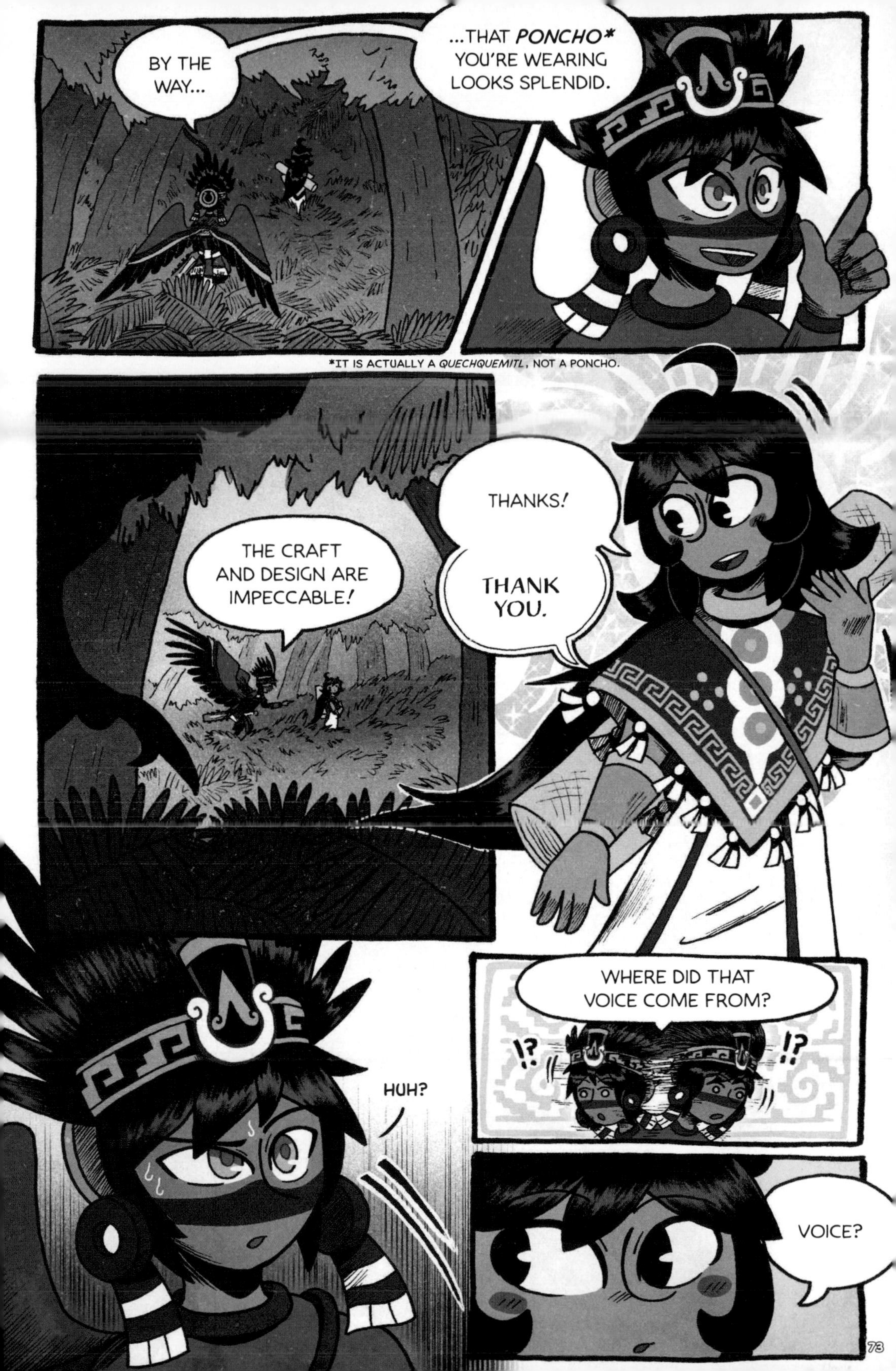
BY THE WAY...
...THAT *PONCHO** YOU'RE WEARING LOOKS SPLENDID.
*IT IS ACTUALLY A *QUECHQUEMITL*, NOT A PONCHO.
THE CRAFT AND DESIGN ARE IMPECCABLE!
THANKS!
THANK YOU.
HUH?
WHERE DID THAT VOICE COME FROM?
!?
!?
VOICE?

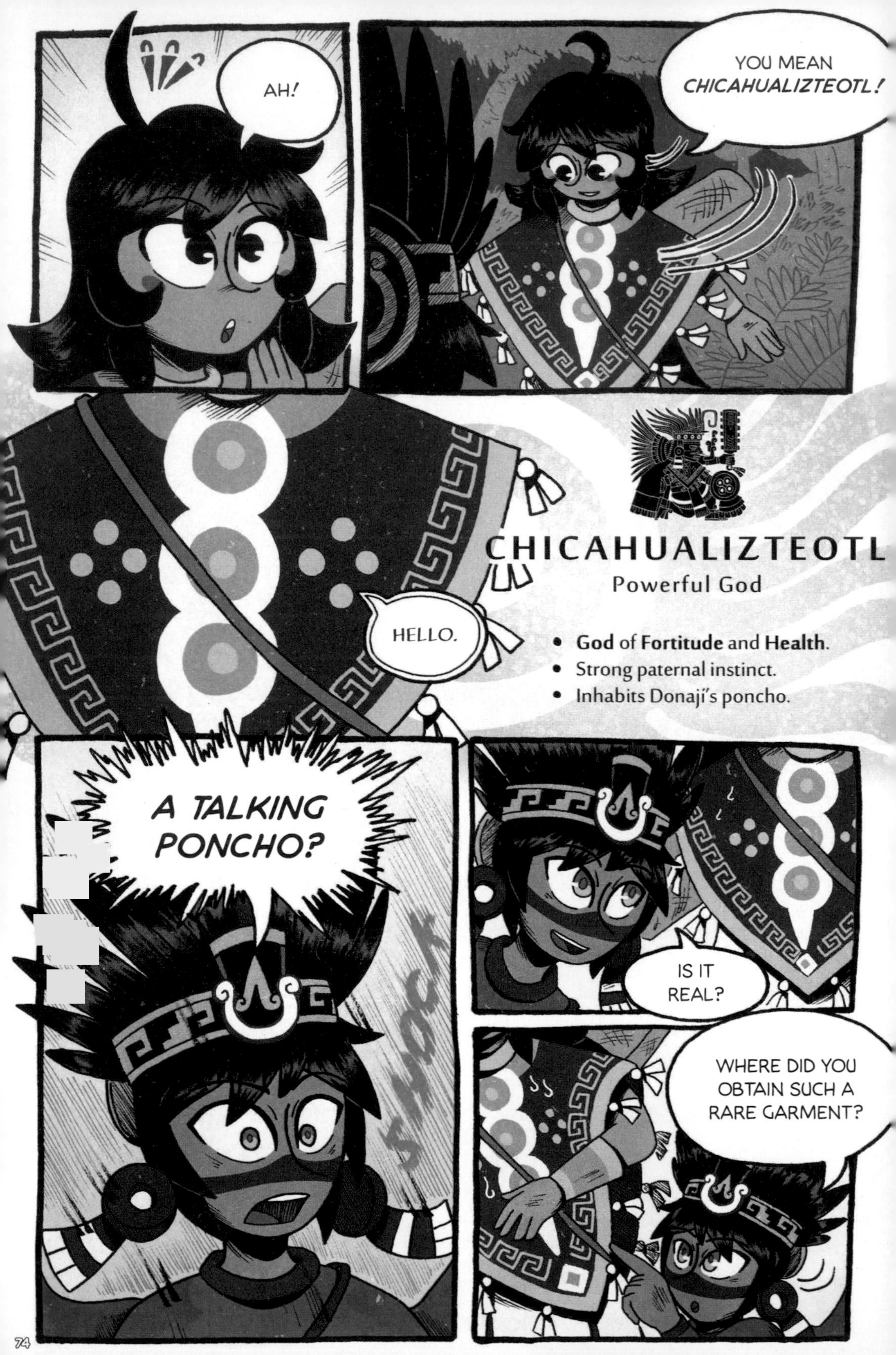
AH!
YOU MEAN CHICAHUALIZTEOTL!
CHICAHUALIZTEOTL
Powerful God
HELLO.
• God of Fortitude and Health.
• Strong paternal instinct.
• Inhabits Donají's poncho.
A TALKING PONCHO?
SHOCK
IS IT REAL?
WHERE DID YOU OBTAIN SUCH A RARE GARMENT?

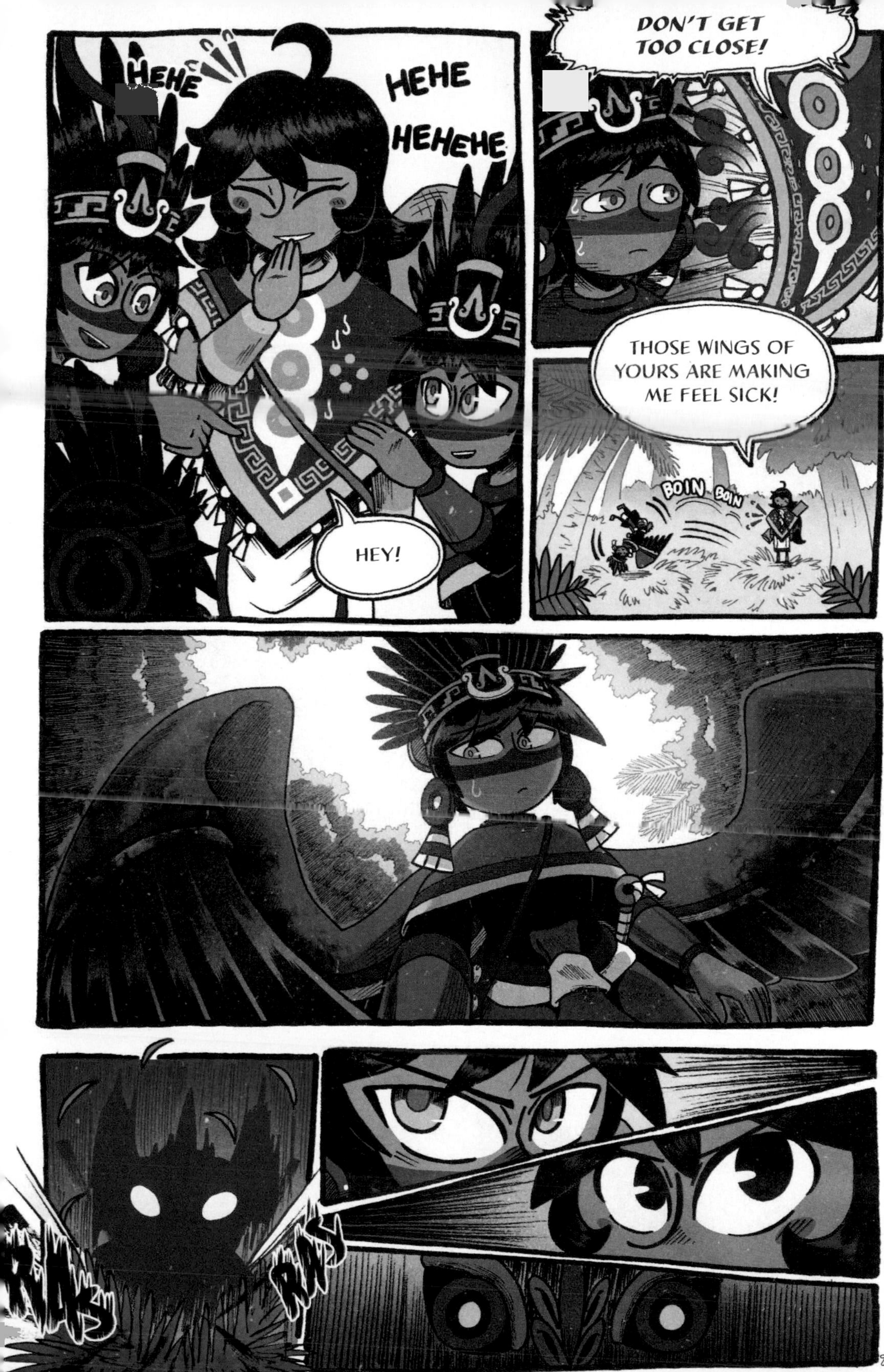
HEHE
HEHE
HEHEHE
HEY!
DON'T GET TOO CLOSE!
THOSE WINGS OF YOURS ARE MAKING ME FEEL SICK!
BOIN BOIN

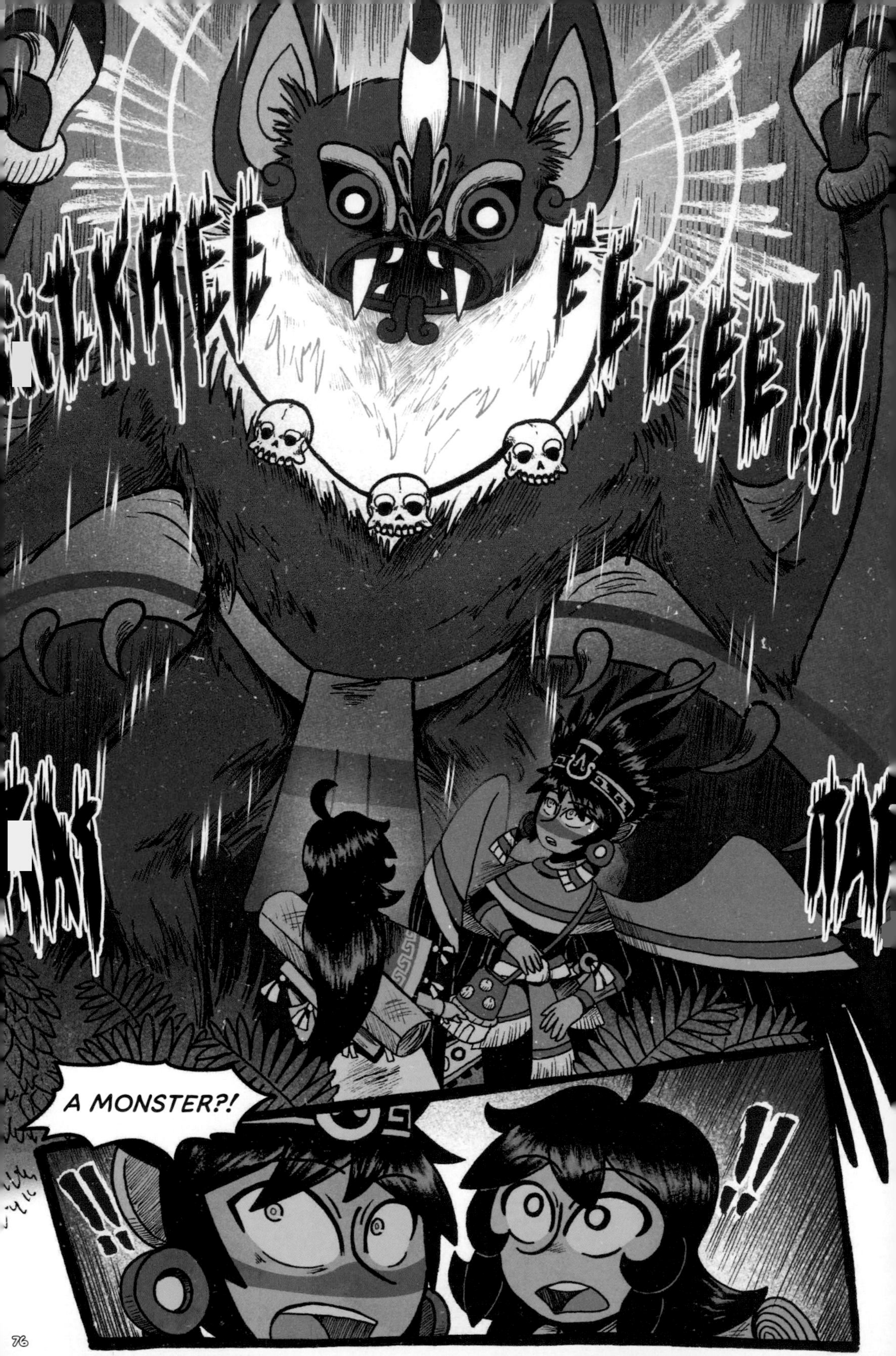
A MONSTER?!
!!
!!

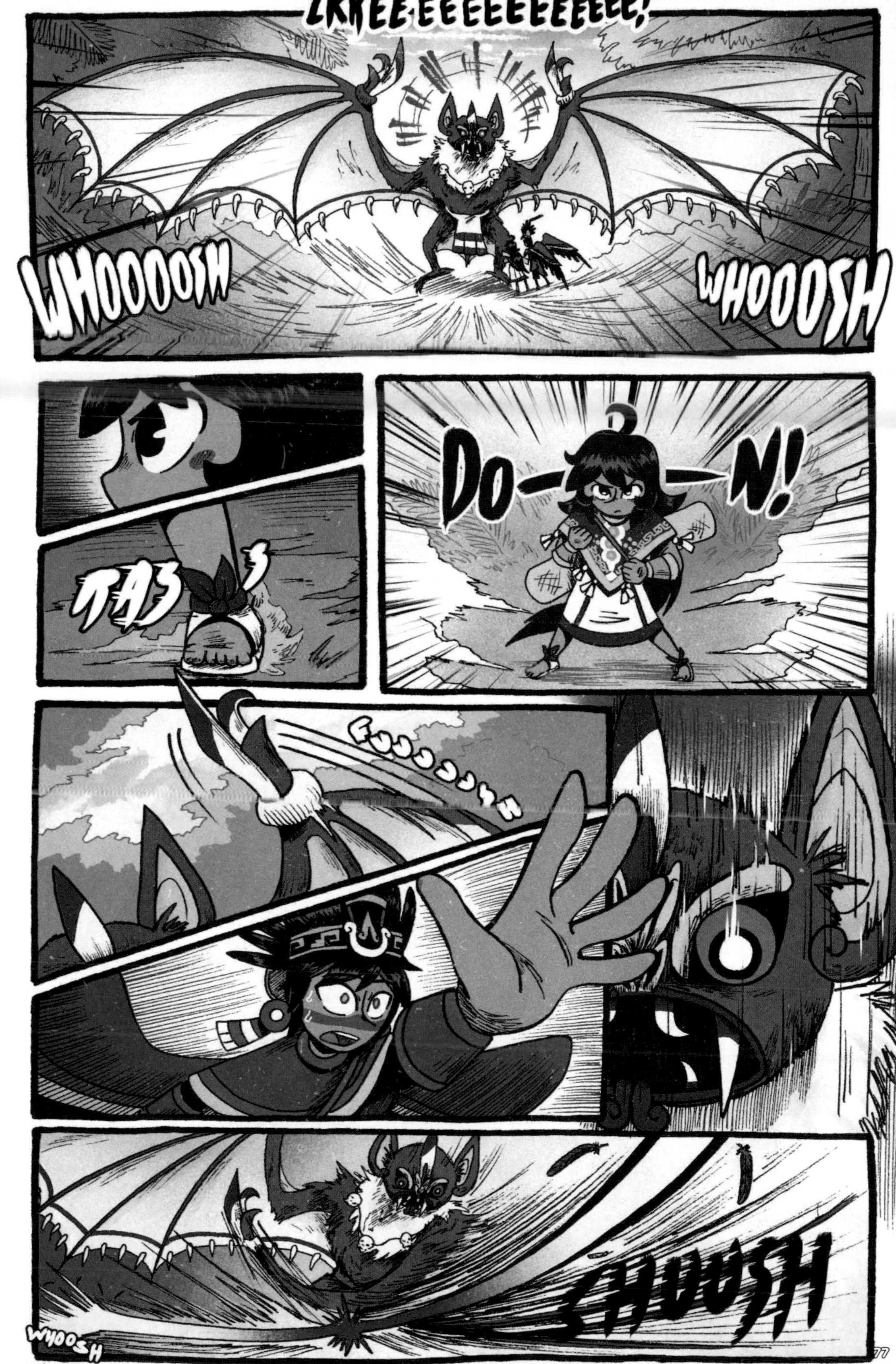
ZKREE-EEEEEEEEEEE!
WHOOOOSH
WHOOOSH
TAS
DO—N!
FUUUUUSH
SHUUSH
WHOOSH

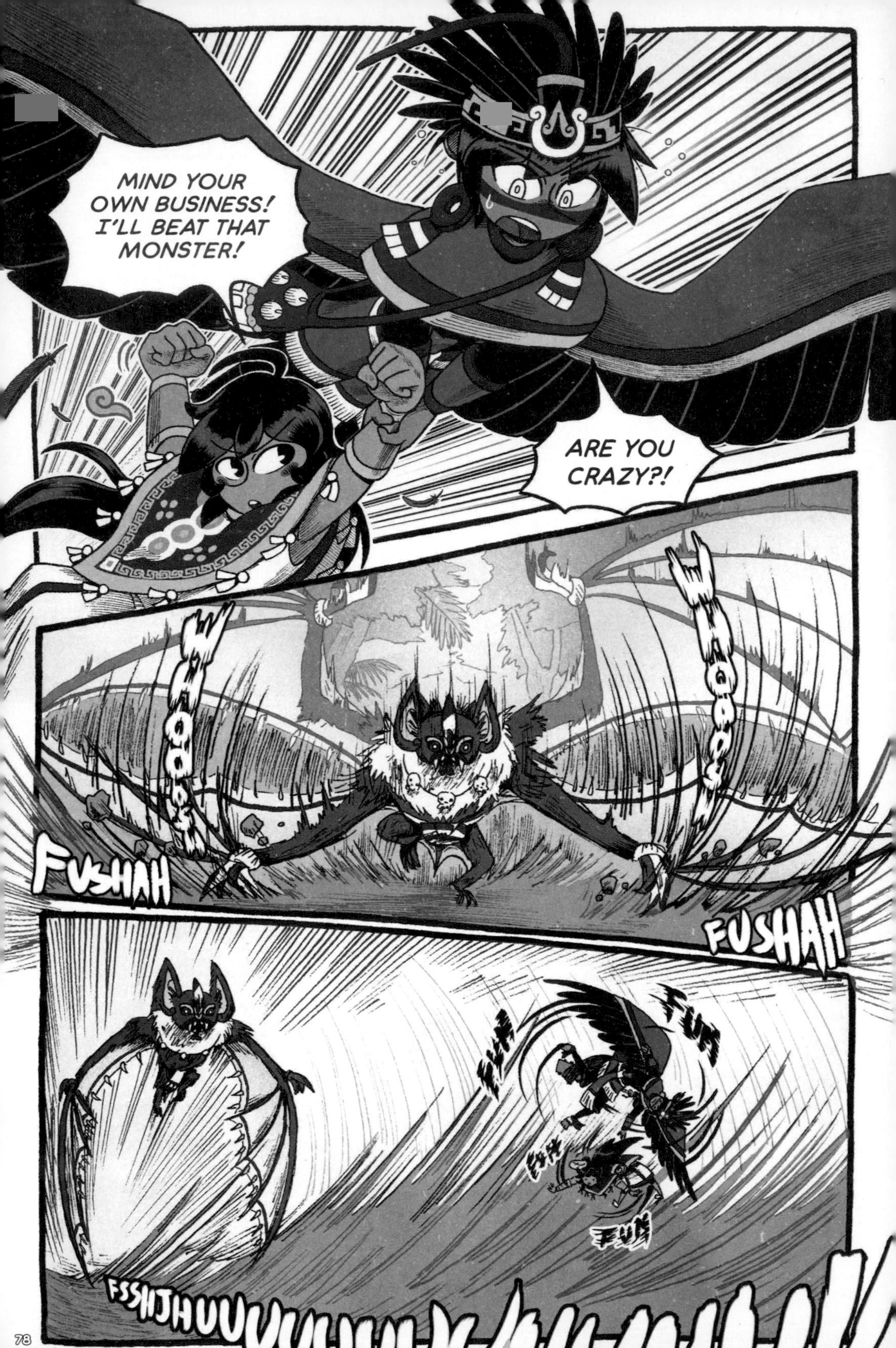
MIND YOUR OWN BUSINESS! I'LL BEAT THAT MONSTER!
ARE YOU CRAZY?!
FUSHAH
FUSHAH
FSSHJHUUUUUUUU

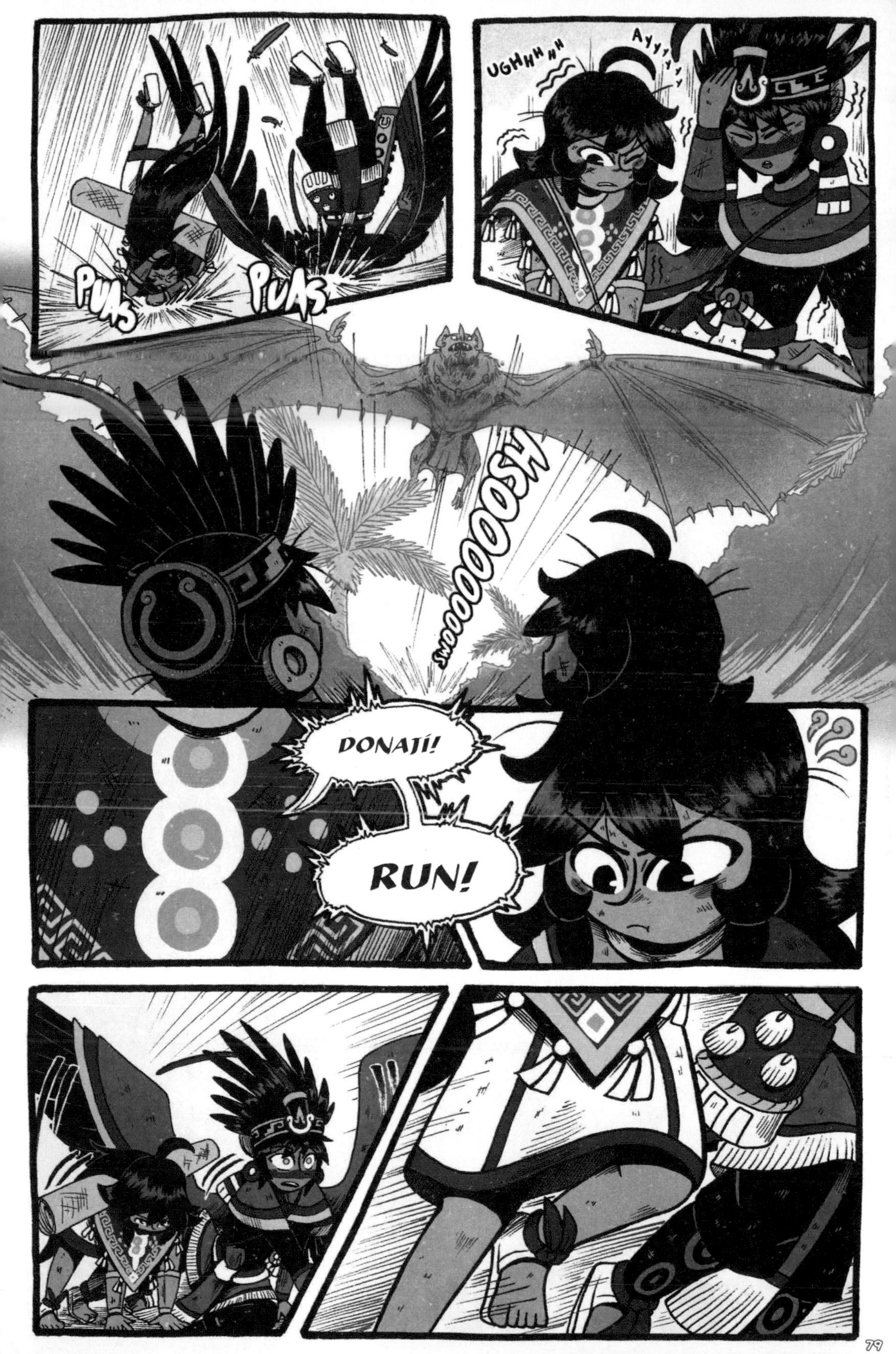
PUAS
PUAS
UGHHHHH
Ayyyyyy
SHOOOOOOOOOOOOWS
DONAJÍ!
RUN!

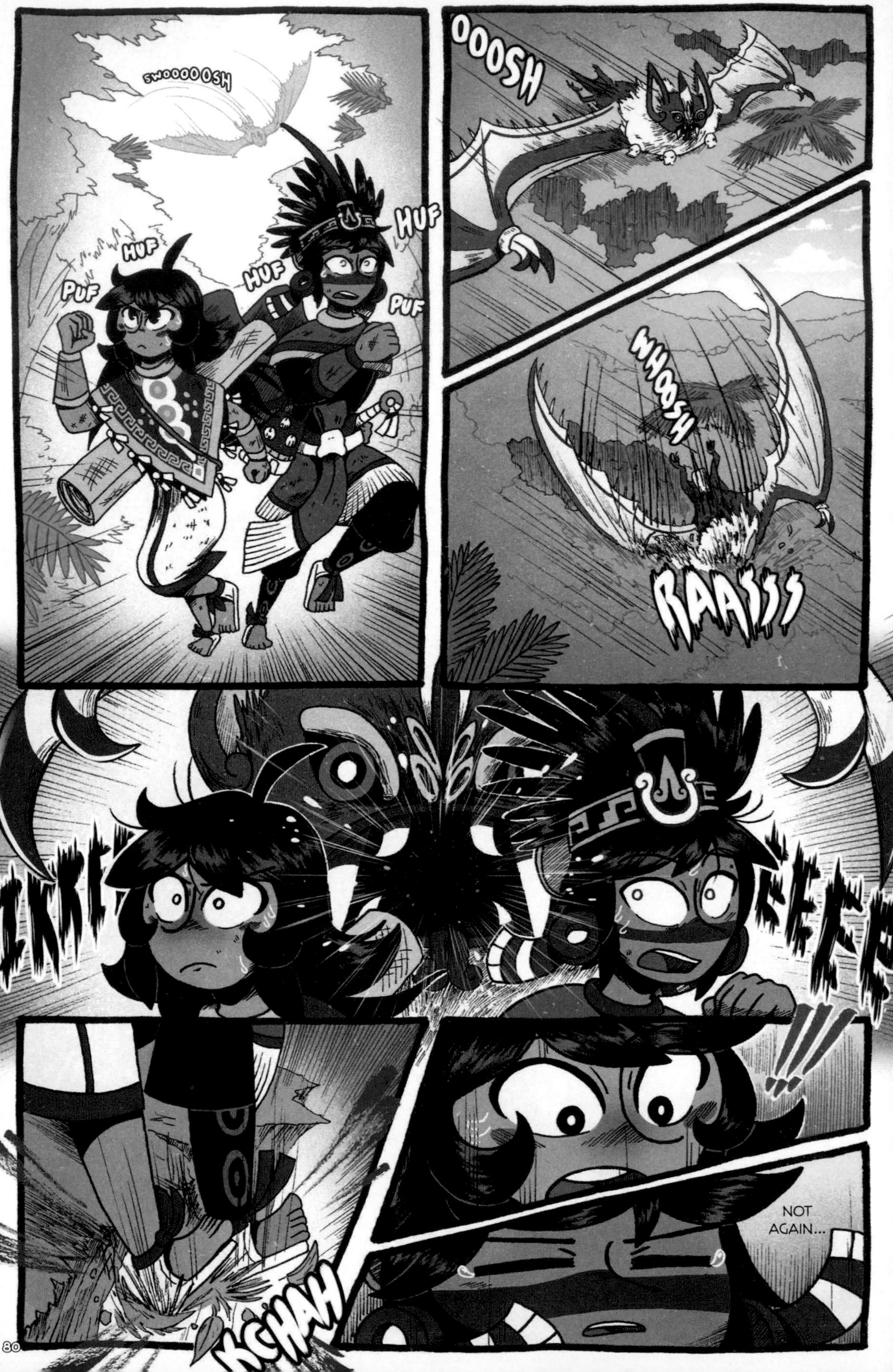
SWOOOOOOSH
HUF
PUF
HUF
HUF
PUF
OOOSH
WHOOSH
RAASSS
IKREEEEEEE
!!!
NOT AGAIN...
KCHAH

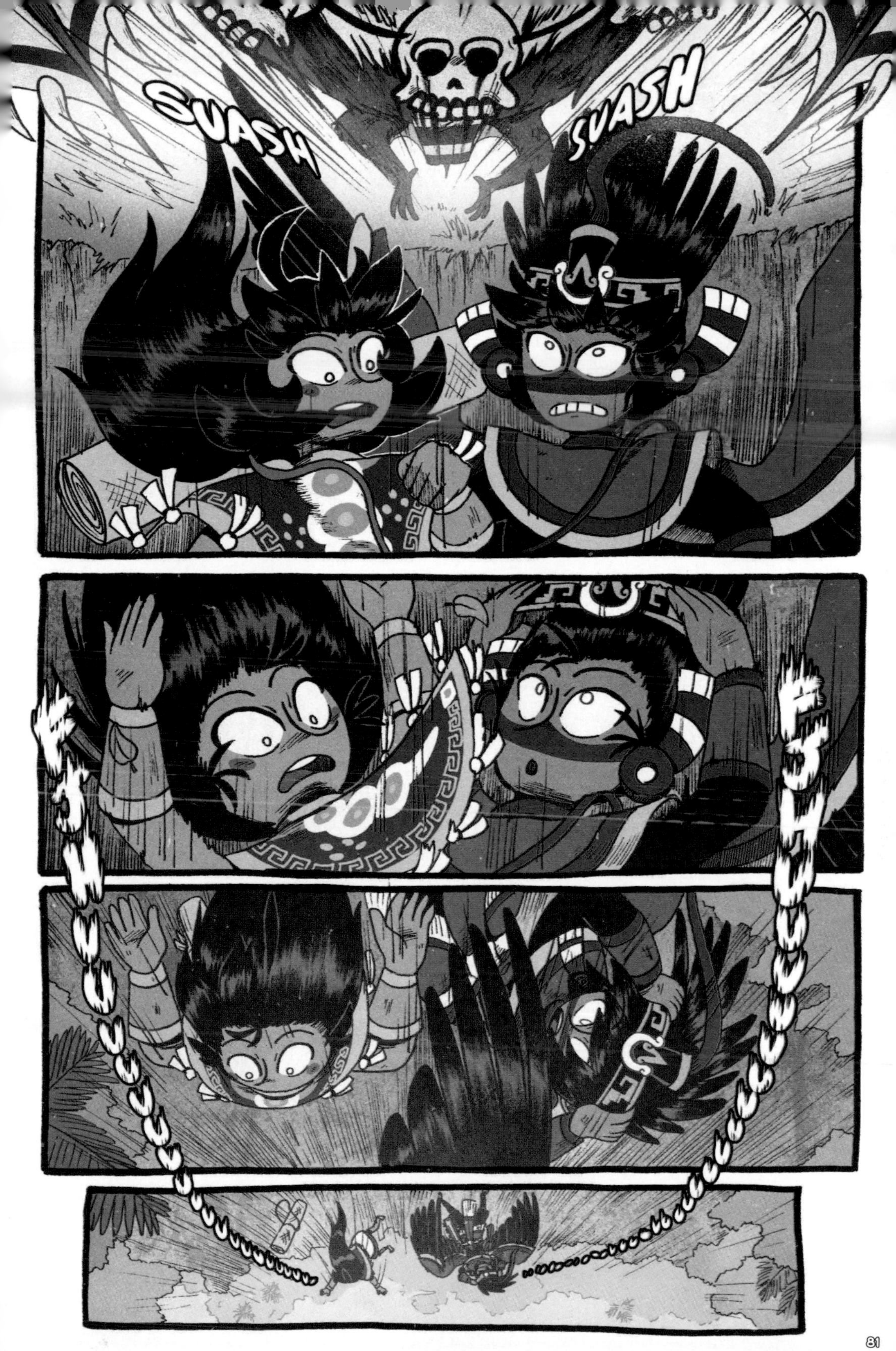
SUASH
SUASH

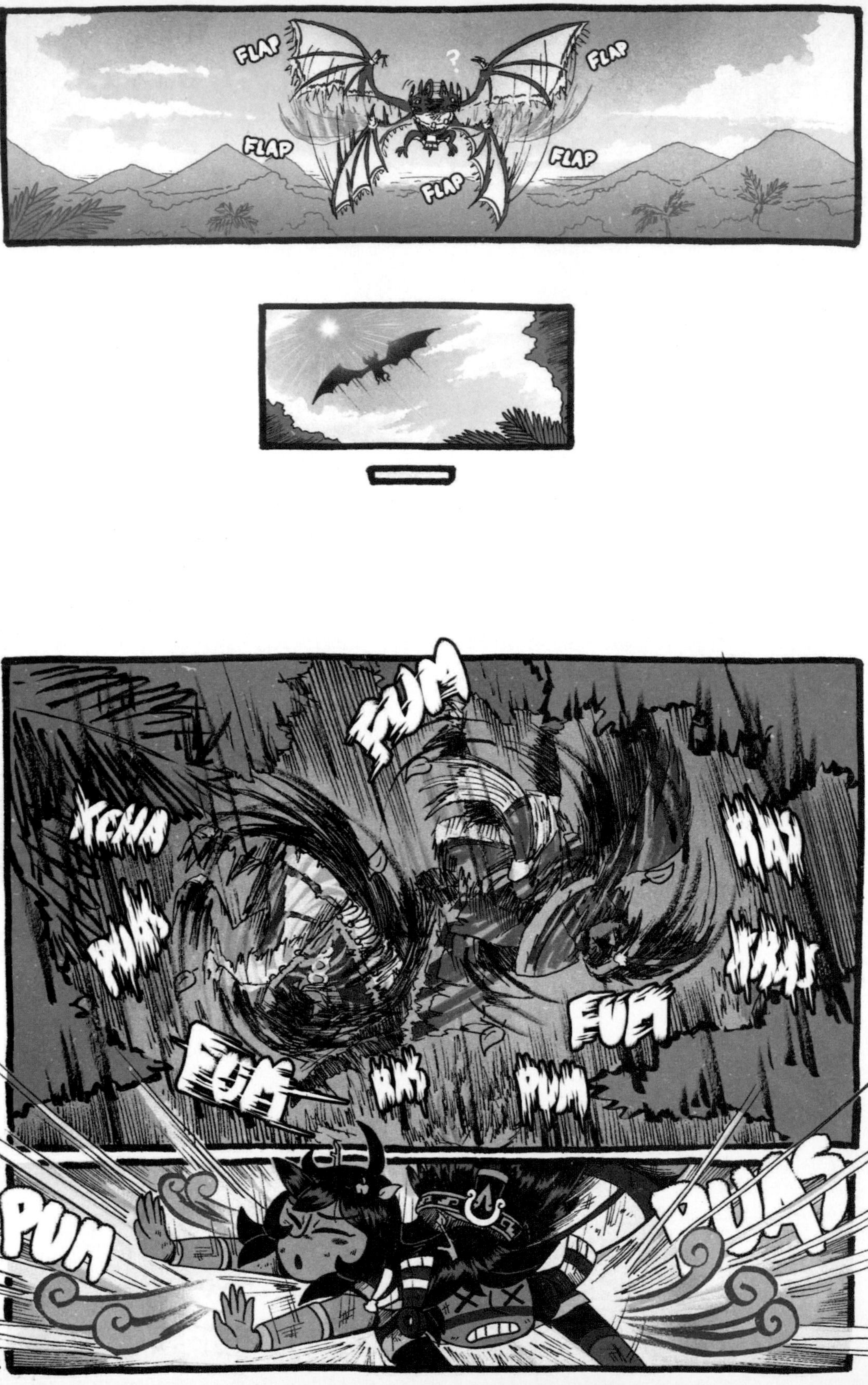
FLAP
FLAP
?
FLAP
FLAP
FLAP
FUM
XCHA
PUAS
RAS
KRAS
FUM
FUM
RAS
PUM
PUM
PUAS

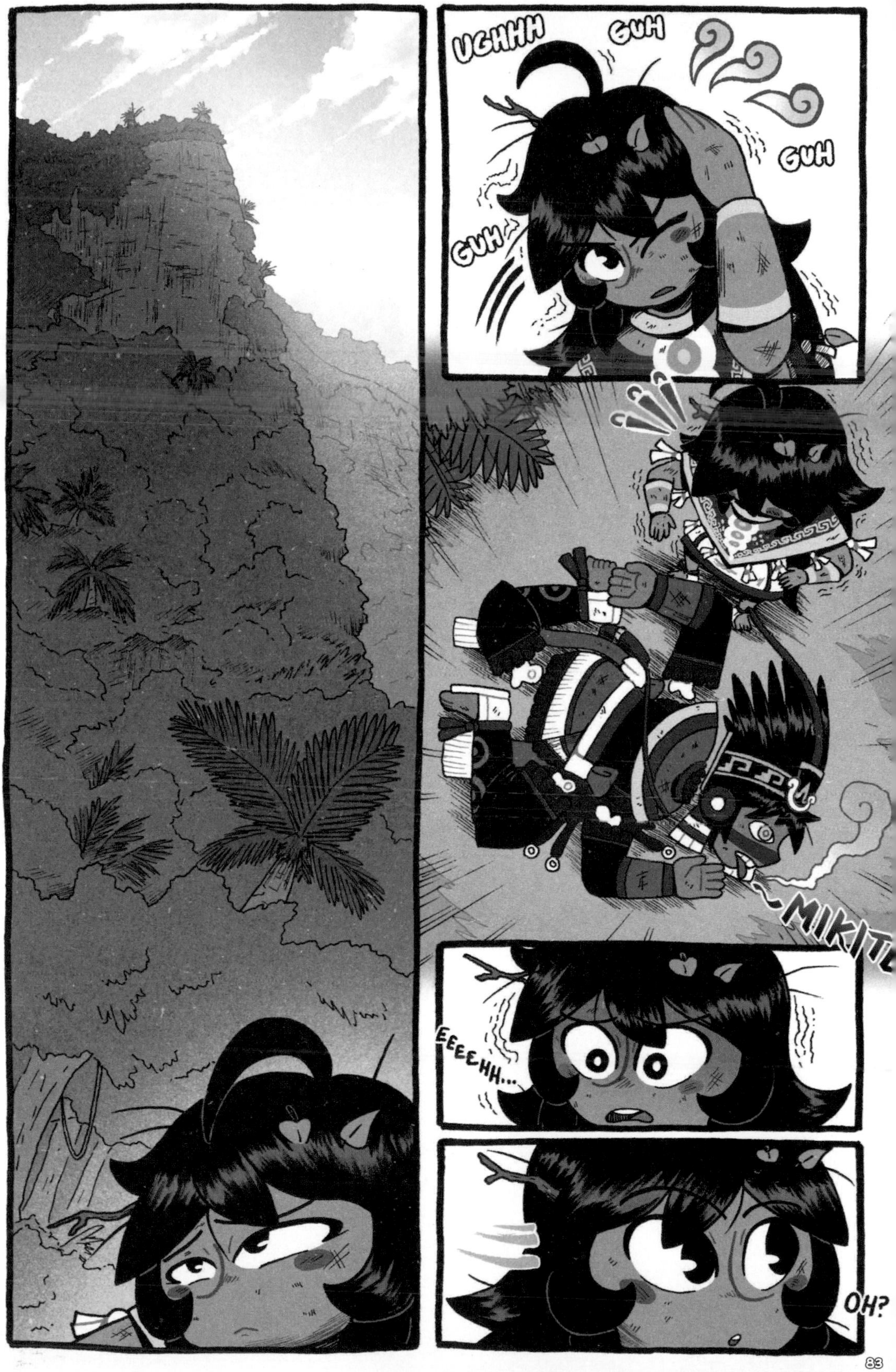
UGHHH
GUH
GUH
GUH
~MIKITL
EEEEHH...
OH?

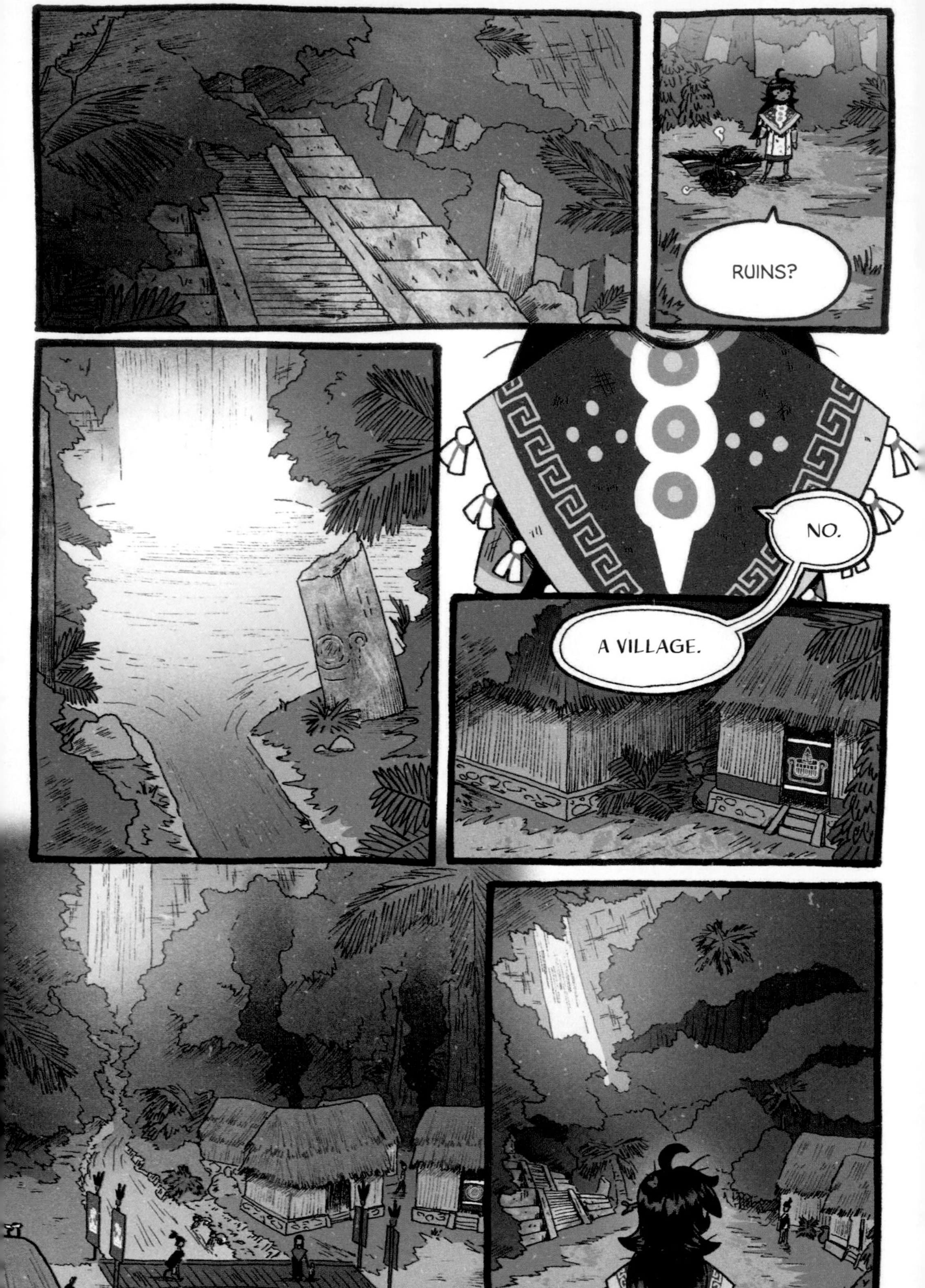
RUINS?
NO.
A VILLAGE.

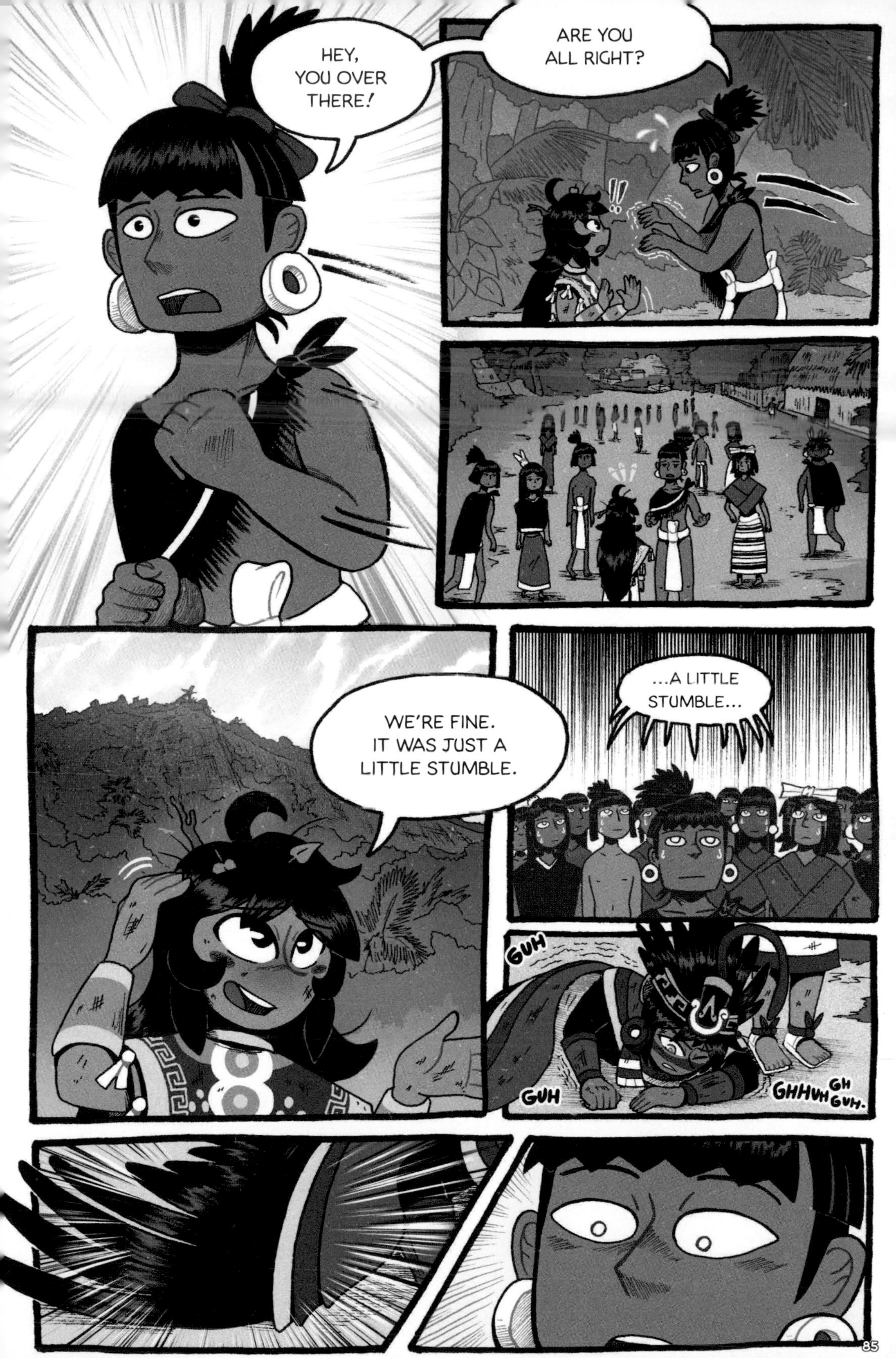
HEY, YOU OVER THERE!
ARE YOU ALL RIGHT?
!!
WE'RE FINE. IT WAS JUST A LITTLE STUMBLE.
...A LITTLE STUMBLE...
GUH
GUH
GHHUH GH GUH.

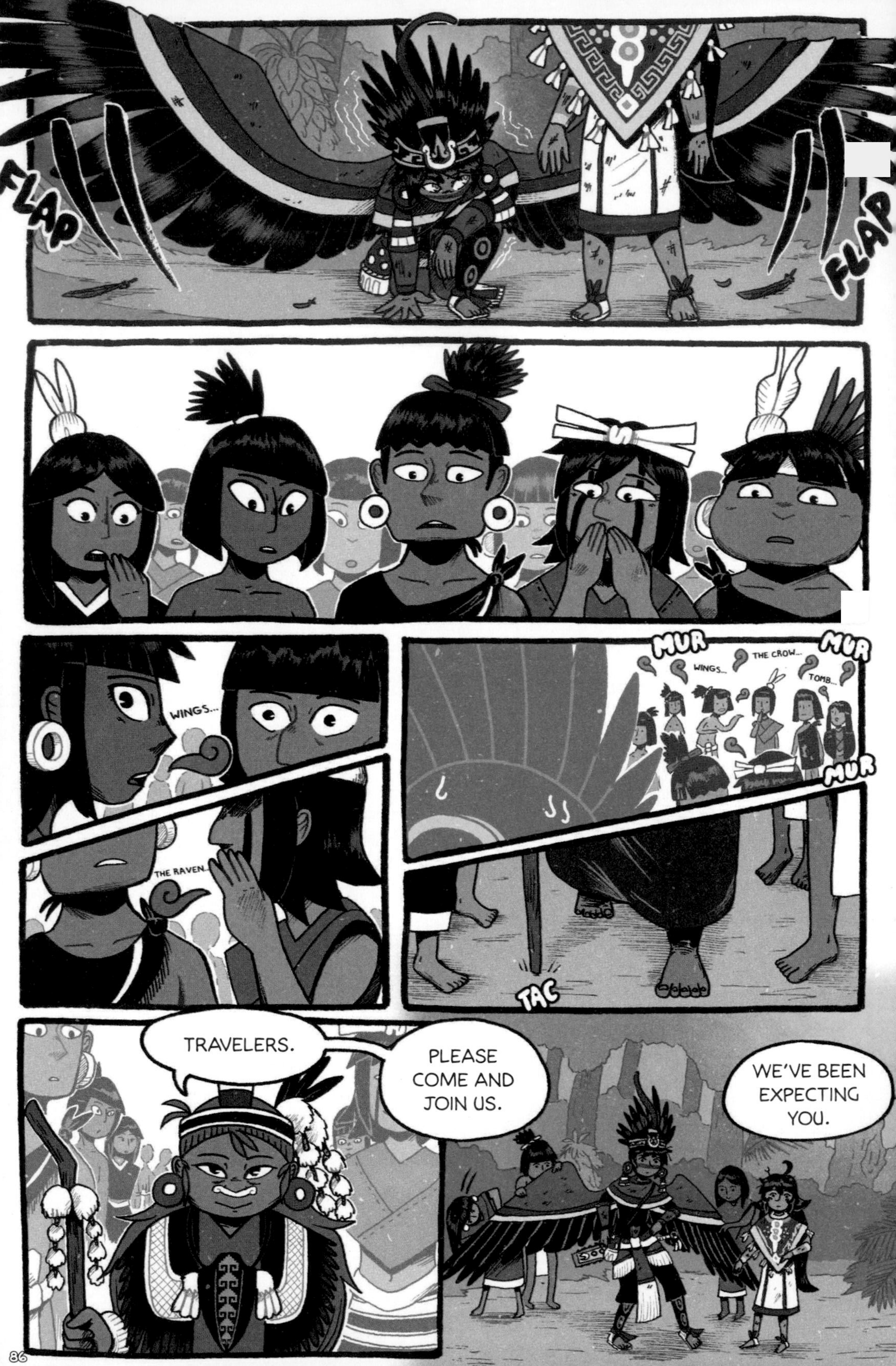
FLAP
FLAP
WINGS...
THE RAVEN...
MUR
MUR
WINGS...
THE CROW...
TOMB...
MUR
TAC
TRAVELERS.
PLEASE COME AND JOIN US.
WE'VE BEEN EXPECTING YOU.

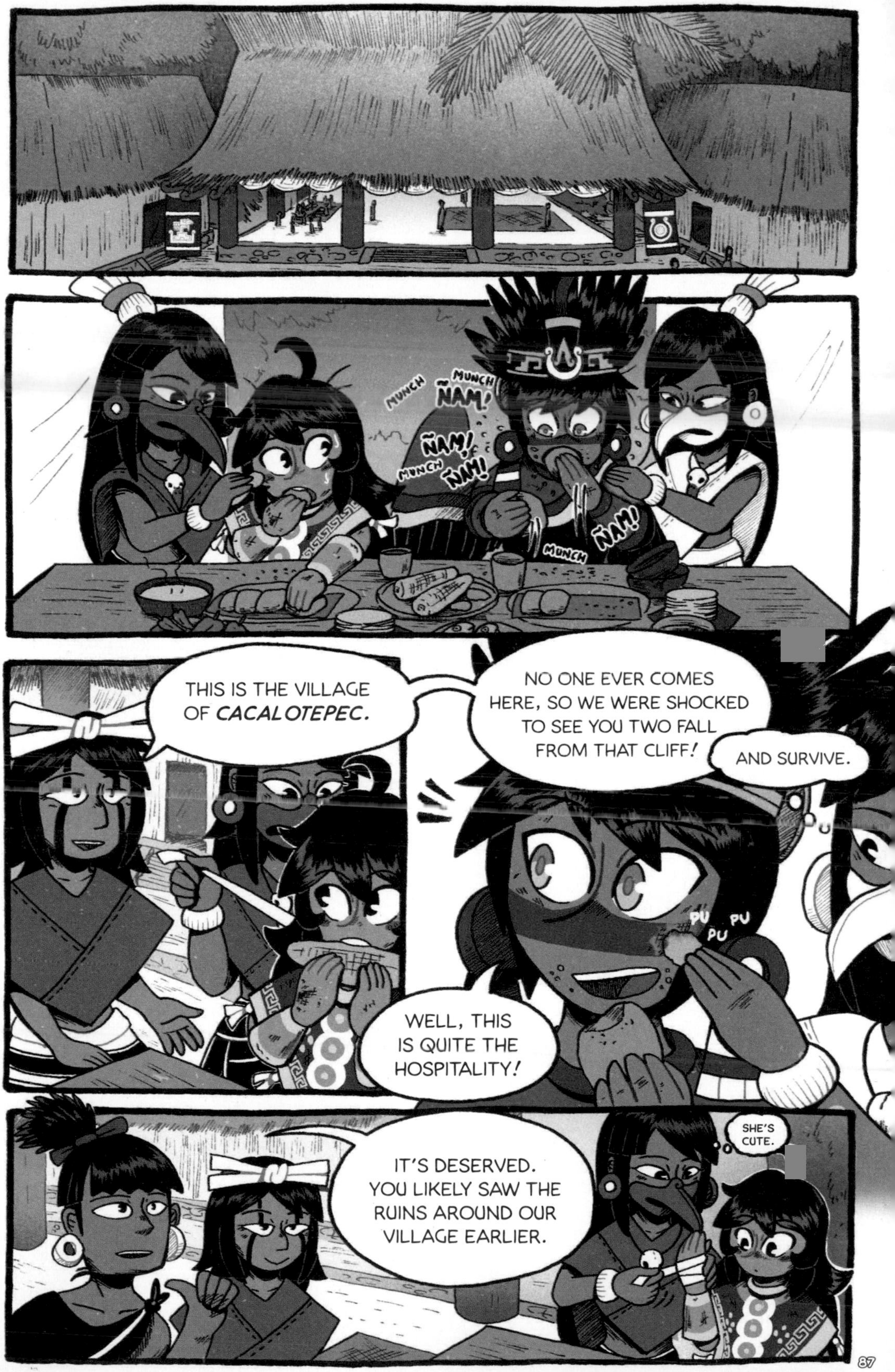
MUNCH
MUNCH
ÑAM!
ÑAM!
MUNCH
ÑAM!
ÑAM!
MUNCH
THIS IS THE VILLAGE OF *CACALOTEPEC.*
NO ONE EVER COMES HERE, SO WE WERE SHOCKED TO SEE YOU TWO FALL FROM THAT CLIFF!
AND SURVIVE.
PU PU PU
WELL, THIS IS QUITE THE HOSPITALITY!
IT'S DESERVED. YOU LIKELY SAW THE RUINS AROUND OUR VILLAGE EARLIER.
SHE'S CUTE.

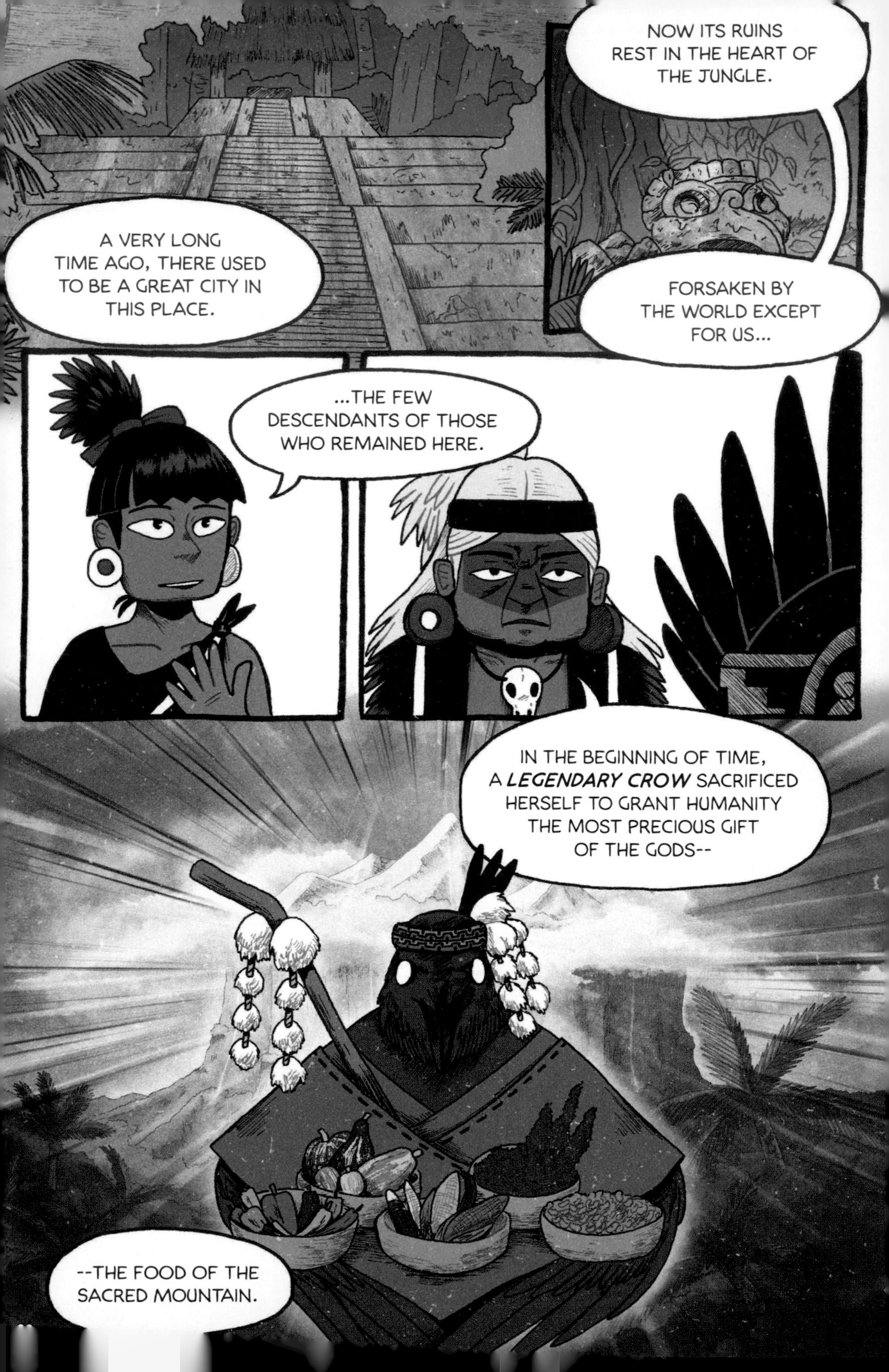
A VERY LONG TIME AGO, THERE USED TO BE A GREAT CITY IN THIS PLACE.
NOW ITS RUINS REST IN THE HEART OF THE JUNGLE.
FORSAKEN BY THE WORLD EXCEPT FOR US...
...THE FEW DESCENDANTS OF THOSE WHO REMAINED HERE.
IN THE BEGINNING OF TIME, A *LEGENDARY CROW* SACRIFICED HERSELF TO GRANT HUMANITY THE MOST PRECIOUS GIFT OF THE GODS--
--THE FOOD OF THE SACRED MOUNTAIN.

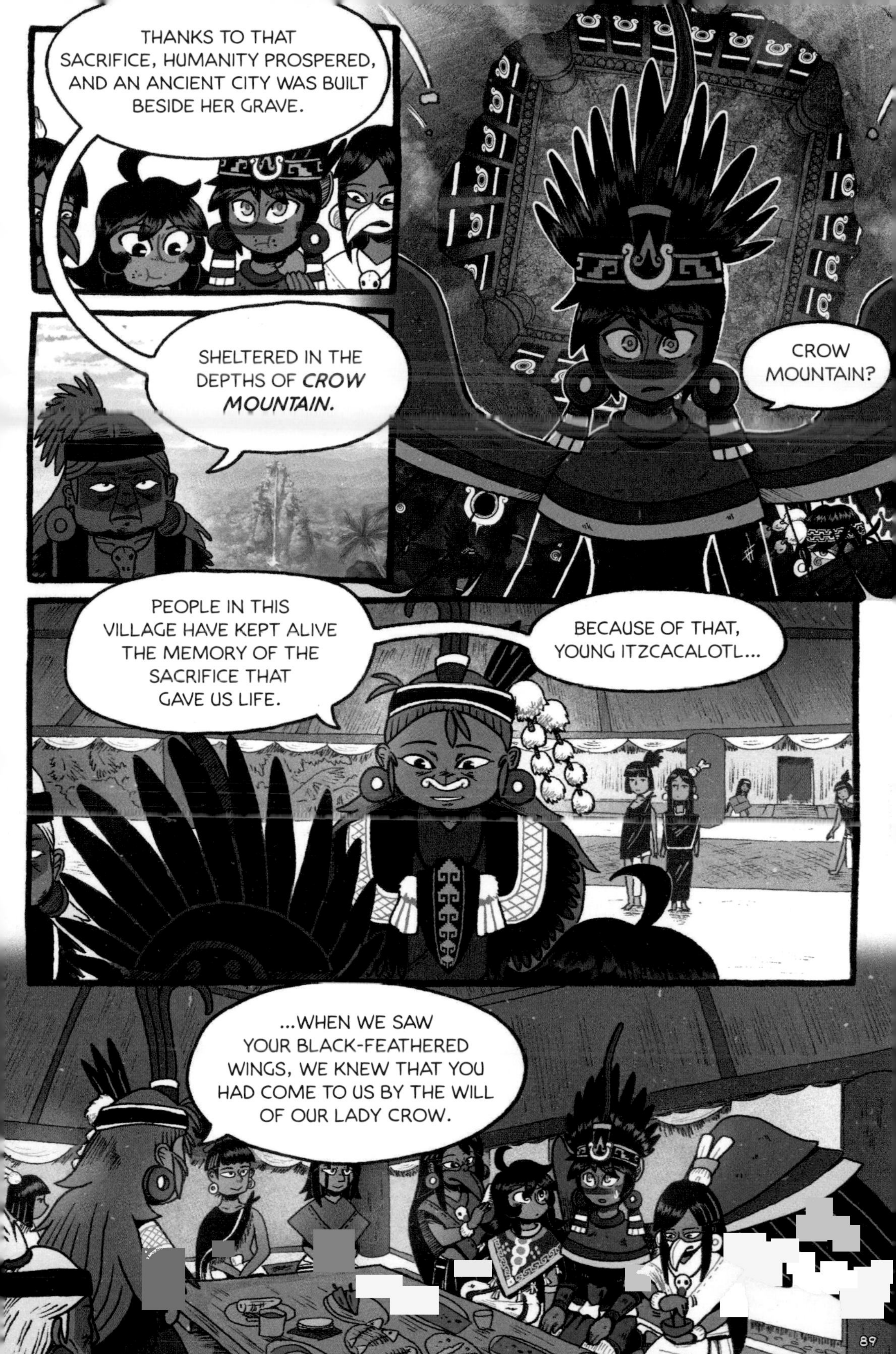
THANKS TO THAT SACRIFICE, HUMANITY PROSPERED, AND AN ANCIENT CITY WAS BUILT BESIDE HER GRAVE.
SHELTERED IN THE DEPTHS OF *CROW MOUNTAIN.*
CROW MOUNTAIN?
PEOPLE IN THIS VILLAGE HAVE KEPT ALIVE THE MEMORY OF THE SACRIFICE THAT GAVE US LIFE.
BECAUSE OF THAT, YOUNG ITZCACALOTL...
...WHEN WE SAW YOUR BLACK-FEATHERED WINGS, WE KNEW THAT YOU HAD COME TO US BY THE WILL OF OUR LADY CROW.

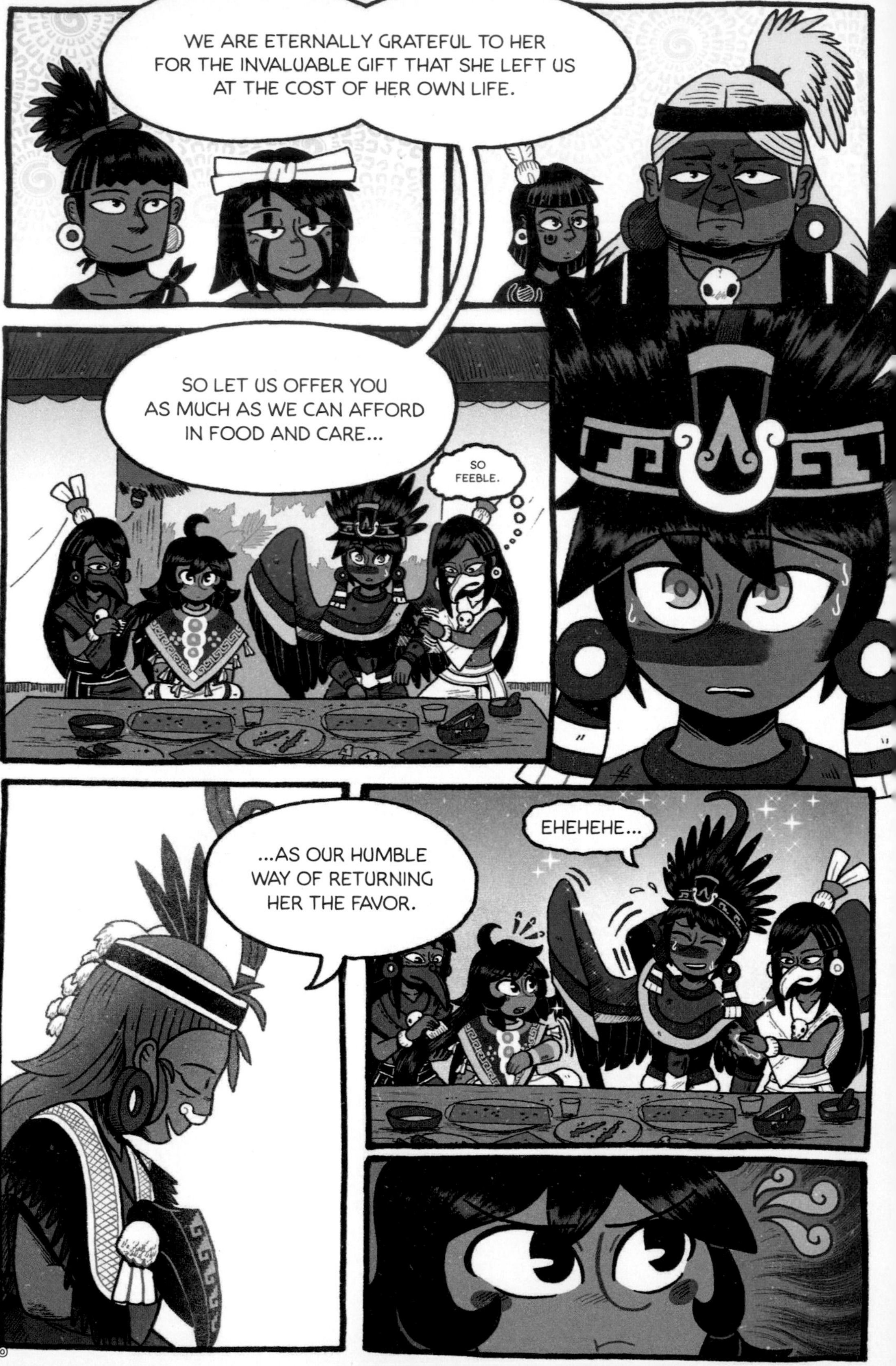
WE ARE ETERNALLY GRATEFUL TO HER FOR THE INVALUABLE GIFT THAT SHE LEFT US AT THE COST OF HER OWN LIFE.
SO LET US OFFER YOU AS MUCH AS WE CAN AFFORD IN FOOD AND CARE...
SO FEEBLE.
...AS OUR HUMBLE WAY OF RETURNING HER THE FAVOR.
EHEHEHE...

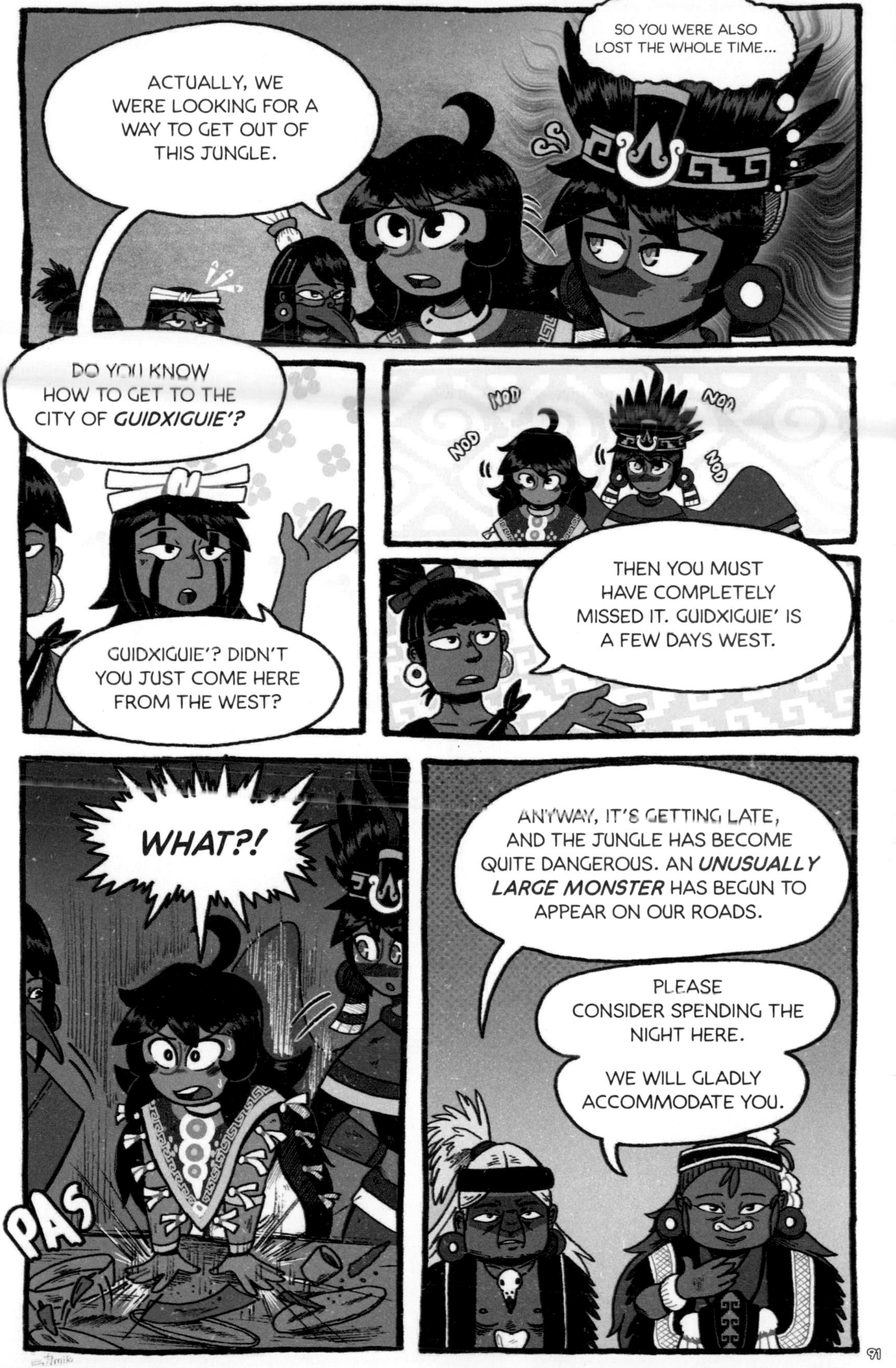
ACTUALLY, WE WERE LOOKING FOR A WAY TO GET OUT OF THIS JUNGLE.
SO YOU WERE ALSO LOST THE WHOLE TIME...
DO YOU KNOW HOW TO GET TO THE CITY OF ***GUIDXIGUIE'?***
GUIDXIGUIE'? DIDN'T YOU JUST COME HERE FROM THE WEST?
NOD
NOD
NOD
NOD
THEN YOU MUST HAVE COMPLETELY MISSED IT. GUIDXIGUIE' IS A FEW DAYS WEST.
WHAT?!
PAS
ANYWAY, IT'S GETTING LATE, AND THE JUNGLE HAS BECOME QUITE DANGEROUS. AN ***UNUSUALLY LARGE MONSTER*** HAS BEGUN TO APPEAR ON OUR ROADS.
PLEASE CONSIDER SPENDING THE NIGHT HERE.
WE WILL GLADLY ACCOMMODATE YOU.

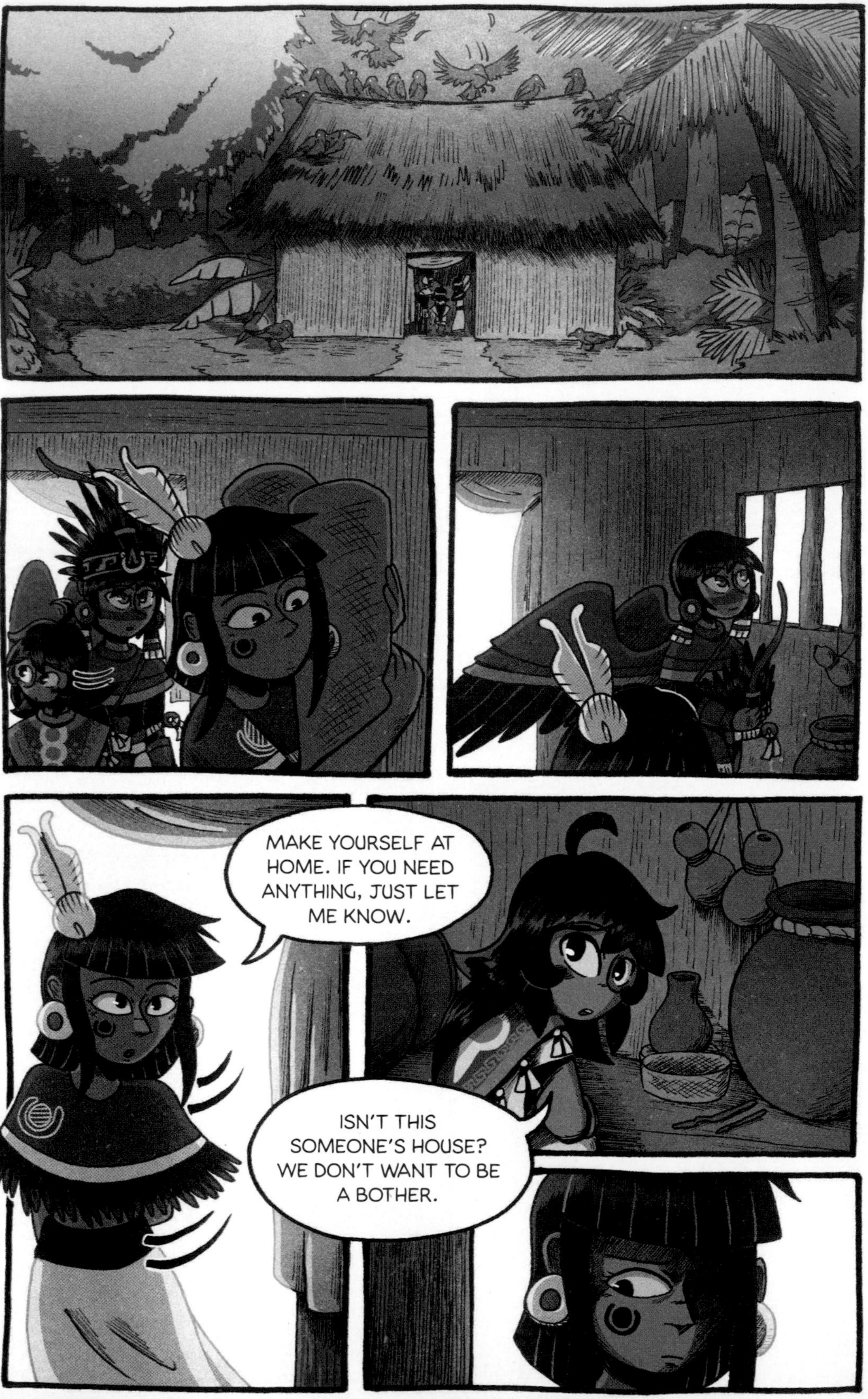
MAKE YOURSELF AT HOME. IF YOU NEED ANYTHING, JUST LET ME KNOW.
ISN'T THIS SOMEONE'S HOUSE? WE DON'T WANT TO BE A BOTHER.

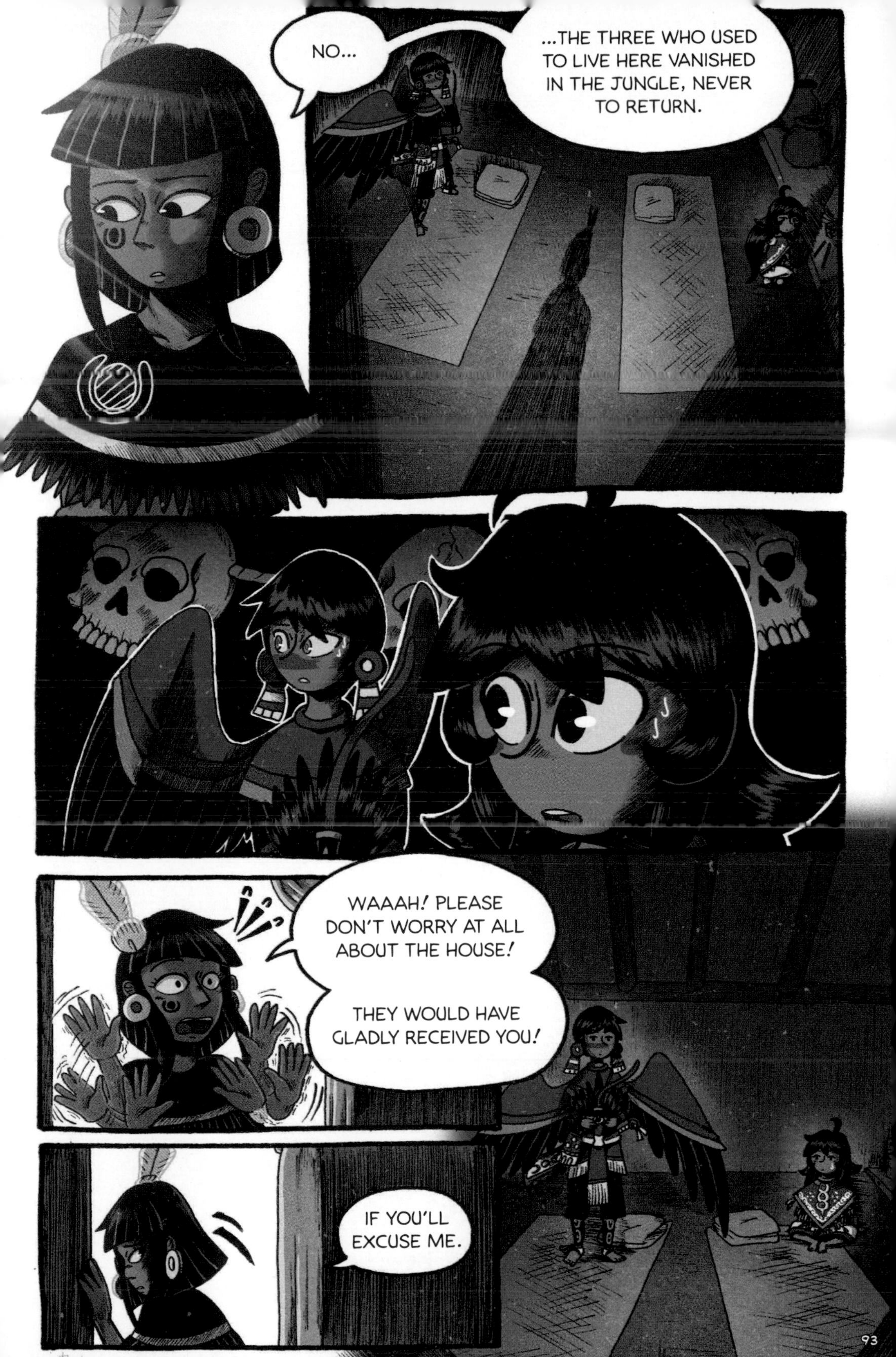
NO...
...THE THREE WHO USED TO LIVE HERE VANISHED IN THE JUNGLE, NEVER TO RETURN.
WAAAH! PLEASE DON'T WORRY AT ALL ABOUT THE HOUSE!
THEY WOULD HAVE GLADLY RECEIVED YOU!
IF YOU'LL EXCUSE ME.

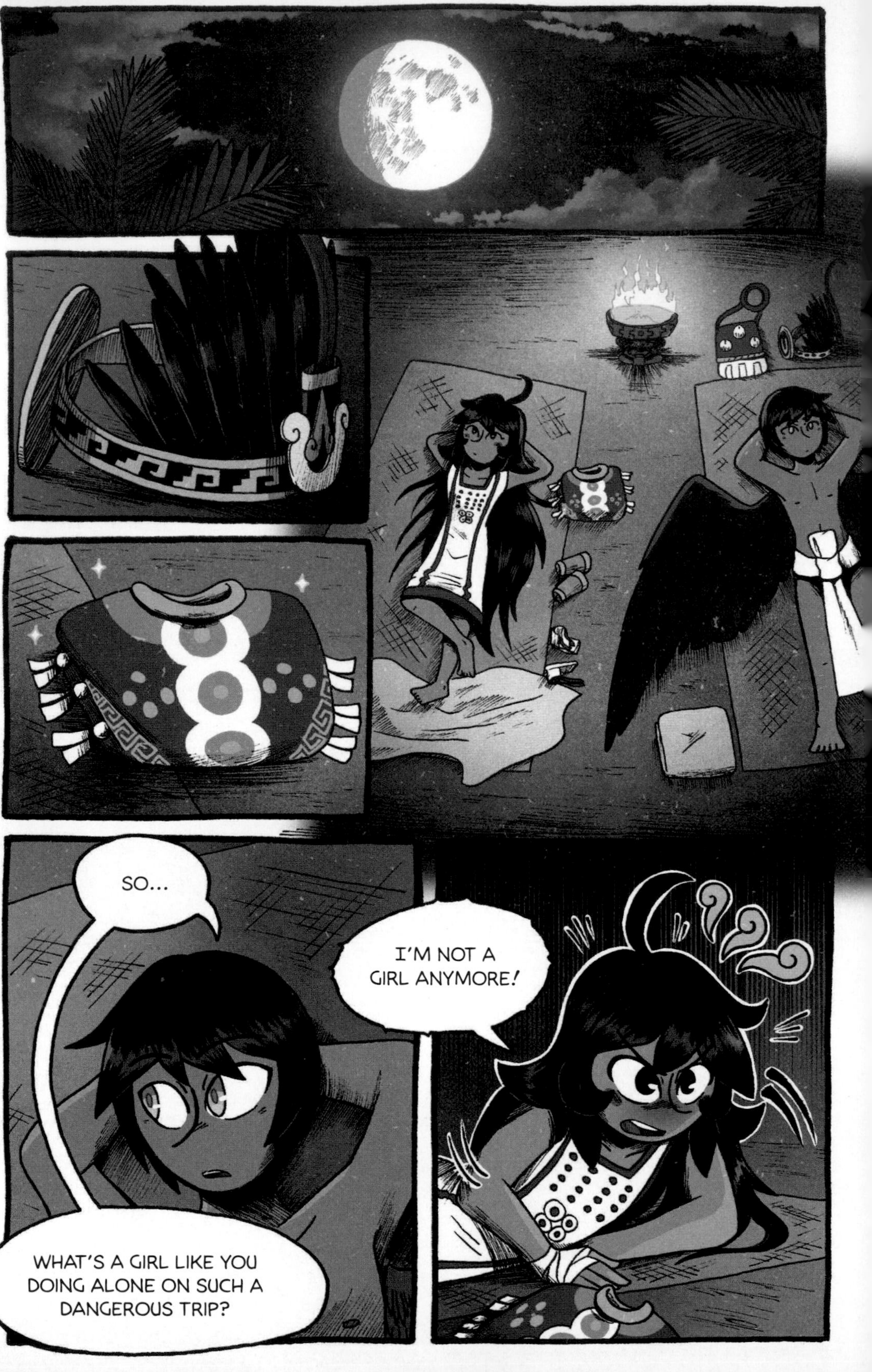
SO...
WHAT'S A GIRL LIKE YOU DOING ALONE ON SUCH A DANGEROUS TRIP?
I'M NOT A GIRL ANYMORE!

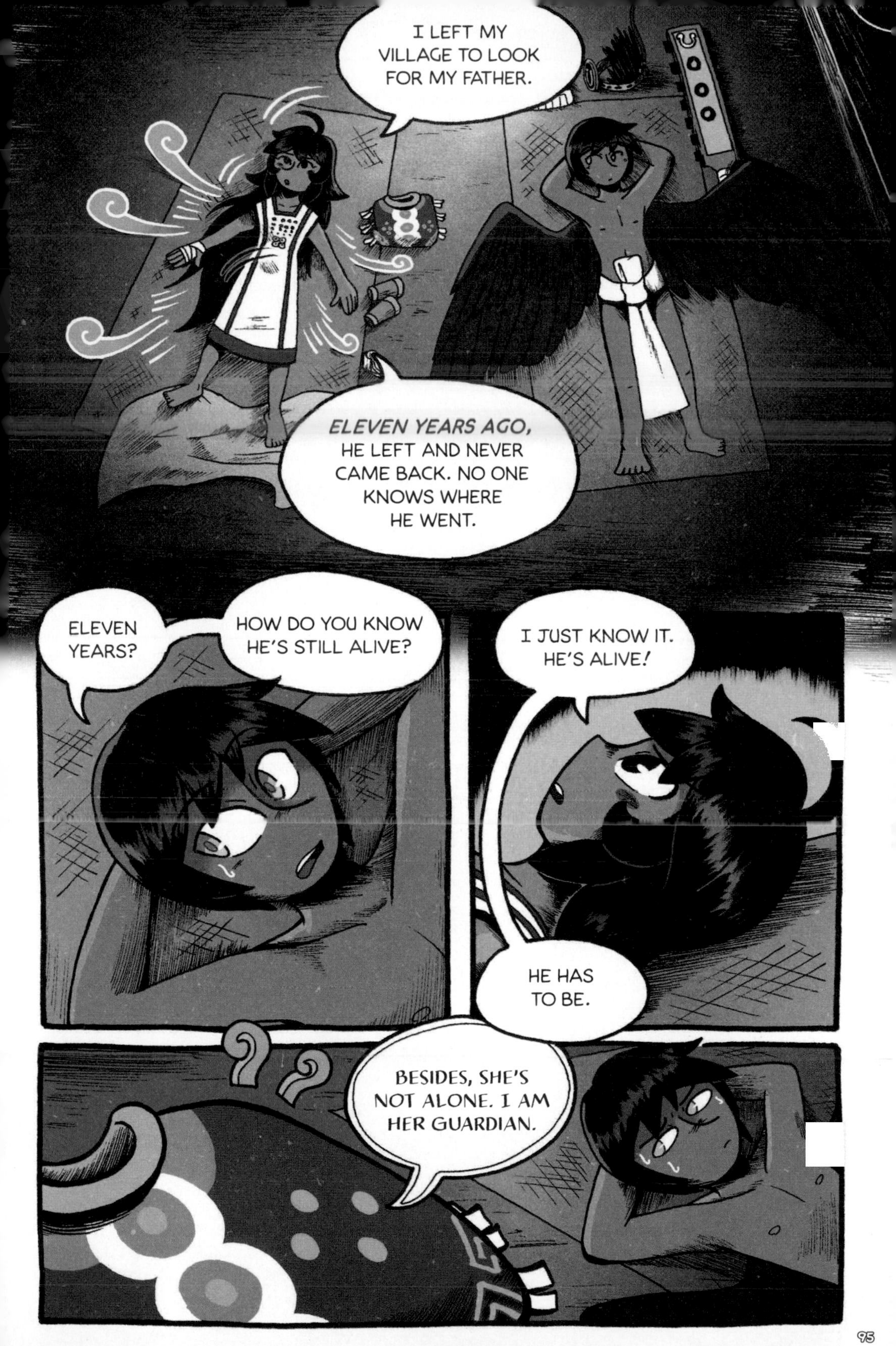
I LEFT MY VILLAGE TO LOOK FOR MY FATHER.
ELEVEN YEARS AGO, HE LEFT AND NEVER CAME BACK. NO ONE KNOWS WHERE HE WENT.
ELEVEN YEARS?
HOW DO YOU KNOW HE'S STILL ALIVE?
I JUST KNOW IT. HE'S ALIVE!
HE HAS TO BE.
BESIDES, SHE'S NOT ALONE. I AM HER GUARDIAN.

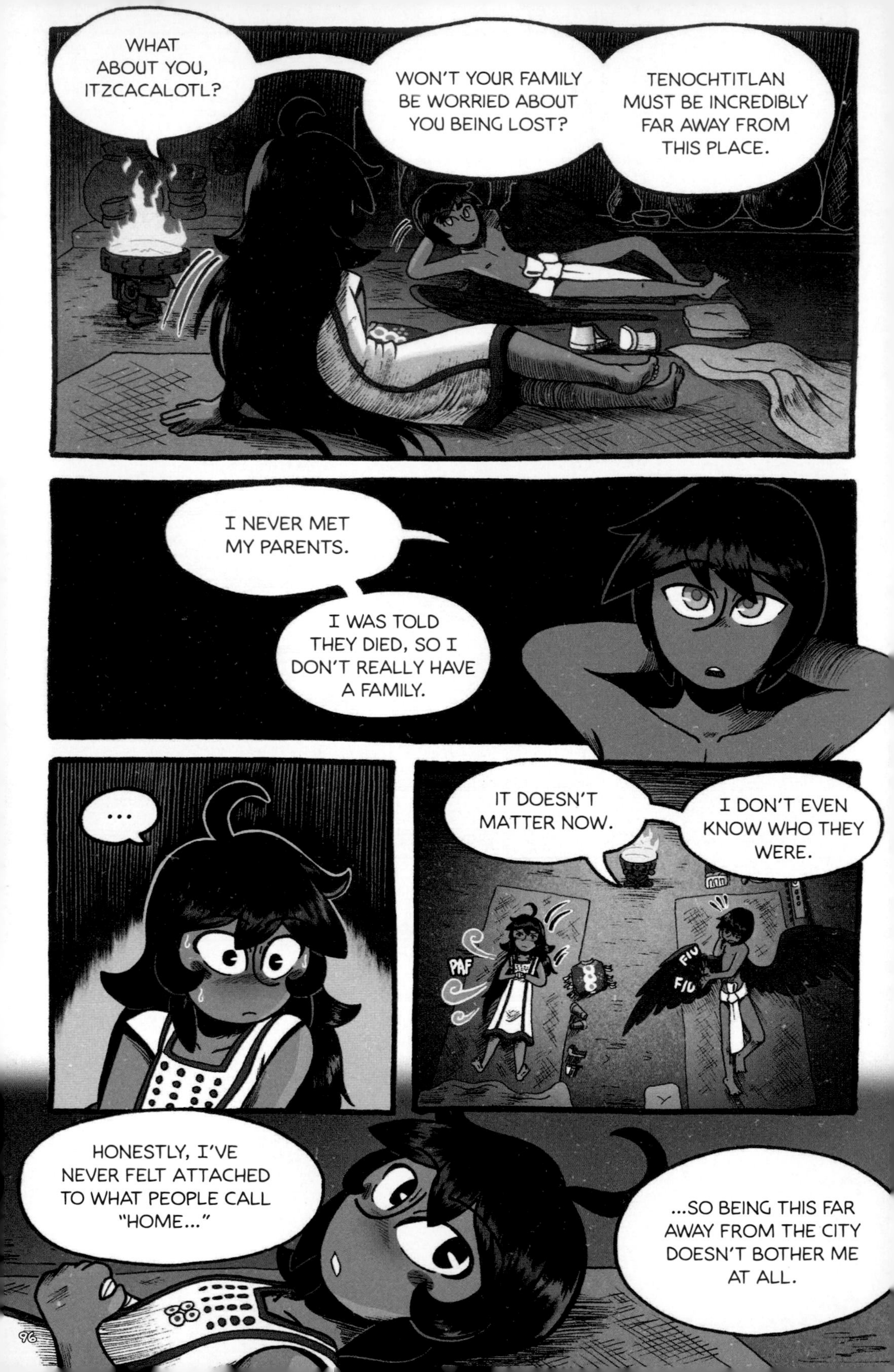
WHAT ABOUT YOU, ITZCACALOTL?
WON'T YOUR FAMILY BE WORRIED ABOUT YOU BEING LOST?
TENOCHTITLAN MUST BE INCREDIBLY FAR AWAY FROM THIS PLACE.
I NEVER MET MY PARENTS.
I WAS TOLD THEY DIED, SO I DON'T REALLY HAVE A FAMILY.
...
IT DOESN'T MATTER NOW.
I DON'T EVEN KNOW WHO THEY WERE.
PAF
FIU
FIU
HONESTLY, I'VE NEVER FELT ATTACHED TO WHAT PEOPLE CALL "HOME..."
...SO BEING THIS FAR AWAY FROM THE CITY DOESN'T BOTHER ME AT ALL.

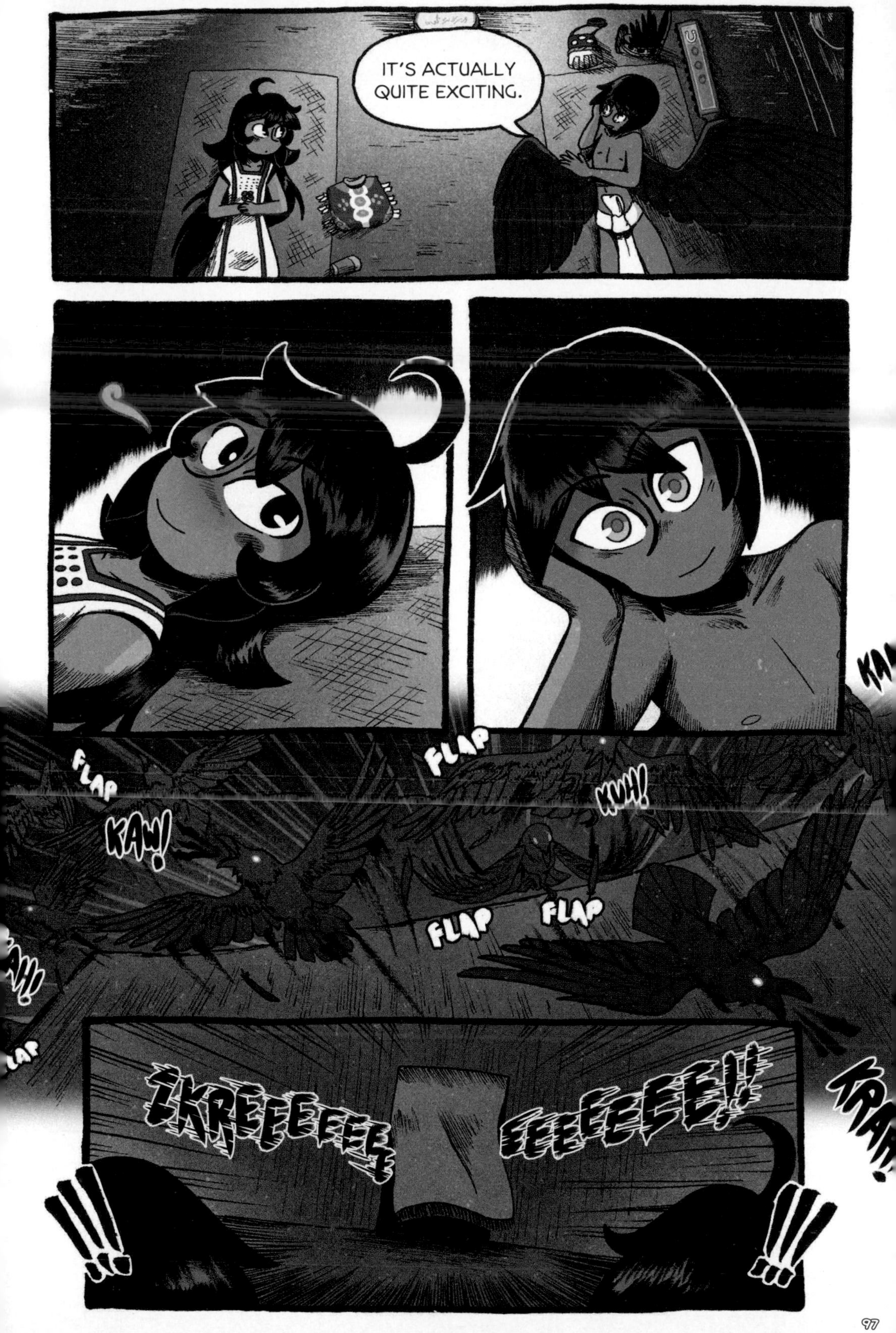
IT'S ACTUALLY QUITE EXCITING.
FLAP
FLAP
KAW!
KUH!
FLAP
FLAP
KAW
KRAH!
SKREEEEEEEEEEEEEEEEE!!
KRAH!
!!!
!!!

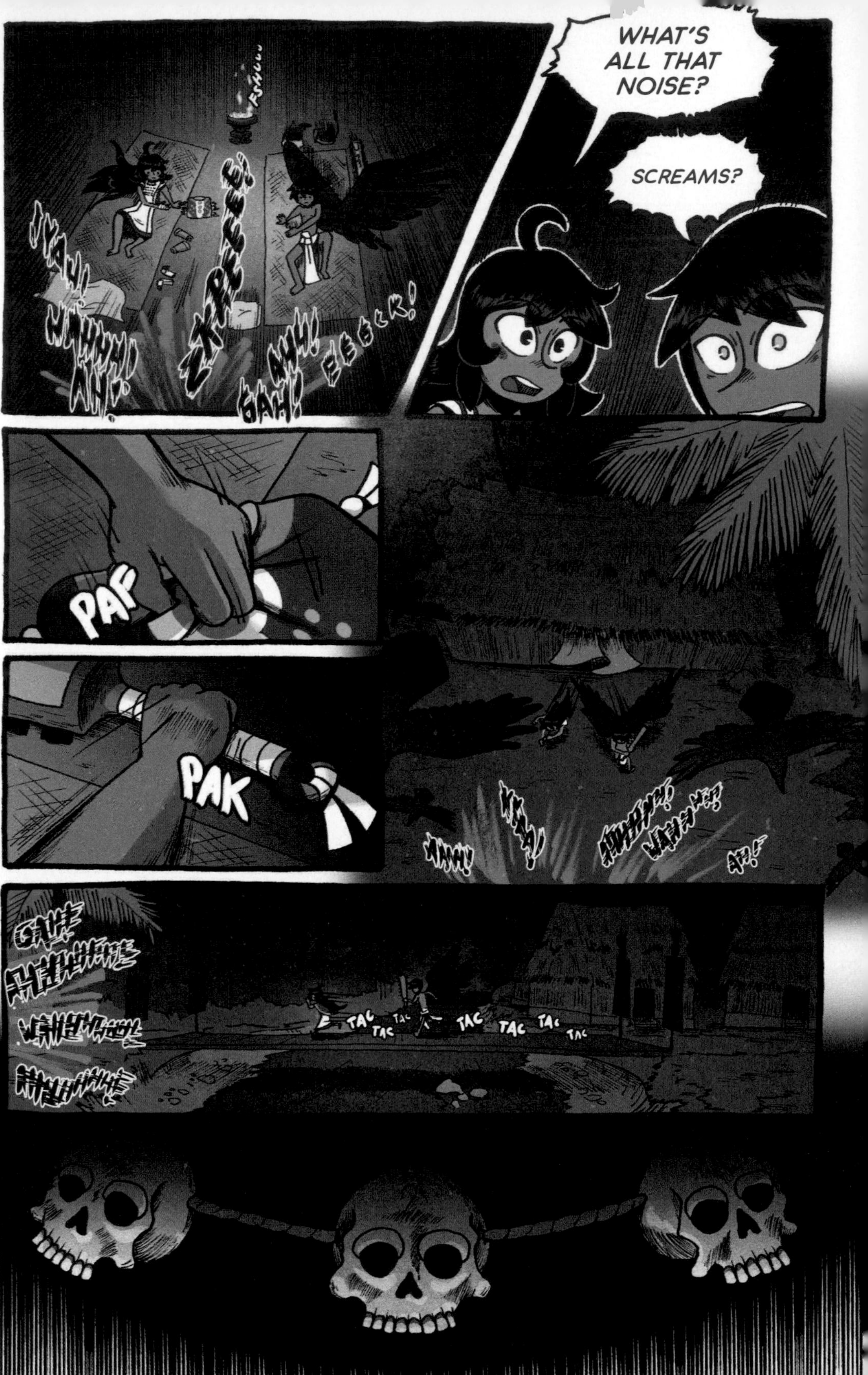

WHAT'S ALL THAT NOISE?
SCREAMS?
GAH!
AHH!
PAP
PAK
TAC TAC TAC TAC TAC TAC

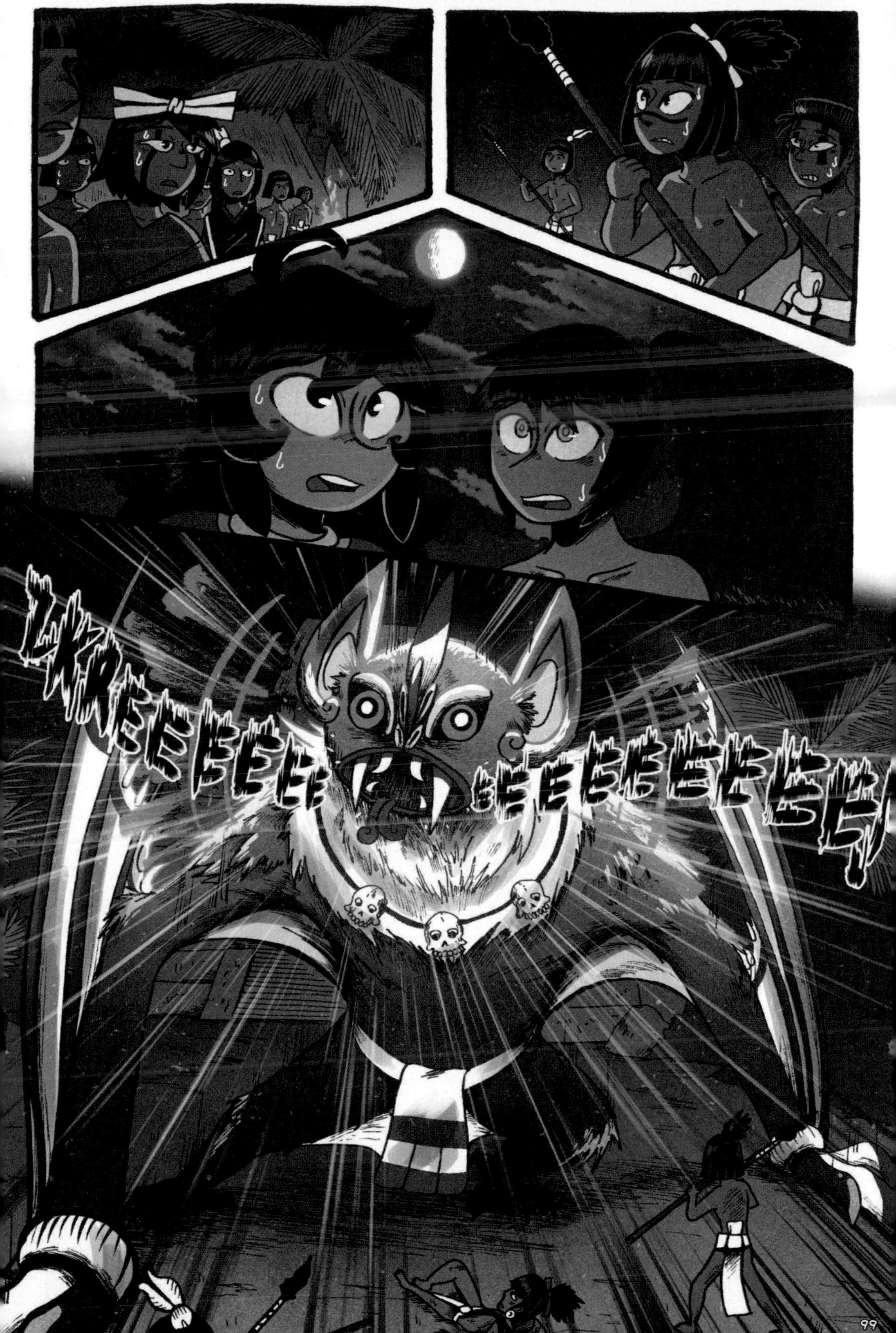
ZKREEEEEEEEEEEEEEEEE!

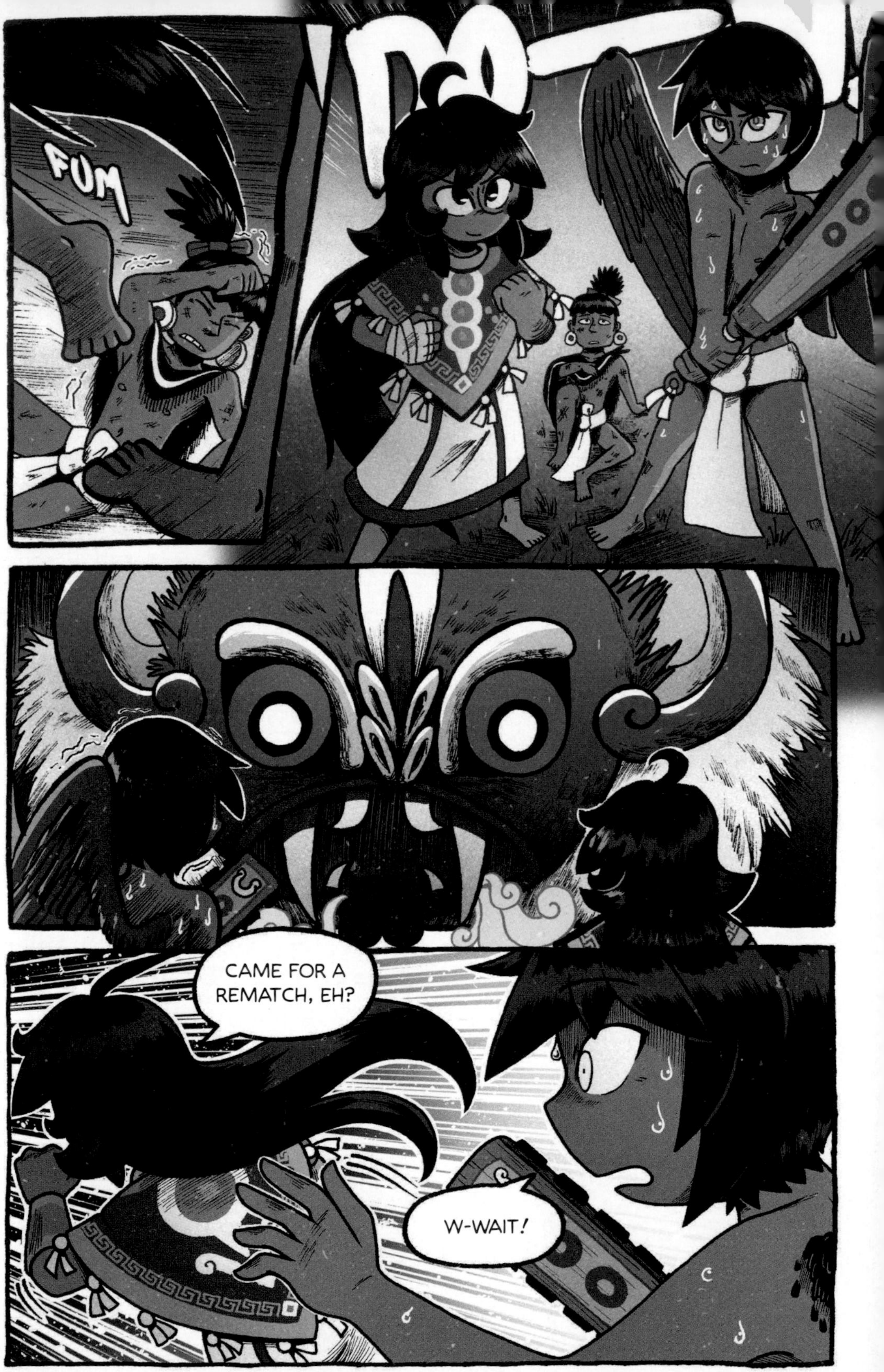

FUM
CAME FOR A REMATCH, EH?
W-WAIT!

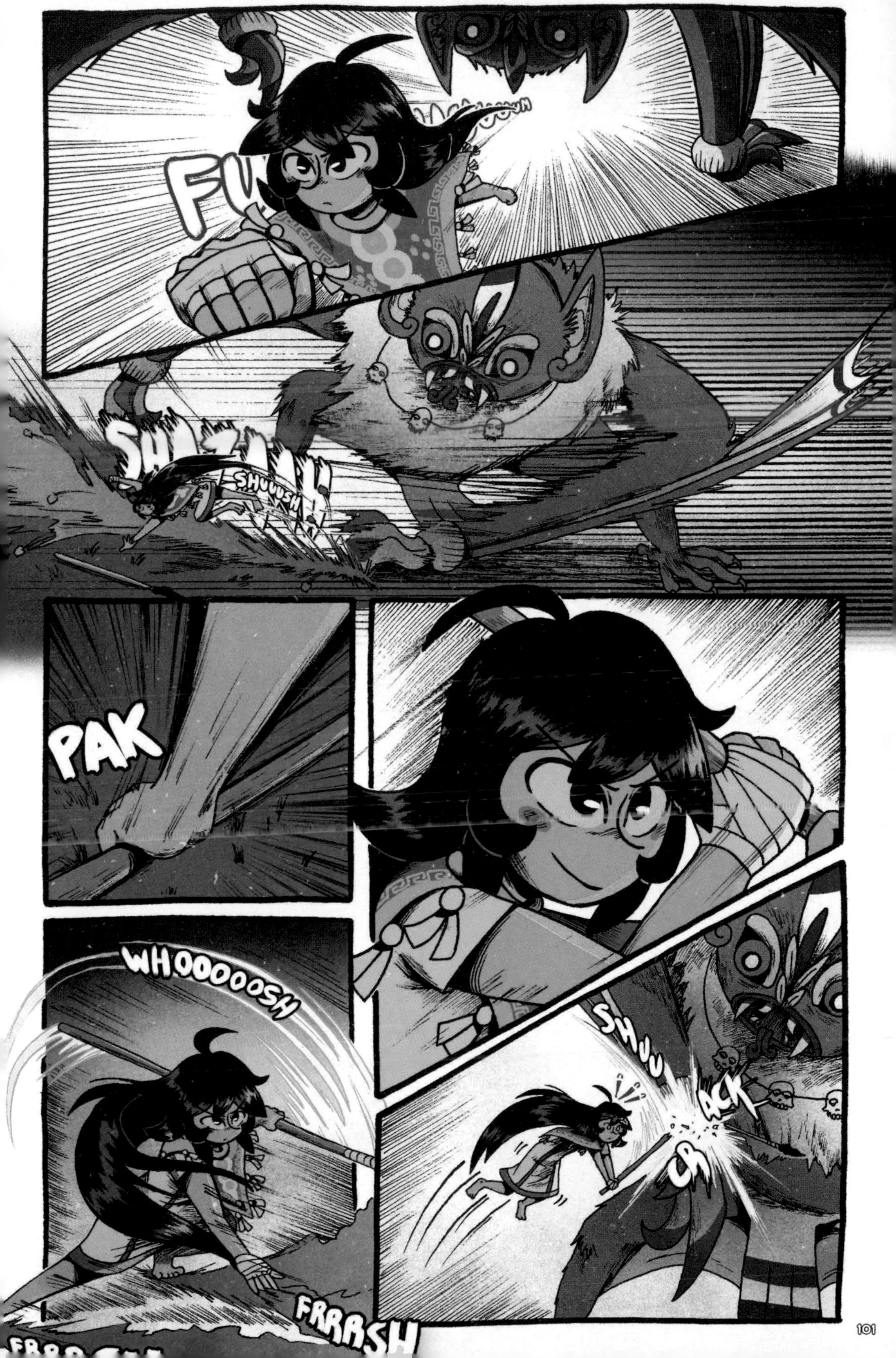
SHUUUSH
PAK
WHOOOOOOSH
SHUU
CRACK
FRRRSH

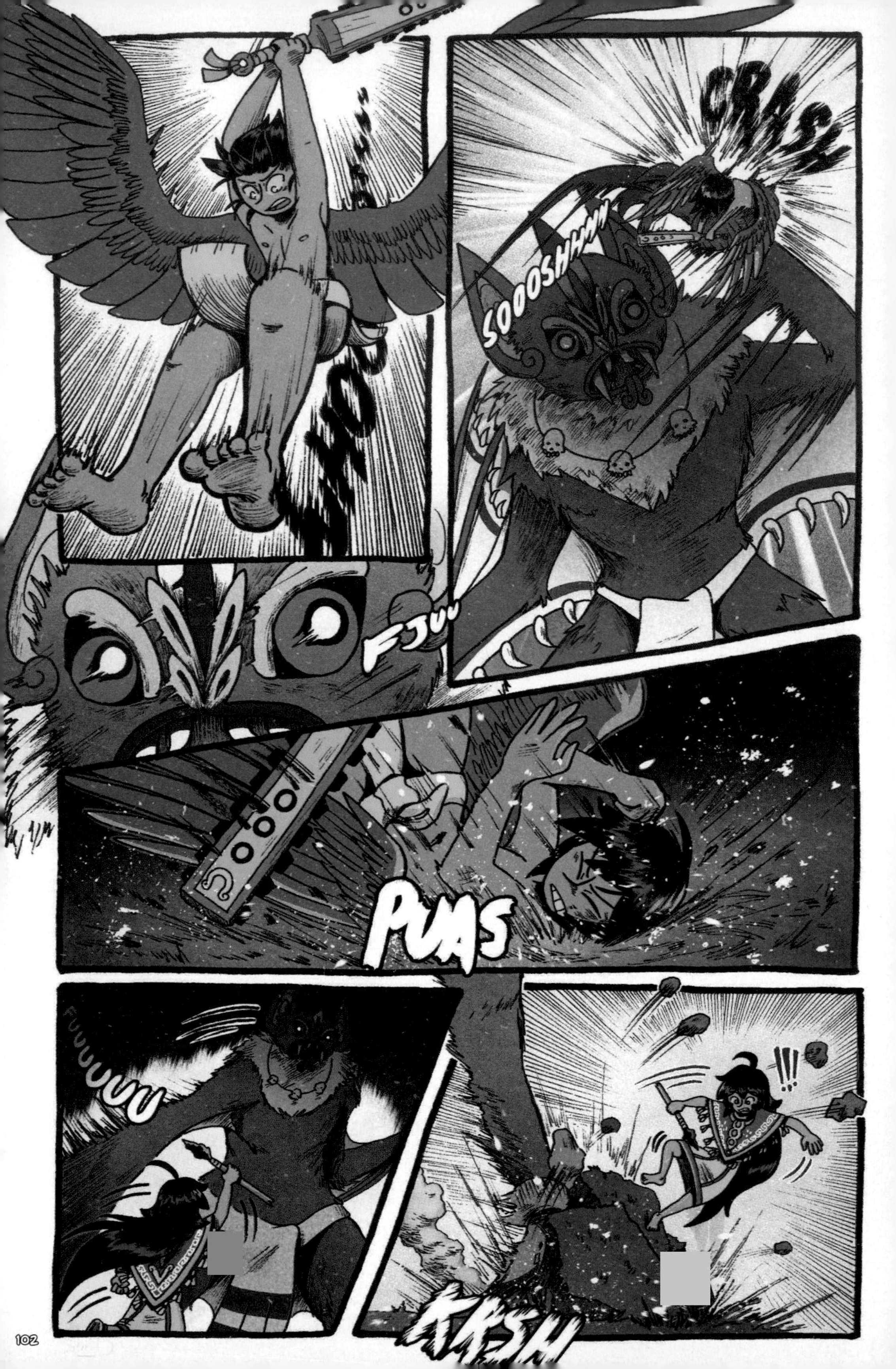
CRASH
SOOOSHHHH
FJUU
PUAS
FUUUUUUU
!!!
KRSH

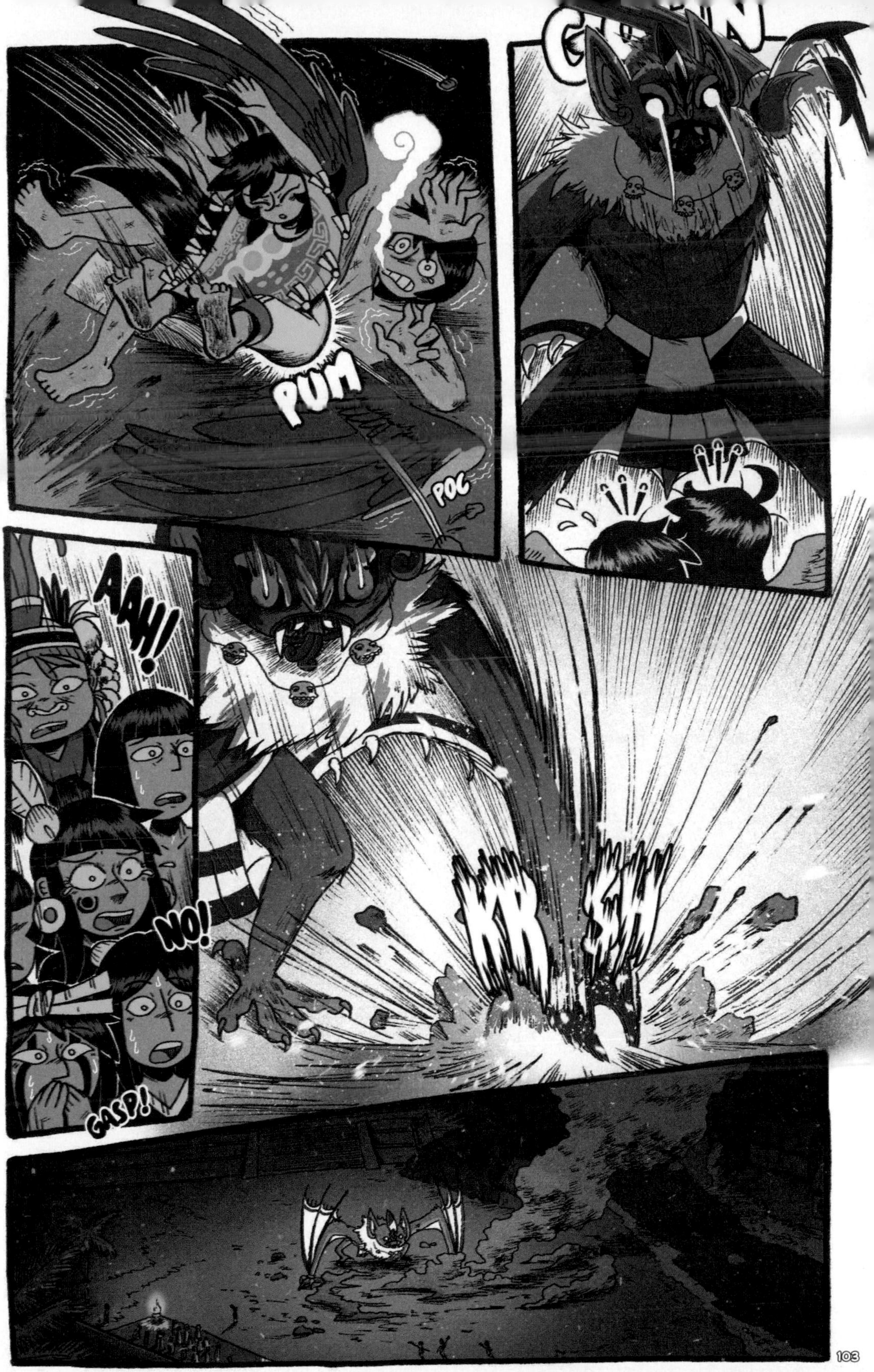

PUM
POC
AAH!
NO!
GASP!
KR SH

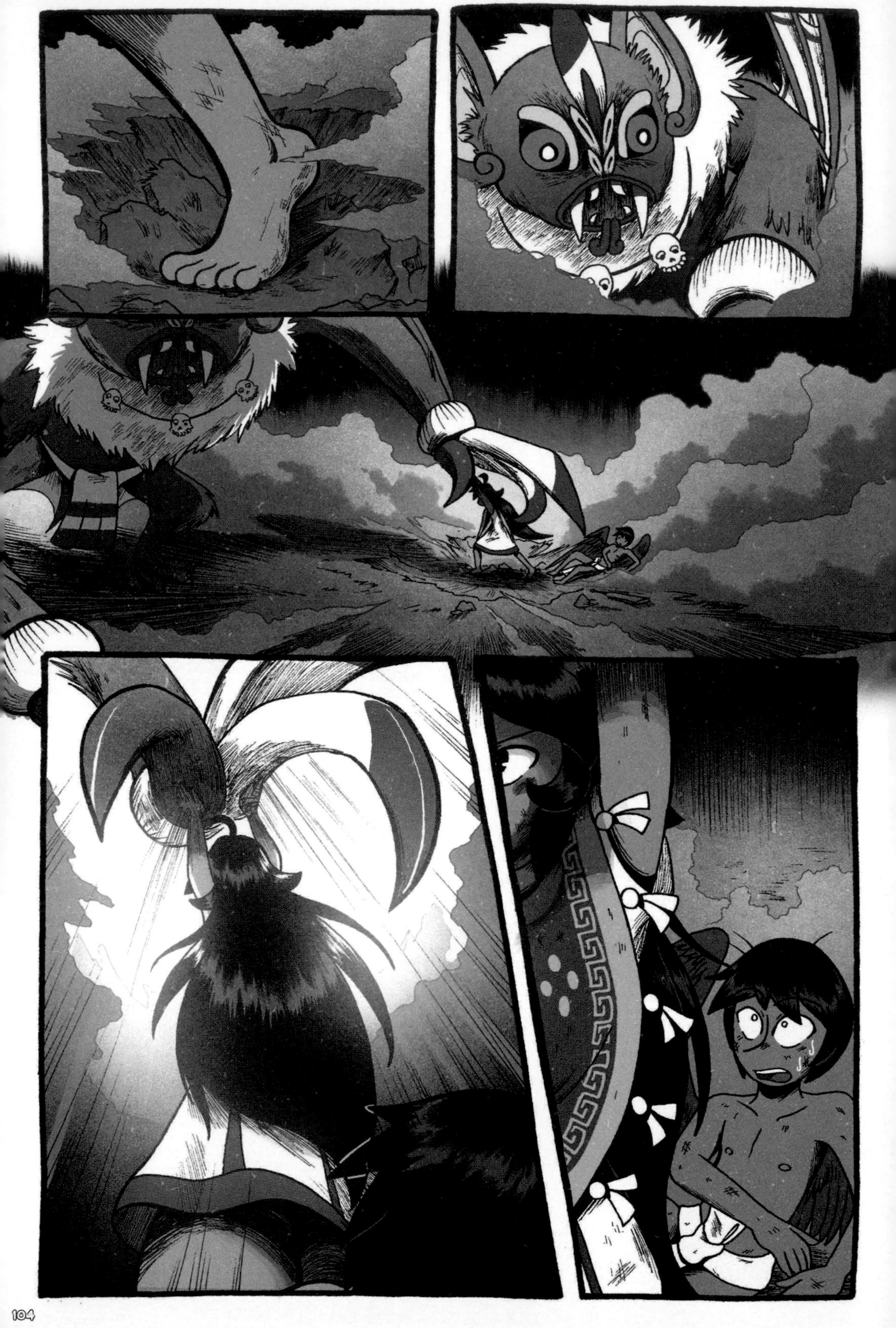

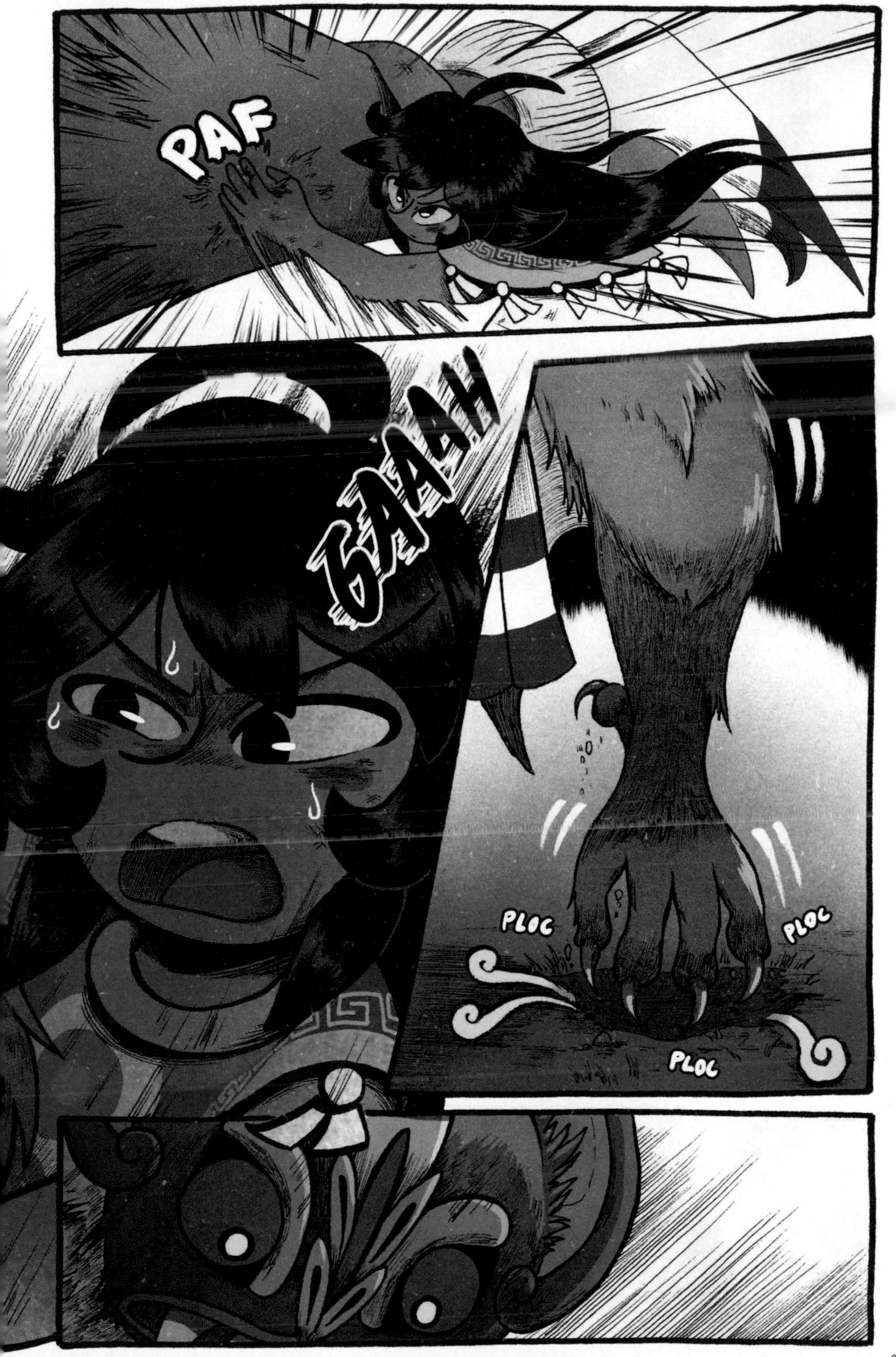
PAF
GAAAH
PLOC
PLOC
PLOC

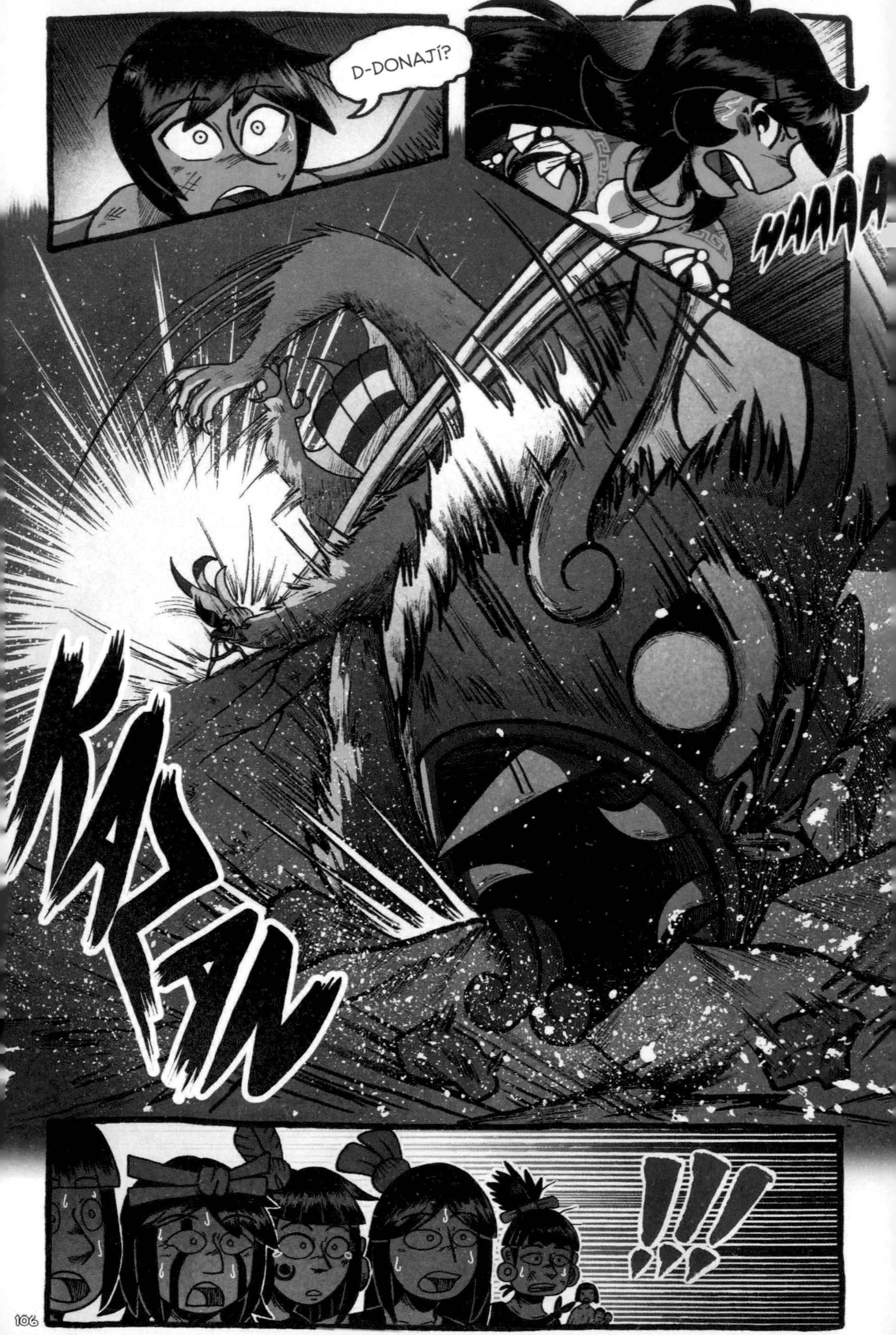
D-DONAJÍ?
HAAAAA
KABAM
!!!

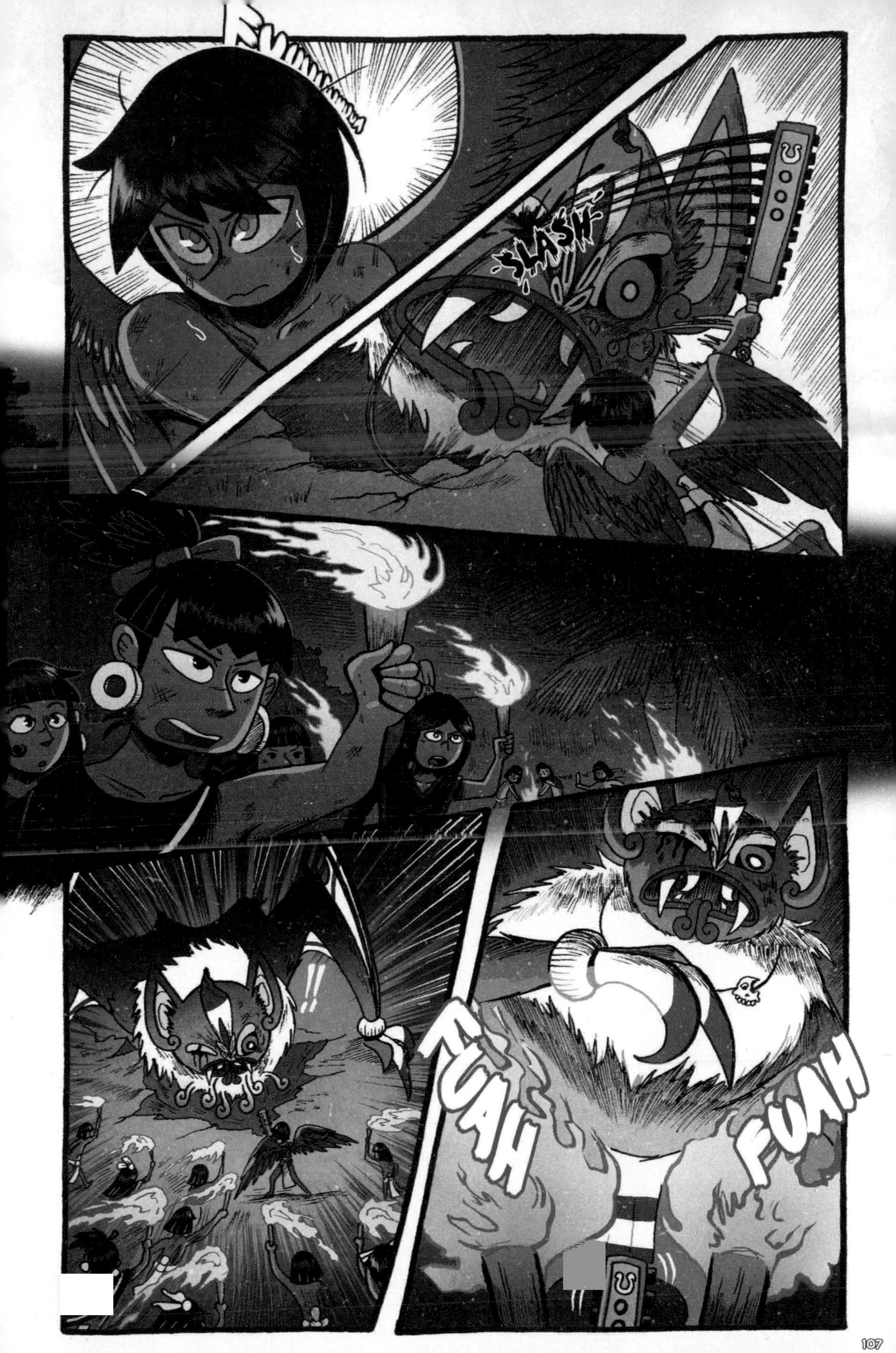

SLASH
!!
FUAH
FUAH

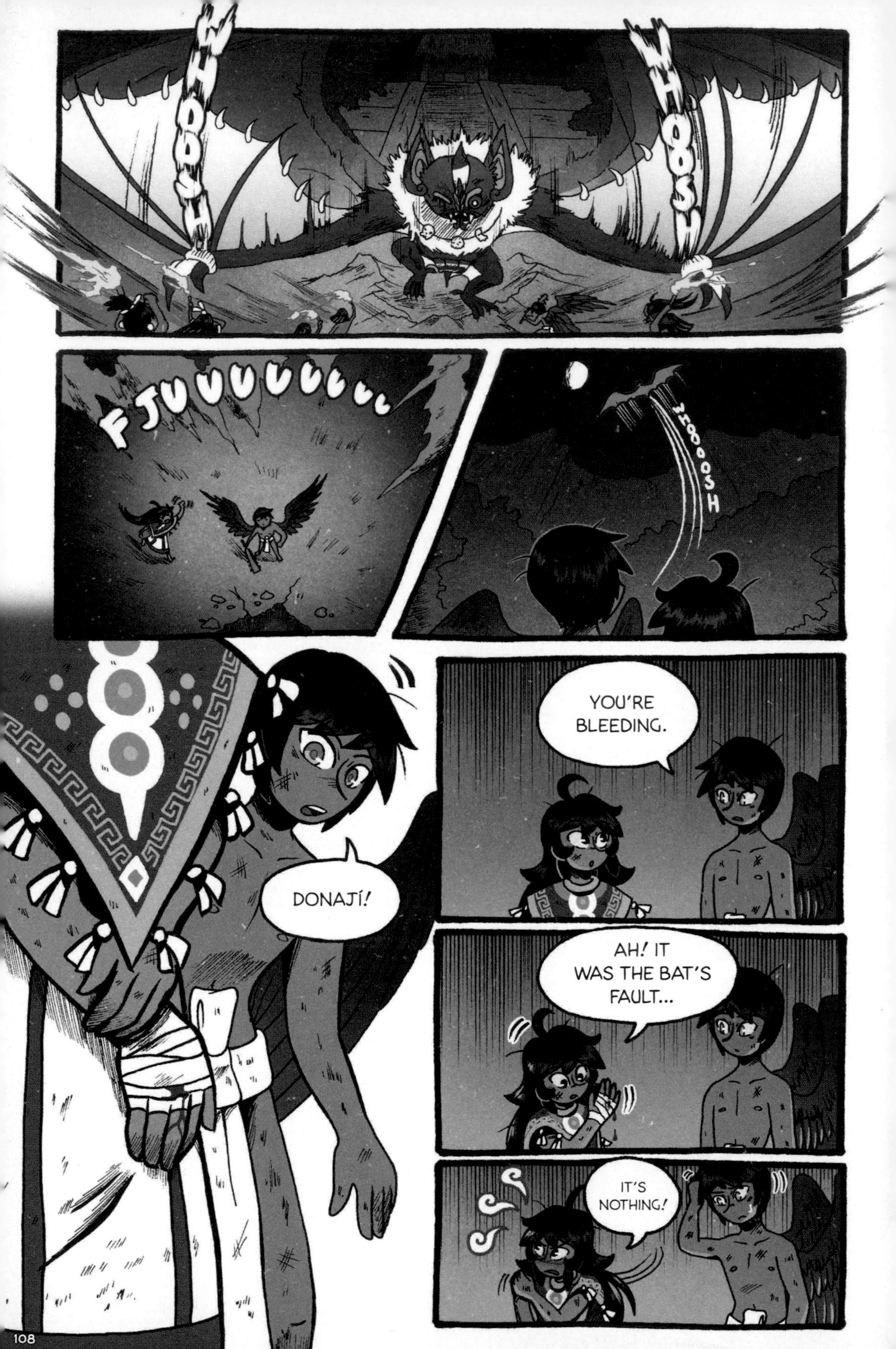
WHOOSH
WHOOSH
FJUUUUUUUU
WHOOOOSH
DONAJÍ!
YOU'RE BLEEDING.
AH! IT WAS THE BAT'S FAULT...
IT'S NOTHING!

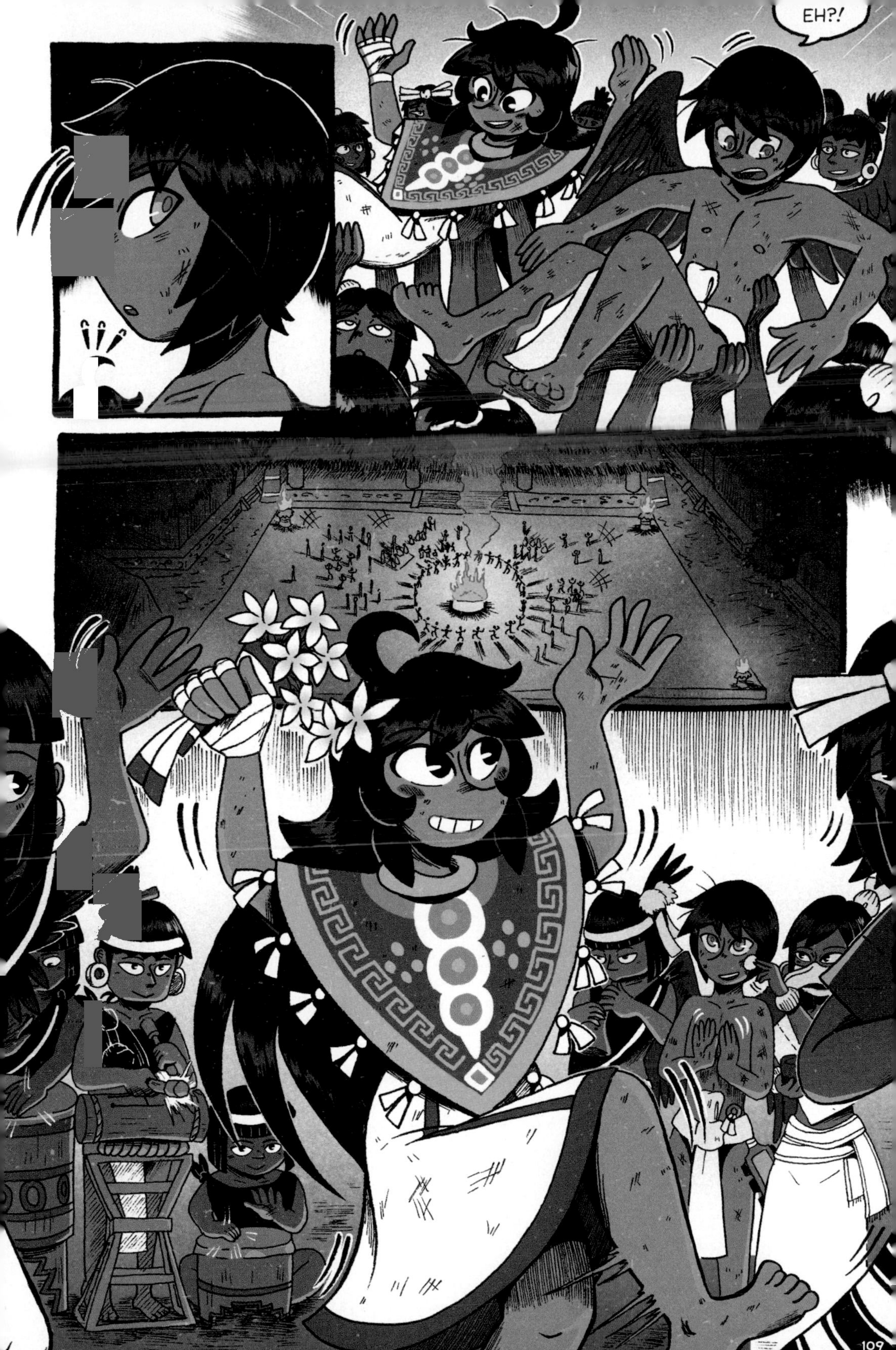
EH?!

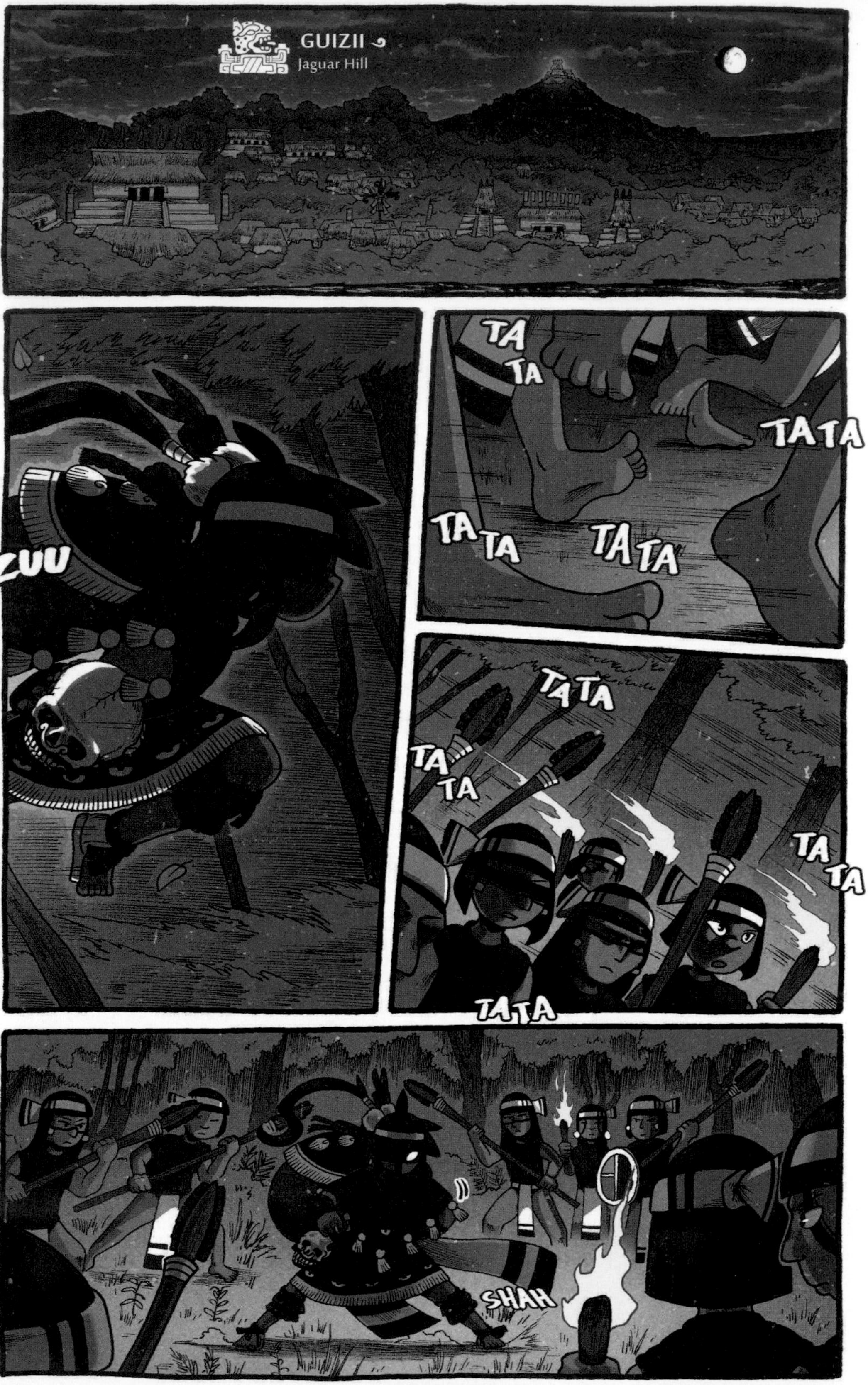
GUIZII
Jaguar Hill
ZUU
TA
TA
TATA
TATA
TATA
TATA
TA
TA
TA
TA
TATA
SHAH

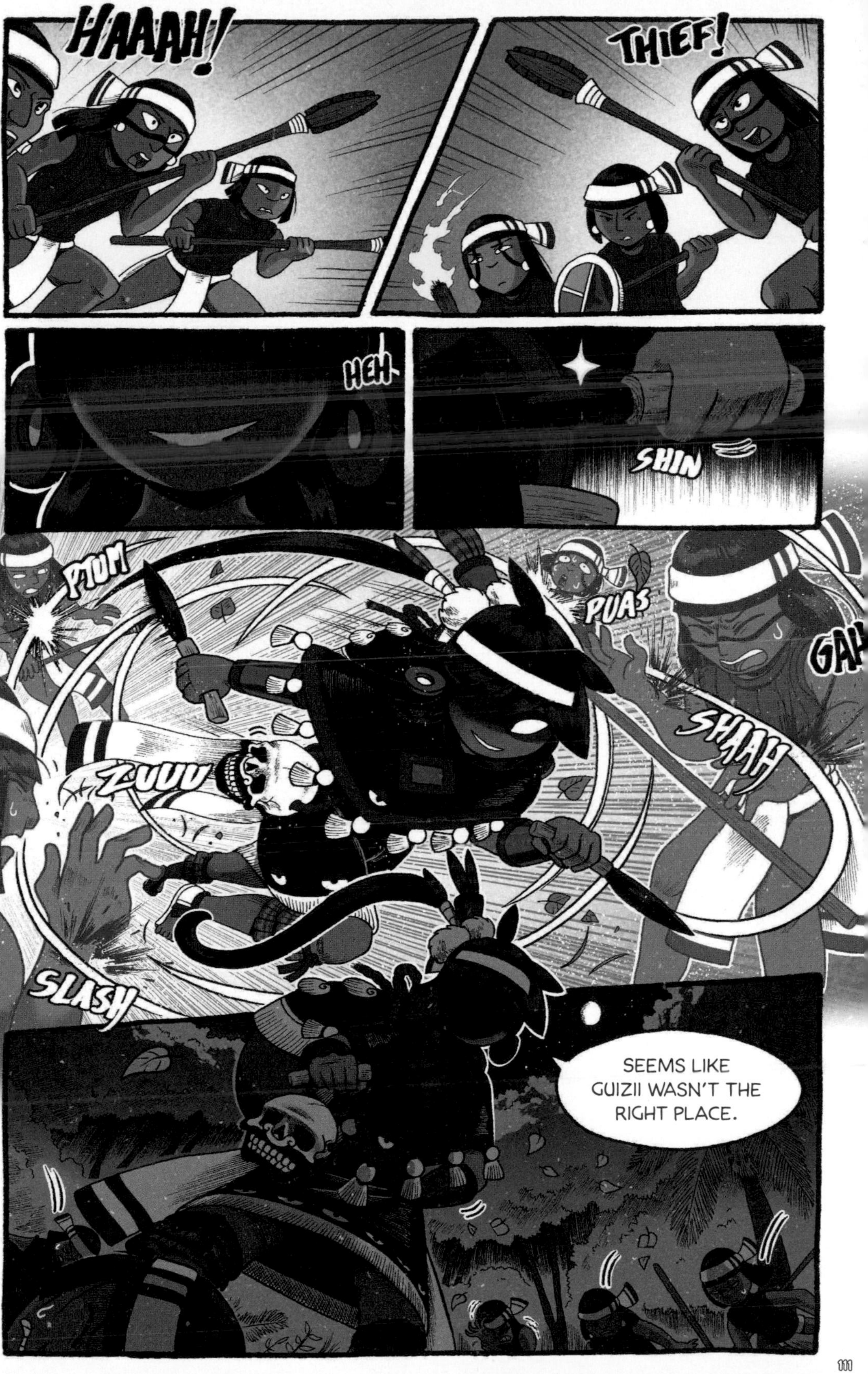
HAAAH!
THIEF!
HEH
SHIN
PTUM
PUAS
GAH
SHAAH
ZUUU
SLASH
SEEMS LIKE GUIZII WASN'T THE RIGHT PLACE.

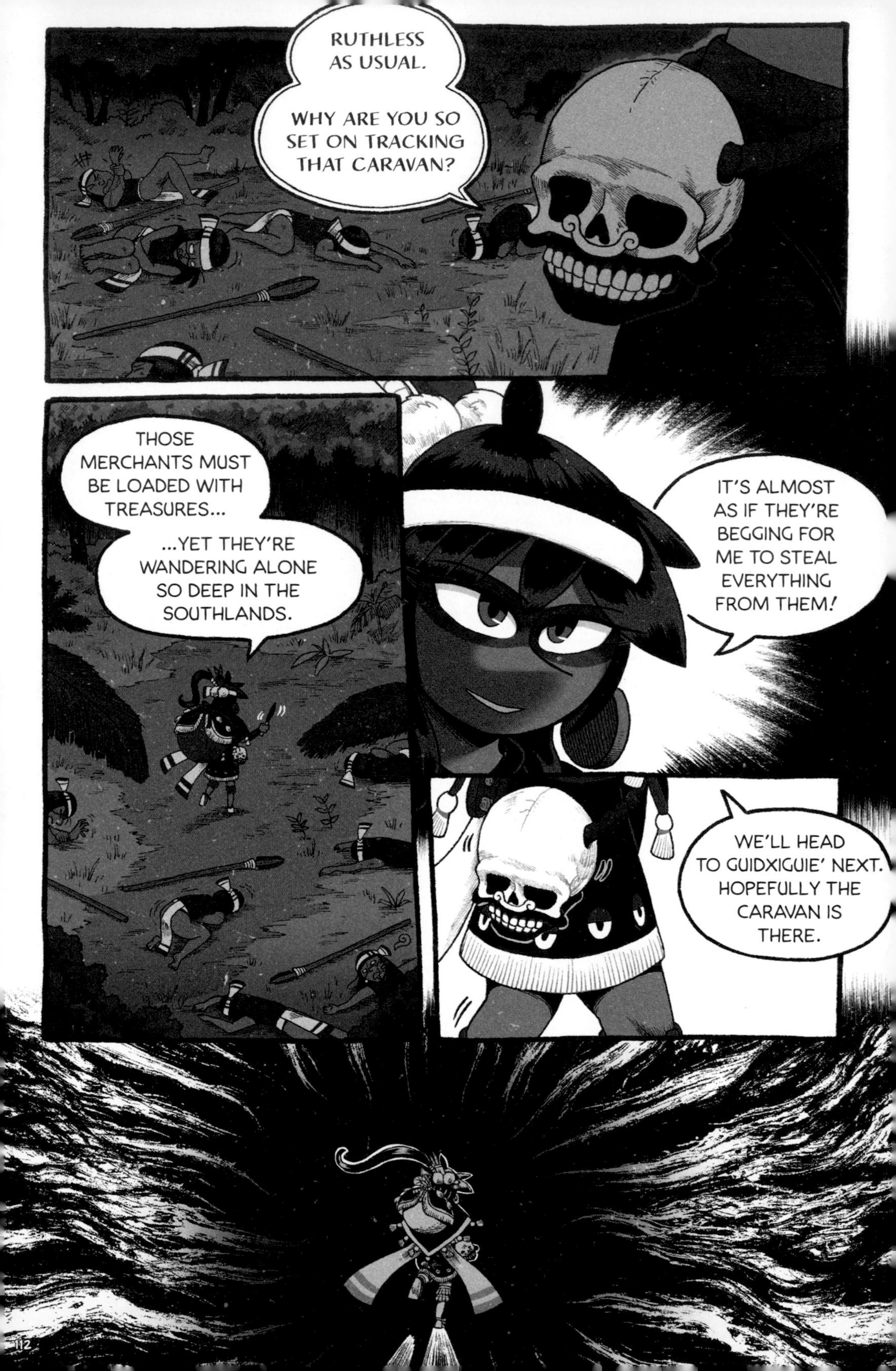
RUTHLESS AS USUAL.
WHY ARE YOU SO SET ON TRACKING THAT CARAVAN?
THOSE MERCHANTS MUST BE LOADED WITH TREASURES...
...YET THEY'RE WANDERING ALONE SO DEEP IN THE SOUTHLANDS.
IT'S ALMOST AS IF THEY'RE BEGGING FOR ME TO STEAL EVERYTHING FROM THEM!
WE'LL HEAD TO GUIDXIGUIE' NEXT. HOPEFULLY THE CARAVAN IS THERE.

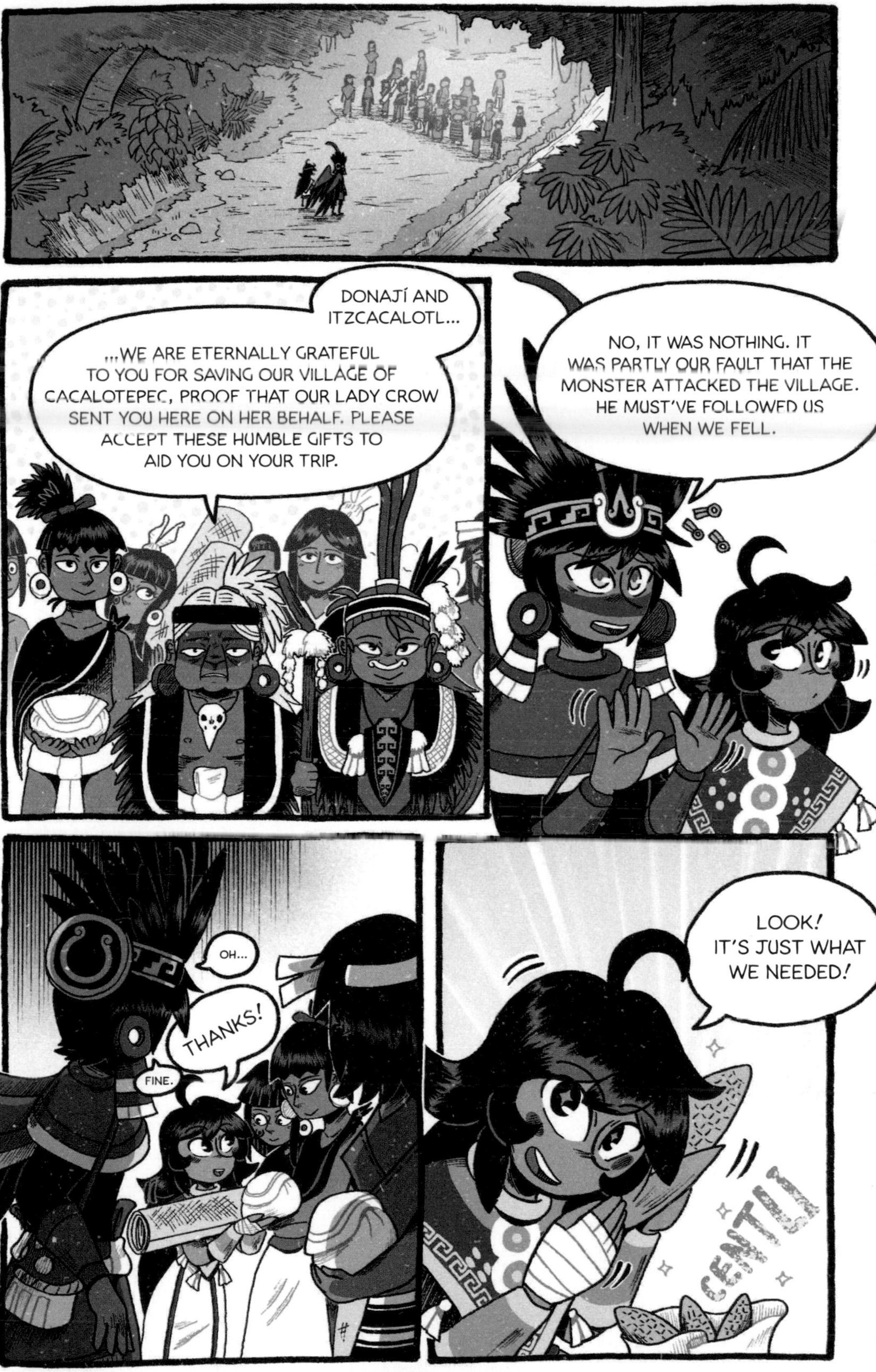
DONAJÍ AND ITZCACALOTL...
...WE ARE ETERNALLY GRATEFUL TO YOU FOR SAVING OUR VILLAGE OF CACALOTEPEC, PROOF THAT OUR LADY CROW SENT YOU HERE ON HER BEHALF. PLEASE ACCEPT THESE HUMBLE GIFTS TO AID YOU ON YOUR TRIP.
NO, IT WAS NOTHING. IT WAS PARTLY OUR FAULT THAT THE MONSTER ATTACKED THE VILLAGE. HE MUST'VE FOLLOWED US WHEN WE FELL.
OH...
THANKS!
FINE.
LOOK! IT'S JUST WHAT WE NEEDED!
CENTLI

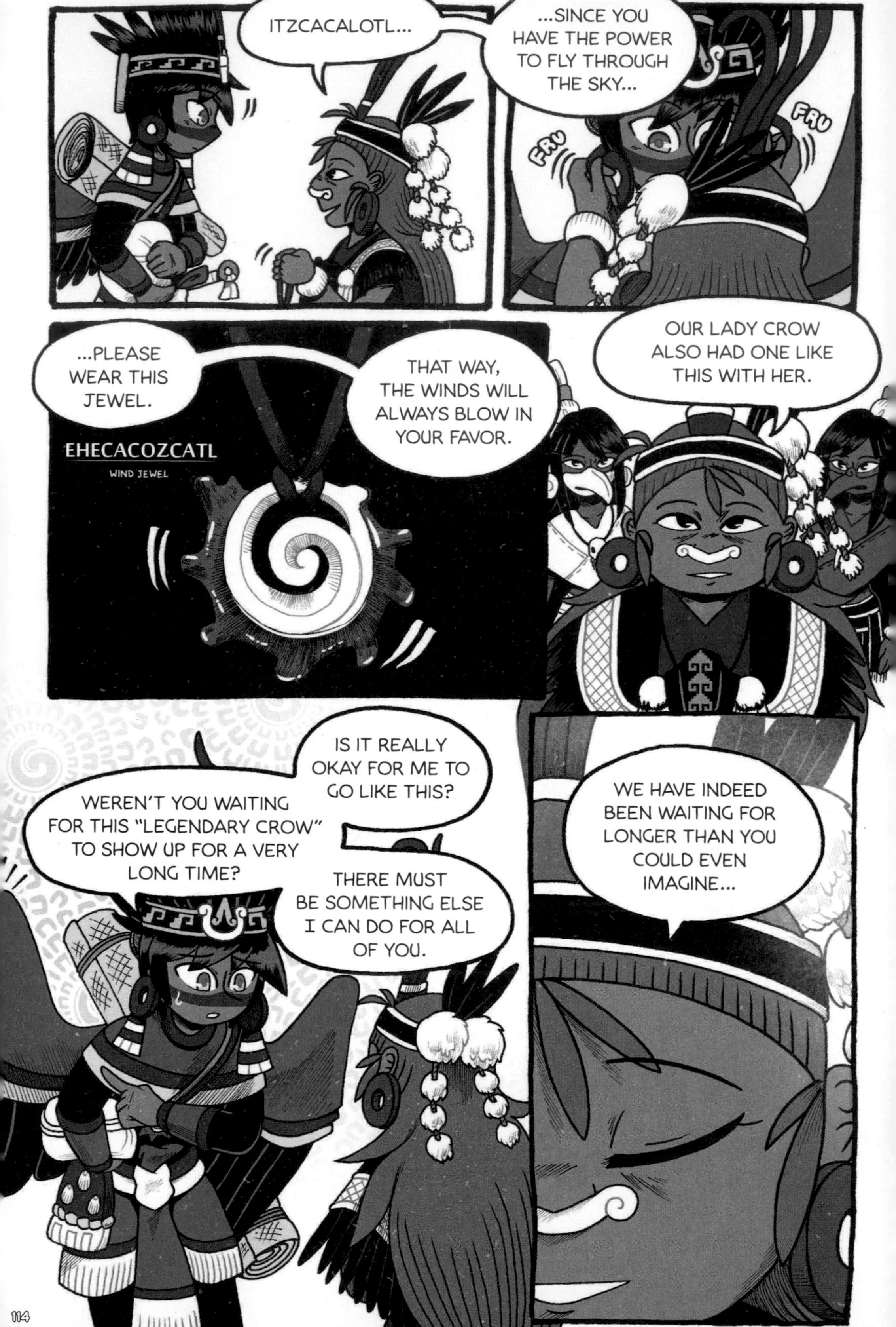

ITZCACALOTL...
...SINCE YOU HAVE THE POWER TO FLY THROUGH THE SKY...
FRU
FRU
...PLEASE WEAR THIS JEWEL.
THAT WAY, THE WINDS WILL ALWAYS BLOW IN YOUR FAVOR.
EHECACOZCATL
WIND JEWEL
OUR LADY CROW ALSO HAD ONE LIKE THIS WITH HER.
IS IT REALLY OKAY FOR ME TO GO LIKE THIS?
WEREN'T YOU WAITING FOR THIS "LEGENDARY CROW" TO SHOW UP FOR A VERY LONG TIME?
THERE MUST BE SOMETHING ELSE I CAN DO FOR ALL OF YOU.
WE HAVE INDEED BEEN WAITING FOR LONGER THAN YOU COULD EVEN IMAGINE...

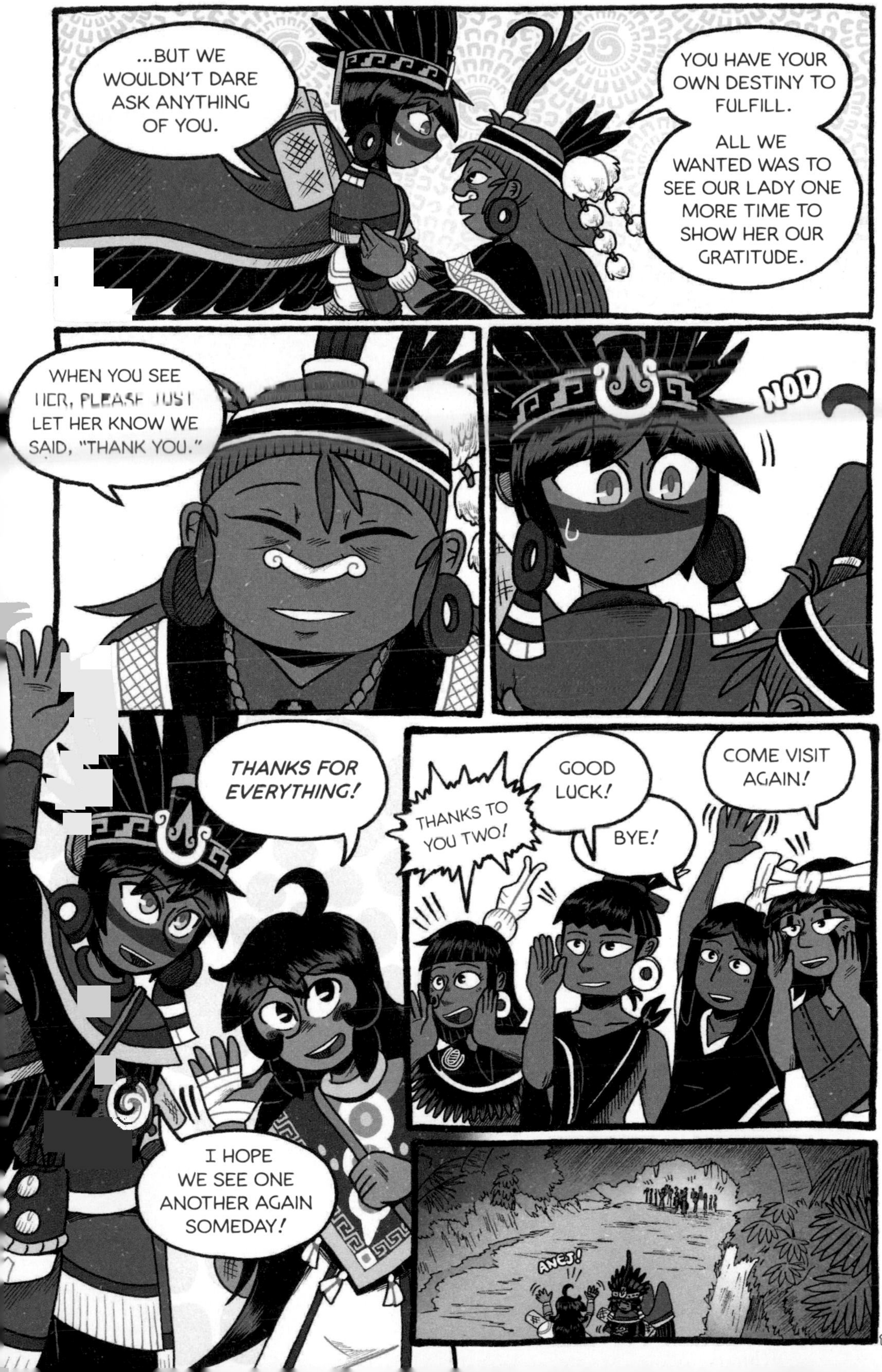

...BUT WE WOULDN'T DARE ASK ANYTHING OF YOU.
YOU HAVE YOUR OWN DESTINY TO FULFILL.
ALL WE WANTED WAS TO SEE OUR LADY ONE MORE TIME TO SHOW HER OUR GRATITUDE.
WHEN YOU SEE HER, PLEASE JUST LET HER KNOW WE SAID, "THANK YOU."
NOD
THANKS FOR EVERYTHING!
I HOPE WE SEE ONE ANOTHER AGAIN SOMEDAY!
THANKS TO YOU TWO!
GOOD LUCK!
BYE!
COME VISIT AGAIN!
ANEJ!

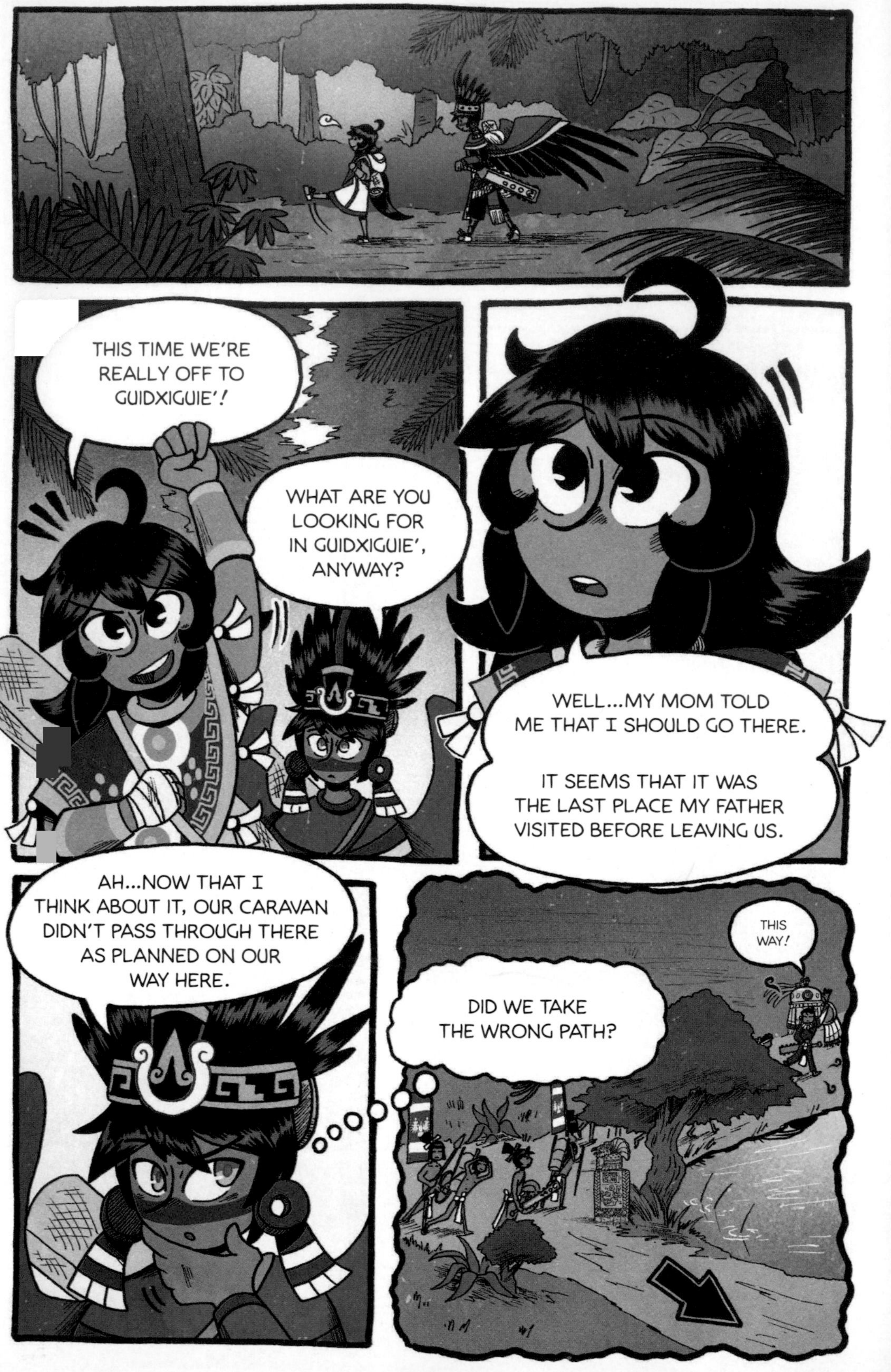
THIS TIME WE'RE REALLY OFF TO GUIDXIGUIE'!
WHAT ARE YOU LOOKING FOR IN GUIDXIGUIE', ANYWAY?
WELL...MY MOM TOLD ME THAT I SHOULD GO THERE.
IT SEEMS THAT IT WAS THE LAST PLACE MY FATHER VISITED BEFORE LEAVING US.
AH...NOW THAT I THINK ABOUT IT, OUR CARAVAN DIDN'T PASS THROUGH THERE AS PLANNED ON OUR WAY HERE.
DID WE TAKE THE WRONG PATH?
THIS WAY!

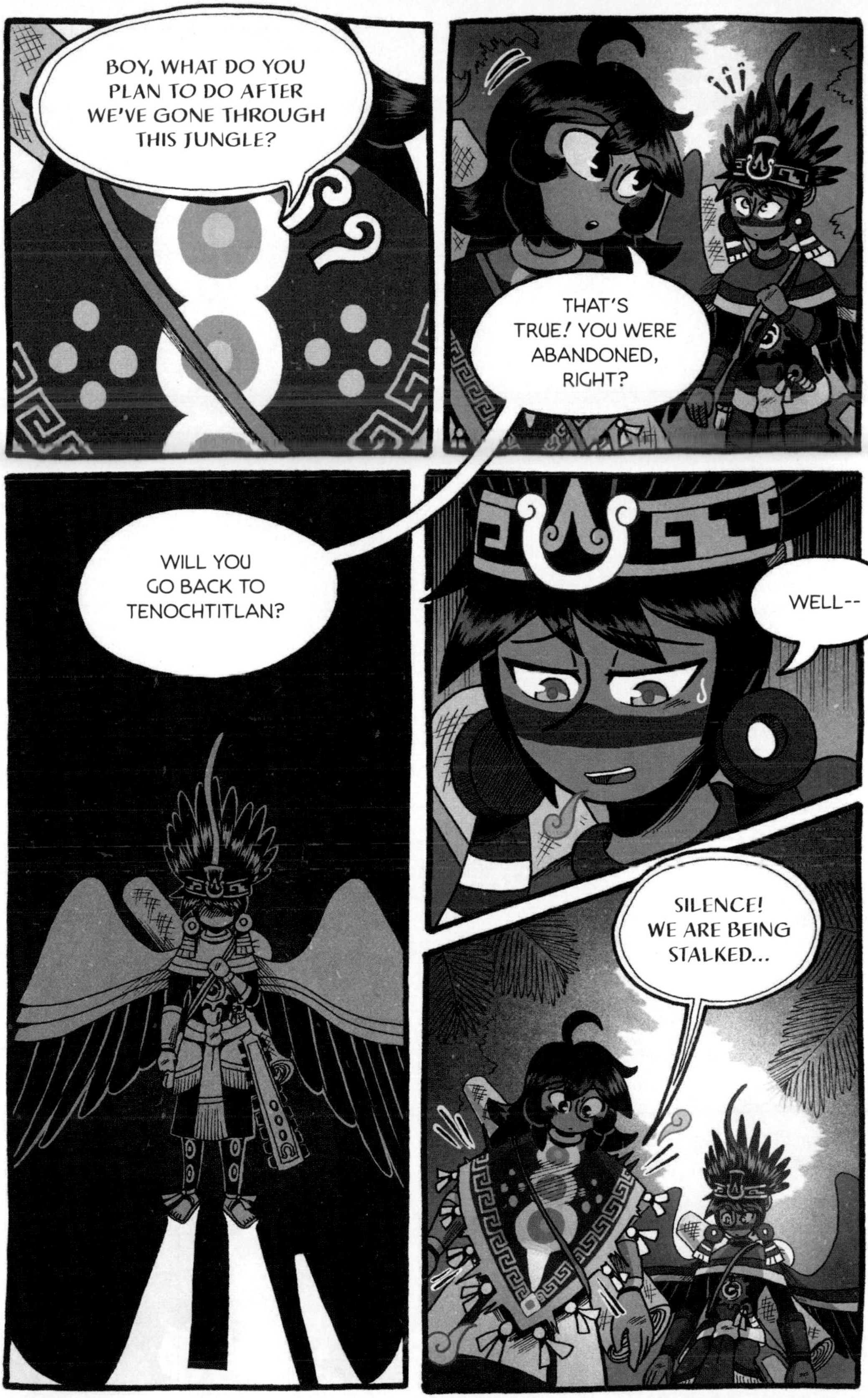
BOY, WHAT DO YOU PLAN TO DO AFTER WE'VE GONE THROUGH THIS JUNGLE?
THAT'S TRUE! YOU WERE ABANDONED, RIGHT?
WILL YOU GO BACK TO TENOCHTITLAN?
WELL--
SILENCE! WE ARE BEING STALKED...

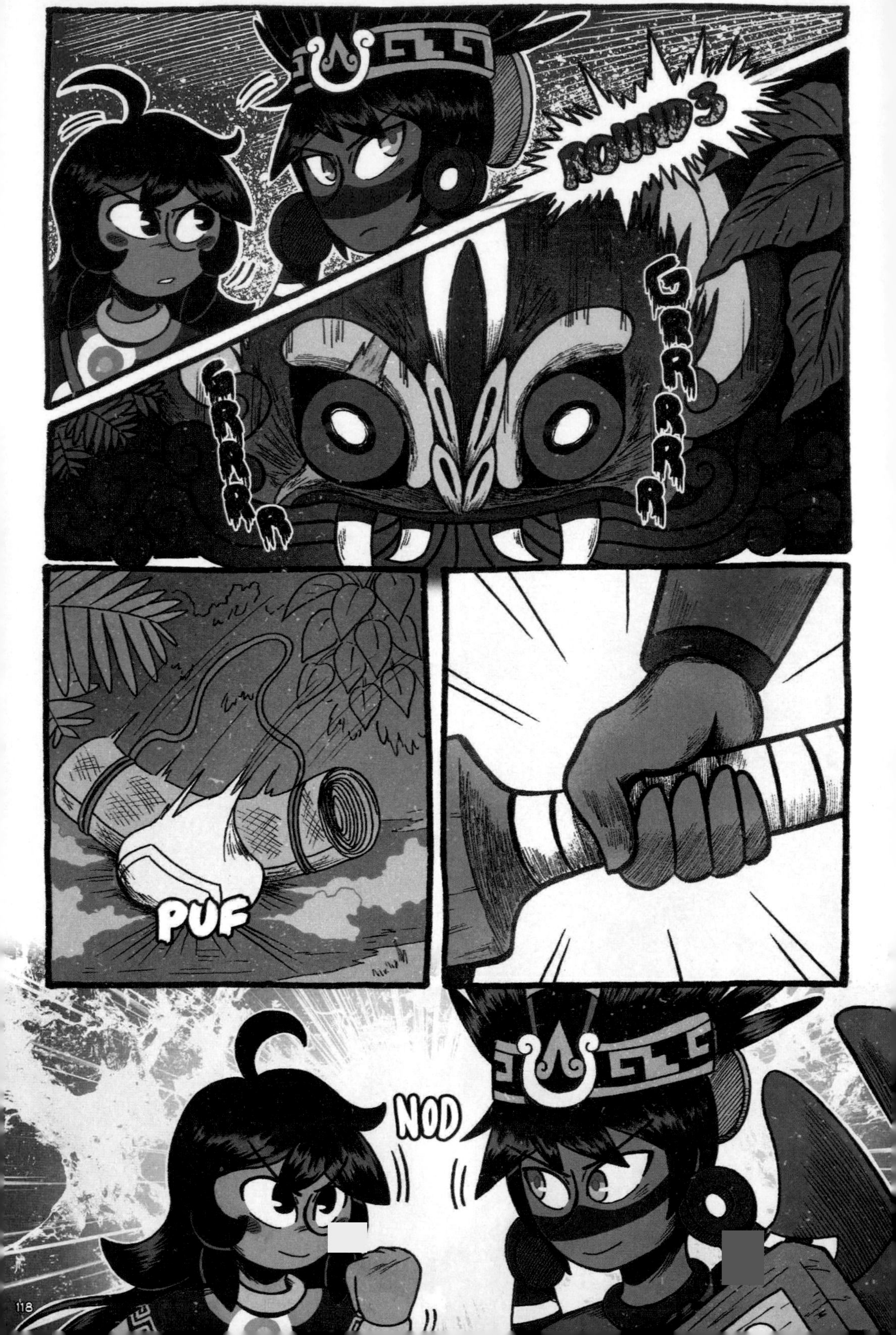
ROUND 3
GRRRRR
GRRRRRR
PUF
NOD

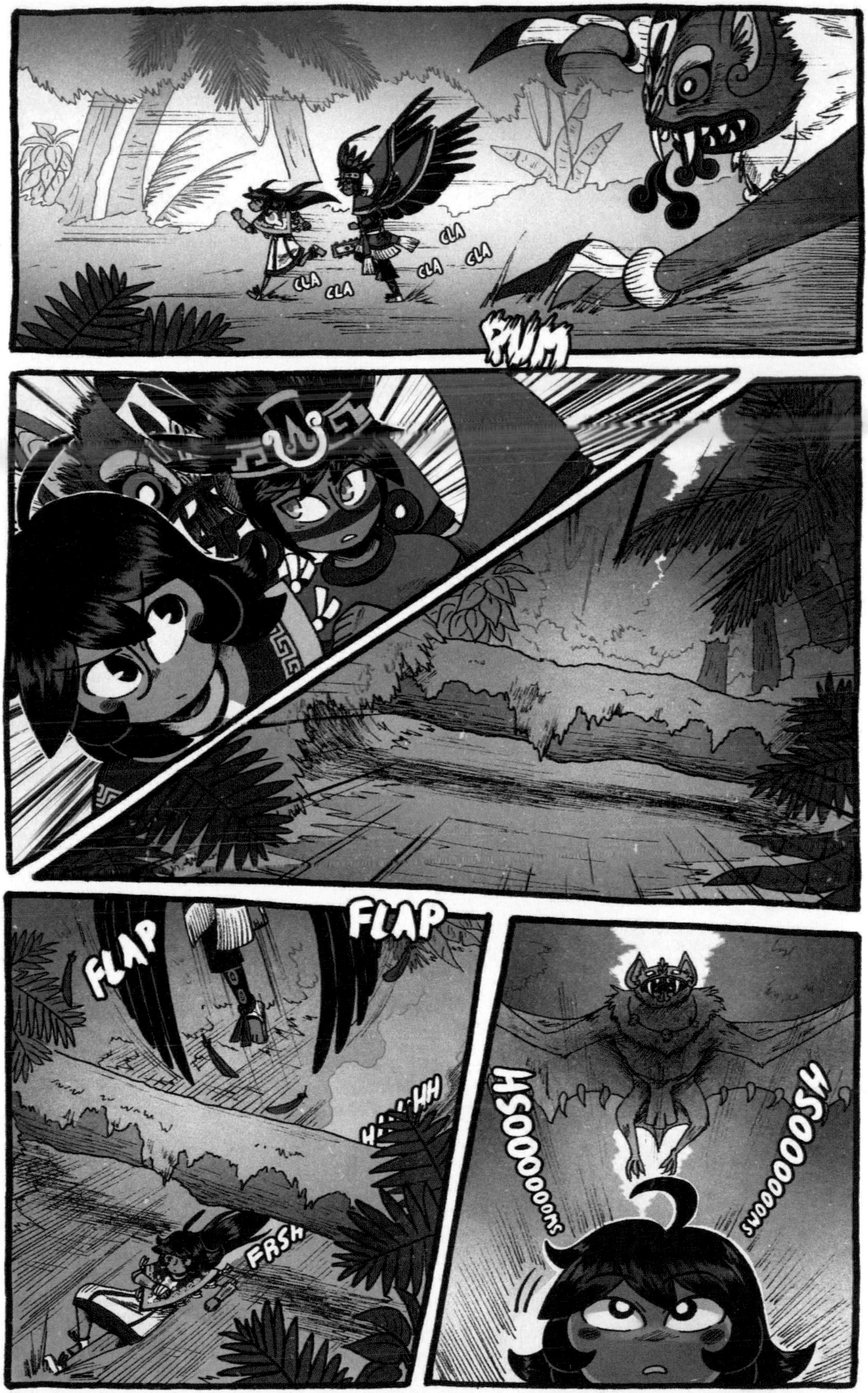
CLA
CLA
CLA
CLA
CLA
CLA
PUM
FLAP
FLAP
FRSH
SWOOOOOOSH
SWOOOOOOSH

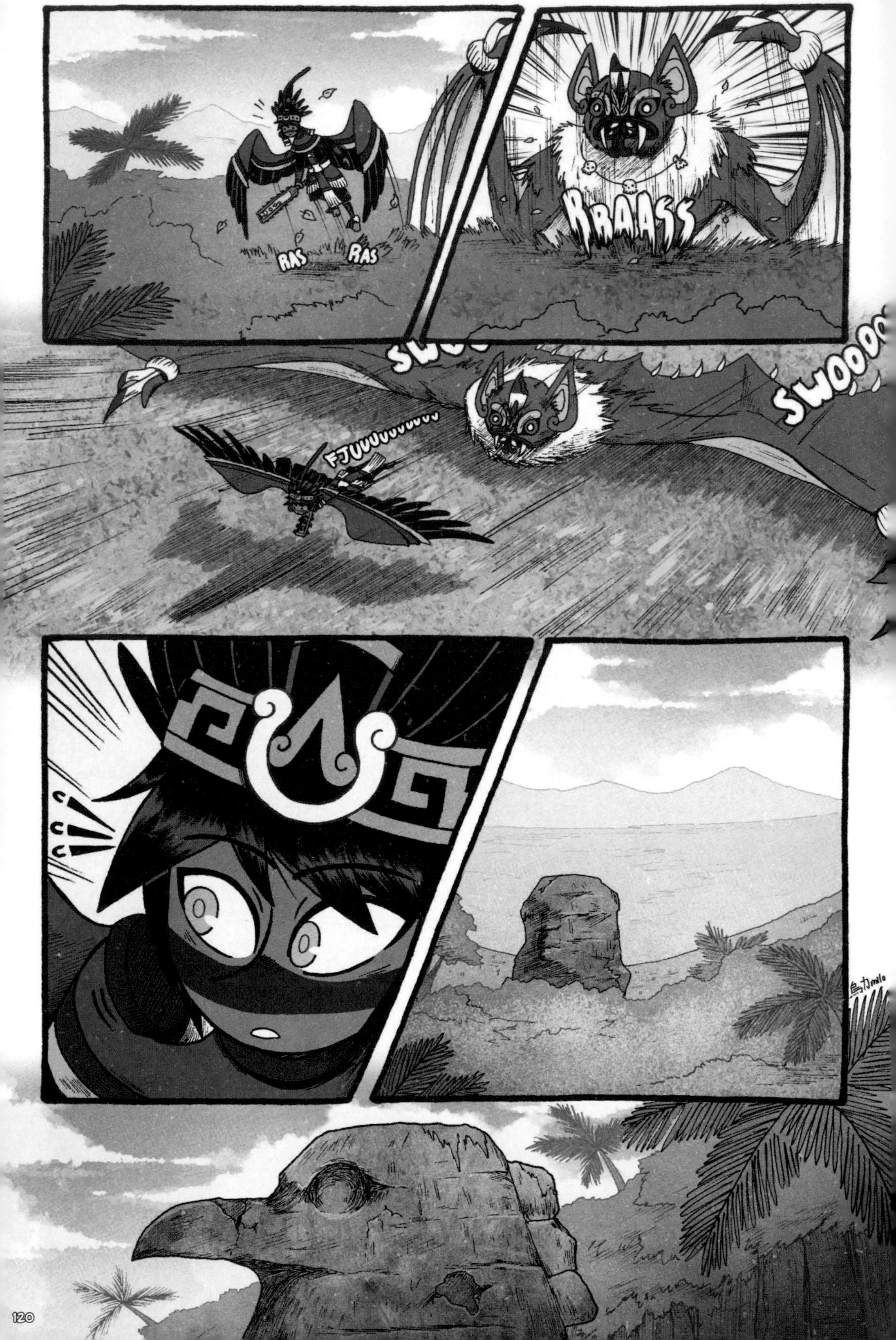
RAS
RAS
RBAASS
SWOO
SWOOO
FJUUUUUUUU
¡¡!!

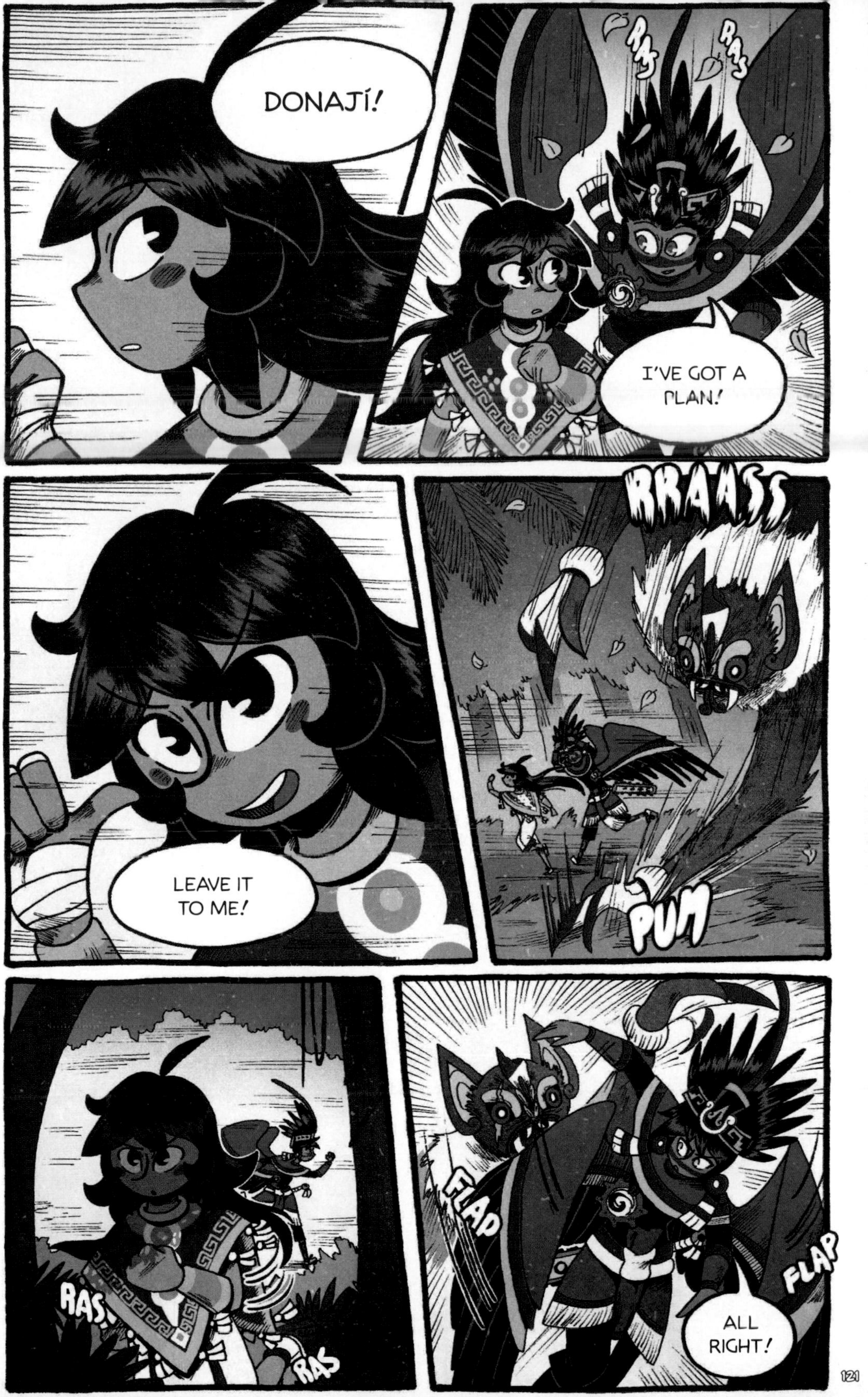
DONAJÍ!
RAS
RAS
I'VE GOT A PLAN!
LEAVE IT TO ME!
BRAASS
PUM
RAS
RAS
FLAP
FLAP
ALL RIGHT!

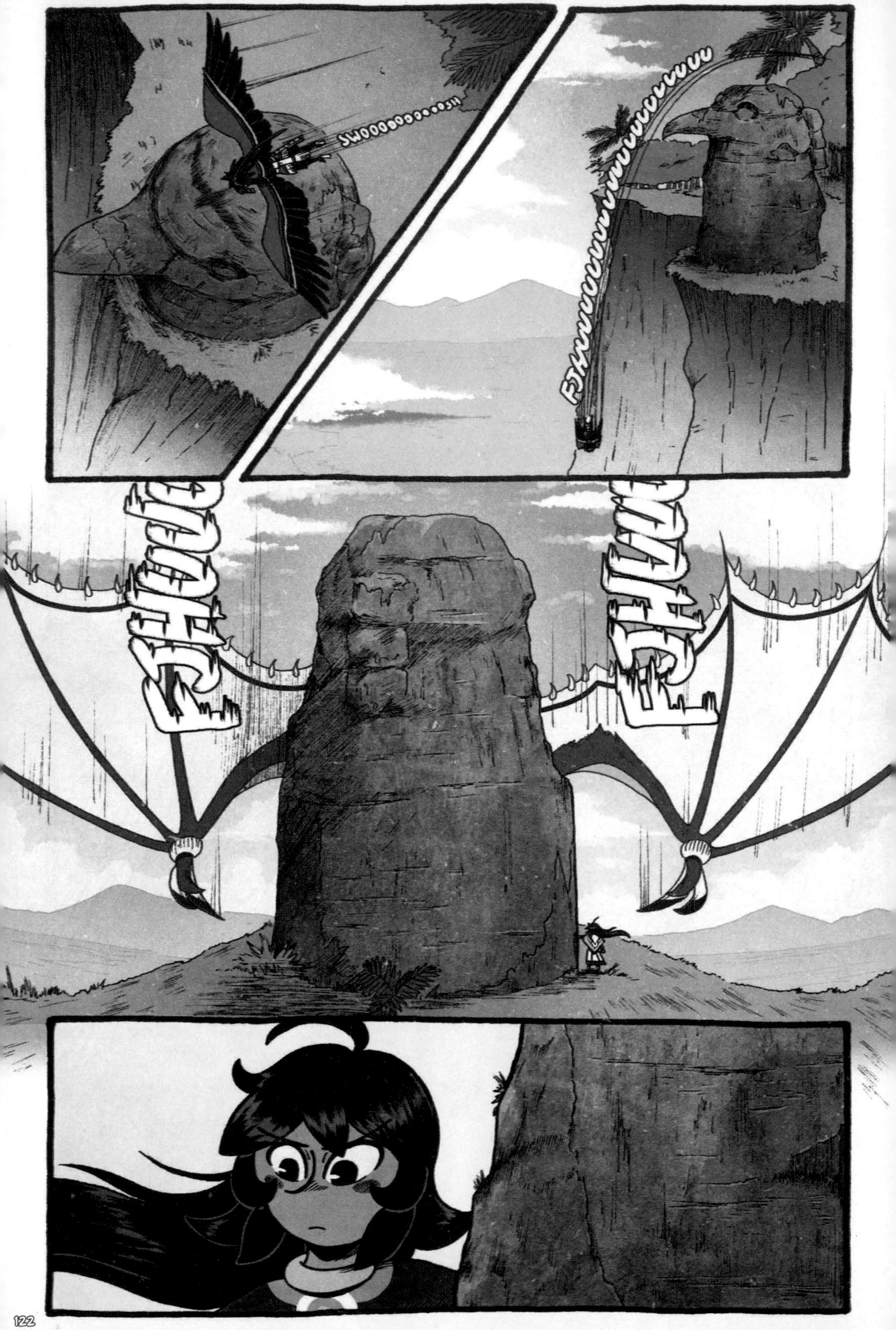
SWOOOoooooooosH
FSHUUUUUUUUUUUUUUUUUUUUUUUU
FSHUU
FSHUU

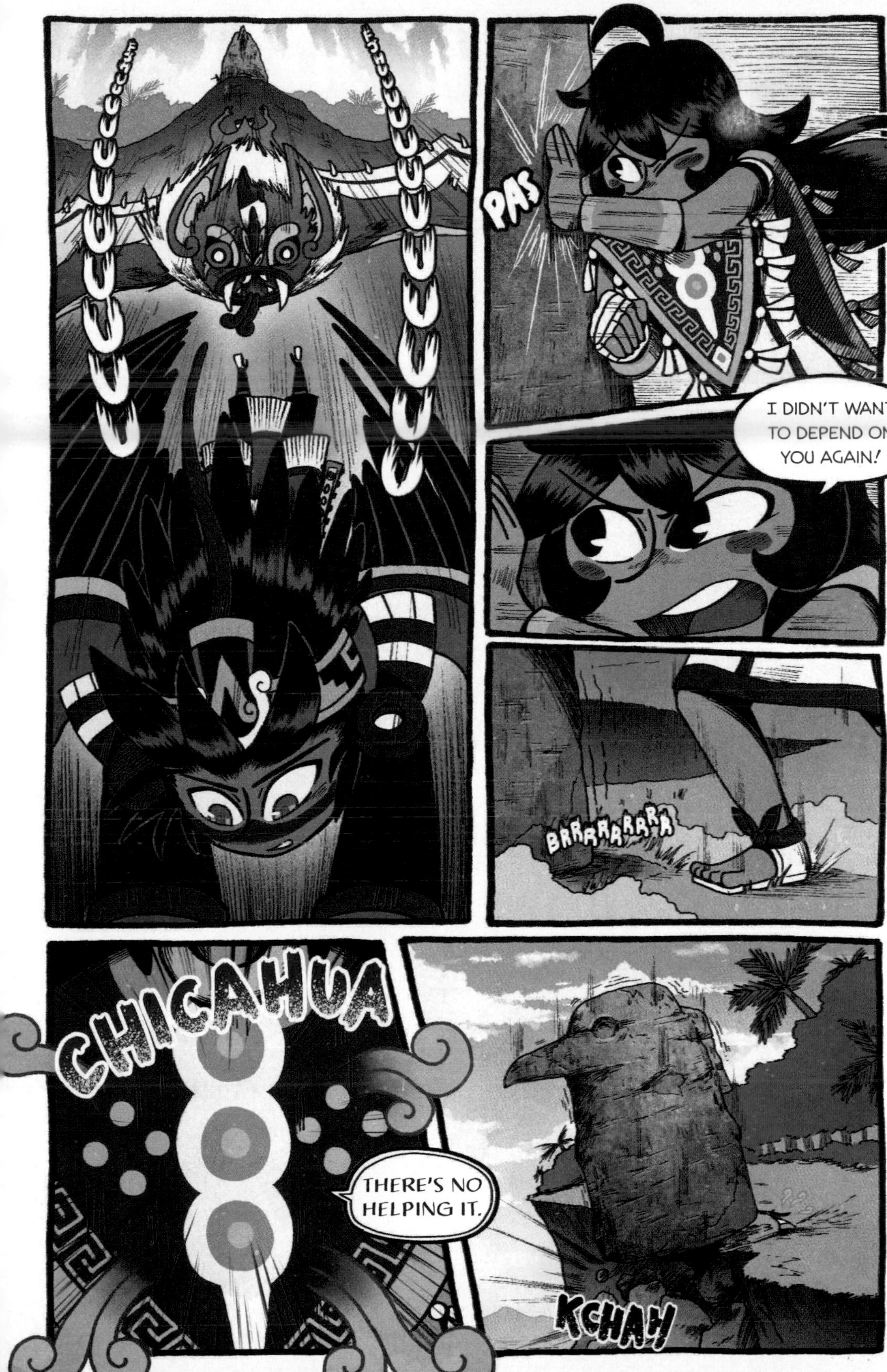

PAS
I DIDN'T WANT TO DEPEND ON YOU AGAIN!
BRRRRRRRRR
CHICAHUA
THERE'S NO HELPING IT.
KCHAH

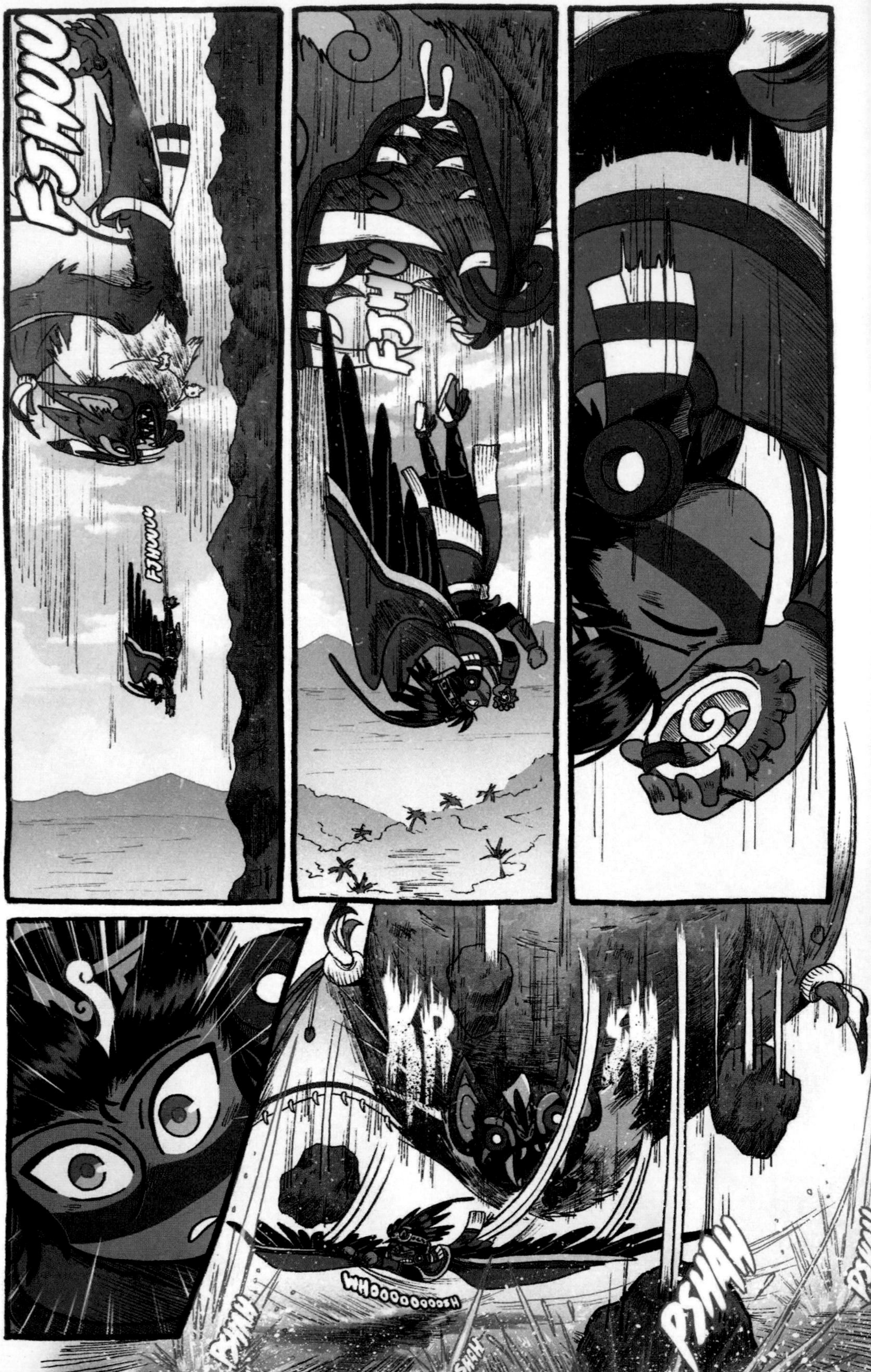
FSHOOO
FSHUUUU
FSHO
KR
SH
WHOOOOOOOOOSH
PSHAH

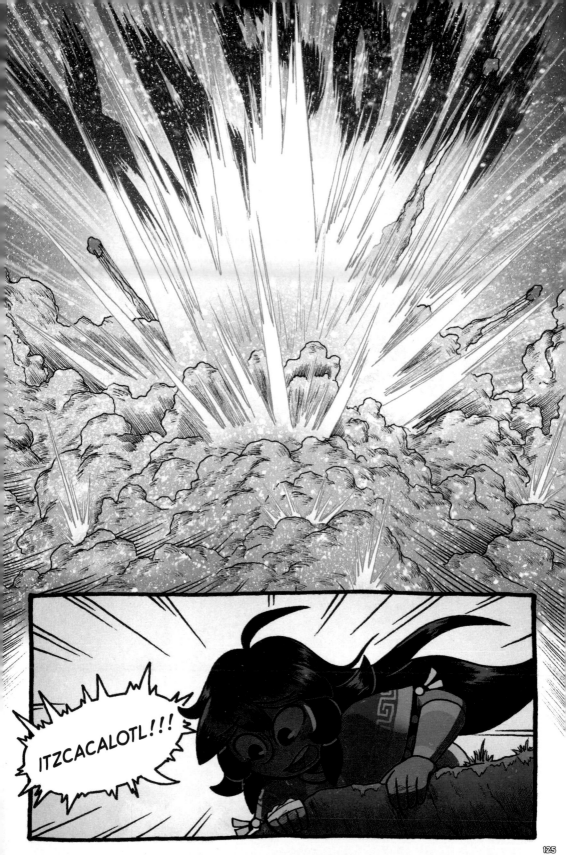

ITZCACALOTL!!!

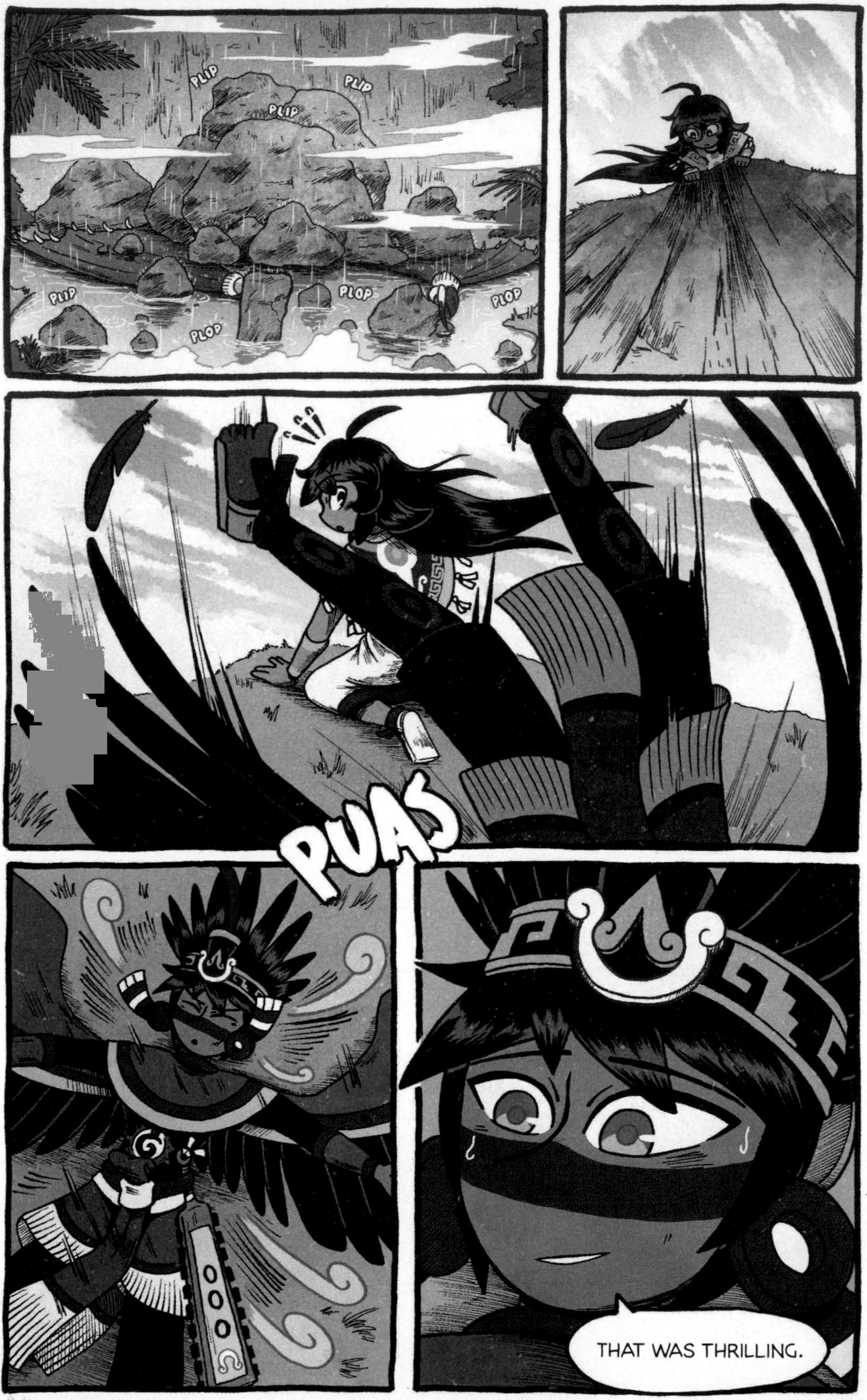
PLIP
PLIP
PLIP
PLIP
PLOP
PLOP
PLOP
PUAS
THAT WAS THRILLING.

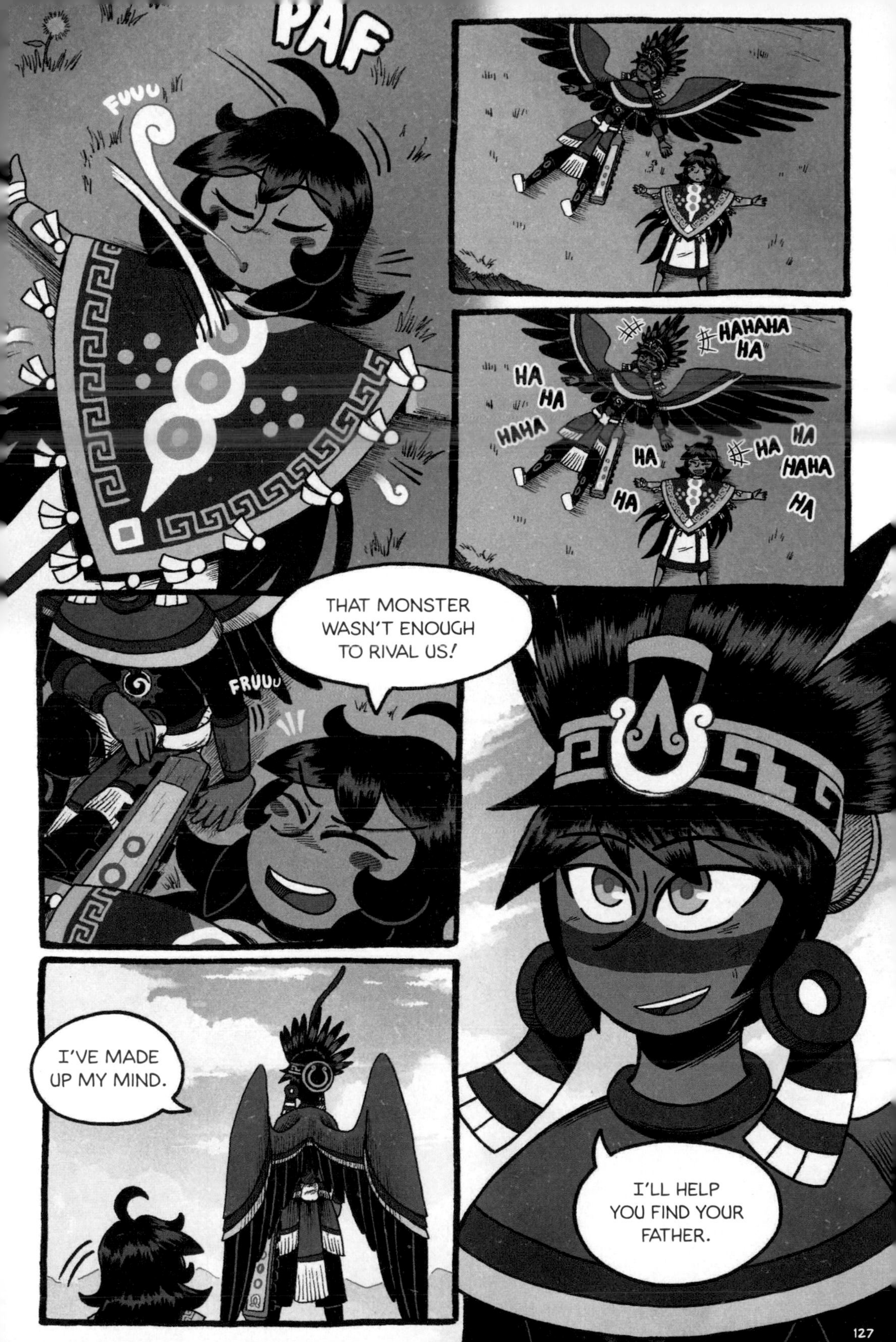
PAF
FUUU
HAHAHA
HA
HA
HA
HAHA
HA
HA
HA
HAHA
HA
HA
THAT MONSTER WASN'T ENOUGH TO RIVAL US!
FRUUU
I'VE MADE UP MY MIND.
I'LL HELP YOU FIND YOUR FATHER.

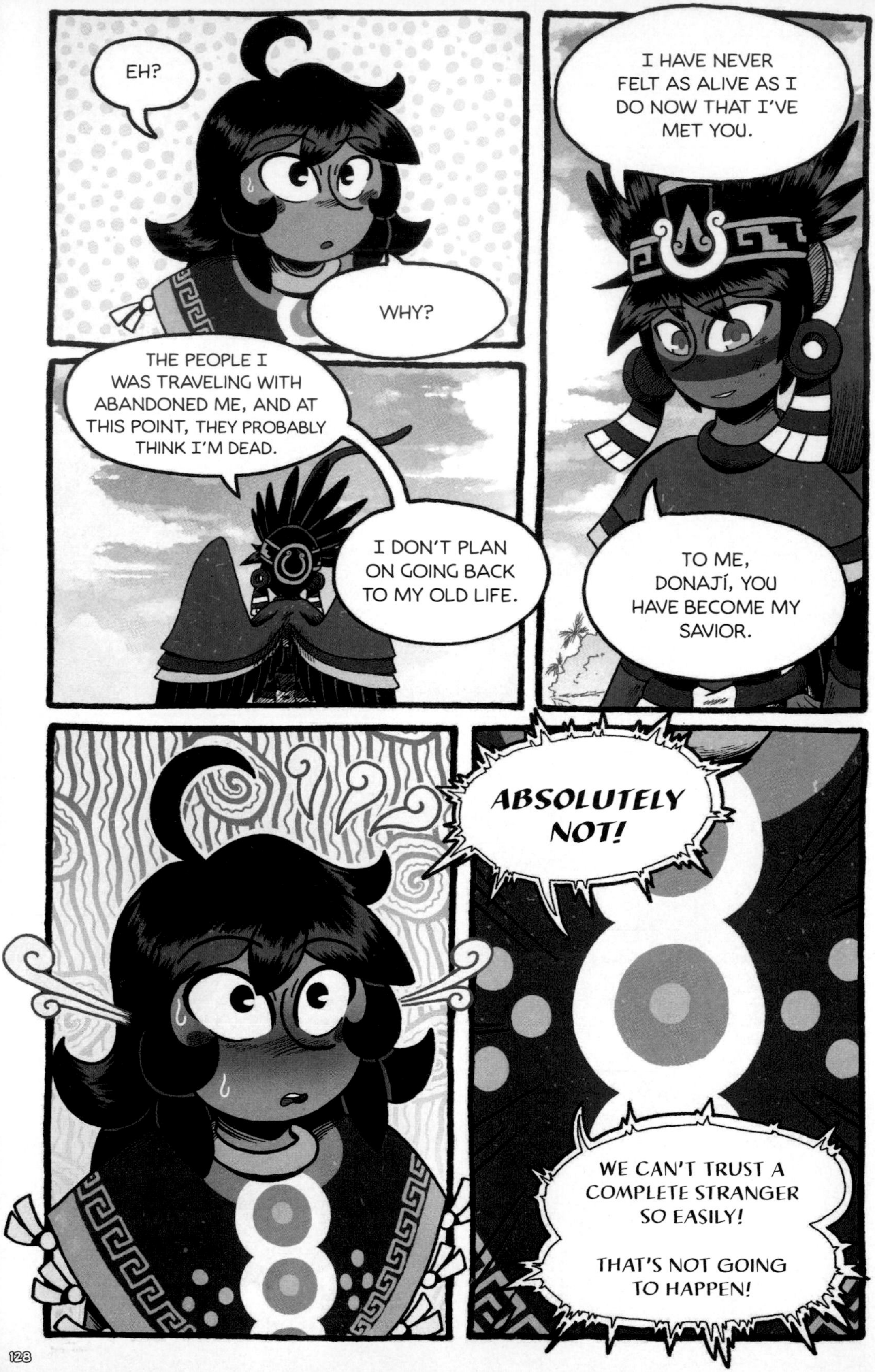
EH?
WHY?
I HAVE NEVER FELT AS ALIVE AS I DO NOW THAT I'VE MET YOU.
THE PEOPLE I WAS TRAVELING WITH ABANDONED ME, AND AT THIS POINT, THEY PROBABLY THINK I'M DEAD.
I DON'T PLAN ON GOING BACK TO MY OLD LIFE.
TO ME, DONAJÍ, YOU HAVE BECOME MY SAVIOR.
ABSOLUTELY NOT!
WE CAN'T TRUST A COMPLETE STRANGER SO EASILY!
THAT'S NOT GOING TO HAPPEN!

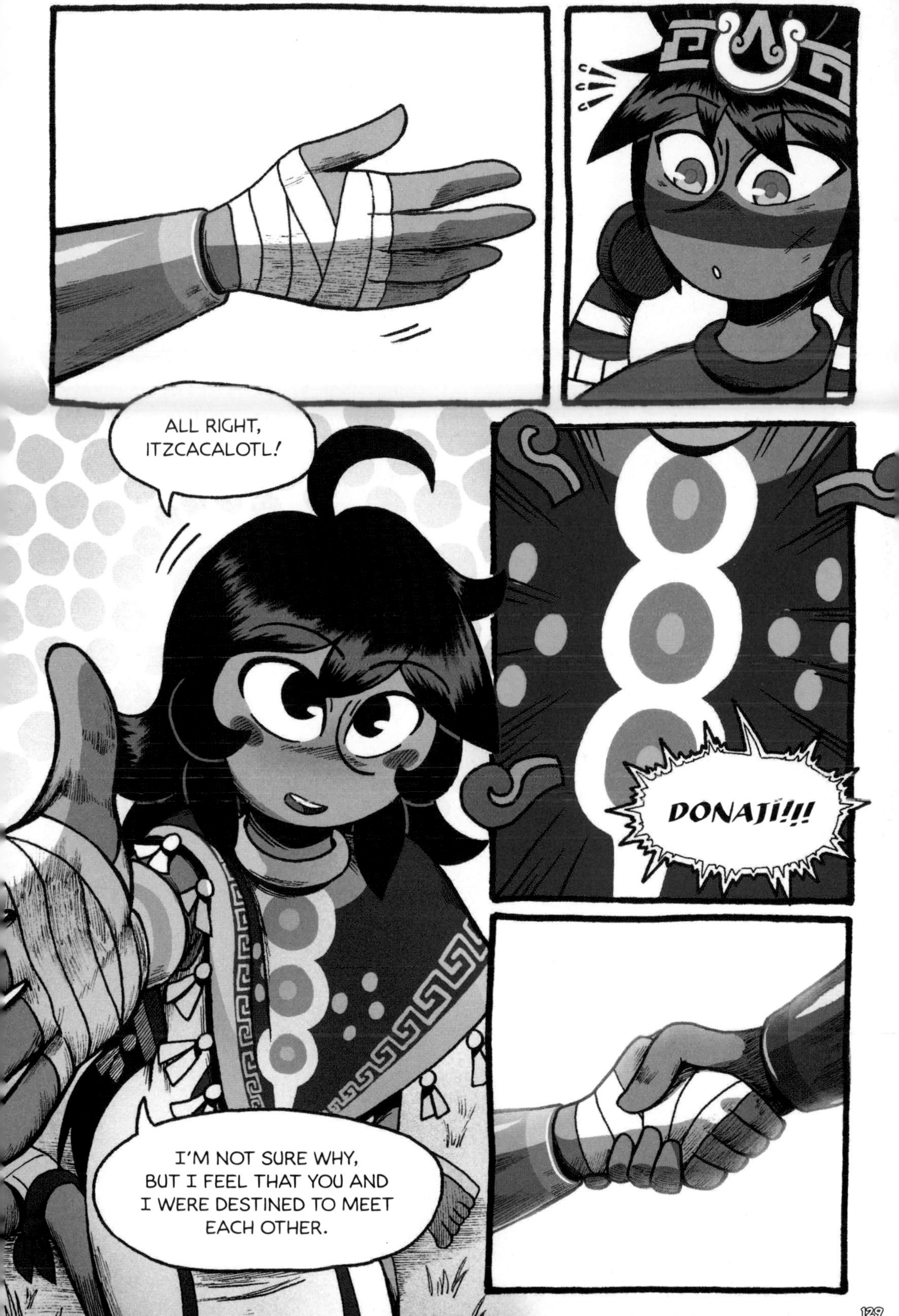
ALL RIGHT, ITZCACALOTL!
DONAJI!!!
I'M NOT SURE WHY, BUT I FEEL THAT YOU AND I WERE DESTINED TO MEET EACH OTHER.

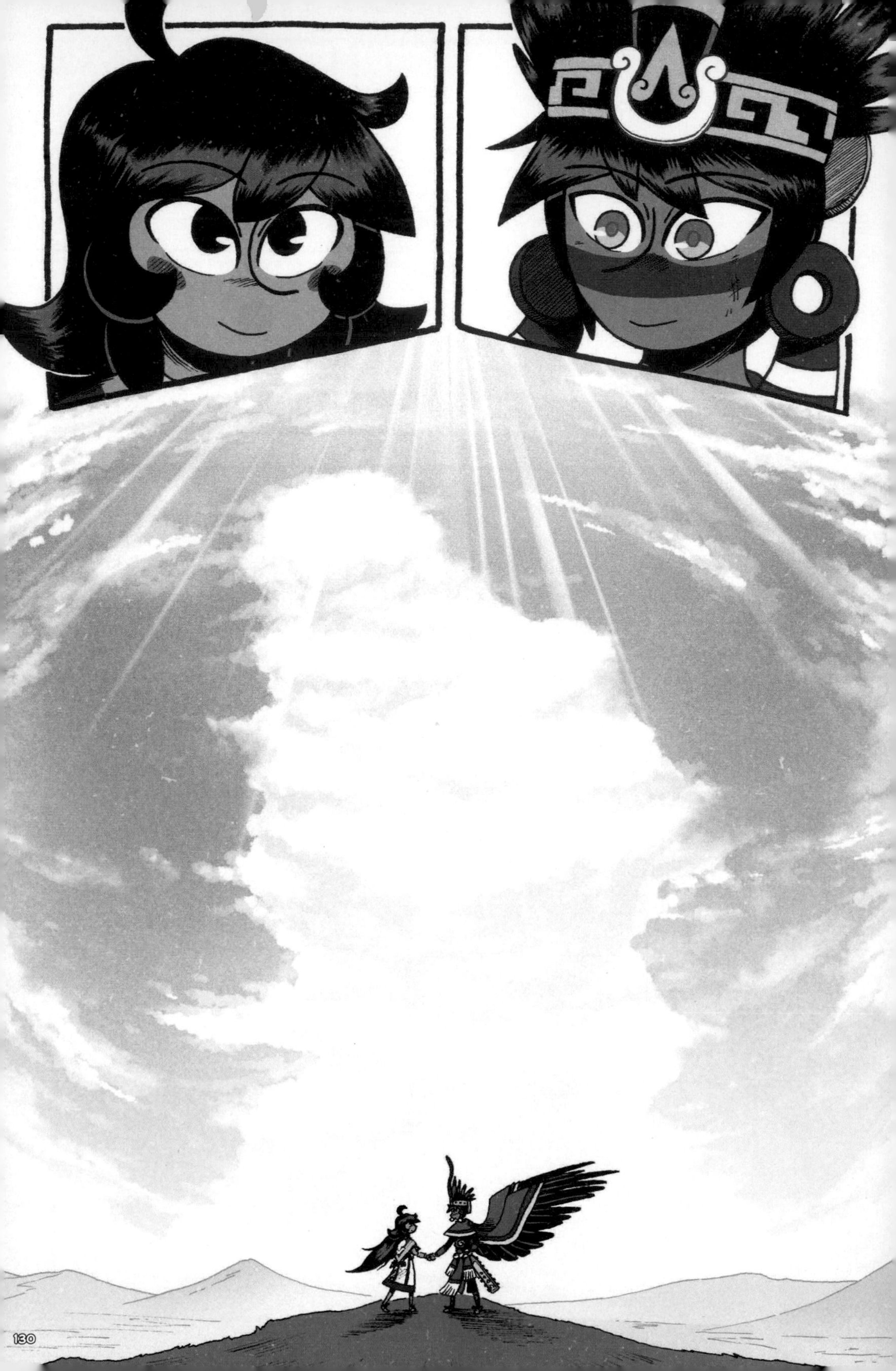

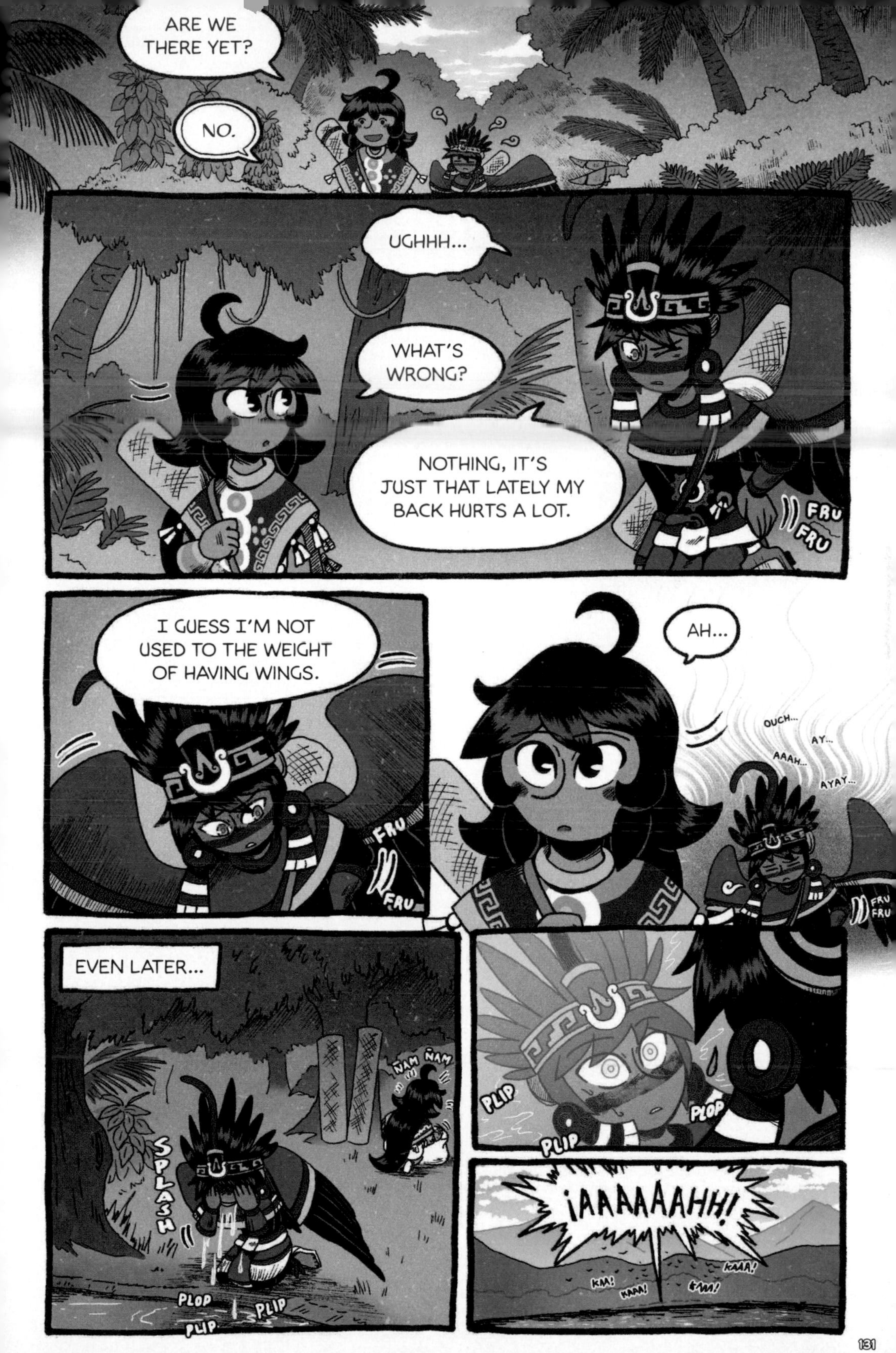
ARE WE THERE YET?
NO.
UGHHH...
WHAT'S WRONG?
NOTHING, IT'S JUST THAT LATELY MY BACK HURTS A LOT.
FRU FRU
I GUESS I'M NOT USED TO THE WEIGHT OF HAVING WINGS.
FRU
FRU
AH...
OUCH...
AY...
AAAH...
AYAY...
FRU FRU
EVEN LATER...
ÑAM ÑAM
SPLASH
PLOP
PLIP
PLIP
PLIP
PLOP
PLIP
¡AAAAAAHH!
KAA!
KAAA!
KAAA!
KAAA!

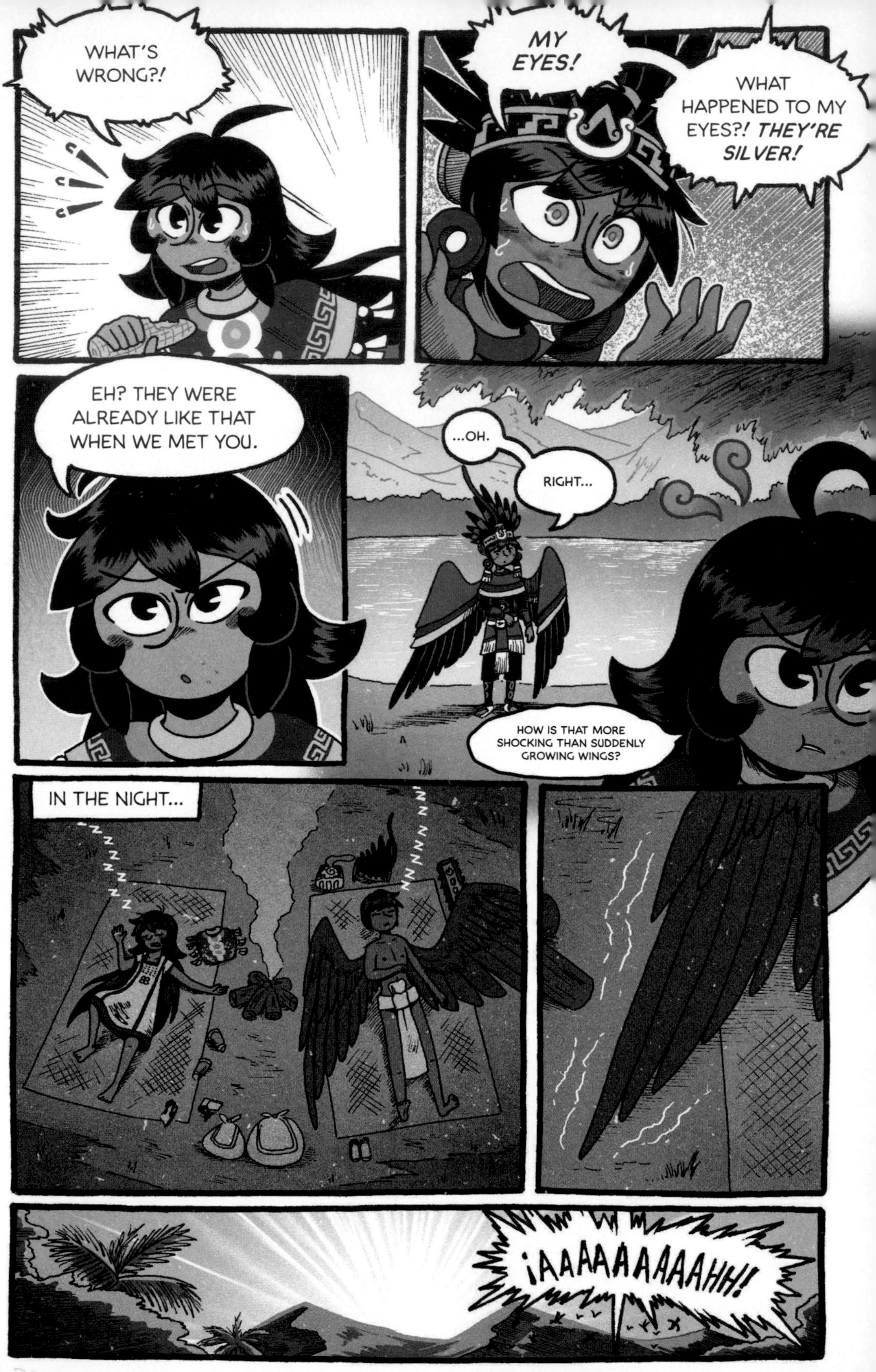
WHAT'S WRONG?!
MY EYES!
WHAT HAPPENED TO MY EYES?! THEY'RE SILVER!
EH? THEY WERE ALREADY LIKE THAT WHEN WE MET YOU.
...OH.
RIGHT...
HOW IS THAT MORE SHOCKING THAN SUDDENLY GROWING WINGS?
IN THE NIGHT...
¡AAAAAAAAAAHH!

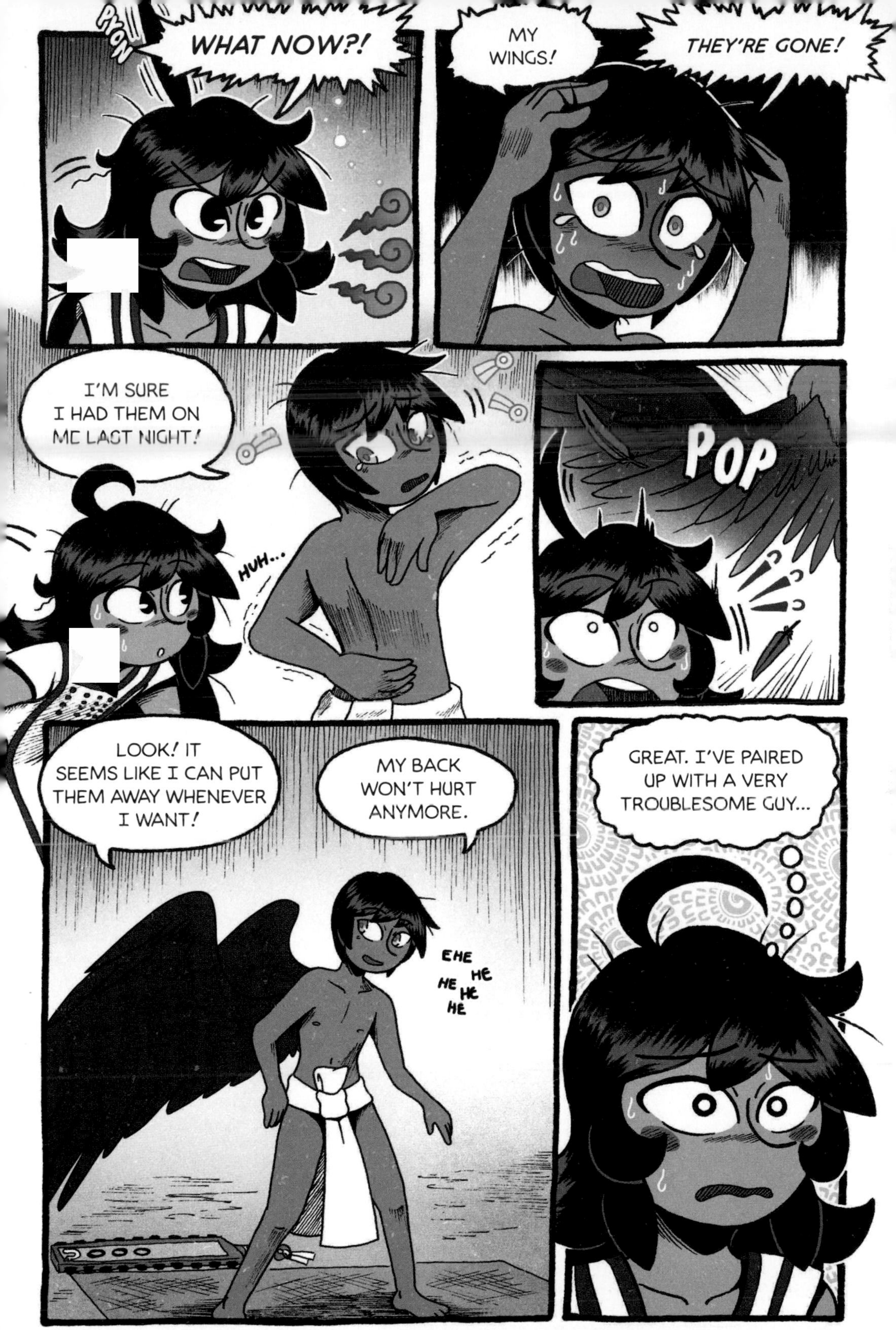
PYON
WHAT NOW?!
MY WINGS!
THEY'RE GONE!
I'M SURE I HAD THEM ON ME LAST NIGHT!
HUH...
POP
LOOK! IT SEEMS LIKE I CAN PUT THEM AWAY WHENEVER I WANT!
MY BACK WON'T HURT ANYMORE.
EHE HE HE HE HE
GREAT. I'VE PAIRED UP WITH A VERY TROUBLESOME GUY...

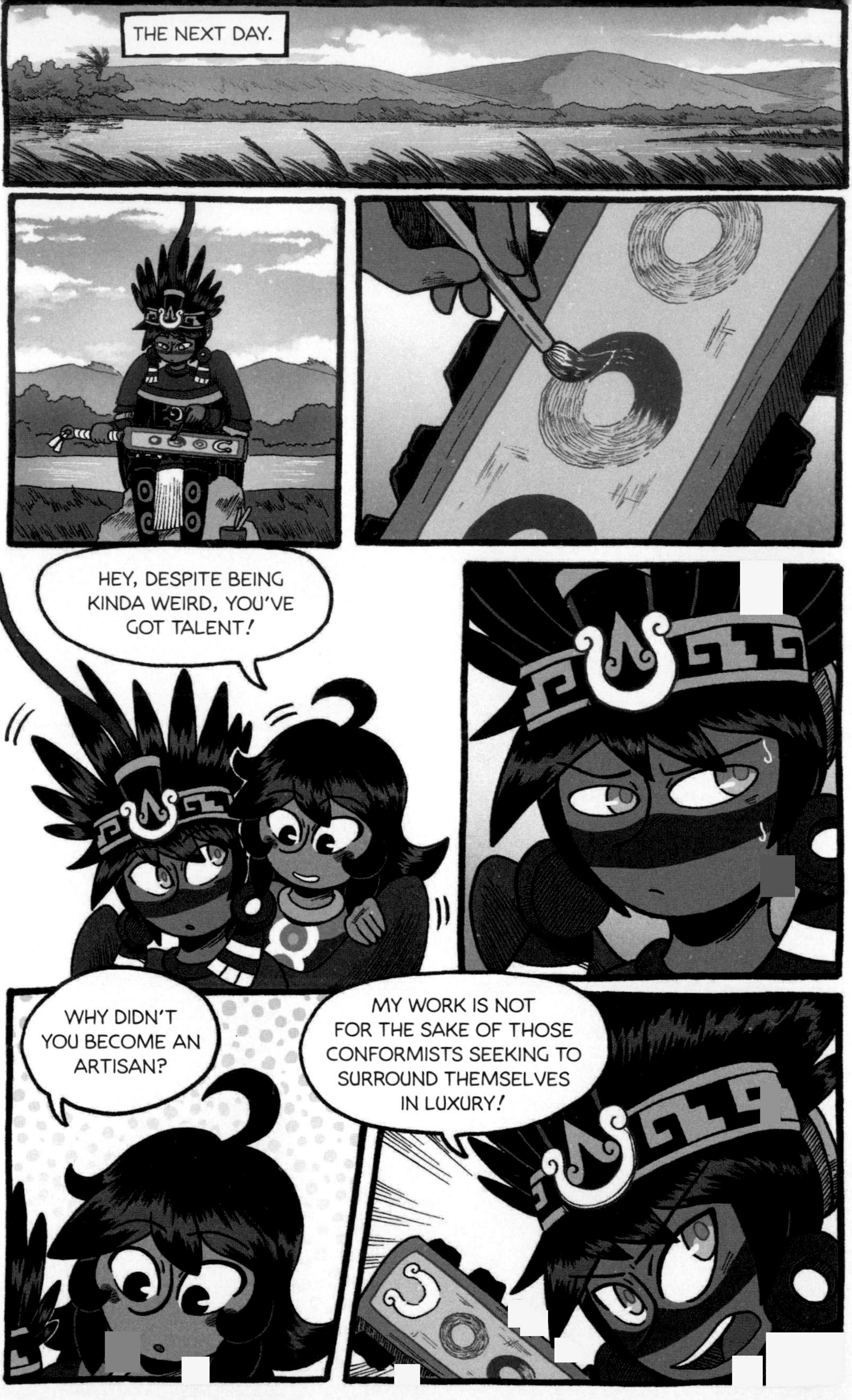
THE NEXT DAY.
HEY, DESPITE BEING KINDA WEIRD, YOU'VE GOT TALENT!
WHY DIDN'T YOU BECOME AN ARTISAN?
MY WORK IS NOT FOR THE SAKE OF THOSE CONFORMISTS SEEKING TO SURROUND THEMSELVES IN LUXURY!

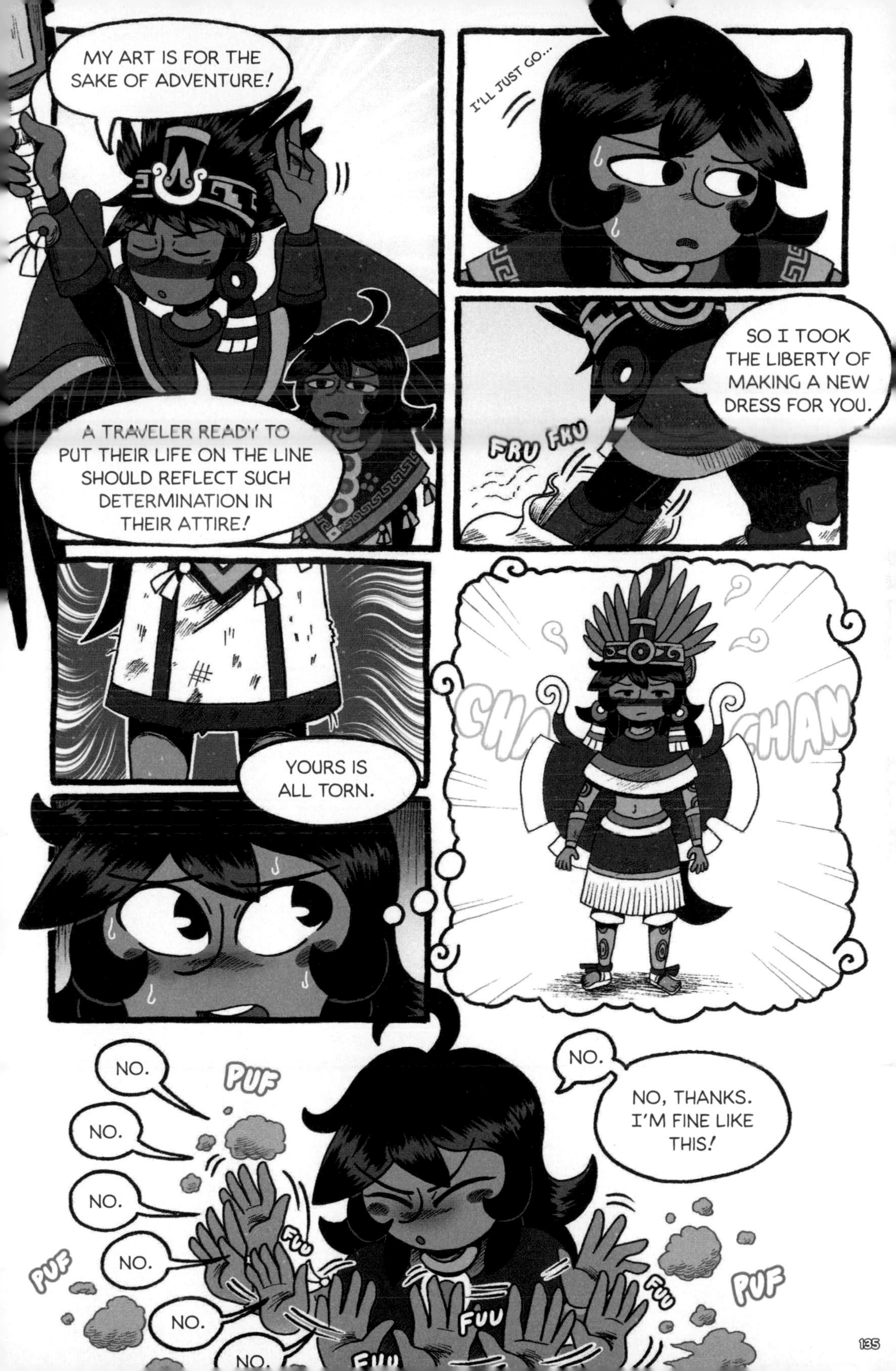

MY ART IS FOR THE SAKE OF ADVENTURE!
I'LL JUST GO...
A TRAVELER READY TO PUT THEIR LIFE ON THE LINE SHOULD REFLECT SUCH DETERMINATION IN THEIR ATTIRE!
SO I TOOK THE LIBERTY OF MAKING A NEW DRESS FOR YOU.
FRU FRU
YOURS IS ALL TORN.
CHAN
CHAN
NO.
PUF
NO.
NO.
NO.
PUF
NO.
NO.
NO.
NO, THANKS. I'M FINE LIKE THIS!
FUU
FUU
FUU
PUF

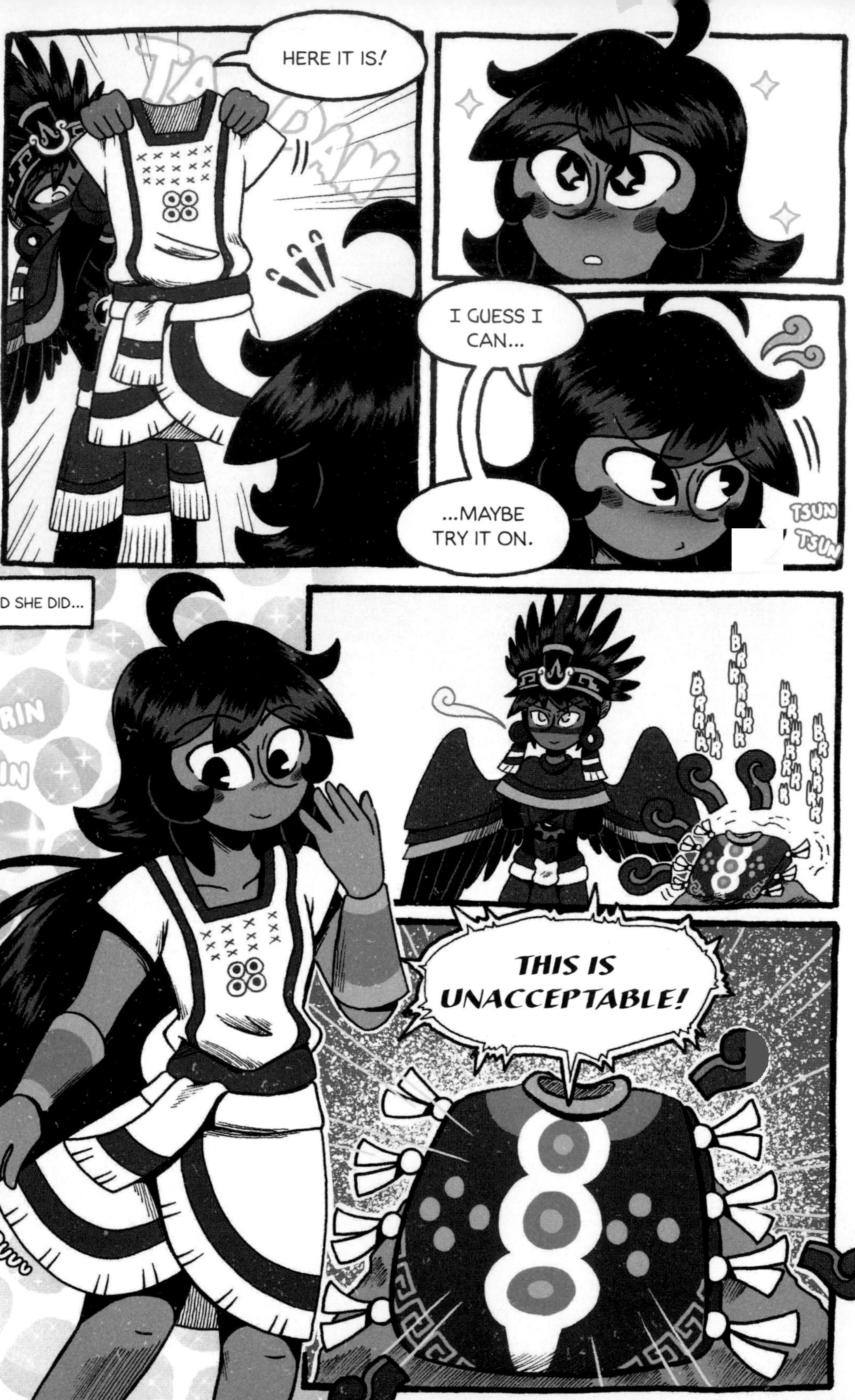
HERE IT IS!
TA-DAM
I GUESS I CAN...
...MAYBE TRY IT ON.
TSUN
TSUN
AND SHE DID...
PRIN
PRIN
FRUUU
BRRRR
BRRRRRR
BRRRRRRRR
BRRRRRRR
THIS IS UNACCEPTABLE!

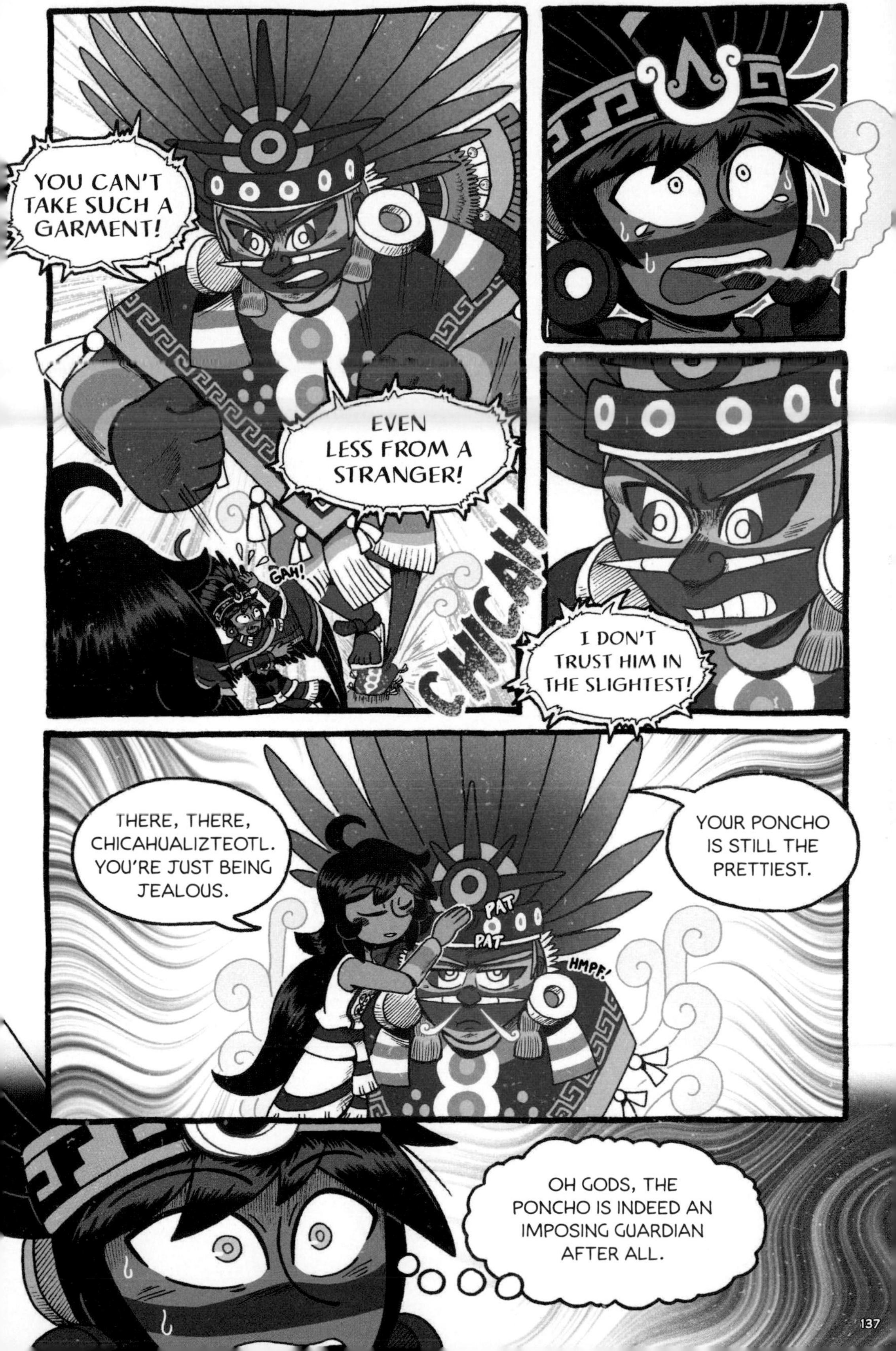
YOU CAN'T TAKE SUCH A GARMENT!
EVEN LESS FROM A STRANGER!
GAH!
CHICAH
I DON'T TRUST HIM IN THE SLIGHTEST!
THERE, THERE, CHICAHUALIZTEOTL. YOU'RE JUST BEING JEALOUS.
PAT
PAT
YOUR PONCHO IS STILL THE PRETTIEST.
HMPF!
OH GODS, THE PONCHO IS INDEED AN IMPOSING GUARDIAN AFTER ALL.

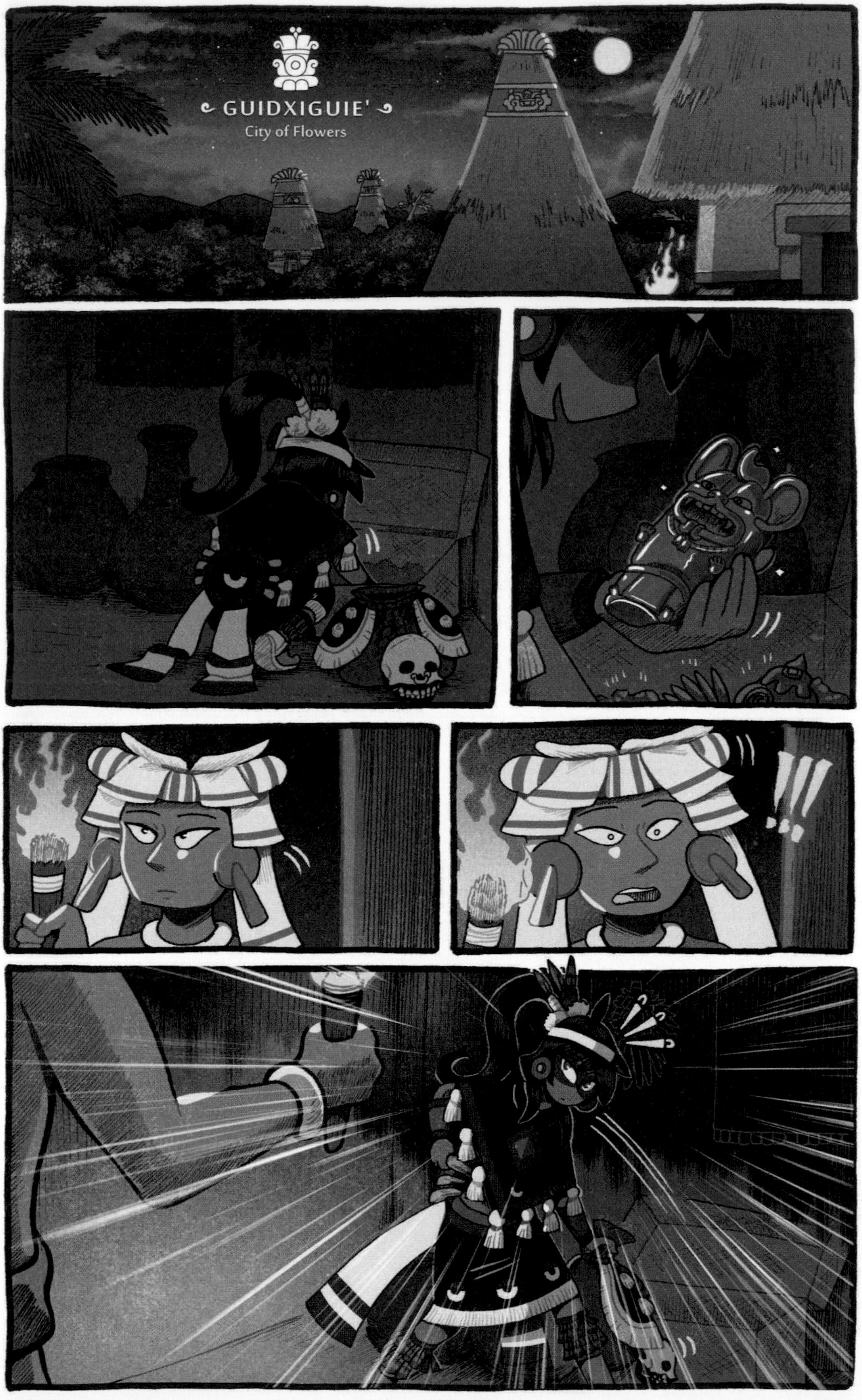
GUIDXIGUIE'
City of Flowers

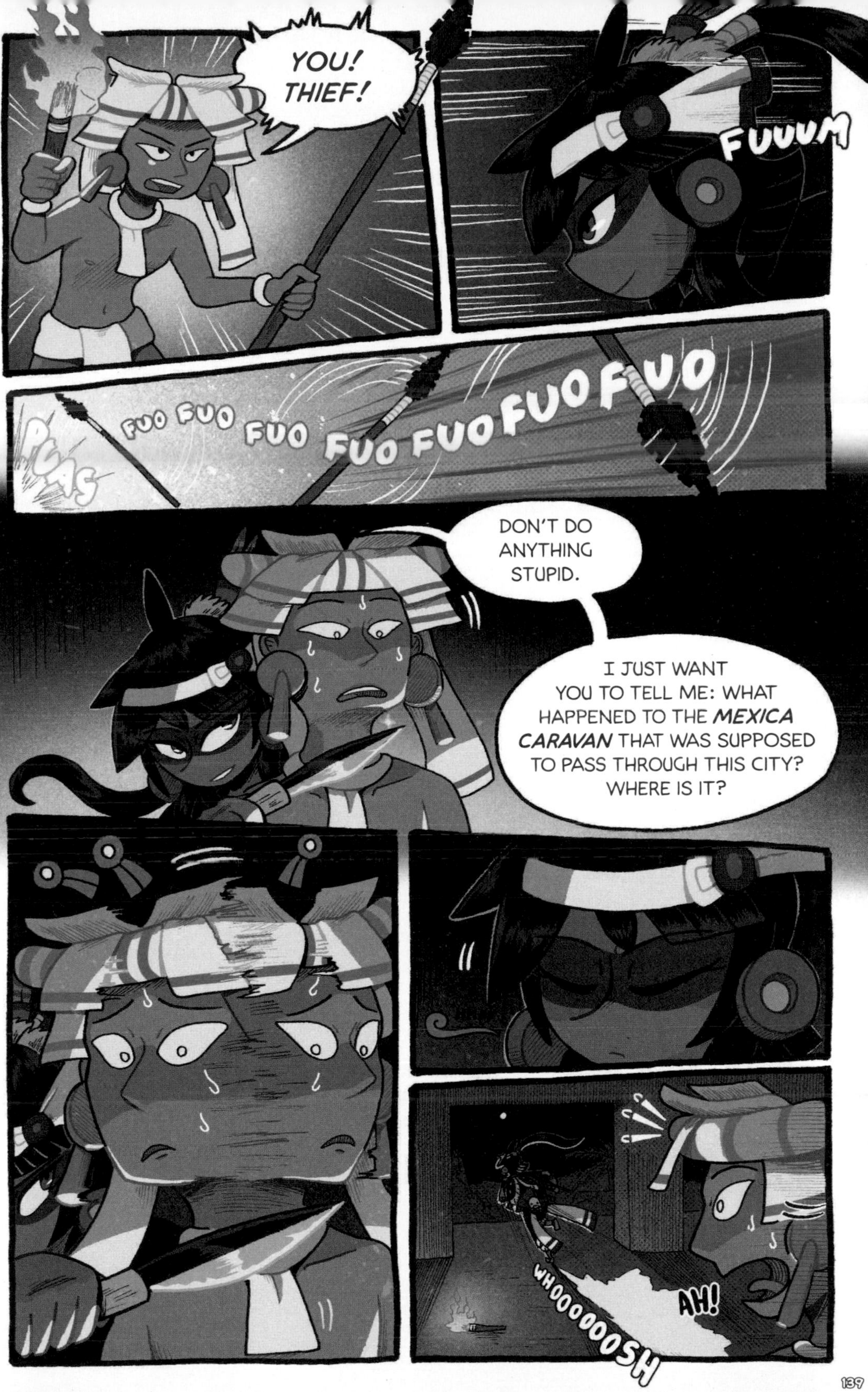

YOU! THIEF!
FUUUM
PLAS
FUO FUO FUO FUO FUO FUO FUO
DON'T DO ANYTHING STUPID.
I JUST WANT YOU TO TELL ME: WHAT HAPPENED TO THE *MEXICA CARAVAN* THAT WAS SUPPOSED TO PASS THROUGH THIS CITY? WHERE IS IT?
WHOOOOOOSH
AH!

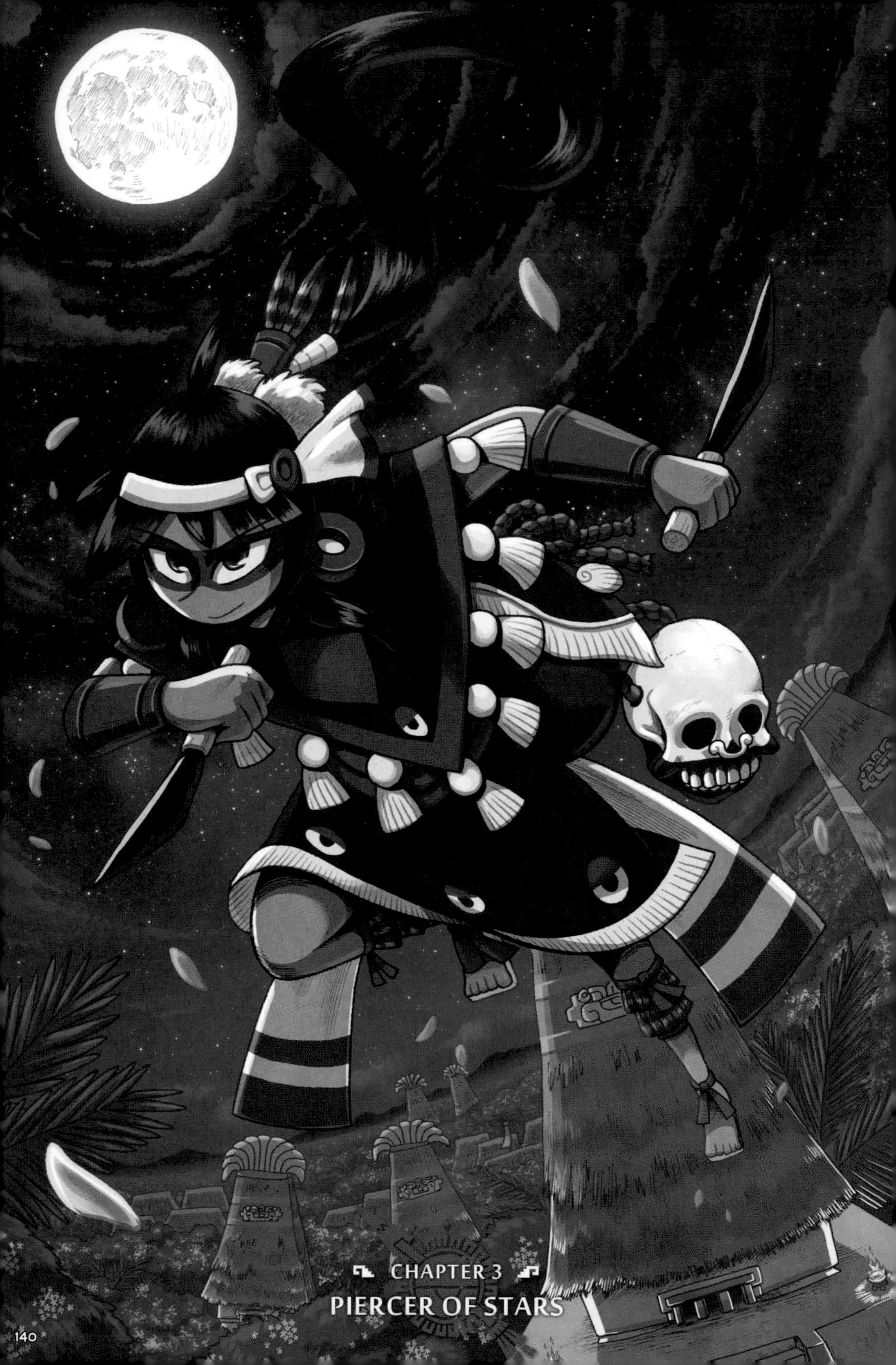

CHAPTER 3
PIERCER OF STARS

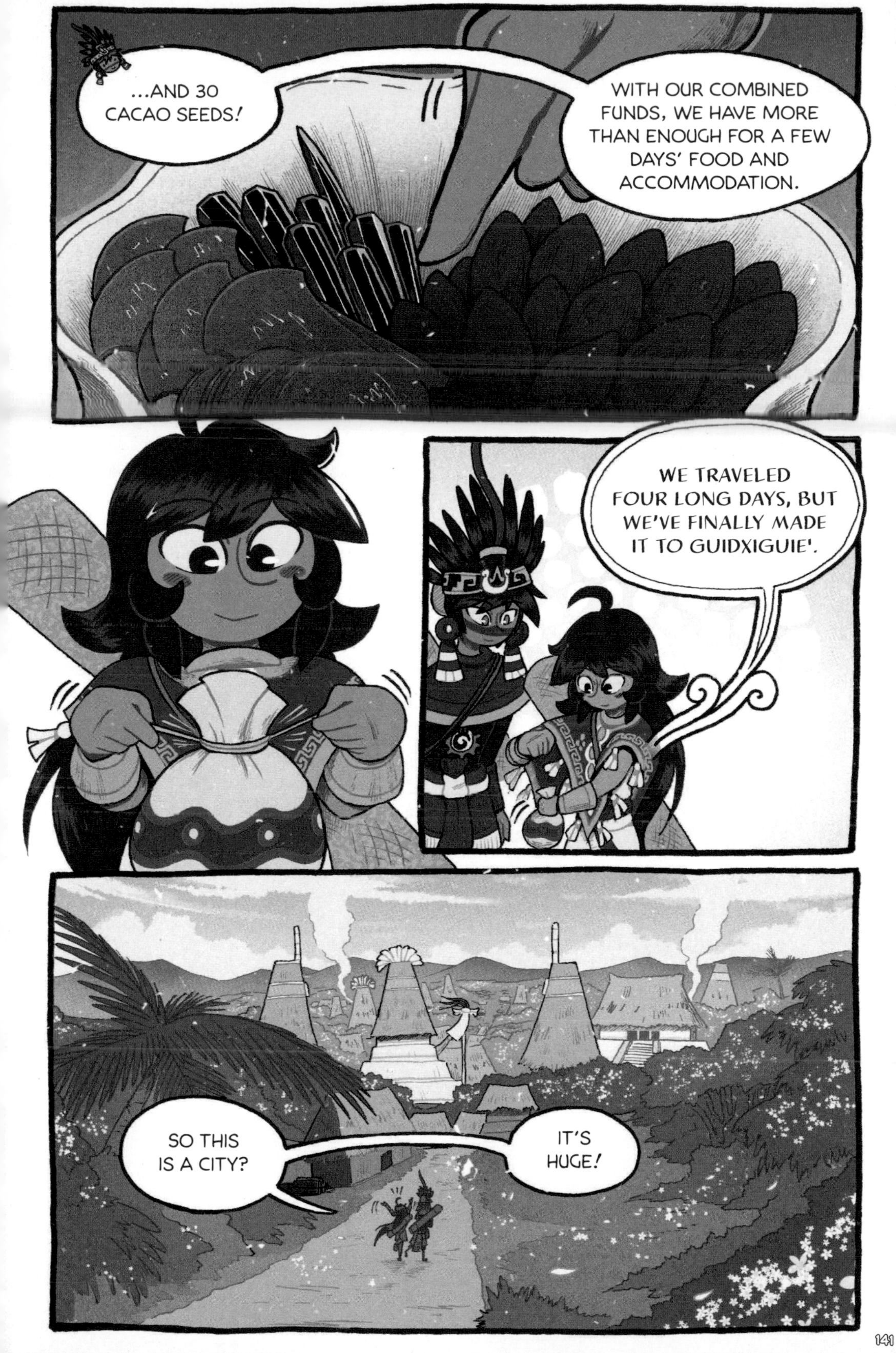
...AND 30 CACAO SEEDS!
WITH OUR COMBINED FUNDS, WE HAVE MORE THAN ENOUGH FOR A FEW DAYS' FOOD AND ACCOMMODATION.
WE TRAVELED FOUR LONG DAYS, BUT WE'VE FINALLY MADE IT TO GUIDXIGUIE'.
SO THIS IS A CITY?
IT'S HUGE!

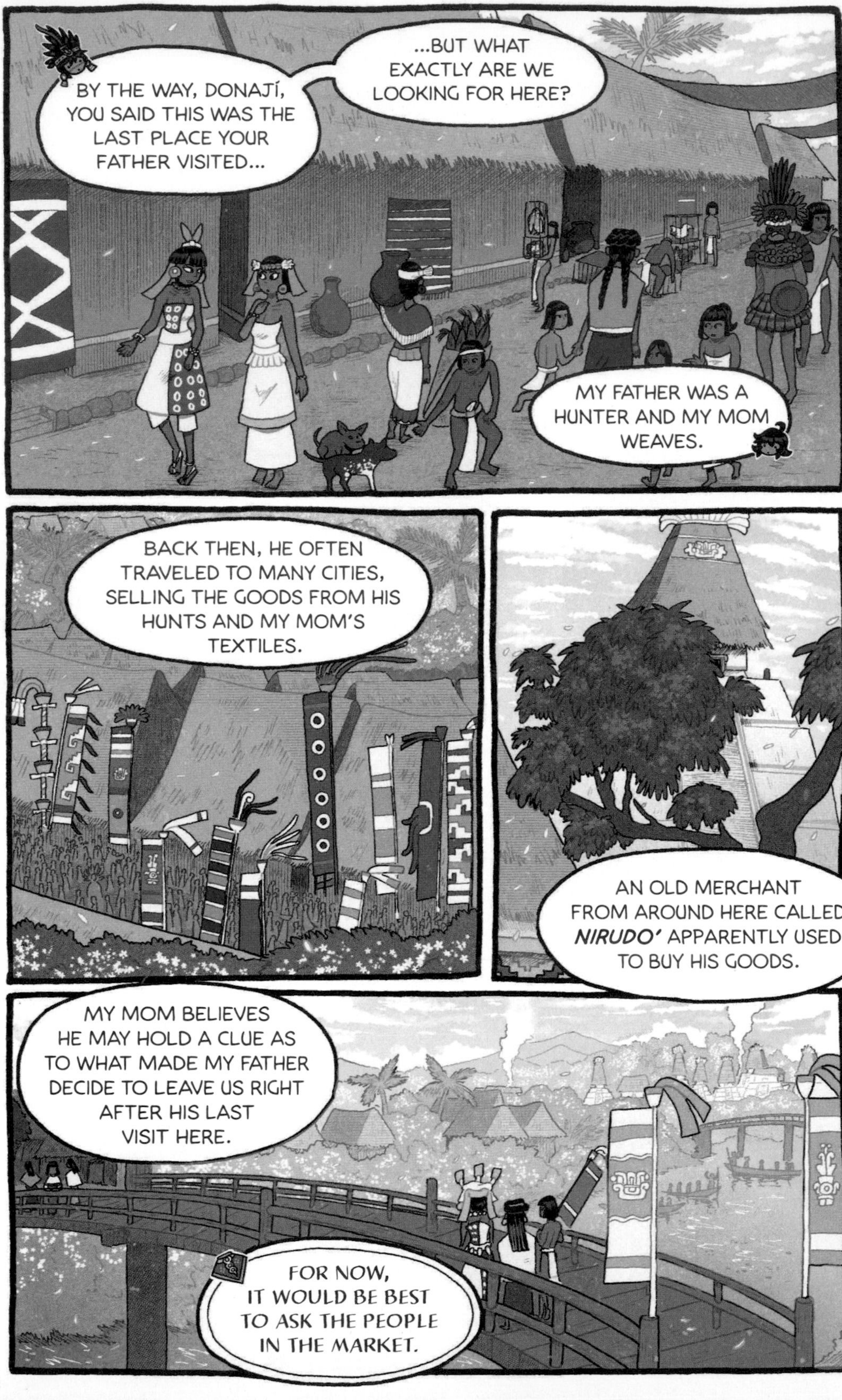
BY THE WAY, DONAJÍ, YOU SAID THIS WAS THE LAST PLACE YOUR FATHER VISITED...
...BUT WHAT EXACTLY ARE WE LOOKING FOR HERE?
MY FATHER WAS A HUNTER AND MY MOM WEAVES.
BACK THEN, HE OFTEN TRAVELED TO MANY CITIES, SELLING THE GOODS FROM HIS HUNTS AND MY MOM'S TEXTILES.
AN OLD MERCHANT FROM AROUND HERE CALLED *NIRUDO'* APPARENTLY USED TO BUY HIS GOODS.
MY MOM BELIEVES HE MAY HOLD A CLUE AS TO WHAT MADE MY FATHER DECIDE TO LEAVE US RIGHT AFTER HIS LAST VISIT HERE.
FOR NOW, IT WOULD BE BEST TO ASK THE PEOPLE IN THE MARKET.

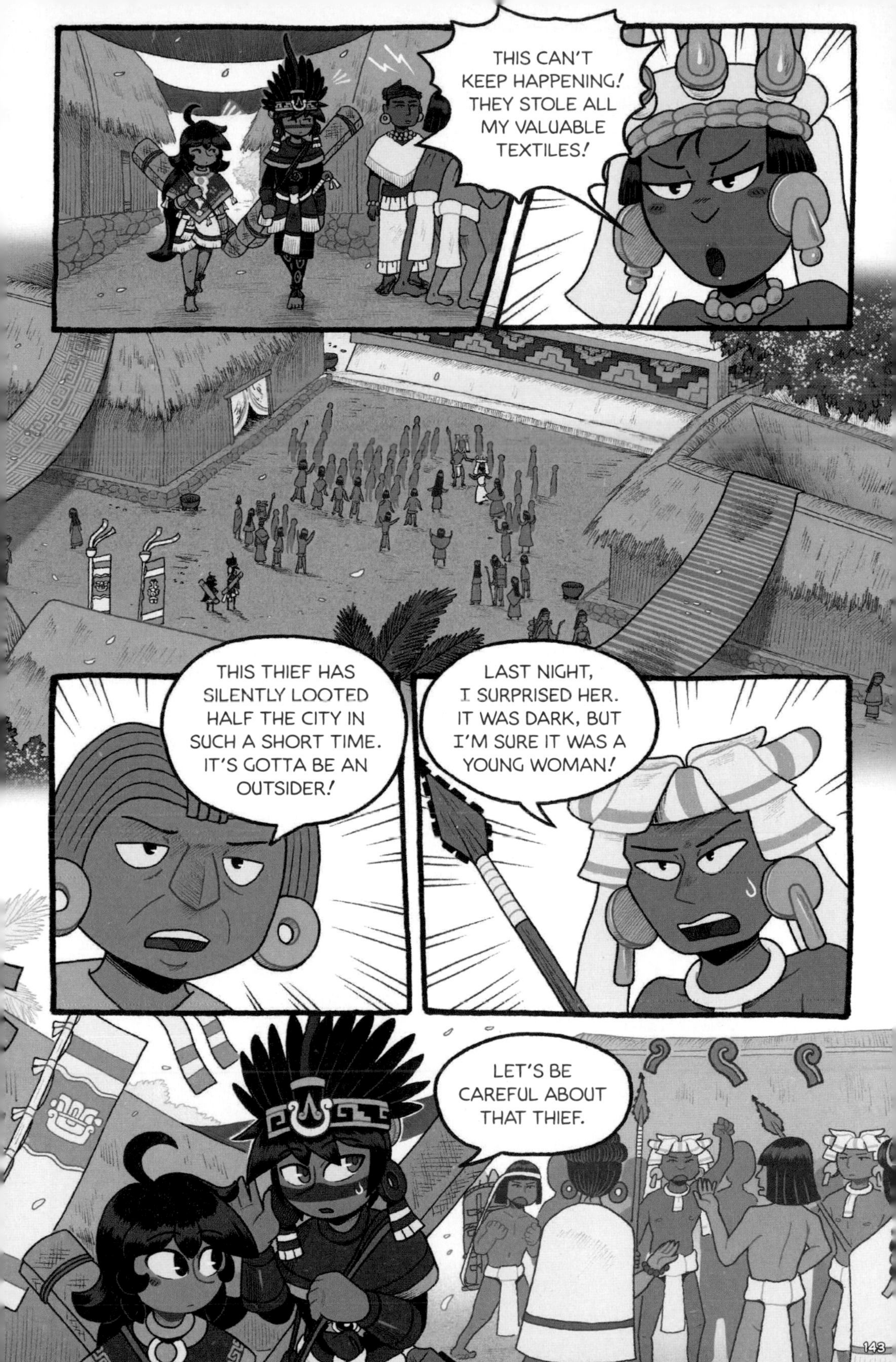
THIS CAN'T KEEP HAPPENING! THEY STOLE ALL MY VALUABLE TEXTILES!
THIS THIEF HAS SILENTLY LOOTED HALF THE CITY IN SUCH A SHORT TIME. IT'S GOTTA BE AN OUTSIDER!
LAST NIGHT, I SURPRISED HER. IT WAS DARK, BUT I'M SURE IT WAS A YOUNG WOMAN!
LET'S BE CAREFUL ABOUT THAT THIEF.

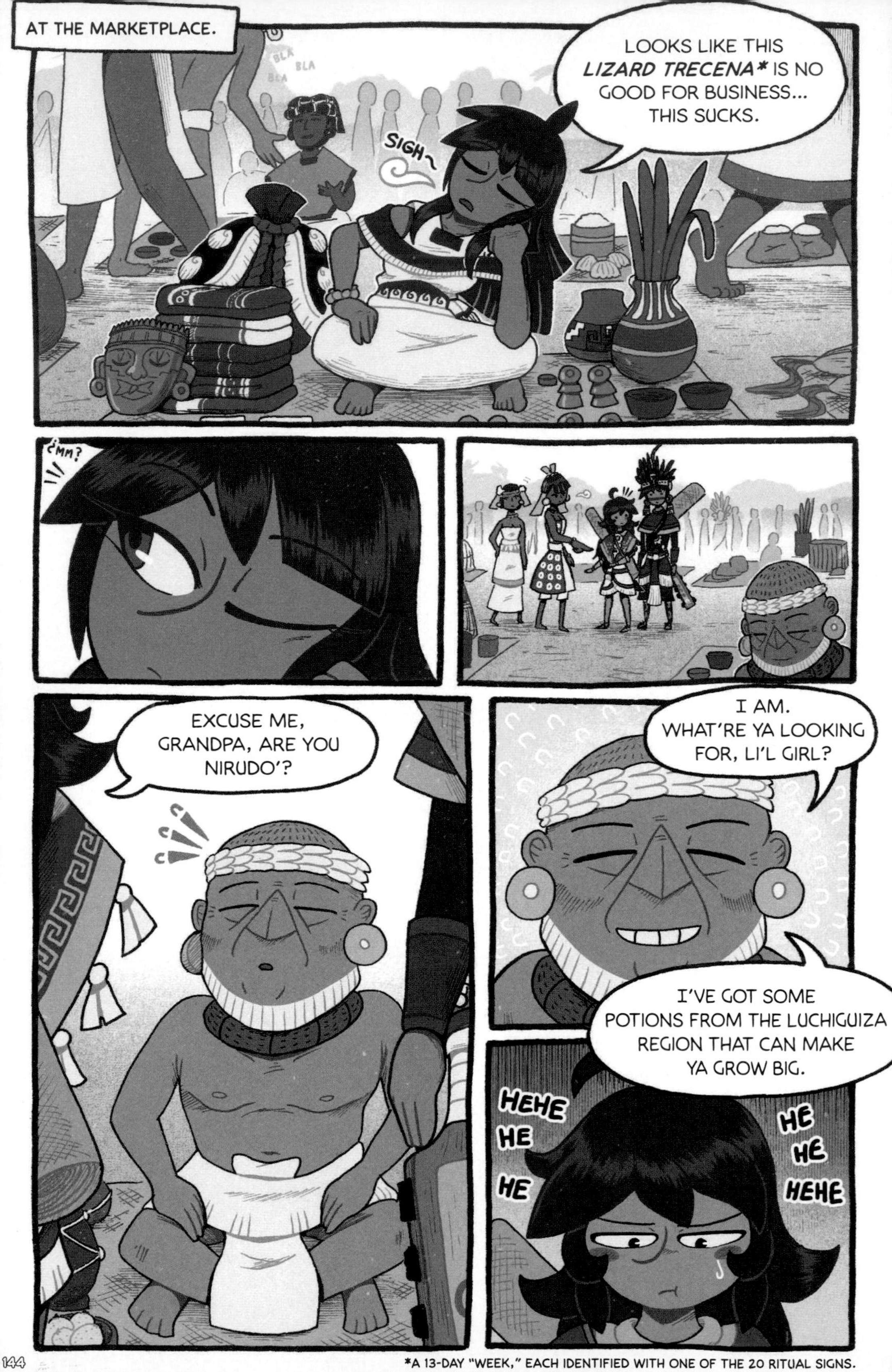
AT THE MARKETPLACE.
BLA
BLA
BLA
LOOKS LIKE THIS LIZARD TRECENA* IS NO GOOD FOR BUSINESS... THIS SUCKS.
SIGH
¿MM?
EXCUSE ME, GRANDPA, ARE YOU NIRUDO'?
I AM. WHAT'RE YA LOOKING FOR, LI'L GIRL?
I'VE GOT SOME POTIONS FROM THE LUCHIGUIZA REGION THAT CAN MAKE YA GROW BIG.
HEHE HE HE
HE HE HEHE

*A 13-DAY "WEEK," EACH IDENTIFIED WITH ONE OF THE 20 RITUAL SIGNS.

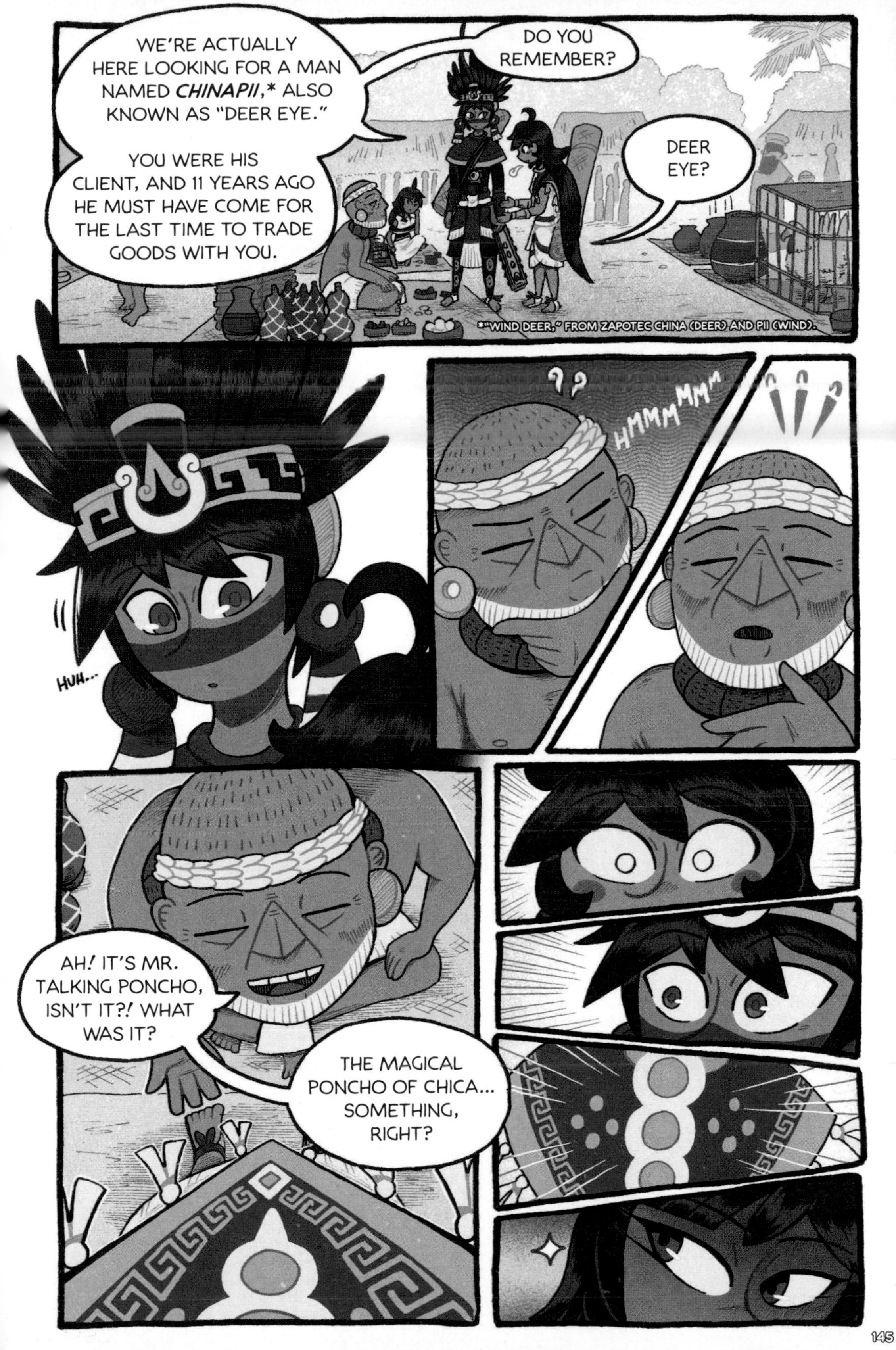
WE'RE ACTUALLY HERE LOOKING FOR A MAN NAMED *CHINAPII*,* ALSO KNOWN AS "DEER EYE."
YOU WERE HIS CLIENT, AND 11 YEARS AGO HE MUST HAVE COME FOR THE LAST TIME TO TRADE GOODS WITH YOU.
DO YOU REMEMBER?
DEER EYE?
*"WIND DEER," FROM ZAPOTEC CHINA (DEER) AND PII (WIND).
HUH...
HMMMMMM
AH! IT'S MR. TALKING PONCHO, ISN'T IT?! WHAT WAS IT?
THE MAGICAL PONCHO OF CHICA... SOMETHING, RIGHT?

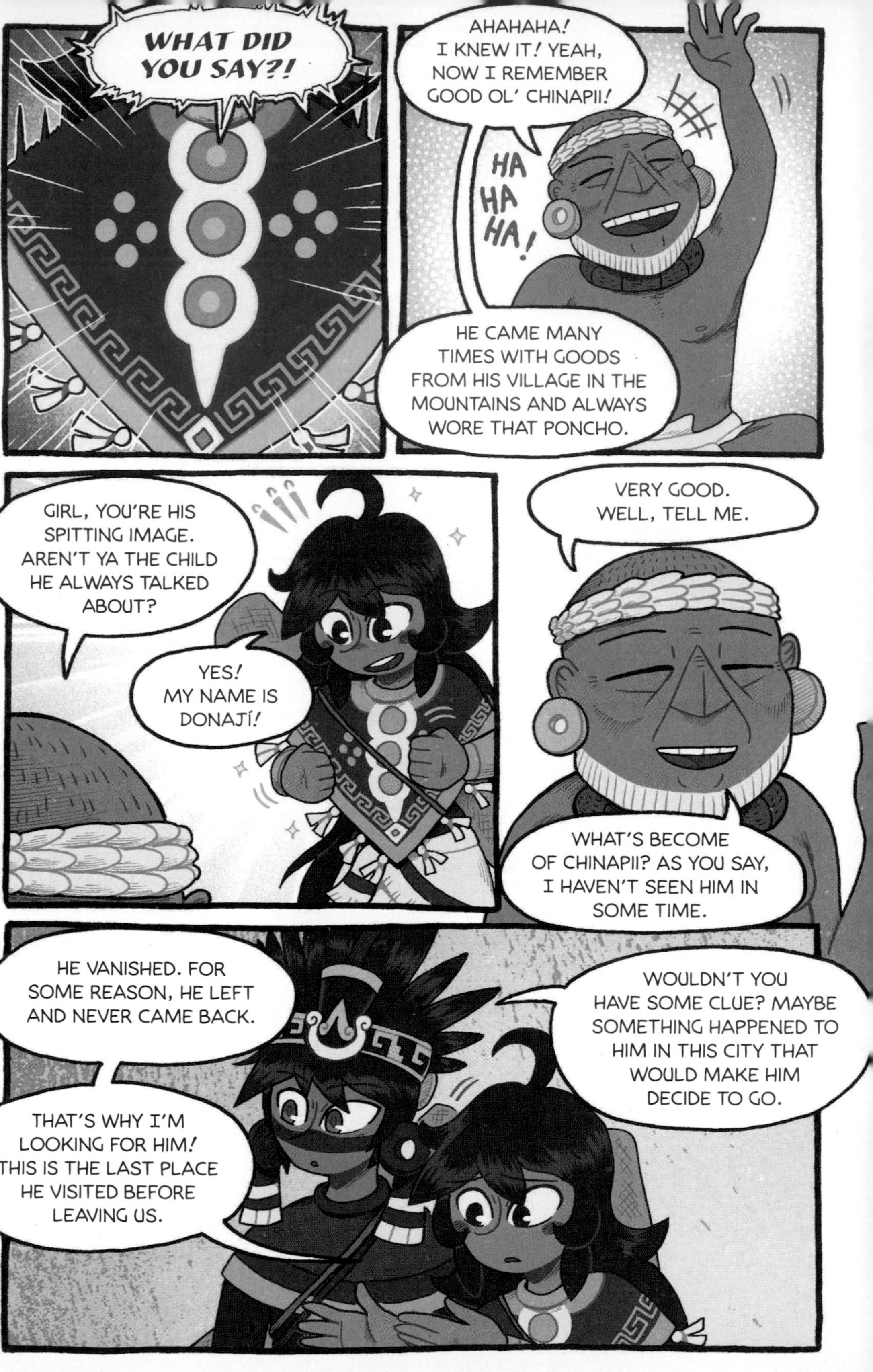
WHAT DID YOU SAY?!
AHAHAHA! I KNEW IT! YEAH, NOW I REMEMBER GOOD OL' CHINAPII!
HA HA HA!
HE CAME MANY TIMES WITH GOODS FROM HIS VILLAGE IN THE MOUNTAINS AND ALWAYS WORE THAT PONCHO.
GIRL, YOU'RE HIS SPITTING IMAGE. AREN'T YA THE CHILD HE ALWAYS TALKED ABOUT?
YES! MY NAME IS DONAJÍ!
VERY GOOD. WELL, TELL ME.
WHAT'S BECOME OF CHINAPII? AS YOU SAY, I HAVEN'T SEEN HIM IN SOME TIME.
HE VANISHED. FOR SOME REASON, HE LEFT AND NEVER CAME BACK.
THAT'S WHY I'M LOOKING FOR HIM! THIS IS THE LAST PLACE HE VISITED BEFORE LEAVING US.
WOULDN'T YOU HAVE SOME CLUE? MAYBE SOMETHING HAPPENED TO HIM IN THIS CITY THAT WOULD MAKE HIM DECIDE TO GO.

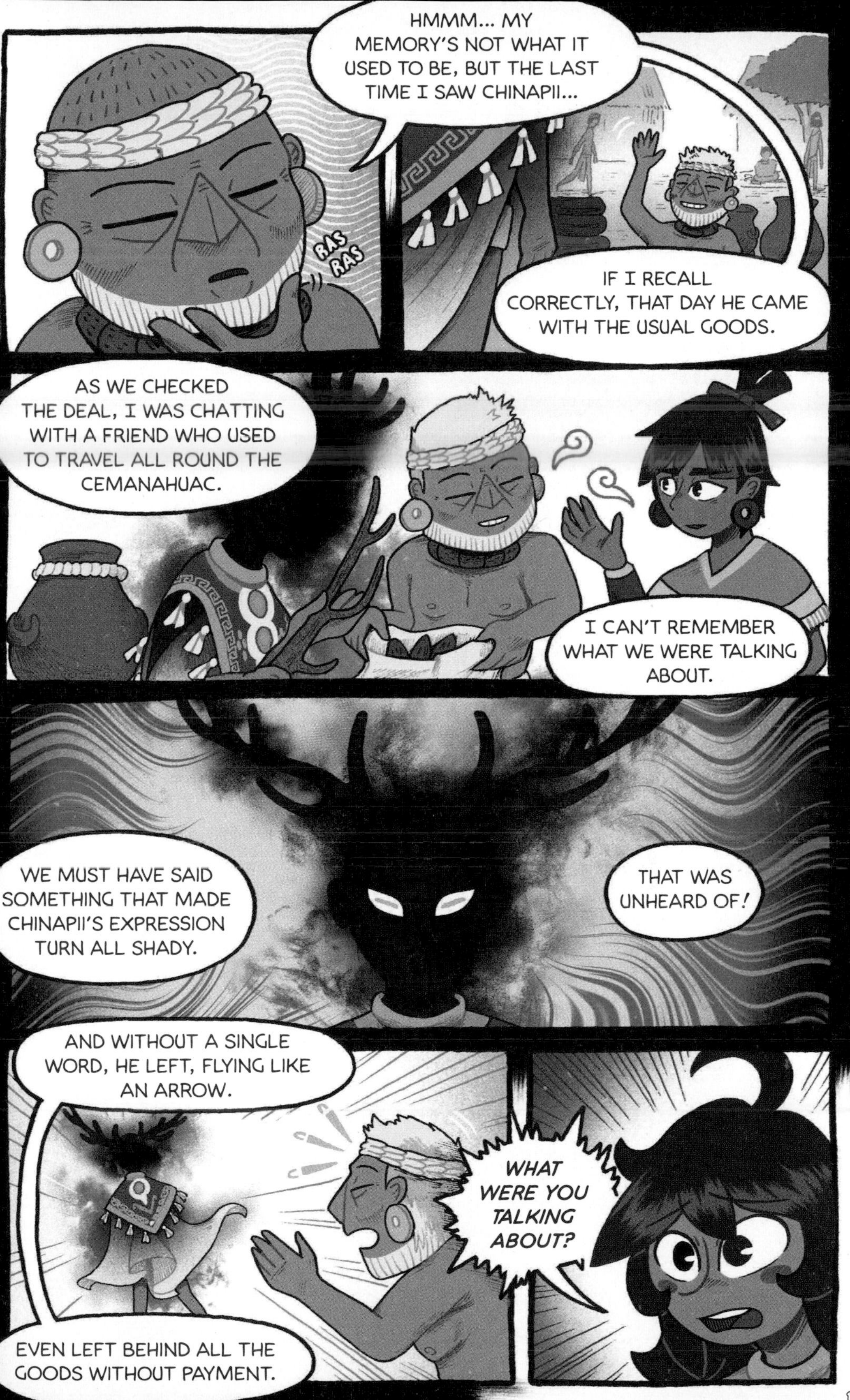
HMMM... MY MEMORY'S NOT WHAT IT USED TO BE, BUT THE LAST TIME I SAW CHINAPII...
RAS RAS
IF I RECALL CORRECTLY, THAT DAY HE CAME WITH THE USUAL GOODS.
AS WE CHECKED THE DEAL, I WAS CHATTING WITH A FRIEND WHO USED TO TRAVEL ALL ROUND THE CEMANAHUAC.
I CAN'T REMEMBER WHAT WE WERE TALKING ABOUT.
WE MUST HAVE SAID SOMETHING THAT MADE CHINAPII'S EXPRESSION TURN ALL SHADY.
THAT WAS UNHEARD OF!
AND WITHOUT A SINGLE WORD, HE LEFT, FLYING LIKE AN ARROW.
EVEN LEFT BEHIND ALL THE GOODS WITHOUT PAYMENT.
WHAT WERE YOU TALKING ABOUT?

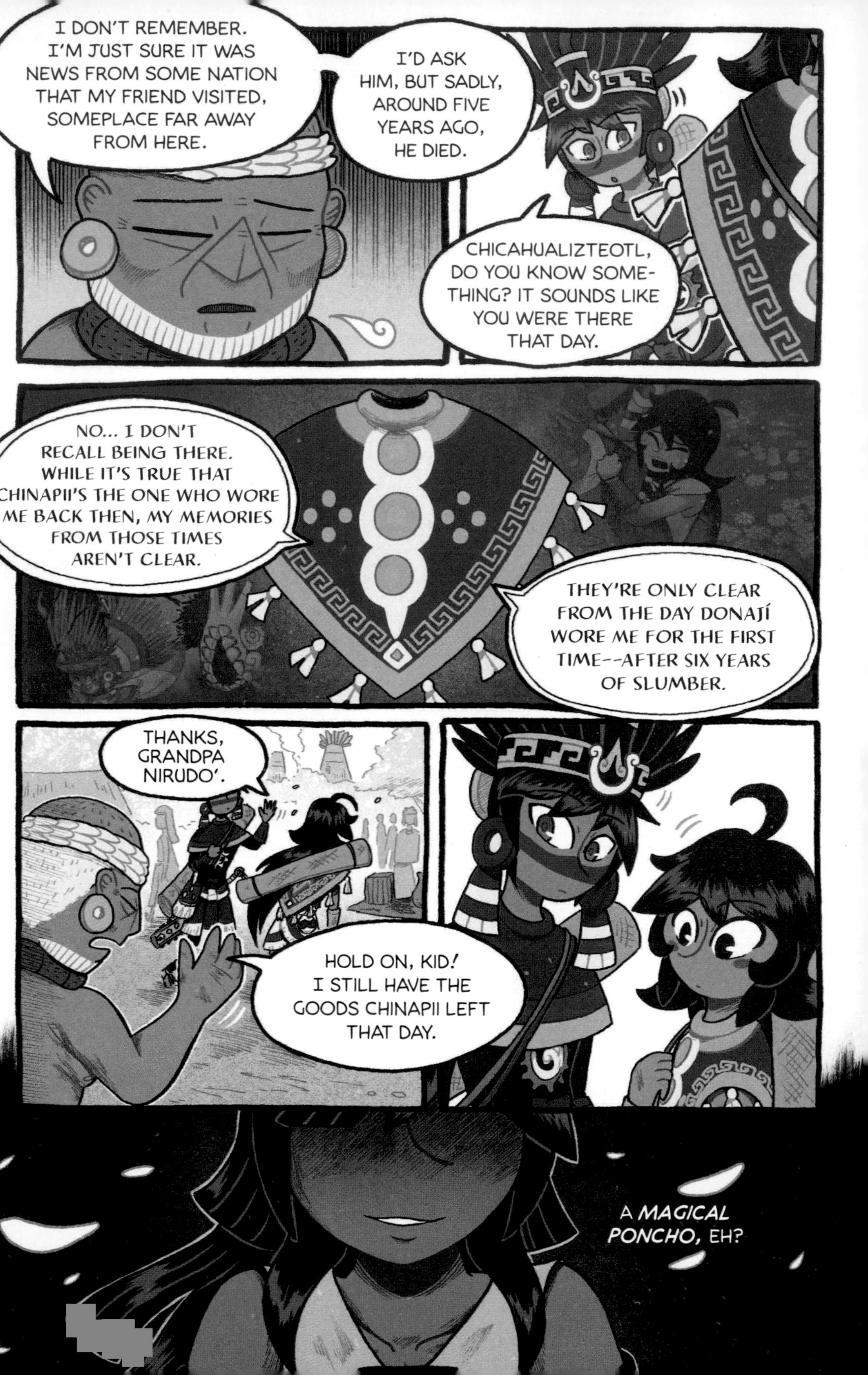
I DON'T REMEMBER. I'M JUST SURE IT WAS NEWS FROM SOME NATION THAT MY FRIEND VISITED, SOMEPLACE FAR AWAY FROM HERE.
I'D ASK HIM, BUT SADLY, AROUND FIVE YEARS AGO, HE DIED.
CHICAHUALIZTEOTL, DO YOU KNOW SOME-THING? IT SOUNDS LIKE YOU WERE THERE THAT DAY.
NO... I DON'T RECALL BEING THERE. WHILE IT'S TRUE THAT CHINAPII'S THE ONE WHO WORE ME BACK THEN, MY MEMORIES FROM THOSE TIMES AREN'T CLEAR.
THEY'RE ONLY CLEAR FROM THE DAY DONAJÍ WORE ME FOR THE FIRST TIME--AFTER SIX YEARS OF SLUMBER.
THANKS, GRANDPA NIRUDO'.
HOLD ON, KID! I STILL HAVE THE GOODS CHINAPII LEFT THAT DAY.
A *MAGICAL PONCHO*, EH?

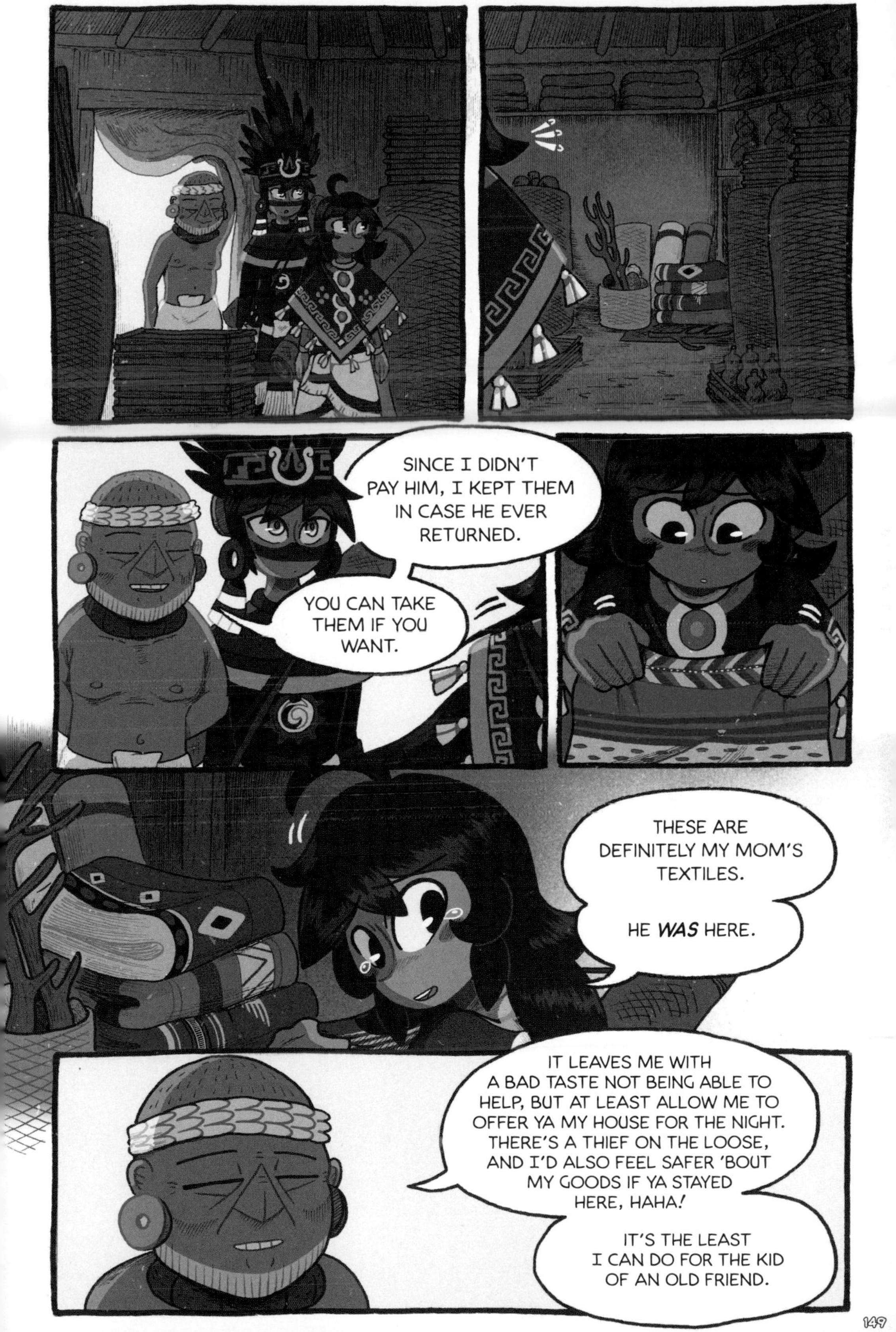
SINCE I DIDN'T PAY HIM, I KEPT THEM IN CASE HE EVER RETURNED.
YOU CAN TAKE THEM IF YOU WANT.
THESE ARE DEFINITELY MY MOM'S TEXTILES.
HE *WAS* HERE.
IT LEAVES ME WITH A BAD TASTE NOT BEING ABLE TO HELP, BUT AT LEAST ALLOW ME TO OFFER YA MY HOUSE FOR THE NIGHT. THERE'S A THIEF ON THE LOOSE, AND I'D ALSO FEEL SAFER 'BOUT MY GOODS IF YA STAYED HERE, HAHA!
IT'S THE LEAST I CAN DO FOR THE KID OF AN OLD FRIEND.

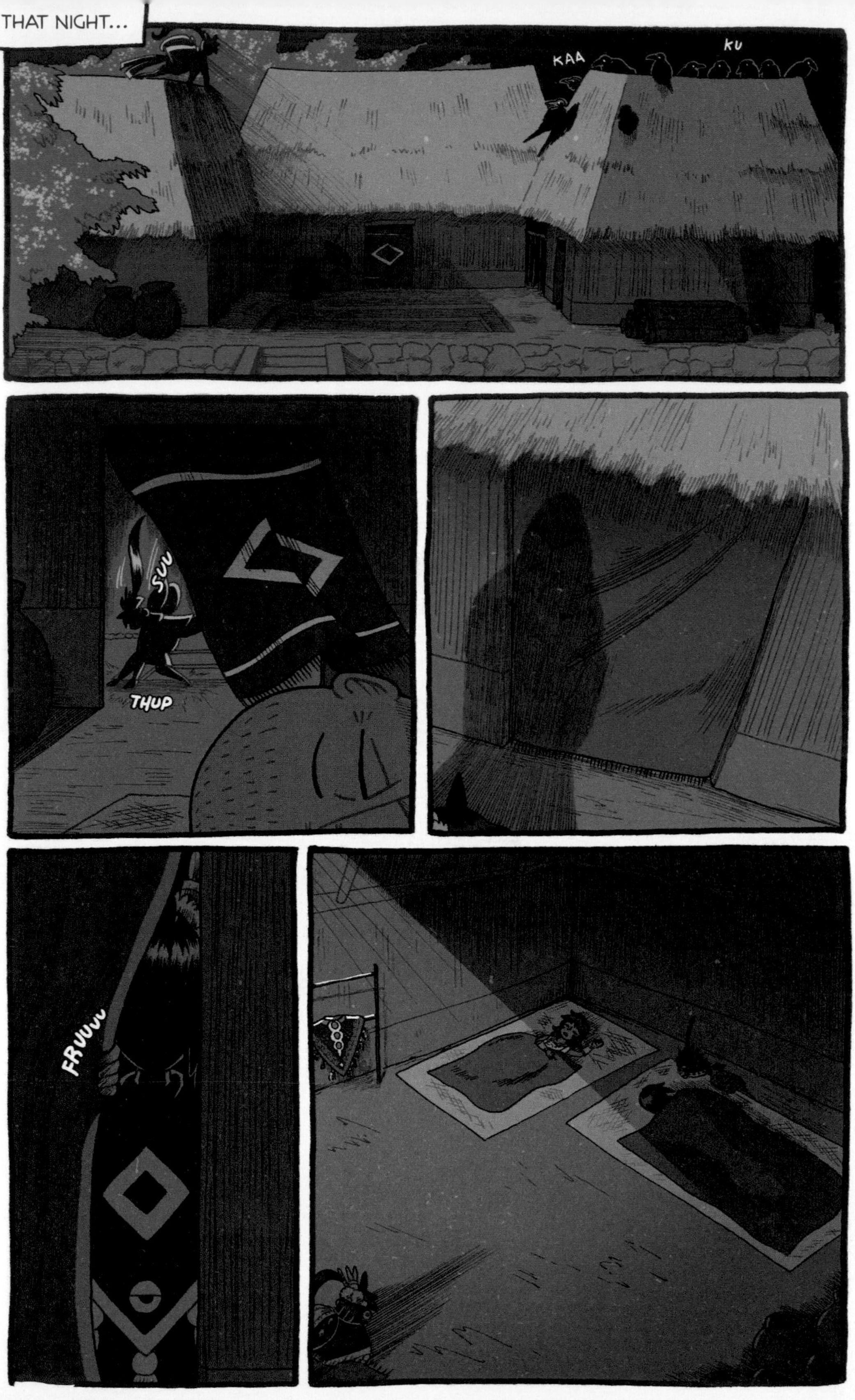
THAT NIGHT...
KAA
KU
SUU
THUP
FRUUUU

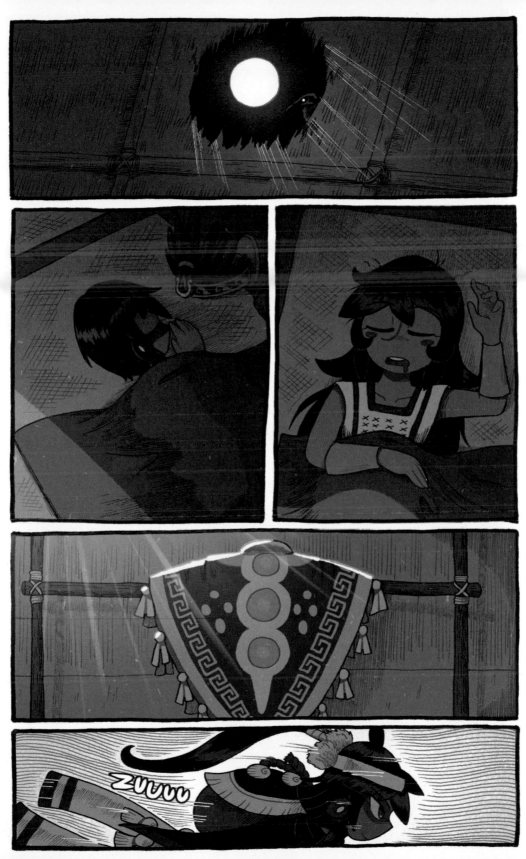

ZUUUU

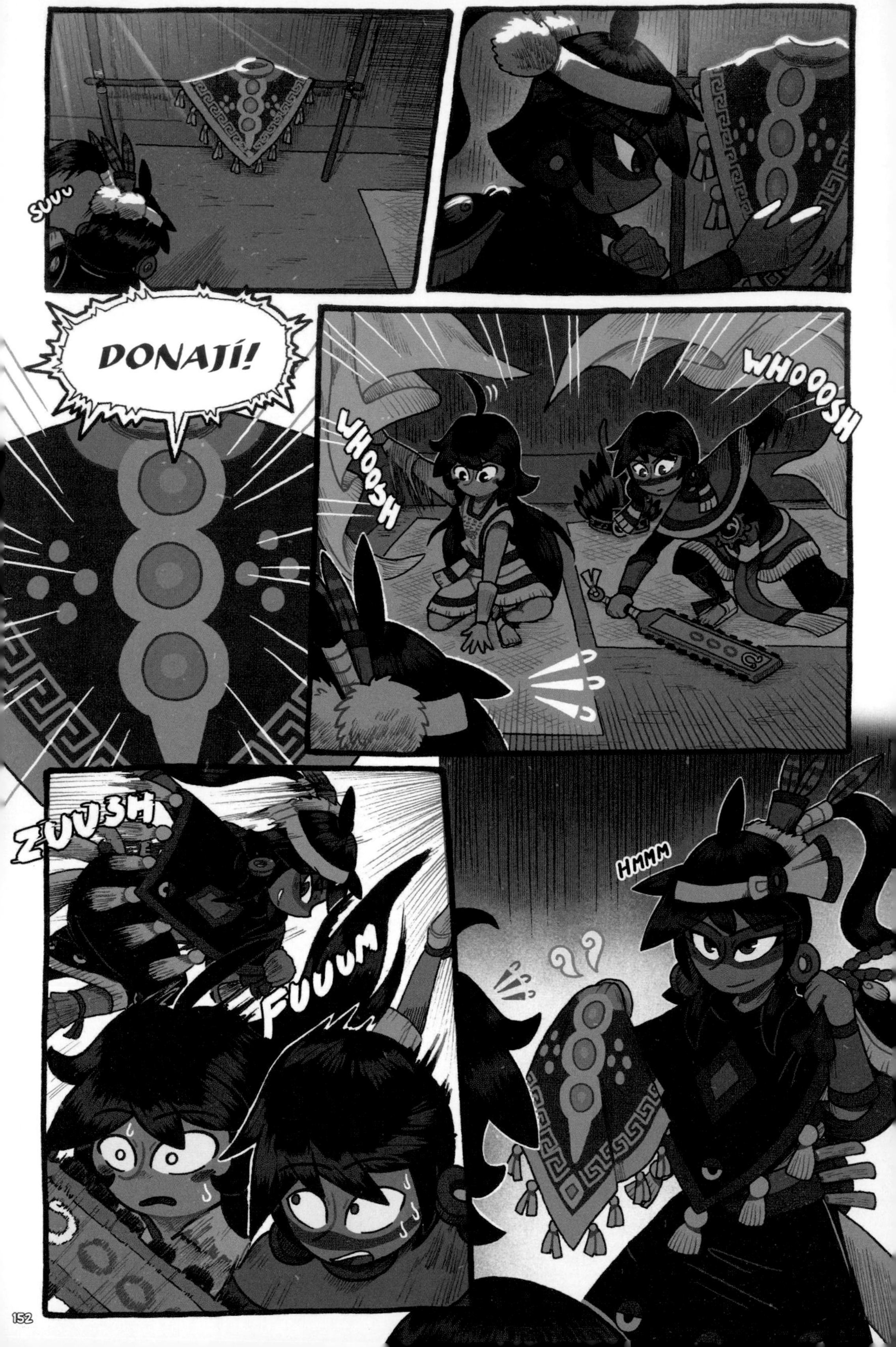
SUUU
DONAJÍ!
WHOOSH
WHOOOSH
ZUUSH
FUUUM
HMMM

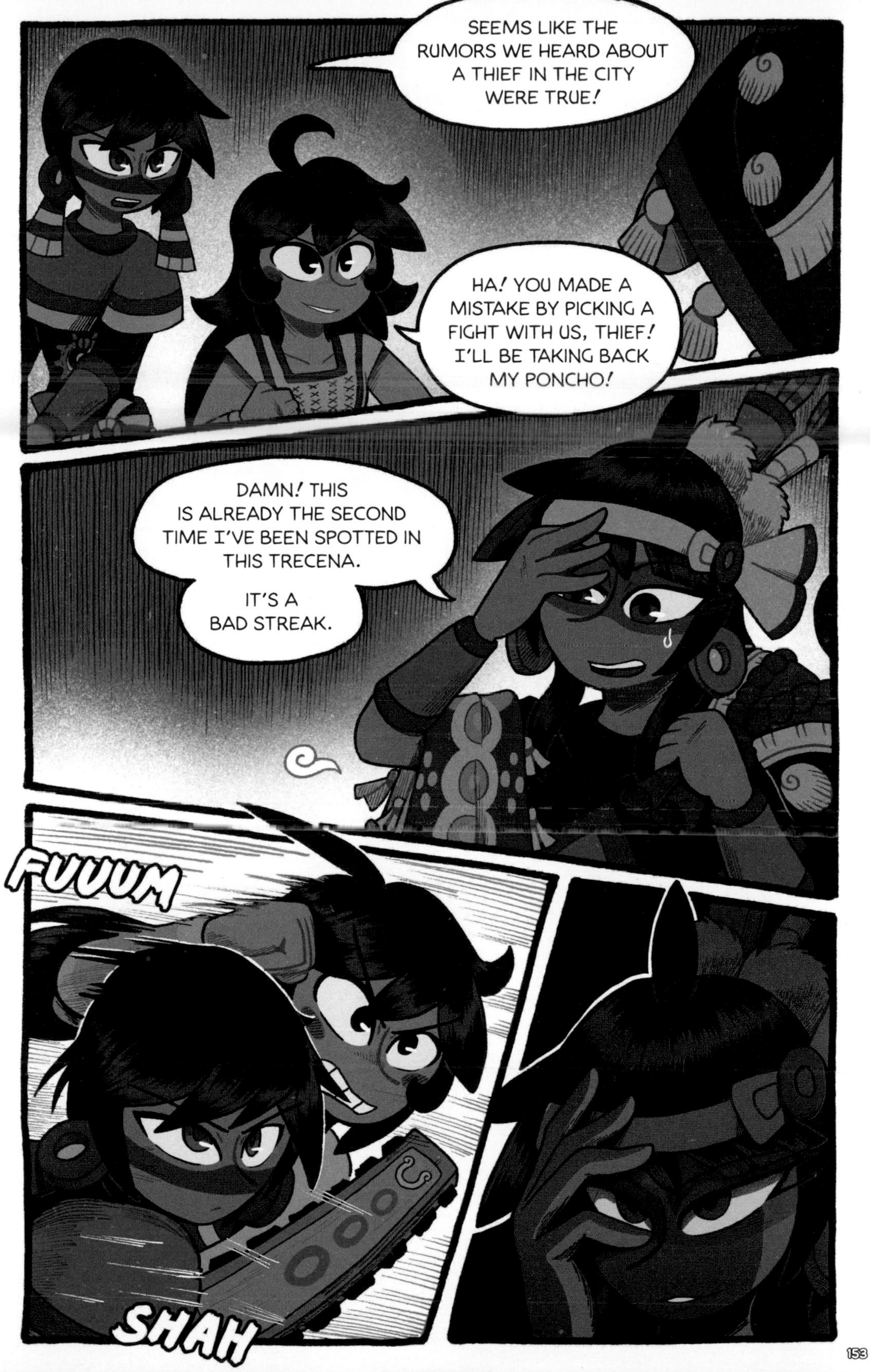
SEEMS LIKE THE RUMORS WE HEARD ABOUT A THIEF IN THE CITY WERE TRUE!
HA! YOU MADE A MISTAKE BY PICKING A FIGHT WITH US, THIEF! I'LL BE TAKING BACK MY PONCHO!
DAMN! THIS IS ALREADY THE SECOND TIME I'VE BEEN SPOTTED IN THIS TRECENA.
IT'S A BAD STREAK.
FUUUM
SHAH

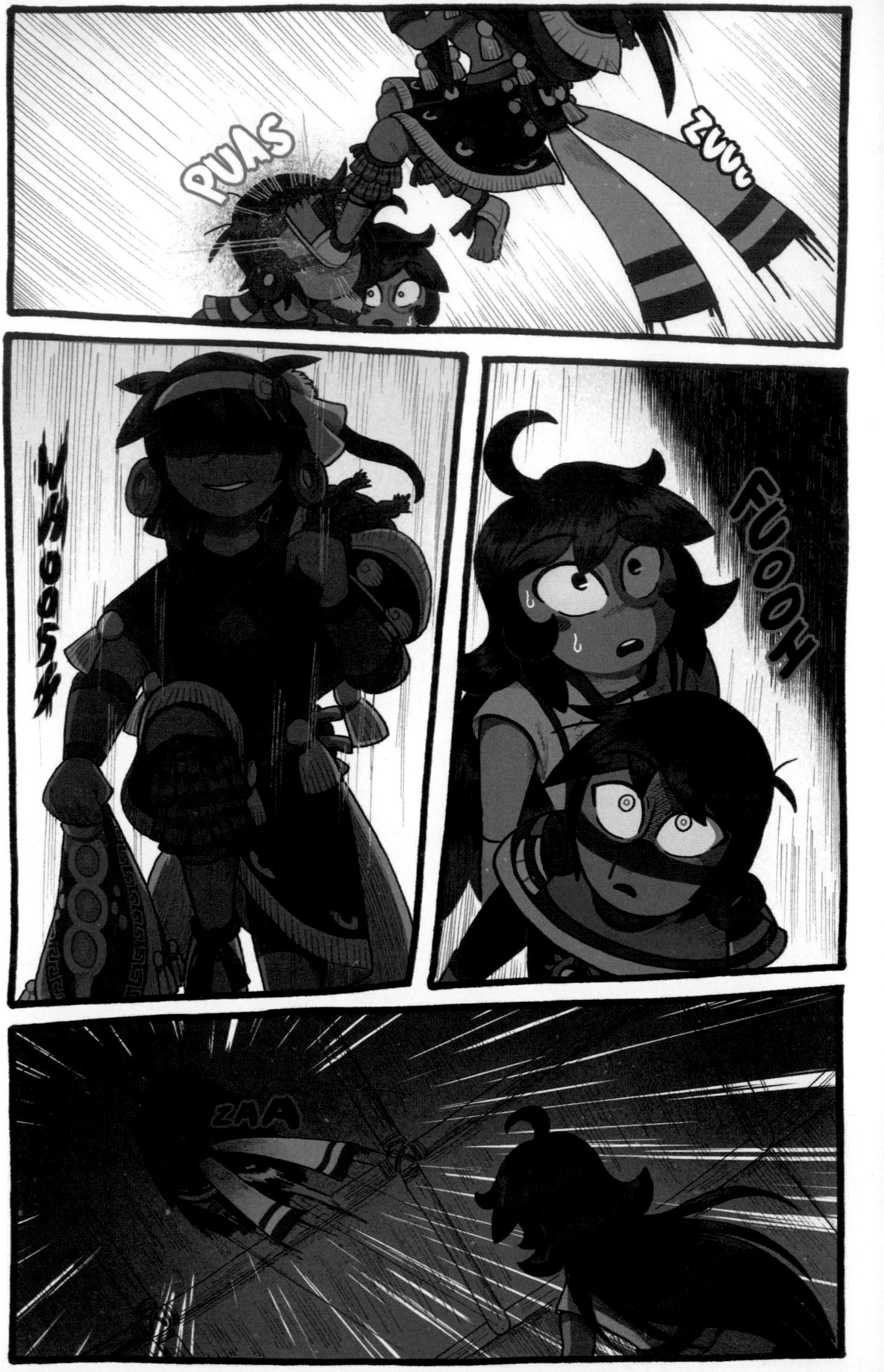
PUAS
ZUUU
WHOOSH
FUOOH
ZAA

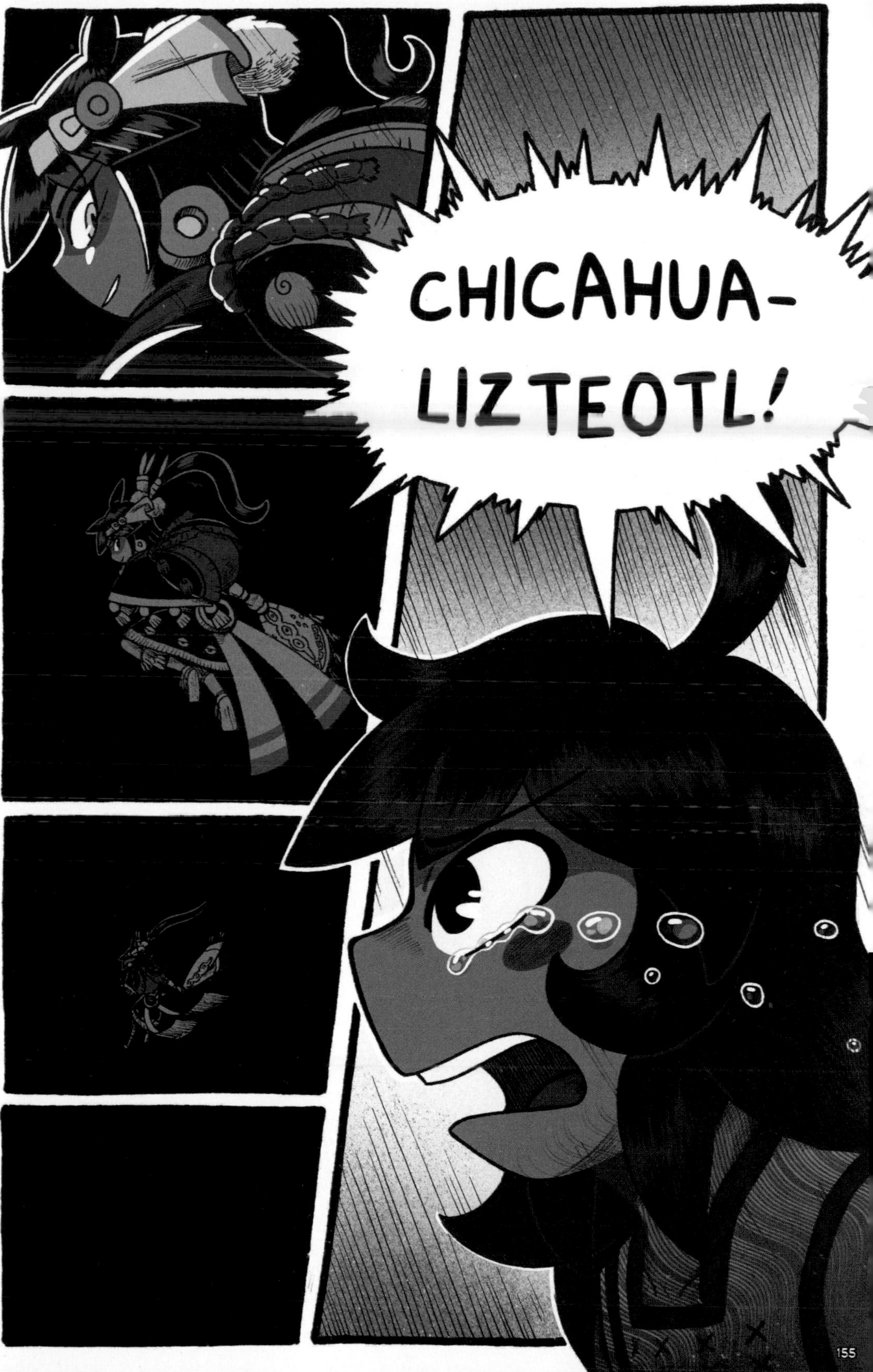
CHICAHUA-
LIZTEOTL!

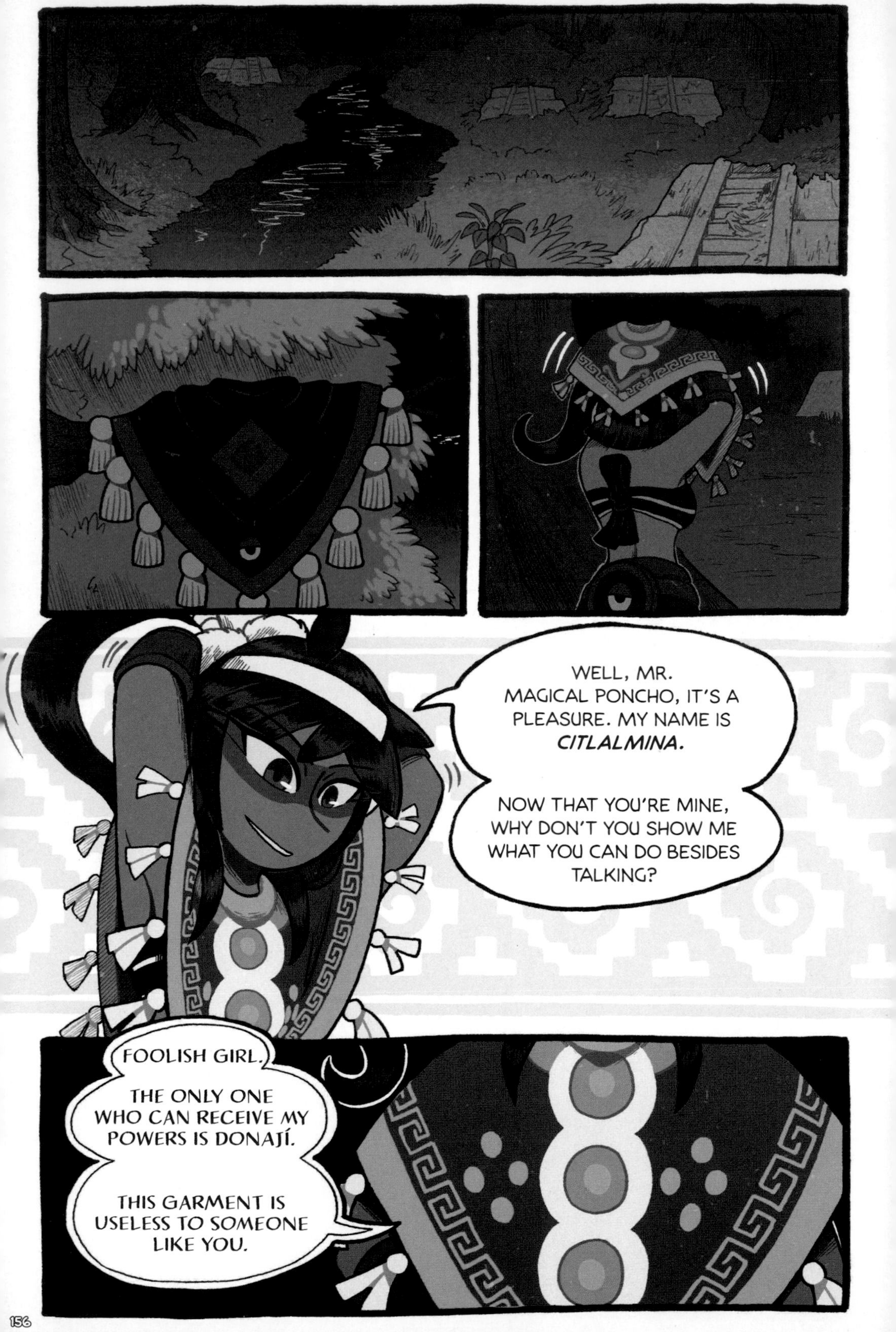
WELL, MR. MAGICAL PONCHO, IT'S A PLEASURE. MY NAME IS *CITLALMINA.*
NOW THAT YOU'RE MINE, WHY DON'T YOU SHOW ME WHAT YOU CAN DO BESIDES TALKING?
FOOLISH GIRL.
THE ONLY ONE WHO CAN RECEIVE MY POWERS IS DONAJÍ.
THIS GARMENT IS USELESS TO SOMEONE LIKE YOU.

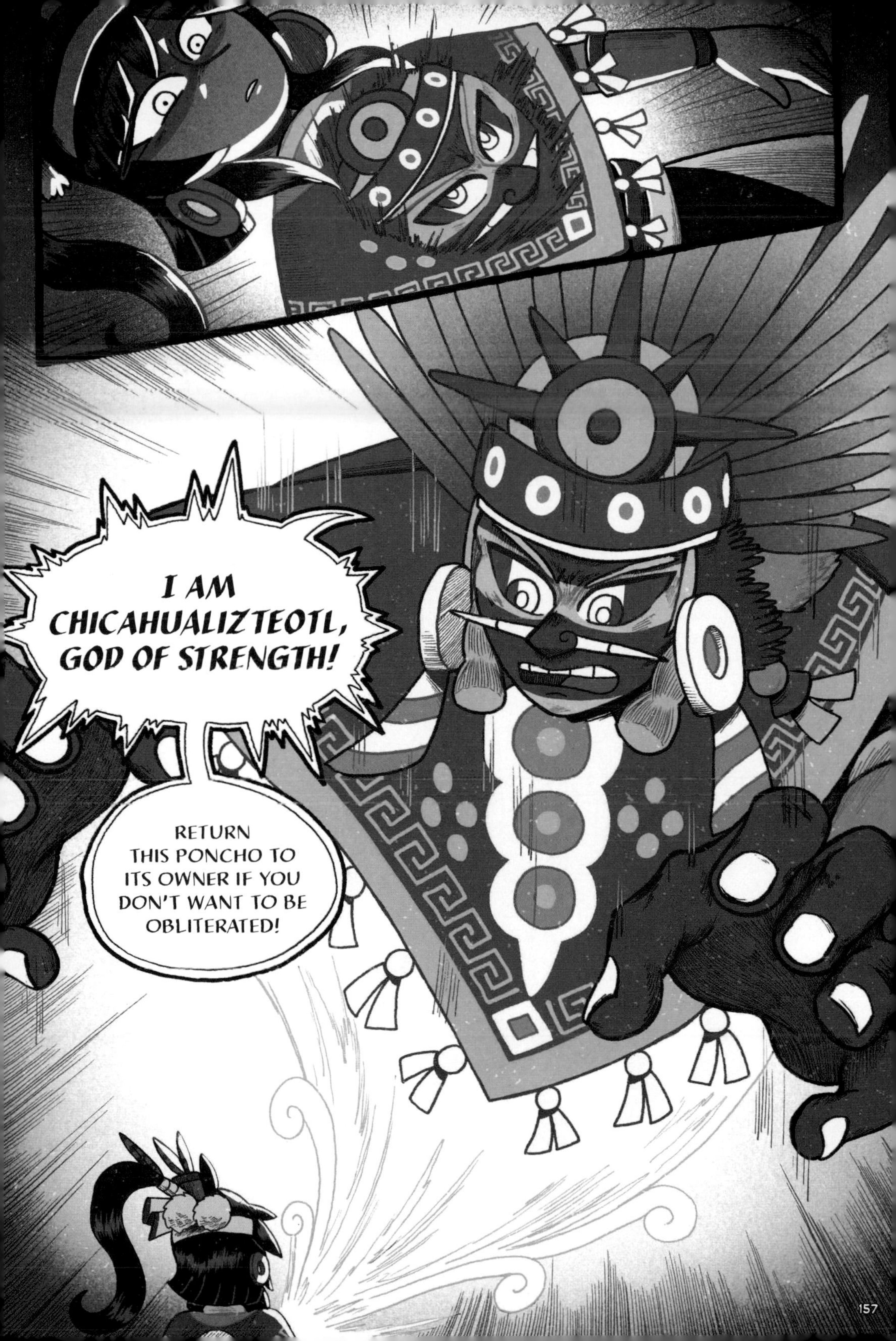
I AM CHICAHUALIZTEOTL, GOD OF STRENGTH!
RETURN THIS PONCHO TO ITS OWNER IF YOU DON'T WANT TO BE OBLITERATED!

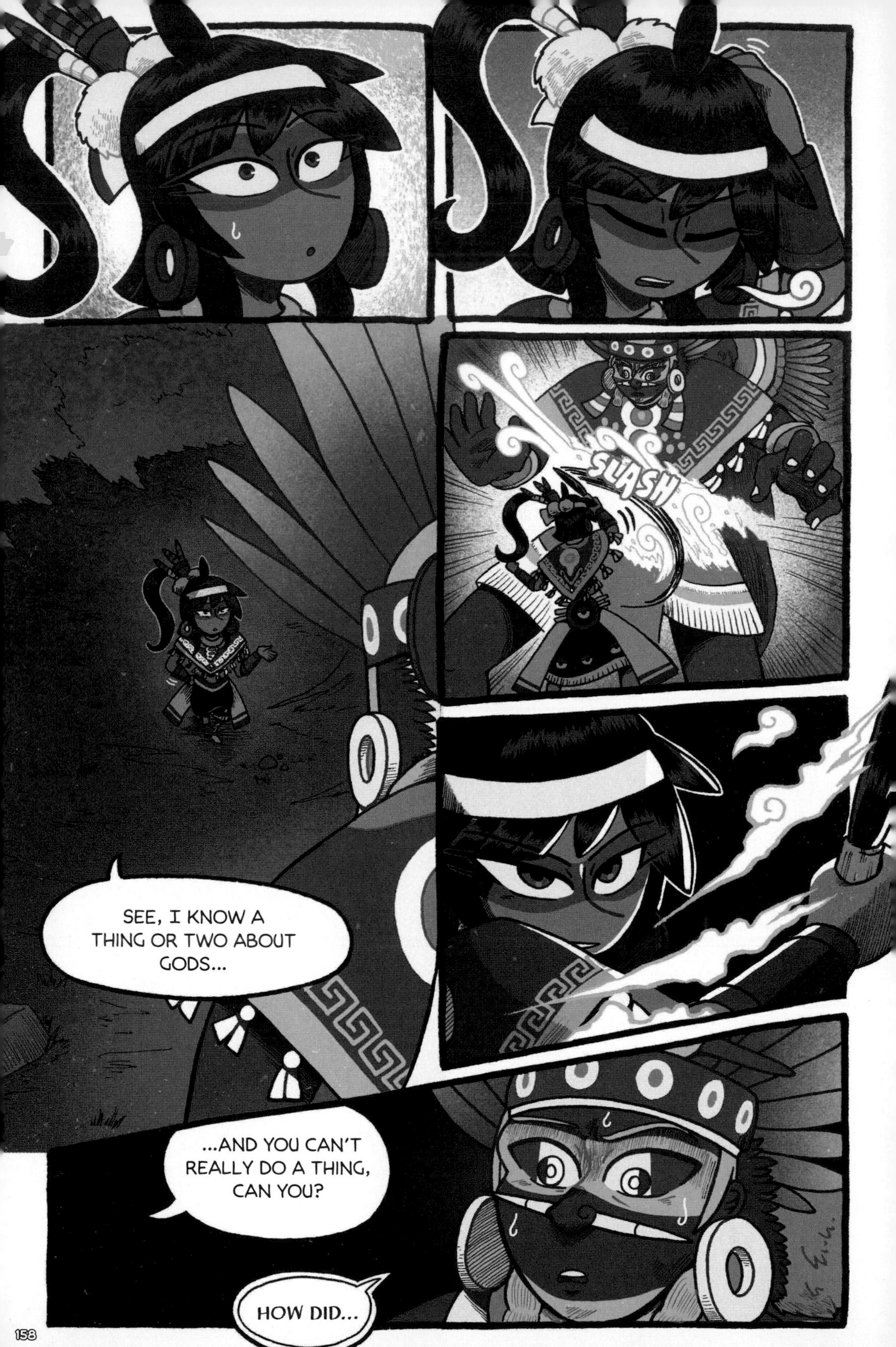
SLASH
SEE, I KNOW A THING OR TWO ABOUT GODS...
...AND YOU CAN'T REALLY DO A THING, CAN YOU?
HOW DID...

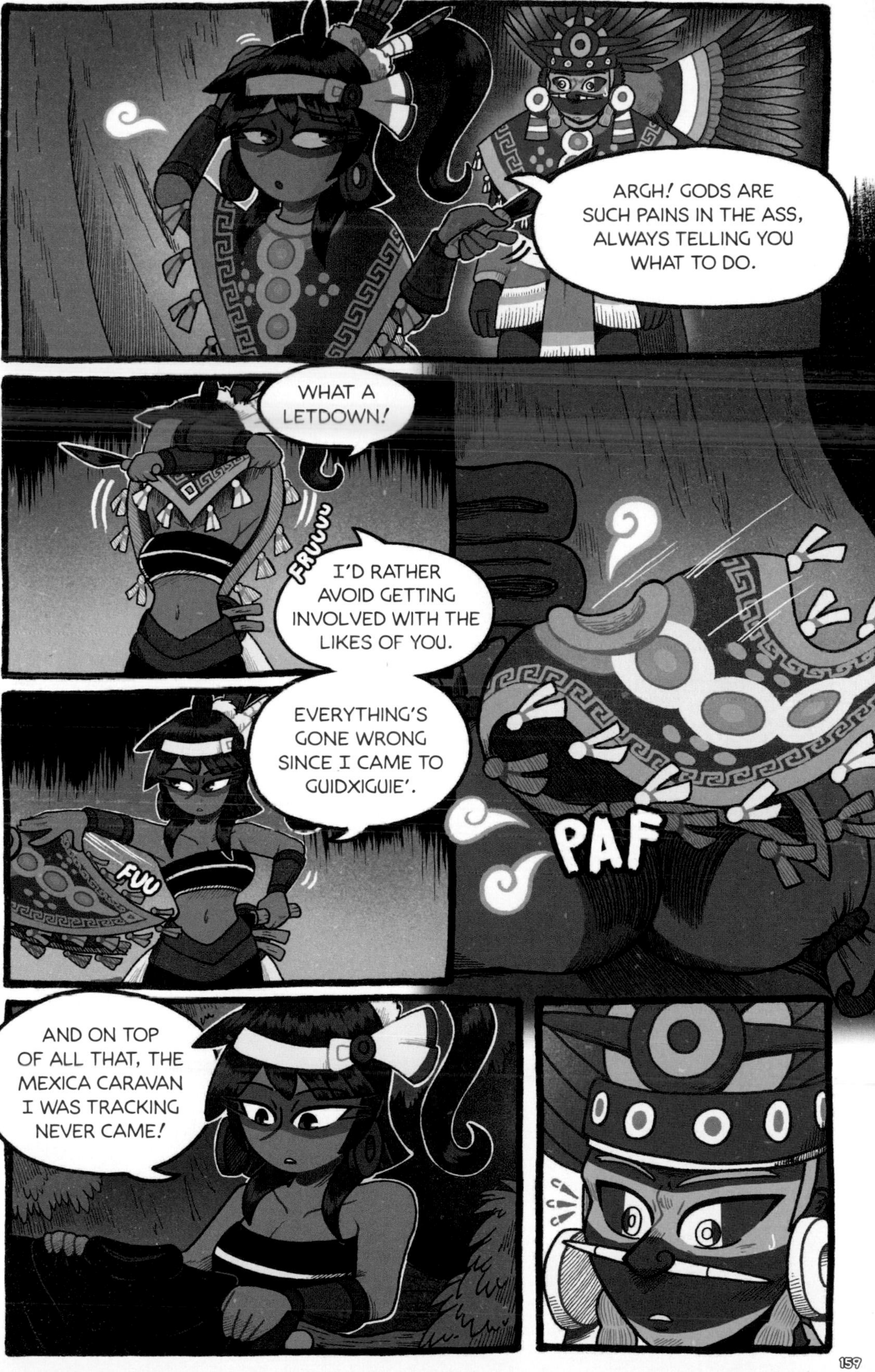
ARGH! GODS ARE SUCH PAINS IN THE ASS, ALWAYS TELLING YOU WHAT TO DO.
WHAT A LETDOWN!
FRUUUU
I'D RATHER AVOID GETTING INVOLVED WITH THE LIKES OF YOU.
EVERYTHING'S GONE WRONG SINCE I CAME TO GUIDXIGUIE'.
FUU
PAF
AND ON TOP OF ALL THAT, THE MEXICA CARAVAN I WAS TRACKING NEVER CAME!

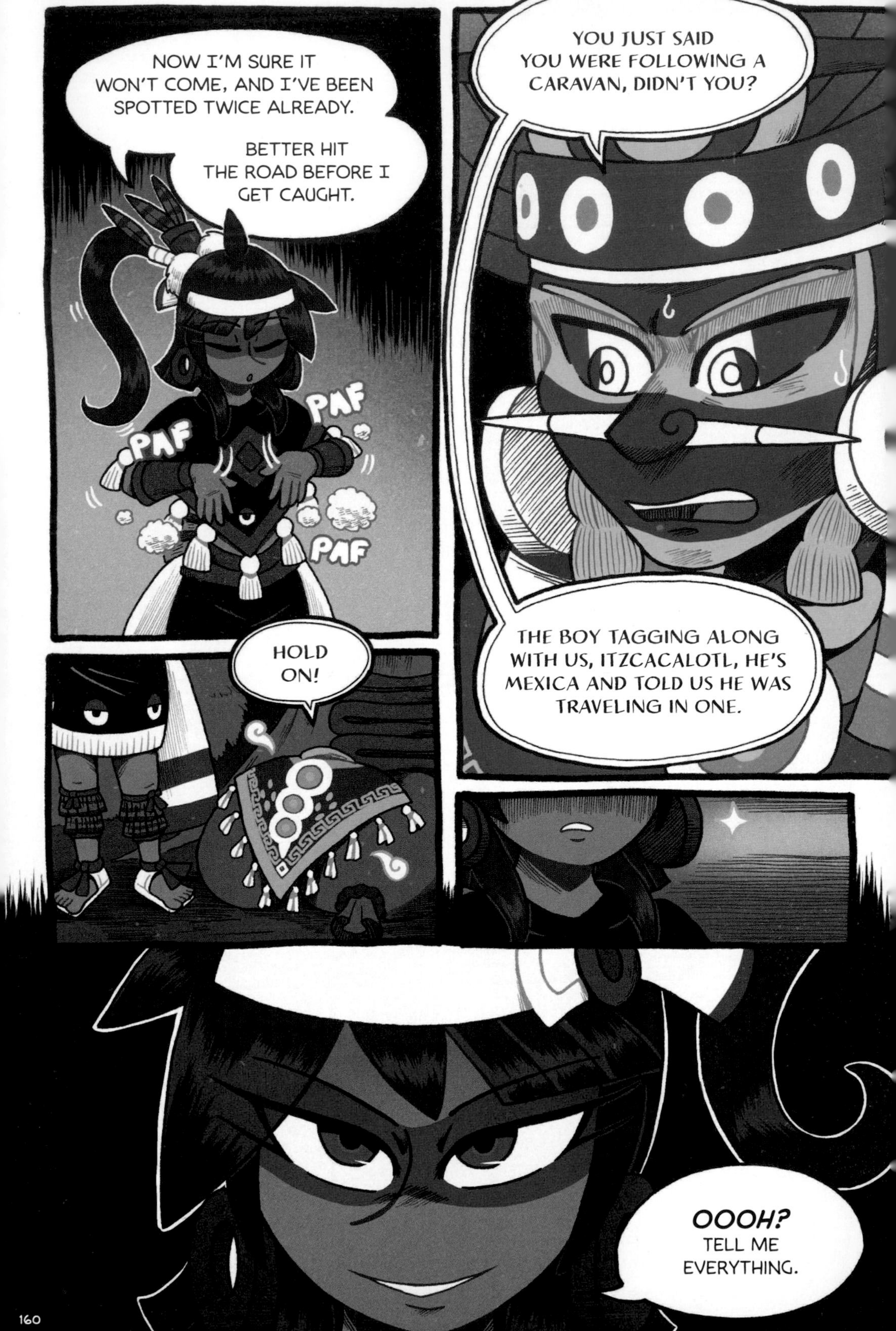
NOW I'M SURE IT WON'T COME, AND I'VE BEEN SPOTTED TWICE ALREADY.
BETTER HIT THE ROAD BEFORE I GET CAUGHT.
PAF
PAF
PAF
YOU JUST SAID YOU WERE FOLLOWING A CARAVAN, DIDN'T YOU?
THE BOY TAGGING ALONG WITH US, ITZCACALOTL, HE'S MEXICA AND TOLD US HE WAS TRAVELING IN ONE.
HOLD ON!
OOOH? TELL ME EVERYTHING.

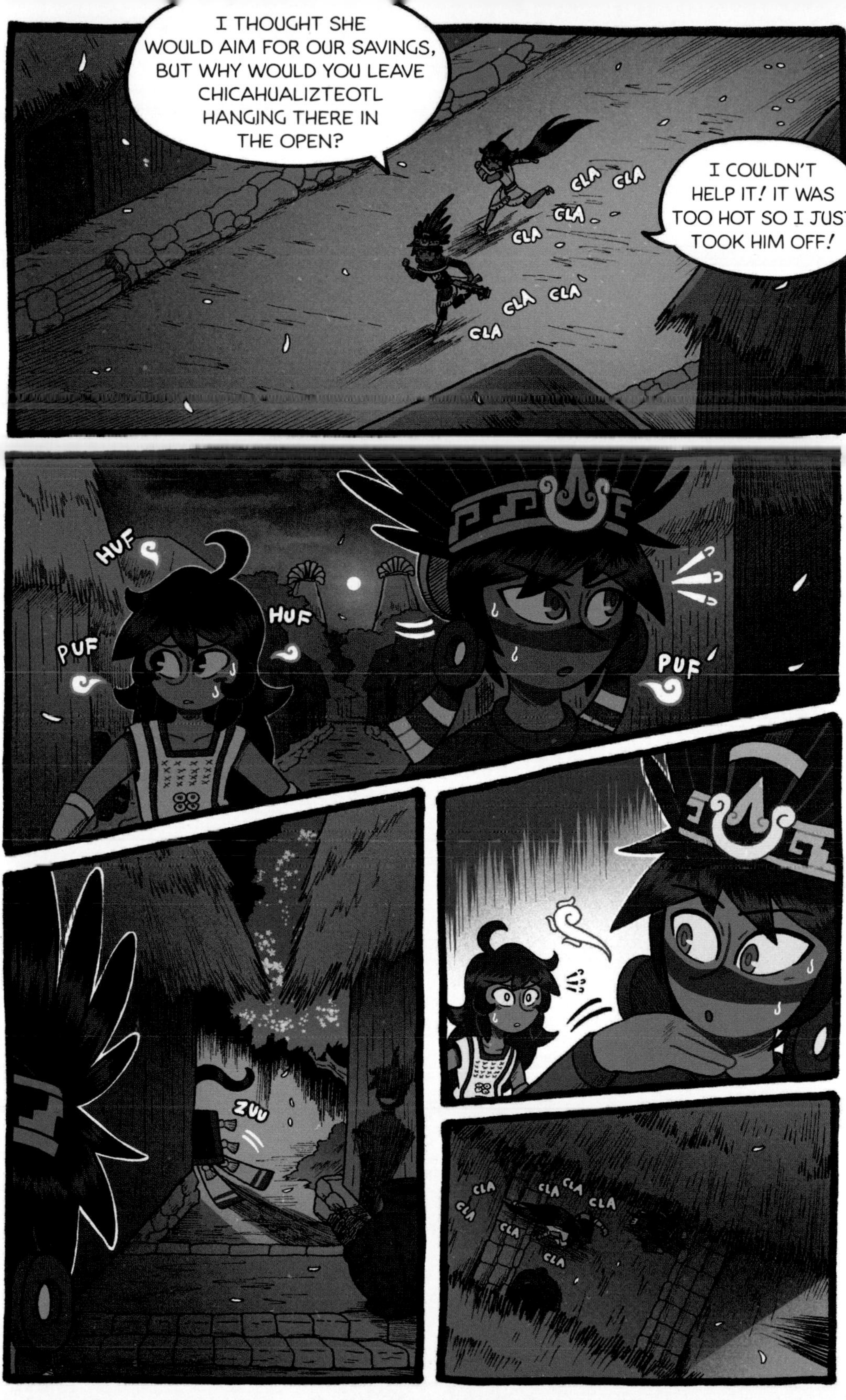
I THOUGHT SHE WOULD AIM FOR OUR SAVINGS, BUT WHY WOULD YOU LEAVE CHICAHUALIZTEOTL HANGING THERE IN THE OPEN?
I COULDN'T HELP IT! IT WAS TOO HOT SO I JUST TOOK HIM OFF!
CLA CLA CLA CLA CLA CLA CLA
HUF HUF PUF PUF
ZUU
CLA CLA CLA CLA CLA CLA CLA

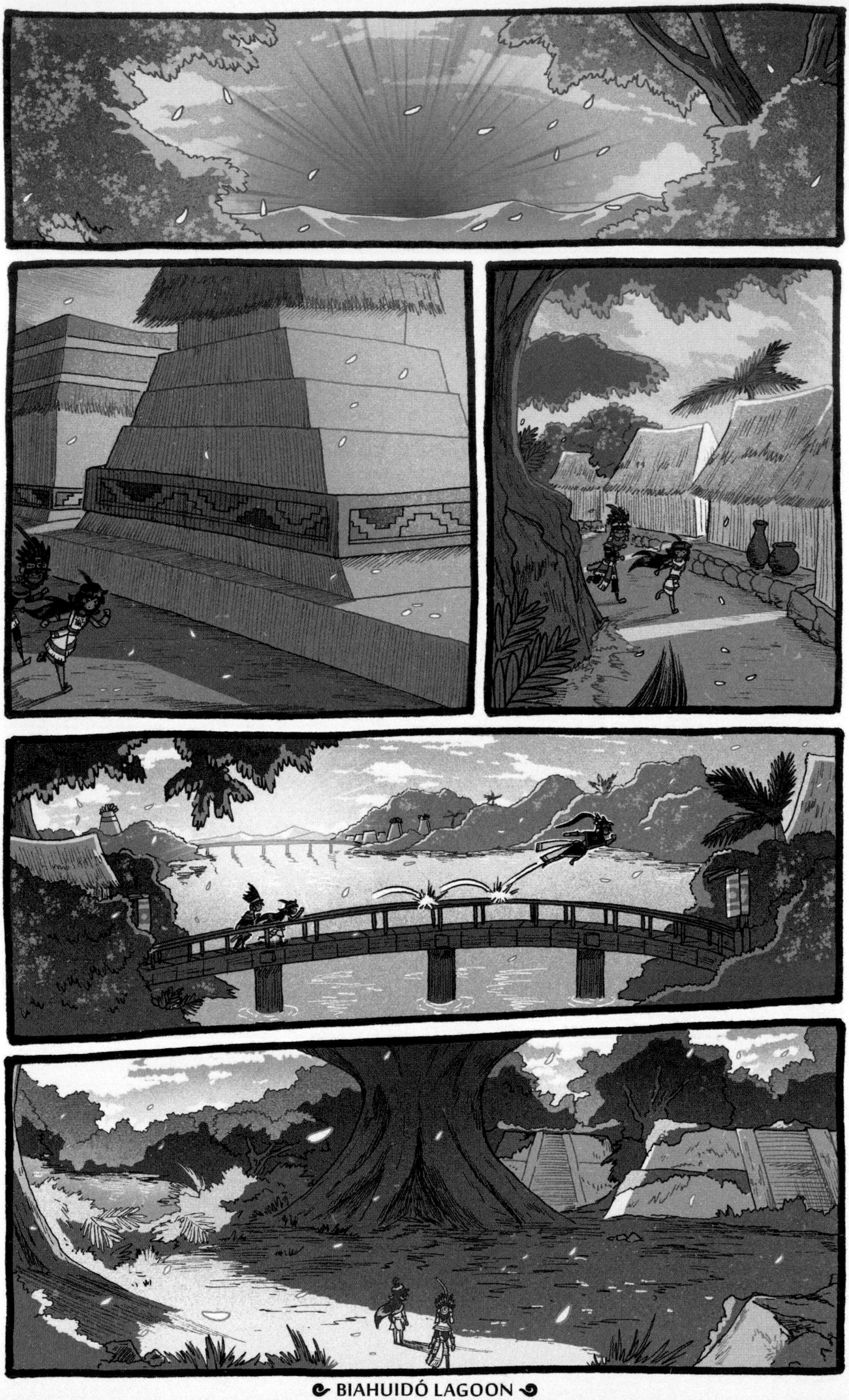

BIAHUIDÓ LAGOON

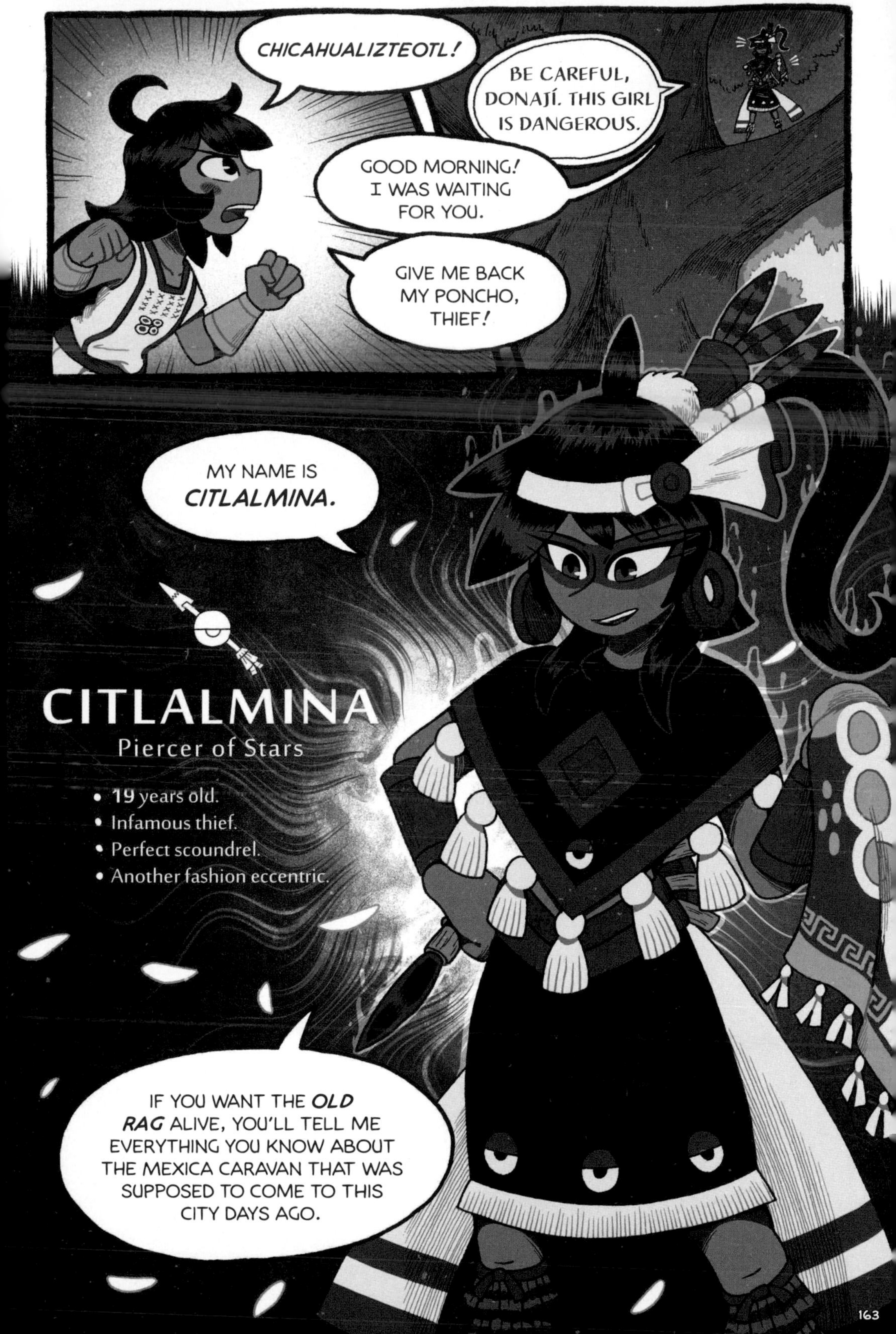
CHICAHUALIZTEOTL!
BE CAREFUL, DONAJÍ. THIS GIRL IS DANGEROUS.
GOOD MORNING! I WAS WAITING FOR YOU.
GIVE ME BACK MY PONCHO, THIEF!
MY NAME IS *CITLALMINA.*
CITLALMINA
Piercer of Stars
• 19 years old.
• Infamous thief.
• Perfect scoundrel.
• Another fashion eccentric.
IF YOU WANT THE *OLD RAG* ALIVE, YOU'LL TELL ME EVERYTHING YOU KNOW ABOUT THE MEXICA CARAVAN THAT WAS SUPPOSED TO COME TO THIS CITY DAYS AGO.

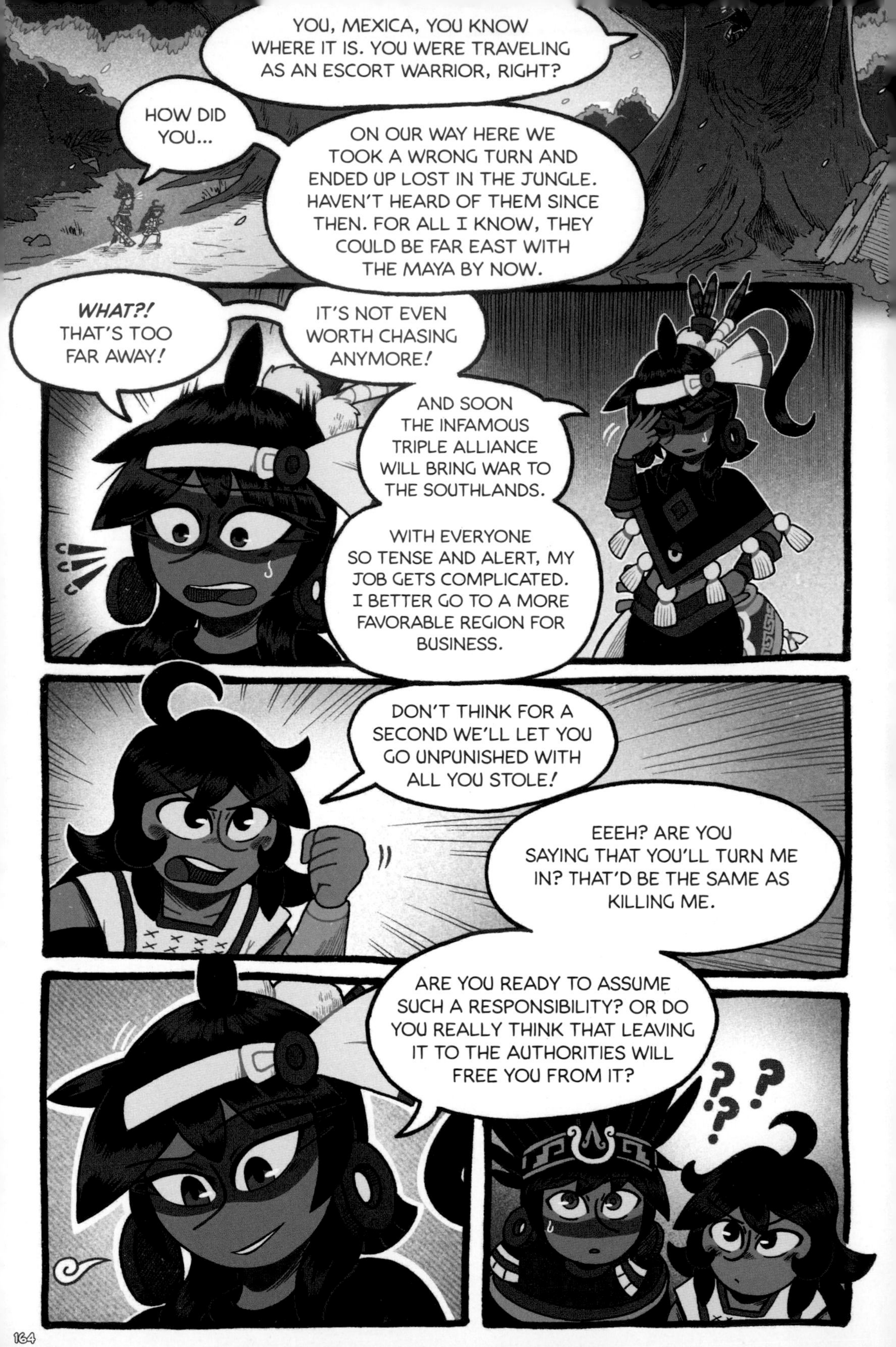
YOU, MEXICA, YOU KNOW WHERE IT IS. YOU WERE TRAVELING AS AN ESCORT WARRIOR, RIGHT?
HOW DID YOU...
ON OUR WAY HERE WE TOOK A WRONG TURN AND ENDED UP LOST IN THE JUNGLE. HAVEN'T HEARD OF THEM SINCE THEN. FOR ALL I KNOW, THEY COULD BE FAR EAST WITH THE MAYA BY NOW.
WHAT?! THAT'S TOO FAR AWAY!
IT'S NOT EVEN WORTH CHASING ANYMORE!
AND SOON THE INFAMOUS TRIPLE ALLIANCE WILL BRING WAR TO THE SOUTHLANDS.
WITH EVERYONE SO TENSE AND ALERT, MY JOB GETS COMPLICATED. I BETTER GO TO A MORE FAVORABLE REGION FOR BUSINESS.
DON'T THINK FOR A SECOND WE'LL LET YOU GO UNPUNISHED WITH ALL YOU STOLE!
EEEH? ARE YOU SAYING THAT YOU'LL TURN ME IN? THAT'D BE THE SAME AS KILLING ME.
ARE YOU READY TO ASSUME SUCH A RESPONSIBILITY? OR DO YOU REALLY THINK THAT LEAVING IT TO THE AUTHORITIES WILL FREE YOU FROM IT?
???

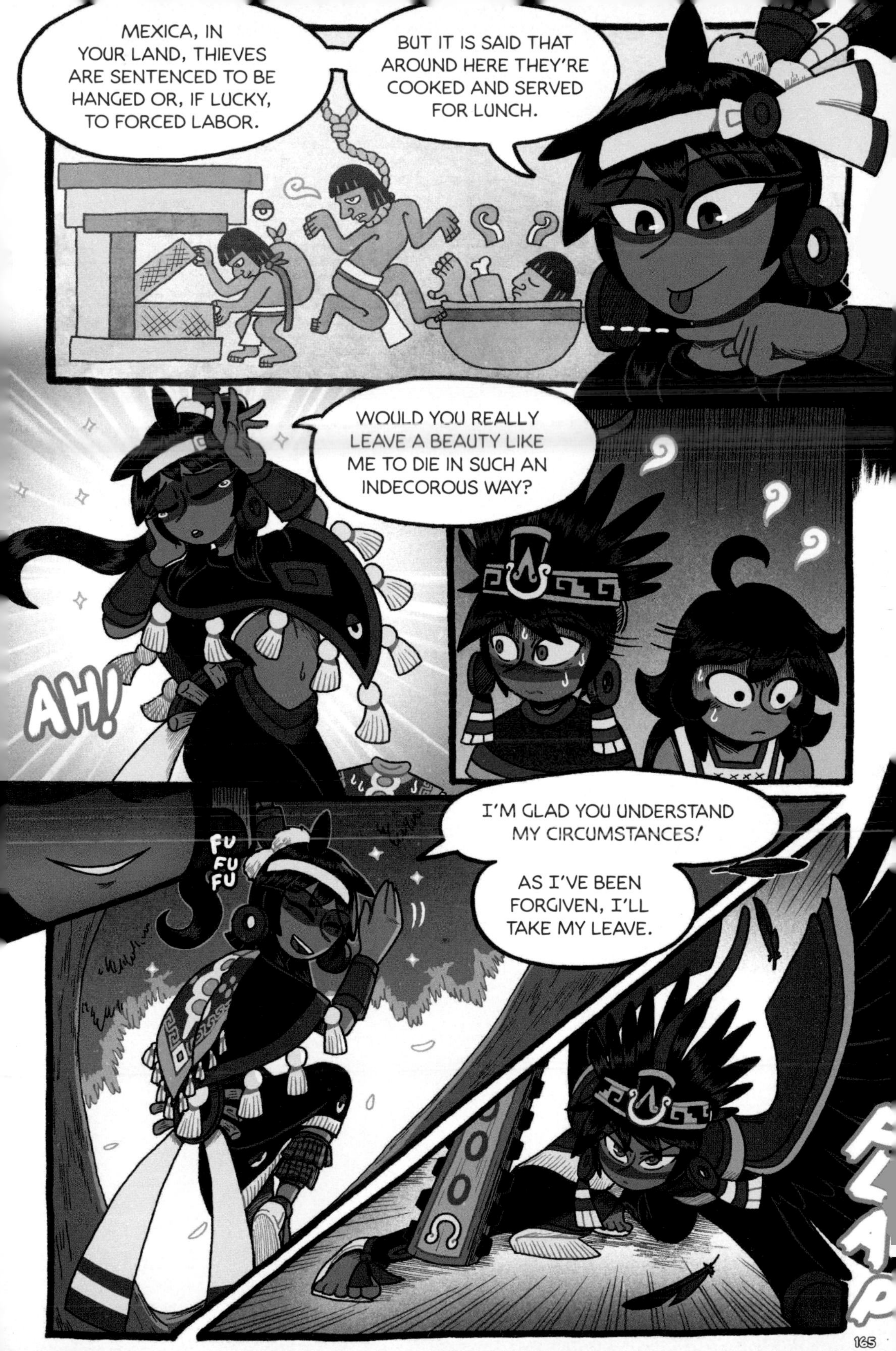
MEXICA, IN YOUR LAND, THIEVES ARE SENTENCED TO BE HANGED OR, IF LUCKY, TO FORCED LABOR.
BUT IT IS SAID THAT AROUND HERE THEY'RE COOKED AND SERVED FOR LUNCH.
WOULD YOU REALLY LEAVE A BEAUTY LIKE ME TO DIE IN SUCH AN INDECOROUS WAY?
AH!
I'M GLAD YOU UNDERSTAND MY CIRCUMSTANCES!
AS I'VE BEEN FORGIVEN, I'LL TAKE MY LEAVE.
FU FU FU
FLAP

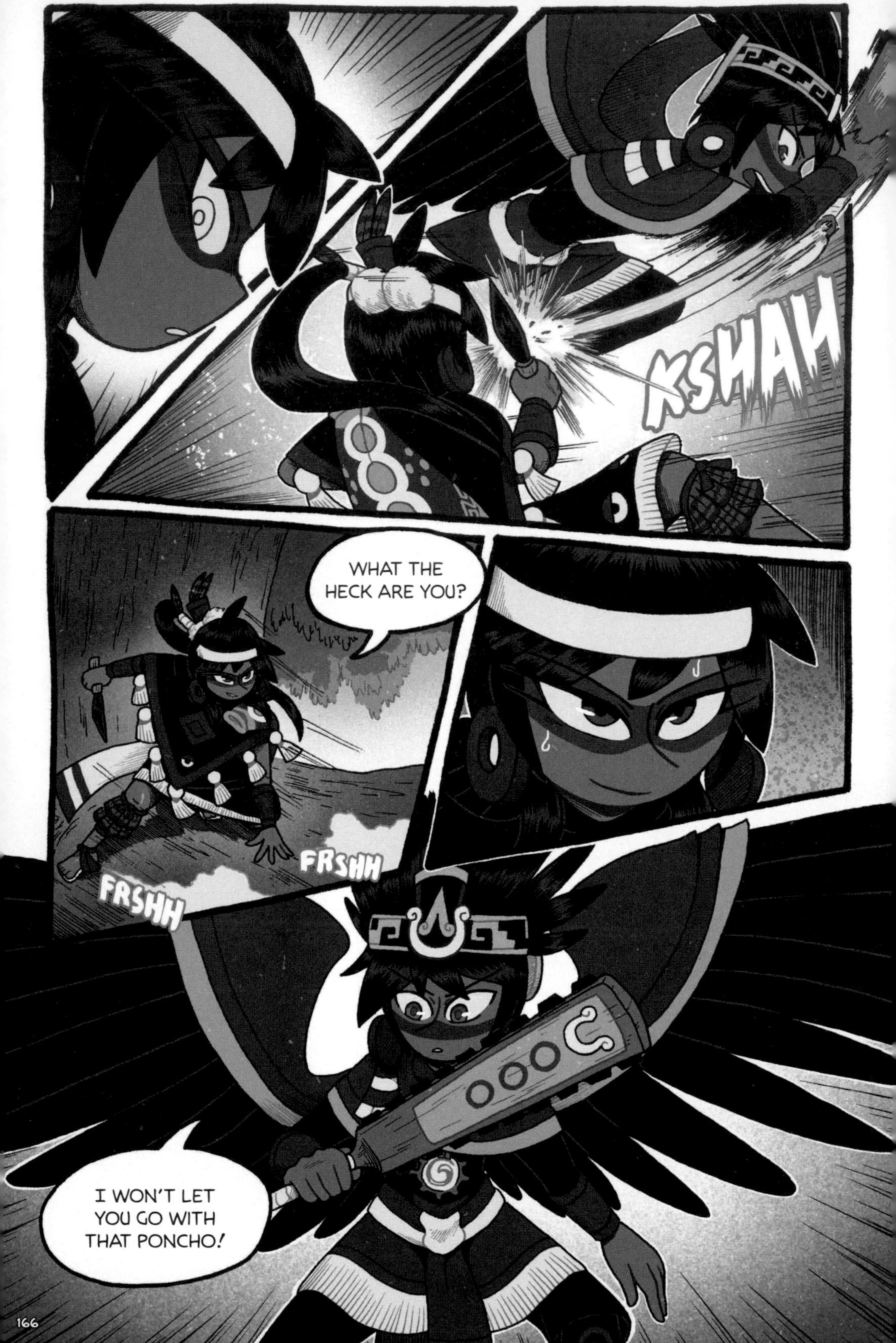
KSHAH
WHAT THE HECK ARE YOU?
FRSHH
FRSHH
I WON'T LET YOU GO WITH THAT PONCHO!

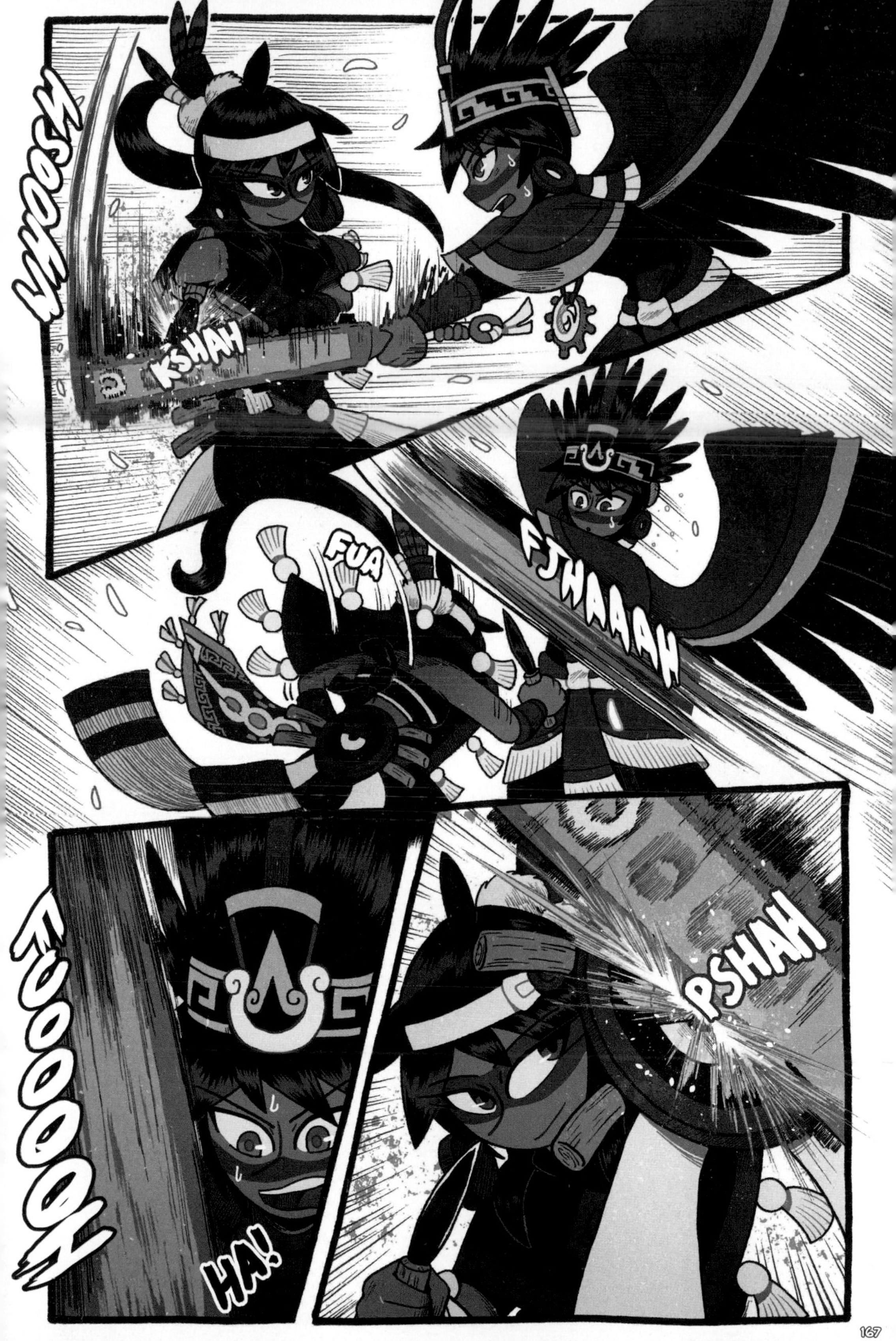

KSHAH
FWOOSH
FUA
FSHAAAAH
PSHAH
FWOOOOSH
HA!

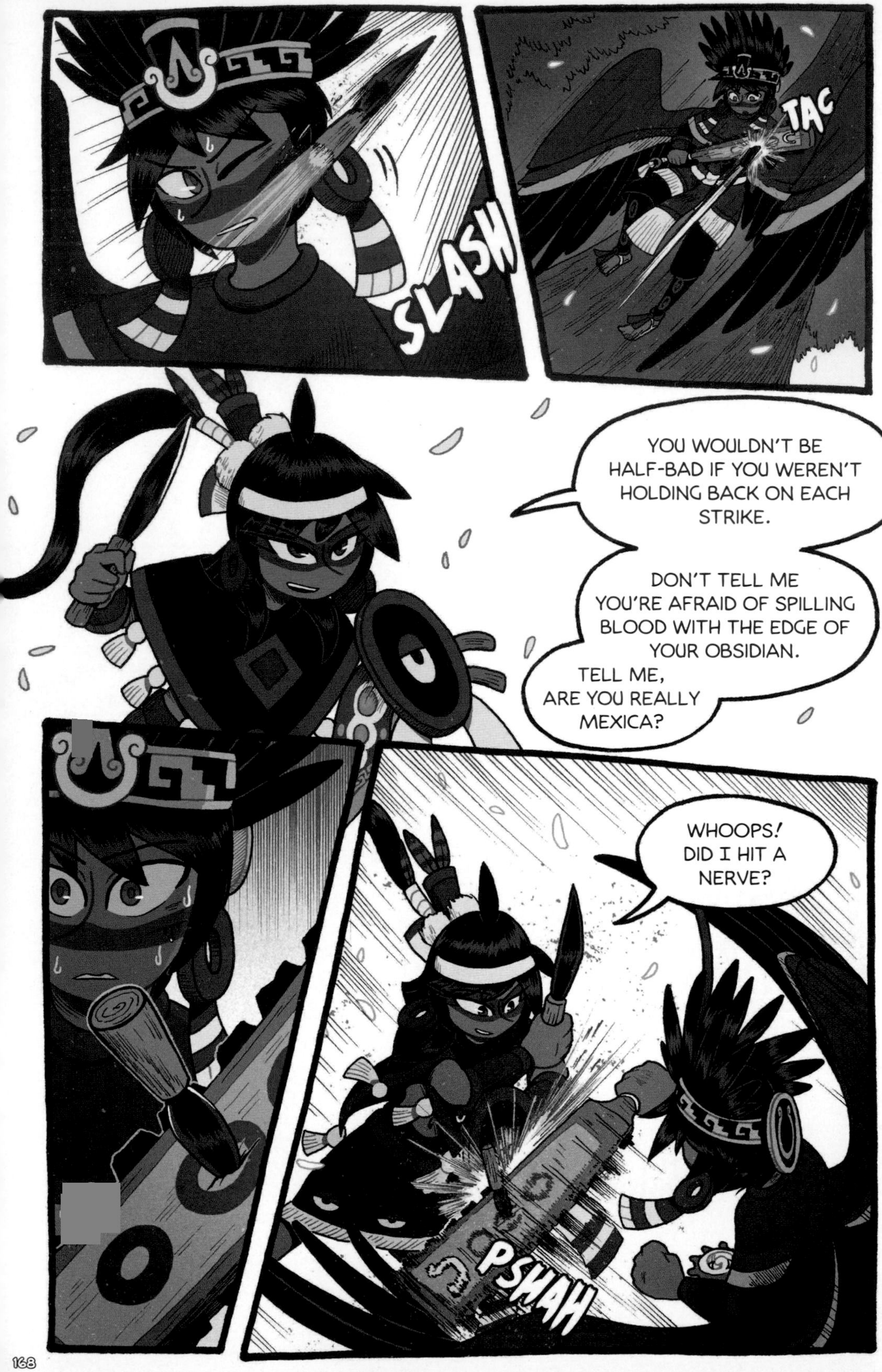
SLASH
TAC
YOU WOULDN'T BE HALF-BAD IF YOU WEREN'T HOLDING BACK ON EACH STRIKE.
DON'T TELL ME YOU'RE AFRAID OF SPILLING BLOOD WITH THE EDGE OF YOUR OBSIDIAN.
TELL ME, ARE YOU REALLY MEXICA?
WHOOPS! DID I HIT A NERVE?
PSHAH

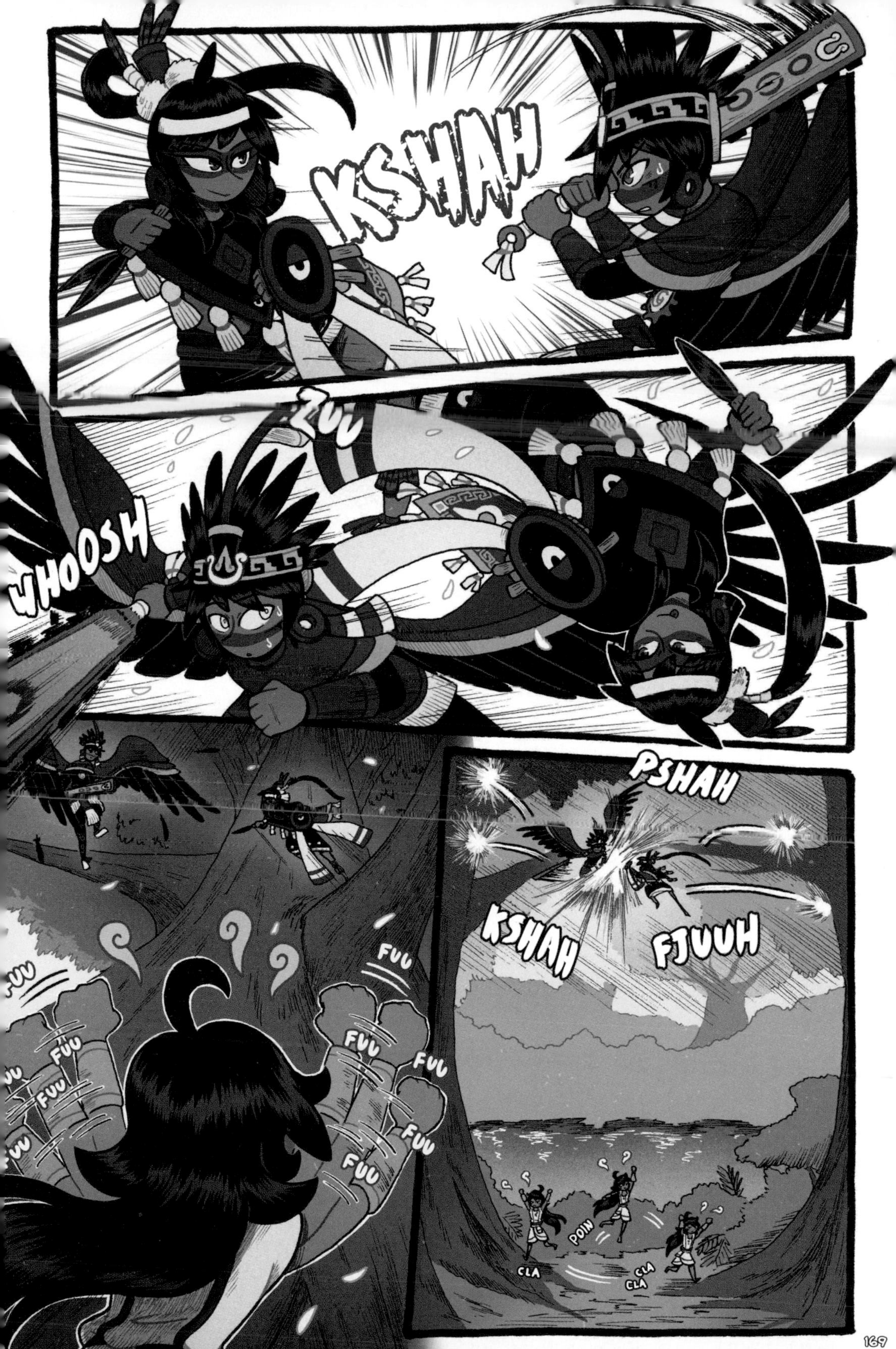
KSHAH
ZUU
WHOOSH
PSHAH
KSHAH
FJUUH
FUU
FUU
FUU
FUU
FUU
FUU
FUU
FUU
FUU
POIN
CLA
CLA
CLA

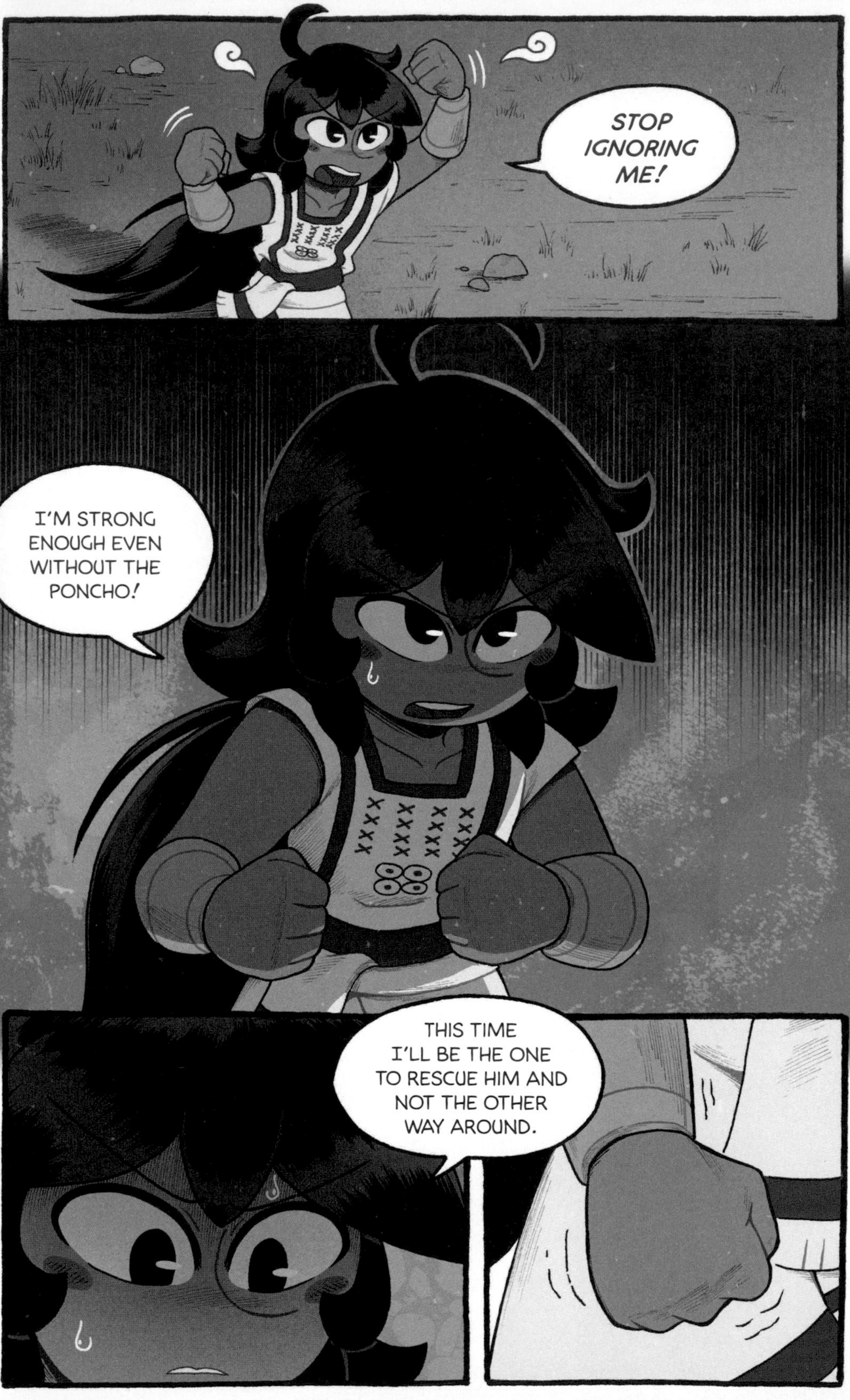

STOP IGNORING ME!
I'M STRONG ENOUGH EVEN WITHOUT THE PONCHO!
THIS TIME I'LL BE THE ONE TO RESCUE HIM AND NOT THE OTHER WAY AROUND.

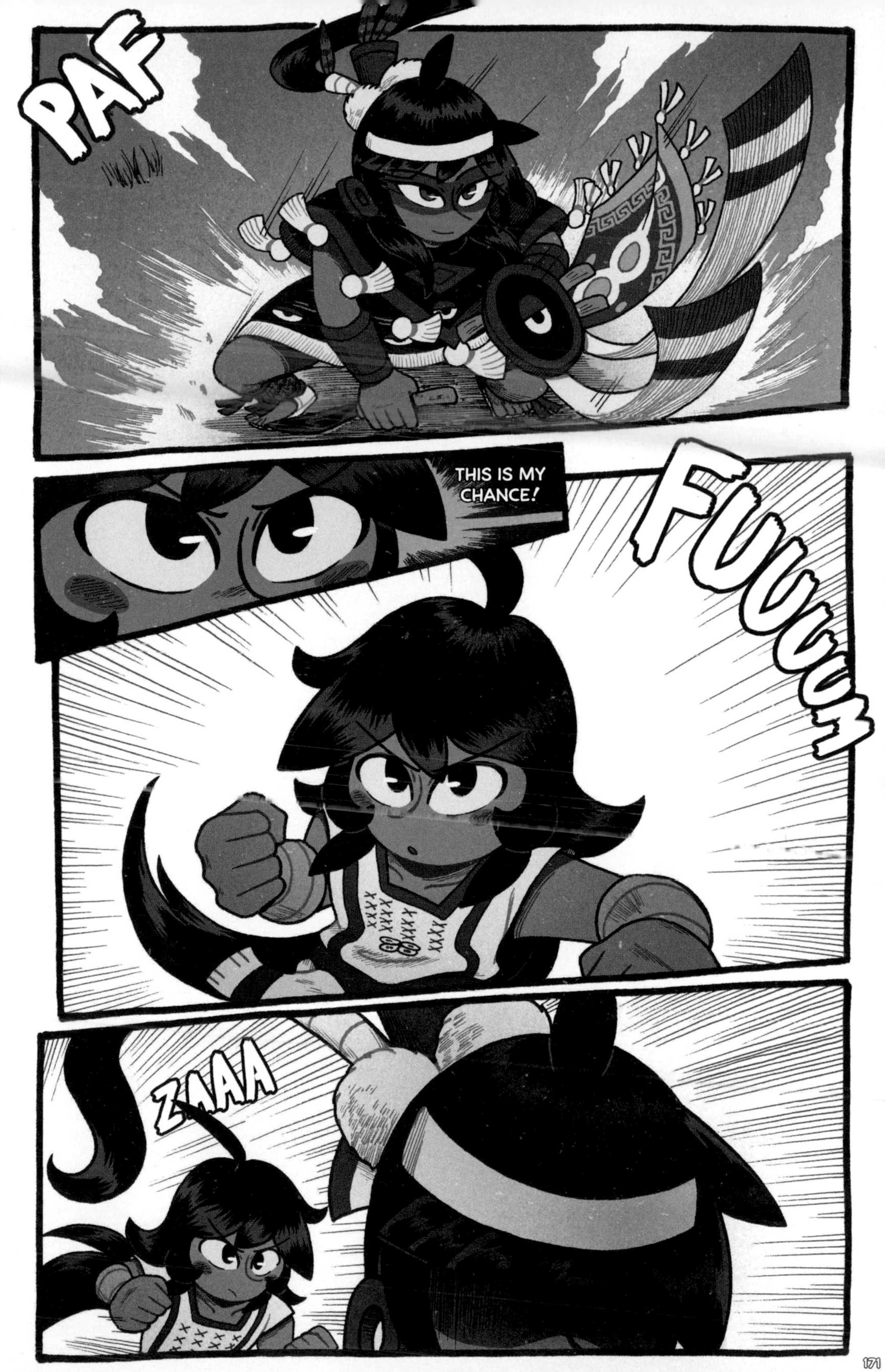
PAF
THIS IS MY CHANCE!
FUUUUM
ZAAA

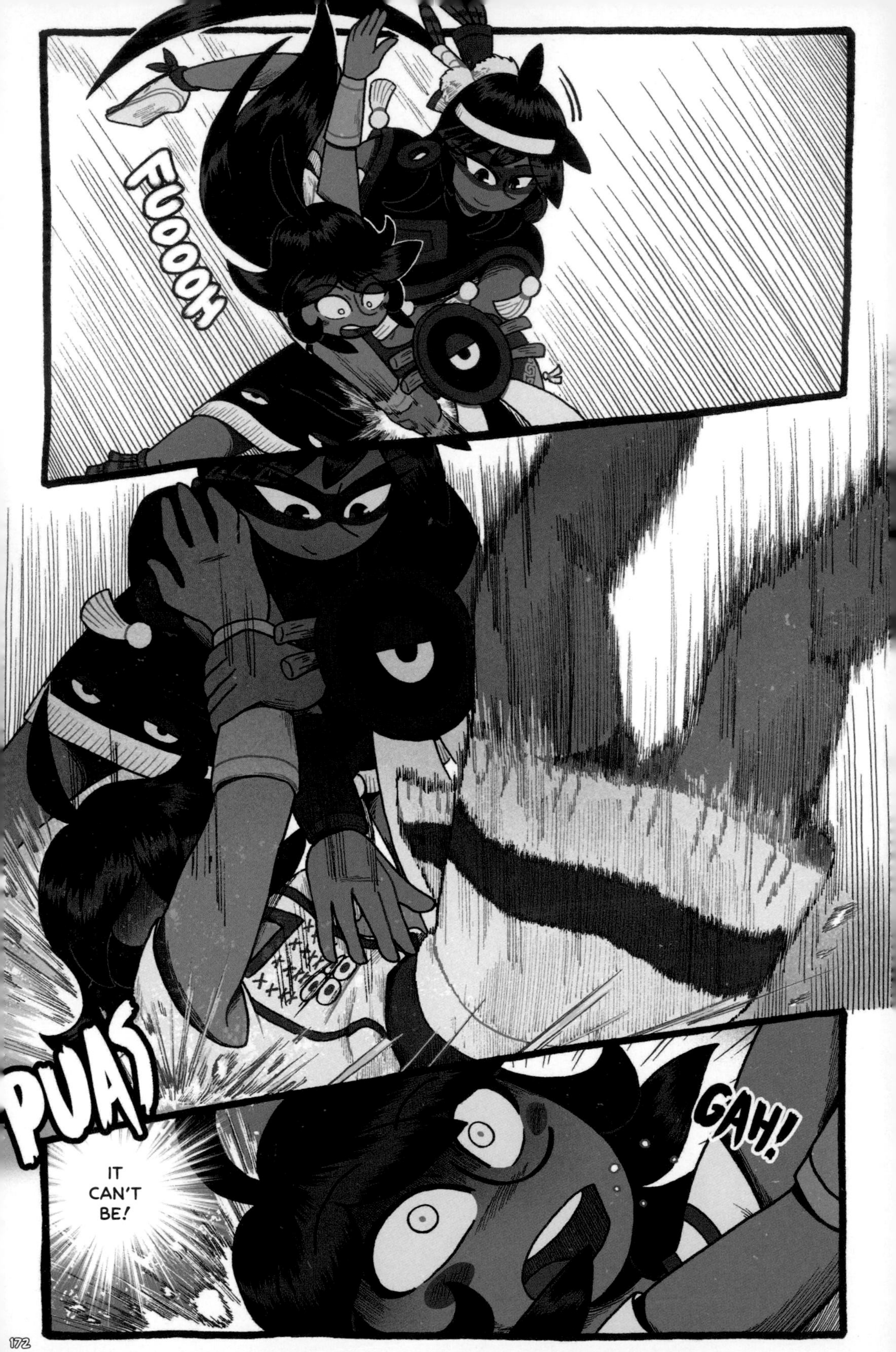
FUOOOOH
PUAS
GAH!
IT CAN'T BE!

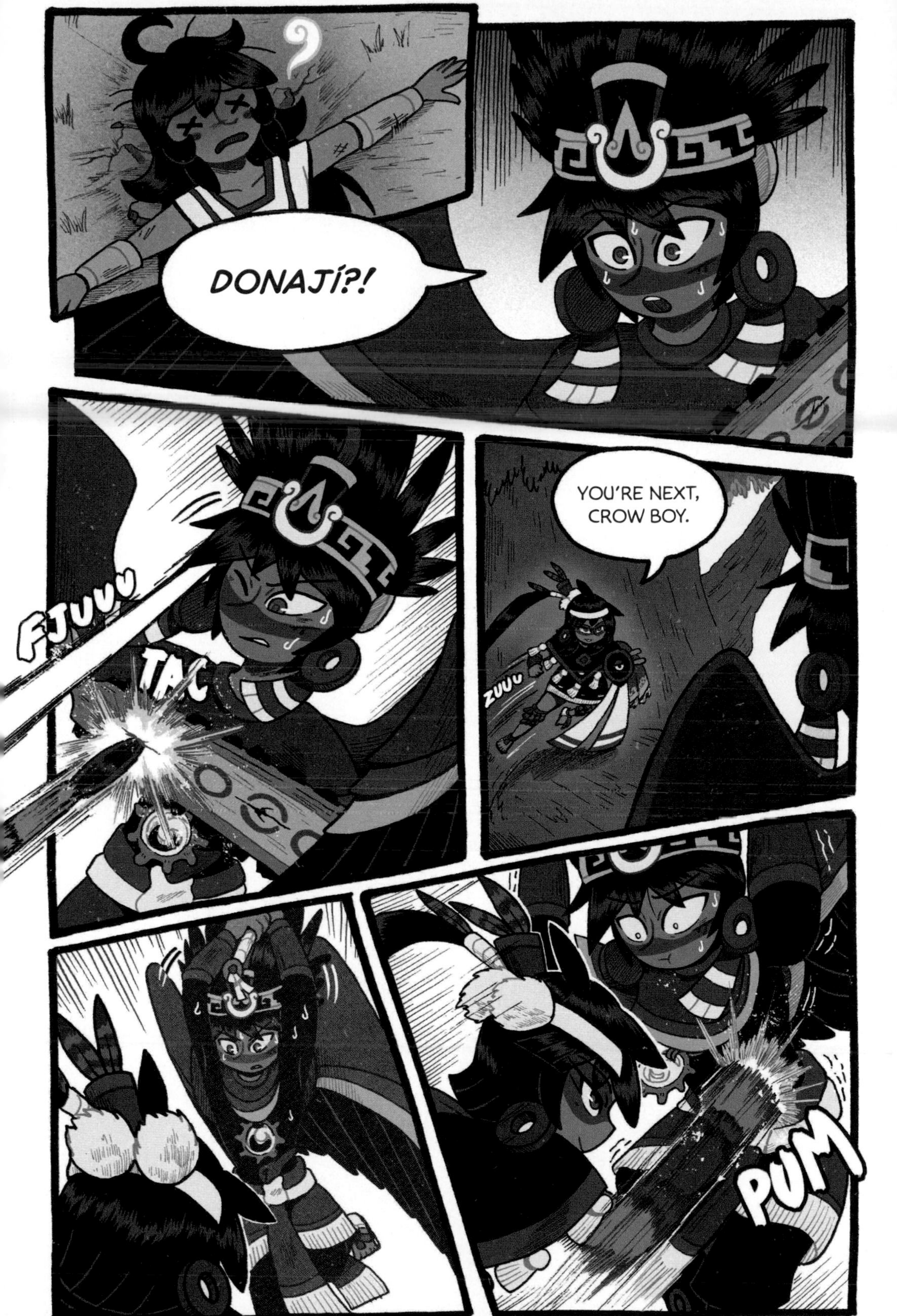
DONAJÍ?!
FJUUU
TAC
YOU'RE NEXT, CROW BOY.
ZUUU
PUM

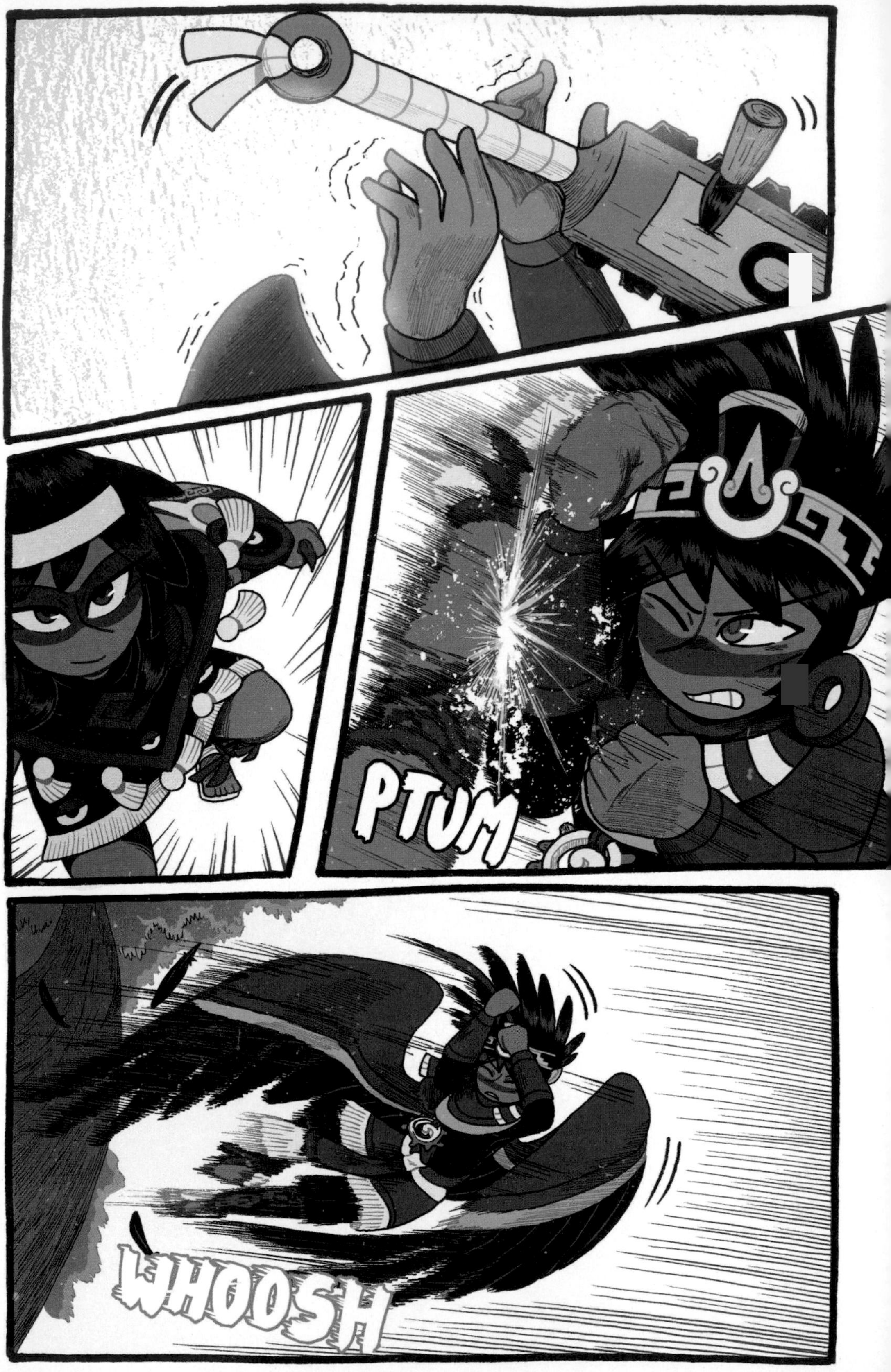
PTUM
WHOOSH

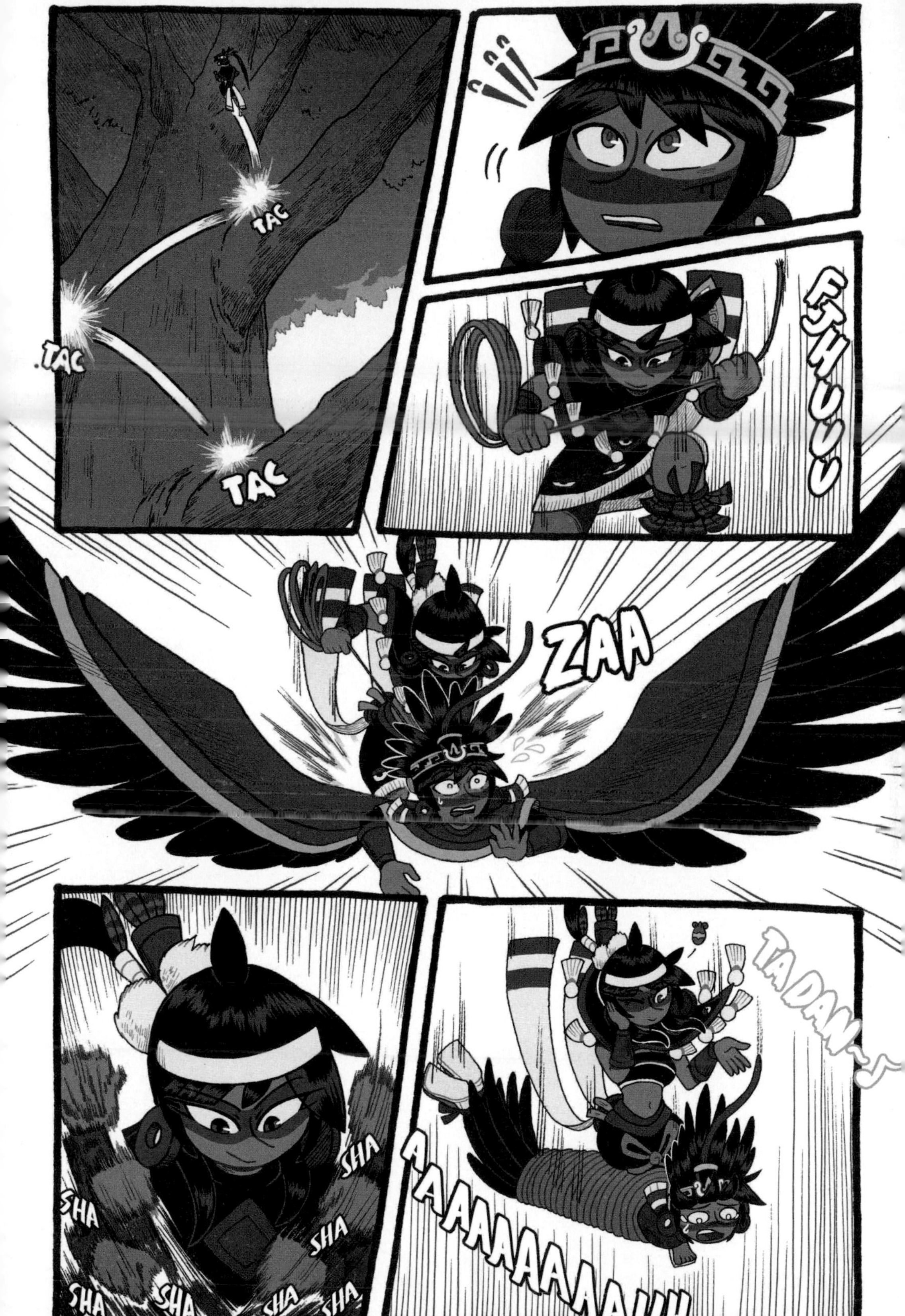
TAC
TAC
TAC
FSHUUUU
ZAA
SHA
SHA
SHA
SHA
SHA
SHA
SHA
TA DAN~♪
AAAAAAAAAAAHH

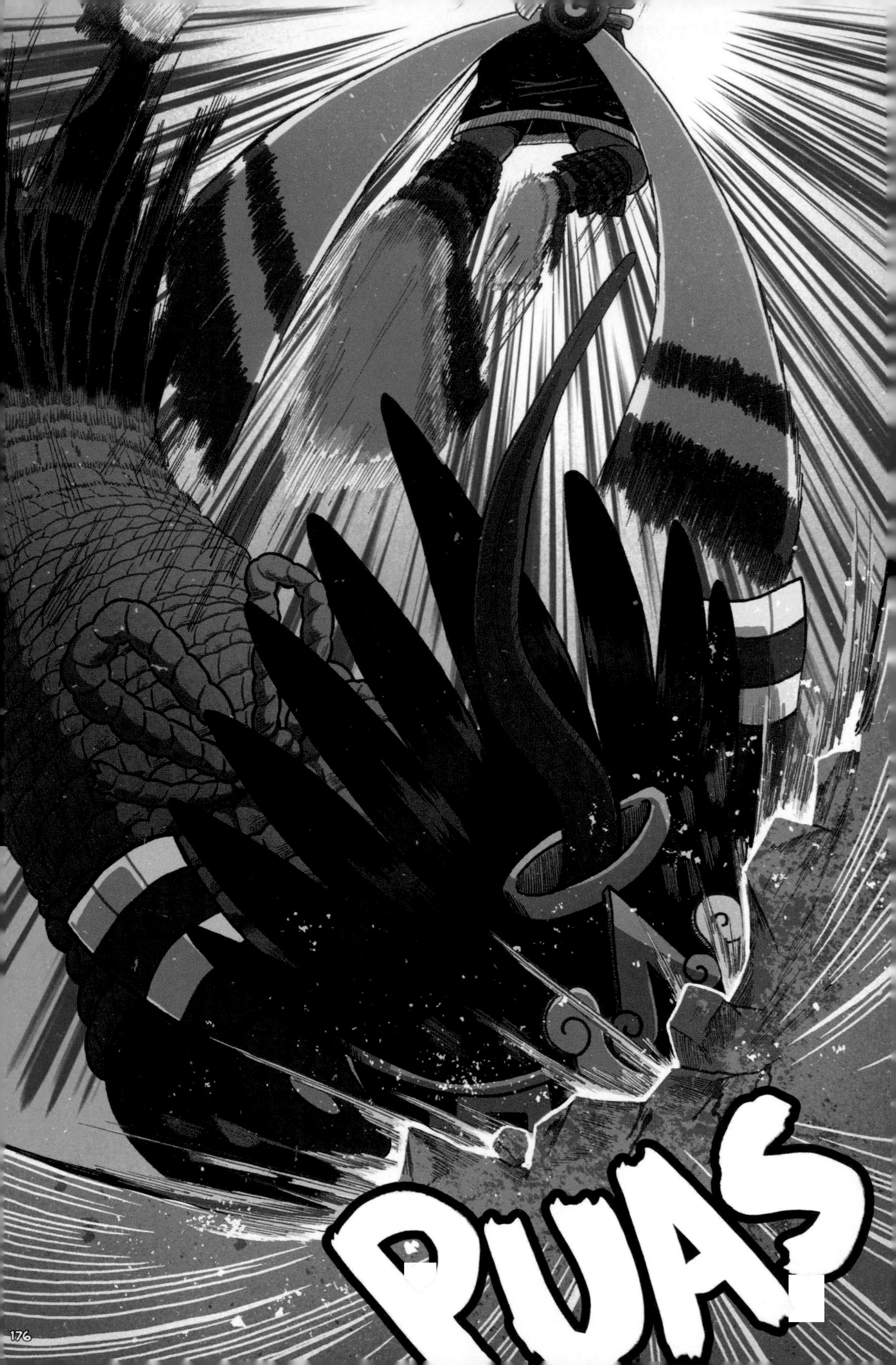
PUAS!

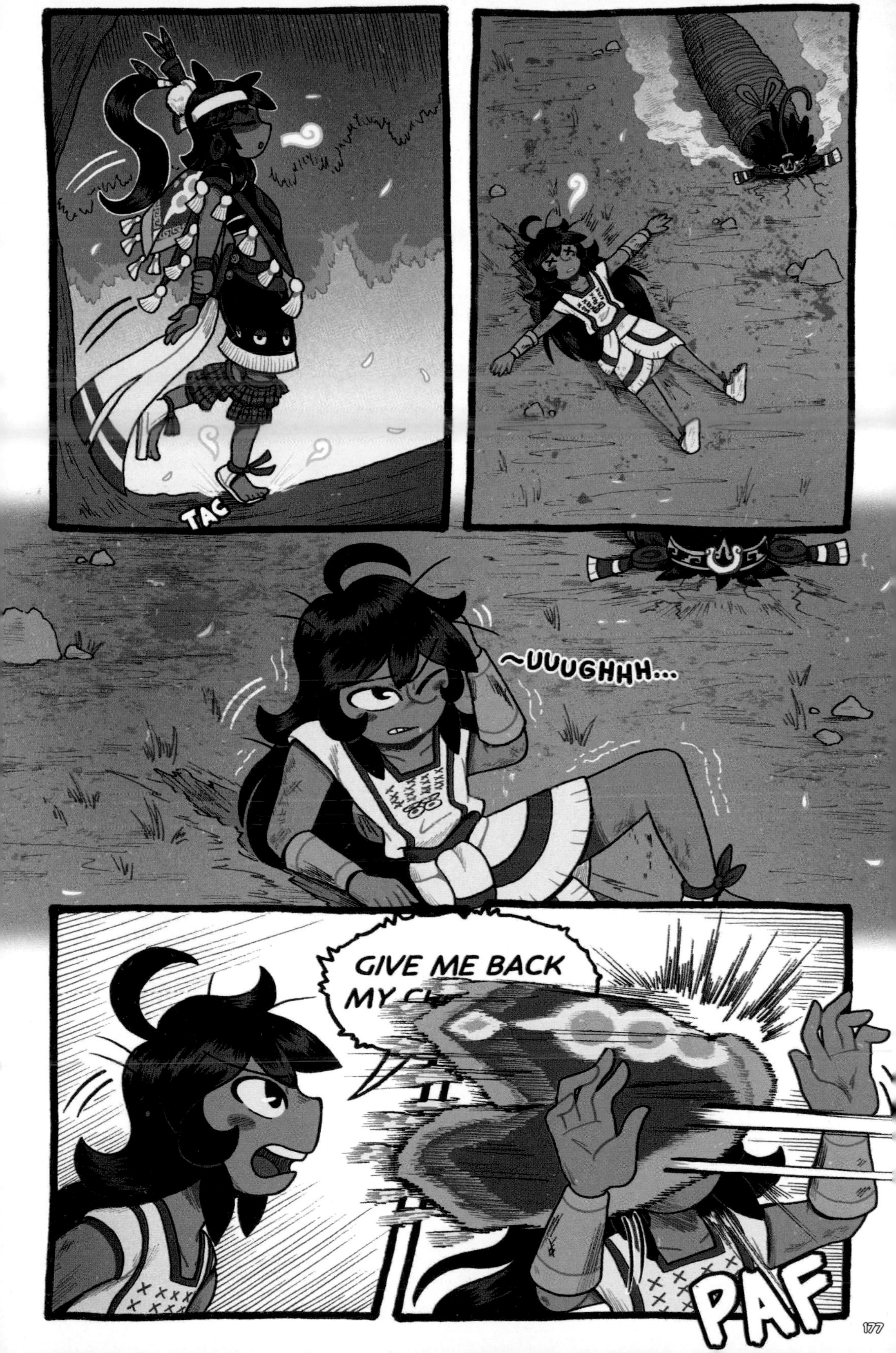
TAC
~UUUGHHH...
GIVE ME BACK
MY CL
PAF

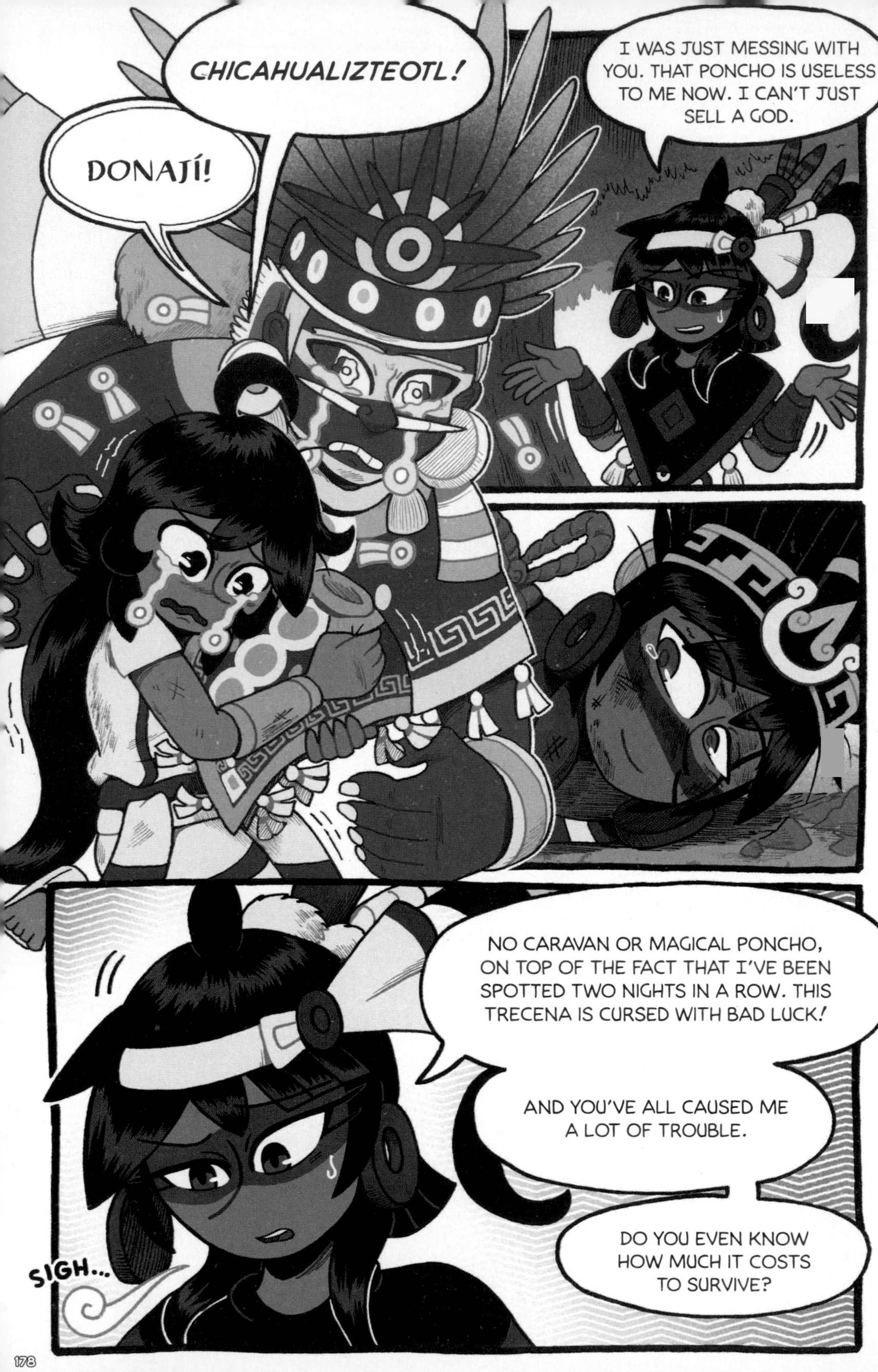
DONAJÍ!
CHICAHUALIZTEOTL!
I WAS JUST MESSING WITH YOU. THAT PONCHO IS USELESS TO ME NOW. I CAN'T JUST SELL A GOD.
NO CARAVAN OR MAGICAL PONCHO, ON TOP OF THE FACT THAT I'VE BEEN SPOTTED TWO NIGHTS IN A ROW. THIS TRECENA IS CURSED WITH BAD LUCK!
AND YOU'VE ALL CAUSED ME A LOT OF TROUBLE.
SIGH...
DO YOU EVEN KNOW HOW MUCH IT COSTS TO SURVIVE?

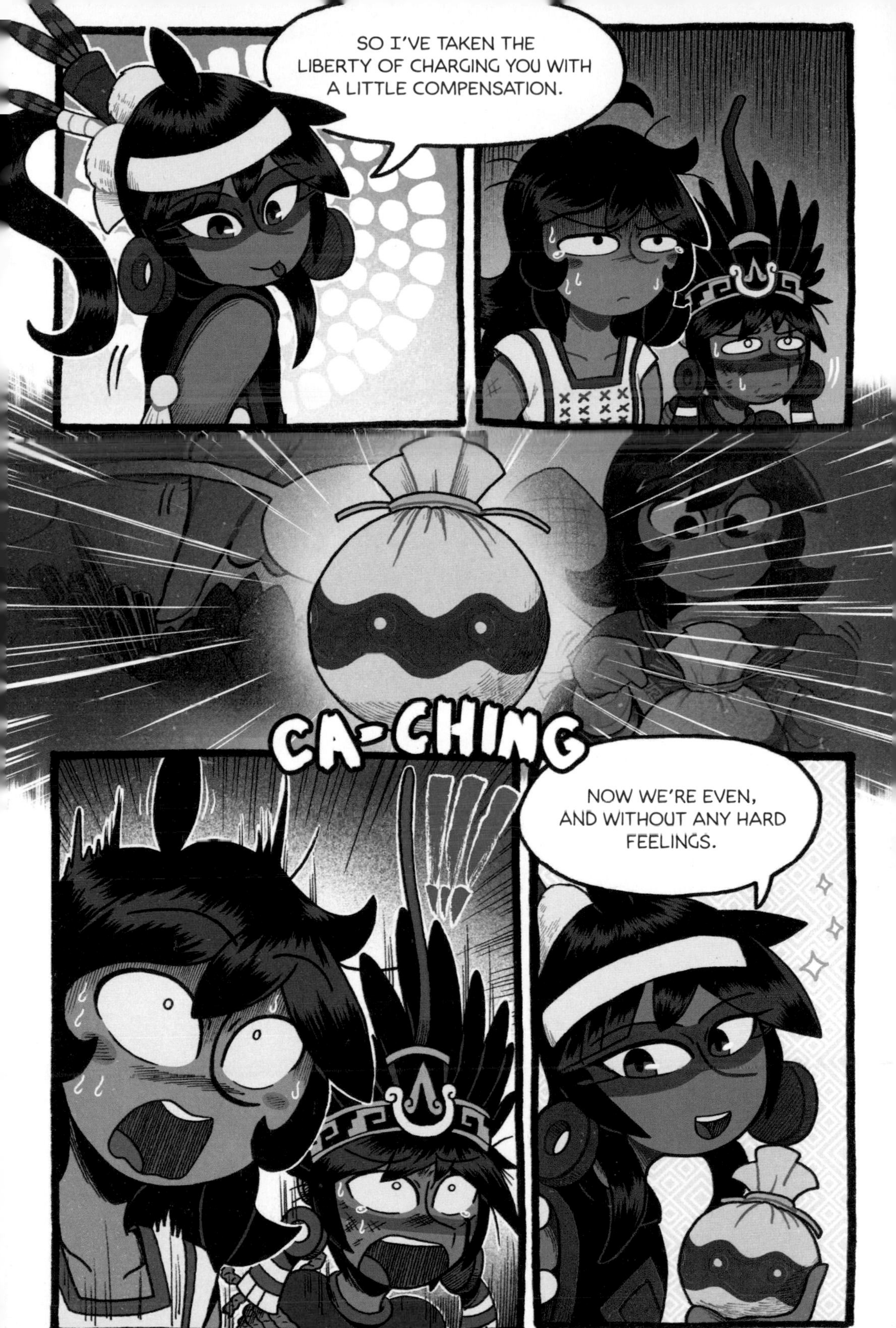
SO I'VE TAKEN THE LIBERTY OF CHARGING YOU WITH A LITTLE COMPENSATION.
CA-CHING
NOW WE'RE EVEN, AND WITHOUT ANY HARD FEELINGS.

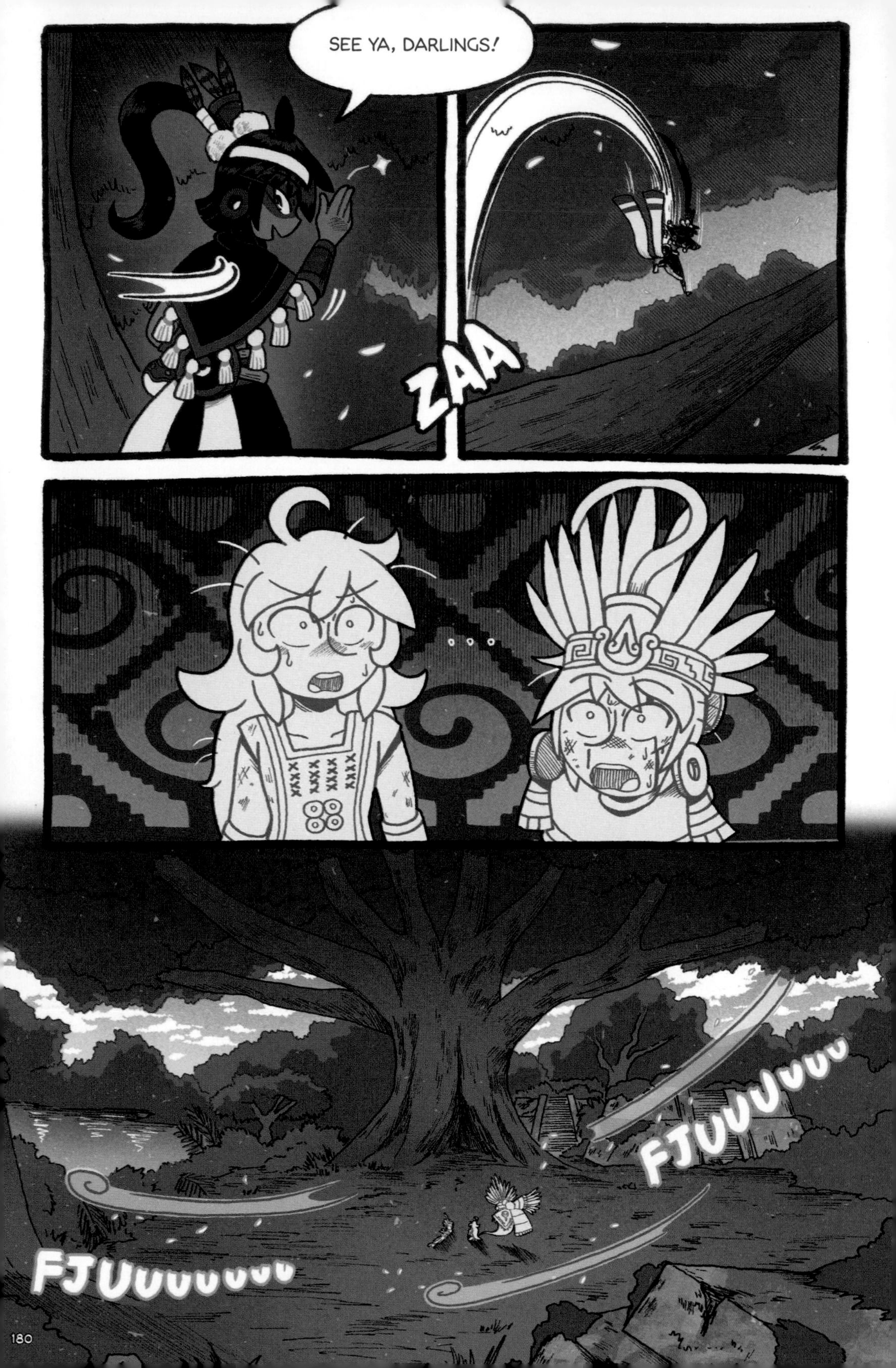
SEE YA, DARLINGS!
ZAA
FJUUUUUUU
FJUUUUUUUU

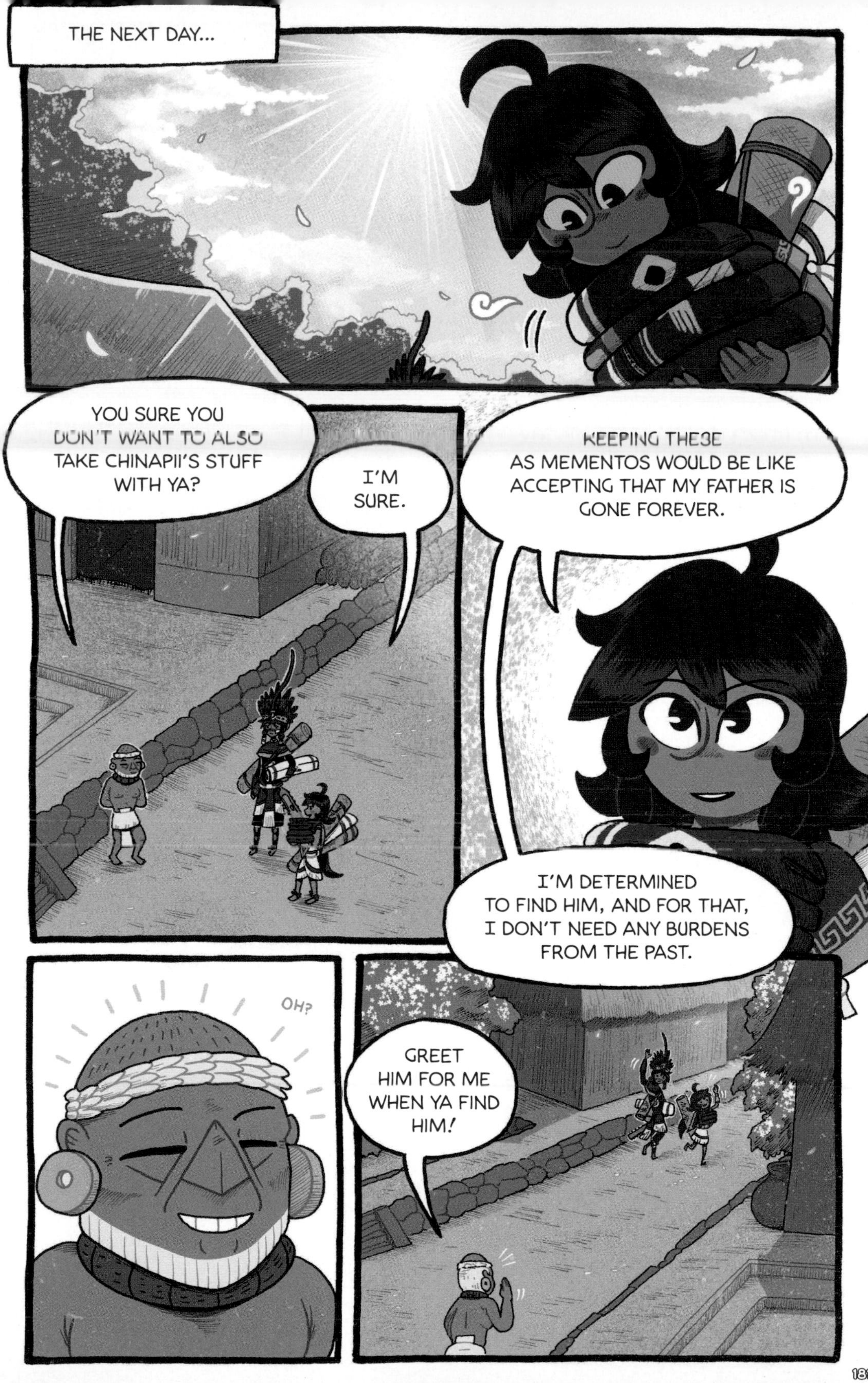
THE NEXT DAY...
YOU SURE YOU DON'T WANT TO ALSO TAKE CHINAPII'S STUFF WITH YA?
I'M SURE.
KEEPING THESE AS MEMENTOS WOULD BE LIKE ACCEPTING THAT MY FATHER IS GONE FOREVER.
I'M DETERMINED TO FIND HIM, AND FOR THAT, I DON'T NEED ANY BURDENS FROM THE PAST.
OH?
GREET HIM FOR ME WHEN YA FIND HIM!

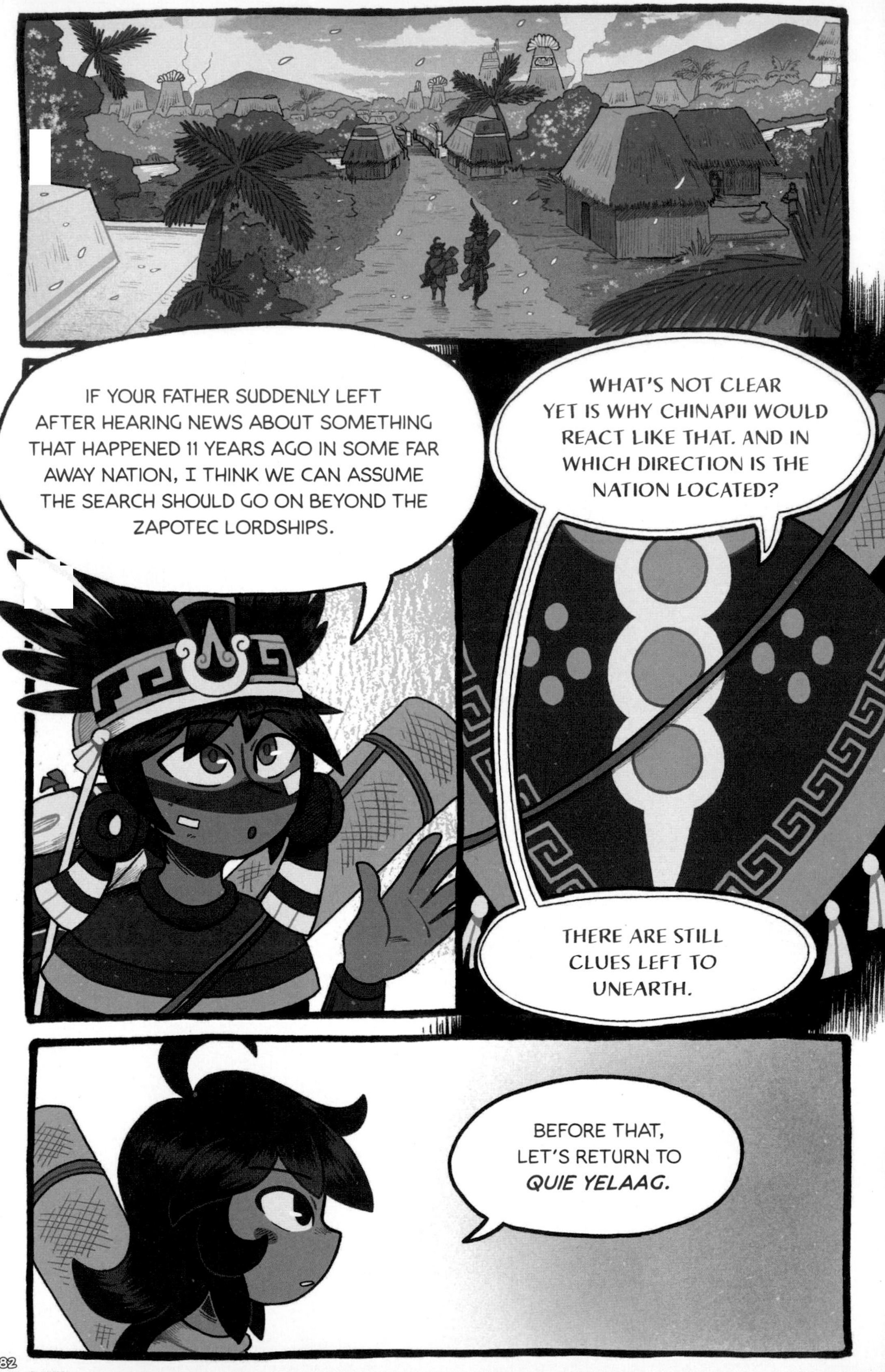
IF YOUR FATHER SUDDENLY LEFT AFTER HEARING NEWS ABOUT SOMETHING THAT HAPPENED 11 YEARS AGO IN SOME FAR AWAY NATION, I THINK WE CAN ASSUME THE SEARCH SHOULD GO ON BEYOND THE ZAPOTEC LORDSHIPS.
WHAT'S NOT CLEAR YET IS WHY CHINAPII WOULD REACT LIKE THAT. AND IN WHICH DIRECTION IS THE NATION LOCATED?
THERE ARE STILL CLUES LEFT TO UNEARTH.
BEFORE THAT, LET'S RETURN TO *QUIE YELAAG.*

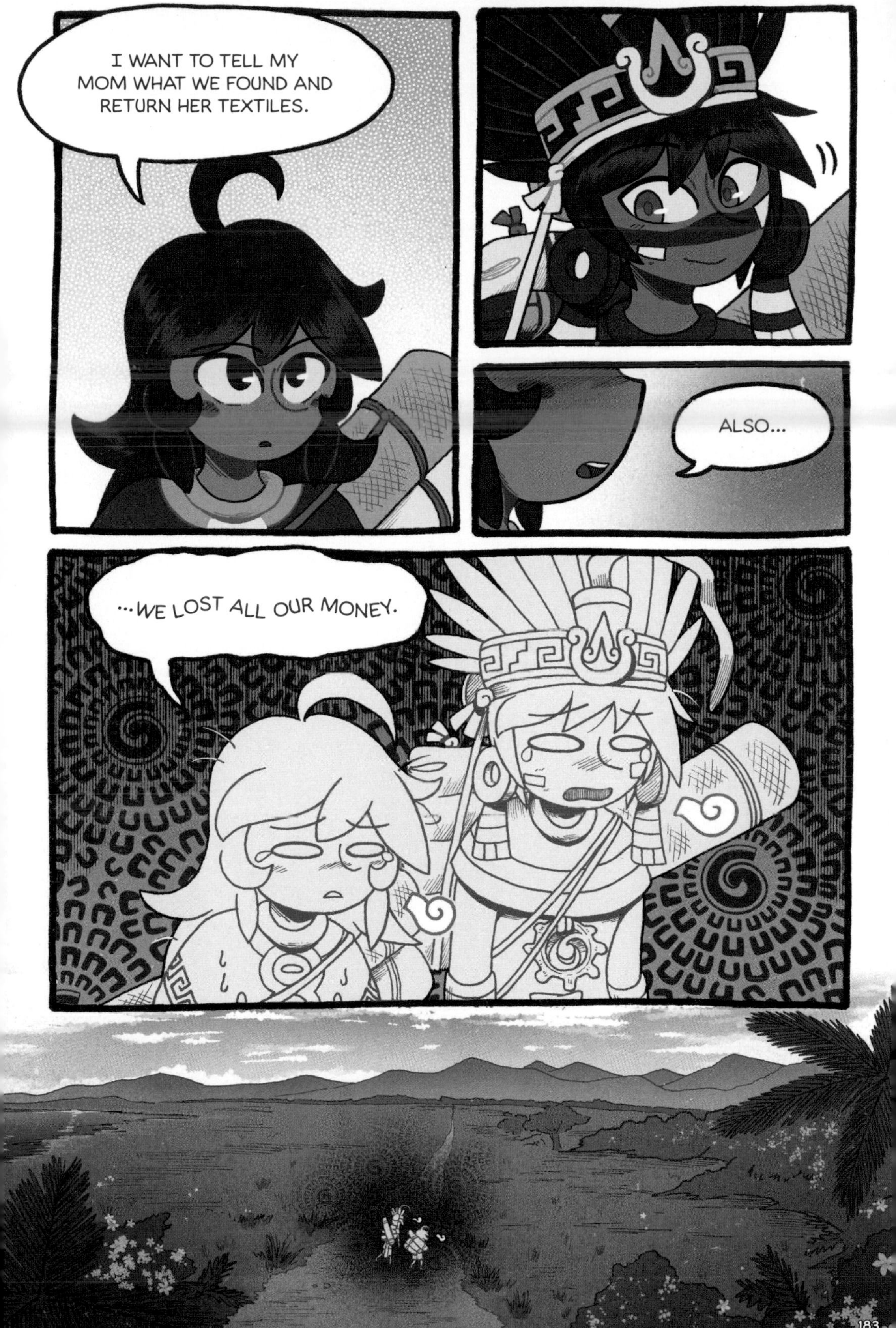
I WANT TO TELL MY MOM WHAT WE FOUND AND RETURN HER TEXTILES.
ALSO...
...WE LOST ALL OUR MONEY.

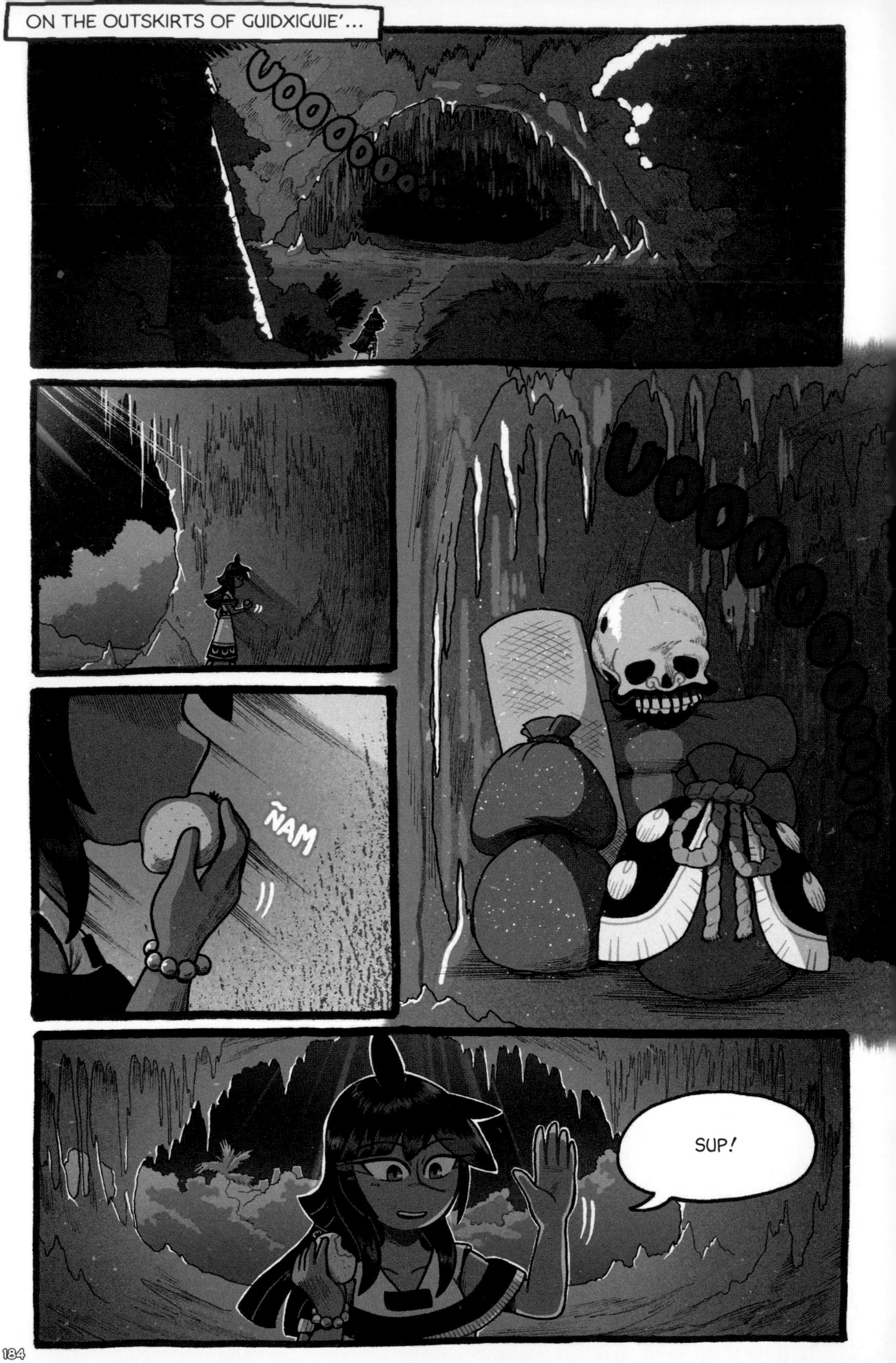
ON THE OUTSKIRTS OF GUIDXIGUIE'...
UOOOOO...
UOOOOOOOOOOOO
ÑAM
SUP!

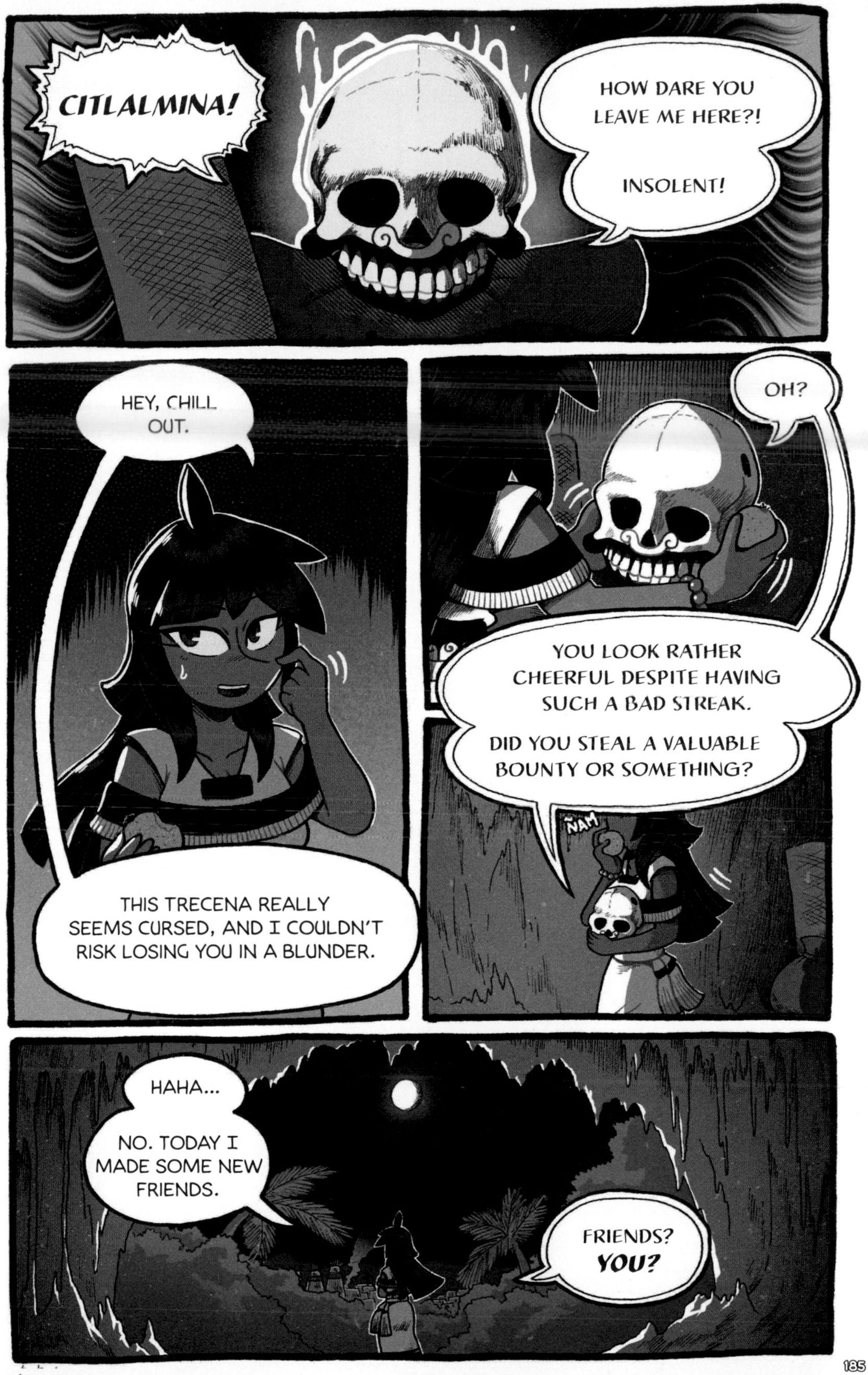
CITLALMINA!
HOW DARE YOU LEAVE ME HERE?!
INSOLENT!
HEY, CHILL OUT.
THIS TRECENA REALLY SEEMS CURSED, AND I COULDN'T RISK LOSING YOU IN A BLUNDER.
OH?
YOU LOOK RATHER CHEERFUL DESPITE HAVING SUCH A BAD STREAK.
DID YOU STEAL A VALUABLE BOUNTY OR SOMETHING?
ÑAM
HAHA...
NO. TODAY I MADE SOME NEW FRIENDS.
FRIENDS? YOU?

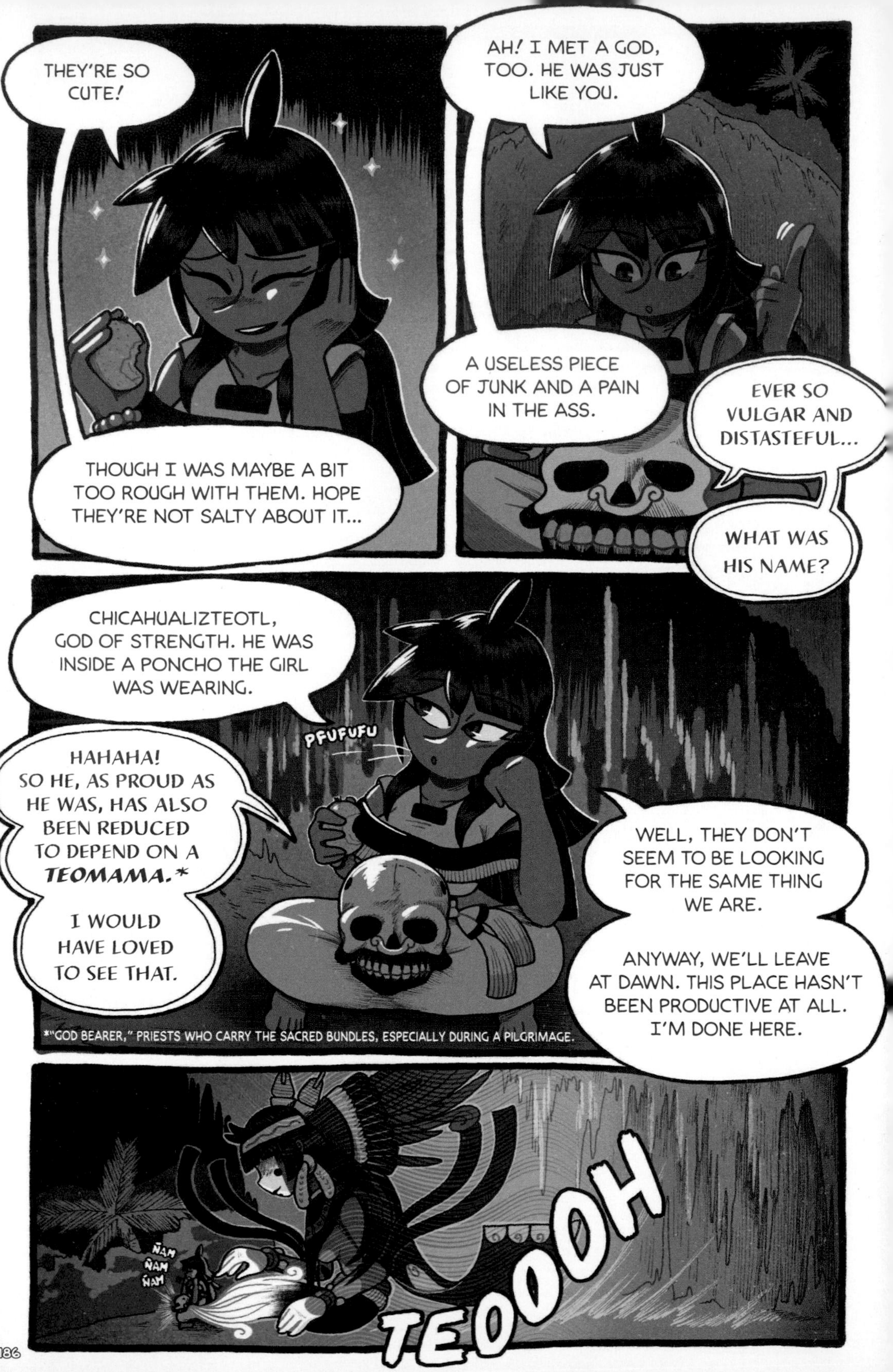
THEY'RE SO CUTE!
THOUGH I WAS MAYBE A BIT TOO ROUGH WITH THEM. HOPE THEY'RE NOT SALTY ABOUT IT...
AH! I MET A GOD, TOO. HE WAS JUST LIKE YOU.
A USELESS PIECE OF JUNK AND A PAIN IN THE ASS.
EVER SO VULGAR AND DISTASTEFUL...
WHAT WAS HIS NAME?
CHICAHUALIZTEOTL, GOD OF STRENGTH. HE WAS INSIDE A PONCHO THE GIRL WAS WEARING.
PFUFUFU
HAHAHA! SO HE, AS PROUD AS HE WAS, HAS ALSO BEEN REDUCED TO DEPEND ON A *TEOMAMA.**
I WOULD HAVE LOVED TO SEE THAT.
WELL, THEY DON'T SEEM TO BE LOOKING FOR THE SAME THING WE ARE.
ANYWAY, WE'LL LEAVE AT DAWN. THIS PLACE HASN'T BEEN PRODUCTIVE AT ALL. I'M DONE HERE.
*"GOD BEARER," PRIESTS WHO CARRY THE SACRED BUNDLES, ESPECIALLY DURING A PILGRIMAGE.
ÑAM ÑAM ÑAM
TEOOOOH

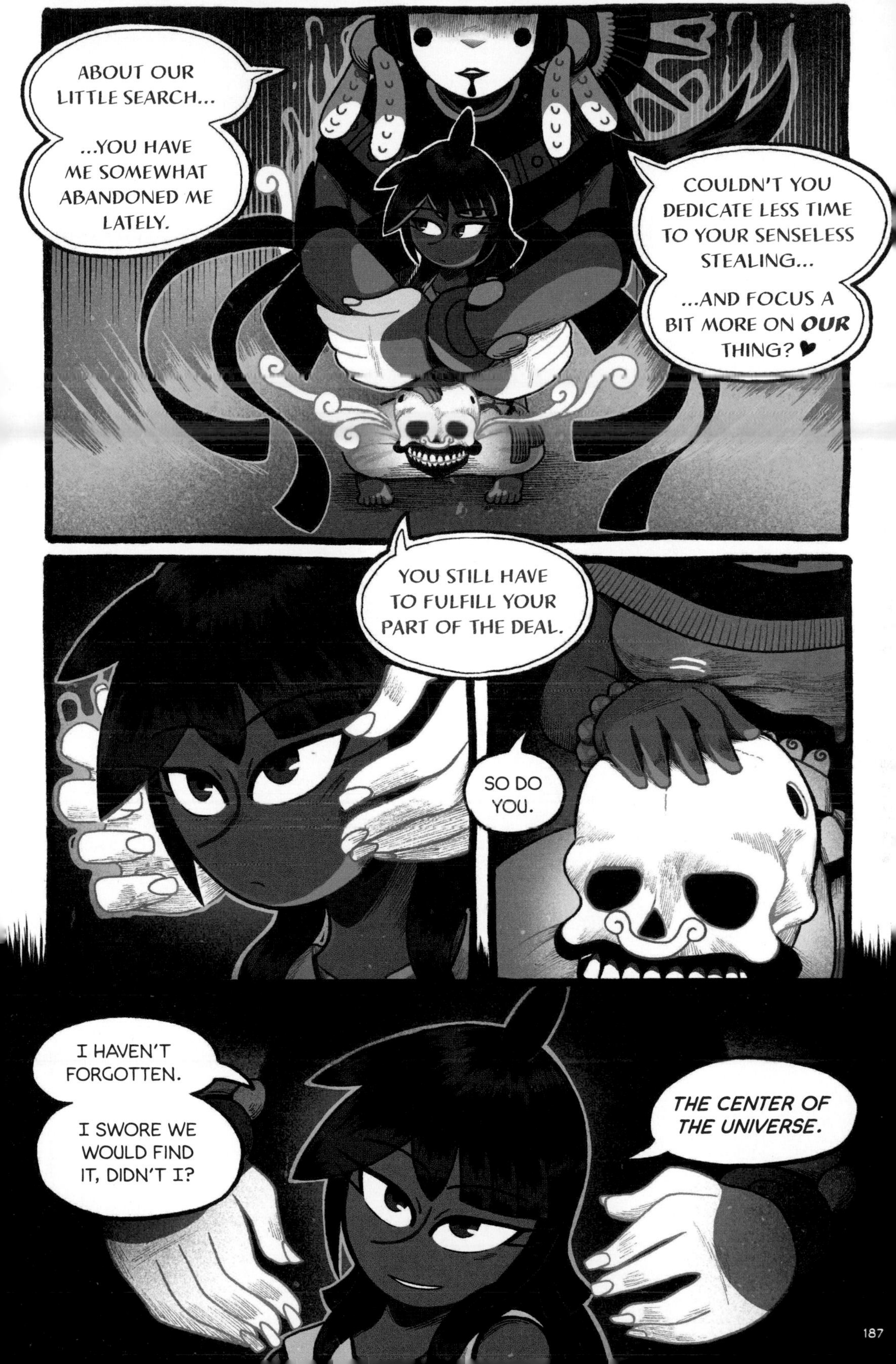
ABOUT OUR LITTLE SEARCH...
...YOU HAVE ME SOMEWHAT ABANDONED ME LATELY.
COULDN'T YOU DEDICATE LESS TIME TO YOUR SENSELESS STEALING...
...AND FOCUS A BIT MORE ON **OUR** THING? ♥
YOU STILL HAVE TO FULFILL YOUR PART OF THE DEAL.
SO DO YOU.
I HAVEN'T FORGOTTEN.
I SWORE WE WOULD FIND IT, DIDN'T I?
THE CENTER OF THE UNIVERSE.

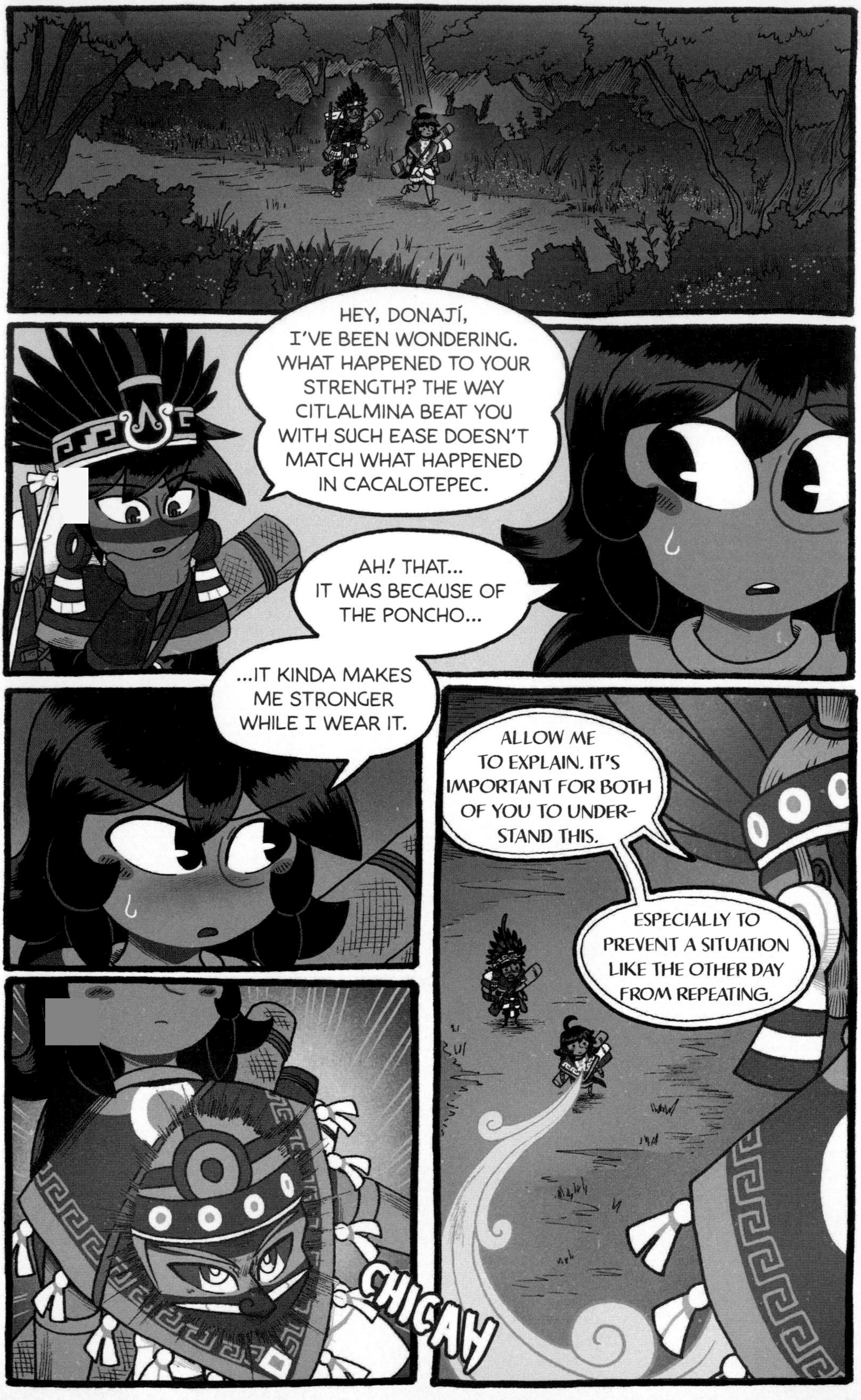
HEY, DONAJÍ, I'VE BEEN WONDERING. WHAT HAPPENED TO YOUR STRENGTH? THE WAY CITLALMINA BEAT YOU WITH SUCH EASE DOESN'T MATCH WHAT HAPPENED IN CACALOTEPEC.
AH! THAT... IT WAS BECAUSE OF THE PONCHO...
...IT KINDA MAKES ME STRONGER WHILE I WEAR IT.
CHICAH
ALLOW ME TO EXPLAIN. IT'S IMPORTANT FOR BOTH OF YOU TO UNDER-STAND THIS.
ESPECIALLY TO PREVENT A SITUATION LIKE THE OTHER DAY FROM REPEATING.

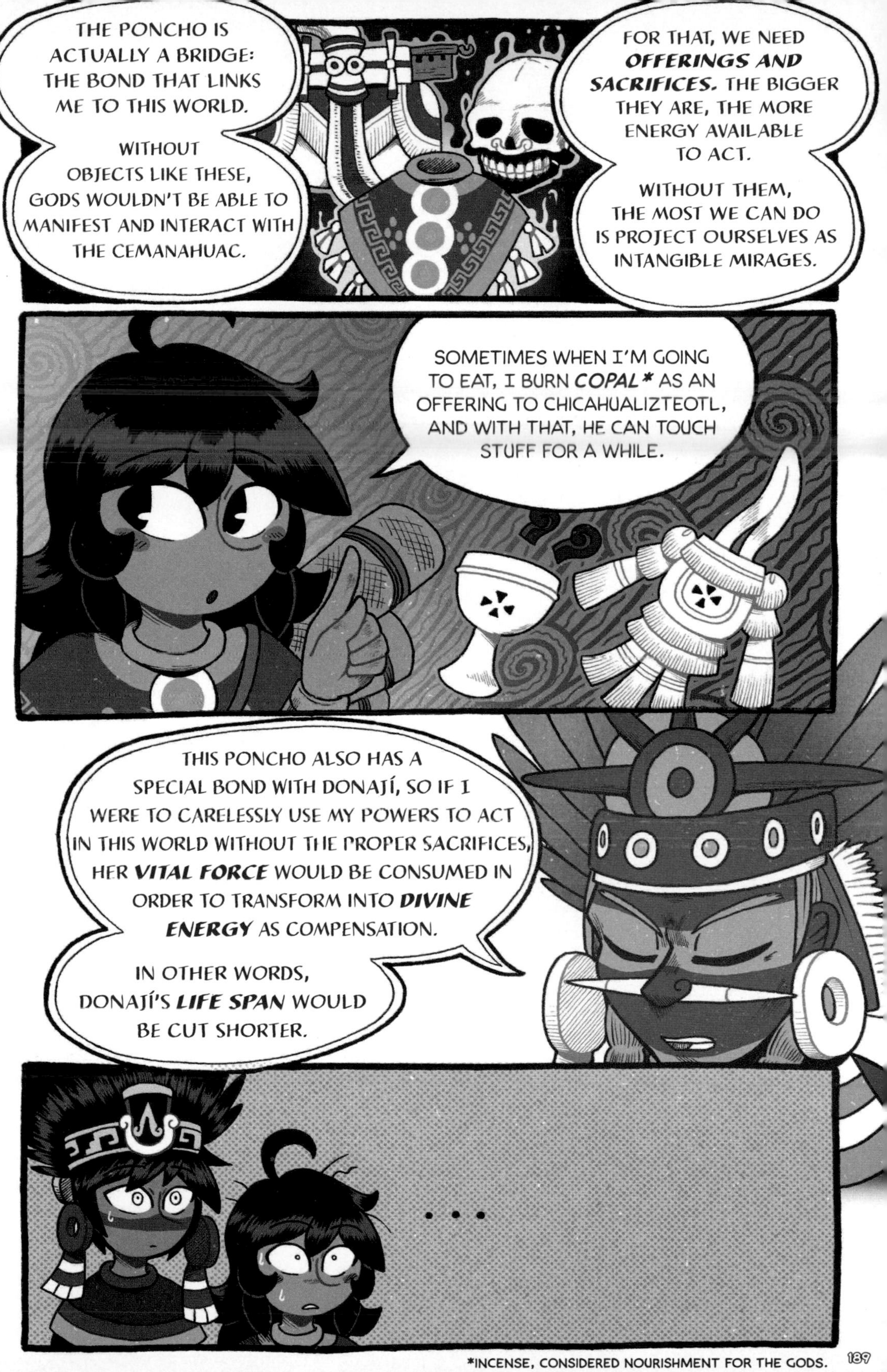
THE PONCHO IS ACTUALLY A BRIDGE: THE BOND THAT LINKS ME TO THIS WORLD.
WITHOUT OBJECTS LIKE THESE, GODS WOULDN'T BE ABLE TO MANIFEST AND INTERACT WITH THE CEMANAHUAC.
FOR THAT, WE NEED **OFFERINGS AND SACRIFICES.** THE BIGGER THEY ARE, THE MORE ENERGY AVAILABLE TO ACT.
WITHOUT THEM, THE MOST WE CAN DO IS PROJECT OURSELVES AS INTANGIBLE MIRAGES.
SOMETIMES WHEN I'M GOING TO EAT, I BURN ***COPAL**** AS AN OFFERING TO CHICAHUALIZTEOTL, AND WITH THAT, HE CAN TOUCH STUFF FOR A WHILE.
THIS PONCHO ALSO HAS A SPECIAL BOND WITH DONAJÍ, SO IF I WERE TO CARELESSLY USE MY POWERS TO ACT IN THIS WORLD WITHOUT THE PROPER SACRIFICES, HER ***VITAL FORCE*** WOULD BE CONSUMED IN ORDER TO TRANSFORM INTO ***DIVINE ENERGY*** AS COMPENSATION.
IN OTHER WORDS, DONAJÍ'S ***LIFE SPAN*** WOULD BE CUT SHORTER.
...

*INCENSE, CONSIDERED NOURISHMENT FOR THE GODS.

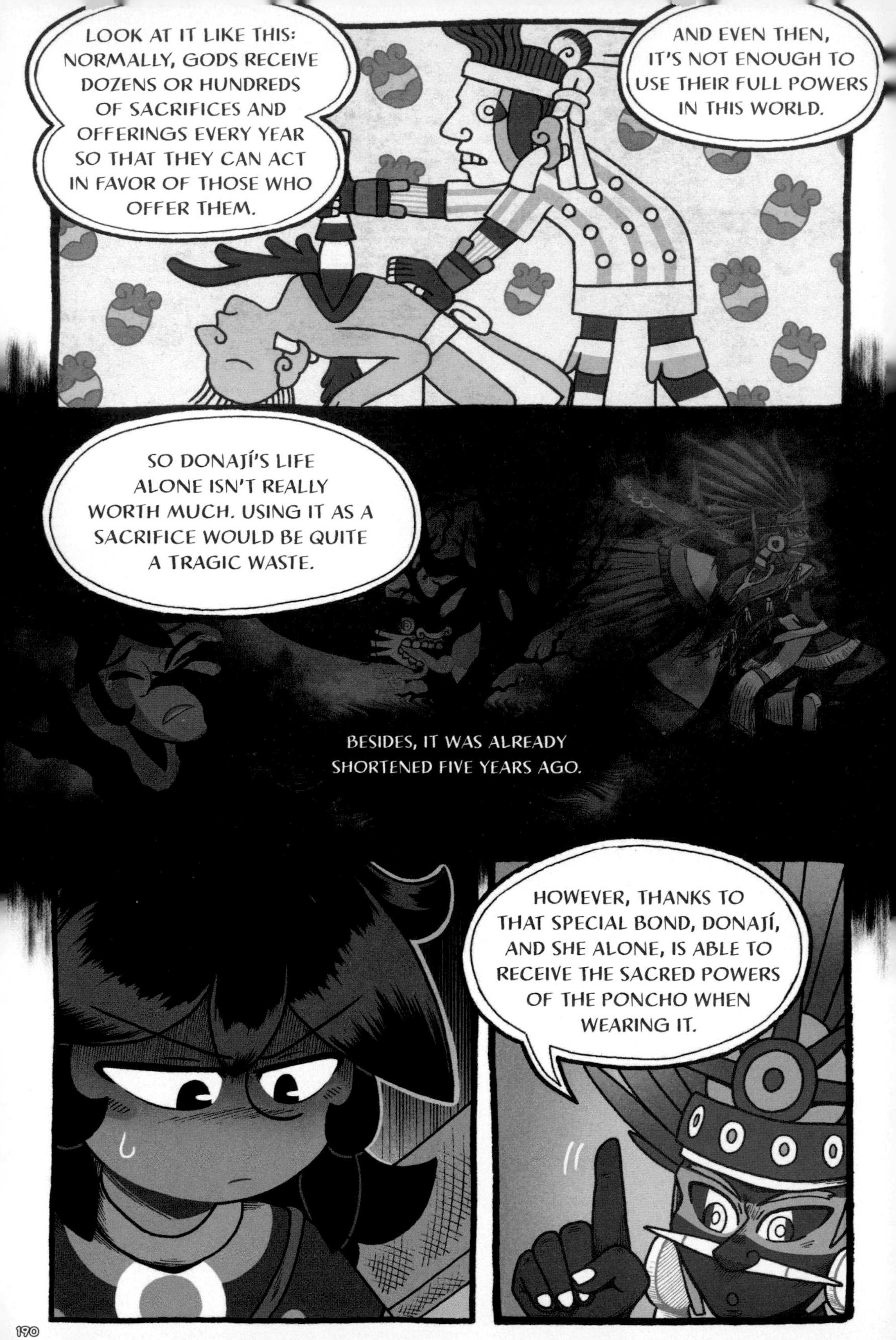
LOOK AT IT LIKE THIS: NORMALLY, GODS RECEIVE DOZENS OR HUNDREDS OF SACRIFICES AND OFFERINGS EVERY YEAR SO THAT THEY CAN ACT IN FAVOR OF THOSE WHO OFFER THEM.
AND EVEN THEN, IT'S NOT ENOUGH TO USE THEIR FULL POWERS IN THIS WORLD.
SO DONAJÍ'S LIFE ALONE ISN'T REALLY WORTH MUCH. USING IT AS A SACRIFICE WOULD BE QUITE A TRAGIC WASTE.
BESIDES, IT WAS ALREADY SHORTENED FIVE YEARS AGO.
HOWEVER, THANKS TO THAT SPECIAL BOND, DONAJÍ, AND SHE ALONE, IS ABLE TO RECEIVE THE SACRED POWERS OF THE PONCHO WHEN WEARING IT.

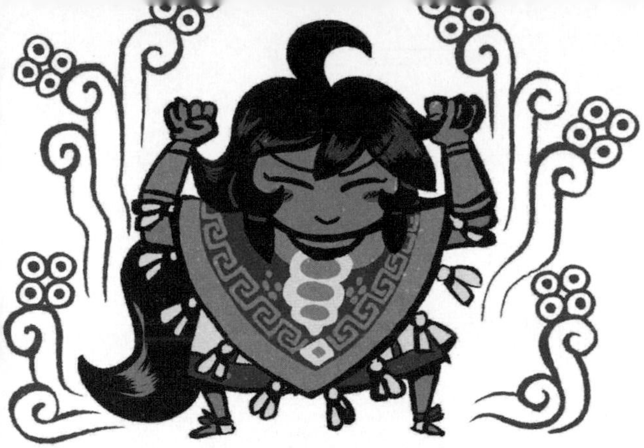

IT GRANTS HER WITH A
SUPERHUMAN STRENGTH
BASED ON THE HEAT OF
HER ***TONALLI.****

(HER ACTIVE PERSONALITY AND AMAZING WILLPOWER ARE UNRELATED TO THE PONCHO, THOUGH.)

*SOUL, HEAT, VITAL ENERGY.

BUT SHE MUST BE CAREFUL NOT TO OVERDO IT, THOUGH, OR SHE WILL FALL INTO A ***STATE OF LETHARGY.***

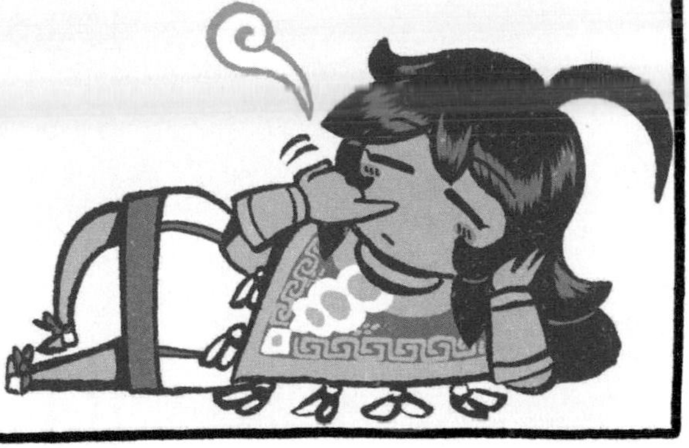

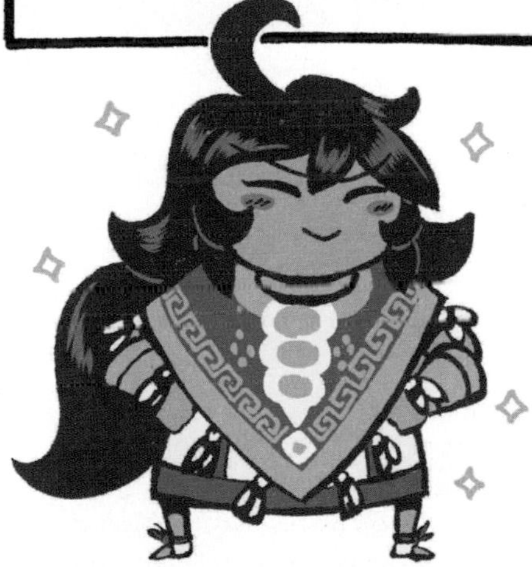

THE PONCHO MAKES HER IMMUNE TO ANY KIND OF ILLNESS THROUGH AN UNWAVERING FORTITUDE.

(THAT'S WHY I'M ALSO CALLED A GOD OF HEALTH.)

IT ALSO PROTECTS HER FROM THE COLD, POISON, TOXIC GASSES, AND ALL KINDS OF SORCERIES THAT ATTEMPT TO WEAKEN HER.

HOWEVER, OTHER THAN THE STRENGTH GRANTED BY IT, THE PONCHO IS ***NOT*** AN IMPREGNABLE SHIELD, AND HER BODY IS STILL AS FRAGILE AS ANY MORTAL'S.

SO SHE'S PARTICULARLY VULNERABLE TO PROJECTILES, SHARP WEAPONS, ETC.

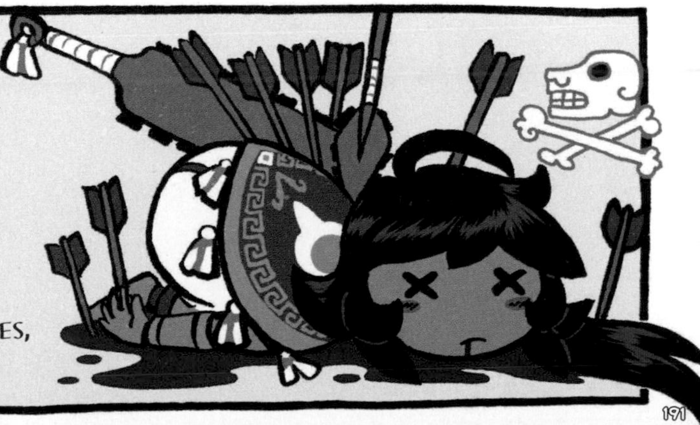

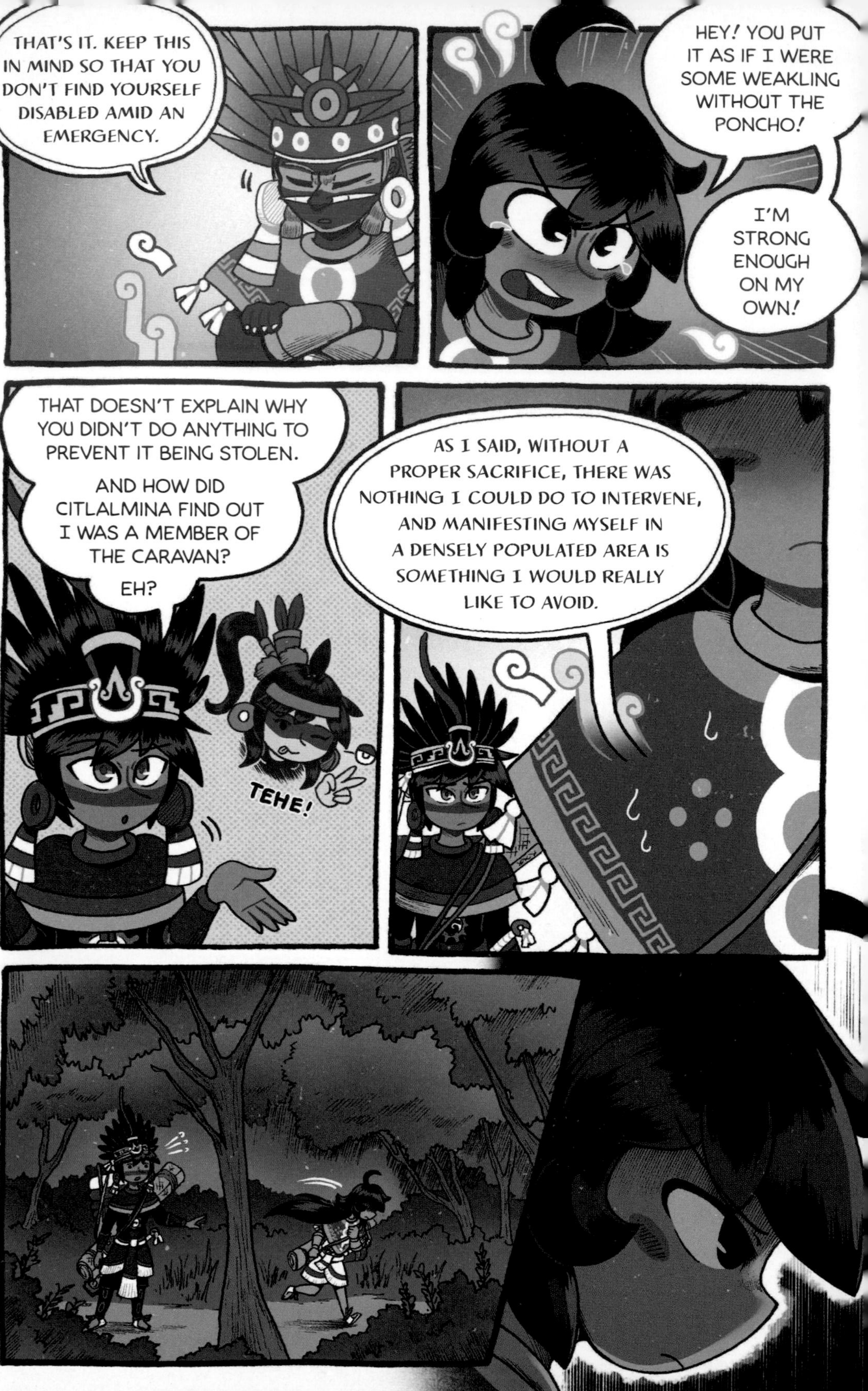
THAT'S IT. KEEP THIS IN MIND SO THAT YOU DON'T FIND YOURSELF DISABLED AMID AN EMERGENCY.
HEY! YOU PUT IT AS IF I WERE SOME WEAKLING WITHOUT THE PONCHO!
I'M STRONG ENOUGH ON MY OWN!
THAT DOESN'T EXPLAIN WHY YOU DIDN'T DO ANYTHING TO PREVENT IT BEING STOLEN.
AND HOW DID CITLALMINA FIND OUT I WAS A MEMBER OF THE CARAVAN?
EH?
TEHE!
AS I SAID, WITHOUT A PROPER SACRIFICE, THERE WAS NOTHING I COULD DO TO INTERVENE, AND MANIFESTING MYSELF IN A DENSELY POPULATED AREA IS SOMETHING I WOULD REALLY LIKE TO AVOID.

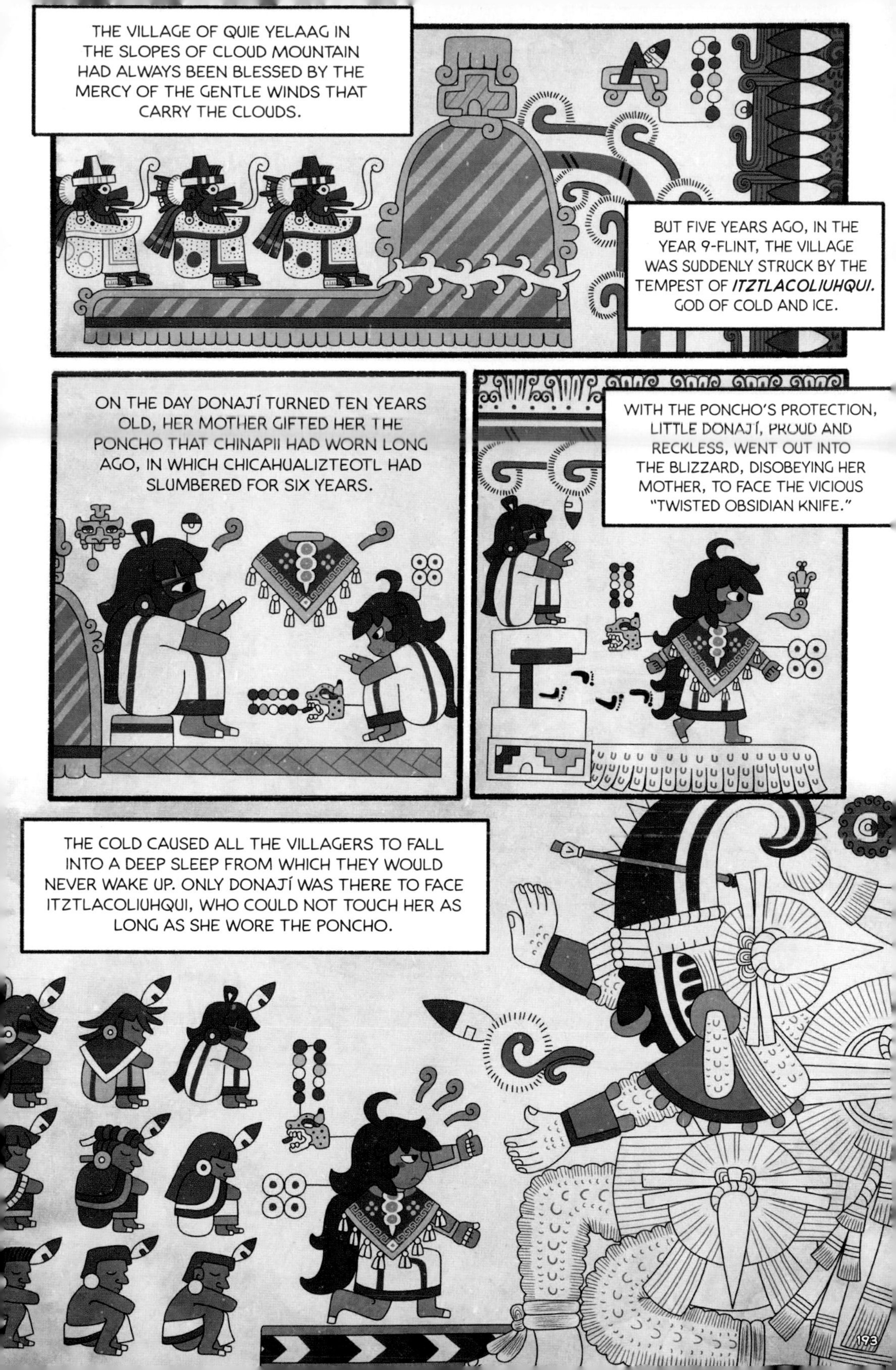
THE VILLAGE OF QUIE YELAAG IN THE SLOPES OF CLOUD MOUNTAIN HAD ALWAYS BEEN BLESSED BY THE MERCY OF THE GENTLE WINDS THAT CARRY THE CLOUDS.
BUT FIVE YEARS AGO, IN THE YEAR 9-FLINT, THE VILLAGE WAS SUDDENLY STRUCK BY THE TEMPEST OF *ITZTLACOLIUHQUI.* GOD OF COLD AND ICE.
ON THE DAY DONAJÍ TURNED TEN YEARS OLD, HER MOTHER GIFTED HER THE PONCHO THAT CHINAPII HAD WORN LONG AGO, IN WHICH CHICAHUALIZTEOTL HAD SLUMBERED FOR SIX YEARS.
WITH THE PONCHO'S PROTECTION, LITTLE DONAJÍ, PROUD AND RECKLESS, WENT OUT INTO THE BLIZZARD, DISOBEYING HER MOTHER, TO FACE THE VICIOUS "TWISTED OBSIDIAN KNIFE."
THE COLD CAUSED ALL THE VILLAGERS TO FALL INTO A DEEP SLEEP FROM WHICH THEY WOULD NEVER WAKE UP. ONLY DONAJÍ WAS THERE TO FACE ITZTLACOLIUHQUI, WHO COULD NOT TOUCH HER AS LONG AS SHE WORE THE PONCHO.

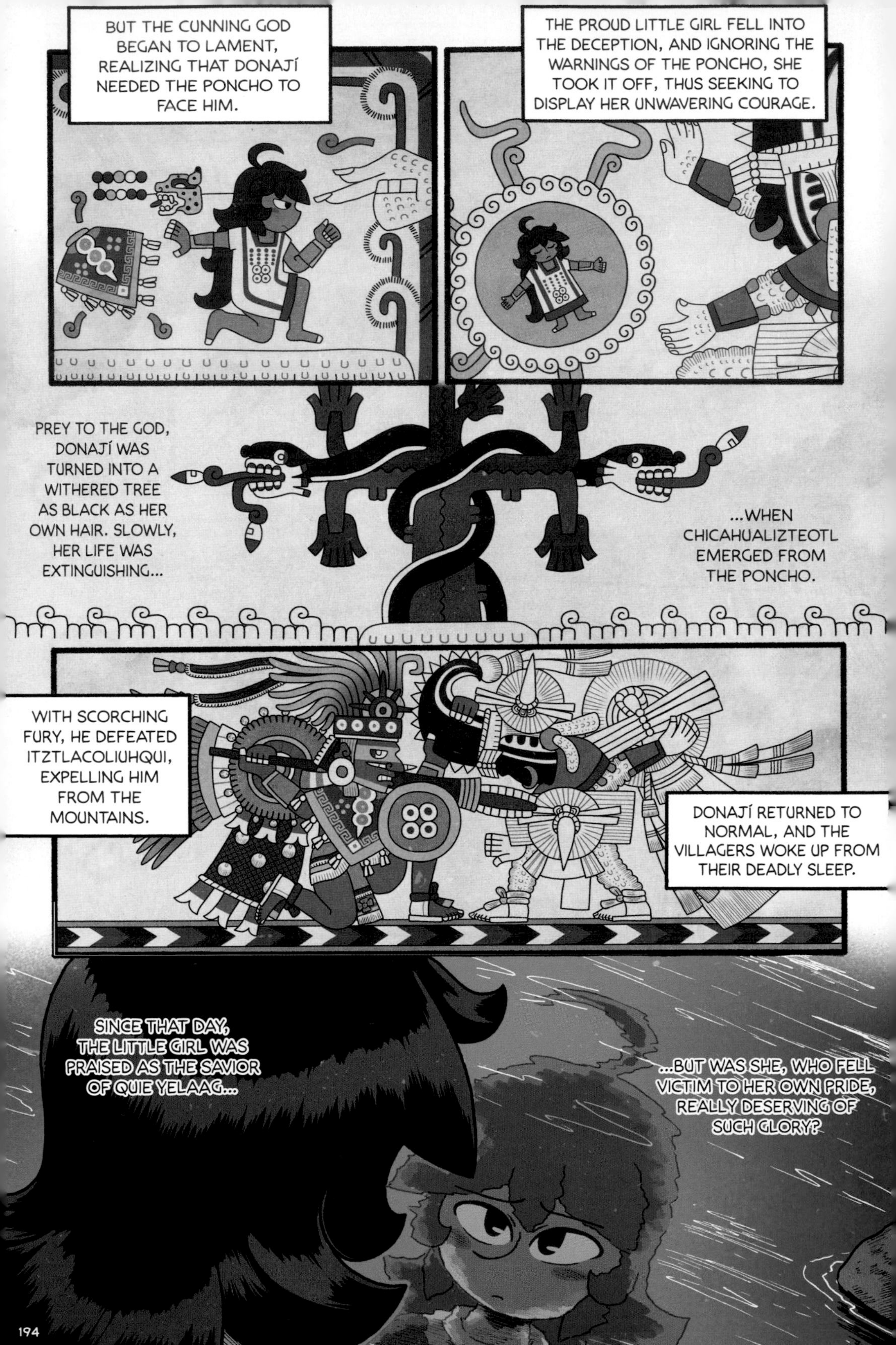
BUT THE CUNNING GOD BEGAN TO LAMENT, REALIZING THAT DONAJÍ NEEDED THE PONCHO TO FACE HIM.
THE PROUD LITTLE GIRL FELL INTO THE DECEPTION, AND IGNORING THE WARNINGS OF THE PONCHO, SHE TOOK IT OFF, THUS SEEKING TO DISPLAY HER UNWAVERING COURAGE.
PREY TO THE GOD, DONAJÍ WAS TURNED INTO A WITHERED TREE AS BLACK AS HER OWN HAIR. SLOWLY, HER LIFE WAS EXTINGUISHING...
...WHEN CHICAHUALIZTEOTL EMERGED FROM THE PONCHO.
WITH SCORCHING FURY, HE DEFEATED ITZTLACOLIUHQUI, EXPELLING HIM FROM THE MOUNTAINS.
DONAJÍ RETURNED TO NORMAL, AND THE VILLAGERS WOKE UP FROM THEIR DEADLY SLEEP.
SINCE THAT DAY, THE LITTLE GIRL WAS PRAISED AS THE SAVIOR OF QUIE YELAAG...
...BUT WAS SHE, WHO FELL VICTIM TO HER OWN PRIDE, REALLY DESERVING OF SUCH GLORY?

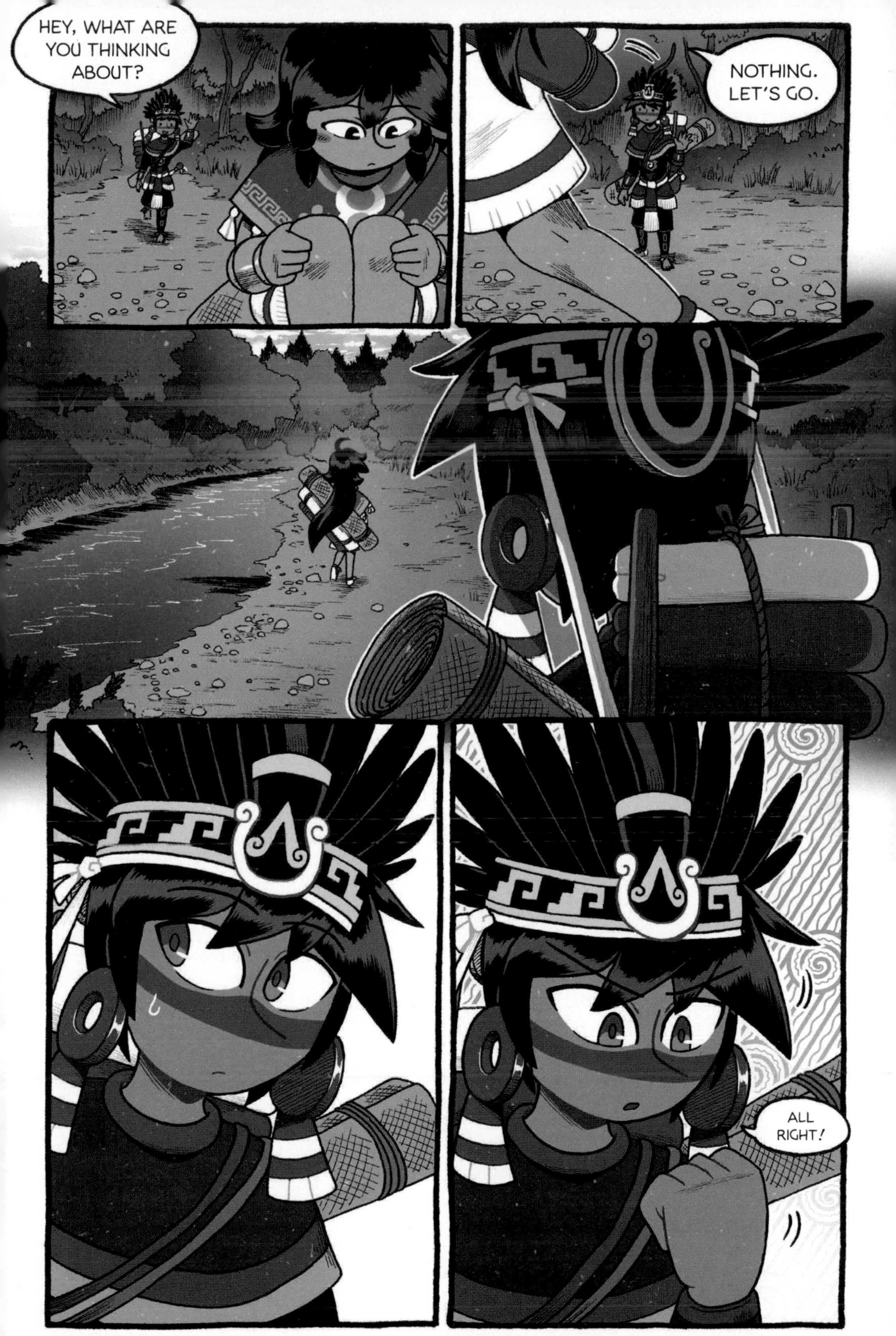
HEY, WHAT ARE YOU THINKING ABOUT?
NOTHING. LET'S GO.
ALL RIGHT!

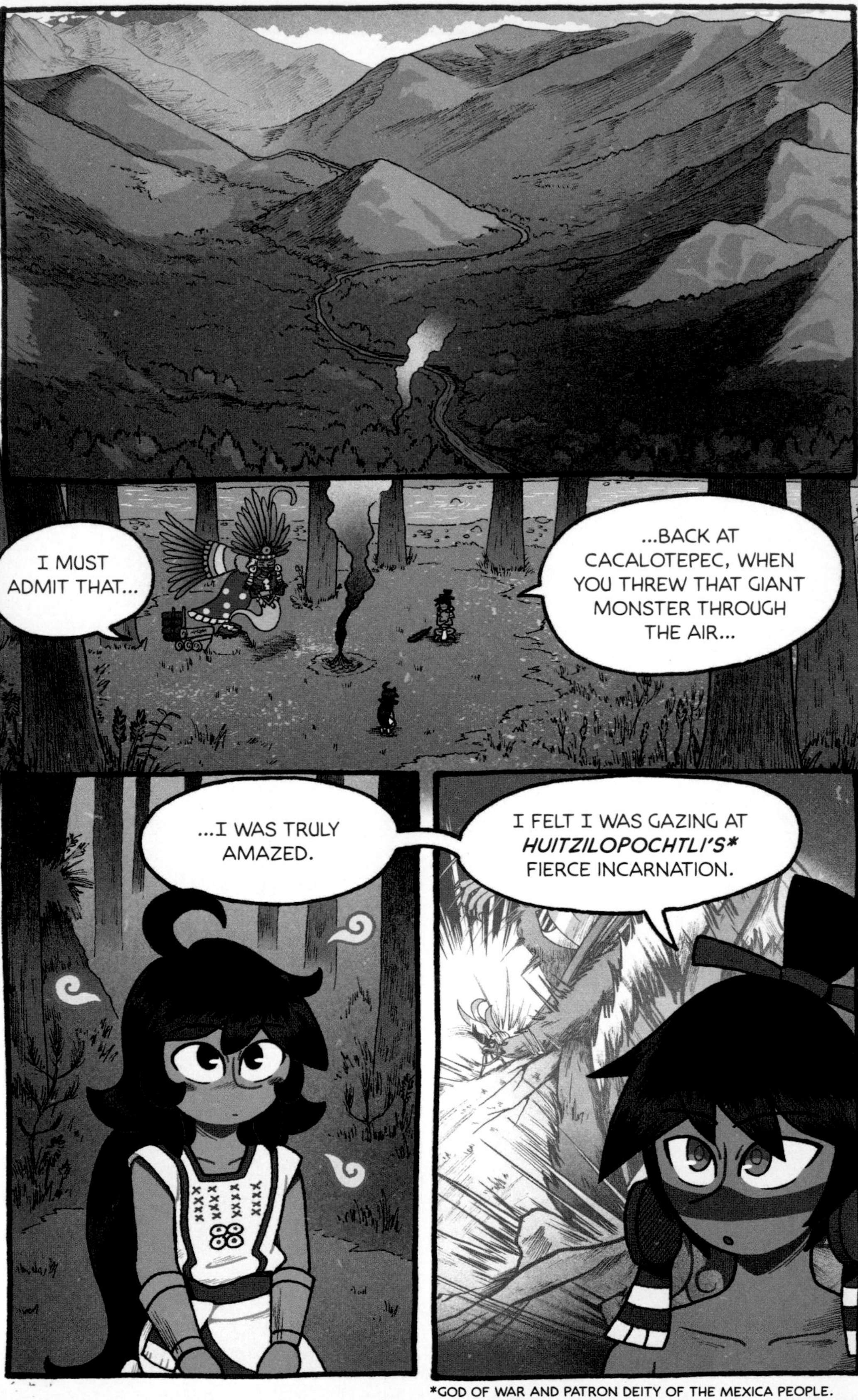
I MUST ADMIT THAT...
...BACK AT CACALOTEPEC, WHEN YOU THREW THAT GIANT MONSTER THROUGH THE AIR...
...I WAS TRULY AMAZED.
I FELT I WAS GAZING AT *HUITZILOPOCHTLI'S** FIERCE INCARNATION.

*GOD OF WAR AND PATRON DEITY OF THE MEXICA PEOPLE.

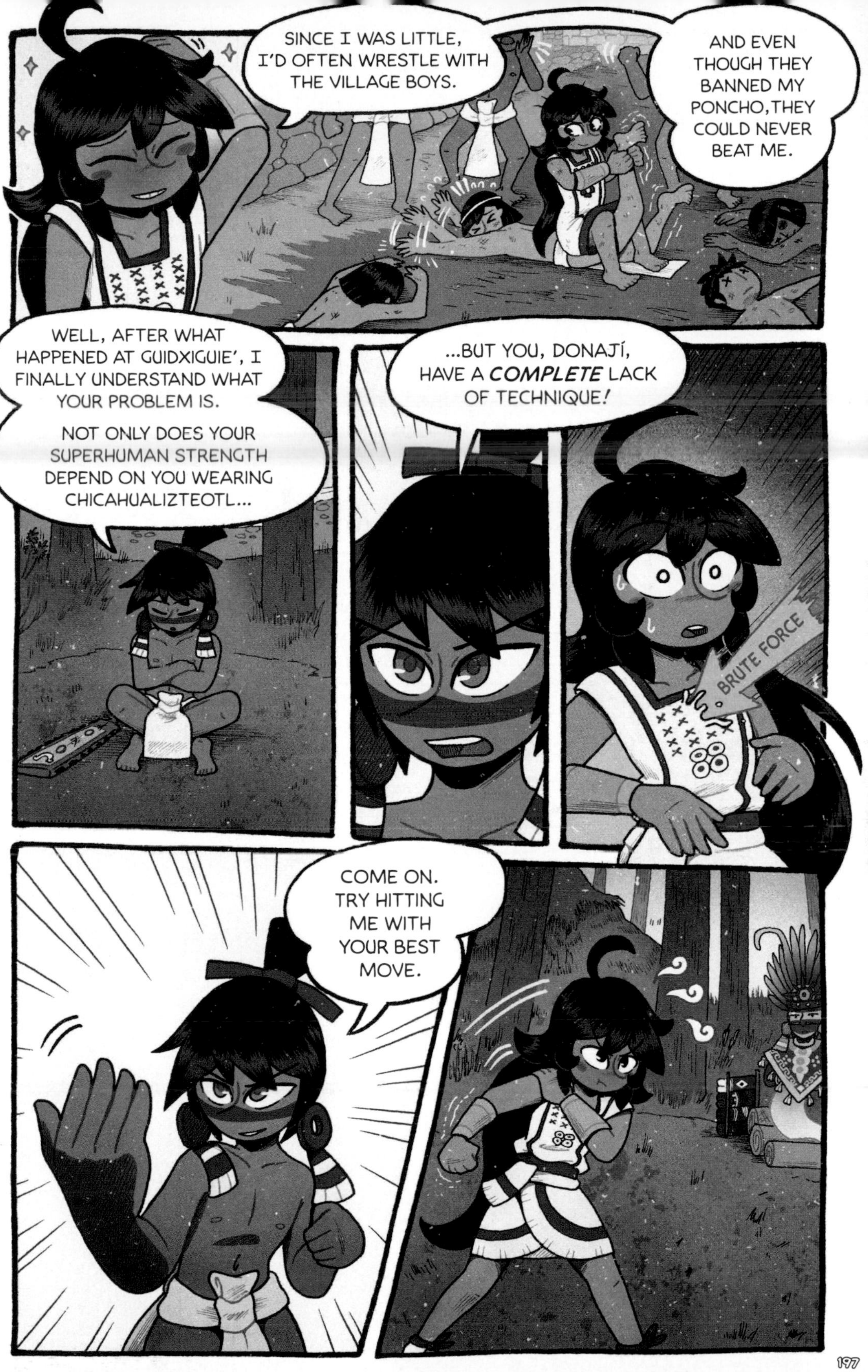
SINCE I WAS LITTLE, I'D OFTEN WRESTLE WITH THE VILLAGE BOYS.
AND EVEN THOUGH THEY BANNED MY PONCHO, THEY COULD NEVER BEAT ME.
WELL, AFTER WHAT HAPPENED AT GUIDXIGUIE', I FINALLY UNDERSTAND WHAT YOUR PROBLEM IS.
NOT ONLY DOES YOUR SUPERHUMAN STRENGTH DEPEND ON YOU WEARING CHICAHUALIZTEOTL...
...BUT YOU, DONAJÍ, HAVE A *COMPLETE* LACK OF TECHNIQUE!
BRUTE FORCE
COME ON. TRY HITTING ME WITH YOUR BEST MOVE.

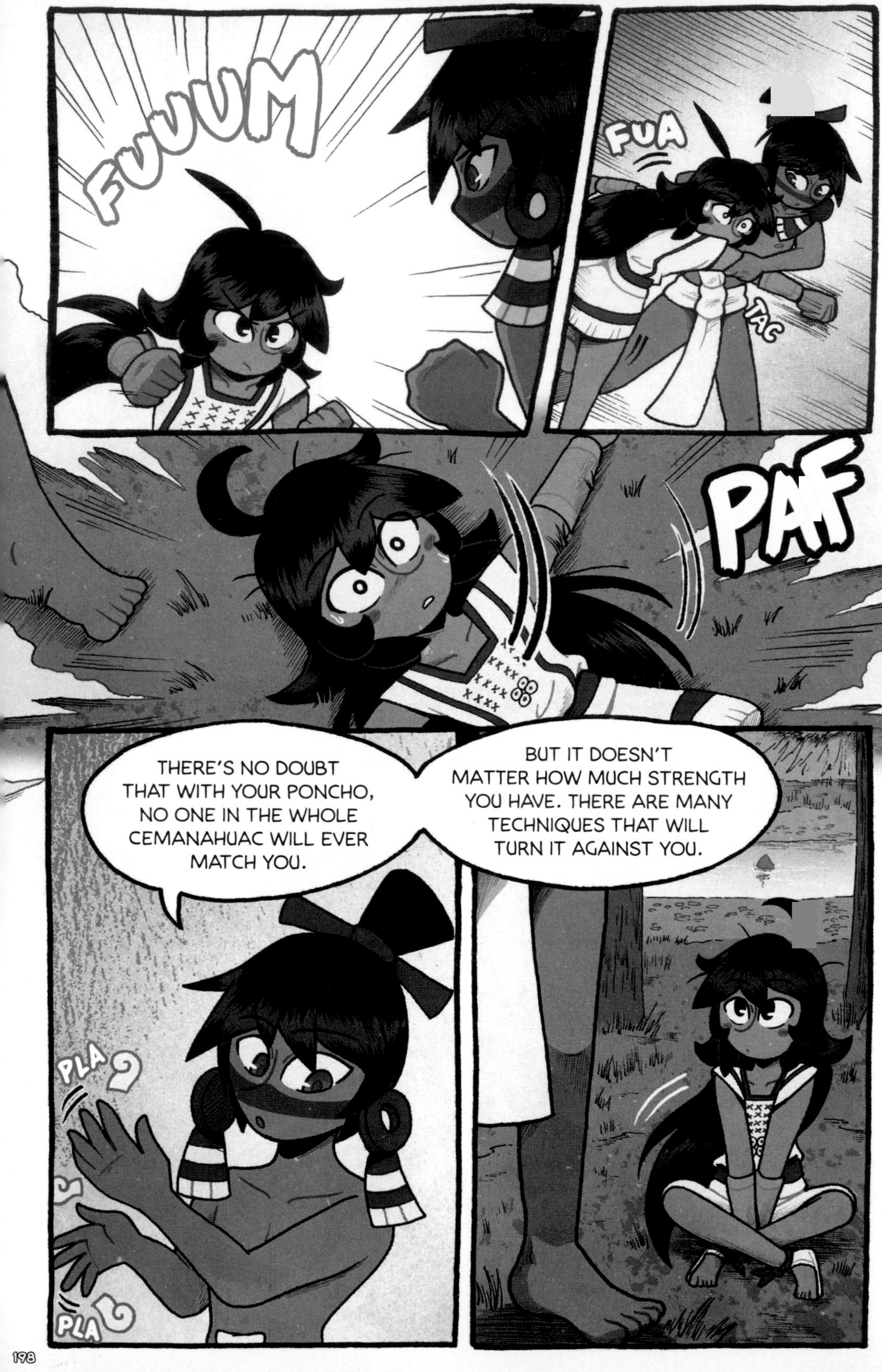
FUUUM
FUA
TAC
PAF
THERE'S NO DOUBT THAT WITH YOUR PONCHO, NO ONE IN THE WHOLE CEMANAHUAC WILL EVER MATCH YOU.
BUT IT DOESN'T MATTER HOW MUCH STRENGTH YOU HAVE. THERE ARE MANY TECHNIQUES THAT WILL TURN IT AGAINST YOU.
PLA
PLA

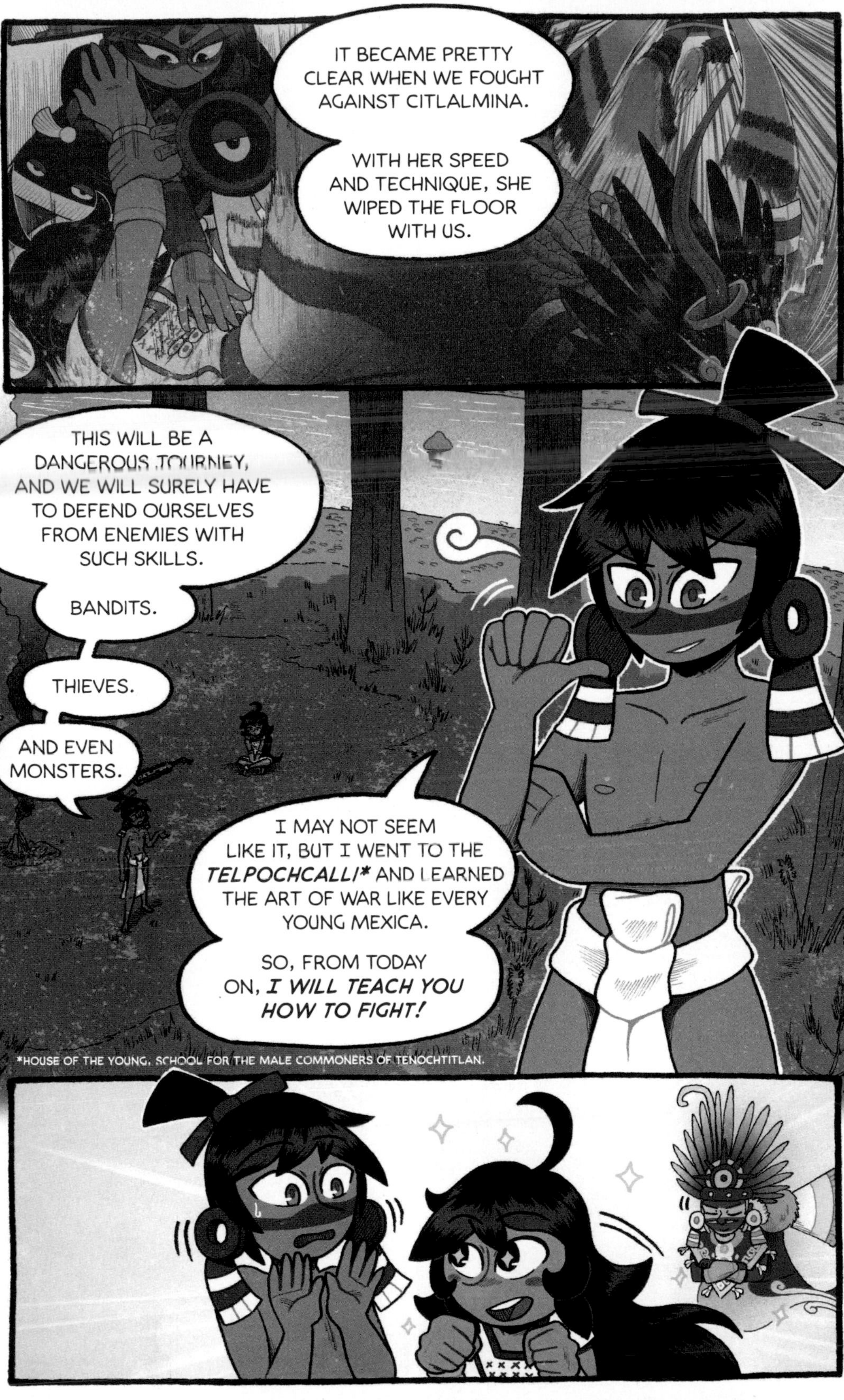
IT BECAME PRETTY CLEAR WHEN WE FOUGHT AGAINST CITLALMINA.
WITH HER SPEED AND TECHNIQUE, SHE WIPED THE FLOOR WITH US.
THIS WILL BE A DANGEROUS JOURNEY, AND WE WILL SURELY HAVE TO DEFEND OURSELVES FROM ENEMIES WITH SUCH SKILLS.
BANDITS.
THIEVES.
AND EVEN MONSTERS.
I MAY NOT SEEM LIKE IT, BUT I WENT TO THE *TELPOCHCALLI** AND LEARNED THE ART OF WAR LIKE EVERY YOUNG MEXICA.
SO, FROM TODAY ON, ***I WILL TEACH YOU HOW TO FIGHT!***
*HOUSE OF THE YOUNG. SCHOOL FOR THE MALE COMMONERS OF TENOCHTITLAN.

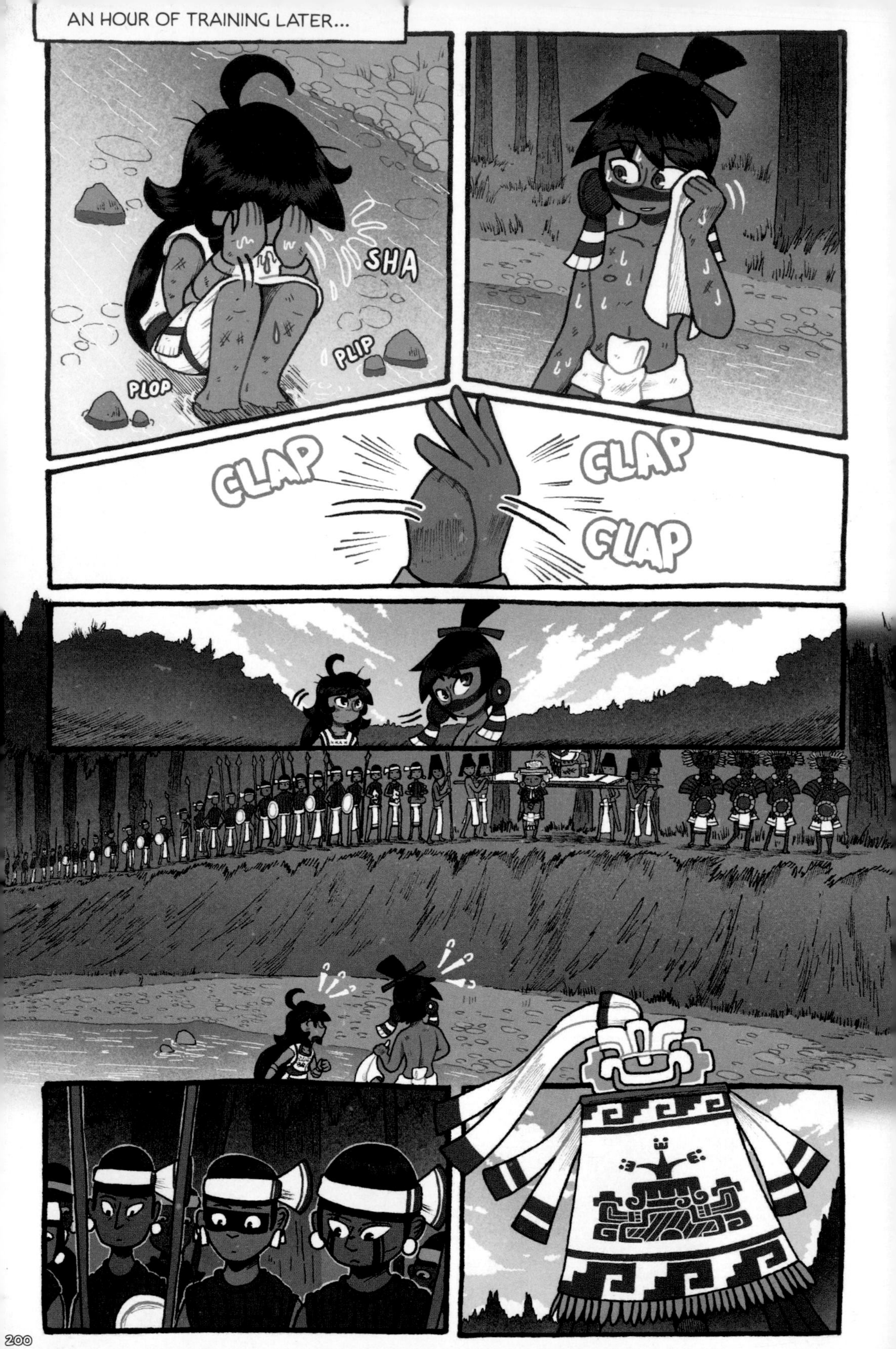
AN HOUR OF TRAINING LATER...
SHA
PLIP
PLOP
CLAP
CLAP
CLAP

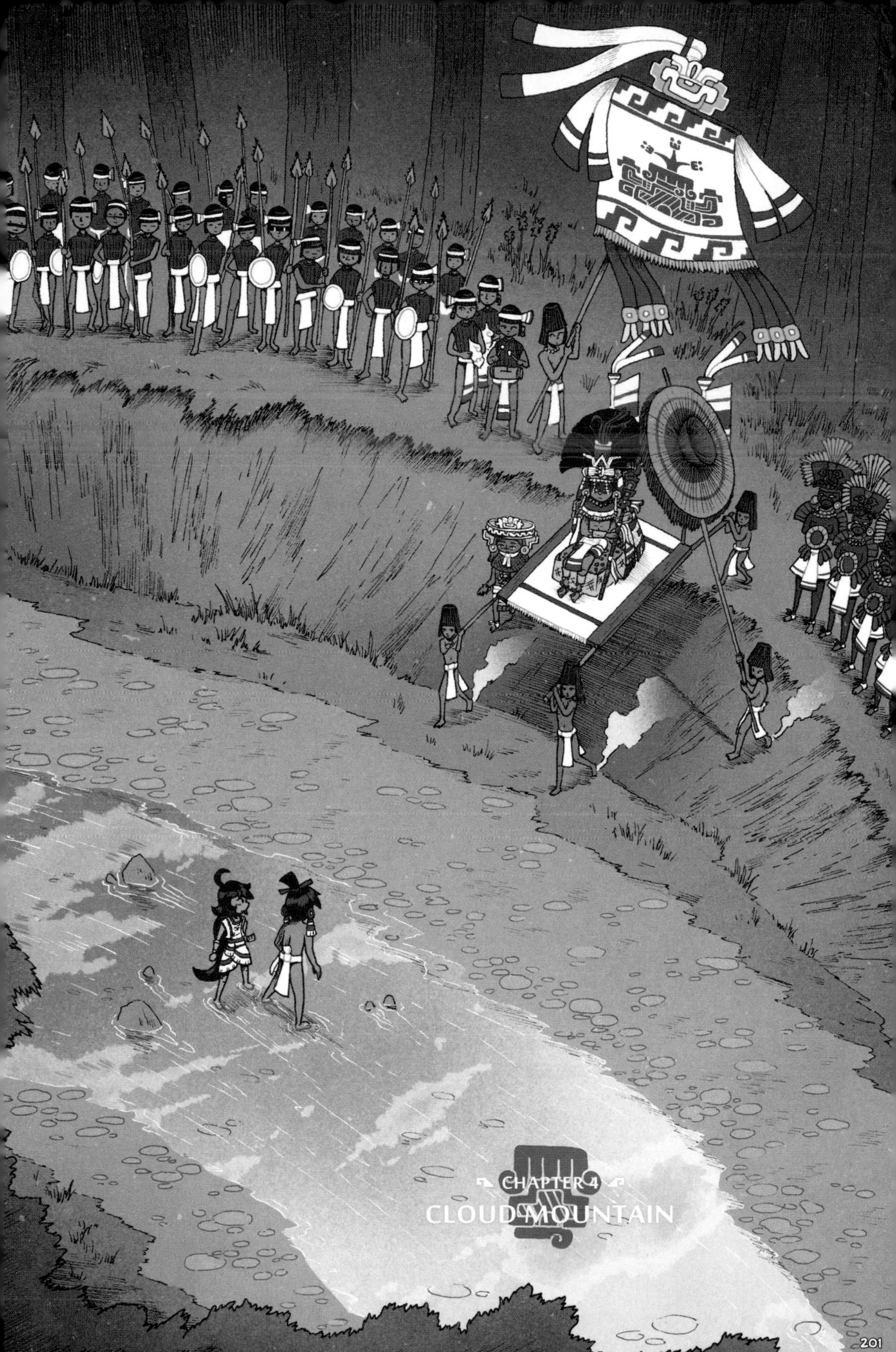
CHAPTER 4
CLOUD MOUNTAIN

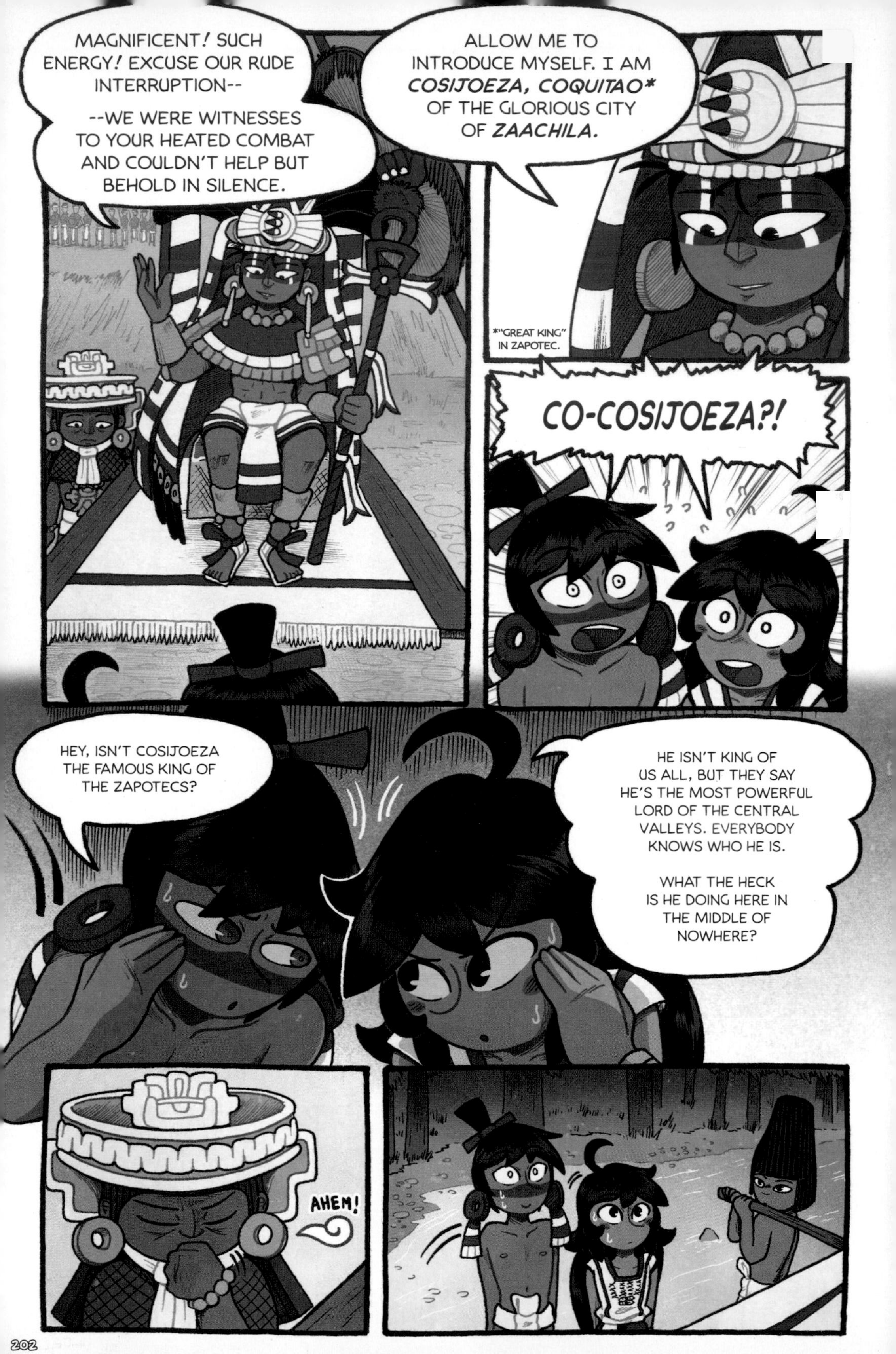
MAGNIFICENT! SUCH ENERGY! EXCUSE OUR RUDE INTERRUPTION--
--WE WERE WITNESSES TO YOUR HEATED COMBAT AND COULDN'T HELP BUT BEHOLD IN SILENCE.
ALLOW ME TO INTRODUCE MYSELF. I AM COSIJOEZA, COQUITAO* OF THE GLORIOUS CITY OF ZAACHILA.
*"GREAT KING" IN ZAPOTEC.
CO-COSIJOEZA?!
HEY, ISN'T COSIJOEZA THE FAMOUS KING OF THE ZAPOTECS?
HE ISN'T KING OF US ALL, BUT THEY SAY HE'S THE MOST POWERFUL LORD OF THE CENTRAL VALLEYS. EVERYBODY KNOWS WHO HE IS.
WHAT THE HECK IS HE DOING HERE IN THE MIDDLE OF NOWHERE?
AHEM!

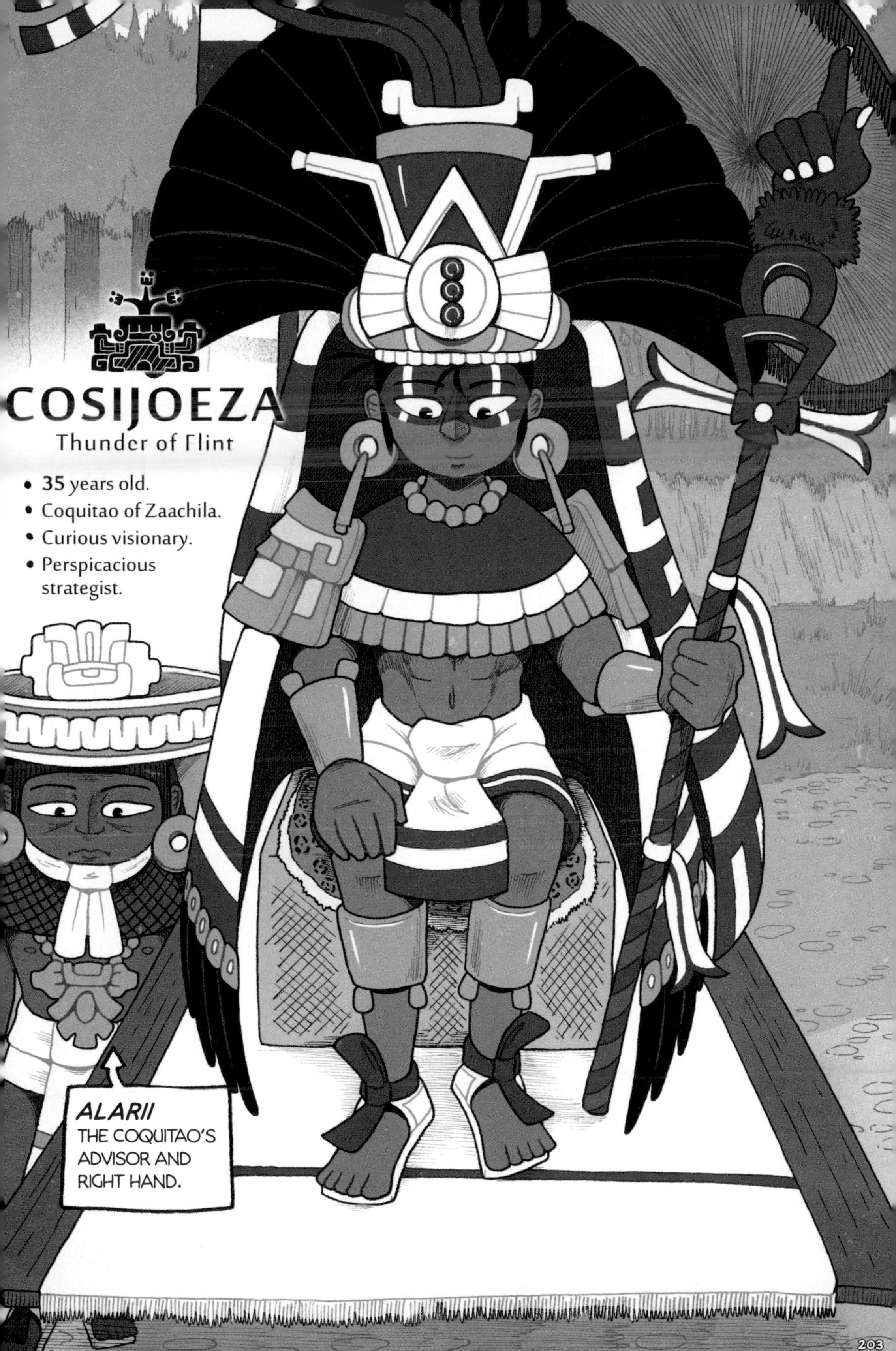
COSIJOEZA
Thunder of Flint
• 35 years old.
• Coquitao of Zaachila.
• Curious visionary.
• Perspicacious strategist.
ALARII
THE COQUITAO'S ADVISOR AND RIGHT HAND.

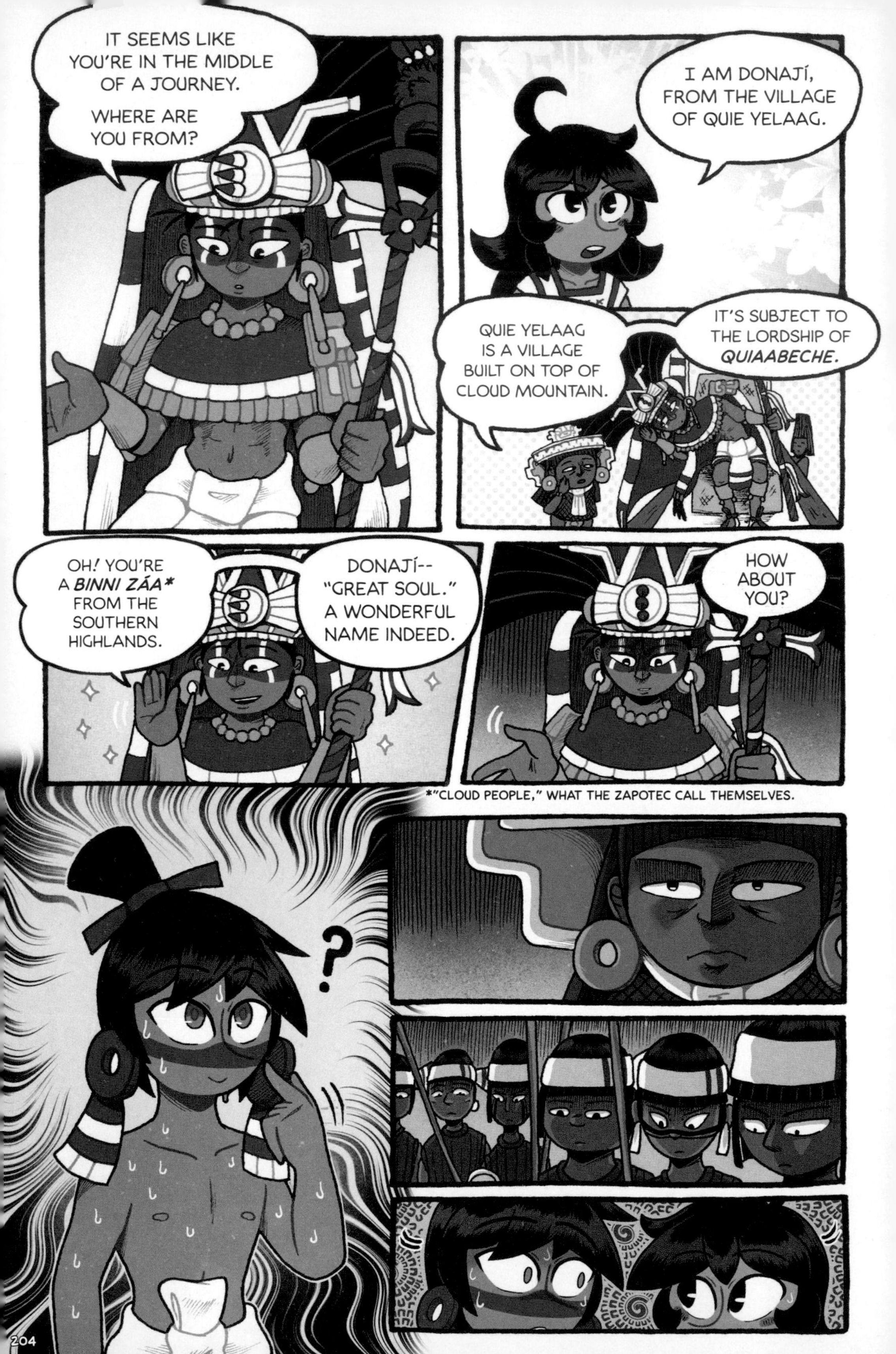
IT SEEMS LIKE YOU'RE IN THE MIDDLE OF A JOURNEY.
WHERE ARE YOU FROM?
I AM DONAJÍ, FROM THE VILLAGE OF QUIE YELAAG.
QUIE YELAAG IS A VILLAGE BUILT ON TOP OF CLOUD MOUNTAIN.
IT'S SUBJECT TO THE LORDSHIP OF *QUIAABECHE.*
OH! YOU'RE A ***BINNI ZÁA**** FROM THE SOUTHERN HIGHLANDS.
DONAJÍ-- "GREAT SOUL." A WONDERFUL NAME INDEED.
HOW ABOUT YOU?
*"CLOUD PEOPLE," WHAT THE ZAPOTEC CALL THEMSELVES.
?

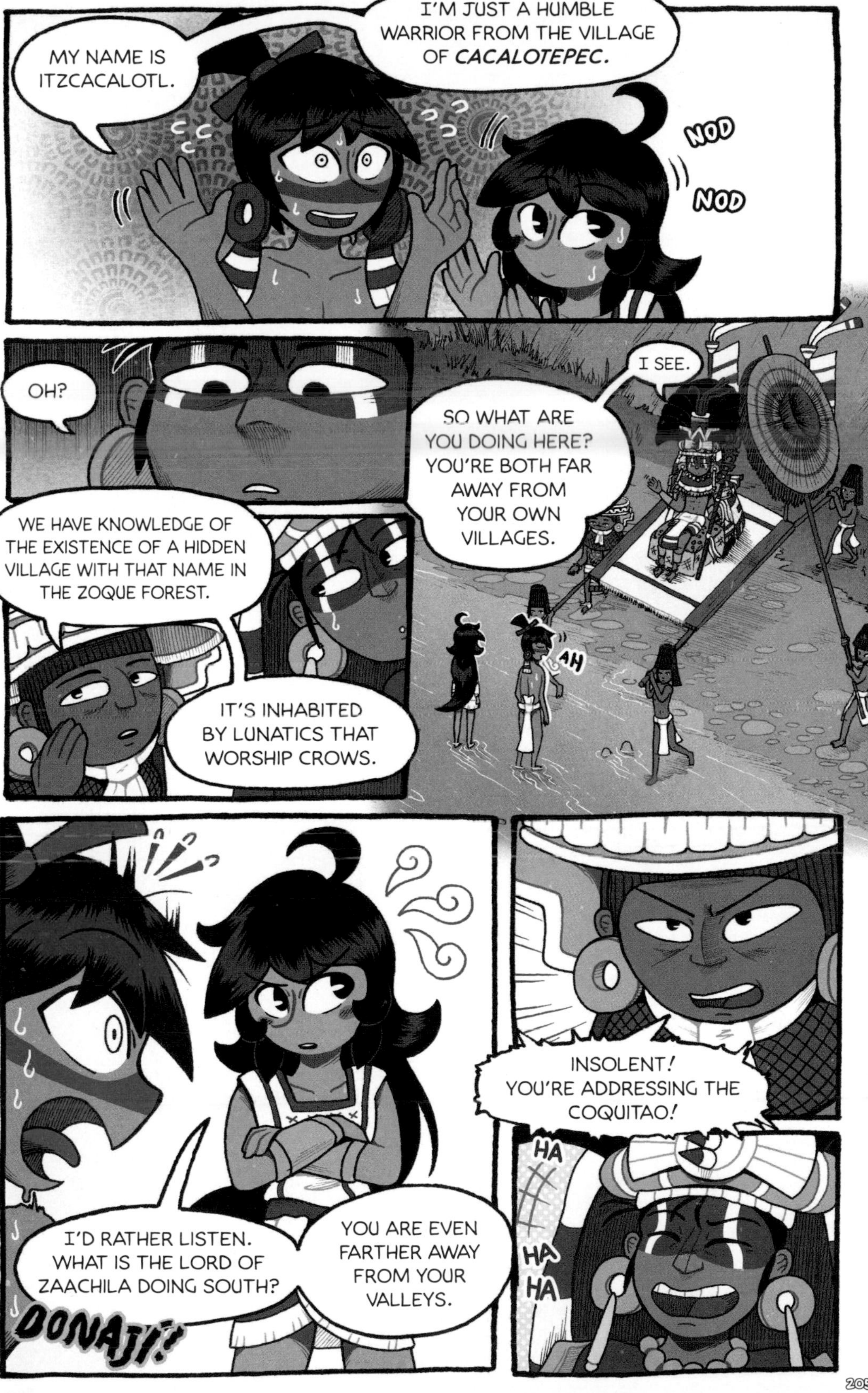

MY NAME IS ITZCACALOTL.
I'M JUST A HUMBLE WARRIOR FROM THE VILLAGE OF *CACALOTEPEC.*
NOD
NOD
OH?
I SEE.
SO WHAT ARE YOU DOING HERE? YOU'RE BOTH FAR AWAY FROM YOUR OWN VILLAGES.
WE HAVE KNOWLEDGE OF THE EXISTENCE OF A HIDDEN VILLAGE WITH THAT NAME IN THE ZOQUE FOREST.
AH
IT'S INHABITED BY LUNATICS THAT WORSHIP CROWS.
I'D RATHER LISTEN. WHAT IS THE LORD OF ZAACHILA DOING SOUTH?
YOU ARE EVEN FARTHER AWAY FROM YOUR VALLEYS.
DONAJI!?
INSOLENT! YOU'RE ADDRESSING THE COQUITAO!
HA
HA
HA

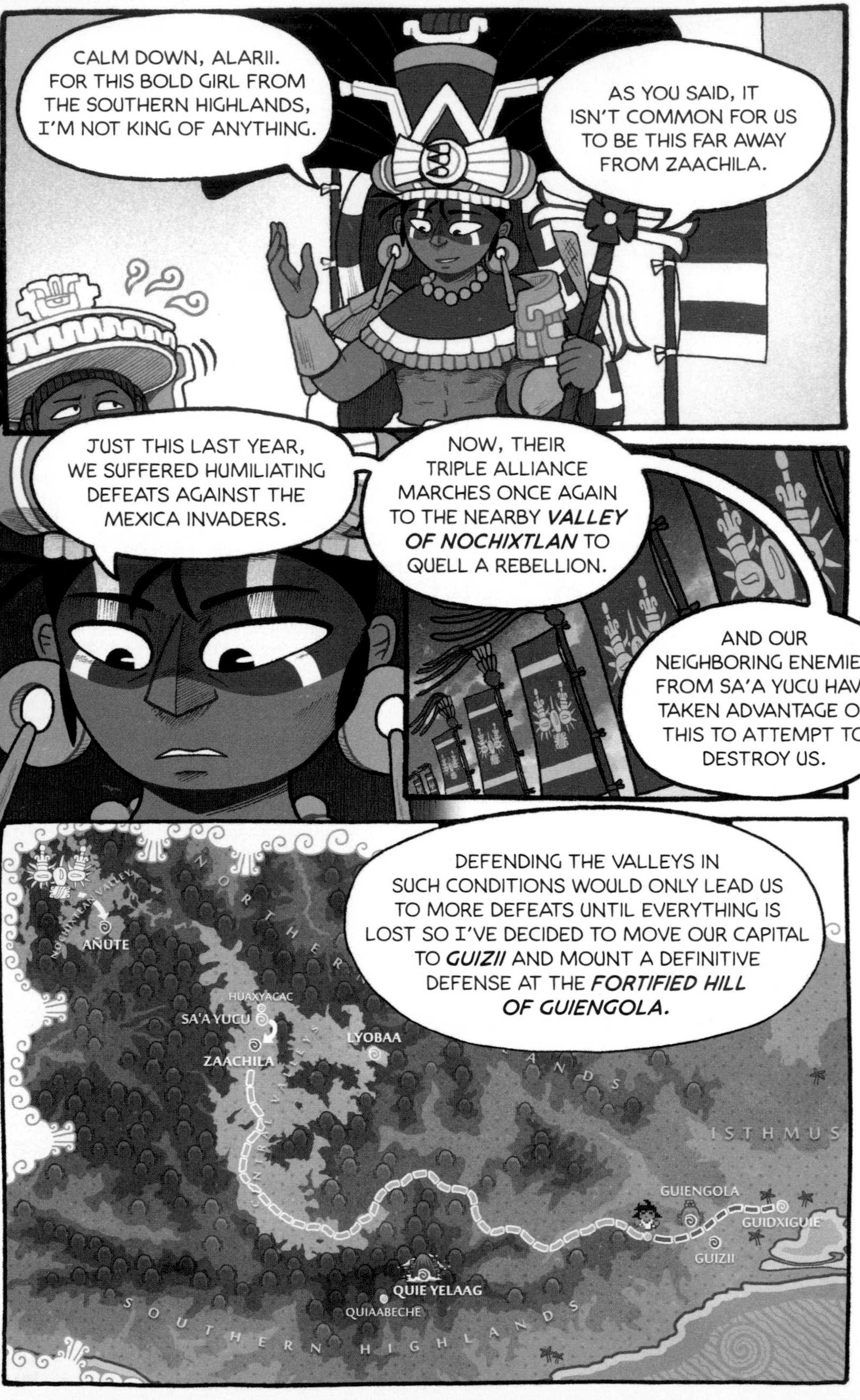
CALM DOWN, ALARII. FOR THIS BOLD GIRL FROM THE SOUTHERN HIGHLANDS, I'M NOT KING OF ANYTHING.
AS YOU SAID, IT ISN'T COMMON FOR US TO BE THIS FAR AWAY FROM ZAACHILA.
JUST THIS LAST YEAR, WE SUFFERED HUMILIATING DEFEATS AGAINST THE MEXICA INVADERS.
NOW, THEIR TRIPLE ALLIANCE MARCHES ONCE AGAIN TO THE NEARBY ***VALLEY OF NOCHIXTLAN*** TO QUELL A REBELLION.
AND OUR NEIGHBORING ENEMIES FROM SA'A YUCU HAVE TAKEN ADVANTAGE OF THIS TO ATTEMPT TO DESTROY US.
DEFENDING THE VALLEYS IN SUCH CONDITIONS WOULD ONLY LEAD US TO MORE DEFEATS UNTIL EVERYTHING IS LOST SO I'VE DECIDED TO MOVE OUR CAPITAL TO ***GUIZII*** AND MOUNT A DEFINITIVE DEFENSE AT THE ***FORTIFIED HILL OF GUIENGOLA.***
NOCHIXTLAN VALLEY
AÑUTE
HUAXYACAC
SA'A YUCU
LYOBAA
ZAACHILA
CENTRAL VALLEYS
ISTHMUS
GUIENGOLA
GUIDXIGUIE
GUIZII
QUIE YELAAG
QUIAABECHE
SOUTHERN HIGHLANDS

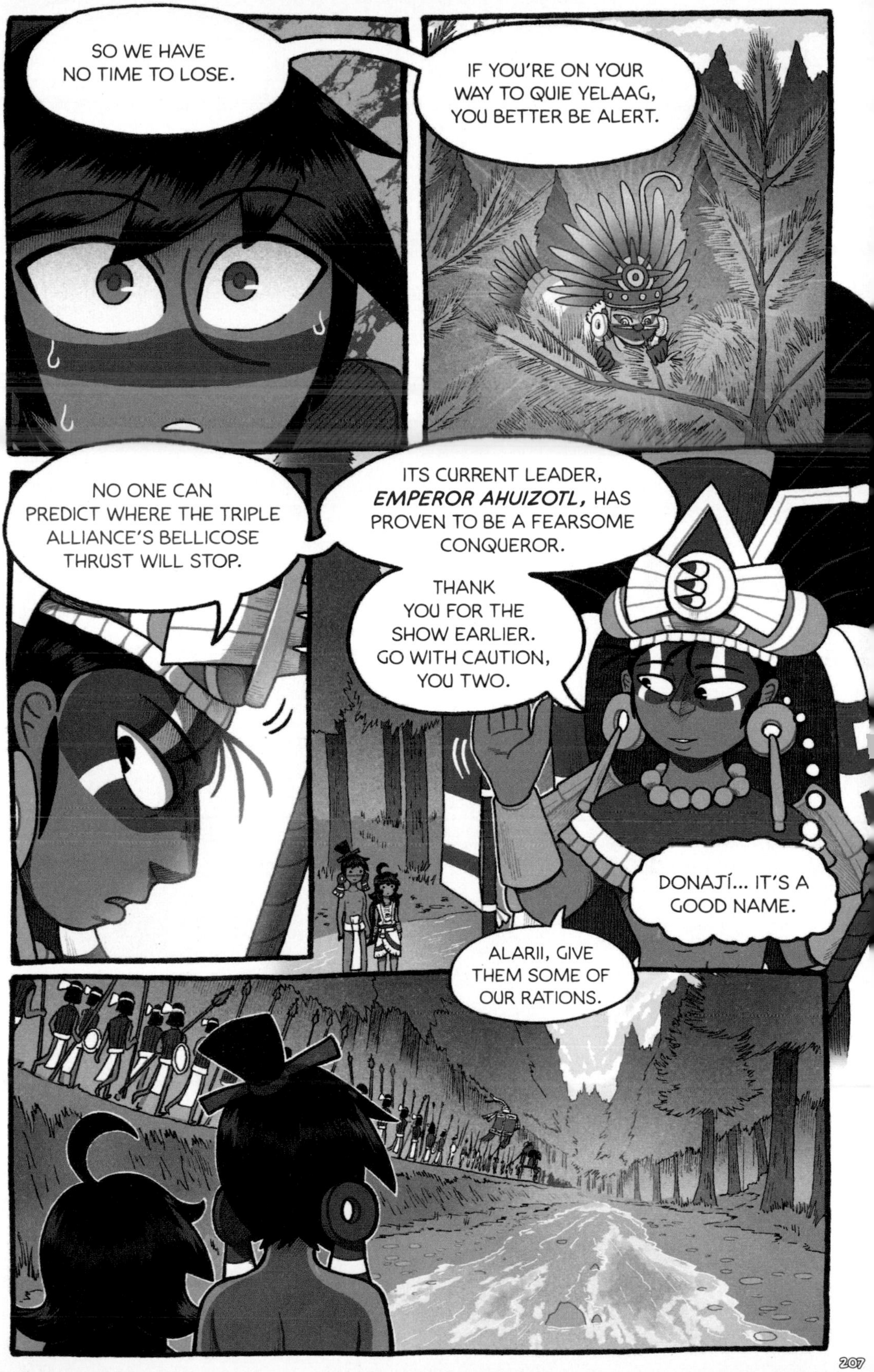
SO WE HAVE NO TIME TO LOSE.
IF YOU'RE ON YOUR WAY TO QUIE YELAAG, YOU BETTER BE ALERT.
NO ONE CAN PREDICT WHERE THE TRIPLE ALLIANCE'S BELLICOSE THRUST WILL STOP.
ITS CURRENT LEADER, ***EMPEROR AHUIZOTL,*** HAS PROVEN TO BE A FEARSOME CONQUEROR.
THANK YOU FOR THE SHOW EARLIER. GO WITH CAUTION, YOU TWO.
DONAJÍ... IT'S A GOOD NAME.
ALARII, GIVE THEM SOME OF OUR RATIONS.

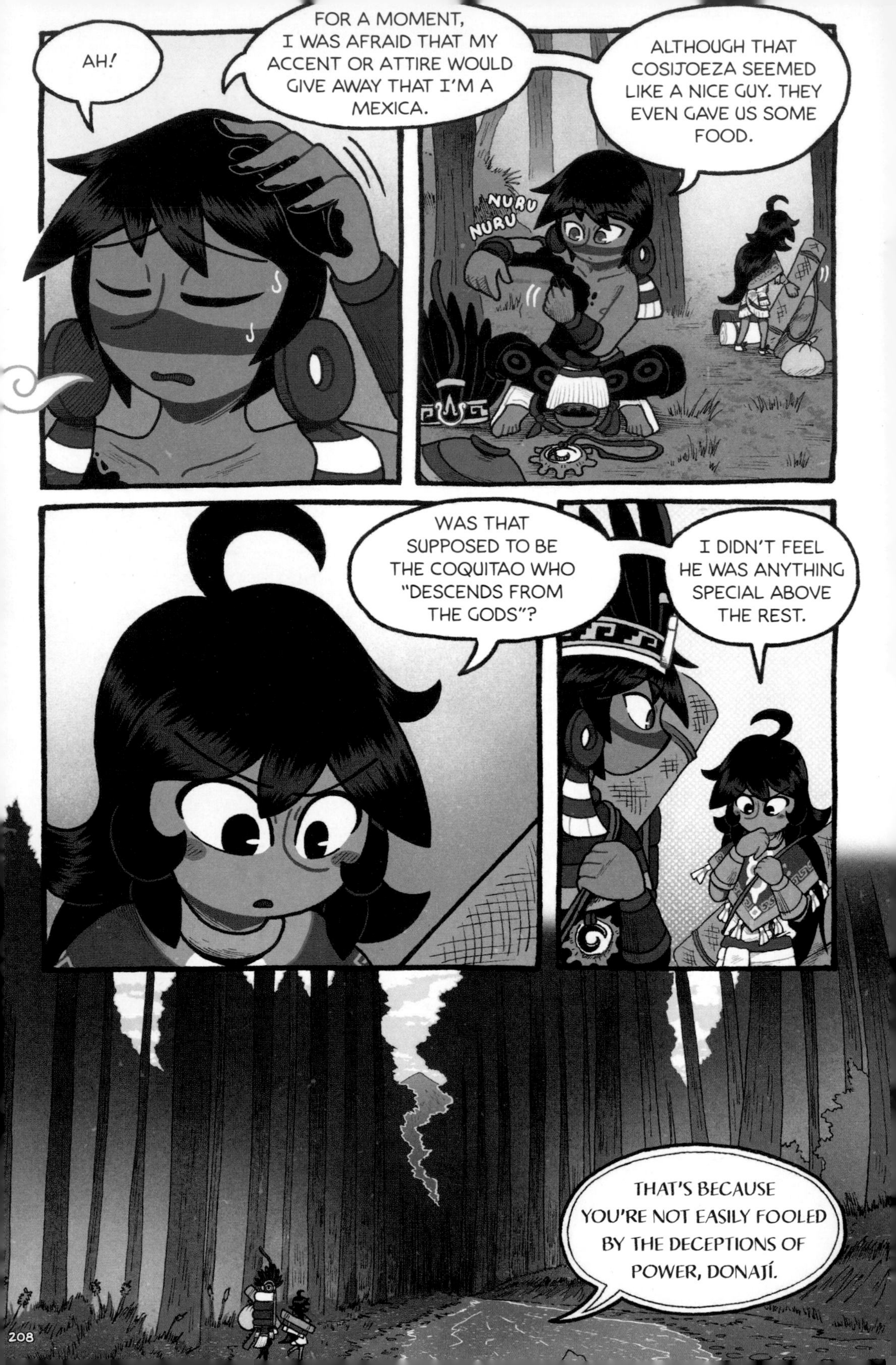
AH!
FOR A MOMENT, I WAS AFRAID THAT MY ACCENT OR ATTIRE WOULD GIVE AWAY THAT I'M A MEXICA.
ALTHOUGH THAT COSIJOEZA SEEMED LIKE A NICE GUY. THEY EVEN GAVE US SOME FOOD.
NURU NURU
WAS THAT SUPPOSED TO BE THE COQUITAO WHO "DESCENDS FROM THE GODS"?
I DIDN'T FEEL HE WAS ANYTHING SPECIAL ABOVE THE REST.
THAT'S BECAUSE YOU'RE NOT EASILY FOOLED BY THE DECEPTIONS OF POWER, DONAJÍ.

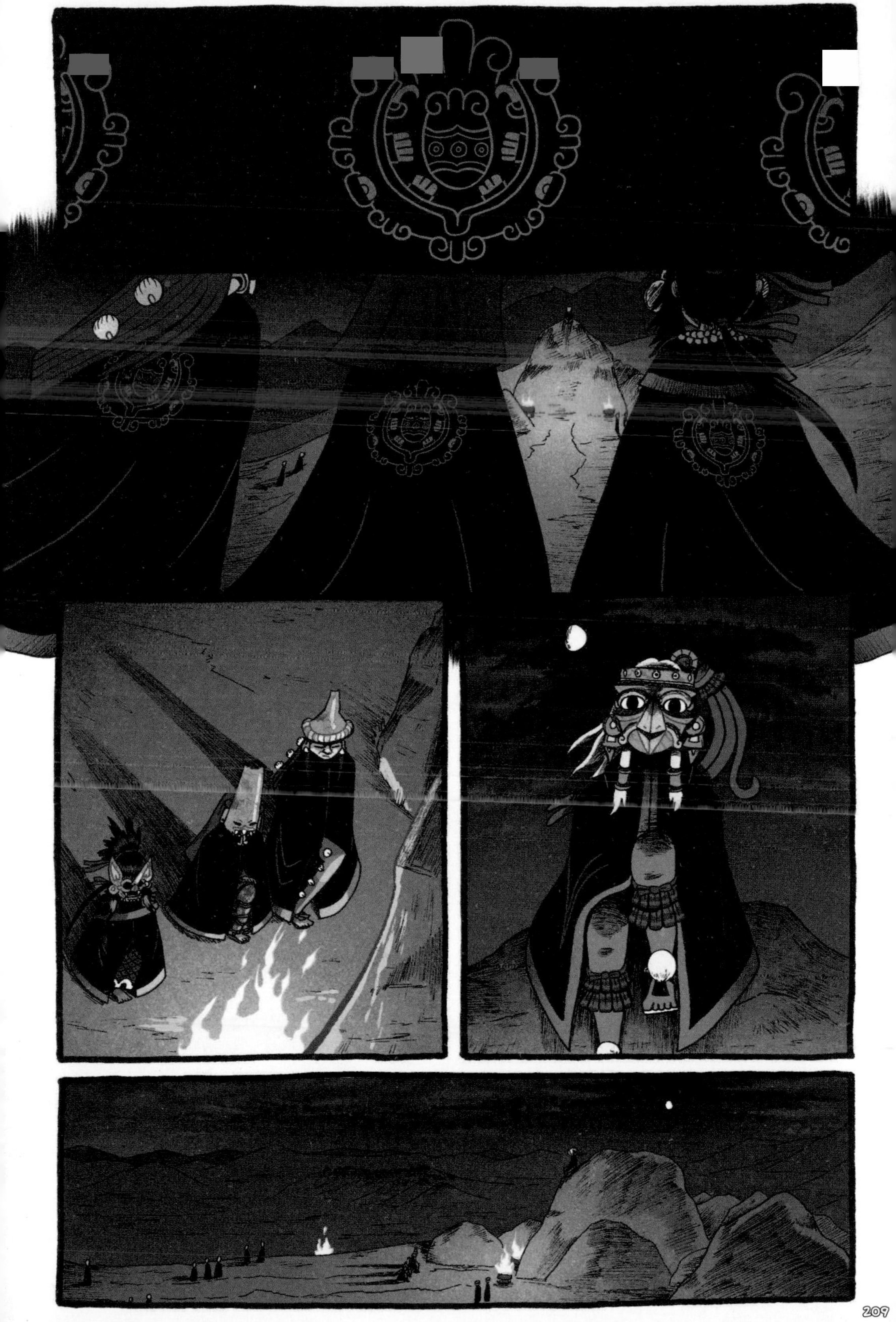

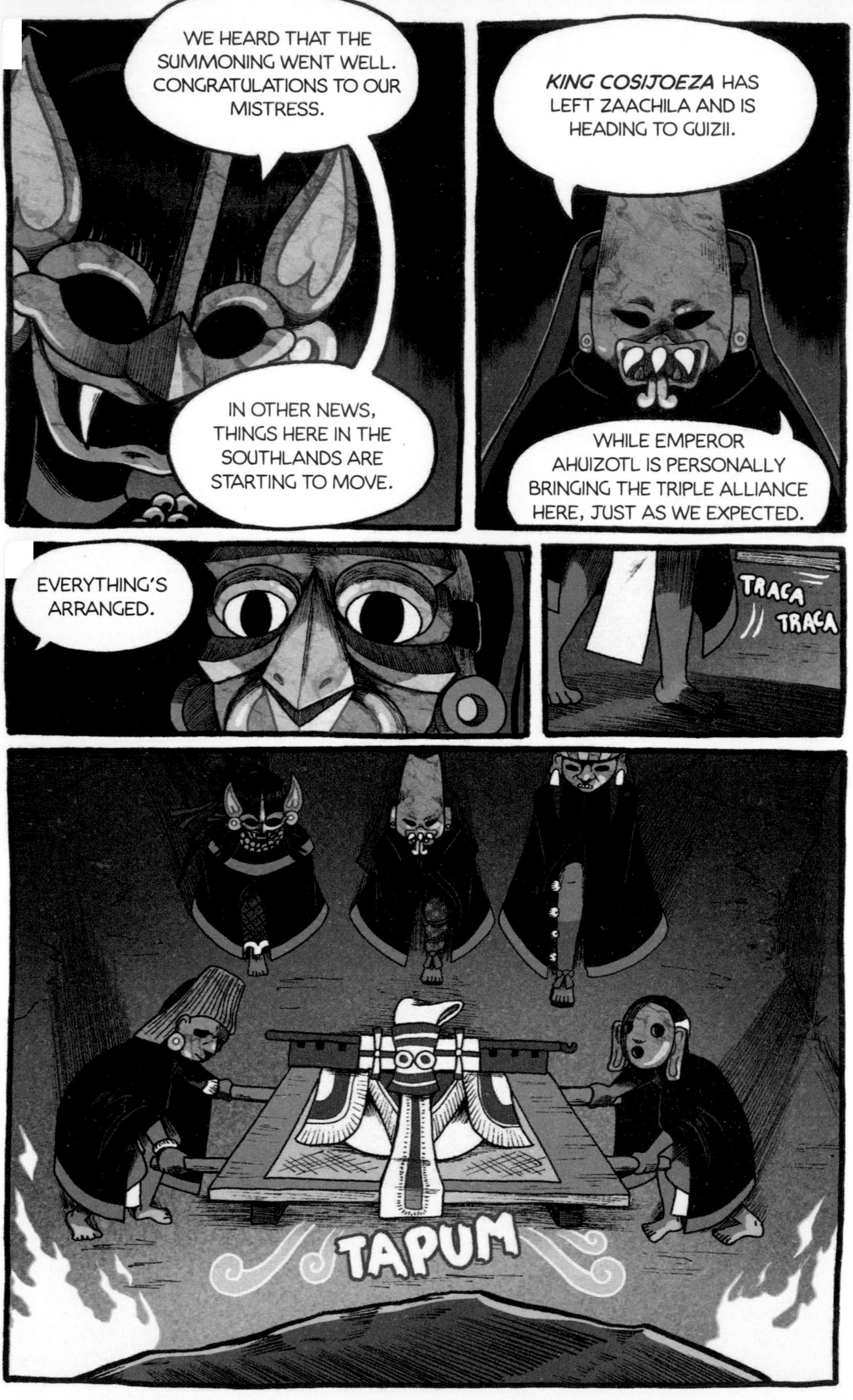

WE HEARD THAT THE SUMMONING WENT WELL. CONGRATULATIONS TO OUR MISTRESS.
IN OTHER NEWS, THINGS HERE IN THE SOUTHLANDS ARE STARTING TO MOVE.
KING COSIJOEZA HAS LEFT ZAACHILA AND IS HEADING TO GUIZII.
WHILE EMPEROR AHUIZOTL IS PERSONALLY BRINGING THE TRIPLE ALLIANCE HERE, JUST AS WE EXPECTED.
EVERYTHING'S ARRANGED.
TRACA TRACA
TAPUM

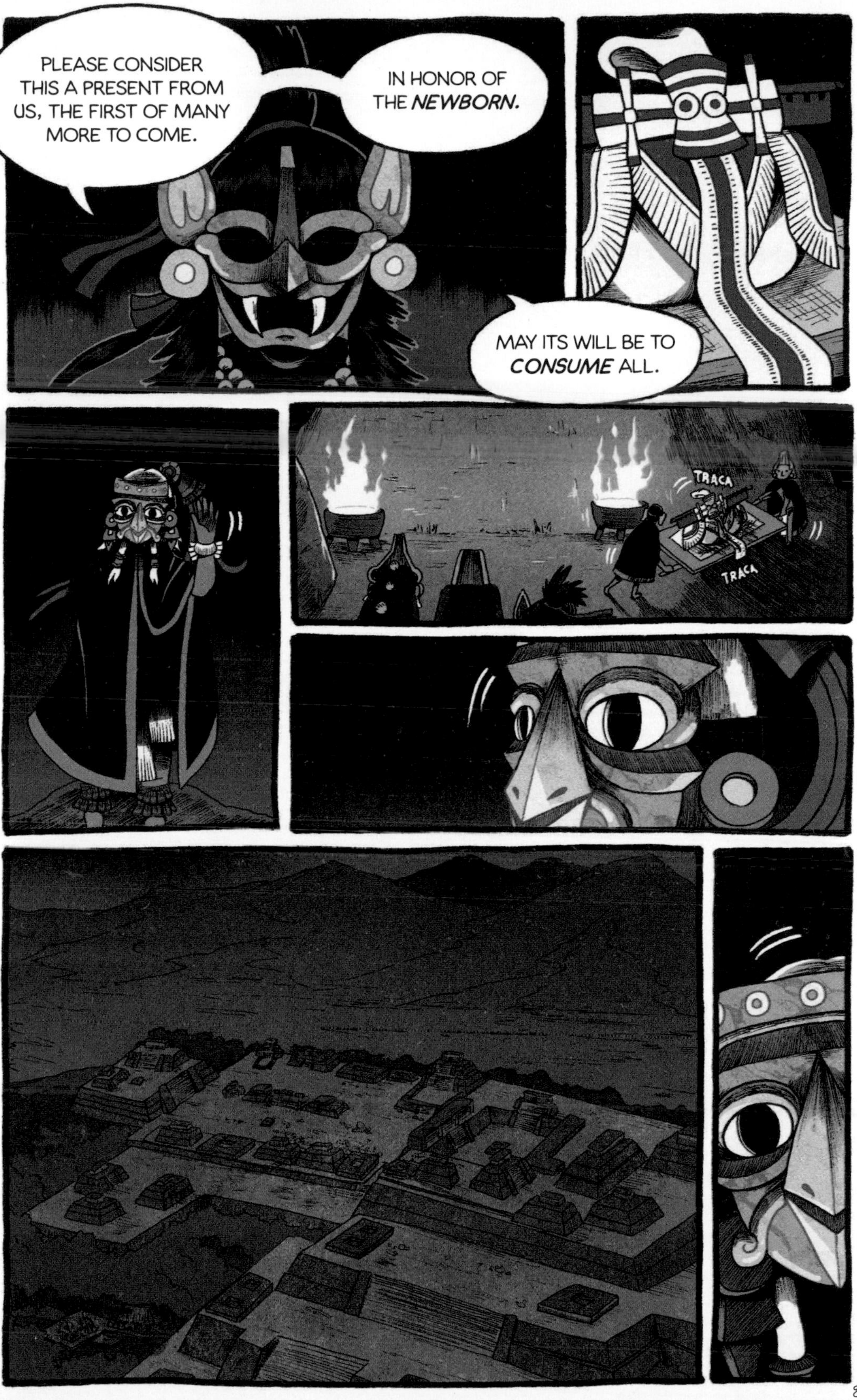
PLEASE CONSIDER THIS A PRESENT FROM US, THE FIRST OF MANY MORE TO COME.
IN HONOR OF THE NEWBORN.
MAY ITS WILL BE TO CONSUME ALL.
TRACA
TRACA

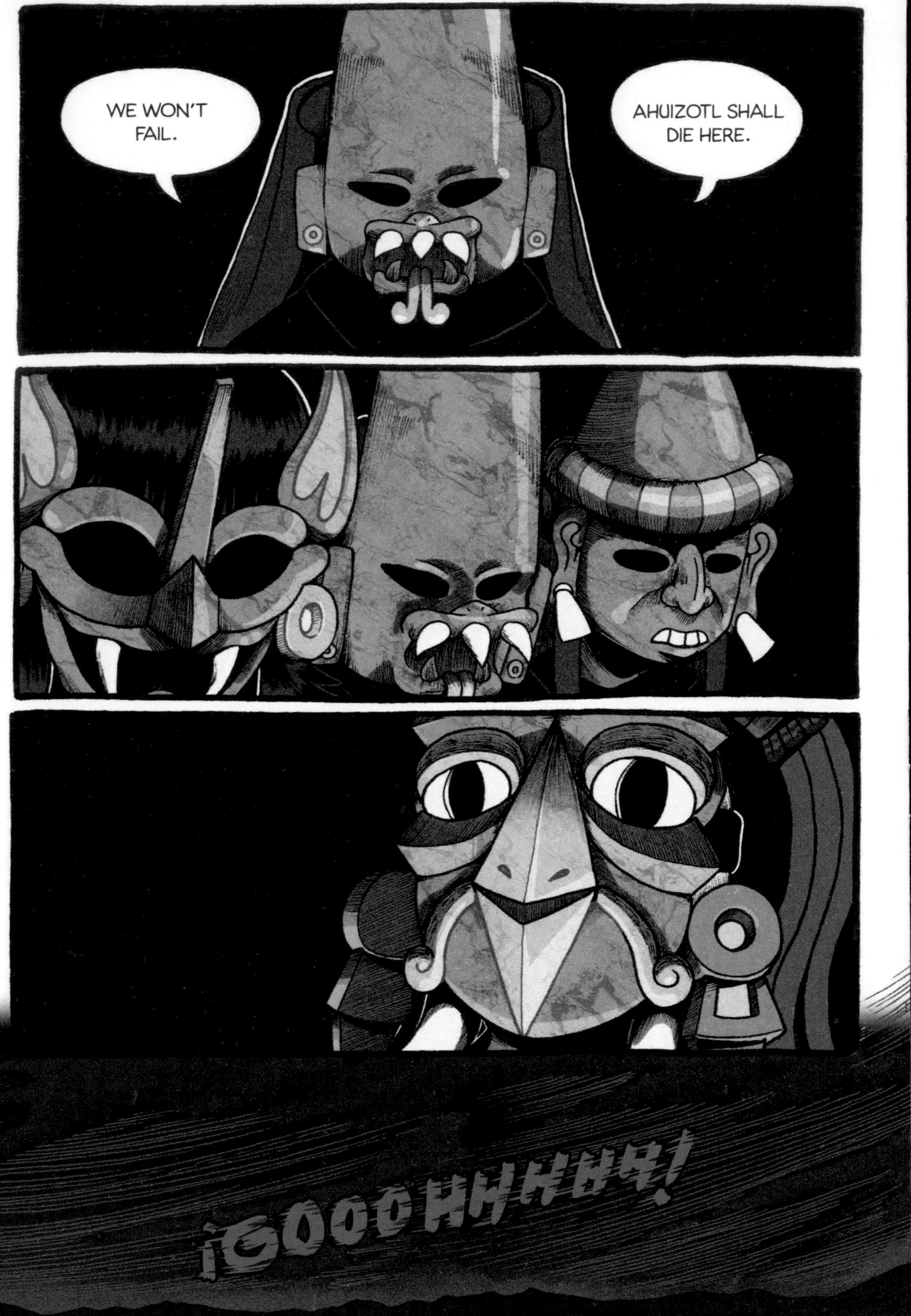
WE WON'T FAIL.
AHUIZOTL SHALL DIE HERE.
¡GOOOHHHHHR!

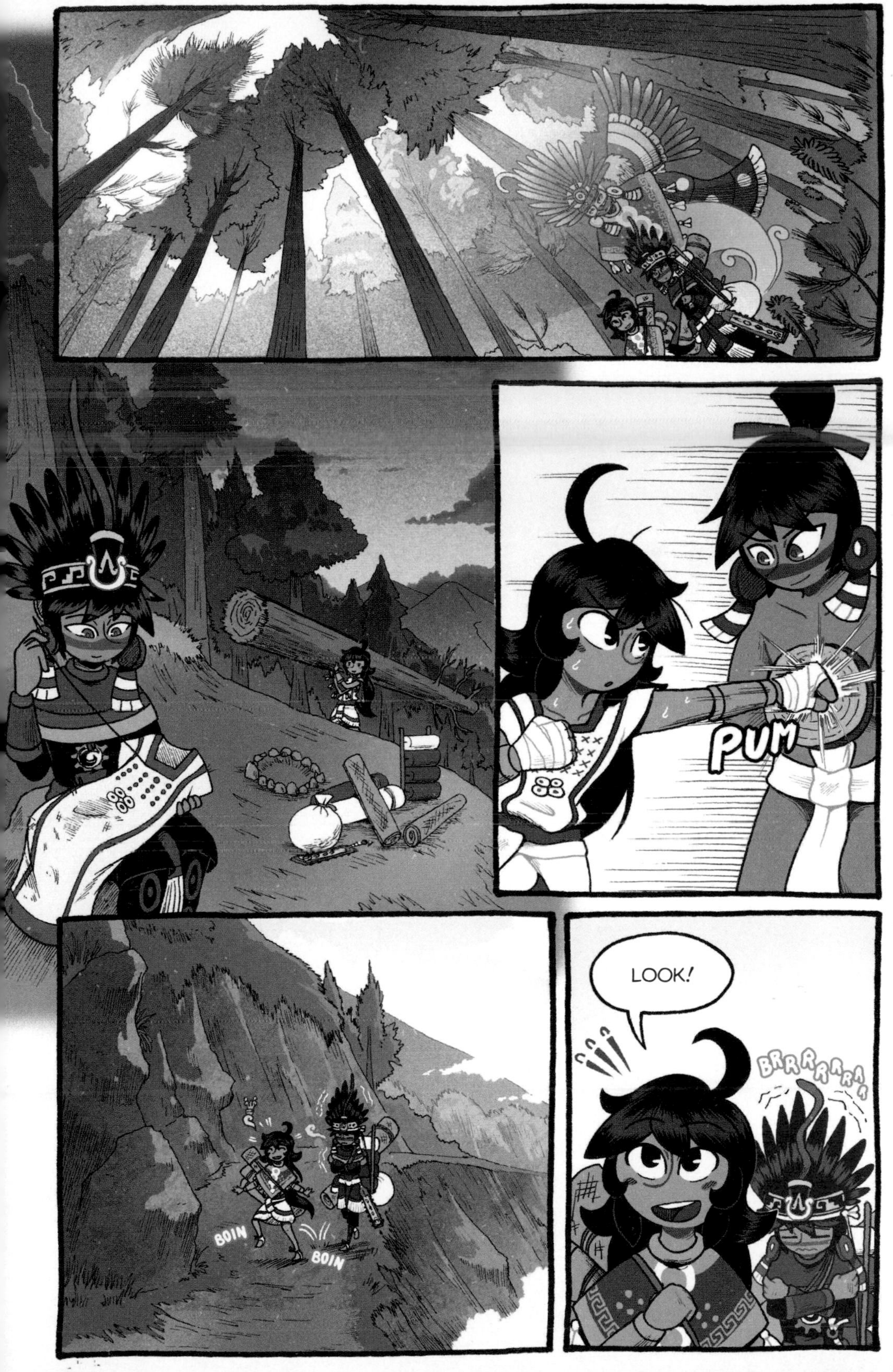
PUM
BOIN
BOIN
LOOK!
BRRRRRRRR

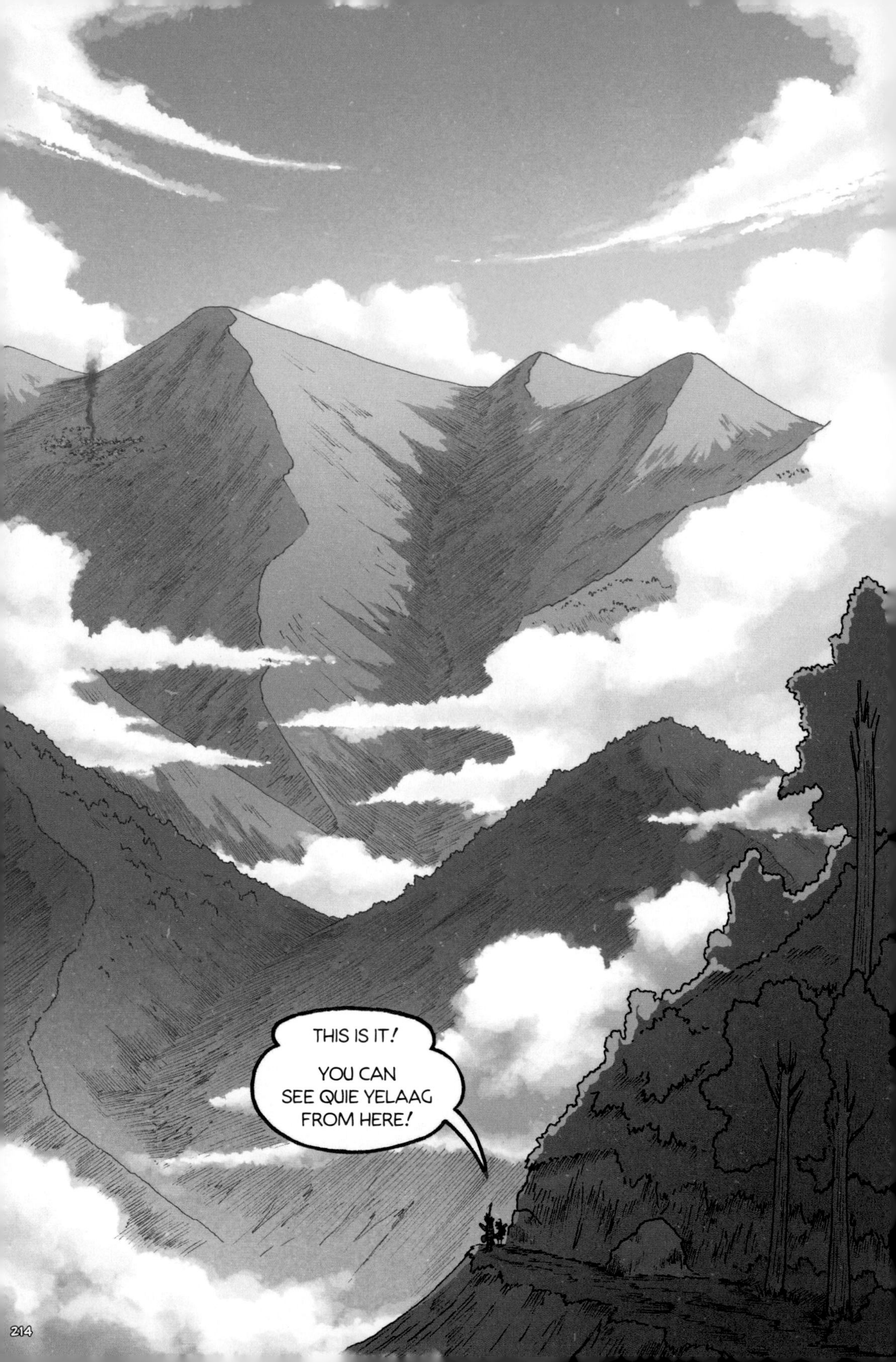
THIS IS IT!
YOU CAN SEE QUIE YELAAG FROM HERE!

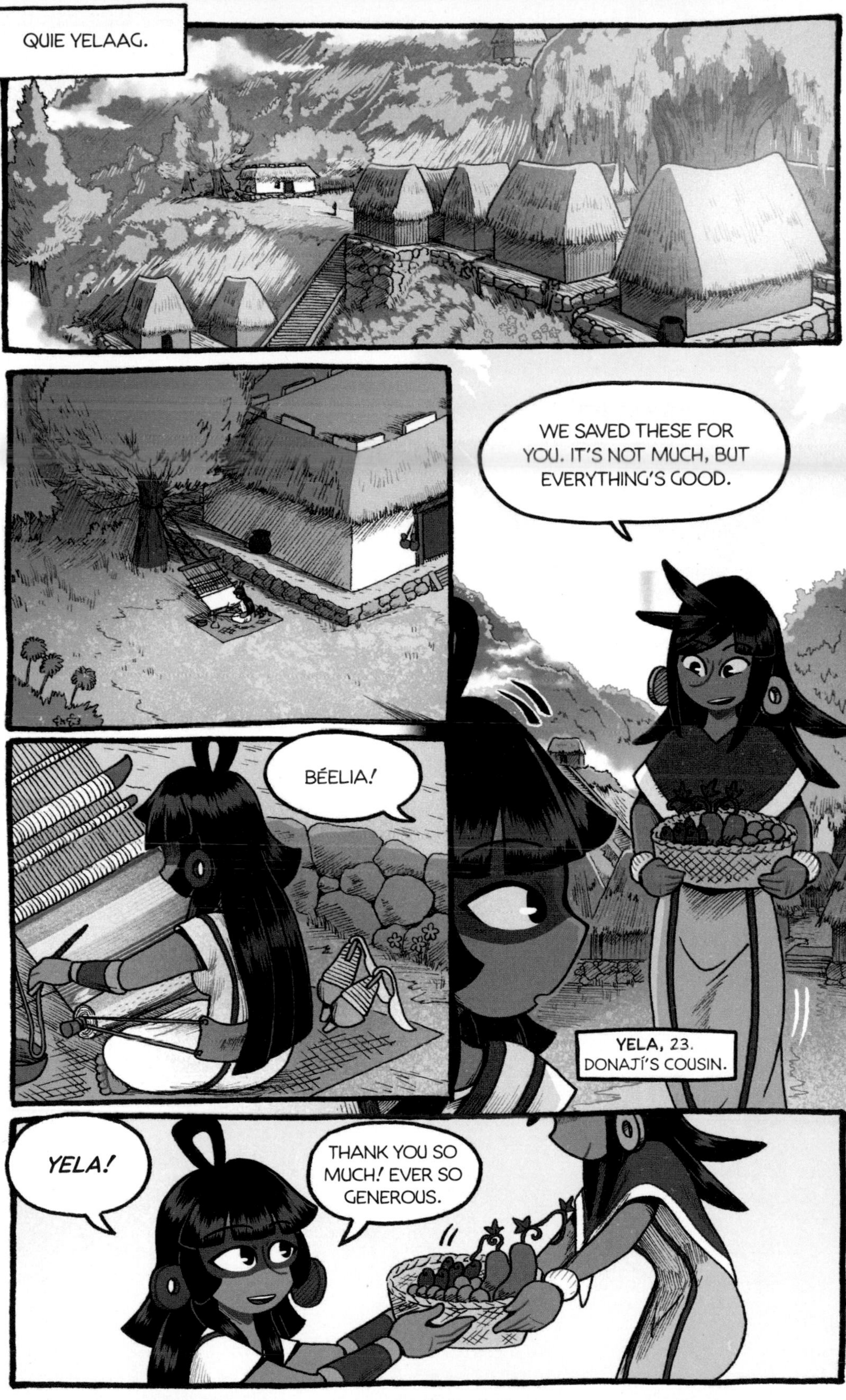
QUIE YELAAG.
WE SAVED THESE FOR YOU. IT'S NOT MUCH, BUT EVERYTHING'S GOOD.
BÉELIA!
YELA, 23. DONAJÍ'S COUSIN.
YELA!
THANK YOU SO MUCH! EVER SO GENEROUS.

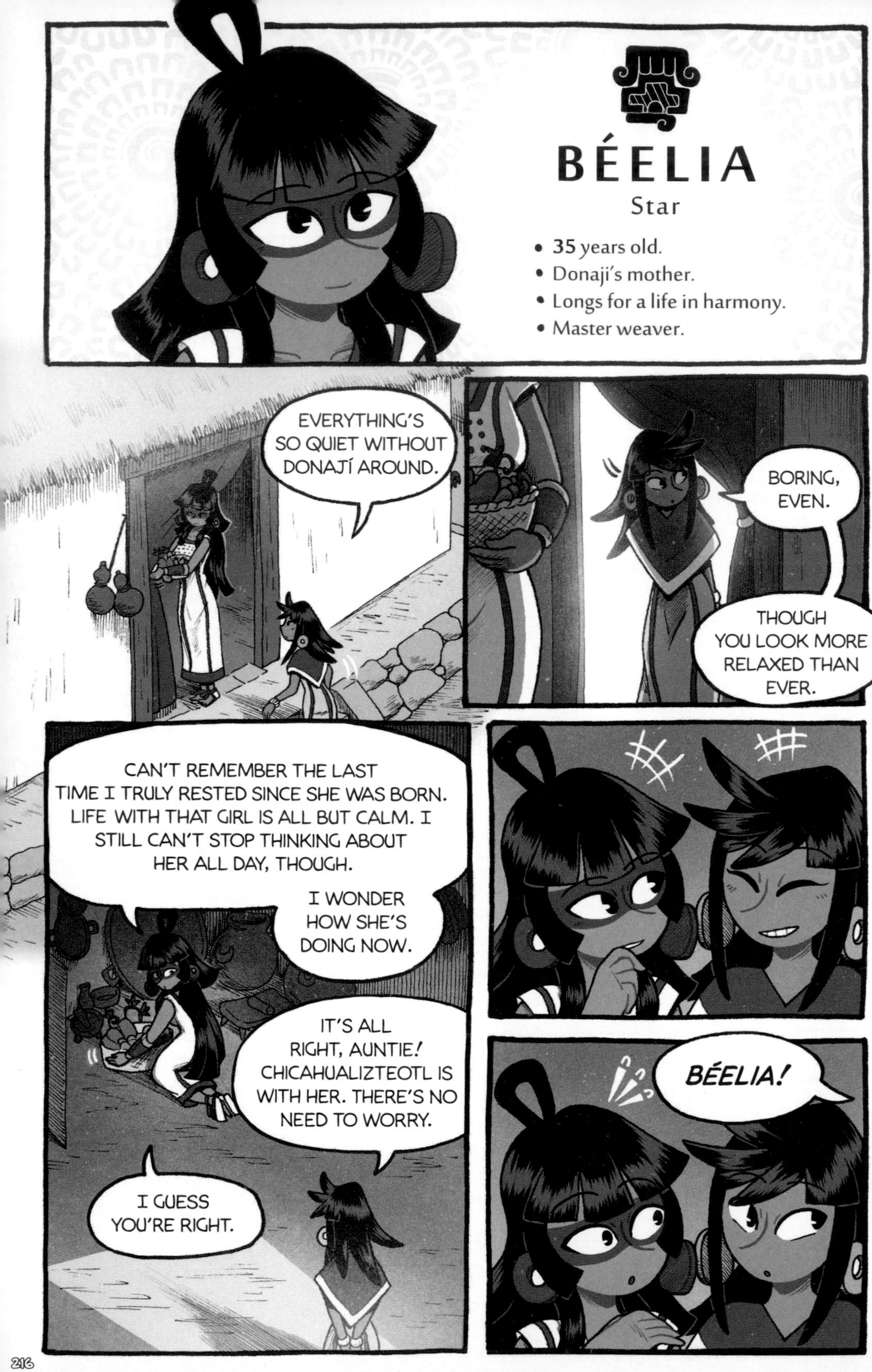
BÉELIA
Star
• 35 years old.
• Donaji's mother.
• Longs for a life in harmony.
• Master weaver.
EVERYTHING'S SO QUIET WITHOUT DONAJÍ AROUND.
BORING, EVEN.
THOUGH YOU LOOK MORE RELAXED THAN EVER.
CAN'T REMEMBER THE LAST TIME I TRULY RESTED SINCE SHE WAS BORN. LIFE WITH THAT GIRL IS ALL BUT CALM. I STILL CAN'T STOP THINKING ABOUT HER ALL DAY, THOUGH.
I WONDER HOW SHE'S DOING NOW.
IT'S ALL RIGHT, AUNTIE! CHICAHUALIZTEOTL IS WITH HER. THERE'S NO NEED TO WORRY.
I GUESS YOU'RE RIGHT.
BÉELIA!

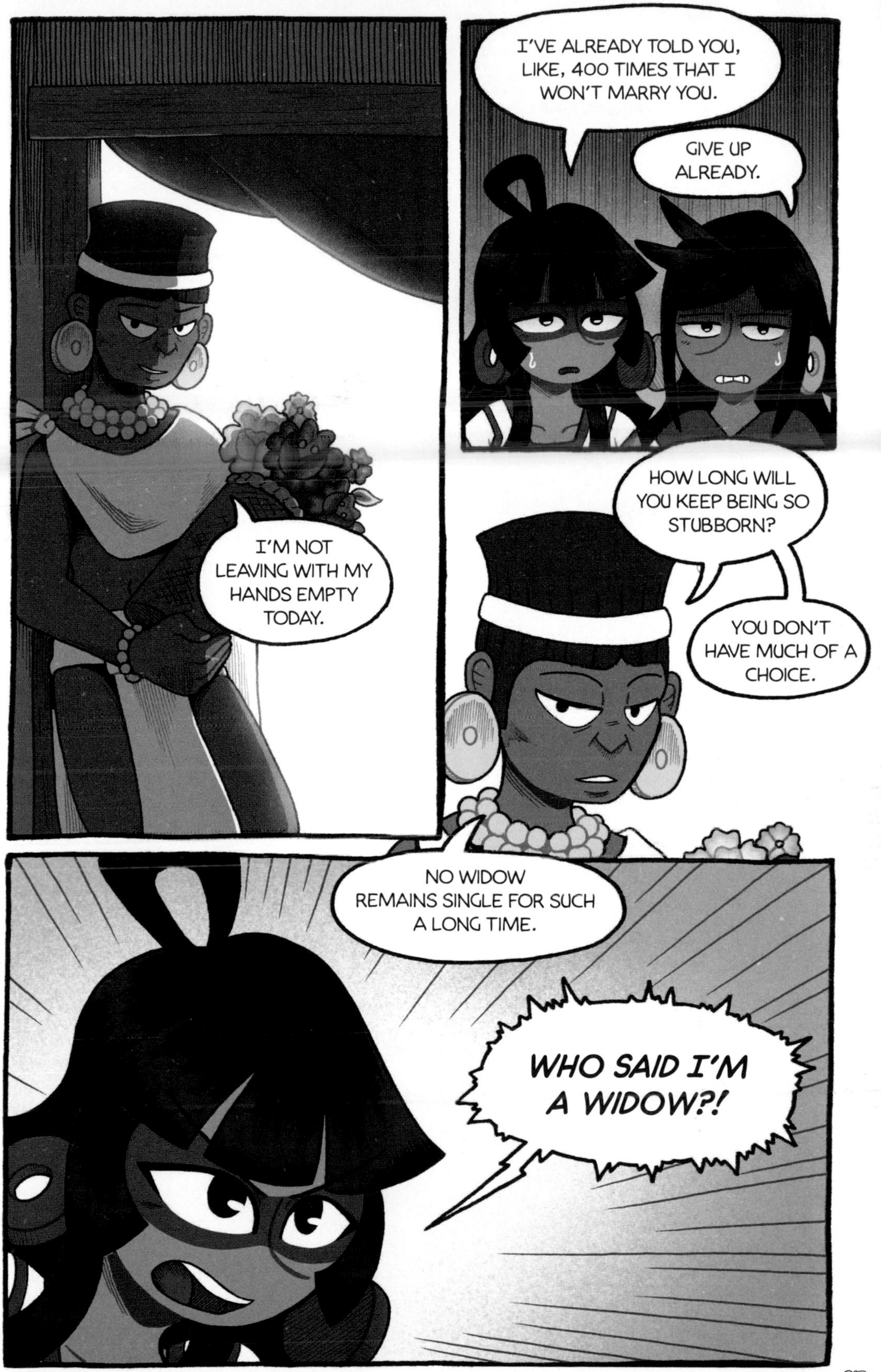
I'VE ALREADY TOLD YOU, LIKE, 400 TIMES THAT I WON'T MARRY YOU.
GIVE UP ALREADY.
I'M NOT LEAVING WITH MY HANDS EMPTY TODAY.
HOW LONG WILL YOU KEEP BEING SO STUBBORN?
YOU DON'T HAVE MUCH OF A CHOICE.
NO WIDOW REMAINS SINGLE FOR SUCH A LONG TIME.
WHO SAID I'M A WIDOW?!

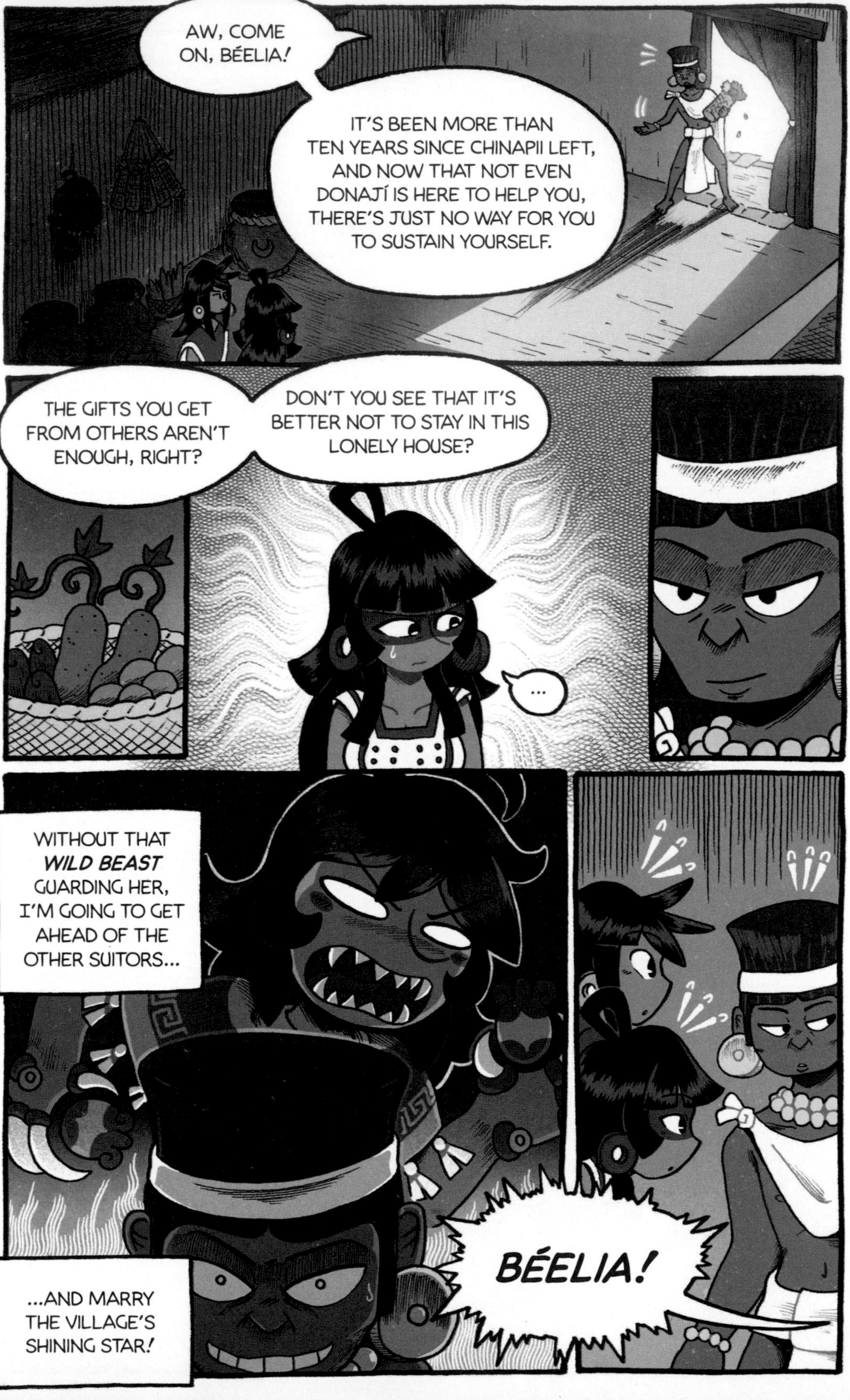
AW, COME ON, BÉELIA!
IT'S BEEN MORE THAN TEN YEARS SINCE CHINAPII LEFT, AND NOW THAT NOT EVEN DONAJÍ IS HERE TO HELP YOU, THERE'S JUST NO WAY FOR YOU TO SUSTAIN YOURSELF.
THE GIFTS YOU GET FROM OTHERS AREN'T ENOUGH, RIGHT?
DON'T YOU SEE THAT IT'S BETTER NOT TO STAY IN THIS LONELY HOUSE?
...
WITHOUT THAT ***WILD BEAST*** GUARDING HER, I'M GOING TO GET AHEAD OF THE OTHER SUITORS...
...AND MARRY THE VILLAGE'S SHINING STAR!
BÉELIA!

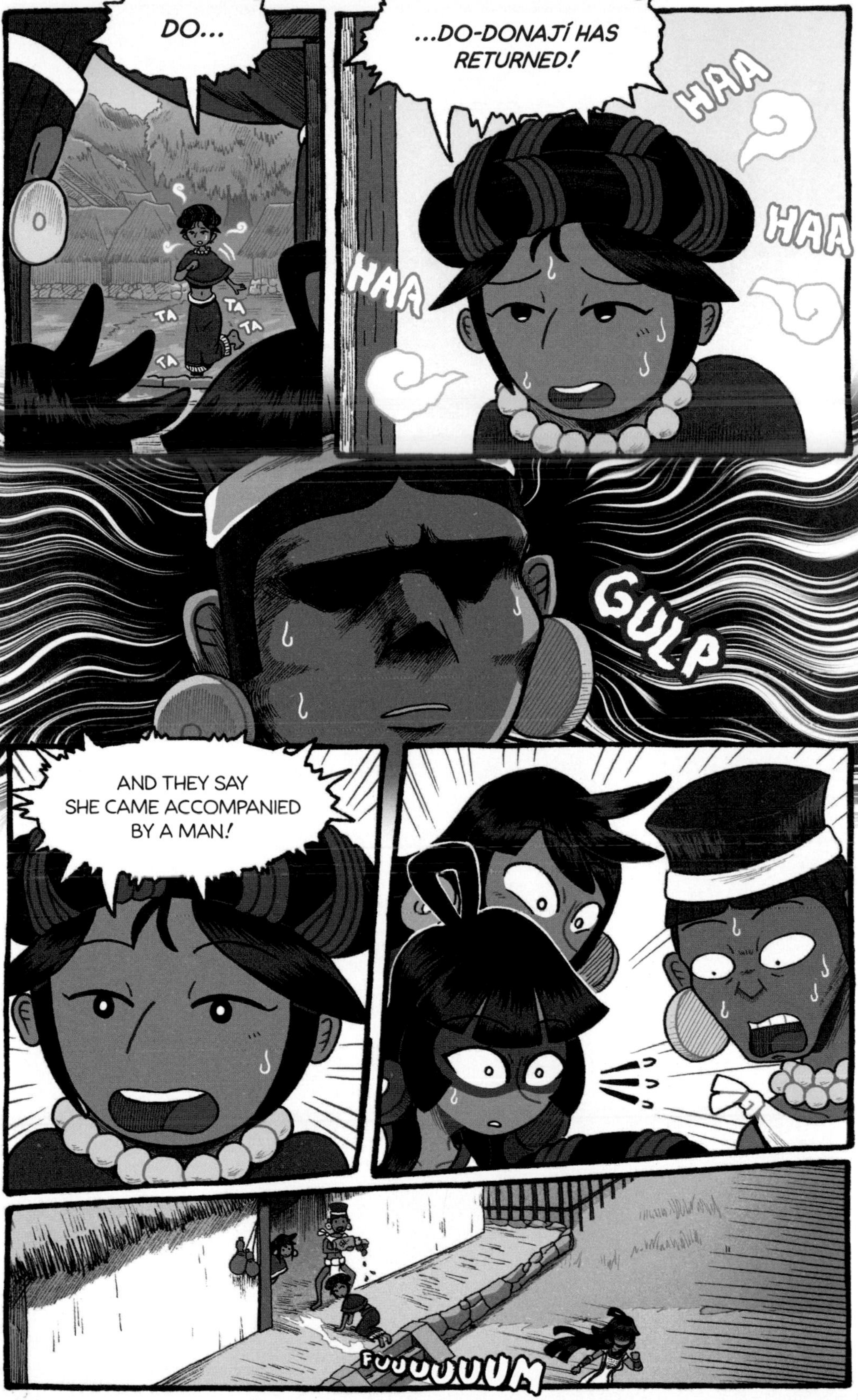
DO...
TA
TA
TA
TA
...DO-DONAJÍ HAS RETURNED!
HAA
HAA
HAA
GULP
AND THEY SAY SHE CAME ACCOMPANIED BY A MAN!
FUUUUUUM

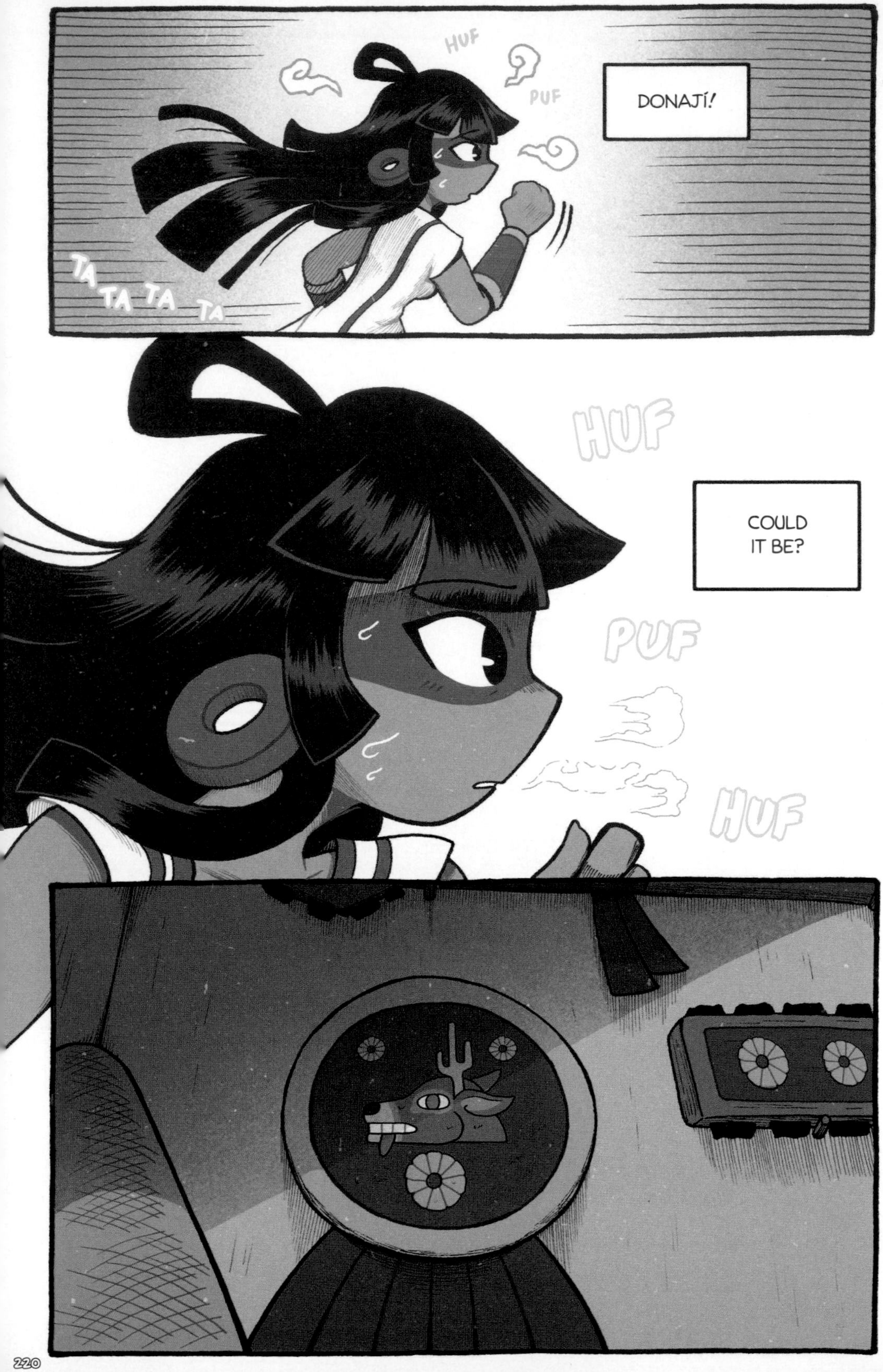
HUF
PUF
DONAJÍ!
TA TA TA TA
HUF
COULD IT BE?
PUF
HUF

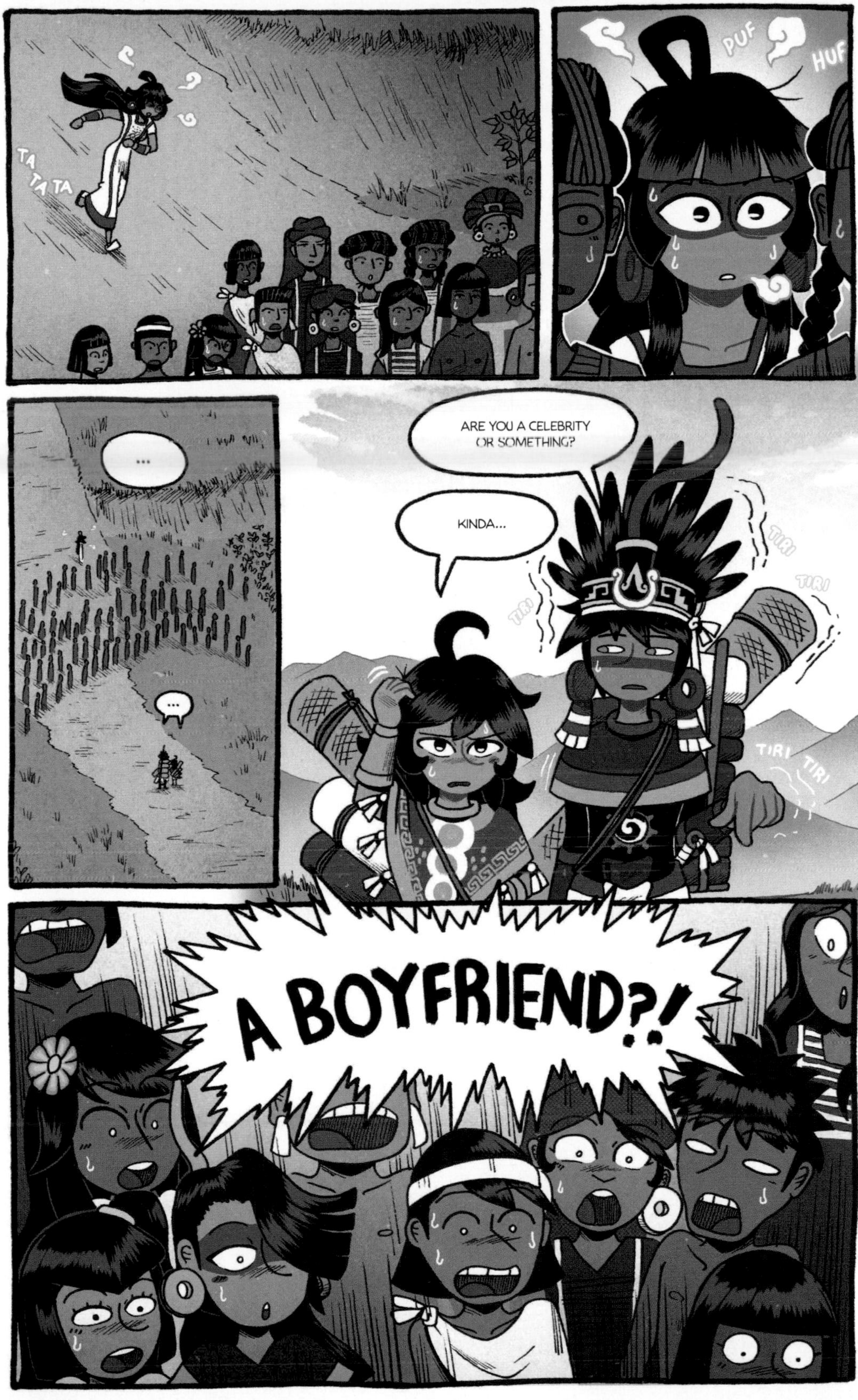
TA TA TA
PUF
HUF
...
...
ARE YOU A CELEBRITY OR SOMETHING?
KINDA...
TIRI
TIRI
TIRI
TIRI
TIRI
A BOYFRIEND?!

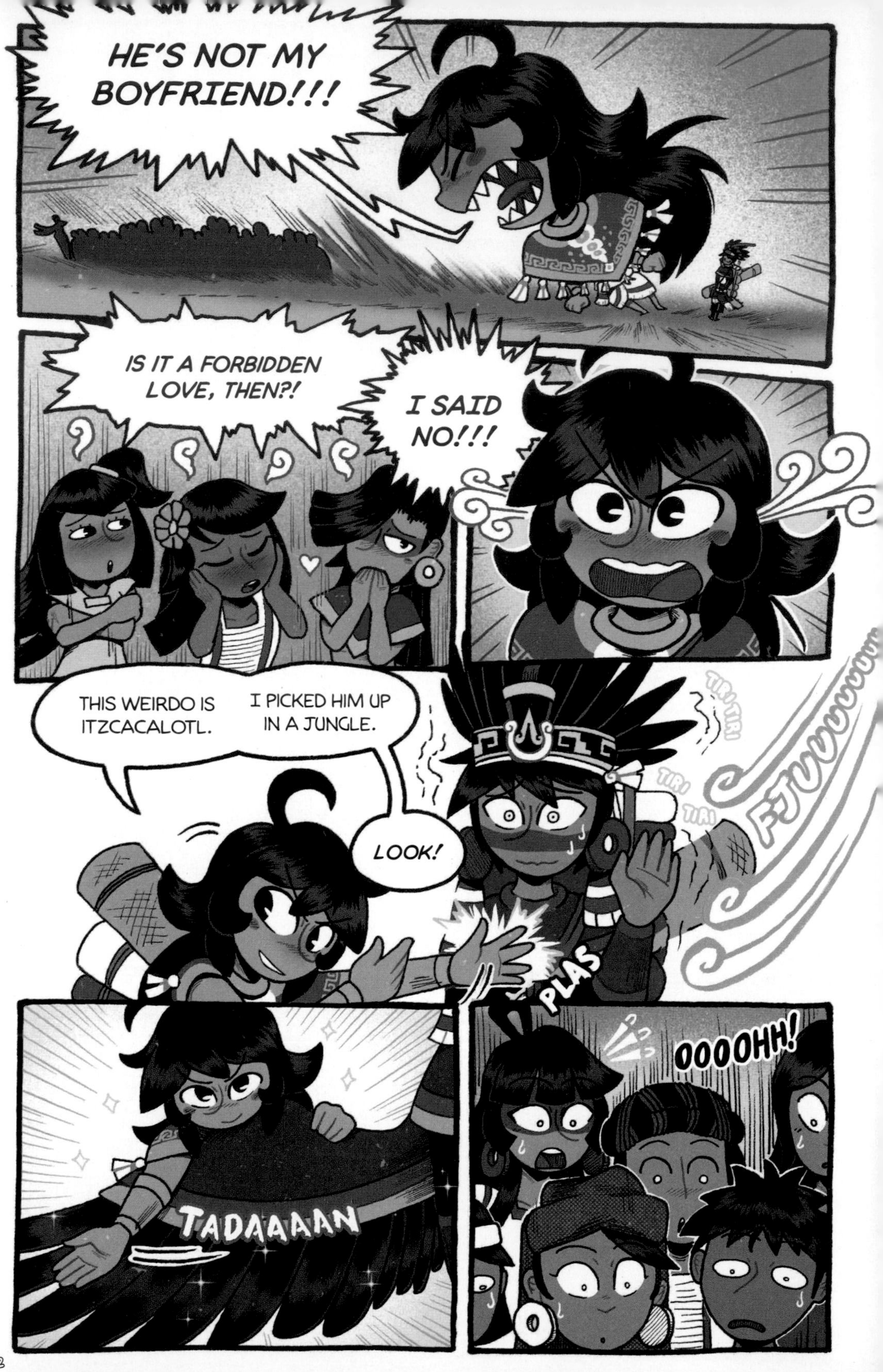

HE'S NOT MY BOYFRIEND!!!
IS IT A FORBIDDEN LOVE, THEN?!
I SAID NO!!!
THIS WEIRDO IS ITZCACALOTL.
I PICKED HIM UP IN A JUNGLE.
LOOK!
TIRI TIRI
TIRI TIRI
FJUUUUUUU
PLAS
TADAAAAN
OOOOHH!

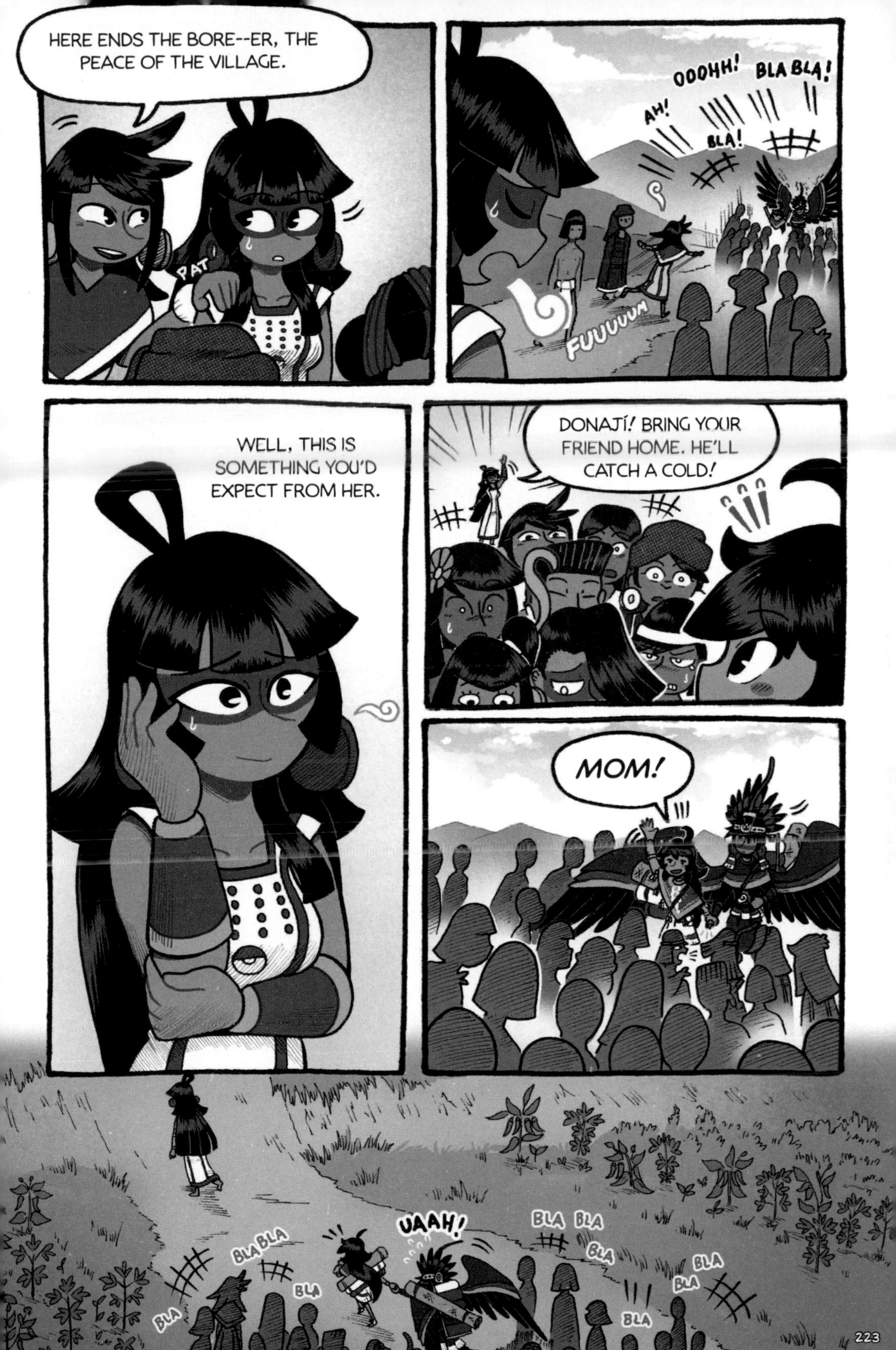
HERE ENDS THE BORE--ER, THE PEACE OF THE VILLAGE.
PAT
OOOHH!
BLA BLA!
AH!
BLA!
FUUUUUM
WELL, THIS IS SOMETHING YOU'D EXPECT FROM HER.
DONAJÍ! BRING YOUR FRIEND HOME. HE'LL CATCH A COLD!
MOM!
UAAH!
BLA BLA
BLA BLA
BLA
BLA
BLA
BLA
BLA
BLA
BLA

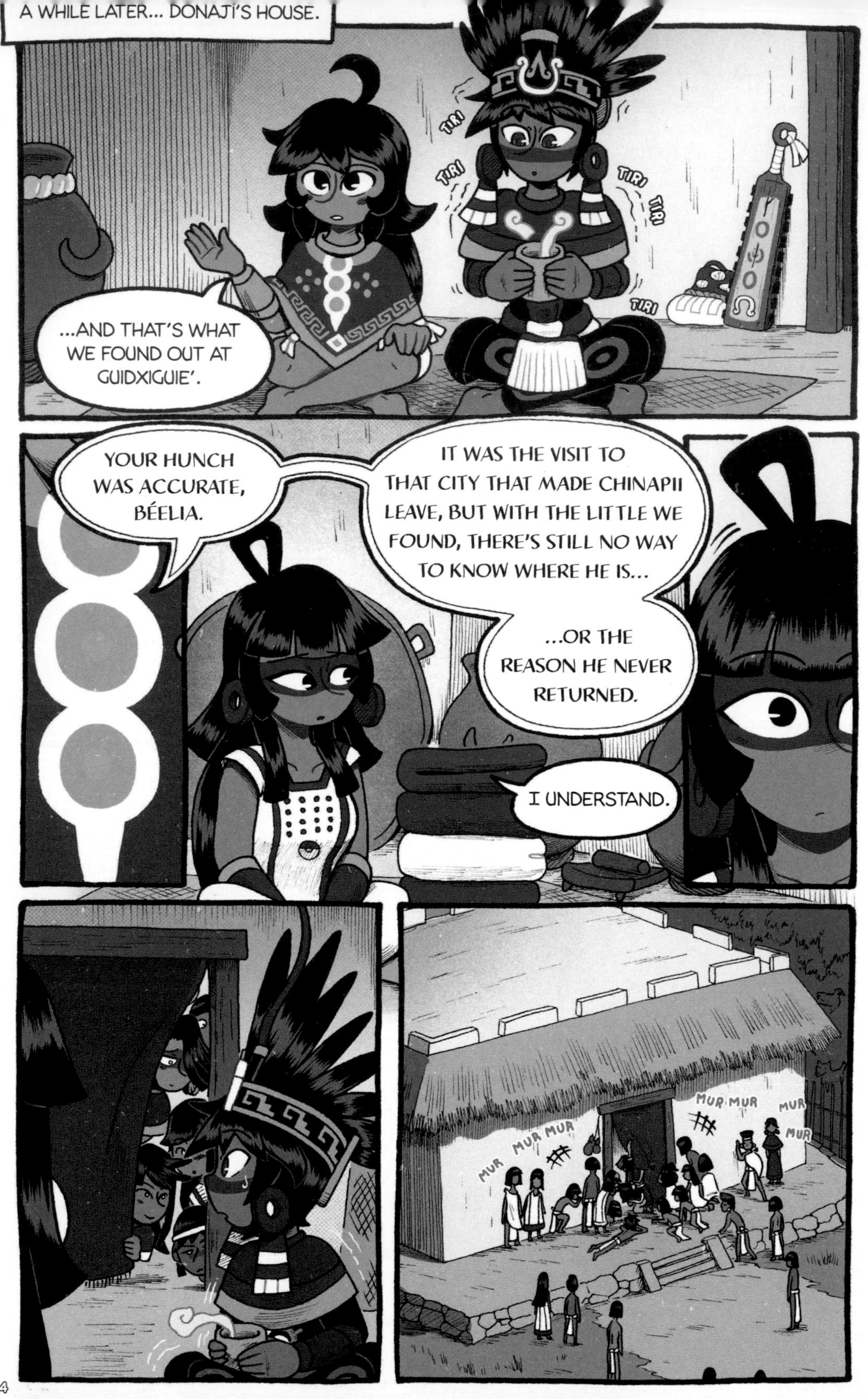
A WHILE LATER... DONAJÍ'S HOUSE.
TIRI
TIRI
TIRI
TIRI
TIRI
...AND THAT'S WHAT WE FOUND OUT AT GUIDXIGUIE'.
YOUR HUNCH WAS ACCURATE, BÉELIA.
IT WAS THE VISIT TO THAT CITY THAT MADE CHINAPII LEAVE, BUT WITH THE LITTLE WE FOUND, THERE'S STILL NO WAY TO KNOW WHERE HE IS...
...OR THE REASON HE NEVER RETURNED.
I UNDERSTAND.
MUR MUR MUR
MUR
MUR MUR
MUR
MUR

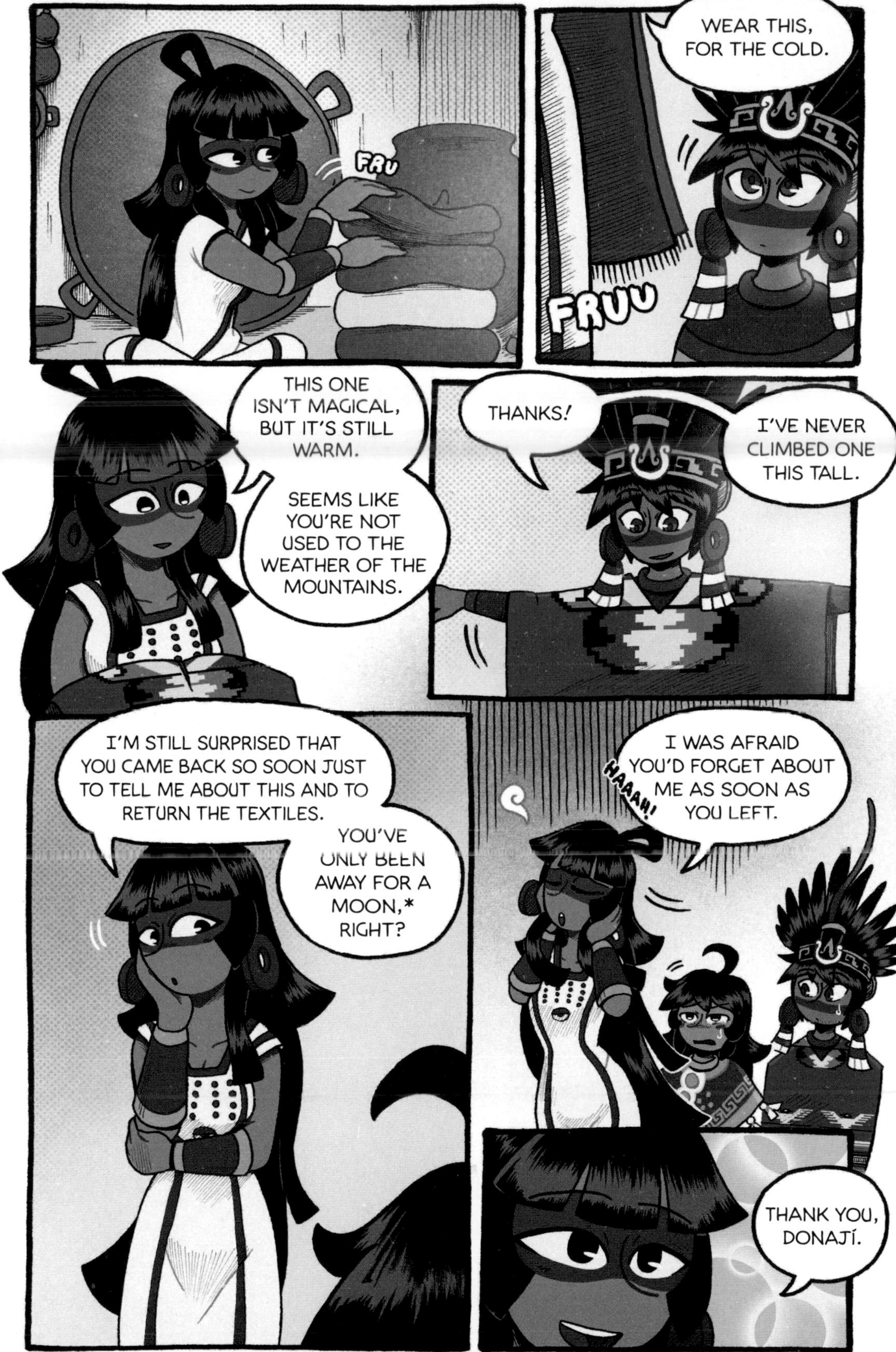

FRU
WEAR THIS, FOR THE COLD.
FRUU
THIS ONE ISN'T MAGICAL, BUT IT'S STILL WARM.
SEEMS LIKE YOU'RE NOT USED TO THE WEATHER OF THE MOUNTAINS.
THANKS!
I'VE NEVER CLIMBED ONE THIS TALL.
I'M STILL SURPRISED THAT YOU CAME BACK SO SOON JUST TO TELL ME ABOUT THIS AND TO RETURN THE TEXTILES.
YOU'VE ONLY BEEN AWAY FOR A MOON,* RIGHT?
I WAS AFRAID YOU'D FORGET ABOUT ME AS SOON AS YOU LEFT.
HAAAH!
THANK YOU, DONAJÍ.

*A 20-DAY "MONTH," AS USED IN CEMANAHUAC.

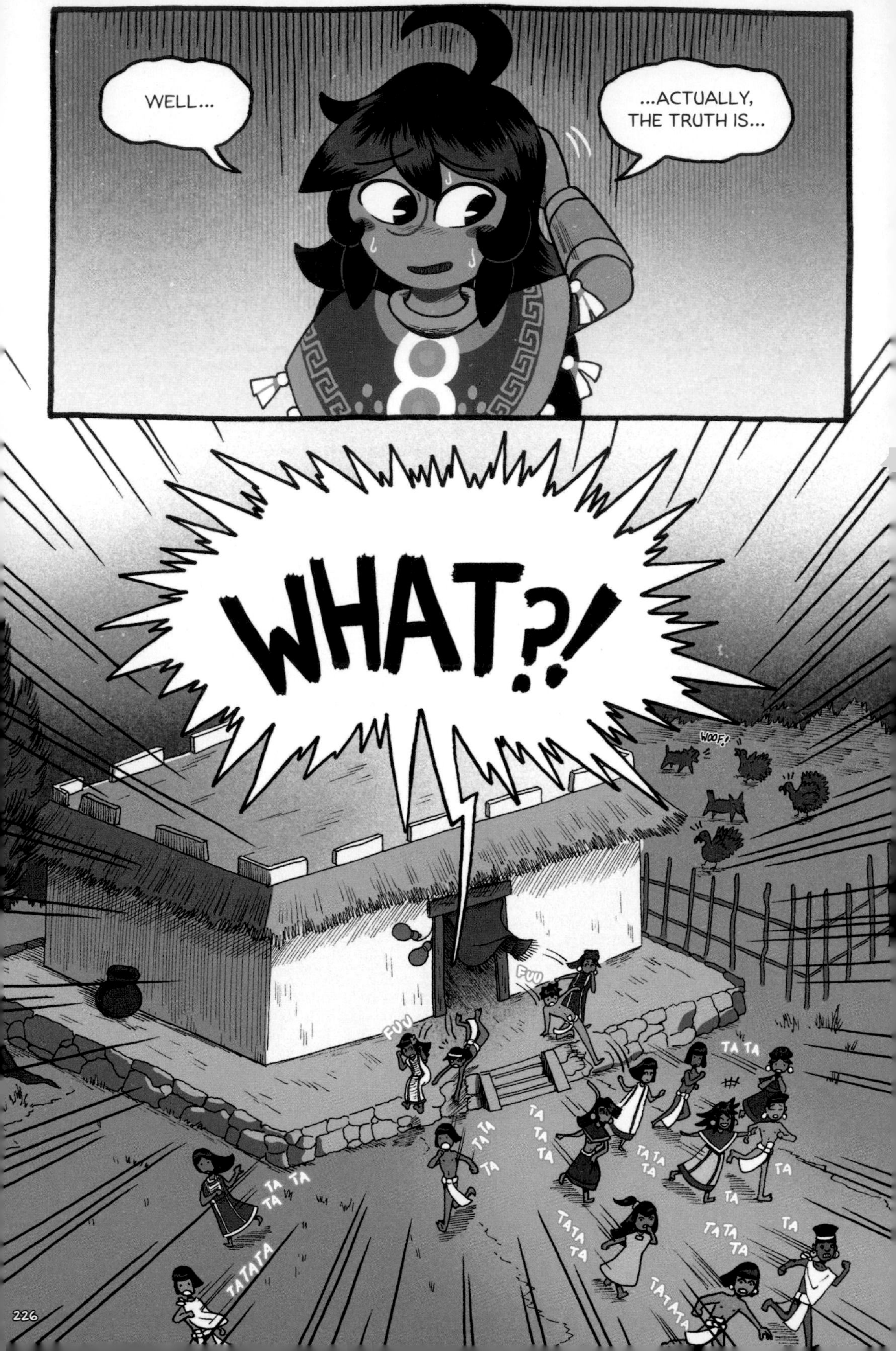
WELL...
...ACTUALLY, THE TRUTH IS...
WHAT?!
WOOF!
FUU
FUU
TA TA
TA TA TA
TA TA TA
TA TA TA
TA TA TA
TA
TA
TA TA TA
TATATA
TA TA TA
TA TA TA
TA
TATATA

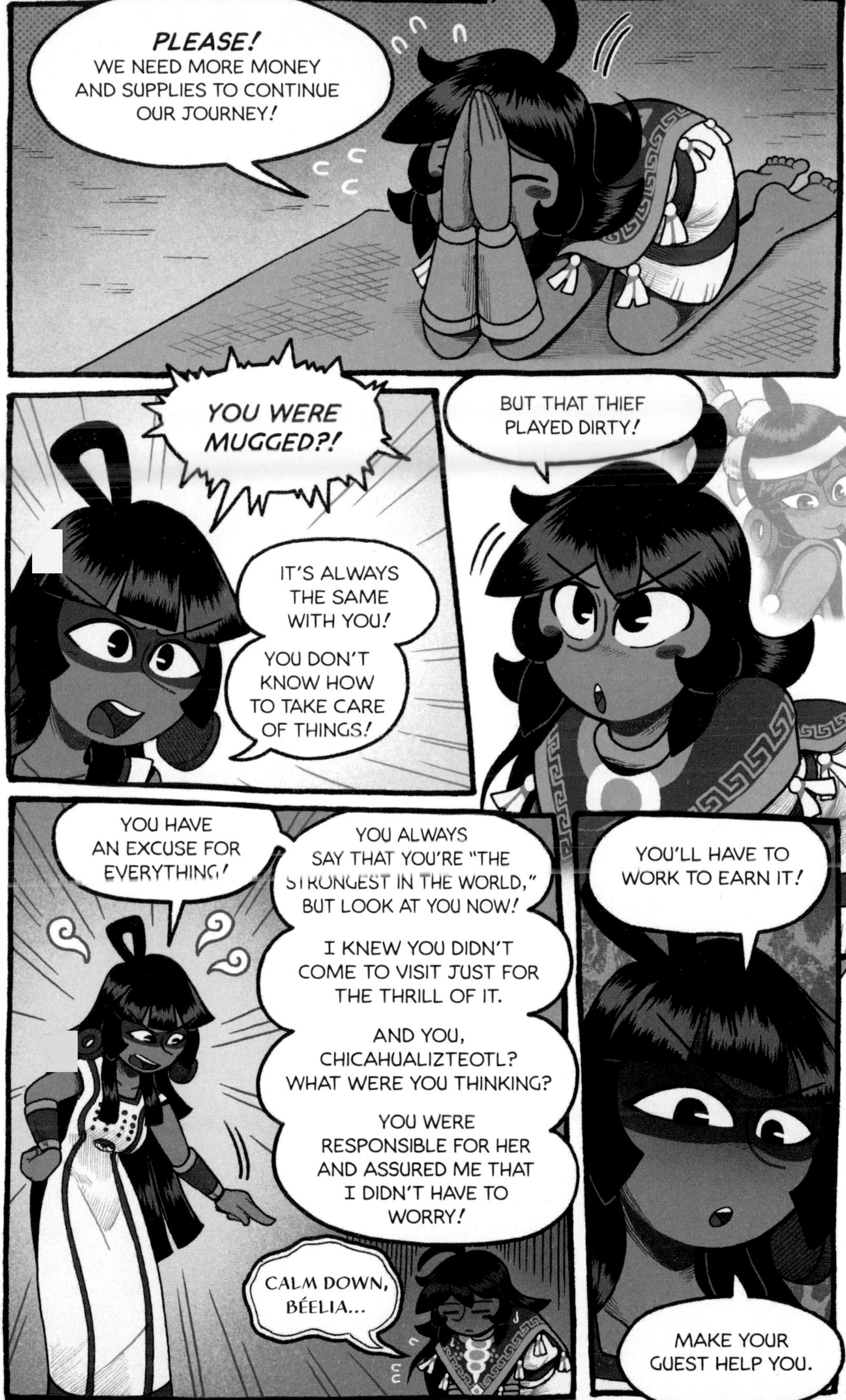
PLEASE! WE NEED MORE MONEY AND SUPPLIES TO CONTINUE OUR JOURNEY!
YOU WERE MUGGED?!
BUT THAT THIEF PLAYED DIRTY!
IT'S ALWAYS THE SAME WITH YOU!
YOU DON'T KNOW HOW TO TAKE CARE OF THINGS!
YOU HAVE AN EXCUSE FOR EVERYTHING!
YOU ALWAYS SAY THAT YOU'RE "THE STRONGEST IN THE WORLD," BUT LOOK AT YOU NOW!
I KNEW YOU DIDN'T COME TO VISIT JUST FOR THE THRILL OF IT.
AND YOU, CHICAHUALIZTEOTL? WHAT WERE YOU THINKING?
YOU WERE RESPONSIBLE FOR HER AND ASSURED ME THAT I DIDN'T HAVE TO WORRY!
CALM DOWN, BÉELIA...
YOU'LL HAVE TO WORK TO EARN IT!
MAKE YOUR GUEST HELP YOU.

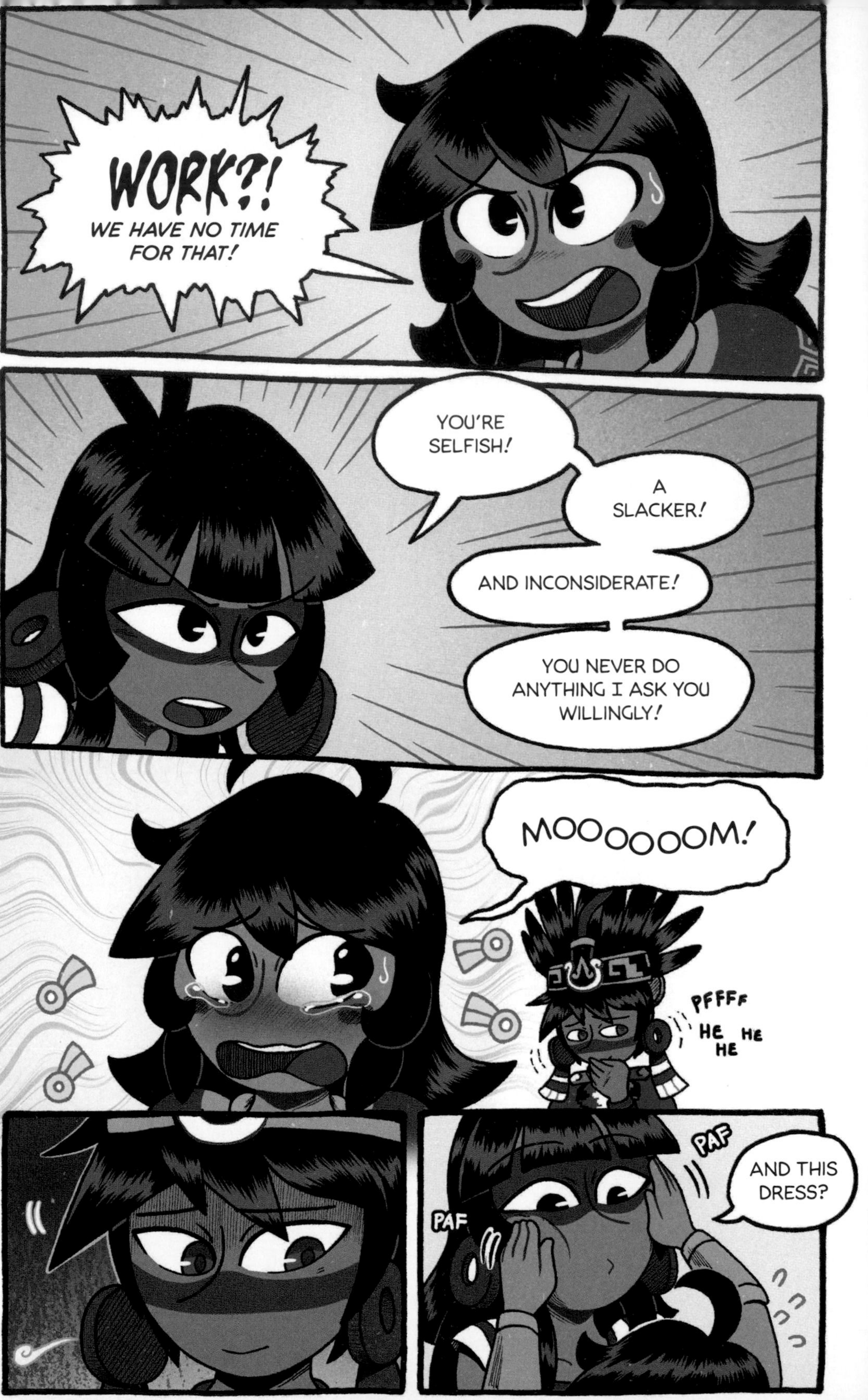
WORK?!
WE HAVE NO TIME FOR THAT!
YOU'RE SELFISH!
A SLACKER!
AND INCONSIDERATE!
YOU NEVER DO ANYTHING I ASK YOU WILLINGLY!
MOOOOOOOM!
PFFFF
HE HE HE
PAF
PAF
AND THIS DRESS?

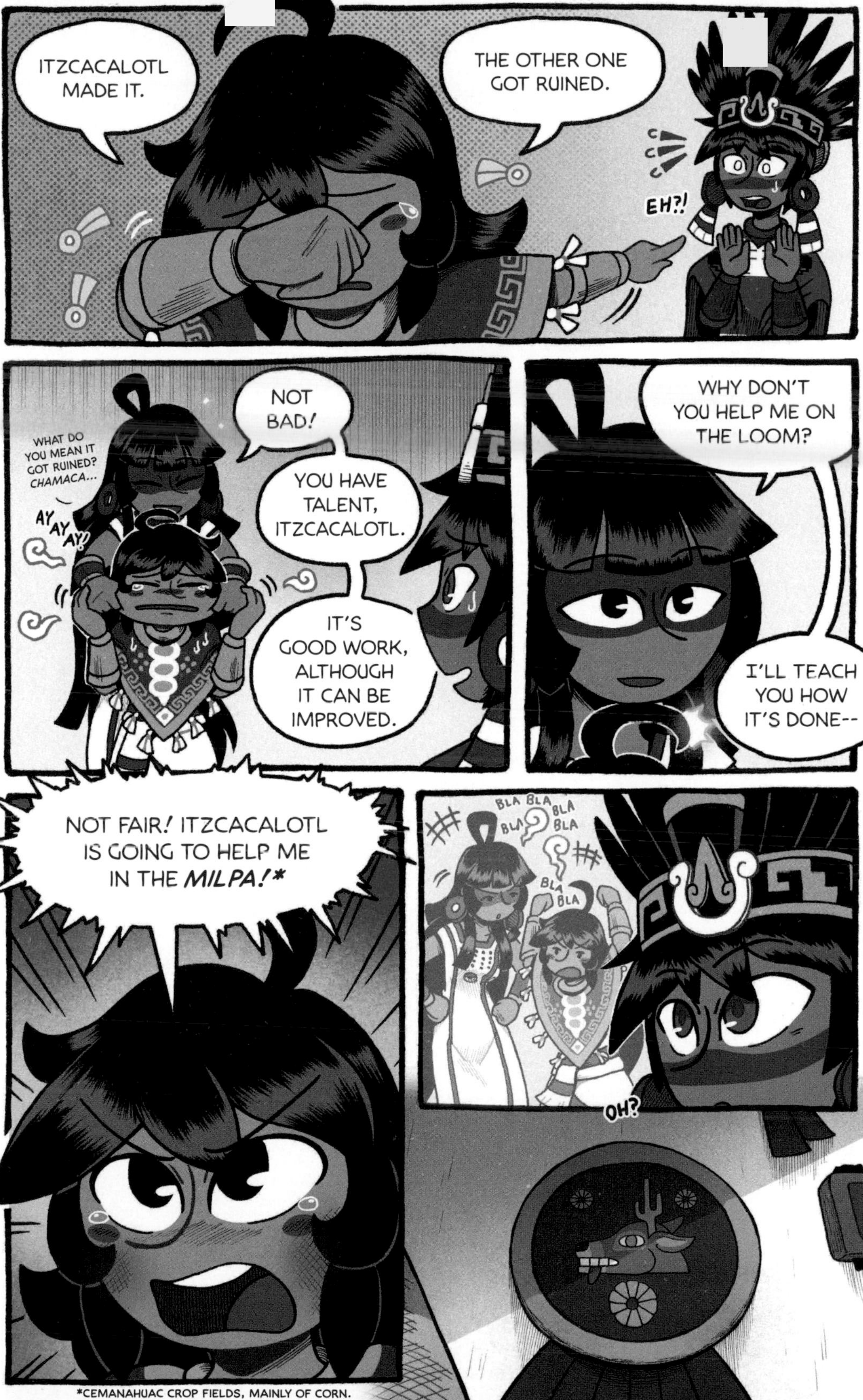
ITZCACALOTL MADE IT.
THE OTHER ONE GOT RUINED.
EH?!
NOT BAD!
YOU HAVE TALENT, ITZCACALOTL.
IT'S GOOD WORK, ALTHOUGH IT CAN BE IMPROVED.
WHAT DO YOU MEAN IT GOT RUINED? CHAMACA...
AY AY AY!
WHY DON'T YOU HELP ME ON THE LOOM?
I'LL TEACH YOU HOW IT'S DONE--
NOT FAIR! ITZCACALOTL IS GOING TO HELP ME IN THE MILPA!*
BLA BLA BLA BLA BLA
BLA BLA
OH?

*CEMANAHUAC CROP FIELDS, MAINLY OF CORN.

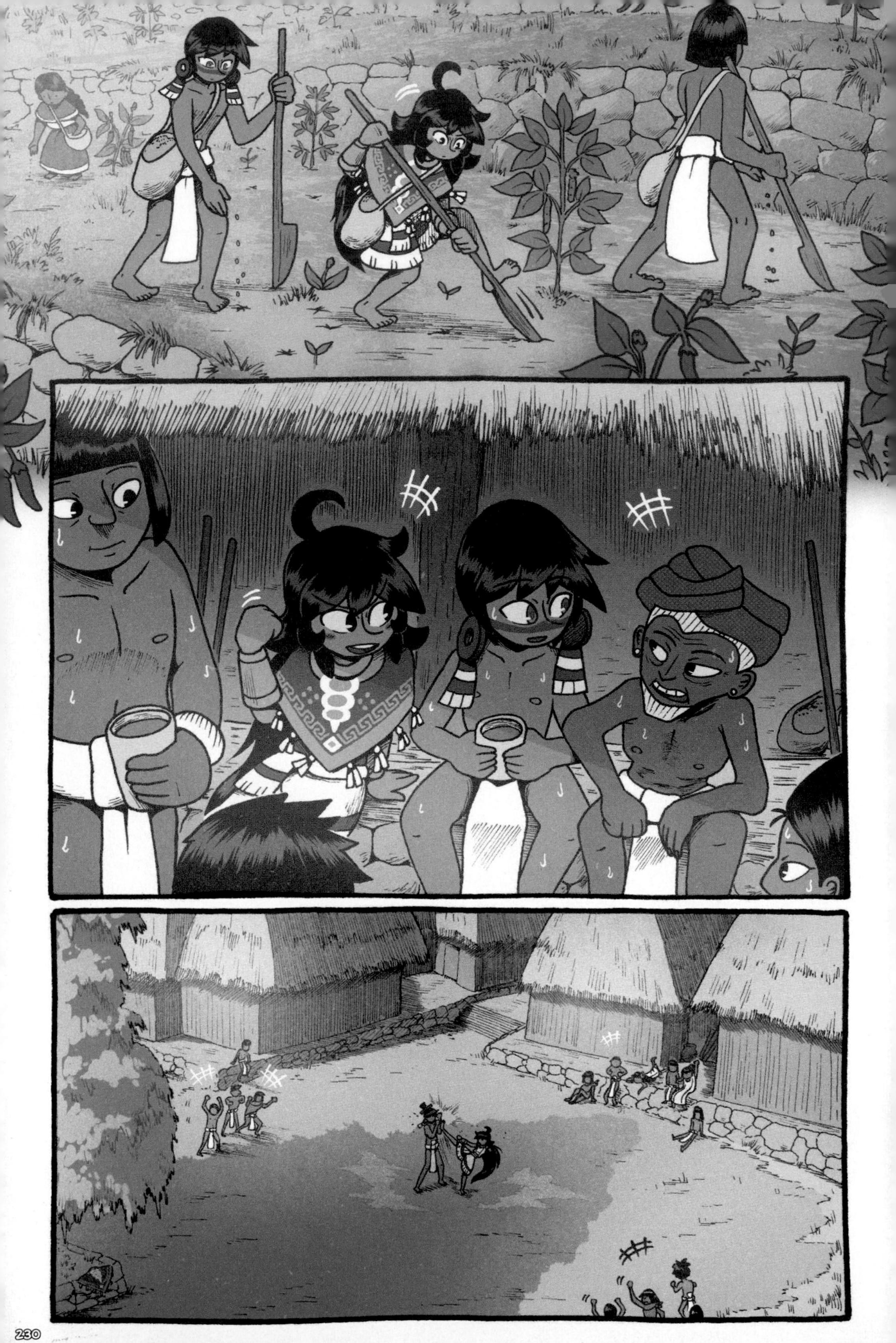

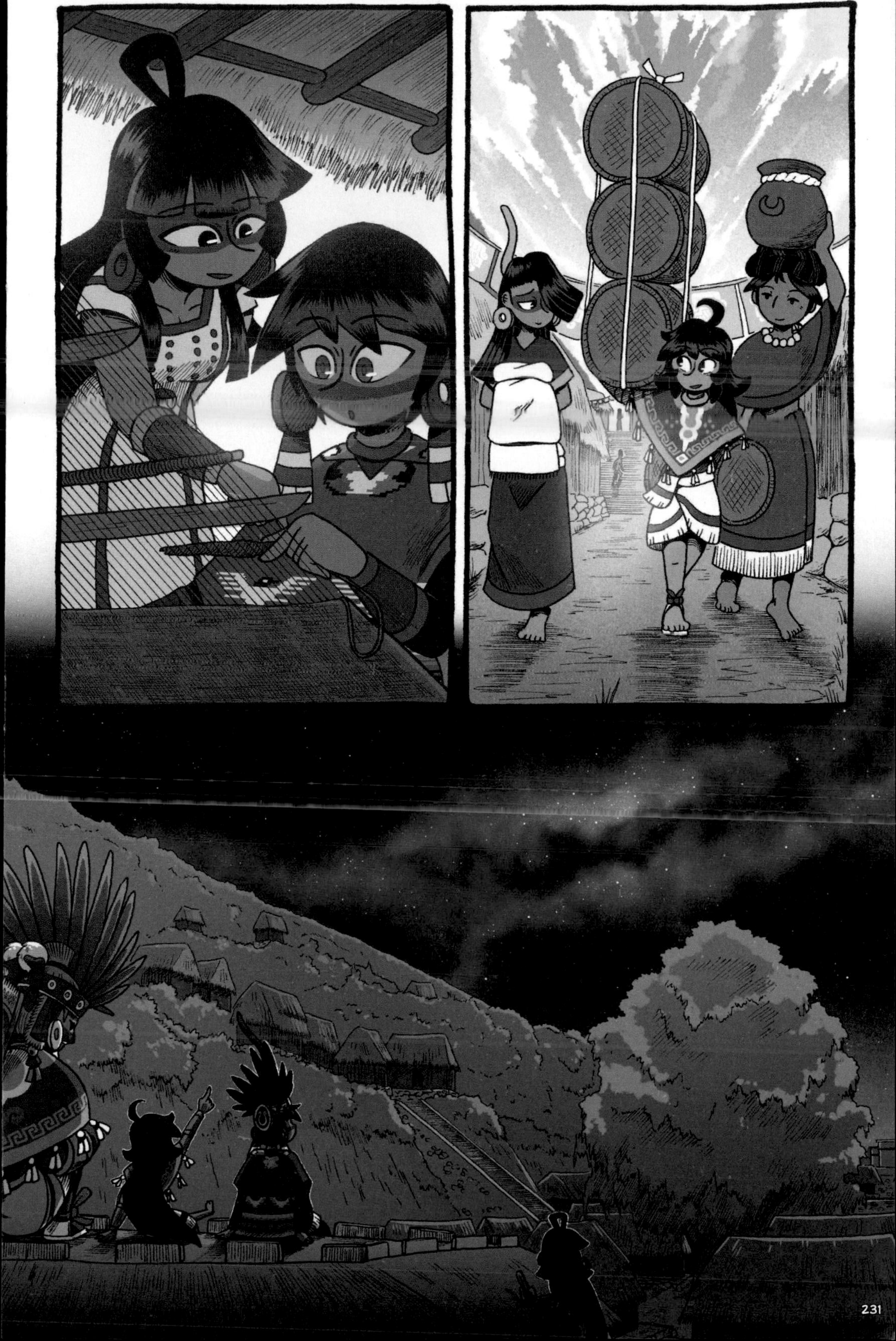

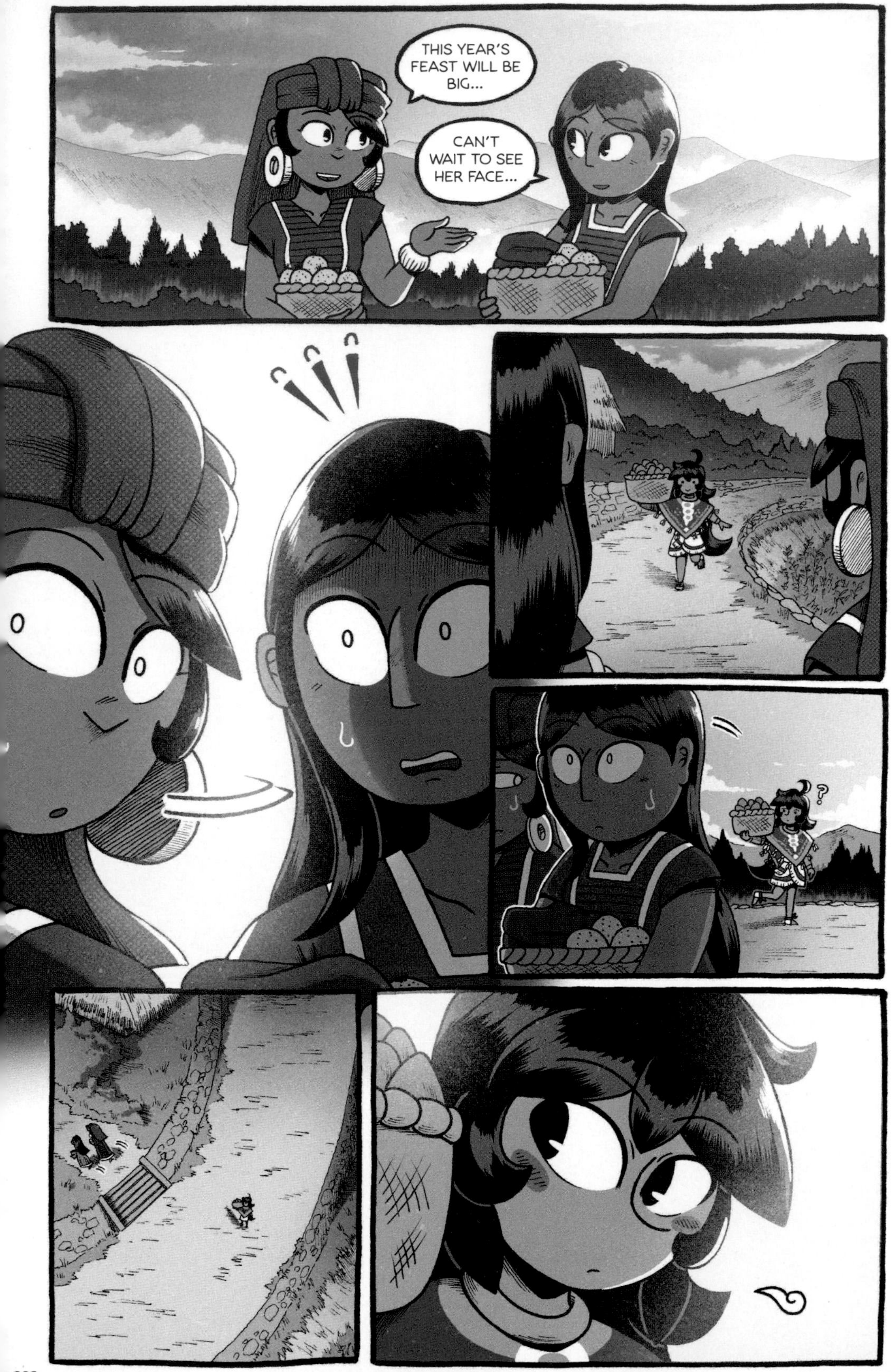

THIS YEAR'S FEAST WILL BE BIG...
CAN'T WAIT TO SEE HER FACE...

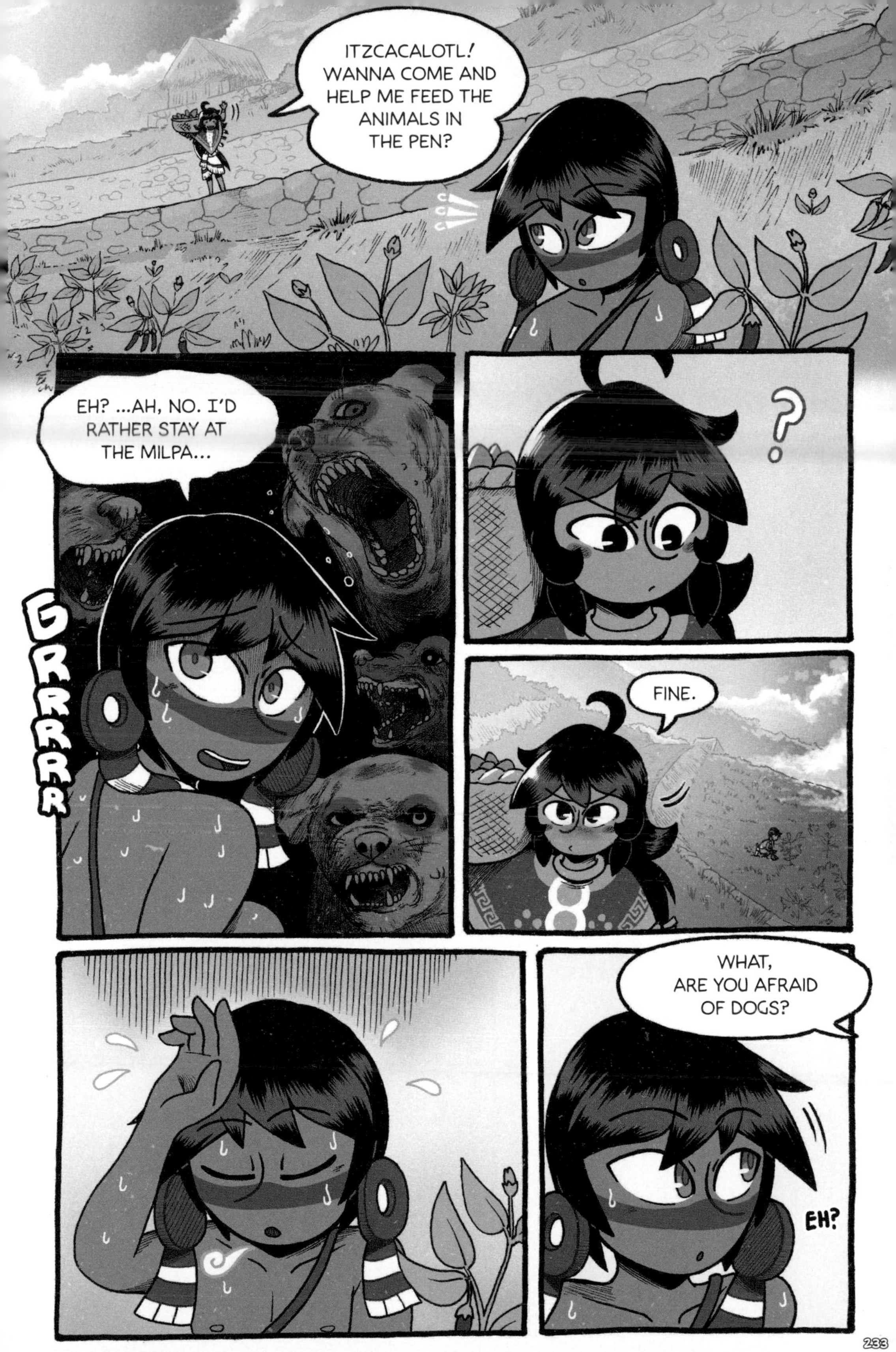
ITZCACALOTL! WANNA COME AND HELP ME FEED THE ANIMALS IN THE PEN?
EH? ...AH, NO. I'D RATHER STAY AT THE MILPA...
GRRRRR
?
FINE.
WHAT, ARE YOU AFRAID OF DOGS?
EH?

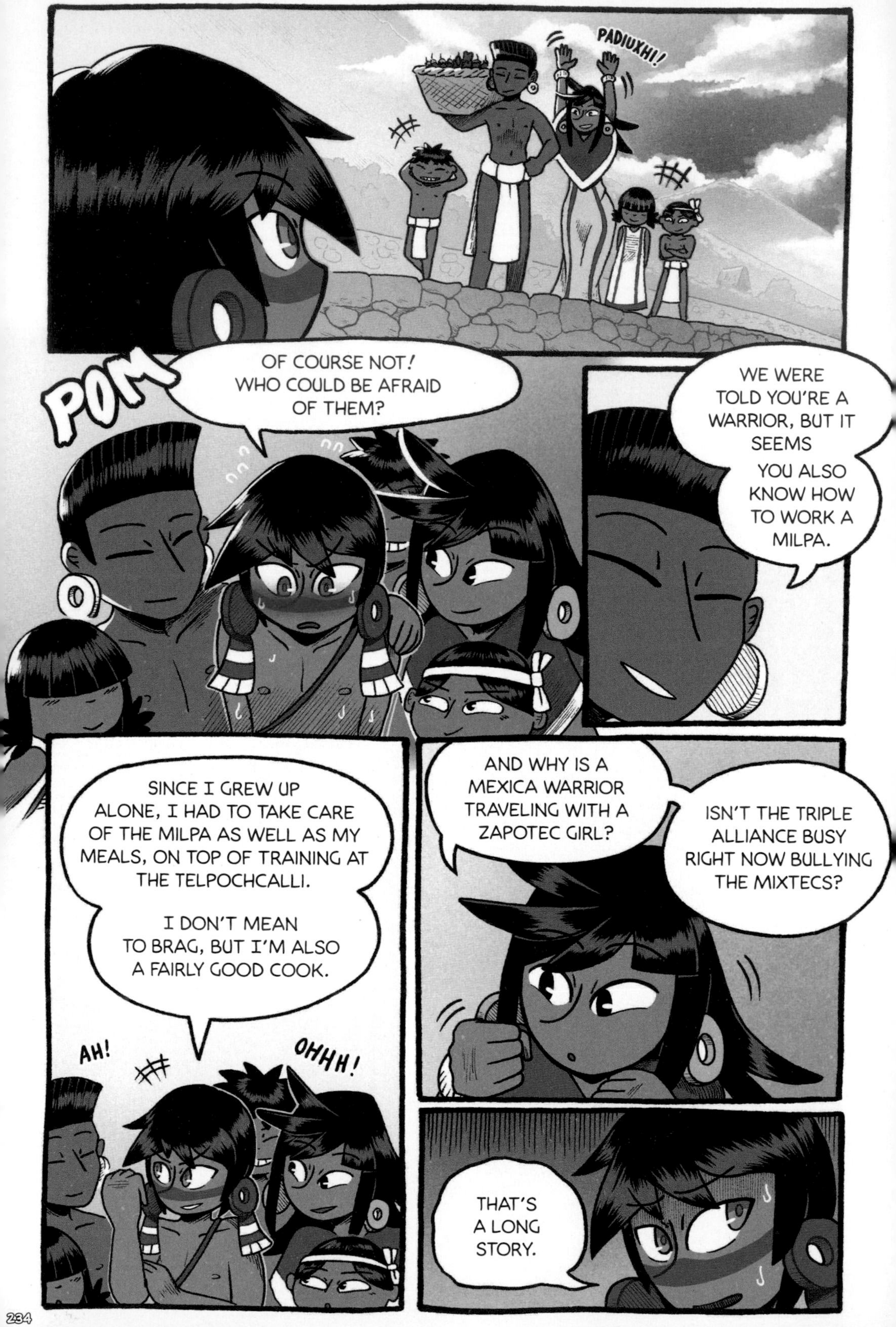
PADIUXHI!
POM
OF COURSE NOT! WHO COULD BE AFRAID OF THEM?
WE WERE TOLD YOU'RE A WARRIOR, BUT IT SEEMS
YOU ALSO KNOW HOW TO WORK A MILPA.
SINCE I GREW UP ALONE, I HAD TO TAKE CARE OF THE MILPA AS WELL AS MY MEALS, ON TOP OF TRAINING AT THE TELPOCHCALLI.
I DON'T MEAN TO BRAG, BUT I'M ALSO A FAIRLY GOOD COOK.
AH!
OHHH!
AND WHY IS A MEXICA WARRIOR TRAVELING WITH A ZAPOTEC GIRL?
ISN'T THE TRIPLE ALLIANCE BUSY RIGHT NOW BULLYING THE MIXTECS?
THAT'S A LONG STORY.

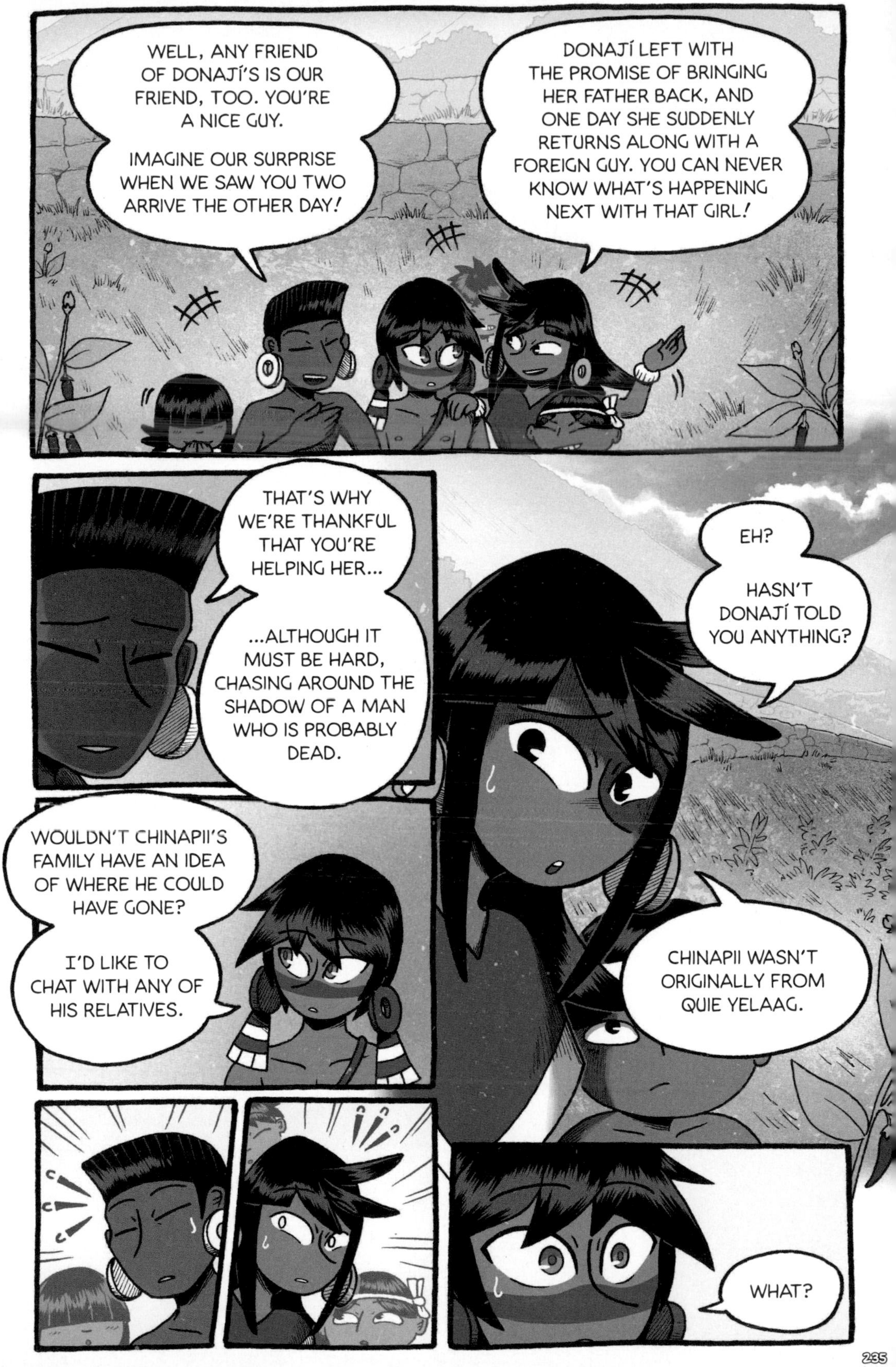

WELL, ANY FRIEND OF DONAJÍ'S IS OUR FRIEND, TOO. YOU'RE A NICE GUY.
IMAGINE OUR SURPRISE WHEN WE SAW YOU TWO ARRIVE THE OTHER DAY!
DONAJÍ LEFT WITH THE PROMISE OF BRINGING HER FATHER BACK, AND ONE DAY SHE SUDDENLY RETURNS ALONG WITH A FOREIGN GUY. YOU CAN NEVER KNOW WHAT'S HAPPENING NEXT WITH THAT GIRL!
THAT'S WHY WE'RE THANKFUL THAT YOU'RE HELPING HER...
...ALTHOUGH IT MUST BE HARD, CHASING AROUND THE SHADOW OF A MAN WHO IS PROBABLY DEAD.
EH?
HASN'T DONAJÍ TOLD YOU ANYTHING?
WOULDN'T CHINAPII'S FAMILY HAVE AN IDEA OF WHERE HE COULD HAVE GONE?
I'D LIKE TO CHAT WITH ANY OF HIS RELATIVES.
CHINAPII WASN'T ORIGINALLY FROM QUIE YELAAG.
WHAT?

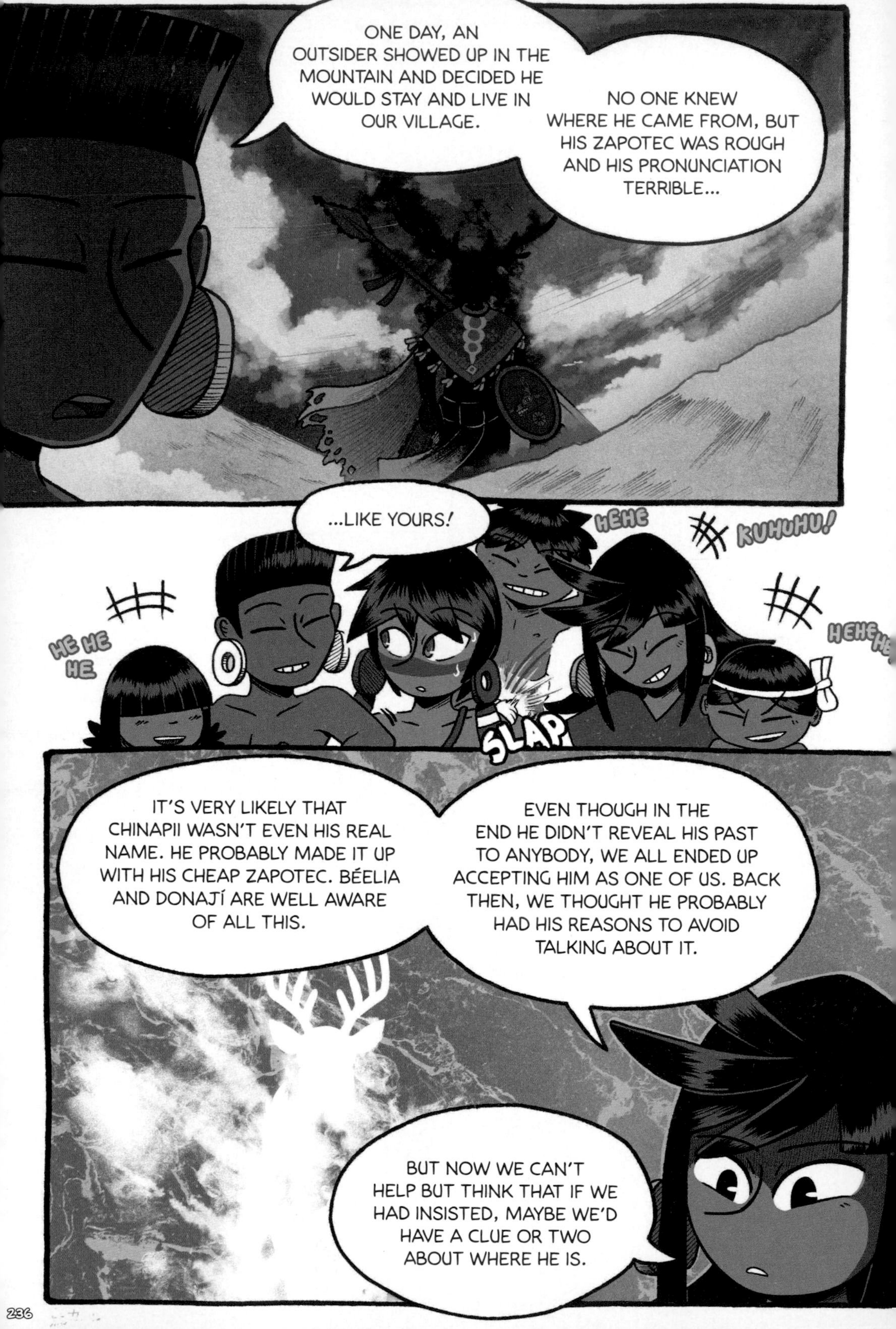
ONE DAY, AN OUTSIDER SHOWED UP IN THE MOUNTAIN AND DECIDED HE WOULD STAY AND LIVE IN OUR VILLAGE.
NO ONE KNEW WHERE HE CAME FROM, BUT HIS ZAPOTEC WAS ROUGH AND HIS PRONUNCIATION TERRIBLE...
...LIKE YOURS!
HEHE
KUHUHU!
HE HE HE
SLAP
IT'S VERY LIKELY THAT CHINAPII WASN'T EVEN HIS REAL NAME. HE PROBABLY MADE IT UP WITH HIS CHEAP ZAPOTEC. BÉELIA AND DONAJÍ ARE WELL AWARE OF ALL THIS.
EVEN THOUGH IN THE END HE DIDN'T REVEAL HIS PAST TO ANYBODY, WE ALL ENDED UP ACCEPTING HIM AS ONE OF US. BACK THEN, WE THOUGHT HE PROBABLY HAD HIS REASONS TO AVOID TALKING ABOUT IT.
BUT NOW WE CAN'T HELP BUT THINK THAT IF WE HAD INSISTED, MAYBE WE'D HAVE A CLUE OR TWO ABOUT WHERE HE IS.

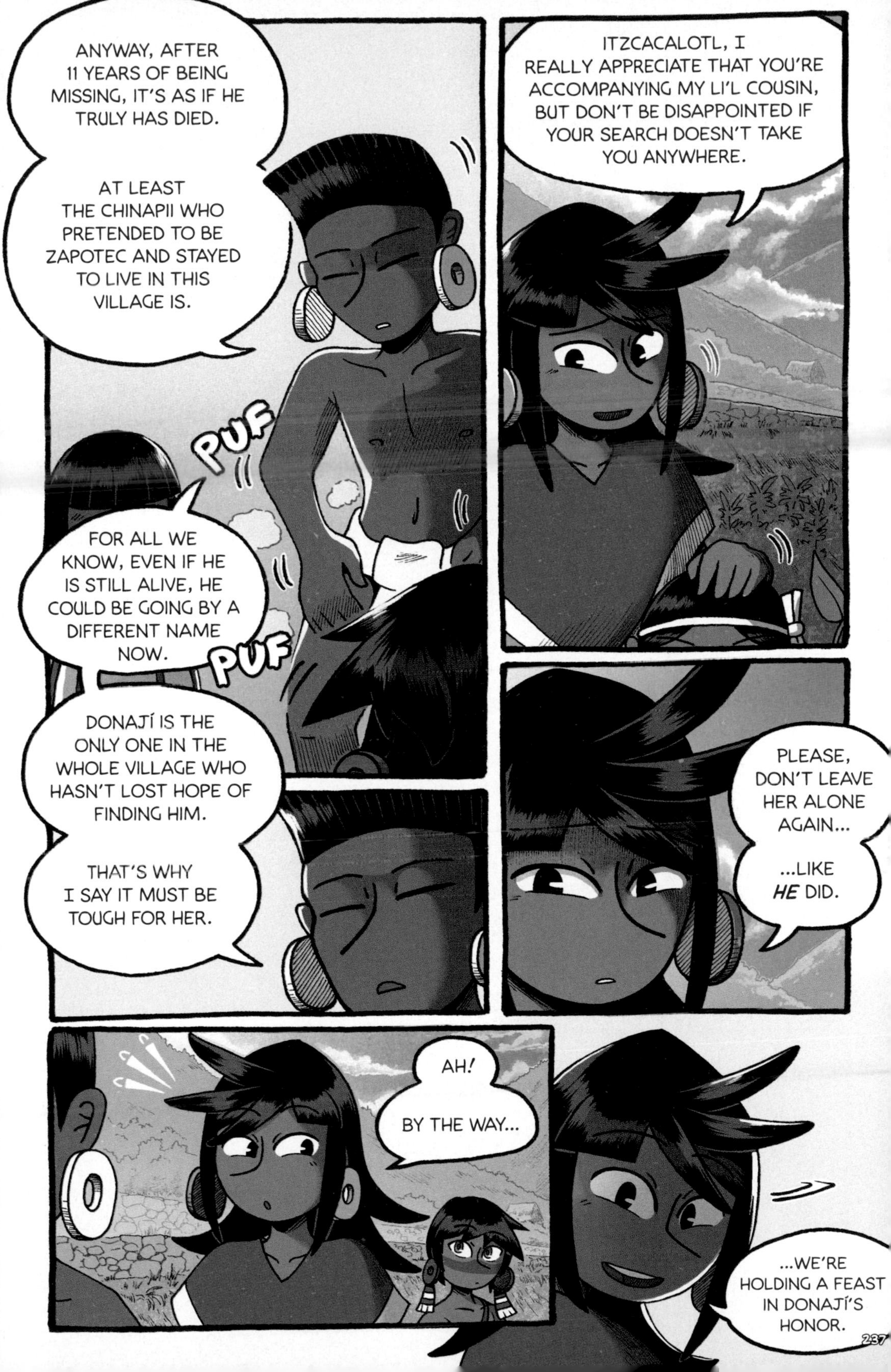
ANYWAY, AFTER 11 YEARS OF BEING MISSING, IT'S AS IF HE TRULY HAS DIED.
AT LEAST THE CHINAPII WHO PRETENDED TO BE ZAPOTEC AND STAYED TO LIVE IN THIS VILLAGE IS.
PUF
FOR ALL WE KNOW, EVEN IF HE IS STILL ALIVE, HE COULD BE GOING BY A DIFFERENT NAME NOW.
PUF
ITZCACALOTL, I REALLY APPRECIATE THAT YOU'RE ACCOMPANYING MY LI'L COUSIN, BUT DON'T BE DISAPPOINTED IF YOUR SEARCH DOESN'T TAKE YOU ANYWHERE.
DONAJÍ IS THE ONLY ONE IN THE WHOLE VILLAGE WHO HASN'T LOST HOPE OF FINDING HIM.
THAT'S WHY I SAY IT MUST BE TOUGH FOR HER.
PLEASE, DON'T LEAVE HER ALONE AGAIN...
...LIKE *HE* DID.
AH!
BY THE WAY...
...WE'RE HOLDING A FEAST IN DONAJÍ'S HONOR.

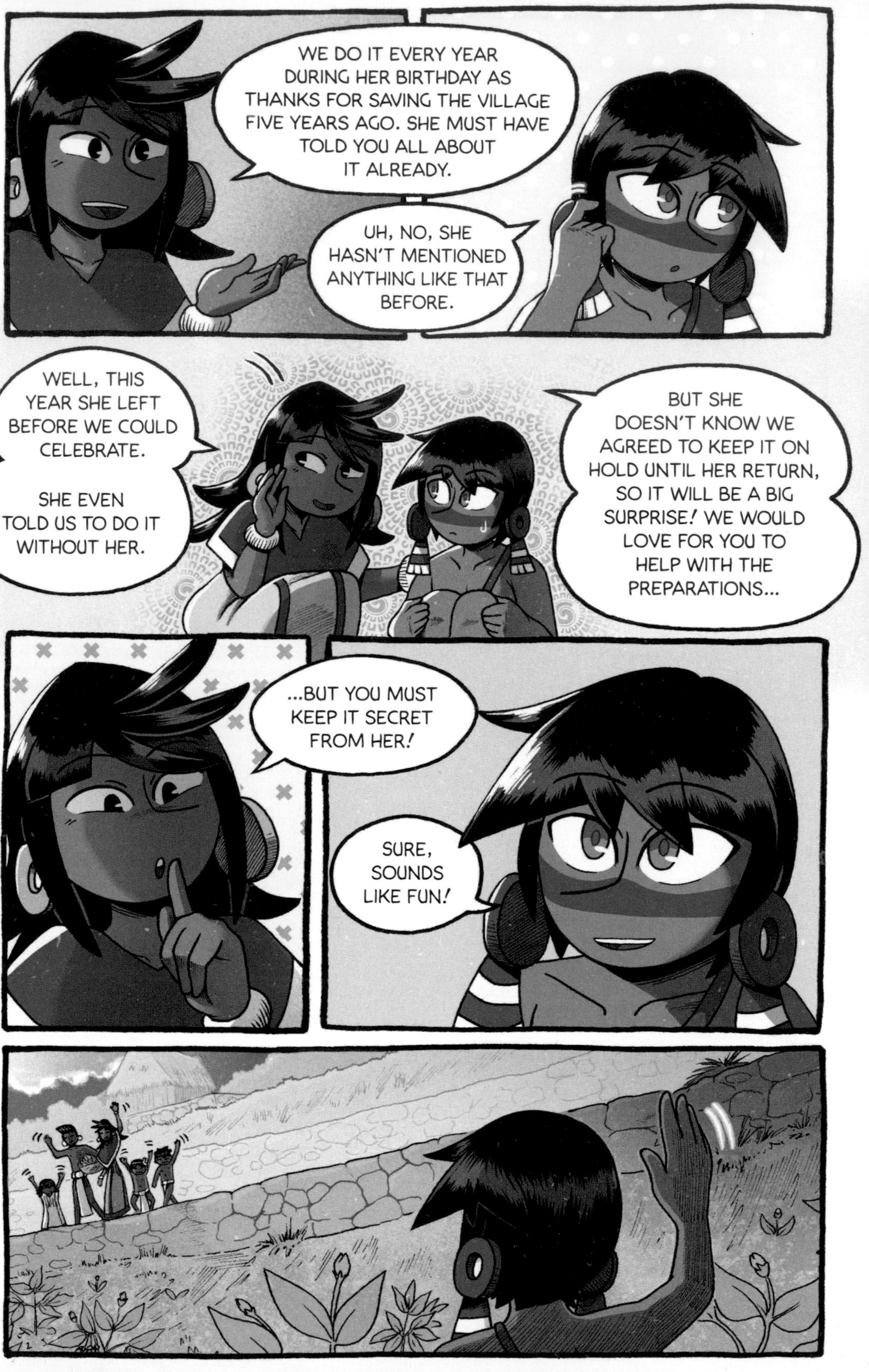
WE DO IT EVERY YEAR DURING HER BIRTHDAY AS THANKS FOR SAVING THE VILLAGE FIVE YEARS AGO. SHE MUST HAVE TOLD YOU ALL ABOUT IT ALREADY.
UH, NO, SHE HASN'T MENTIONED ANYTHING LIKE THAT BEFORE.
WELL, THIS YEAR SHE LEFT BEFORE WE COULD CELEBRATE.
SHE EVEN TOLD US TO DO IT WITHOUT HER.
BUT SHE DOESN'T KNOW WE AGREED TO KEEP IT ON HOLD UNTIL HER RETURN, SO IT WILL BE A BIG SURPRISE! WE WOULD LOVE FOR YOU TO HELP WITH THE PREPARATIONS...
...BUT YOU MUST KEEP IT SECRET FROM HER!
SURE, SOUNDS LIKE FUN!

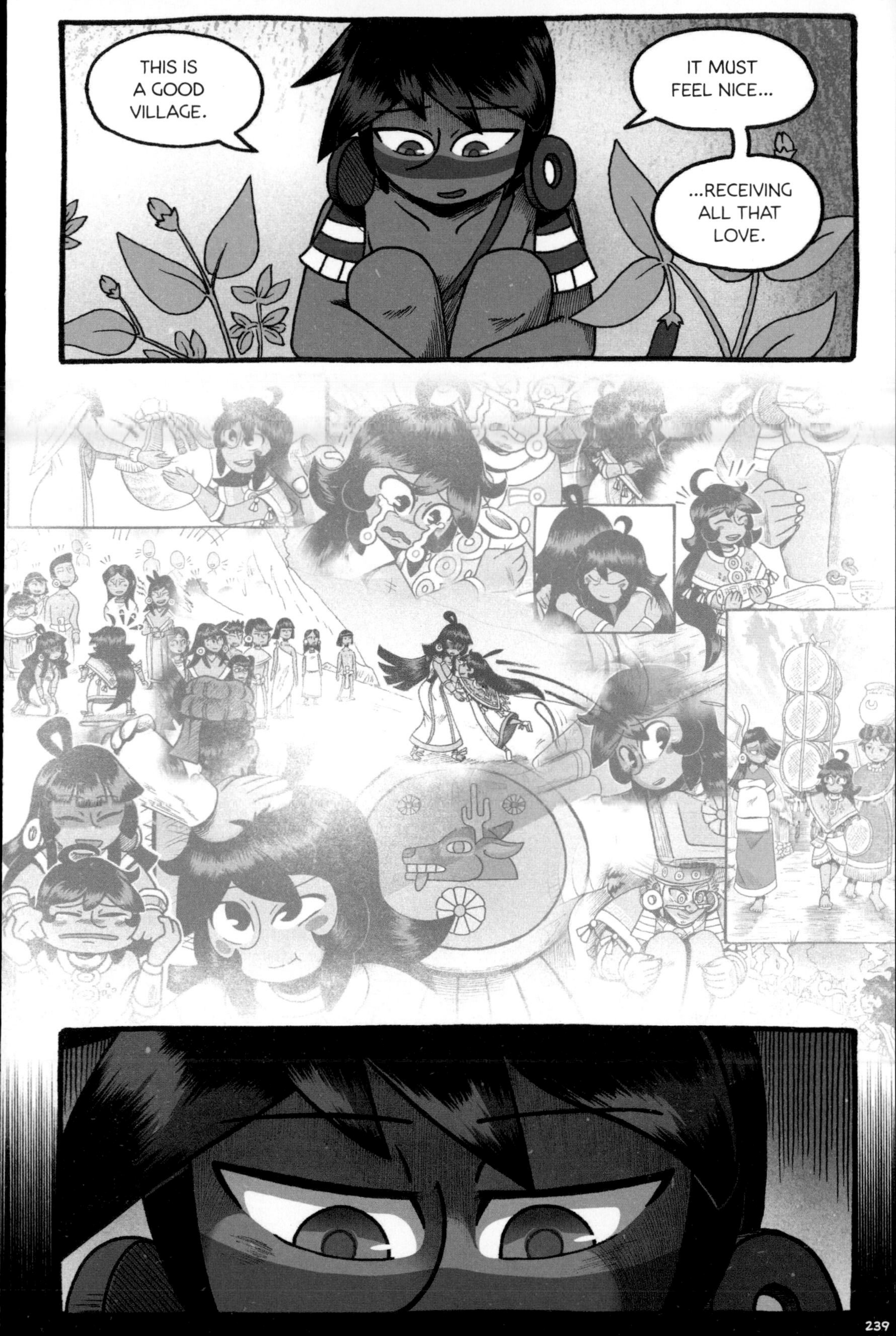
THIS IS A GOOD VILLAGE.
IT MUST FEEL NICE...
...RECEIVING ALL THAT LOVE.

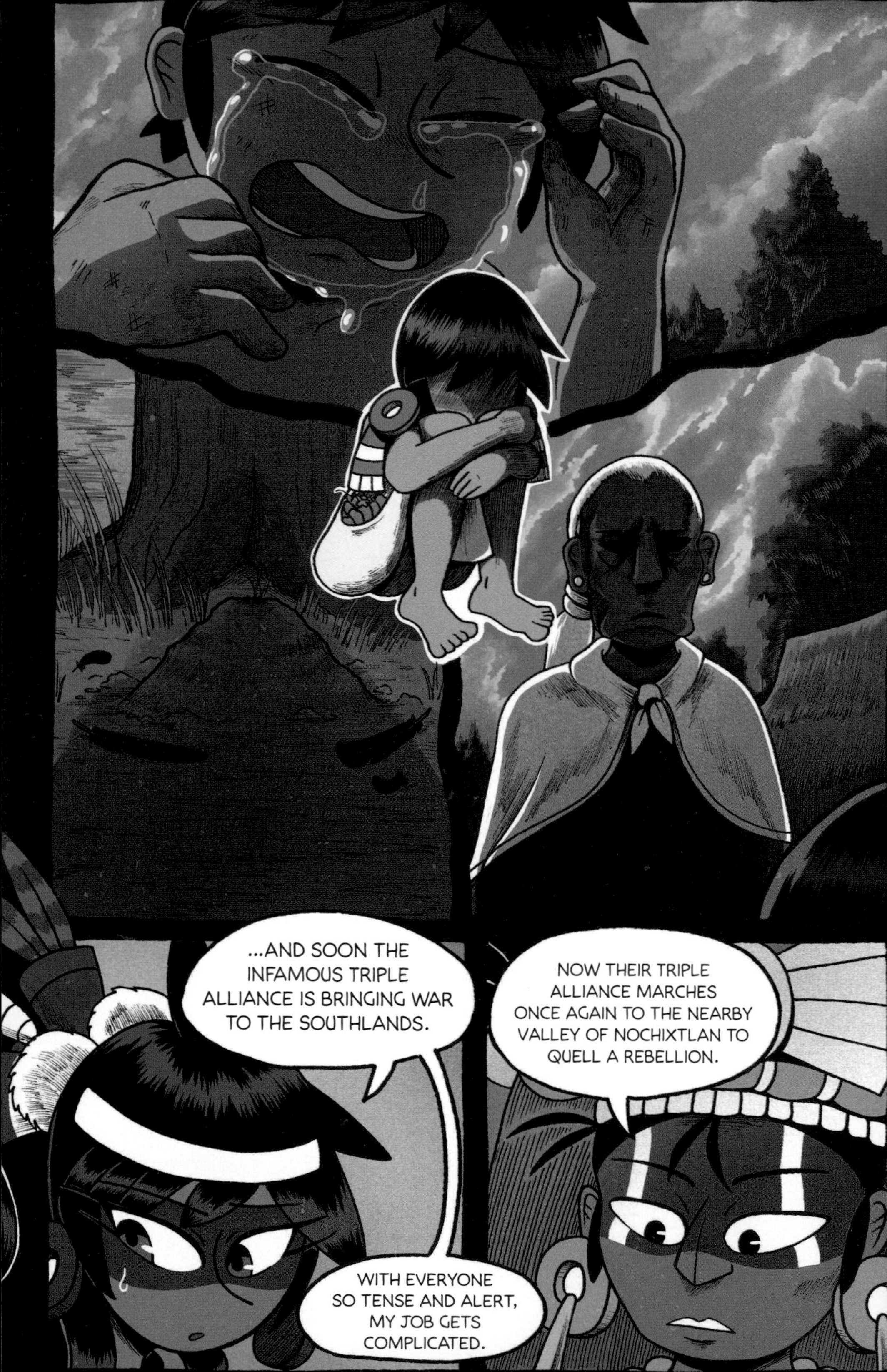
...AND SOON THE INFAMOUS TRIPLE ALLIANCE IS BRINGING WAR TO THE SOUTHLANDS.
NOW THEIR TRIPLE ALLIANCE MARCHES ONCE AGAIN TO THE NEARBY VALLEY OF NOCHIXTLAN TO QUELL A REBELLION.
WITH EVERYONE SO TENSE AND ALERT, MY JOB GETS COMPLICATED.

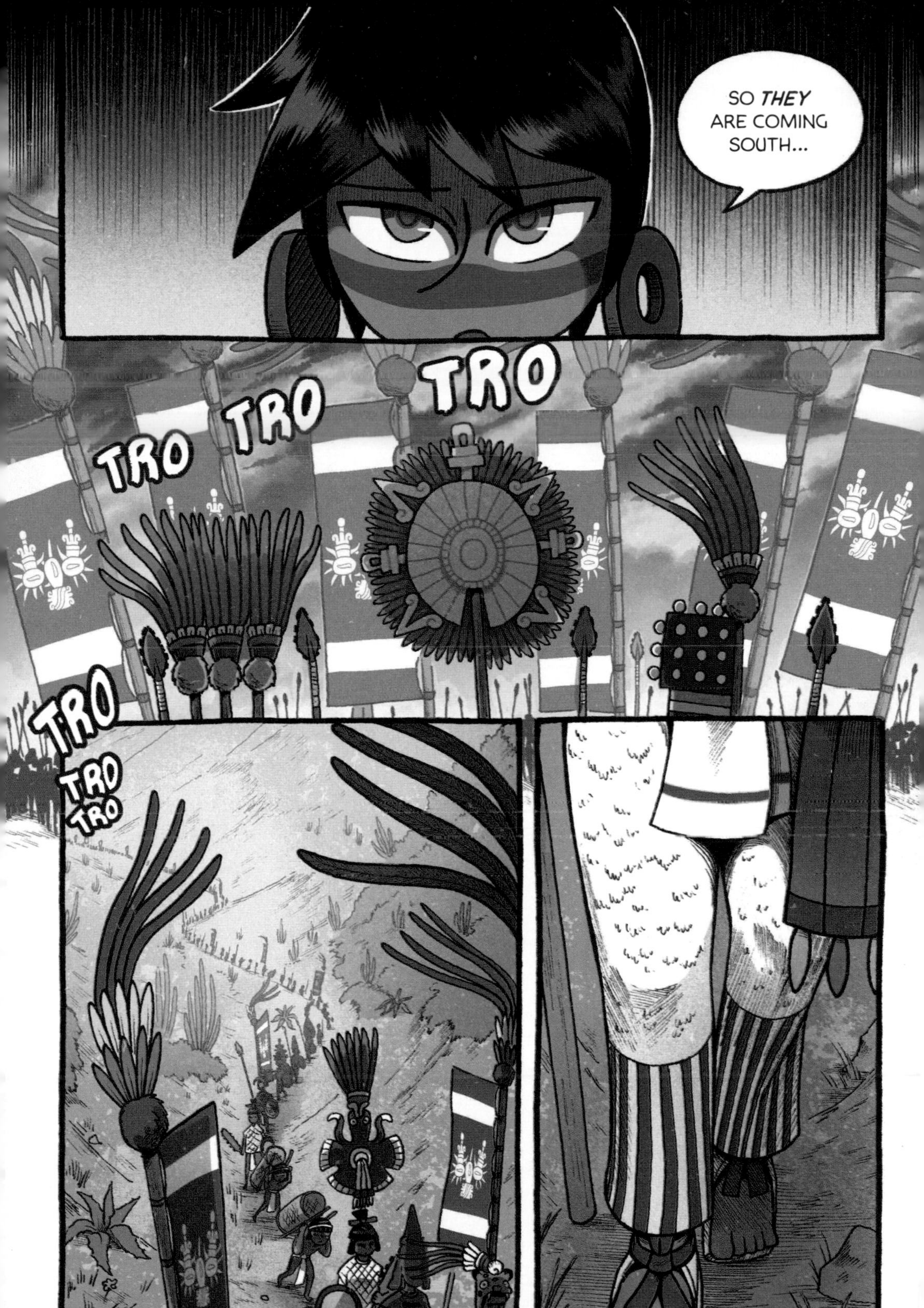
SO *THEY* ARE COMING SOUTH...
TRO TRO TRO
TRO
TRO
TRO

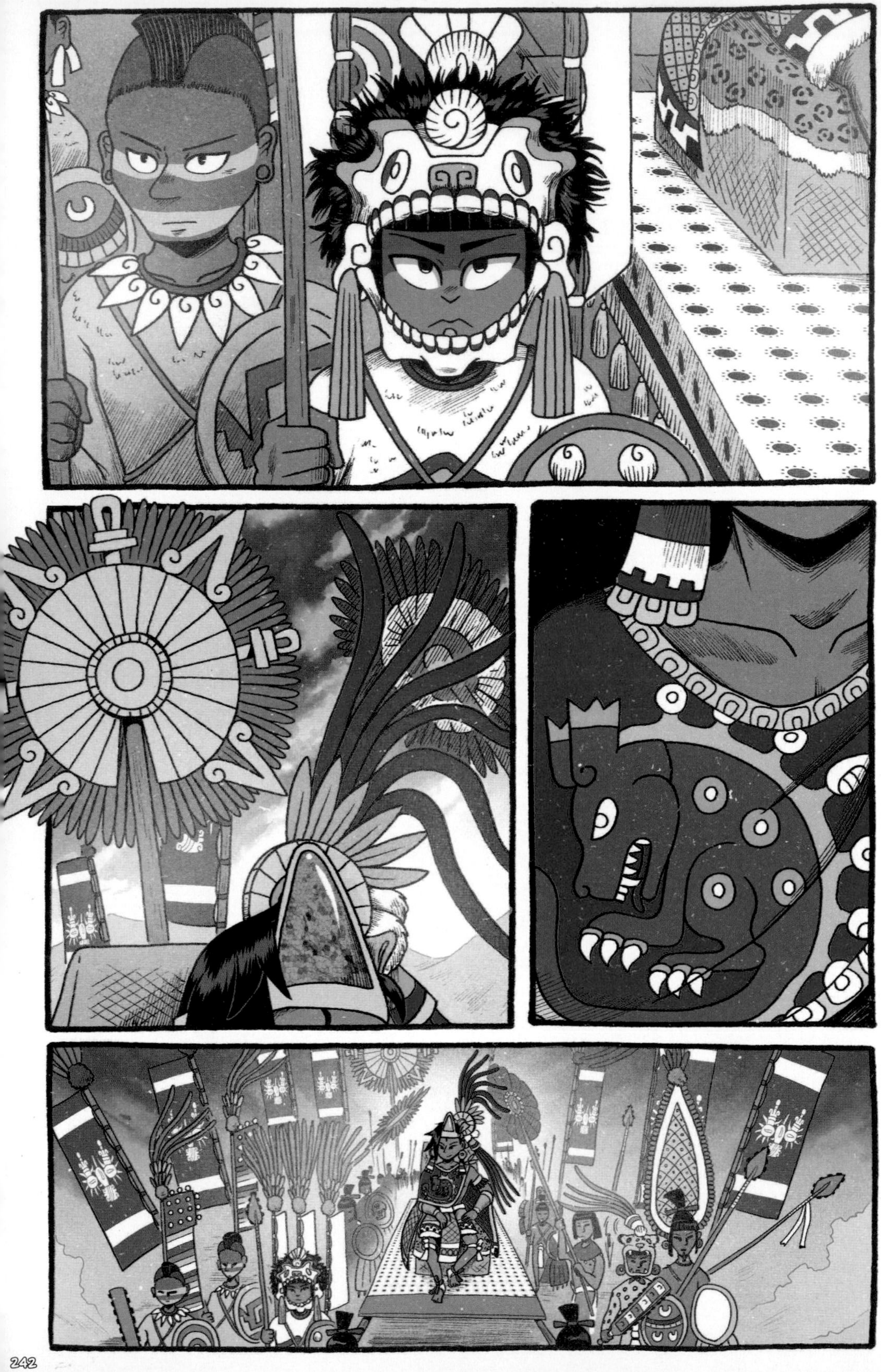

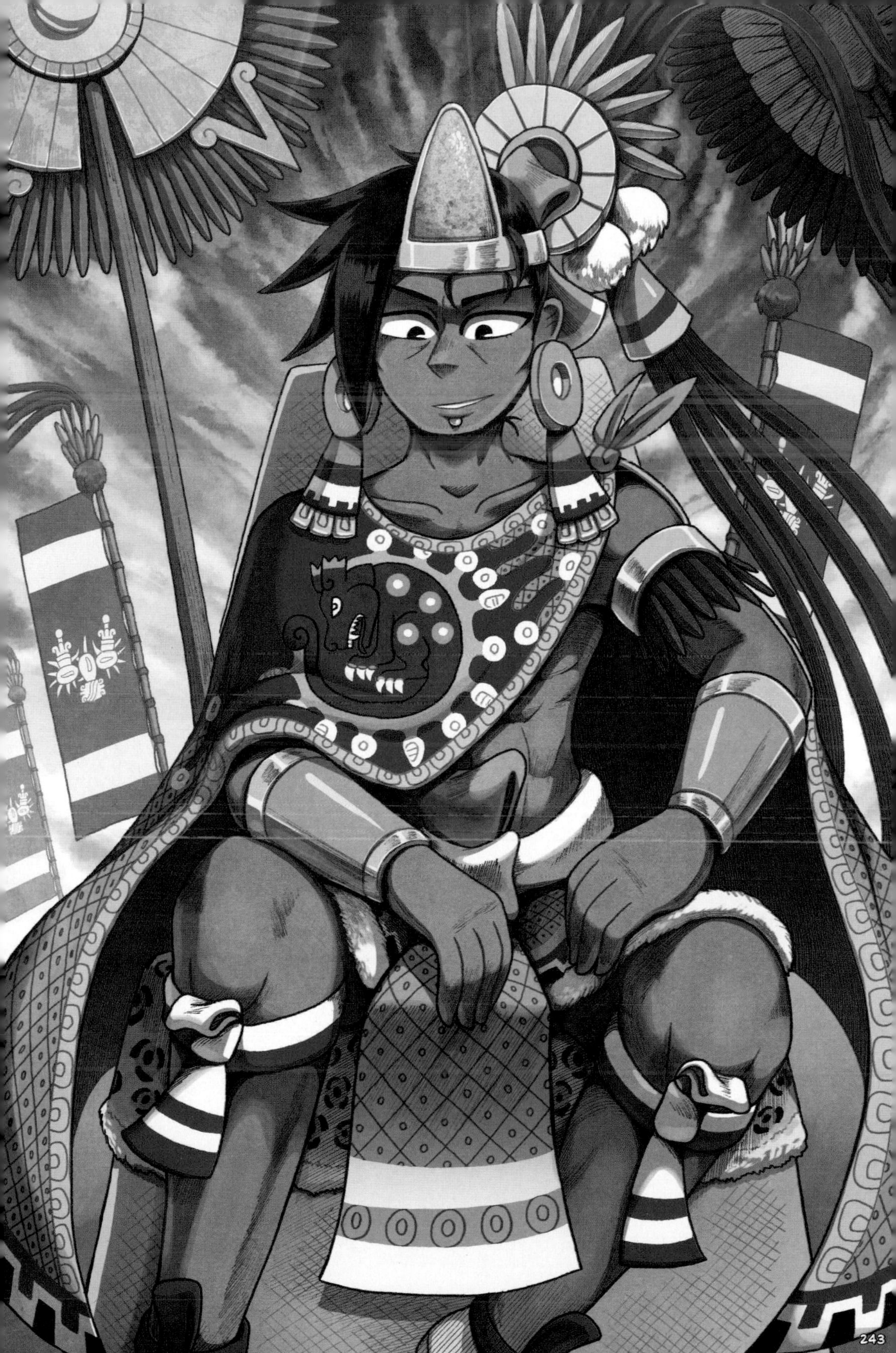

CHAPTER 5

A FIRE AMONG CLOUDS

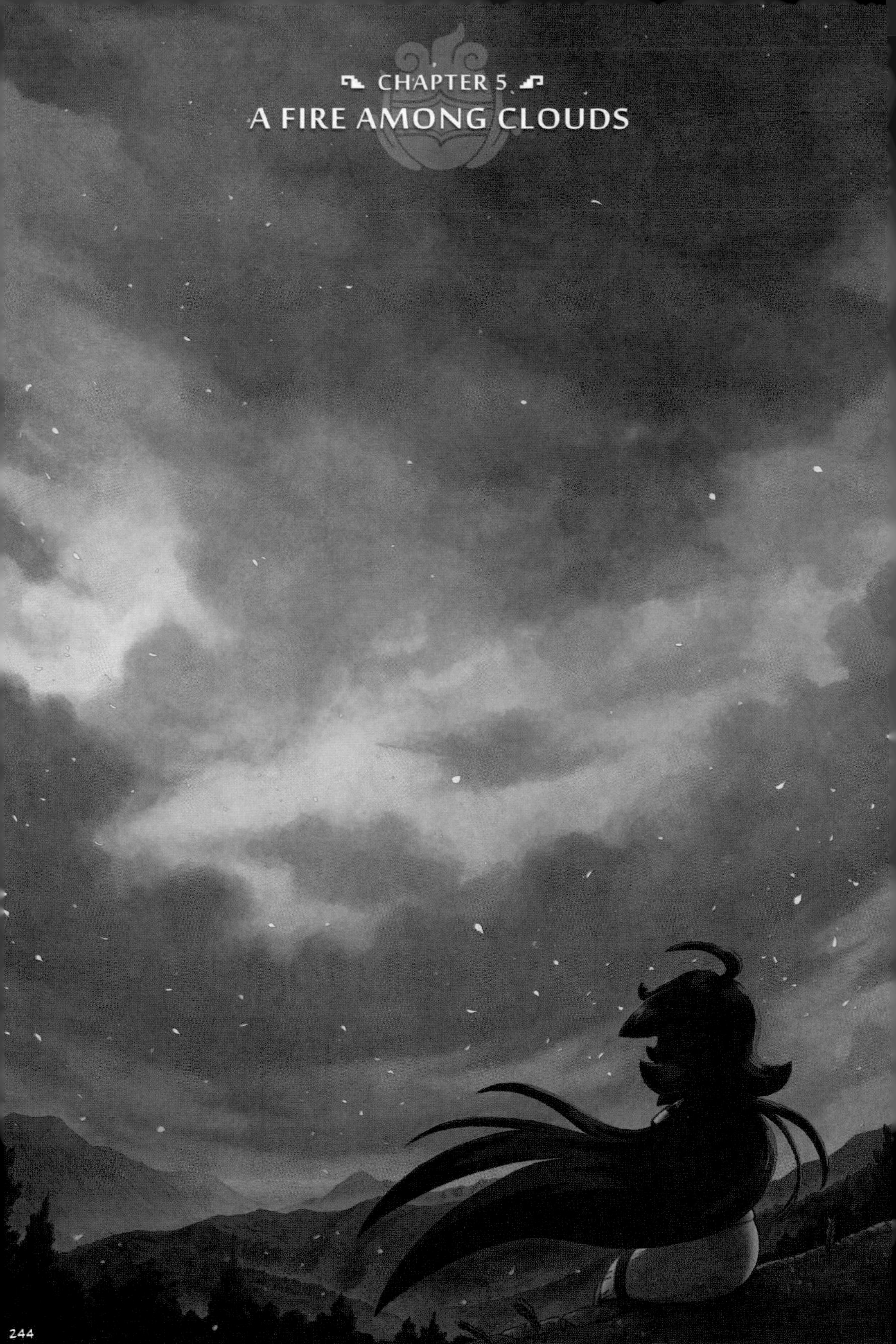

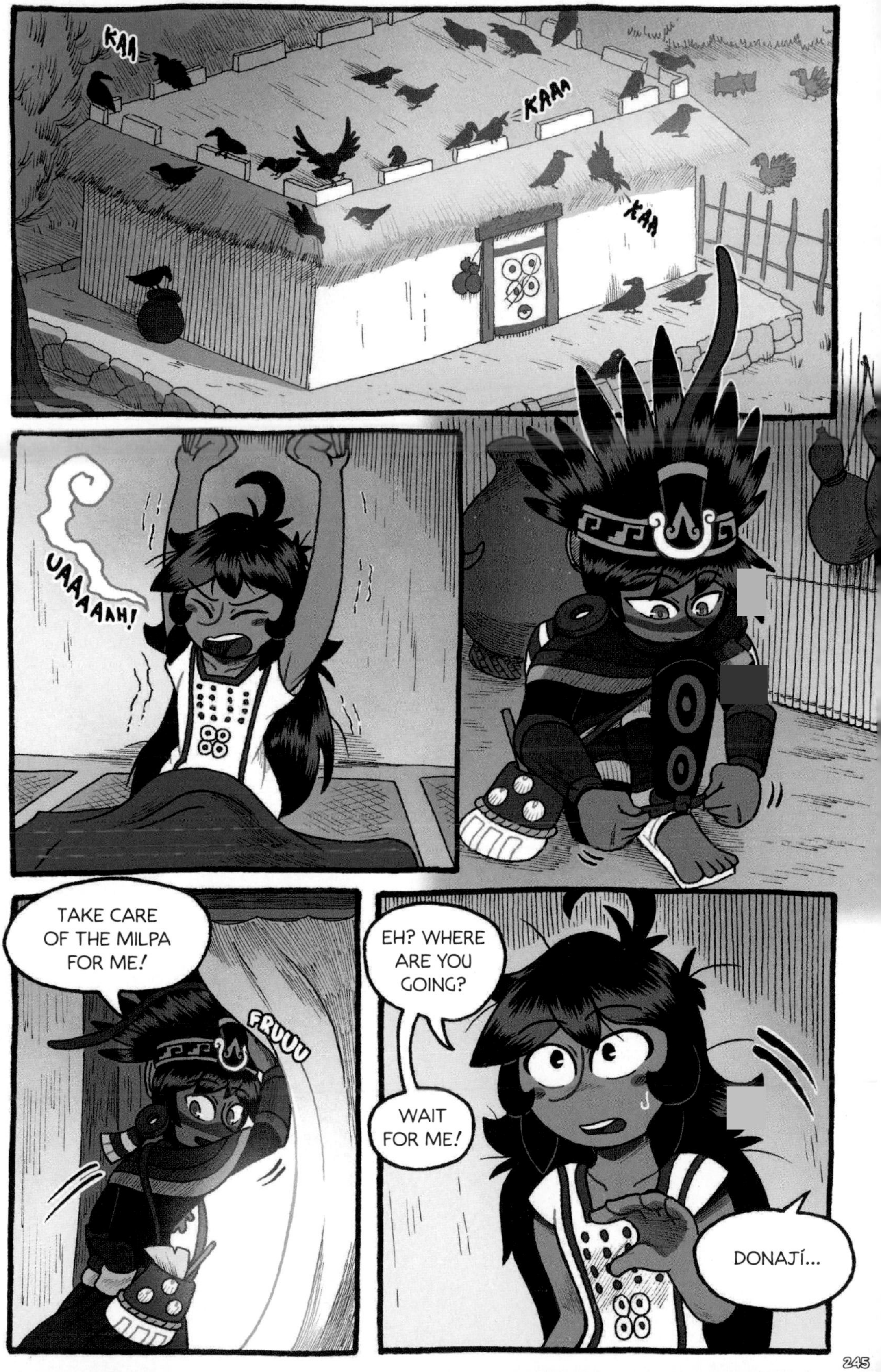
KAA
KAAA
KAA
UAAAAAAH!
TAKE CARE OF THE MILPA FOR ME!
FRUUU
EH? WHERE ARE YOU GOING?
WAIT FOR ME!
DONAJÍ...

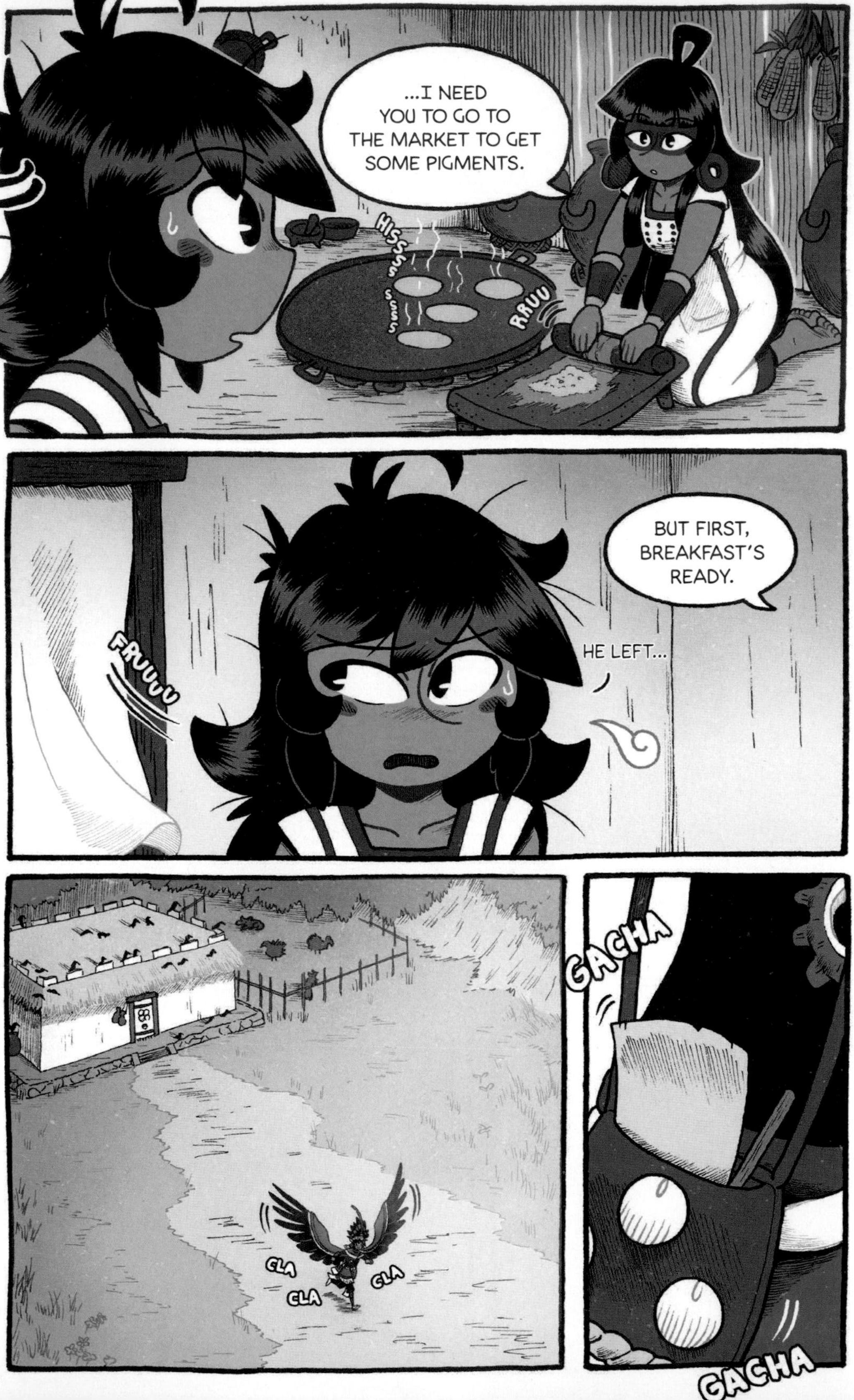
...I NEED YOU TO GO TO THE MARKET TO GET SOME PIGMENTS.
HISSS
SSSS
RRUU
BUT FIRST, BREAKFAST'S READY.
FRUUUU
HE LEFT...
CLA
CLA
CLA
GACHA
GACHA

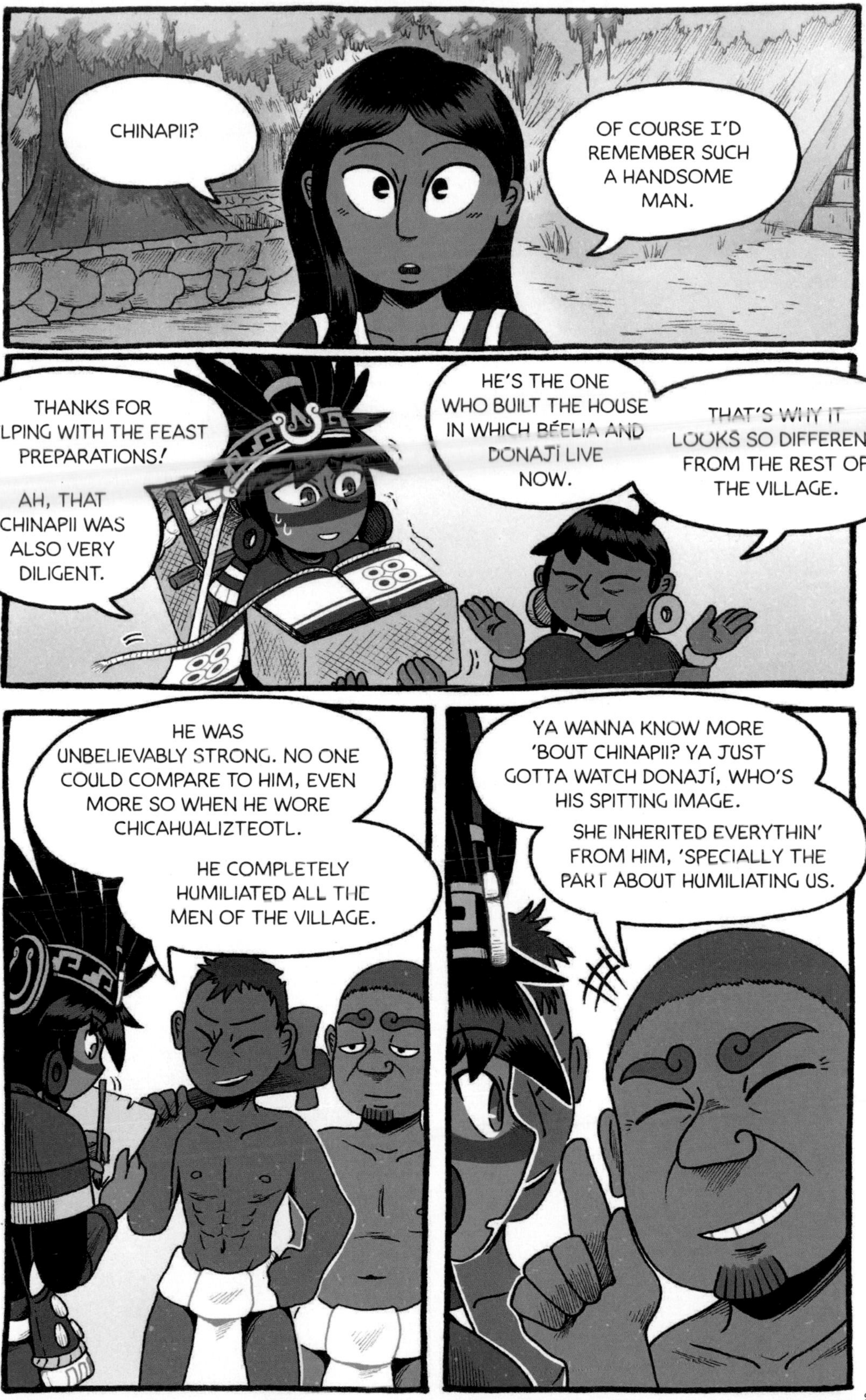
CHINAPII?
OF COURSE I'D REMEMBER SUCH A HANDSOME MAN.
THANKS FOR HELPING WITH THE FEAST PREPARATIONS!
AH, THAT CHINAPII WAS ALSO VERY DILIGENT.
HE'S THE ONE WHO BUILT THE HOUSE IN WHICH BÉELIA AND DONAJÍ LIVE NOW.
THAT'S WHY IT LOOKS SO DIFFERENT FROM THE REST OF THE VILLAGE.
HE WAS UNBELIEVABLY STRONG. NO ONE COULD COMPARE TO HIM, EVEN MORE SO WHEN HE WORE CHICAHUALIZTEOTL.
HE COMPLETELY HUMILIATED ALL THE MEN OF THE VILLAGE.
YA WANNA KNOW MORE 'BOUT CHINAPII? YA JUST GOTTA WATCH DONAJÍ, WHO'S HIS SPITTING IMAGE.
SHE INHERITED EVERYTHIN' FROM HIM, 'SPECIALLY THE PART ABOUT HUMILIATING US.

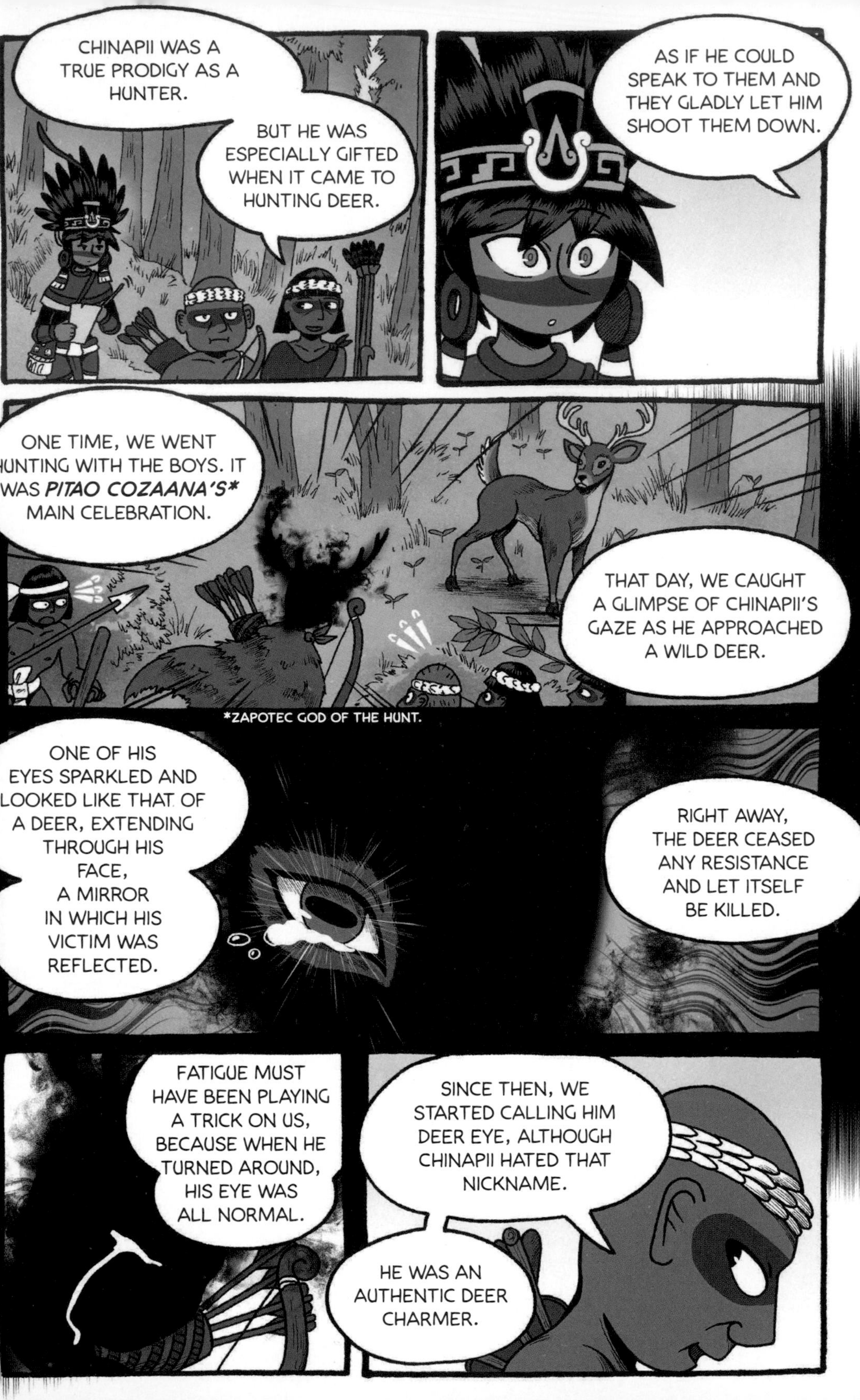
CHINAPII WAS A TRUE PRODIGY AS A HUNTER.
BUT HE WAS ESPECIALLY GIFTED WHEN IT CAME TO HUNTING DEER.
AS IF HE COULD SPEAK TO THEM AND THEY GLADLY LET HIM SHOOT THEM DOWN.
ONE TIME, WE WENT HUNTING WITH THE BOYS. IT WAS *PITAO COZAANA'S** MAIN CELEBRATION.
THAT DAY, WE CAUGHT A GLIMPSE OF CHINAPII'S GAZE AS HE APPROACHED A WILD DEER.
*ZAPOTEC GOD OF THE HUNT.
ONE OF HIS EYES SPARKLED AND LOOKED LIKE THAT OF A DEER, EXTENDING THROUGH HIS FACE, A MIRROR IN WHICH HIS VICTIM WAS REFLECTED.
RIGHT AWAY, THE DEER CEASED ANY RESISTANCE AND LET ITSELF BE KILLED.
FATIGUE MUST HAVE BEEN PLAYING A TRICK ON US, BECAUSE WHEN HE TURNED AROUND, HIS EYE WAS ALL NORMAL.
SINCE THEN, WE STARTED CALLING HIM DEER EYE, ALTHOUGH CHINAPII HATED THAT NICKNAME.
HE WAS AN AUTHENTIC DEER CHARMER.

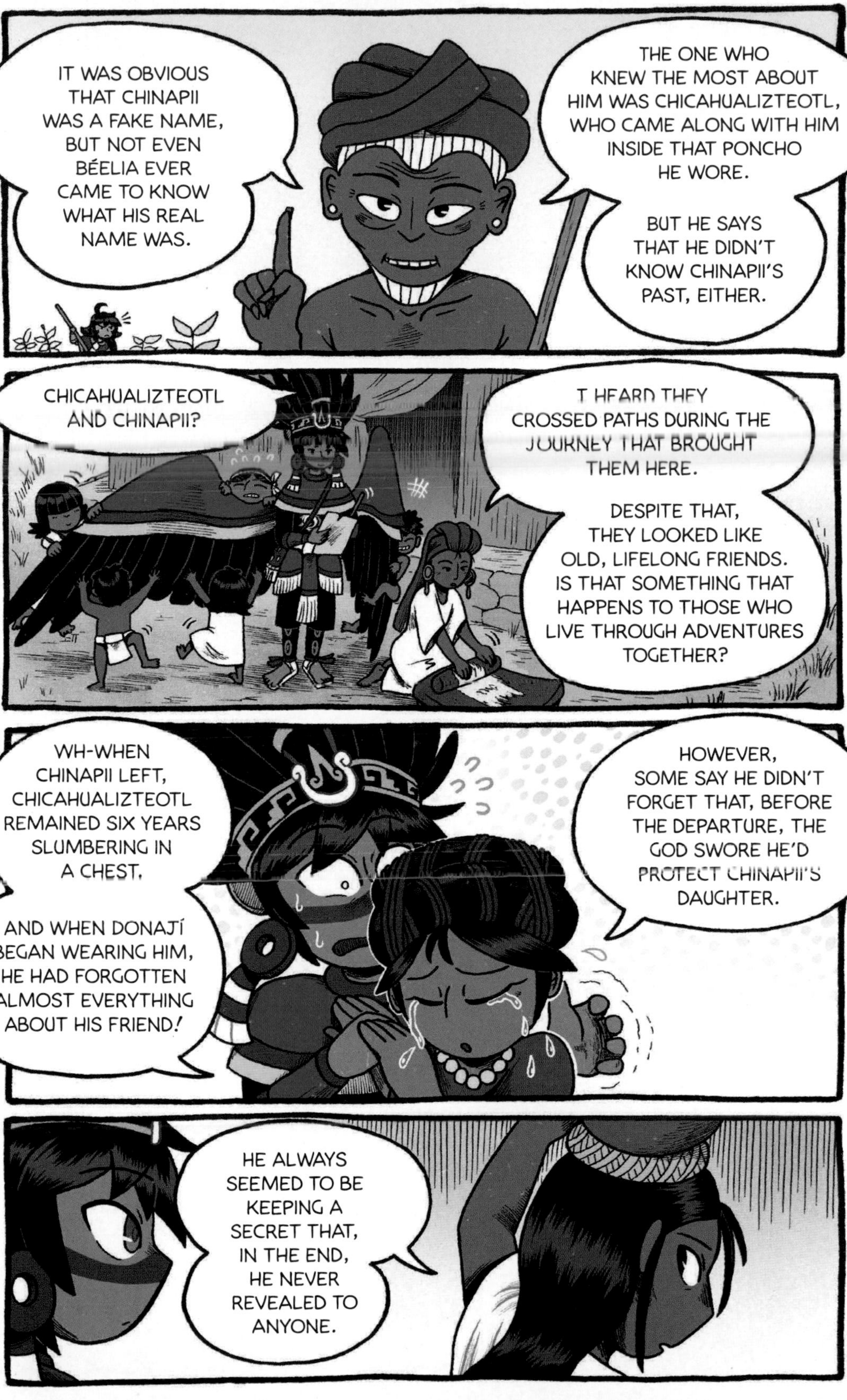
IT WAS OBVIOUS THAT CHINAPII WAS A FAKE NAME, BUT NOT EVEN BÉELIA EVER CAME TO KNOW WHAT HIS REAL NAME WAS.
THE ONE WHO KNEW THE MOST ABOUT HIM WAS CHICAHUALIZTEOTL, WHO CAME ALONG WITH HIM INSIDE THAT PONCHO HE WORE.
BUT HE SAYS THAT HE DIDN'T KNOW CHINAPII'S PAST, EITHER.
CHICAHUALIZTEOTL AND CHINAPII?
I HEARD THEY CROSSED PATHS DURING THE JOURNEY THAT BROUGHT THEM HERE.
DESPITE THAT, THEY LOOKED LIKE OLD, LIFELONG FRIENDS. IS THAT SOMETHING THAT HAPPENS TO THOSE WHO LIVE THROUGH ADVENTURES TOGETHER?
WH-WHEN CHINAPII LEFT, CHICAHUALIZTEOTL REMAINED SIX YEARS SLUMBERING IN A CHEST.
AND WHEN DONAJÍ BEGAN WEARING HIM, HE HAD FORGOTTEN ALMOST EVERYTHING ABOUT HIS FRIEND!
HOWEVER, SOME SAY HE DIDN'T FORGET THAT, BEFORE THE DEPARTURE, THE GOD SWORE HE'D PROTECT CHINAPII'S DAUGHTER.
HE ALWAYS SEEMED TO BE KEEPING A SECRET THAT, IN THE END, HE NEVER REVEALED TO ANYONE.

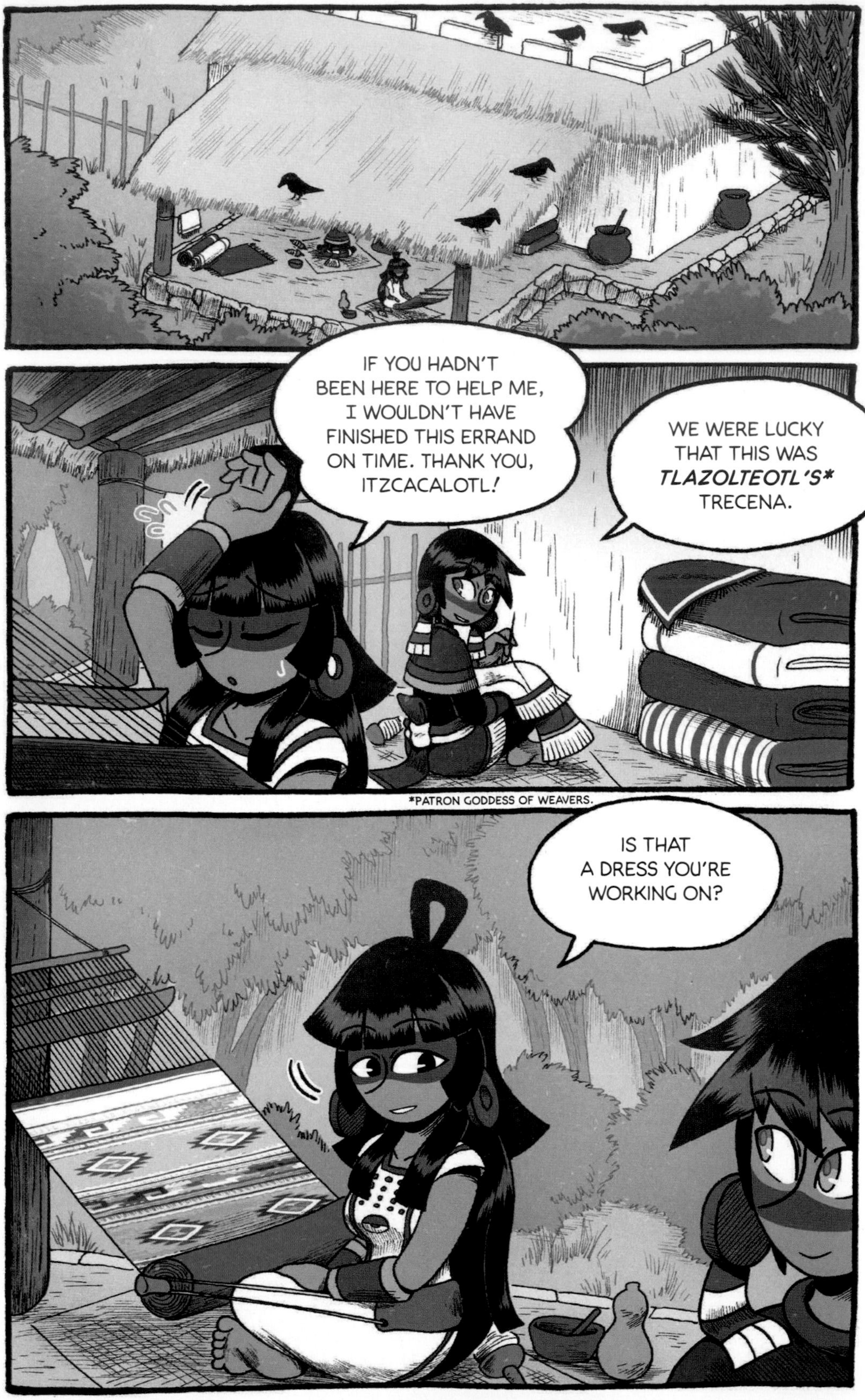
IF YOU HADN'T BEEN HERE TO HELP ME, I WOULDN'T HAVE FINISHED THIS ERRAND ON TIME. THANK YOU, ITZCACALOTL!
WE WERE LUCKY THAT THIS WAS *TLAZOLTEOTL'S** TRECENA.
*PATRON GODDESS OF WEAVERS.
IS THAT A DRESS YOU'RE WORKING ON?

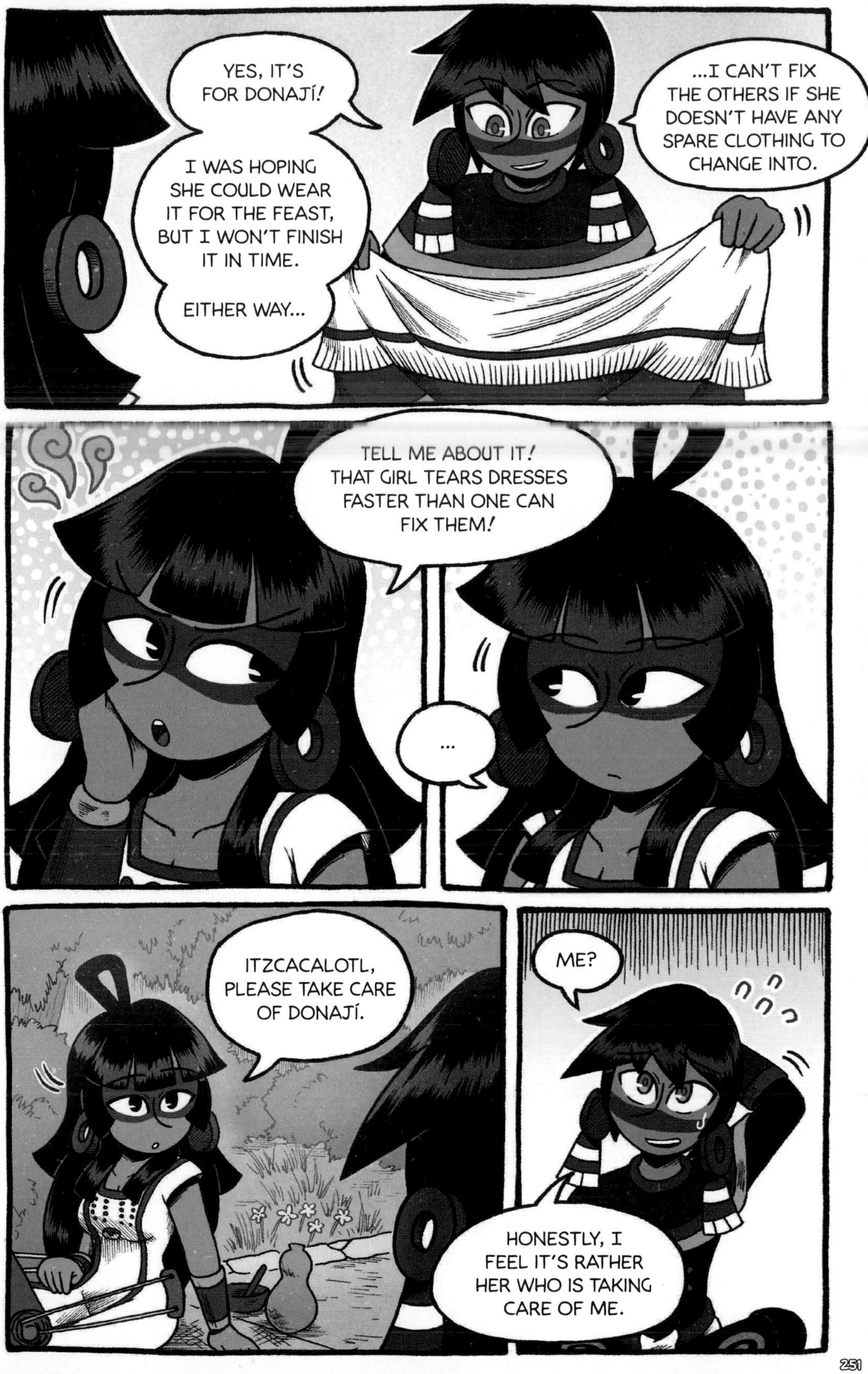
YES, IT'S FOR DONAJÍ!
I WAS HOPING SHE COULD WEAR IT FOR THE FEAST, BUT I WON'T FINISH IT IN TIME.
EITHER WAY...
...I CAN'T FIX THE OTHERS IF SHE DOESN'T HAVE ANY SPARE CLOTHING TO CHANGE INTO.
TELL ME ABOUT IT! THAT GIRL TEARS DRESSES FASTER THAN ONE CAN FIX THEM!
...
ITZCACALOTL, PLEASE TAKE CARE OF DONAJÍ.
ME?
HONESTLY, I FEEL IT'S RATHER HER WHO IS TAKING CARE OF ME.

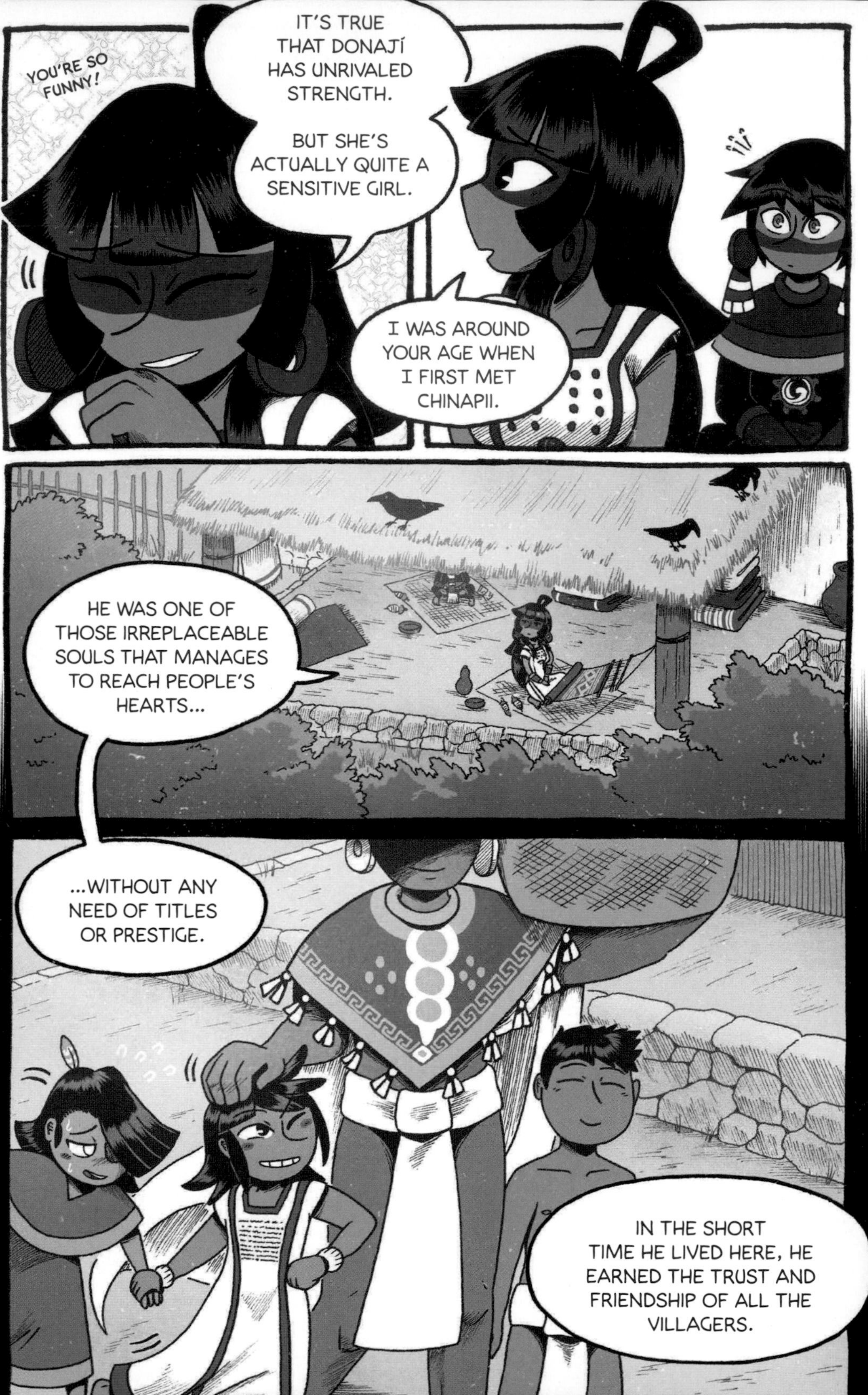

YOU'RE SO FUNNY!
IT'S TRUE THAT DONAJÍ HAS UNRIVALED STRENGTH.
BUT SHE'S ACTUALLY QUITE A SENSITIVE GIRL.
I WAS AROUND YOUR AGE WHEN I FIRST MET CHINAPII.
HE WAS ONE OF THOSE IRREPLACEABLE SOULS THAT MANAGES TO REACH PEOPLE'S HEARTS...
...WITHOUT ANY NEED OF TITLES OR PRESTIGE.
IN THE SHORT TIME HE LIVED HERE, HE EARNED THE TRUST AND FRIENDSHIP OF ALL THE VILLAGERS.

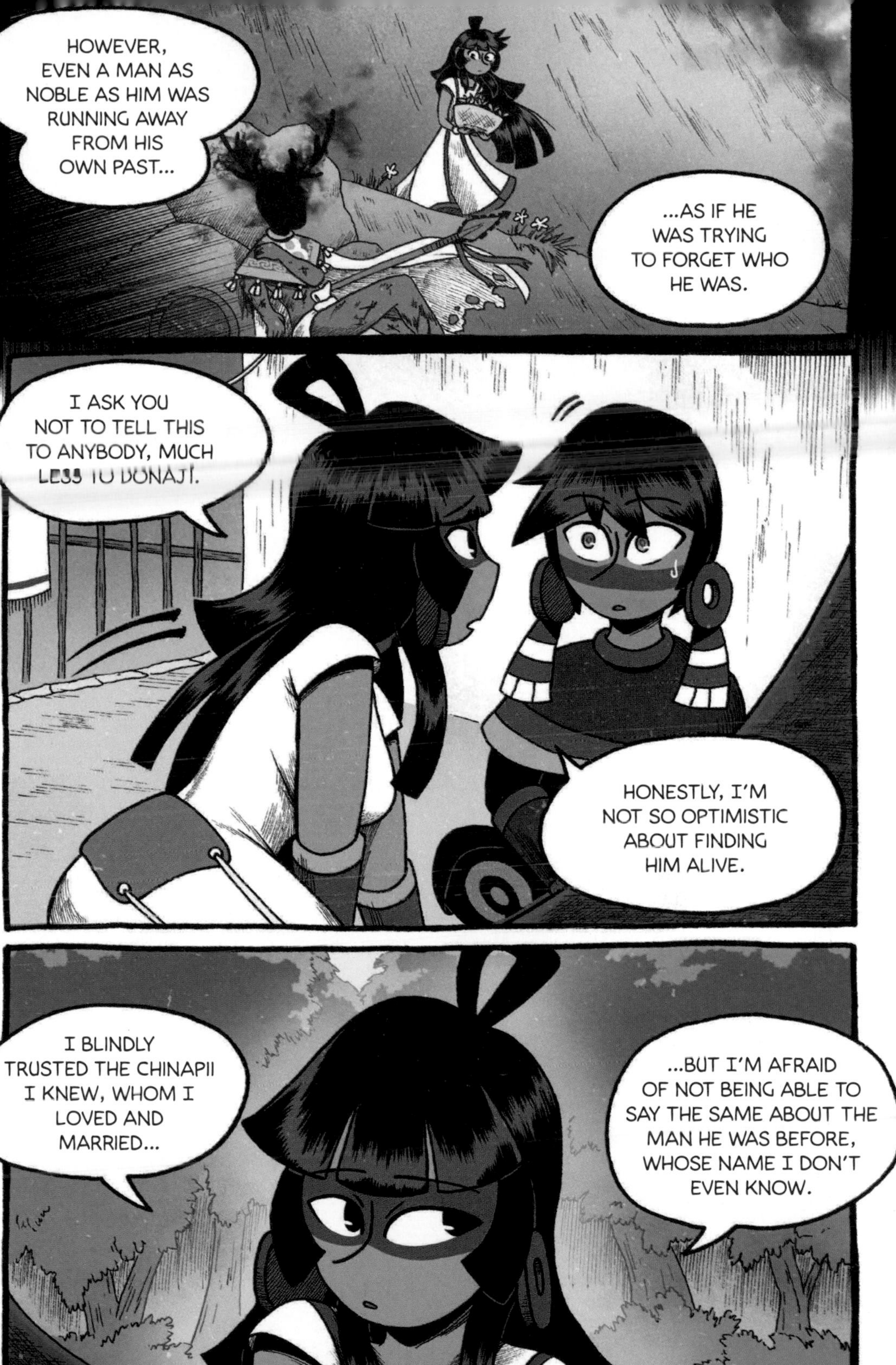
HOWEVER, EVEN A MAN AS NOBLE AS HIM WAS RUNNING AWAY FROM HIS OWN PAST...
...AS IF HE WAS TRYING TO FORGET WHO HE WAS.
I ASK YOU NOT TO TELL THIS TO ANYBODY, MUCH LESS TO DONAJI.
HONESTLY, I'M NOT SO OPTIMISTIC ABOUT FINDING HIM ALIVE.
I BLINDLY TRUSTED THE CHINAPII I KNEW, WHOM I LOVED AND MARRIED...
...BUT I'M AFRAID OF NOT BEING ABLE TO SAY THE SAME ABOUT THE MAN HE WAS BEFORE, WHOSE NAME I DON'T EVEN KNOW.

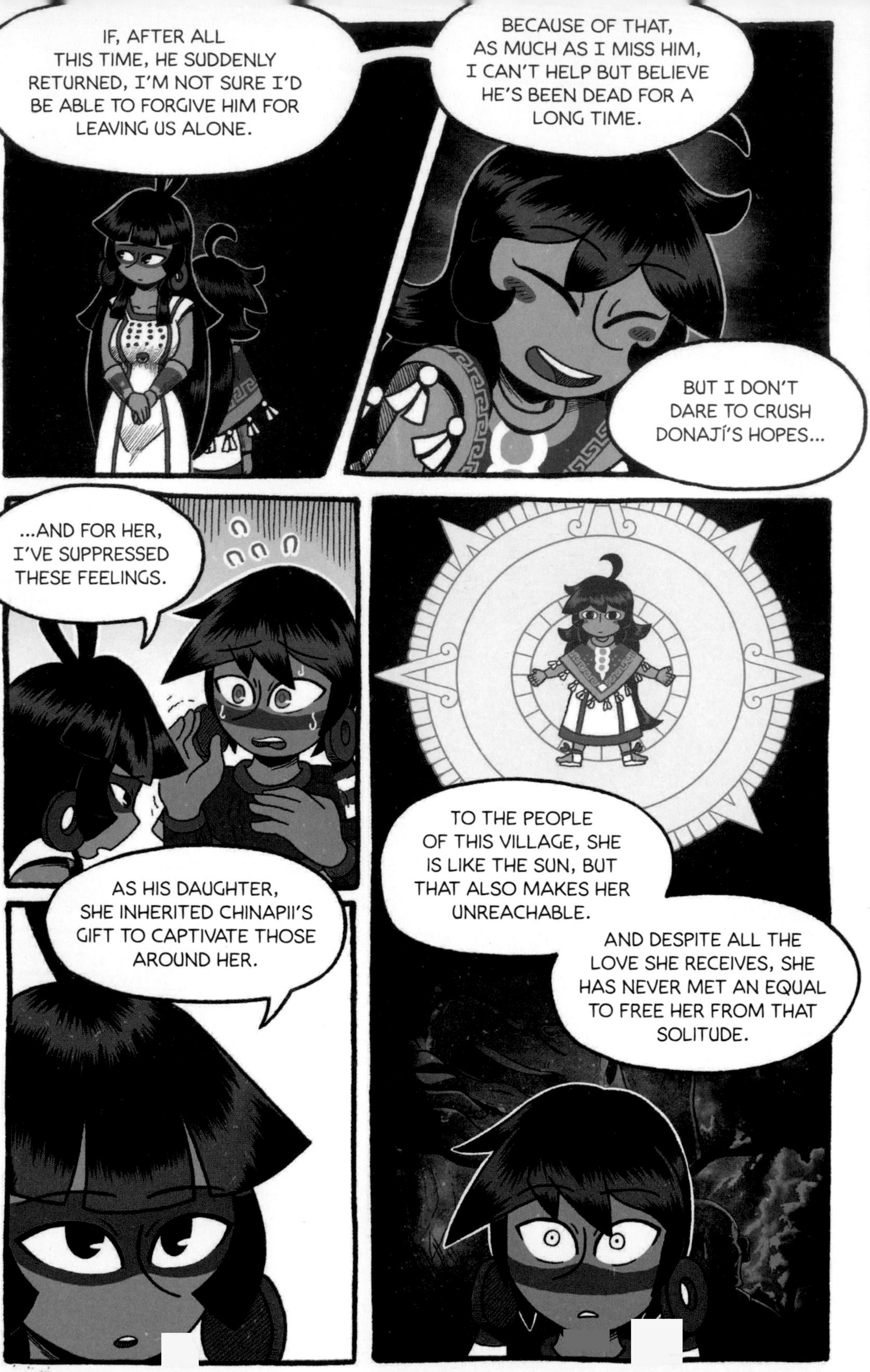
IF, AFTER ALL THIS TIME, HE SUDDENLY RETURNED, I'M NOT SURE I'D BE ABLE TO FORGIVE HIM FOR LEAVING US ALONE.
BECAUSE OF THAT, AS MUCH AS I MISS HIM, I CAN'T HELP BUT BELIEVE HE'S BEEN DEAD FOR A LONG TIME.
BUT I DON'T DARE TO CRUSH DONAJÍ'S HOPES...
...AND FOR HER, I'VE SUPPRESSED THESE FEELINGS.
TO THE PEOPLE OF THIS VILLAGE, SHE IS LIKE THE SUN, BUT THAT ALSO MAKES HER UNREACHABLE.
AS HIS DAUGHTER, SHE INHERITED CHINAPII'S GIFT TO CAPTIVATE THOSE AROUND HER.
AND DESPITE ALL THE LOVE SHE RECEIVES, SHE HAS NEVER MET AN EQUAL TO FREE HER FROM THAT SOLITUDE.

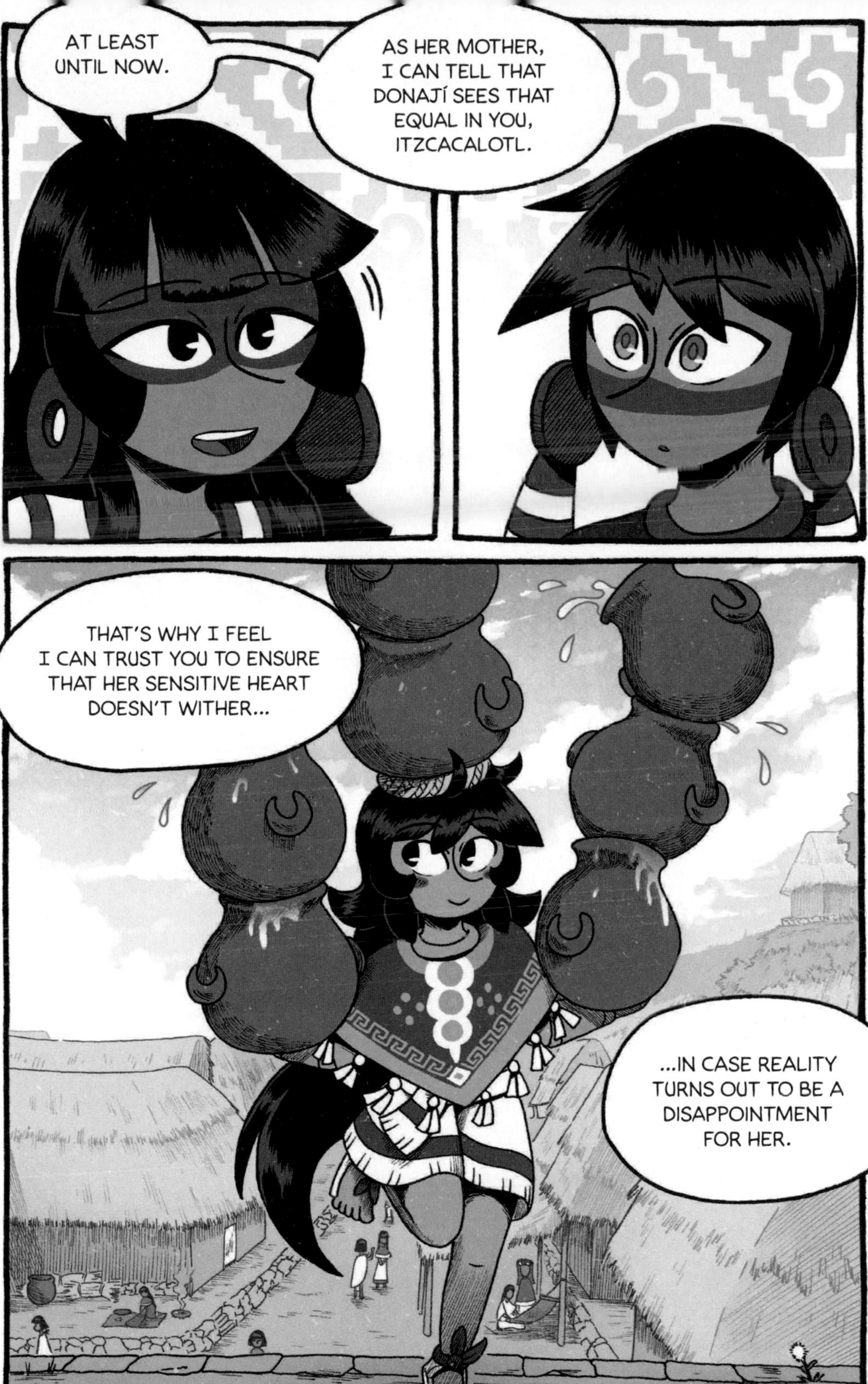

AT LEAST UNTIL NOW.
AS HER MOTHER, I CAN TELL THAT DONAJÍ SEES THAT EQUAL IN YOU, ITZCACALOTL.
THAT'S WHY I FEEL I CAN TRUST YOU TO ENSURE THAT HER SENSITIVE HEART DOESN'T WITHER...
...IN CASE REALITY TURNS OUT TO BE A DISAPPOINTMENT FOR HER.

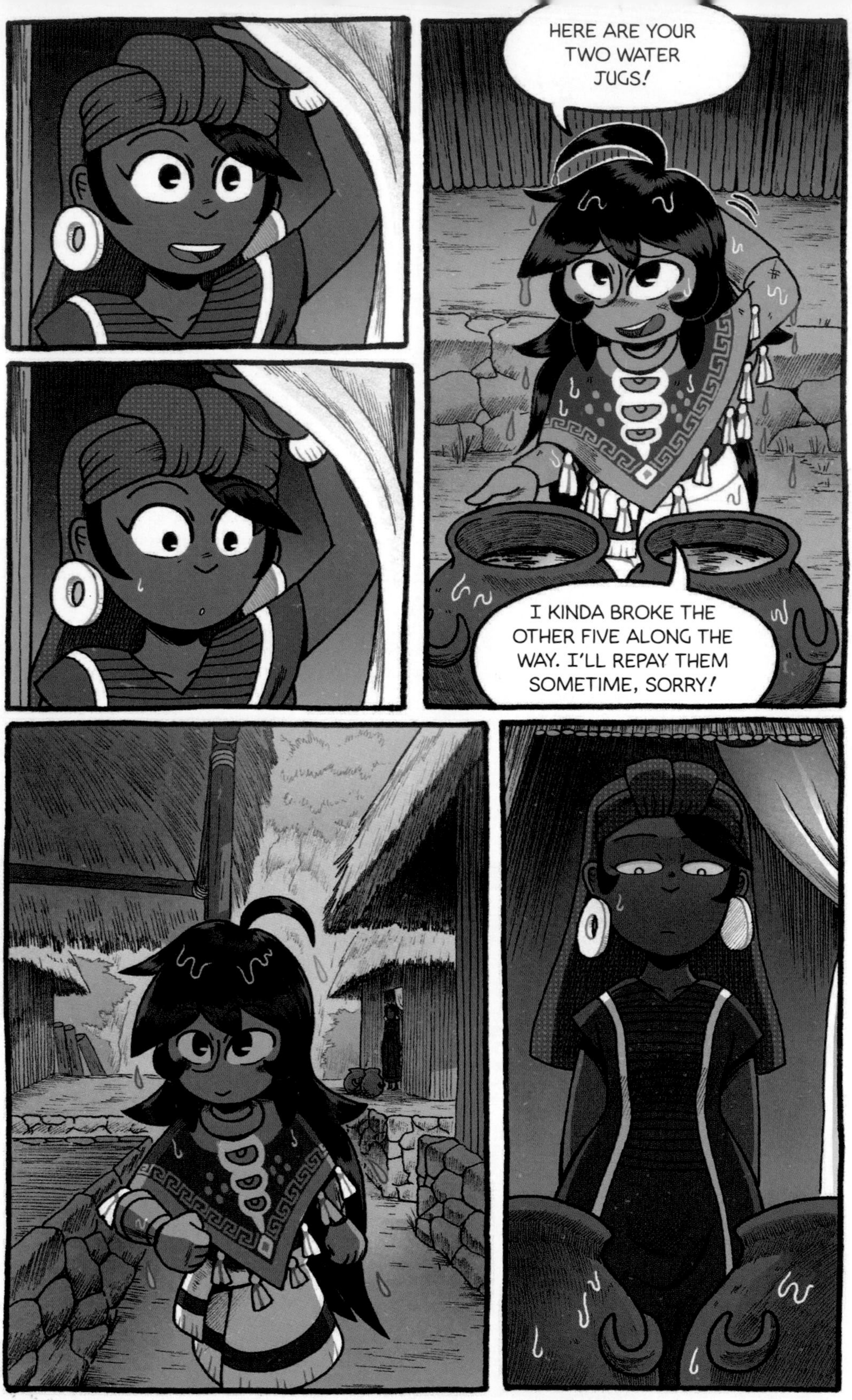
HERE ARE YOUR TWO WATER JUGS!
I KINDA BROKE THE OTHER FIVE ALONG THE WAY. I'LL REPAY THEM SOMETIME, SORRY!

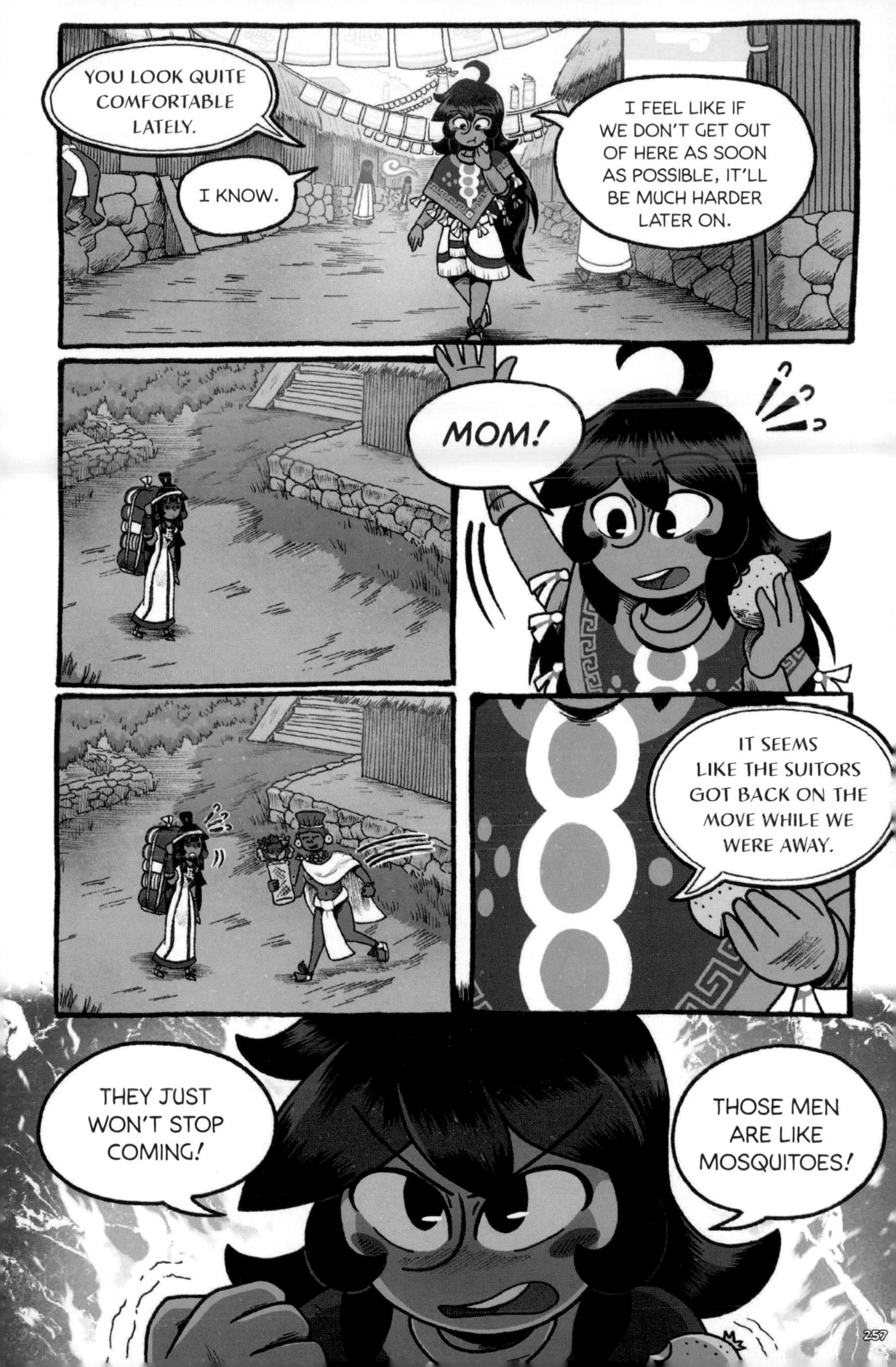
YOU LOOK QUITE COMFORTABLE LATELY.
I KNOW.
I FEEL LIKE IF WE DON'T GET OUT OF HERE AS SOON AS POSSIBLE, IT'LL BE MUCH HARDER LATER ON.
MOM!
IT SEEMS LIKE THE SUITORS GOT BACK ON THE MOVE WHILE WE WERE AWAY.
THEY JUST WON'T STOP COMING!
THOSE MEN ARE LIKE MOSQUITOES!

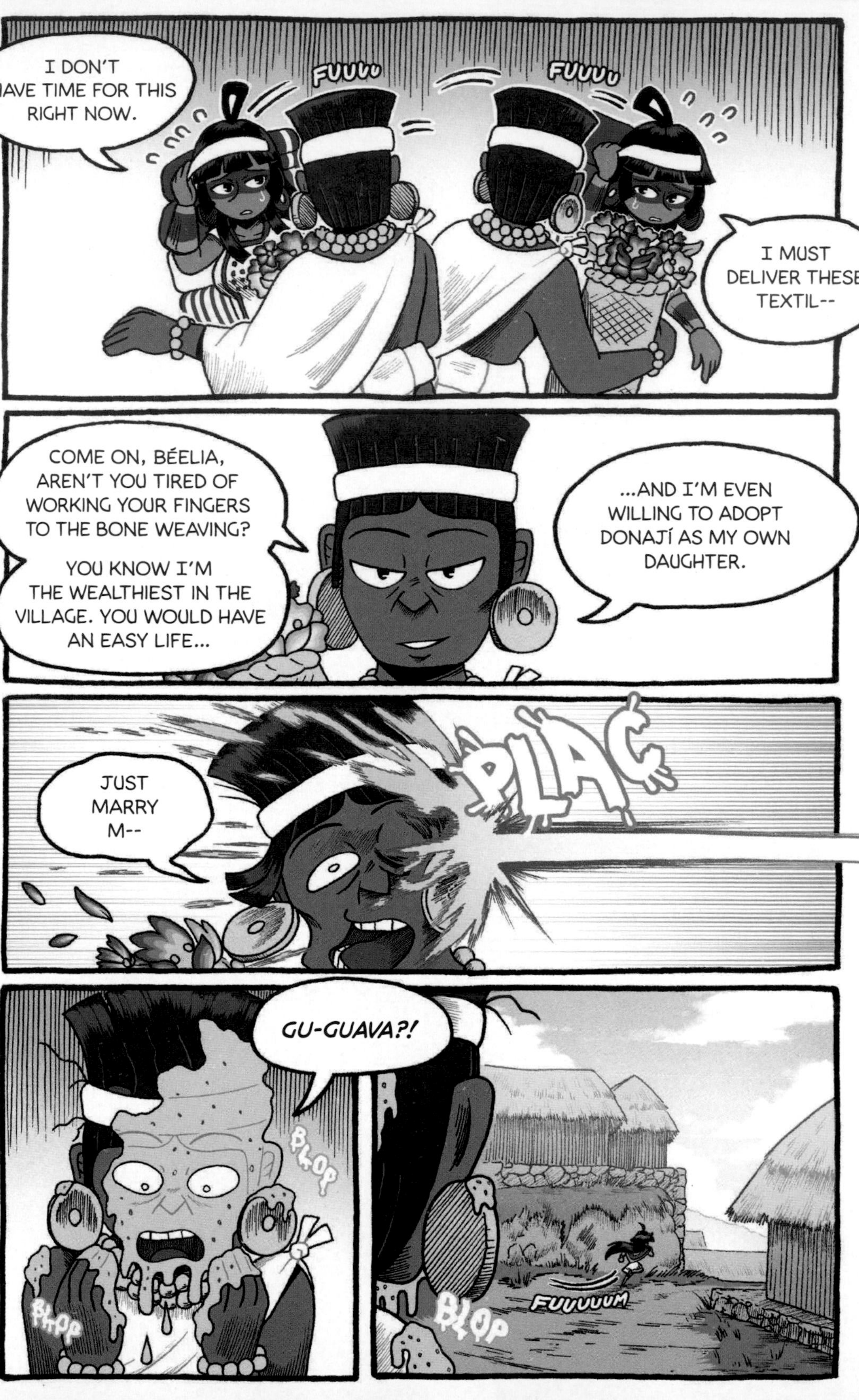
I DON'T HAVE TIME FOR THIS RIGHT NOW.
FUUUU
FUUUU
I MUST DELIVER THESE TEXTIL--
COME ON, BÉELIA, AREN'T YOU TIRED OF WORKING YOUR FINGERS TO THE BONE WEAVING?
YOU KNOW I'M THE WEALTHIEST IN THE VILLAGE. YOU WOULD HAVE AN EASY LIFE...
...AND I'M EVEN WILLING TO ADOPT DONAJÍ AS MY OWN DAUGHTER.
JUST MARRY M--
PLAC
GU-GUAVA?!
BLOP
BLOP
BLOP
FUUUUUM

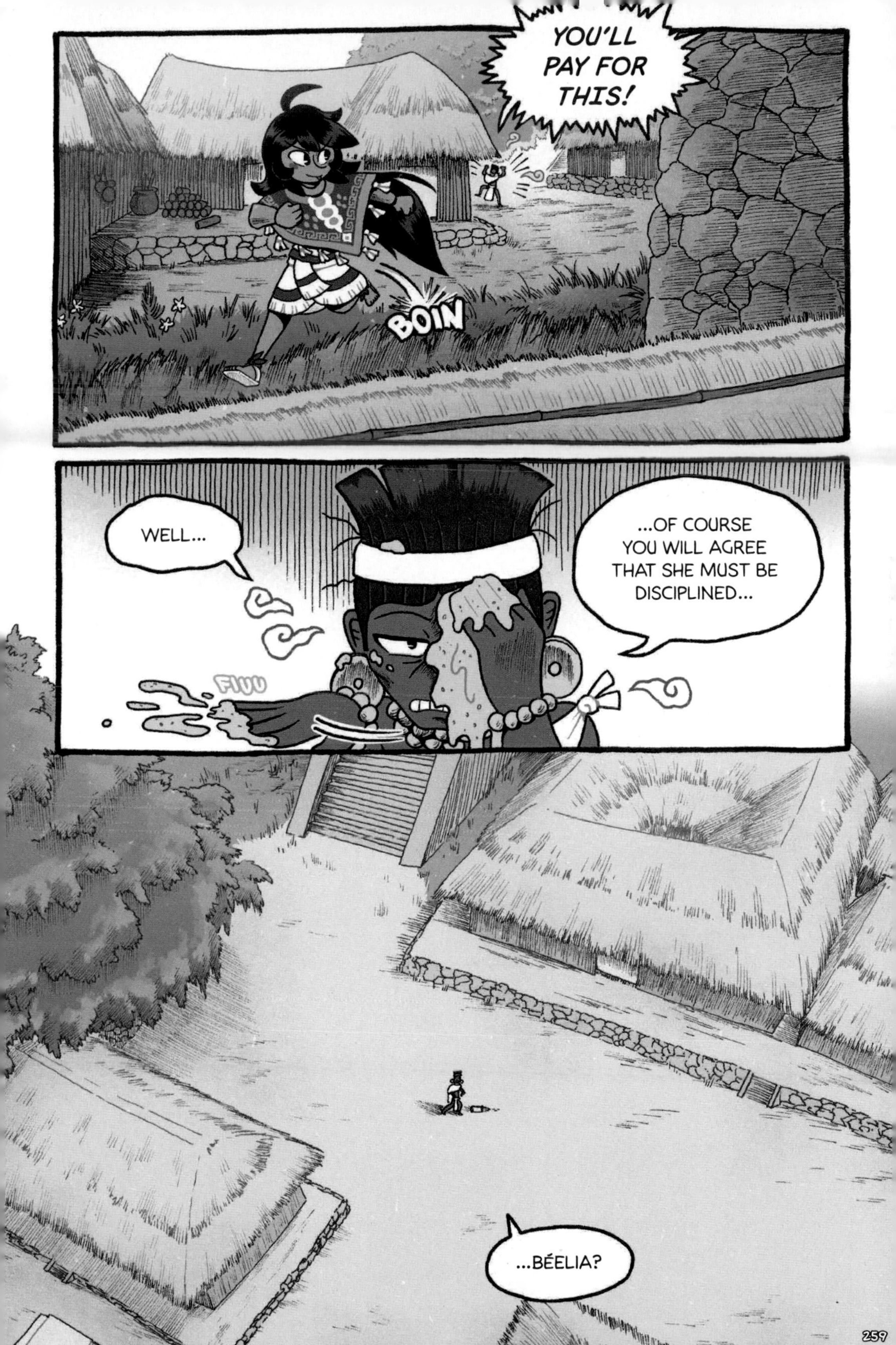
YOU'LL PAY FOR THIS!
BOIN
WELL...
...OF COURSE YOU WILL AGREE THAT SHE MUST BE DISCIPLINED...
FIUU
...BÉELIA?

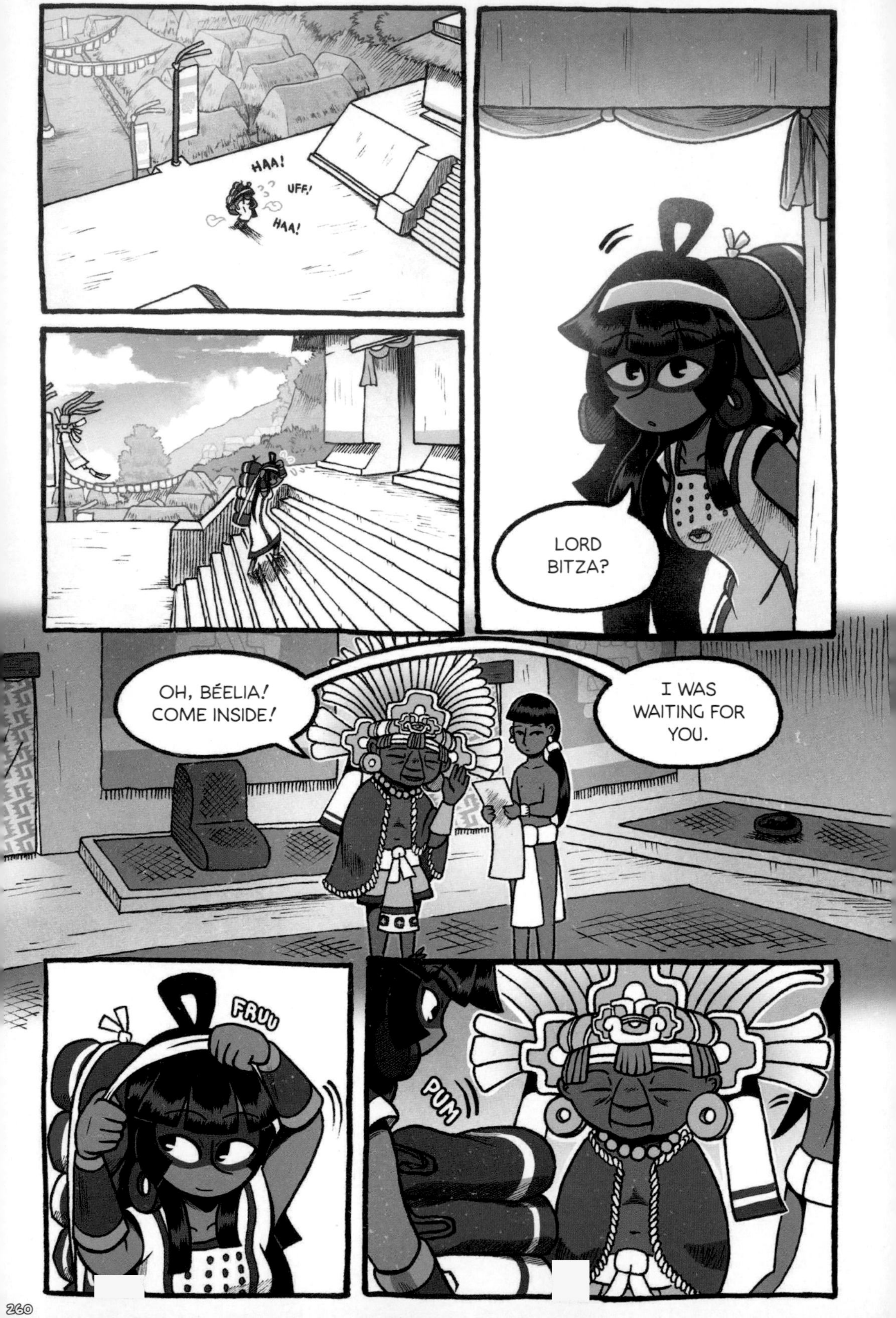
HAA!
UFF!
HAA!
LORD BITZA?
OH, BÉELIA! COME INSIDE!
I WAS WAITING FOR YOU.
FRUU
PUM

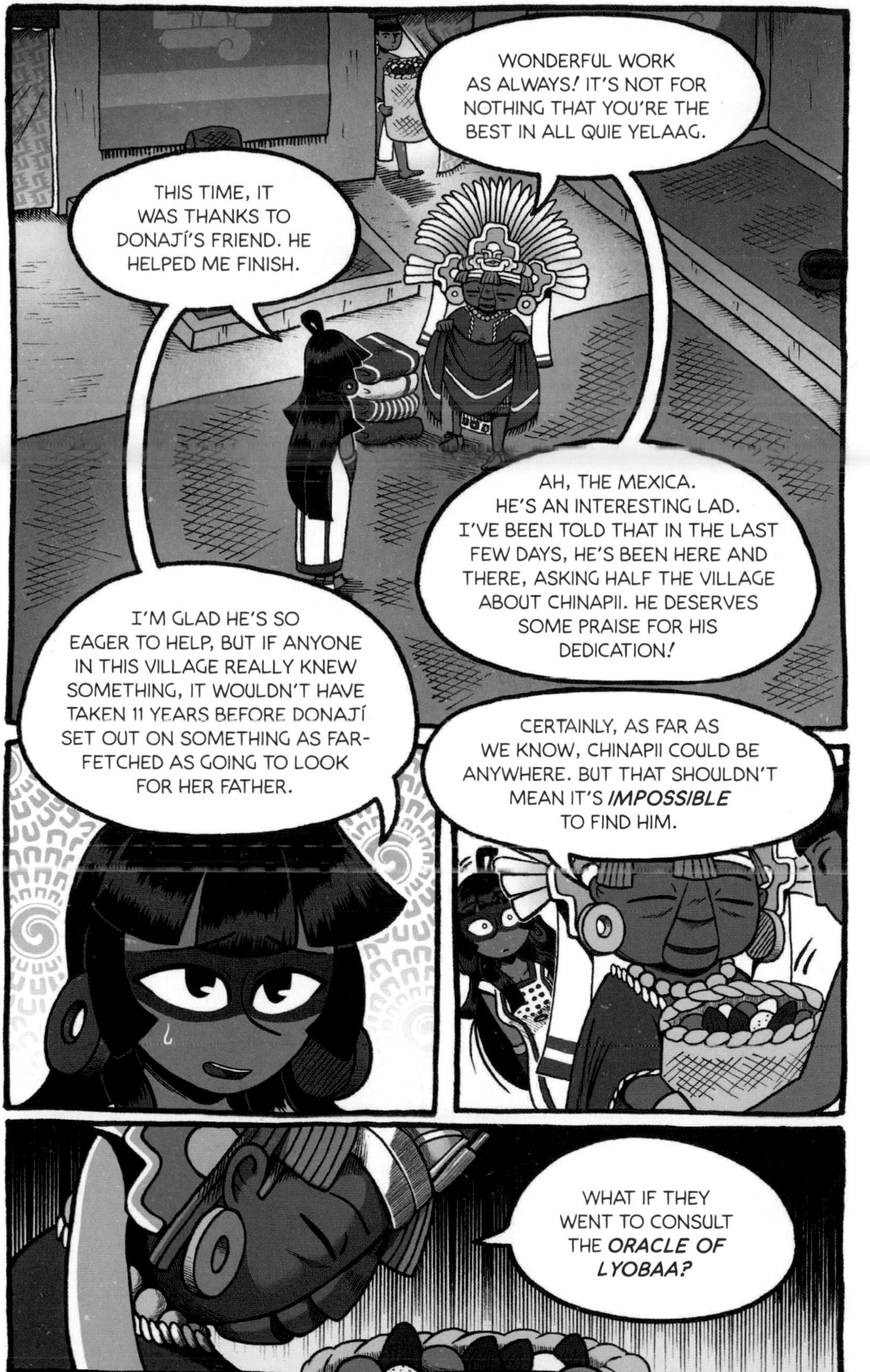
WONDERFUL WORK AS ALWAYS! IT'S NOT FOR NOTHING THAT YOU'RE THE BEST IN ALL QUIE YELAAG.
THIS TIME, IT WAS THANKS TO DONAJÍ'S FRIEND. HE HELPED ME FINISH.
AH, THE MEXICA. HE'S AN INTERESTING LAD. I'VE BEEN TOLD THAT IN THE LAST FEW DAYS, HE'S BEEN HERE AND THERE, ASKING HALF THE VILLAGE ABOUT CHINAPII. HE DESERVES SOME PRAISE FOR HIS DEDICATION!
I'M GLAD HE'S SO EAGER TO HELP, BUT IF ANYONE IN THIS VILLAGE REALLY KNEW SOMETHING, IT WOULDN'T HAVE TAKEN 11 YEARS BEFORE DONAJÍ SET OUT ON SOMETHING AS FAR-FETCHED AS GOING TO LOOK FOR HER FATHER.
CERTAINLY, AS FAR AS WE KNOW, CHINAPII COULD BE ANYWHERE. BUT THAT SHOULDN'T MEAN IT'S *IMPOSSIBLE* TO FIND HIM.
WHAT IF THEY WENT TO CONSULT THE ***ORACLE OF LYOBAA?***

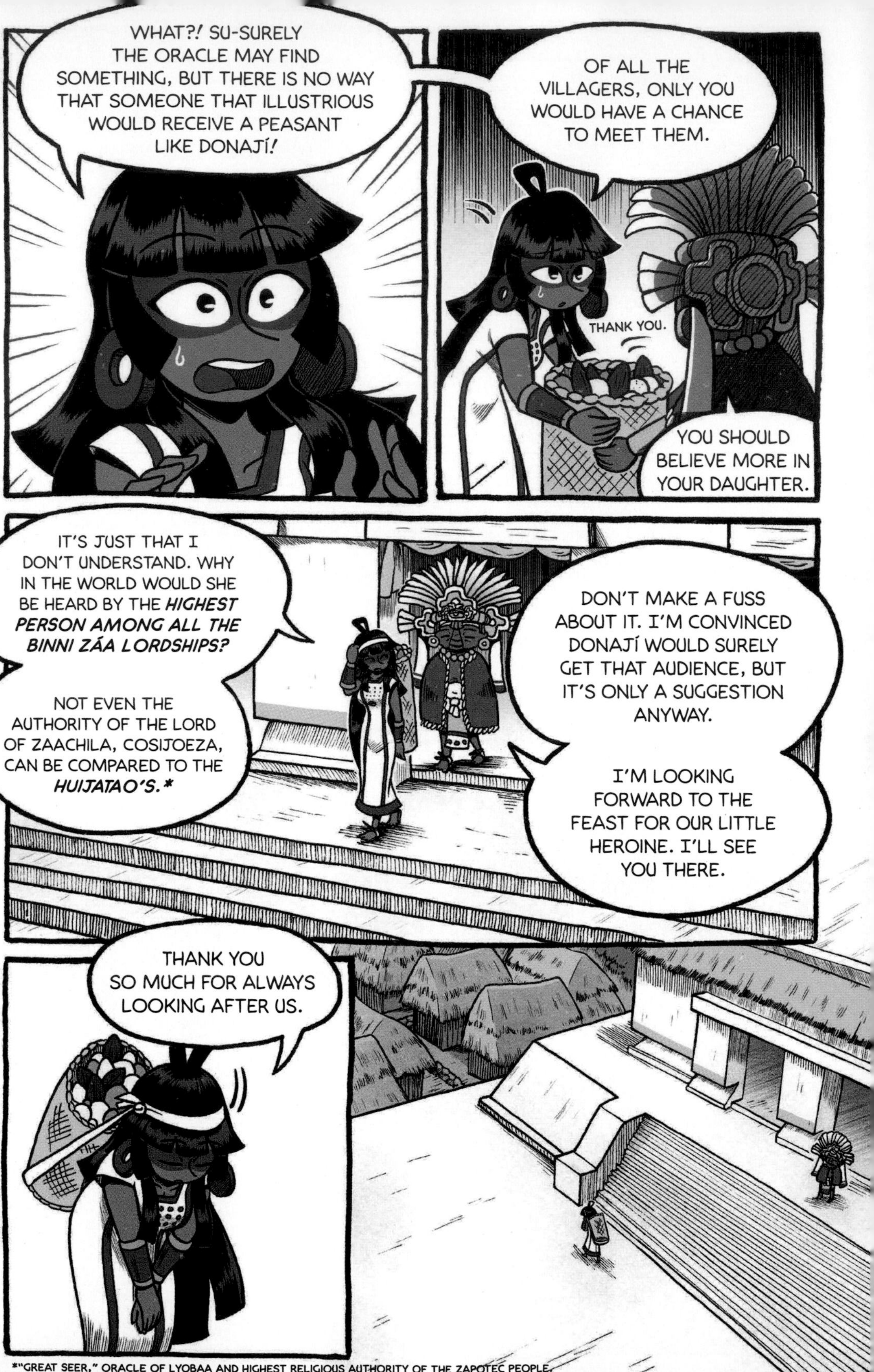
WHAT?! SU-SURELY THE ORACLE MAY FIND SOMETHING, BUT THERE IS NO WAY THAT SOMEONE THAT ILLUSTRIOUS WOULD RECEIVE A PEASANT LIKE DONAJÍ!
OF ALL THE VILLAGERS, ONLY YOU WOULD HAVE A CHANCE TO MEET THEM.
THANK YOU.
YOU SHOULD BELIEVE MORE IN YOUR DAUGHTER.
IT'S JUST THAT I DON'T UNDERSTAND. WHY IN THE WORLD WOULD SHE BE HEARD BY THE HIGHEST PERSON AMONG ALL THE BINNI ZÁA LORDSHIPS?
NOT EVEN THE AUTHORITY OF THE LORD OF ZAACHILA, COSIJOEZA, CAN BE COMPARED TO THE HUIJATAO'S.*
DON'T MAKE A FUSS ABOUT IT. I'M CONVINCED DONAJÍ WOULD SURELY GET THAT AUDIENCE, BUT IT'S ONLY A SUGGESTION ANYWAY.
I'M LOOKING FORWARD TO THE FEAST FOR OUR LITTLE HEROINE. I'LL SEE YOU THERE.
THANK YOU SO MUCH FOR ALWAYS LOOKING AFTER US.

*"GREAT SEER," ORACLE OF LYOBAA AND HIGHEST RELIGIOUS AUTHORITY OF THE ZAPOTEC PEOPLE.

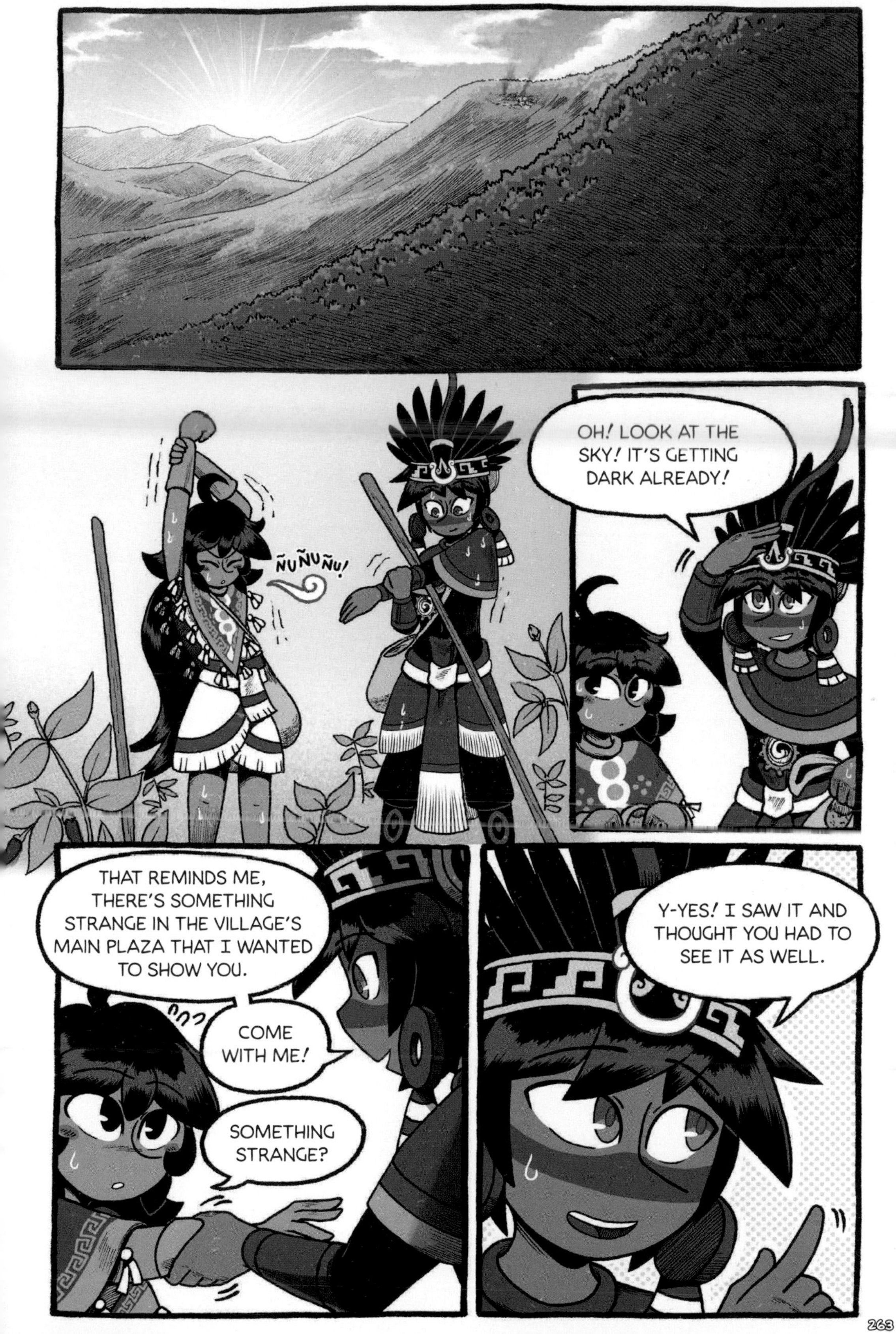
ÑUÑUÑU!
OH! LOOK AT THE SKY! IT'S GETTING DARK ALREADY!
THAT REMINDS ME, THERE'S SOMETHING STRANGE IN THE VILLAGE'S MAIN PLAZA THAT I WANTED TO SHOW YOU.
COME WITH ME!
SOMETHING STRANGE?
Y-YES! I SAW IT AND THOUGHT YOU HAD TO SEE IT AS WELL.

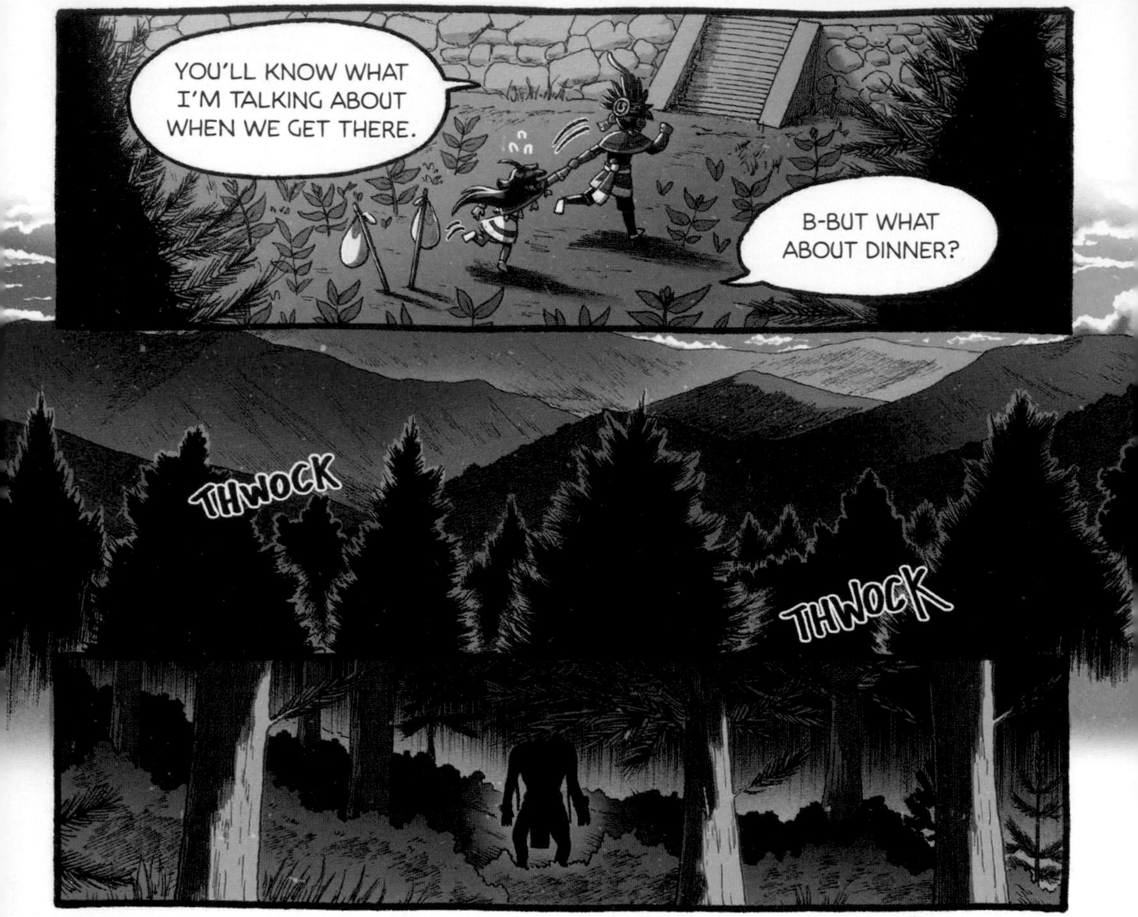
YOU'LL KNOW WHAT I'M TALKING ABOUT WHEN WE GET THERE.
B-BUT WHAT ABOUT DINNER?
THWOCK
THWOCK

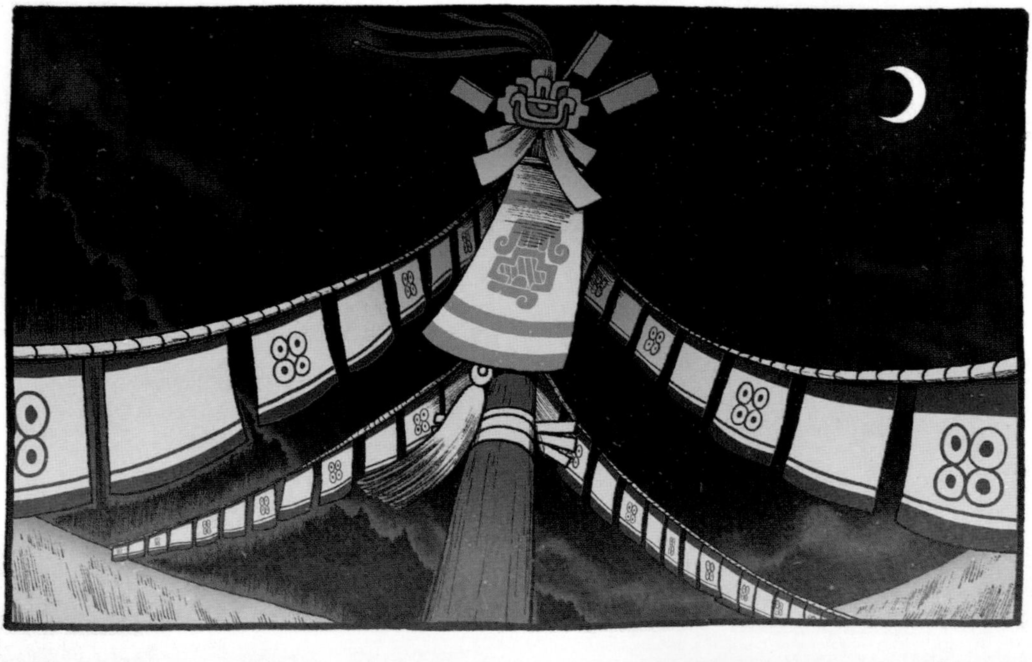

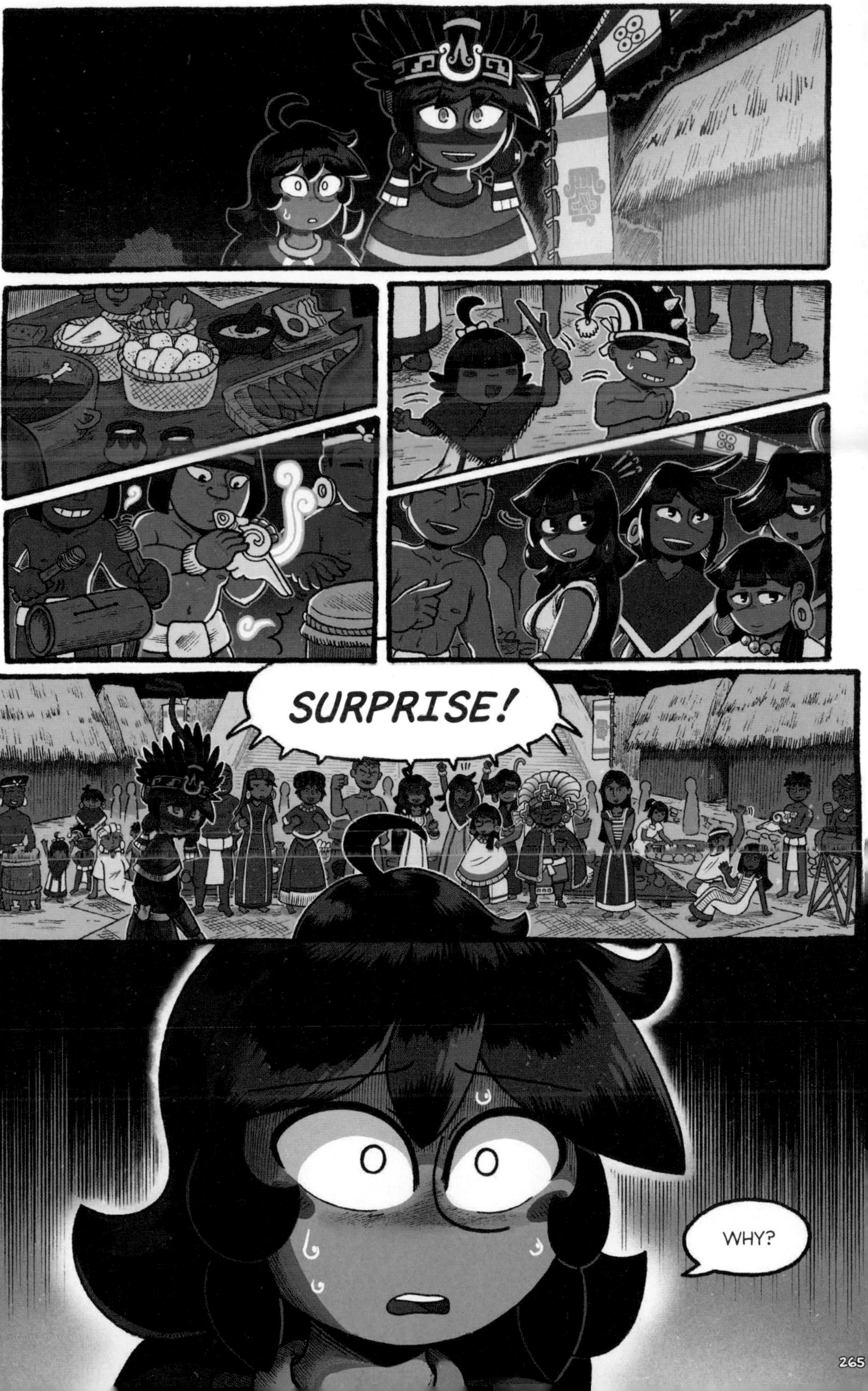
SURPRISE!
WHY?

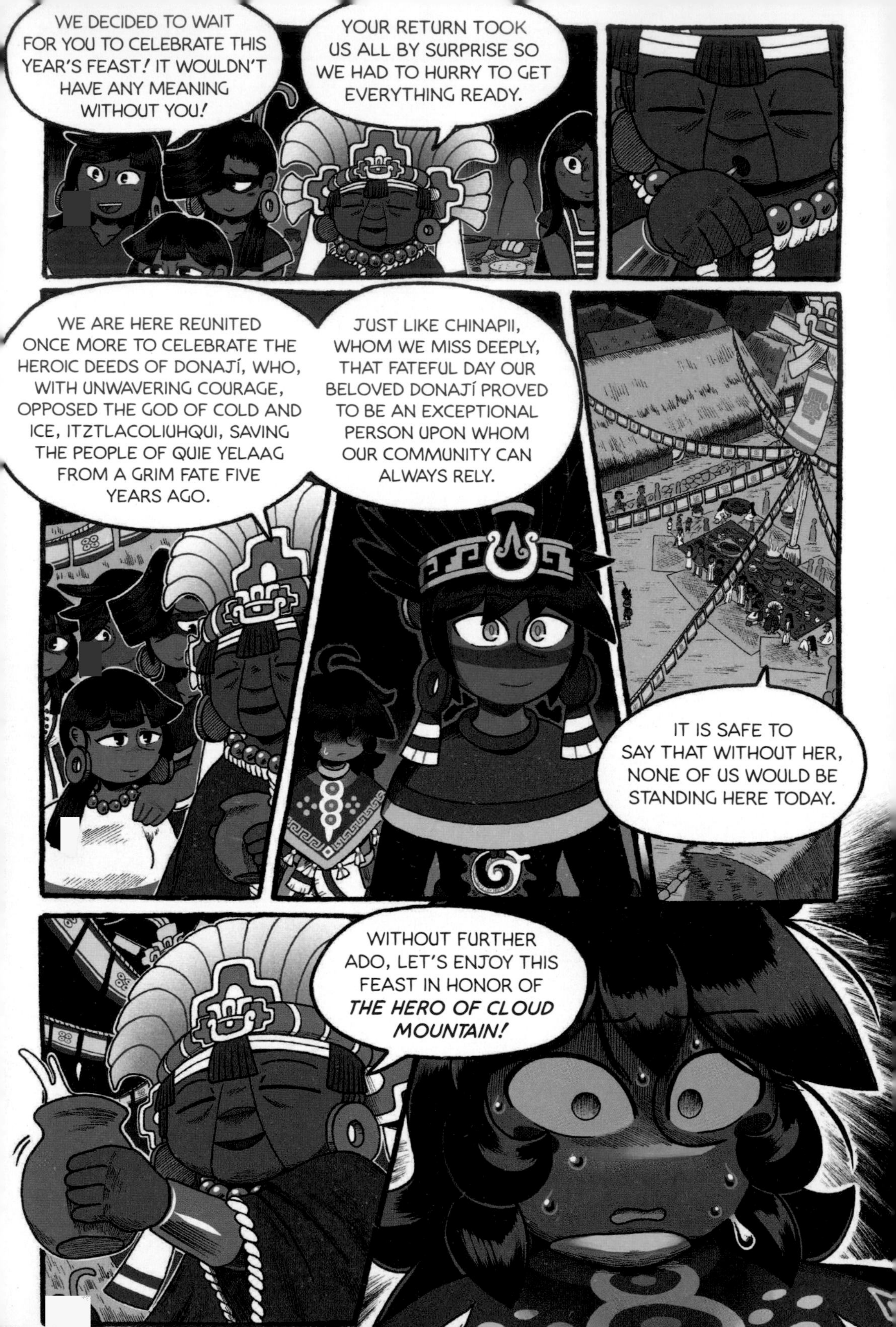
WE DECIDED TO WAIT FOR YOU TO CELEBRATE THIS YEAR'S FEAST! IT WOULDN'T HAVE ANY MEANING WITHOUT YOU!
YOUR RETURN TOOK US ALL BY SURPRISE SO WE HAD TO HURRY TO GET EVERYTHING READY.
WE ARE HERE REUNITED ONCE MORE TO CELEBRATE THE HEROIC DEEDS OF DONAJÍ, WHO, WITH UNWAVERING COURAGE, OPPOSED THE GOD OF COLD AND ICE, ITZTLACOLIUHQUI, SAVING THE PEOPLE OF QUIE YELAAG FROM A GRIM FATE FIVE YEARS AGO.
JUST LIKE CHINAPII, WHOM WE MISS DEEPLY, THAT FATEFUL DAY OUR BELOVED DONAJÍ PROVED TO BE AN EXCEPTIONAL PERSON UPON WHOM OUR COMMUNITY CAN ALWAYS RELY.
IT IS SAFE TO SAY THAT WITHOUT HER, NONE OF US WOULD BE STANDING HERE TODAY.
WITHOUT FURTHER ADO, LET'S ENJOY THIS FEAST IN HONOR OF *THE HERO OF CLOUD MOUNTAIN!*

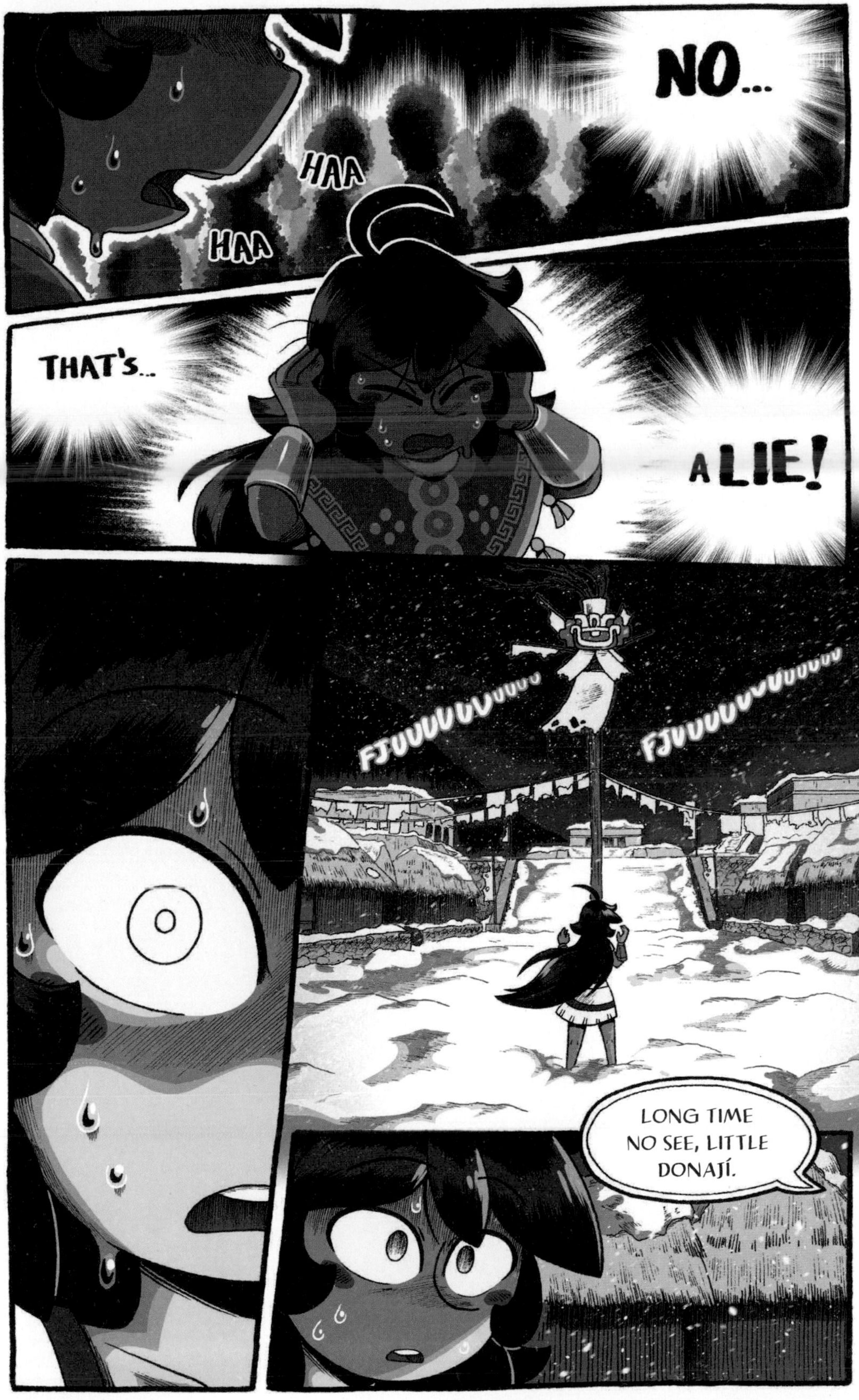
NO...
HAA
HAA
THAT'S...
A LIE!
FJUUUUUUuuuu
FJUUUUUUUuuuuu
LONG TIME NO SEE, LITTLE DONAJÍ.

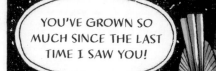

YOU'VE GROWN SO MUCH SINCE THE LAST TIME I SAW YOU!

BUT TO ME, YOU LOOK JUST AS DEFENSELESS AS THAT DAY.

HOW DOES IT FEEL? THE GLORY OF DEFEATING A GOD. OH, WAIT, IF I RECALL CORRECTLY, YOU WERE ABOUT TO DIE THAT DAY, WEREN'T YOU?

SHUT UP! I NEVER SAID IT WAS ME WHO DEFEATED YOU!

BUT YOU DIDN'T SAY OTHERWISE, DID YOU?

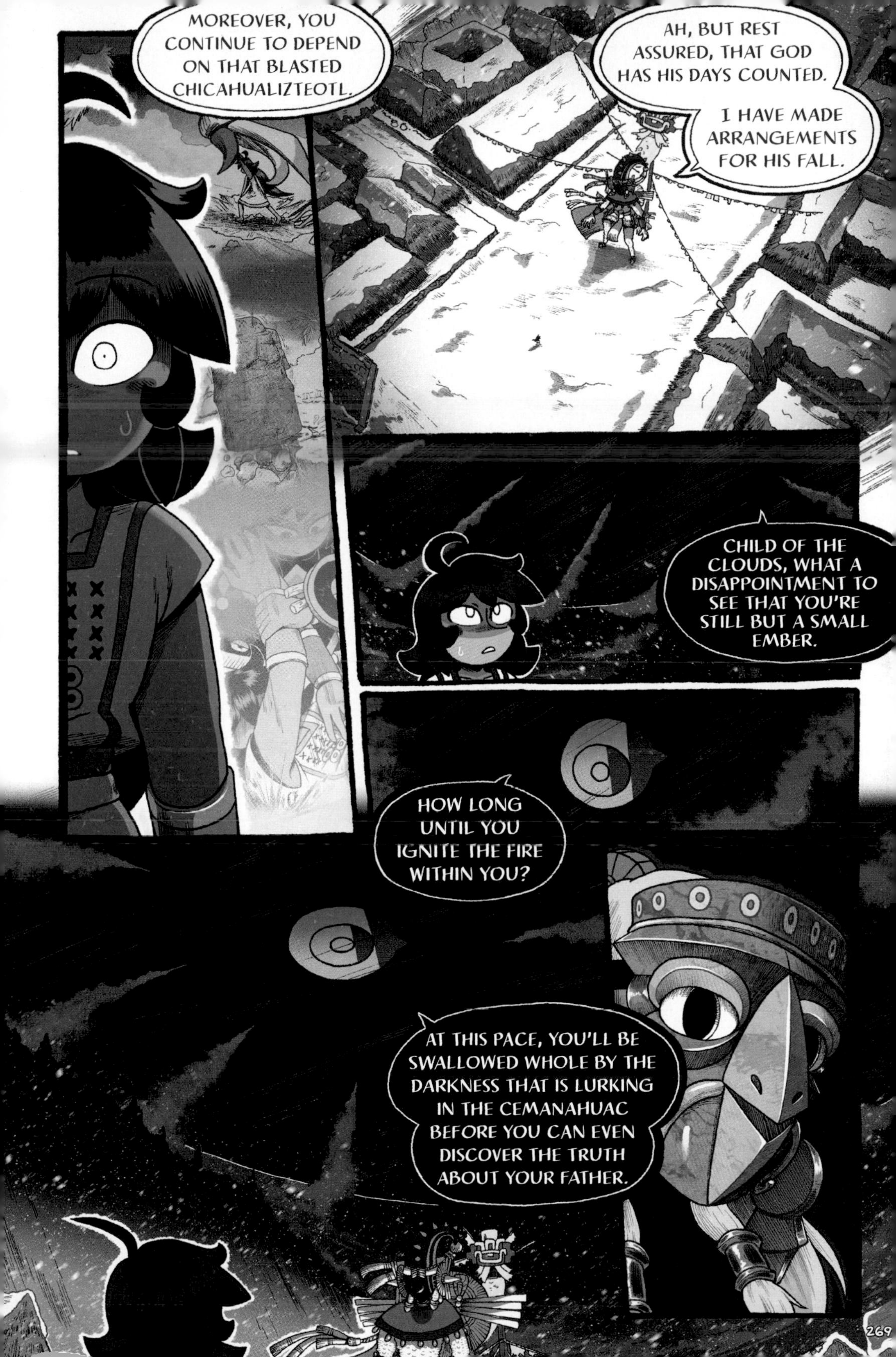
MOREOVER, YOU CONTINUE TO DEPEND ON THAT BLASTED CHICAHUALIZTEOTL.
AH, BUT REST ASSURED, THAT GOD HAS HIS DAYS COUNTED.
I HAVE MADE ARRANGEMENTS FOR HIS FALL.
CHILD OF THE CLOUDS, WHAT A DISAPPOINTMENT TO SEE THAT YOU'RE STILL BUT A SMALL EMBER.
HOW LONG UNTIL YOU IGNITE THE FIRE WITHIN YOU?
AT THIS PACE, YOU'LL BE SWALLOWED WHOLE BY THE DARKNESS THAT IS LURKING IN THE CEMANAHUAC BEFORE YOU CAN EVEN DISCOVER THE TRUTH ABOUT YOUR FATHER.

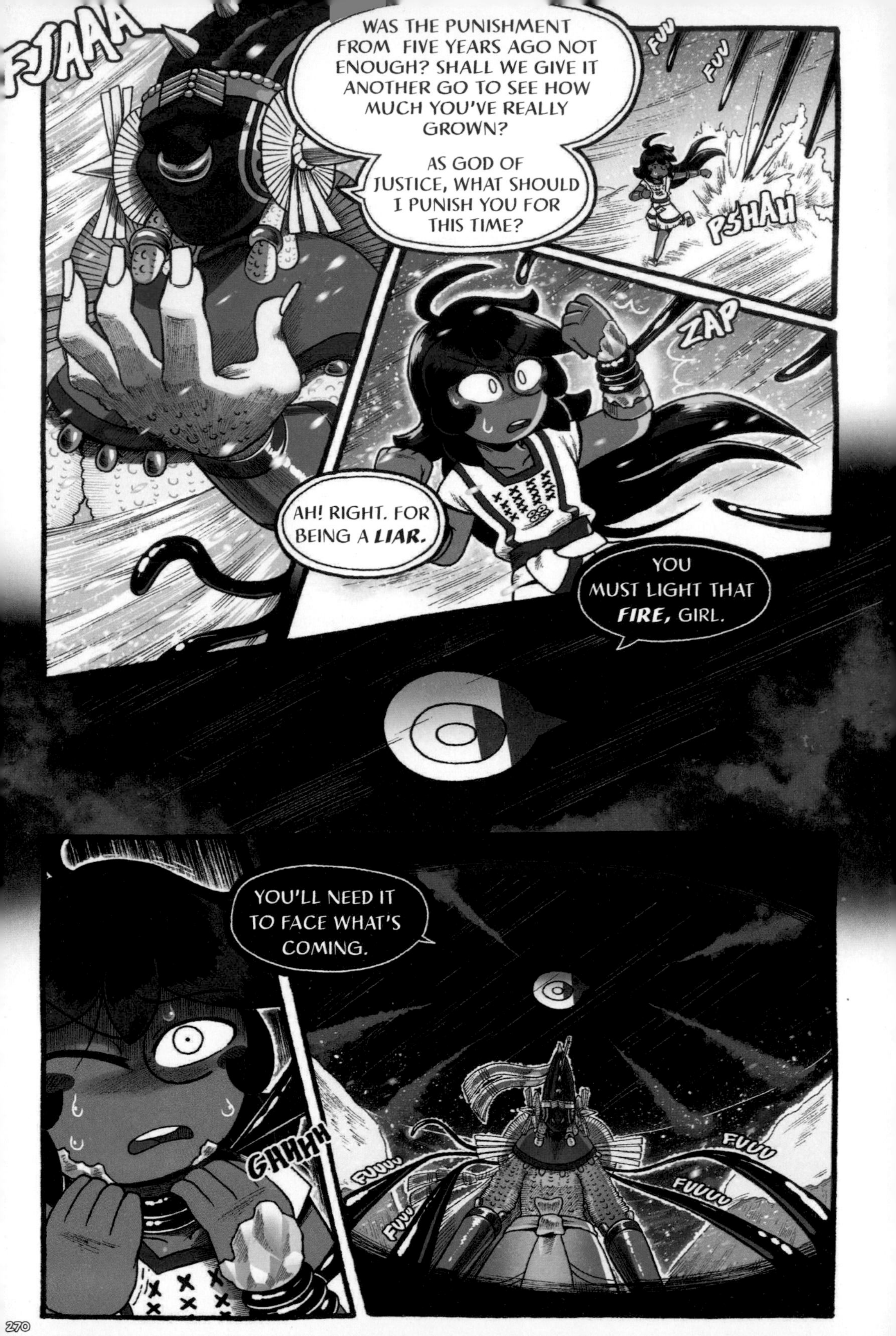
FJAAA
WAS THE PUNISHMENT FROM FIVE YEARS AGO NOT ENOUGH? SHALL WE GIVE IT ANOTHER GO TO SEE HOW MUCH YOU'VE REALLY GROWN?
AS GOD OF JUSTICE, WHAT SHOULD I PUNISH YOU FOR THIS TIME?
FUU
FUU
PSHAH
ZAP
AH! RIGHT. FOR BEING A LIAR.
YOU MUST LIGHT THAT FIRE, GIRL.
YOU'LL NEED IT TO FACE WHAT'S COMING.
GAHHH
FUUU
FUUU
FUUU
FUUU

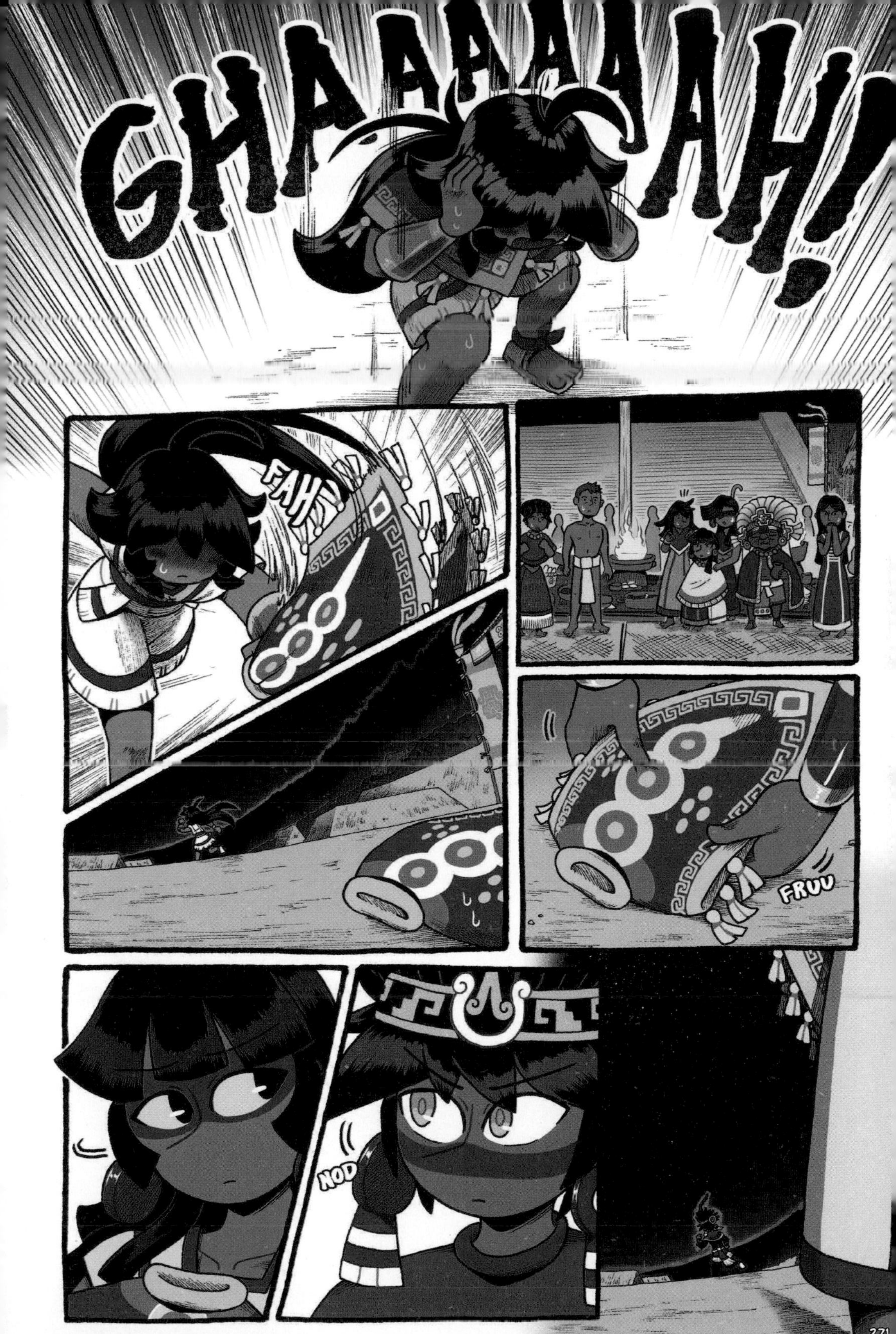
GHAAAAAAH!!
FAH
FRUU
NOD

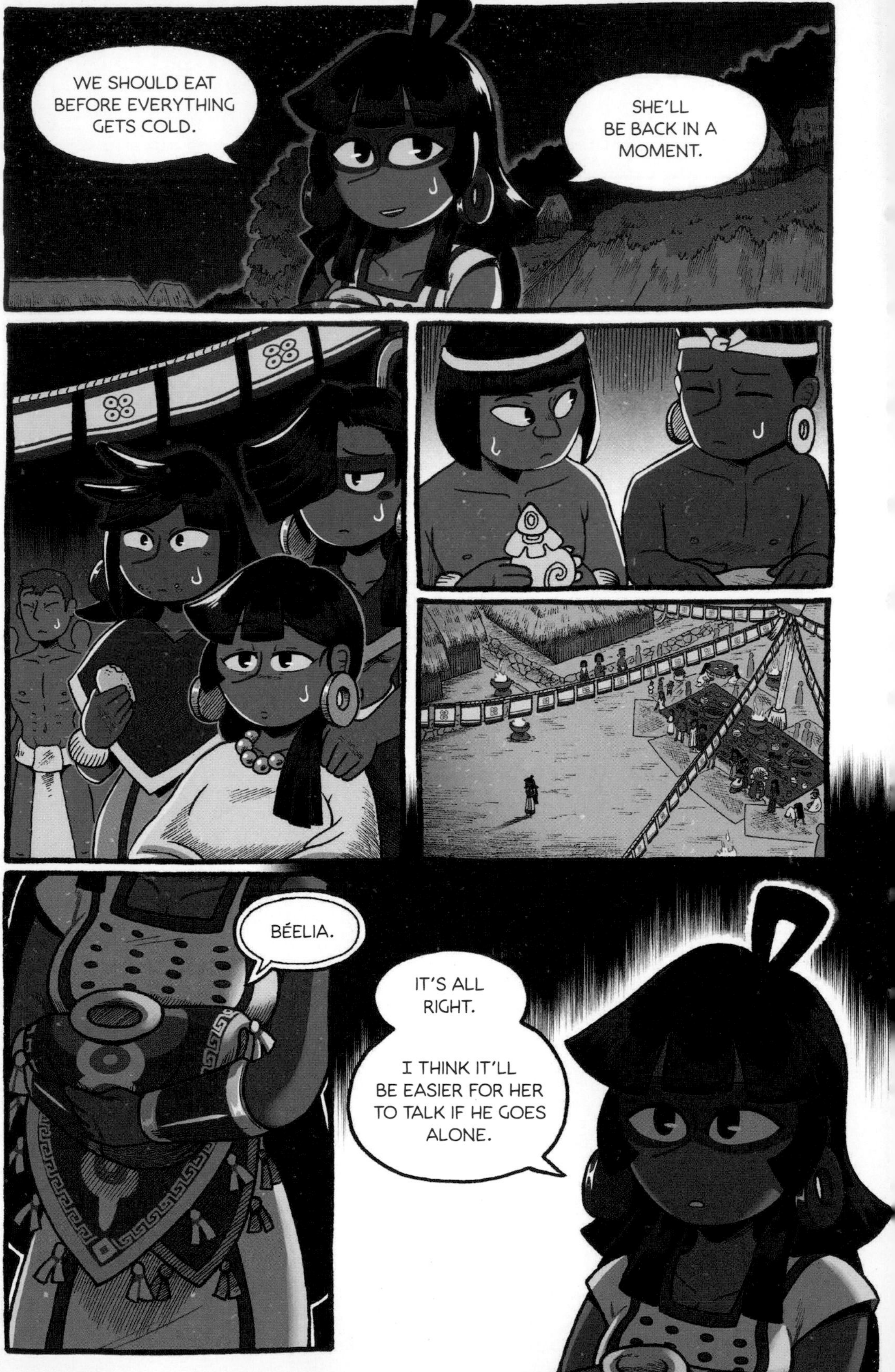
WE SHOULD EAT BEFORE EVERYTHING GETS COLD.
SHE'LL BE BACK IN A MOMENT.
BÉELIA.
IT'S ALL RIGHT.
I THINK IT'LL BE EASIER FOR HER TO TALK IF HE GOES ALONE.

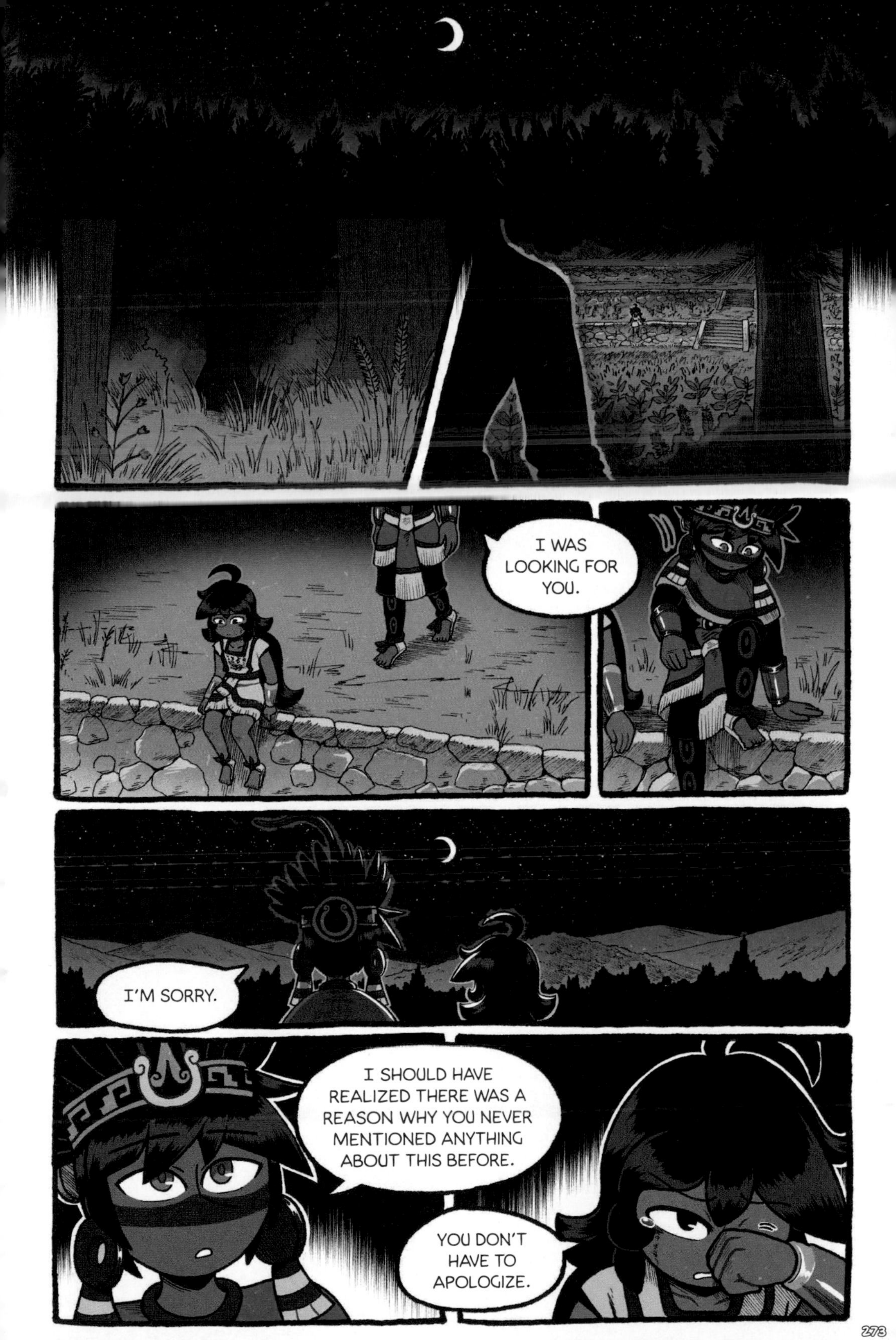
I WAS LOOKING FOR YOU.
I'M SORRY.
I SHOULD HAVE REALIZED THERE WAS A REASON WHY YOU NEVER MENTIONED ANYTHING ABOUT THIS BEFORE.
YOU DON'T HAVE TO APOLOGIZE.

THEY TOLD YOU WHAT THEY THINK IS TRUE...
...BUT THEY DON'T KNOW WHAT REALLY HAPPENED. IT'S MY FAULT, THOUGH. I'VE BEEN LIVING A LIE ALL THESE YEARS.
THAT DAY, I FAILED MISERABLY.
I GOT CARRIED AWAY, AND IF IT WEREN'T FOR CHICAHUALIZTEOTL...
...I WOULD HAVE DIED ALONG WITH EVERYONE ELSE.
THEY RECEIVED ME AS A HERO, BUT I COULDN'T BRING MYSELF TO TELL THEM WHAT REALLY HAPPENED...
...AND WITH TIME IT BECAME EVEN HARDER.
NOW IT FEELS ALMOST IMPOSSIBLE.
WHAT WILL THEY SAY WHEN THEY FIND OUT I'M A FRAUD?
I WAS SO TIRED OF THIS. THAT'S WHY I LEFT ON MY BIRTHDAY. I THOUGHT THEY WOULD HAVE CELEBRATED WITHOUT ME AND I WOULD SPARE MYSELF FROM RELIVING THOSE MEMORIES YET AGAIN.
NO ONE KNOWS THE TRUTH BUT CHICAHUALIZTEOTL...
...AND WHEN I LOOK AT HIM, I JUST REMEMBER THAT I CAN'T DO ANYTHING ON MY OWN.

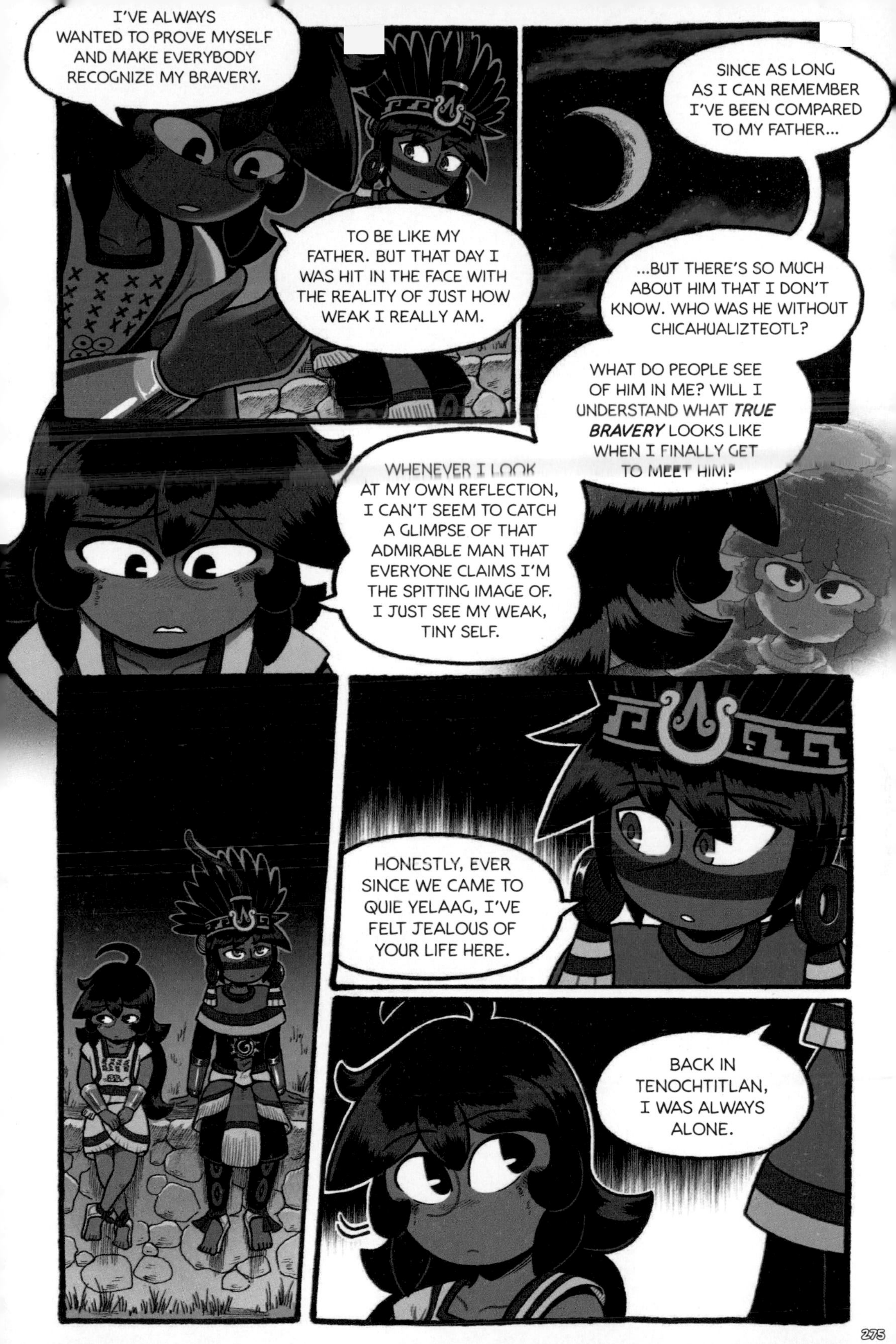
I'VE ALWAYS WANTED TO PROVE MYSELF AND MAKE EVERYBODY RECOGNIZE MY BRAVERY.
TO BE LIKE MY FATHER. BUT THAT DAY I WAS HIT IN THE FACE WITH THE REALITY OF JUST HOW WEAK I REALLY AM.
SINCE AS LONG AS I CAN REMEMBER I'VE BEEN COMPARED TO MY FATHER...
...BUT THERE'S SO MUCH ABOUT HIM THAT I DON'T KNOW. WHO WAS HE WITHOUT CHICAHUALIZTEOTL?
WHAT DO PEOPLE SEE OF HIM IN ME? WILL I UNDERSTAND WHAT TRUE BRAVERY LOOKS LIKE WHEN I FINALLY GET TO MEET HIM?
WHENEVER I LOOK AT MY OWN REFLECTION, I CAN'T SEEM TO CATCH A GLIMPSE OF THAT ADMIRABLE MAN THAT EVERYONE CLAIMS I'M THE SPITTING IMAGE OF. I JUST SEE MY WEAK, TINY SELF.
HONESTLY, EVER SINCE WE CAME TO QUIE YELAAG, I'VE FELT JEALOUS OF YOUR LIFE HERE.
BACK IN TENOCHTITLAN, I WAS ALWAYS ALONE.

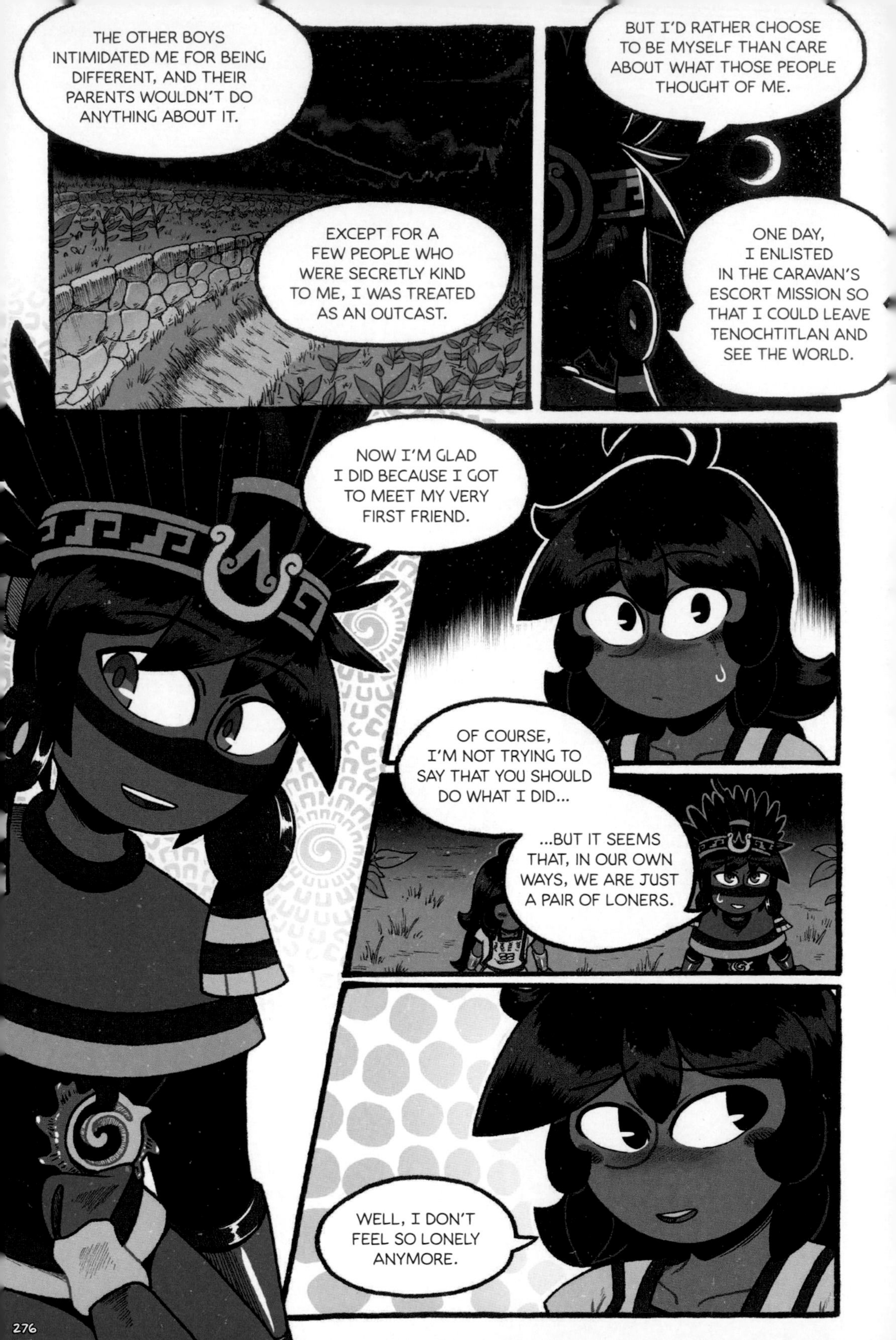
THE OTHER BOYS INTIMIDATED ME FOR BEING DIFFERENT, AND THEIR PARENTS WOULDN'T DO ANYTHING ABOUT IT.
EXCEPT FOR A FEW PEOPLE WHO WERE SECRETLY KIND TO ME, I WAS TREATED AS AN OUTCAST.
BUT I'D RATHER CHOOSE TO BE MYSELF THAN CARE ABOUT WHAT THOSE PEOPLE THOUGHT OF ME.
ONE DAY, I ENLISTED IN THE CARAVAN'S ESCORT MISSION SO THAT I COULD LEAVE TENOCHTITLAN AND SEE THE WORLD.
NOW I'M GLAD I DID BECAUSE I GOT TO MEET MY VERY FIRST FRIEND.
OF COURSE, I'M NOT TRYING TO SAY THAT YOU SHOULD DO WHAT I DID...
...BUT IT SEEMS THAT, IN OUR OWN WAYS, WE ARE JUST A PAIR OF LONERS.
WELL, I DON'T FEEL SO LONELY ANYMORE.

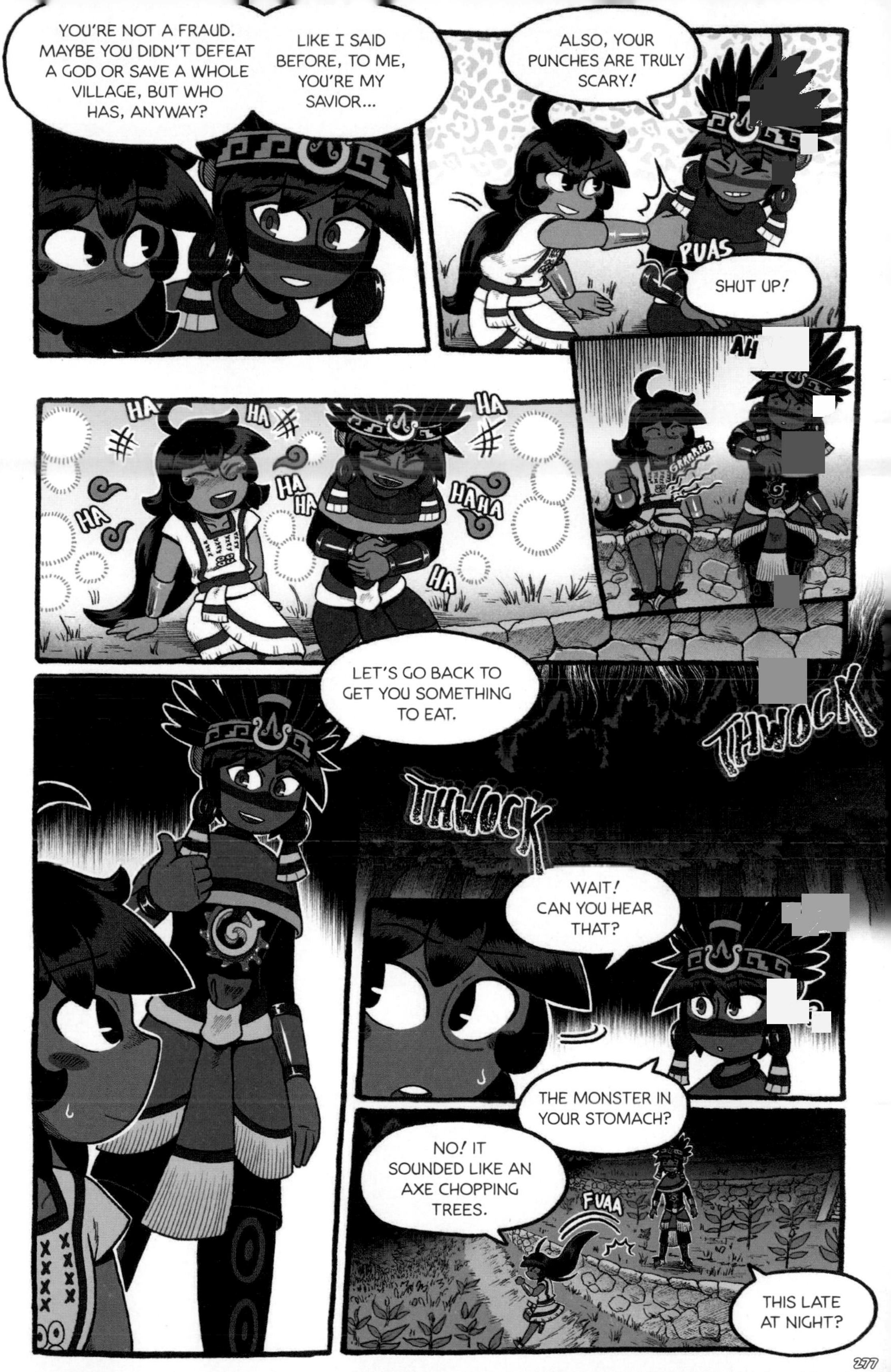
YOU'RE NOT A FRAUD. MAYBE YOU DIDN'T DEFEAT A GOD OR SAVE A WHOLE VILLAGE, BUT WHO HAS, ANYWAY?
LIKE I SAID BEFORE, TO ME, YOU'RE MY SAVIOR...
ALSO, YOUR PUNCHES ARE TRULY SCARY!
PUAS
SHUT UP!
AH
HA
HA
HA
HA HA
HA
HAHA
HA
GRRRRRR
LET'S GO BACK TO GET YOU SOMETHING TO EAT.
THWOCK
THWOCK
WAIT! CAN YOU HEAR THAT?
THE MONSTER IN YOUR STOMACH?
NO! IT SOUNDED LIKE AN AXE CHOPPING TREES.
FUAA
THIS LATE AT NIGHT?

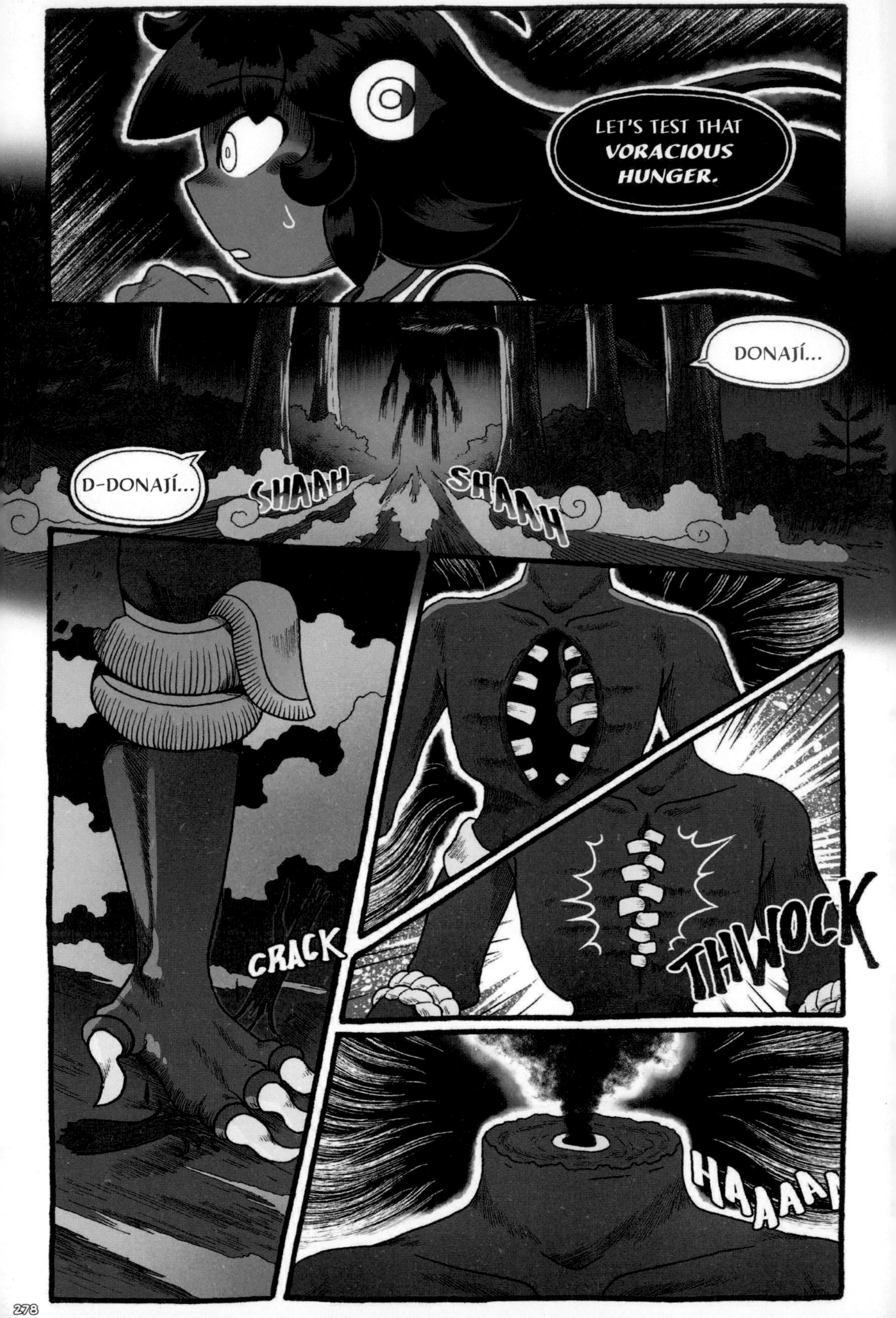
LET'S TEST THAT VORACIOUS HUNGER.
DONAJÍ...
D-DONAJÍ...
SHAAH
SHAAAH
CRACK
THWOCK
HAAAAA

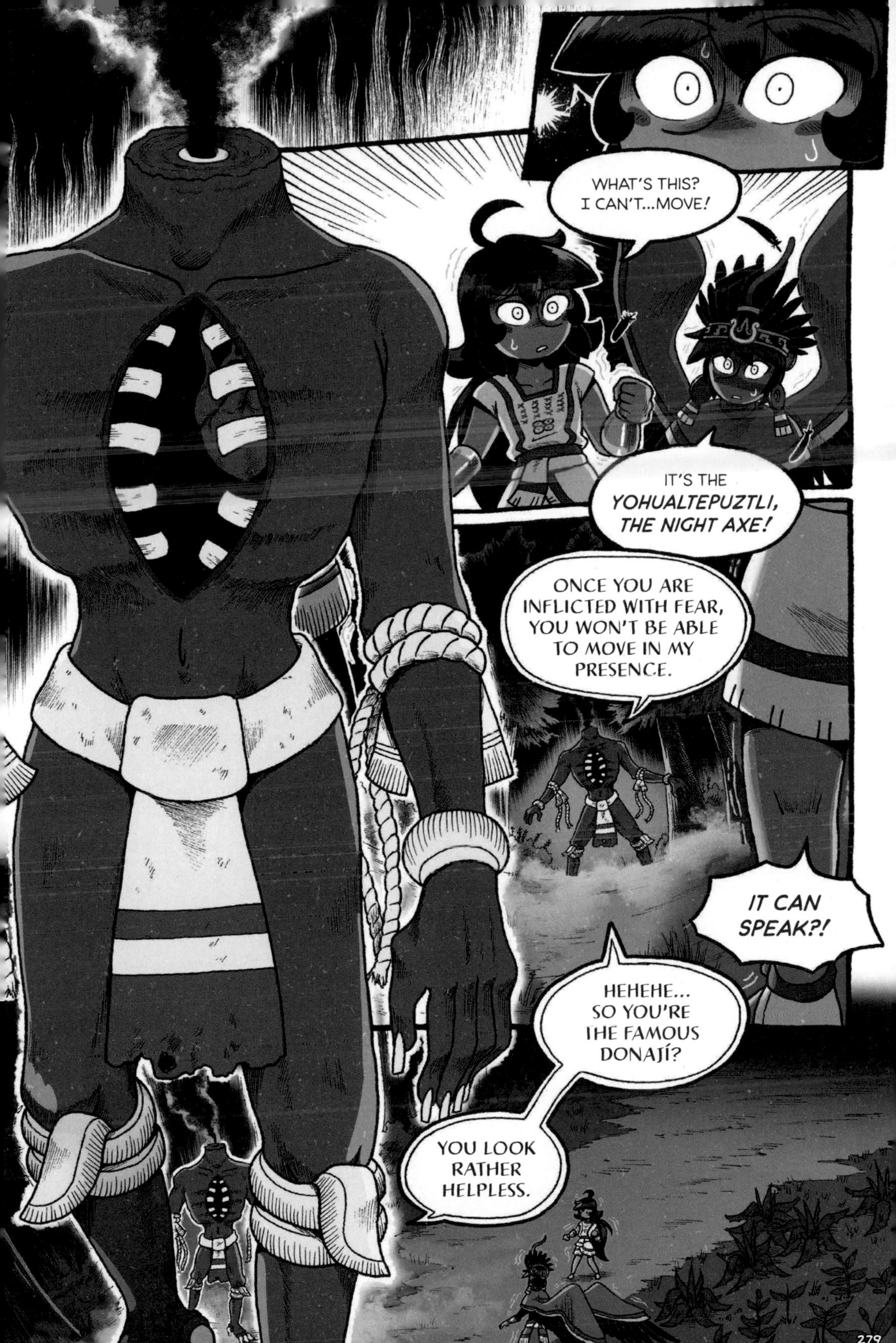
WHAT'S THIS? I CAN'T...MOVE!
IT'S THE *YOHUALTEPUZTLI, THE NIGHT AXE!*
ONCE YOU ARE INFLICTED WITH FEAR, YOU WON'T BE ABLE TO MOVE IN MY PRESENCE.
IT CAN SPEAK?!
HEHEHE... SO YOU'RE THE FAMOUS DONAJÍ?
YOU LOOK RATHER HELPLESS.

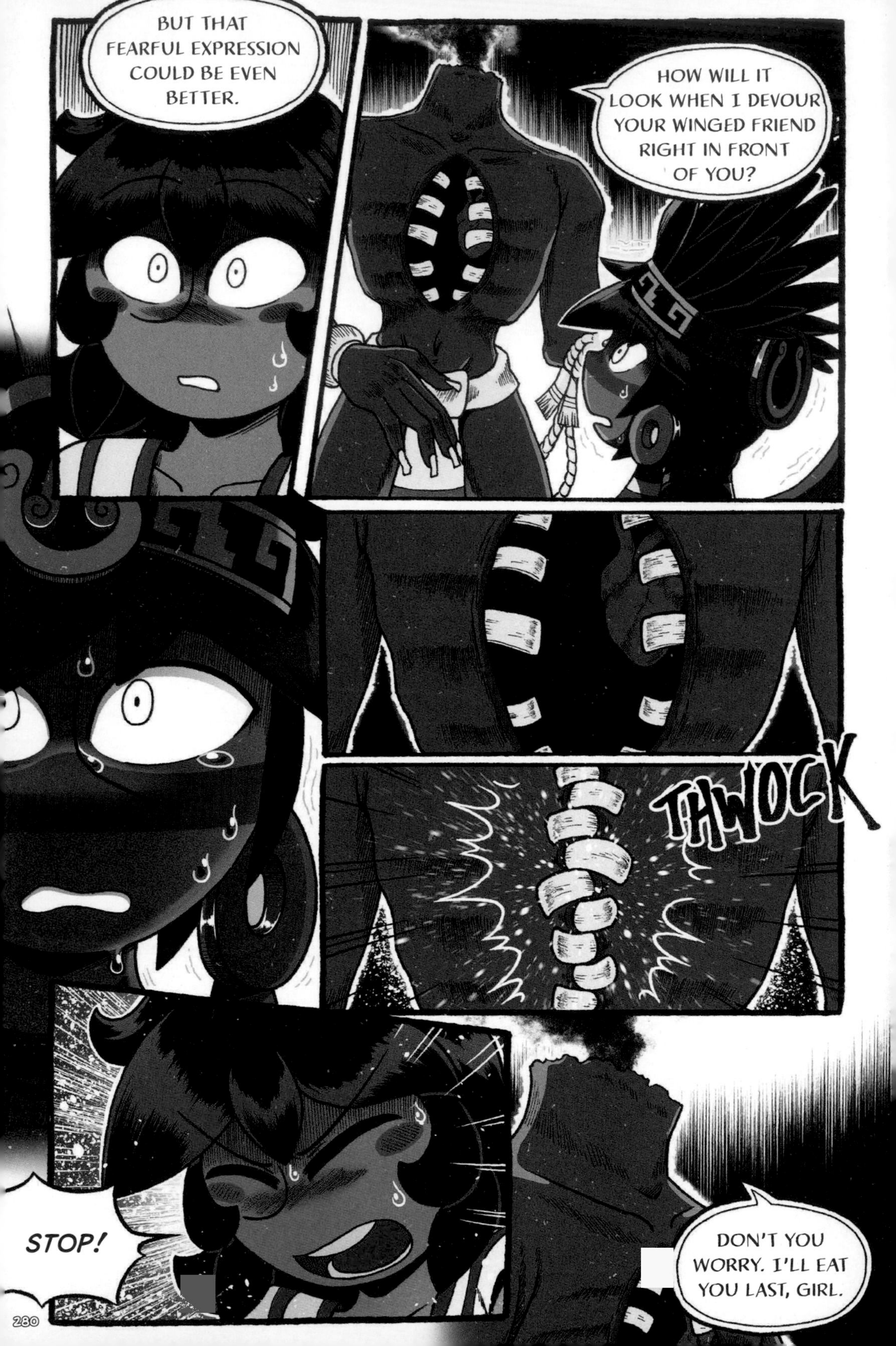
BUT THAT FEARFUL EXPRESSION COULD BE EVEN BETTER.
HOW WILL IT LOOK WHEN I DEVOUR YOUR WINGED FRIEND RIGHT IN FRONT OF YOU?
THWOCK
STOP!
DON'T YOU WORRY. I'LL EAT YOU LAST, GIRL.

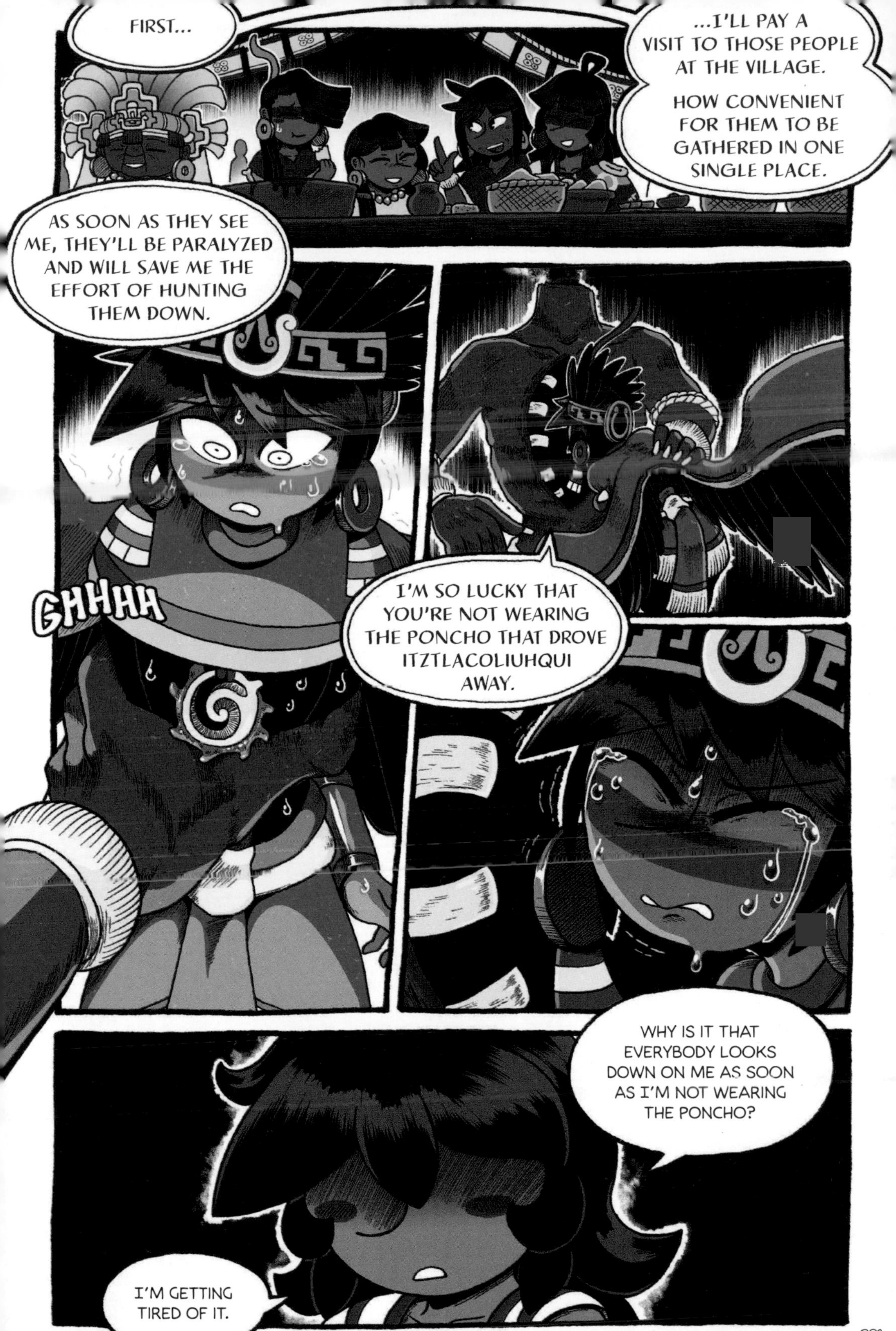
FIRST...
...I'LL PAY A VISIT TO THOSE PEOPLE AT THE VILLAGE.
HOW CONVENIENT FOR THEM TO BE GATHERED IN ONE SINGLE PLACE.
AS SOON AS THEY SEE ME, THEY'LL BE PARALYZED AND WILL SAVE ME THE EFFORT OF HUNTING THEM DOWN.
GHHHA
I'M SO LUCKY THAT YOU'RE NOT WEARING THE PONCHO THAT DROVE ITZTLACOLIUHQUI AWAY.
WHY IS IT THAT EVERYBODY LOOKS DOWN ON ME AS SOON AS I'M NOT WEARING THE PONCHO?
I'M GETTING TIRED OF IT.

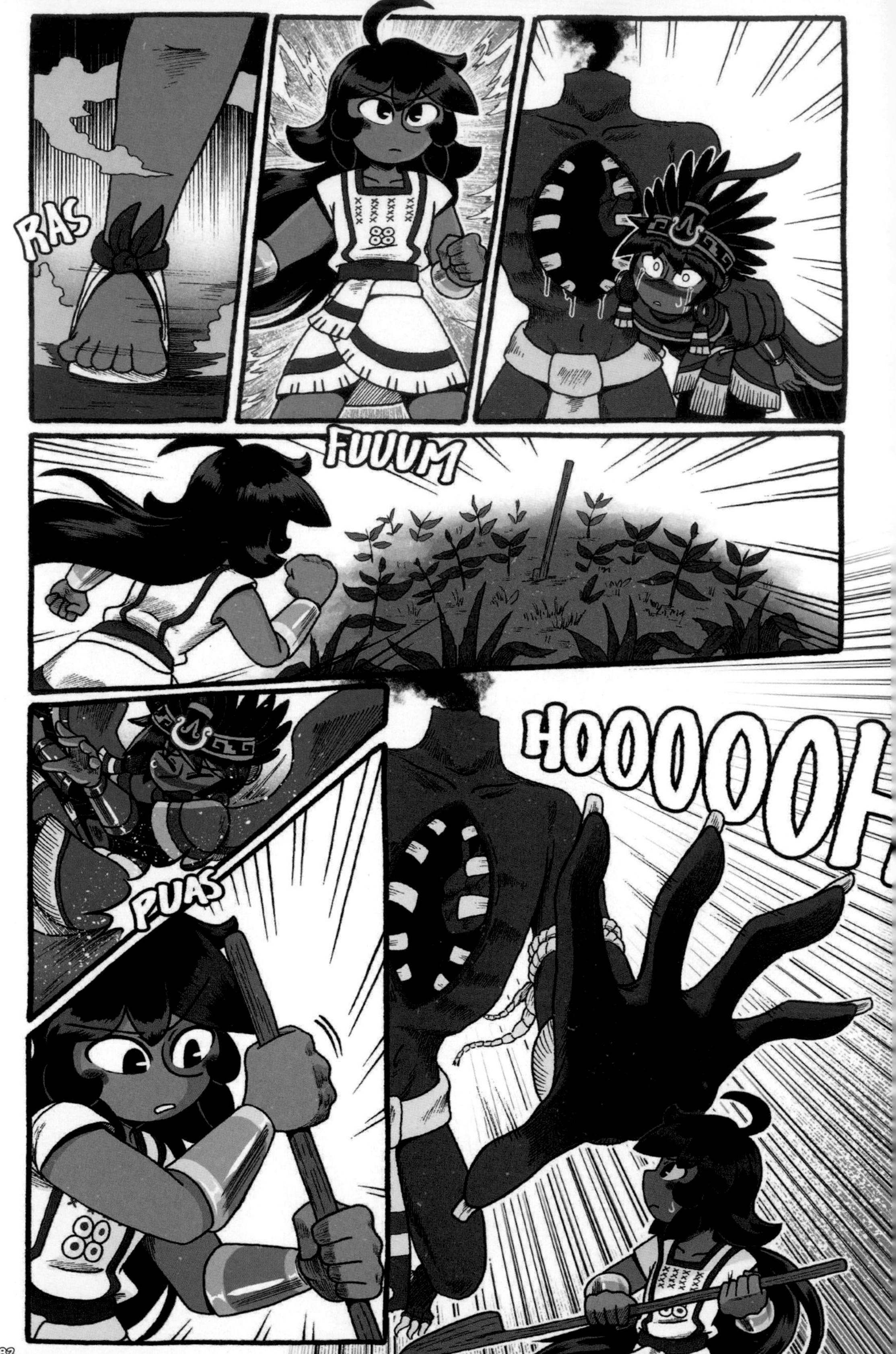
RAS
FUUUM
PUAS
HOOOOOH

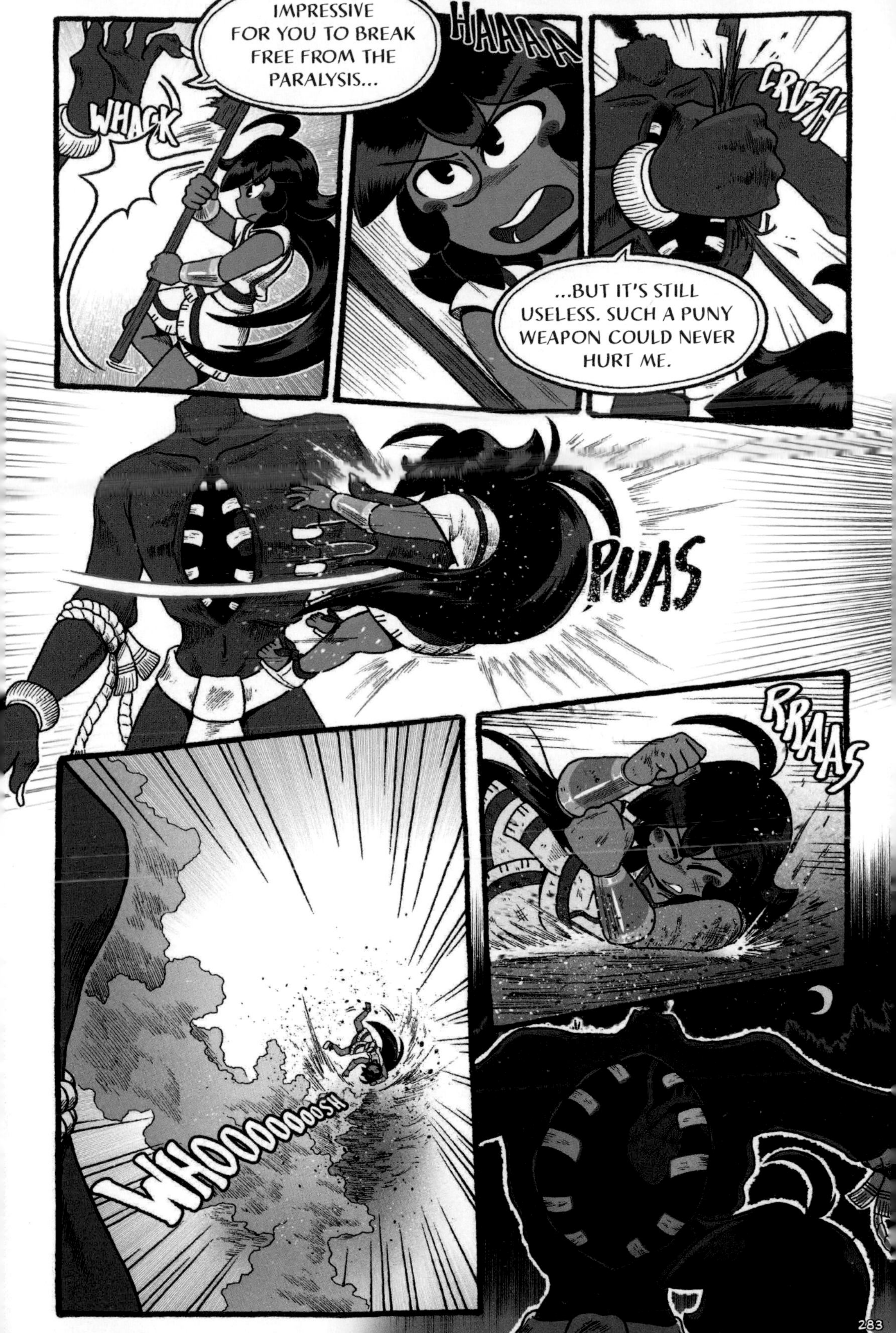
IMPRESSIVE FOR YOU TO BREAK FREE FROM THE PARALYSIS...
WHACK
HAAAAA
CRUSH
...BUT IT'S STILL USELESS. SUCH A PUNY WEAPON COULD NEVER HURT ME.
PUAS
RRAAS
WHOOOOOOOSH

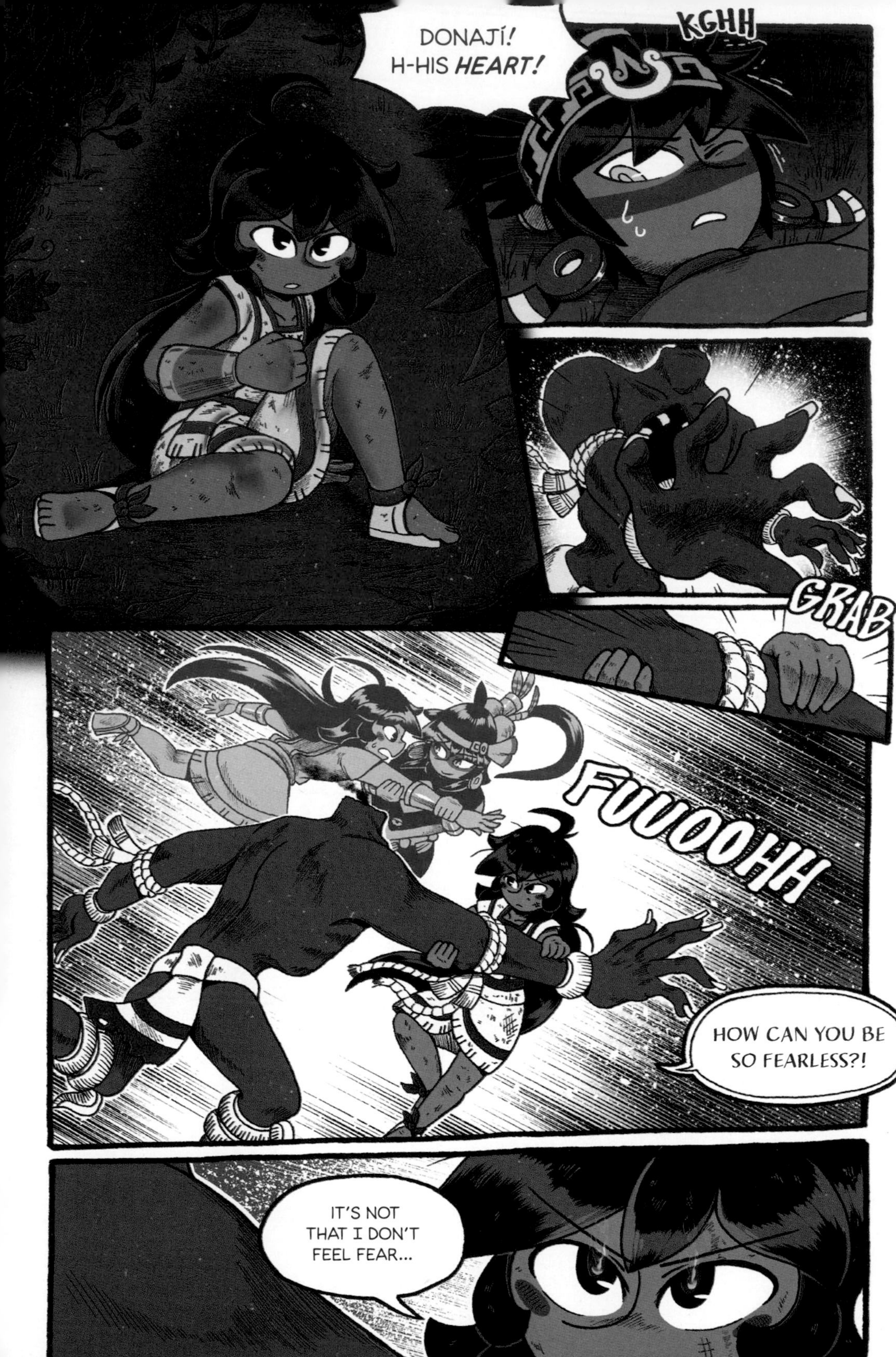
DONAJÍ!
H-HIS *HEART!*
KGHH
GRAB
FUUUOOHH
HOW CAN YOU BE SO FEARLESS?!
IT'S NOT THAT I DON'T FEEL FEAR...

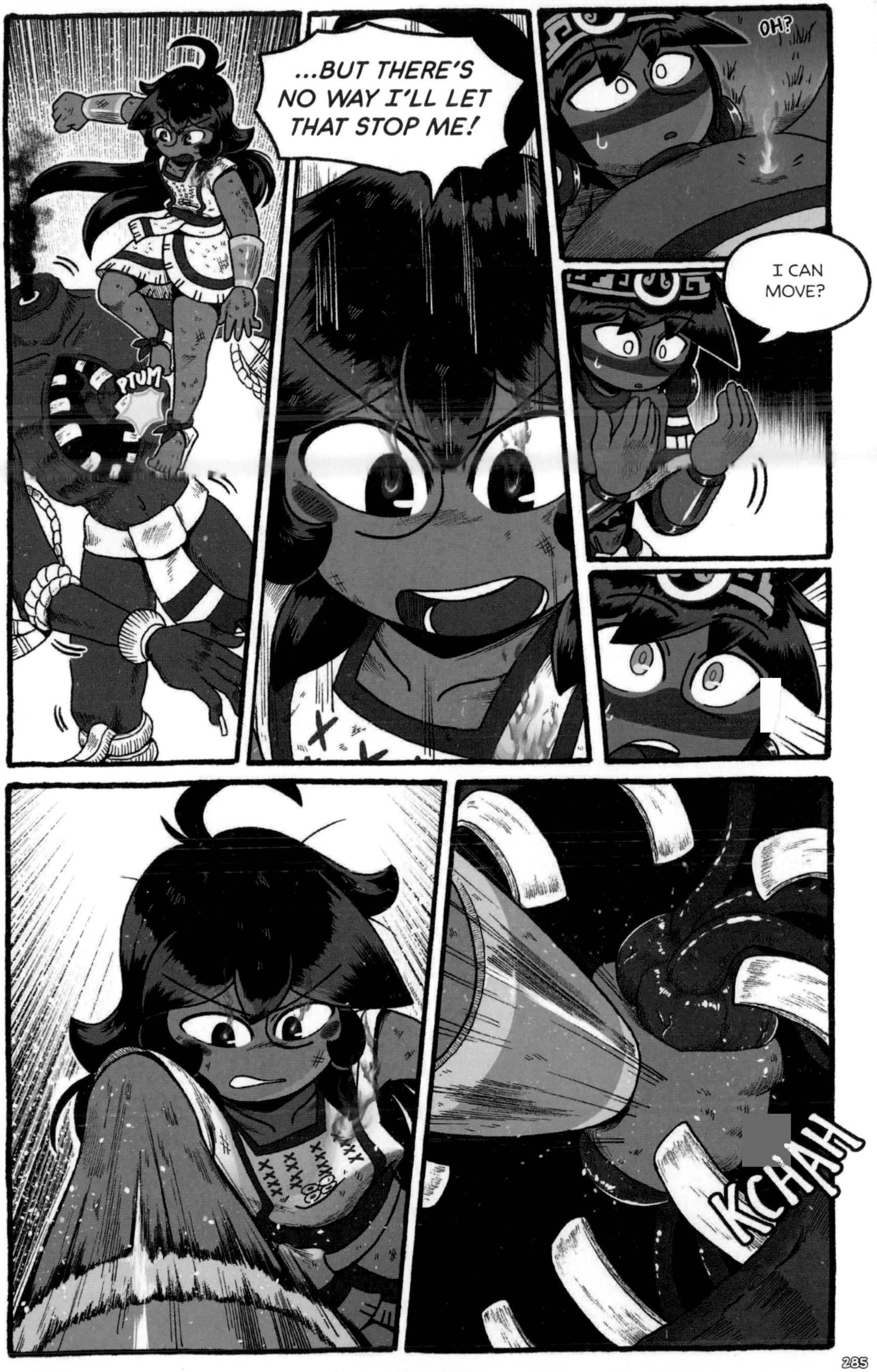
PTUM
...BUT THERE'S NO WAY I'LL LET THAT STOP ME!
OH?
I CAN MOVE?
KCHAH

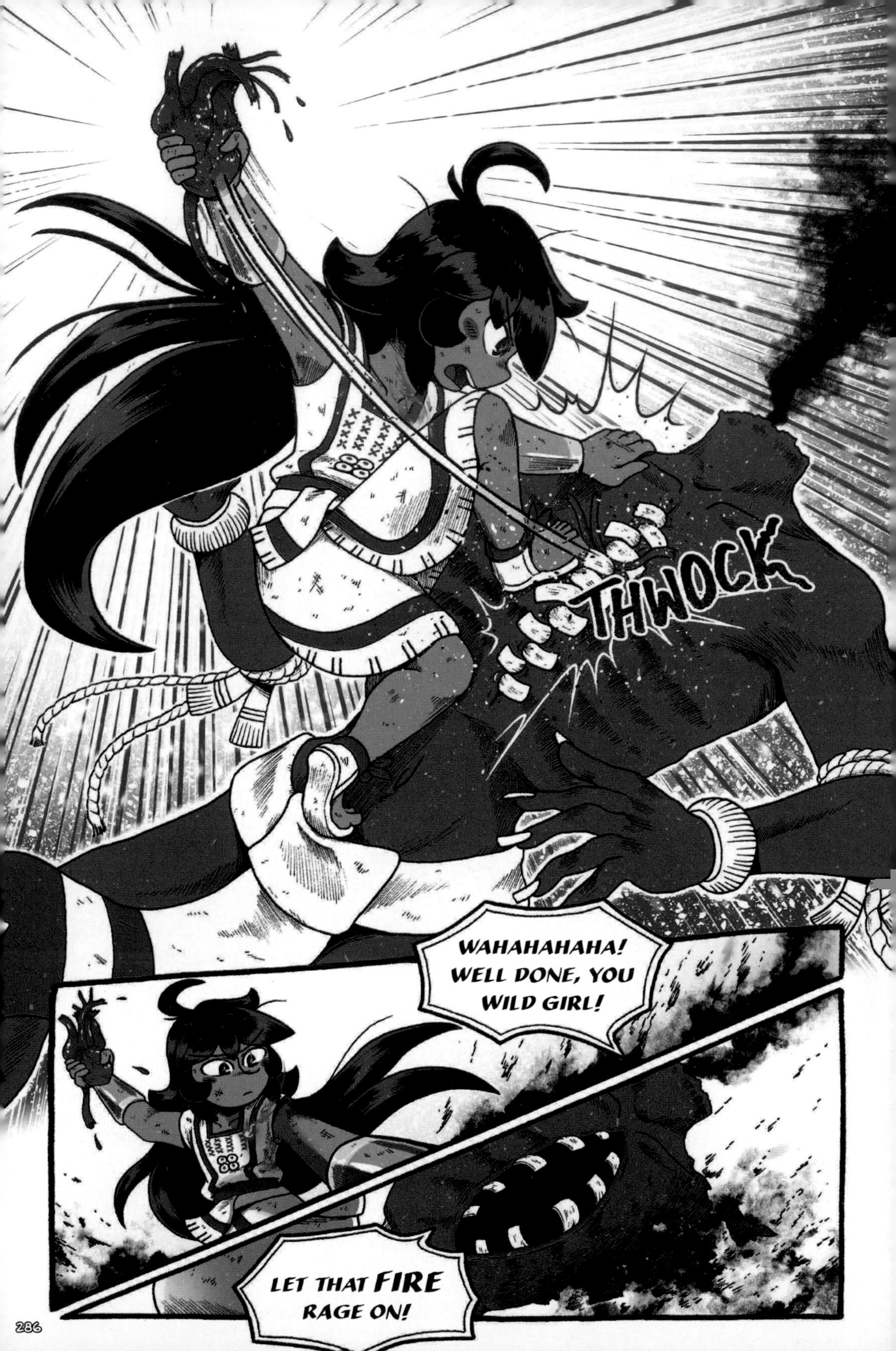
THWOCK
WAHAHAHAHA! WELL DONE, YOU WILD GIRL!
LET THAT FIRE RAGE ON!

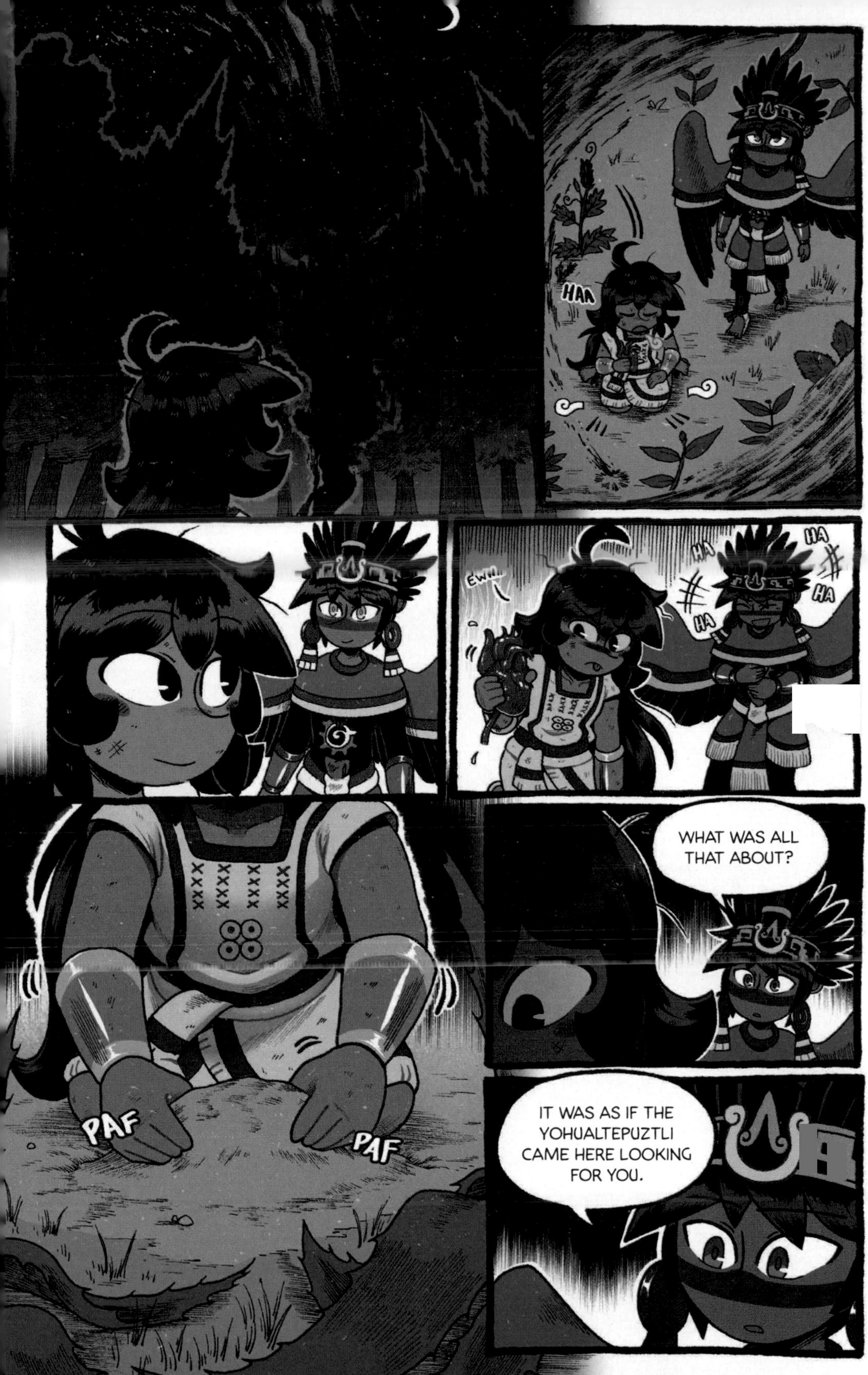
HAA
EWW
HA
HA
HA
HA
WHAT WAS ALL THAT ABOUT?
PAF
PAF
IT WAS AS IF THE YOHUALTEPUZTLI CAME HERE LOOKING FOR YOU.

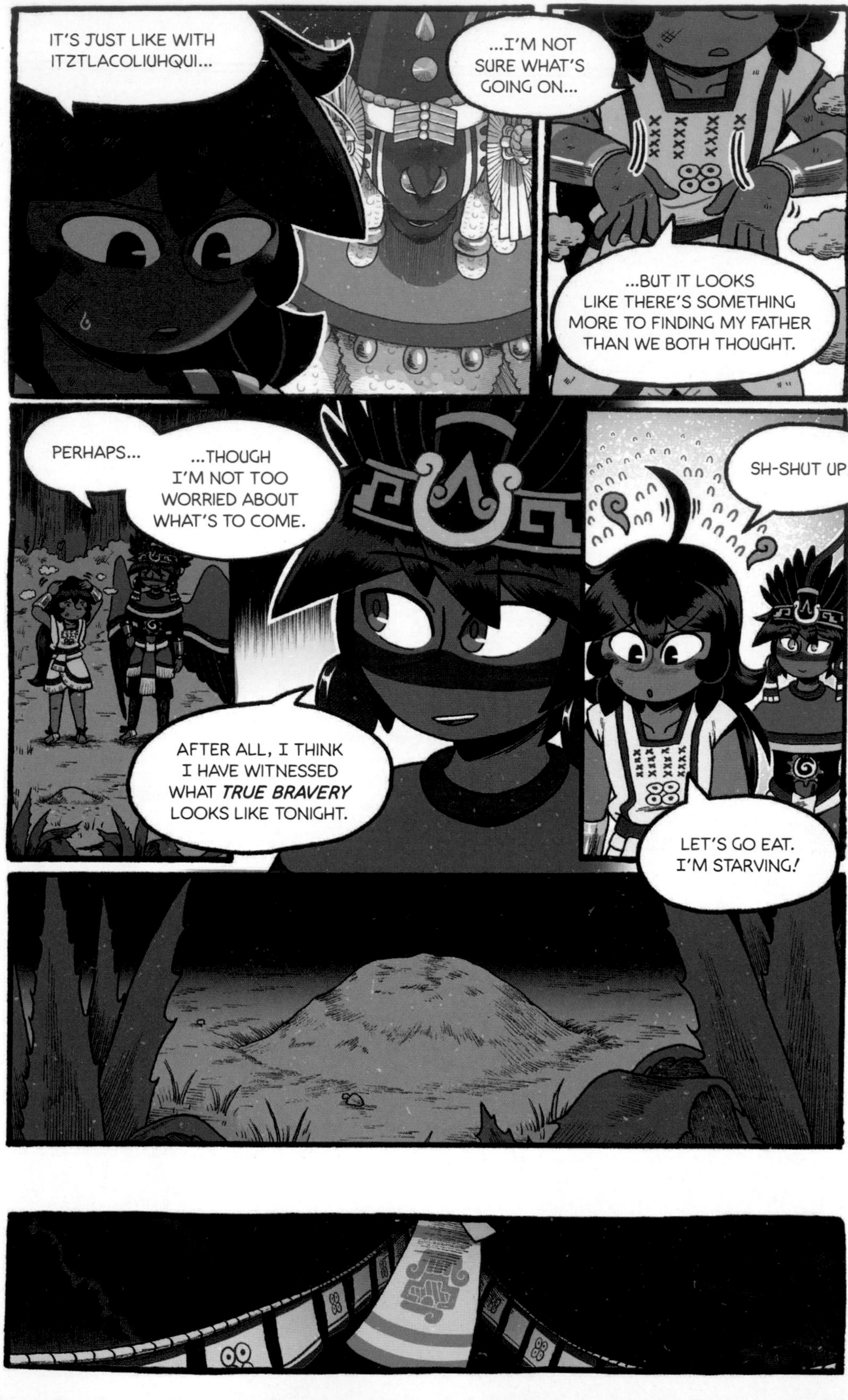
IT'S JUST LIKE WITH ITZTLACOLIUHQUI...
...I'M NOT SURE WHAT'S GOING ON...
...BUT IT LOOKS LIKE THERE'S SOMETHING MORE TO FINDING MY FATHER THAN WE BOTH THOUGHT.
PERHAPS...
...THOUGH I'M NOT TOO WORRIED ABOUT WHAT'S TO COME.
AFTER ALL, I THINK I HAVE WITNESSED WHAT ***TRUE BRAVERY*** LOOKS LIKE TONIGHT.
SH-SHUT UP!
LET'S GO EAT. I'M STARVING!

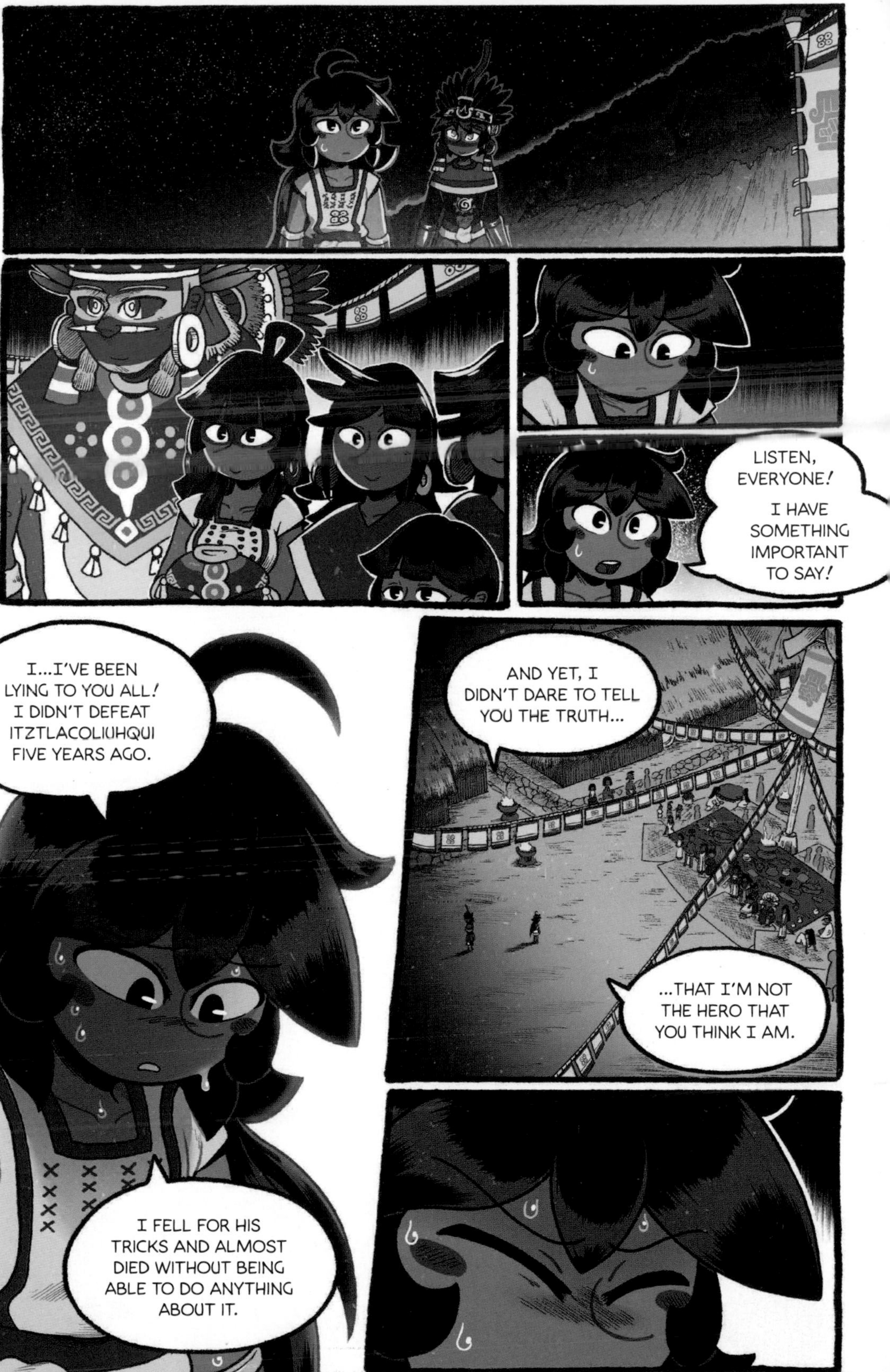
LISTEN, EVERYONE! I HAVE SOMETHING IMPORTANT TO SAY!
I...I'VE BEEN LYING TO YOU ALL! I DIDN'T DEFEAT ITZTLACOLIUHQUI FIVE YEARS AGO.
I FELL FOR HIS TRICKS AND ALMOST DIED WITHOUT BEING ABLE TO DO ANYTHING ABOUT IT.
AND YET, I DIDN'T DARE TO TELL YOU THE TRUTH...
...THAT I'M NOT THE HERO THAT YOU THINK I AM.

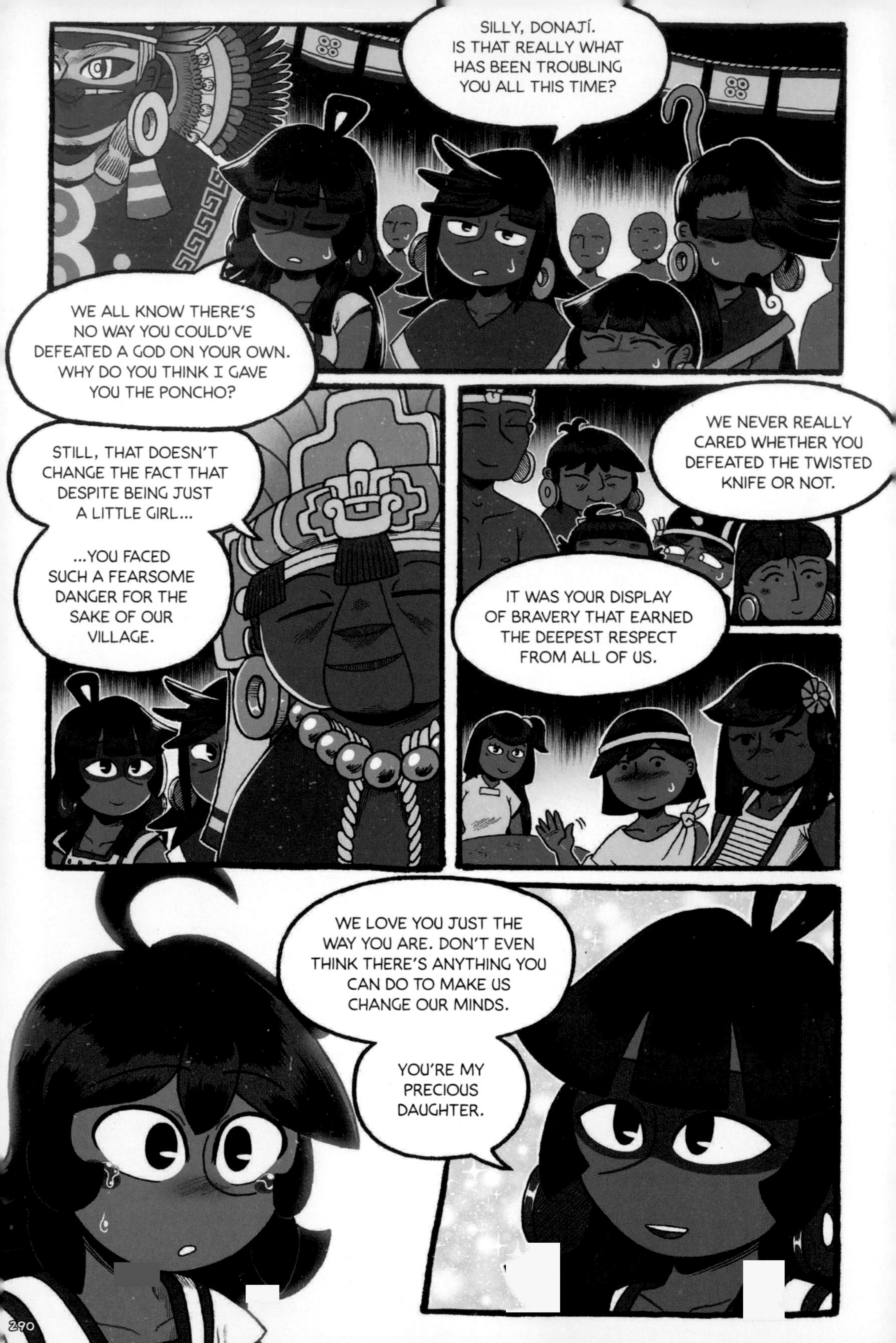
SILLY, DONAJÍ. IS THAT REALLY WHAT HAS BEEN TROUBLING YOU ALL THIS TIME?
WE ALL KNOW THERE'S NO WAY YOU COULD'VE DEFEATED A GOD ON YOUR OWN. WHY DO YOU THINK I GAVE YOU THE PONCHO?
STILL, THAT DOESN'T CHANGE THE FACT THAT DESPITE BEING JUST A LITTLE GIRL...
...YOU FACED SUCH A FEARSOME DANGER FOR THE SAKE OF OUR VILLAGE.
WE NEVER REALLY CARED WHETHER YOU DEFEATED THE TWISTED KNIFE OR NOT.
IT WAS YOUR DISPLAY OF BRAVERY THAT EARNED THE DEEPEST RESPECT FROM ALL OF US.
WE LOVE YOU JUST THE WAY YOU ARE. DON'T EVEN THINK THERE'S ANYTHING YOU CAN DO TO MAKE US CHANGE OUR MINDS.
YOU'RE MY PRECIOUS DAUGHTER.

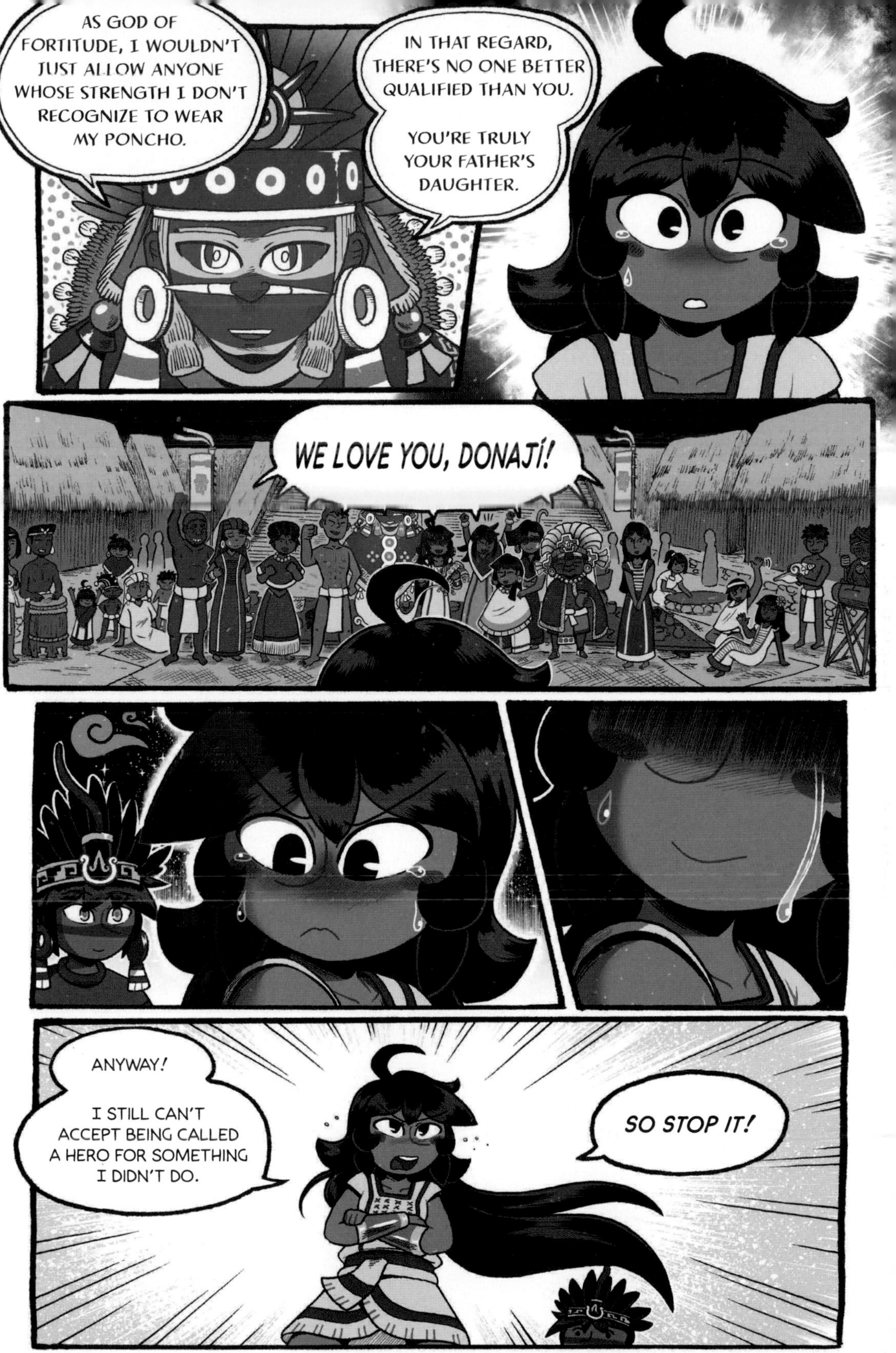
AS GOD OF FORTITUDE, I WOULDN'T JUST ALLOW ANYONE WHOSE STRENGTH I DON'T RECOGNIZE TO WEAR MY PONCHO.
IN THAT REGARD, THERE'S NO ONE BETTER QUALIFIED THAN YOU.
YOU'RE TRULY YOUR FATHER'S DAUGHTER.
WE LOVE YOU, DONAJÍ!
ANYWAY!
I STILL CAN'T ACCEPT BEING CALLED A HERO FOR SOMETHING I DIDN'T DO.
SO STOP IT!

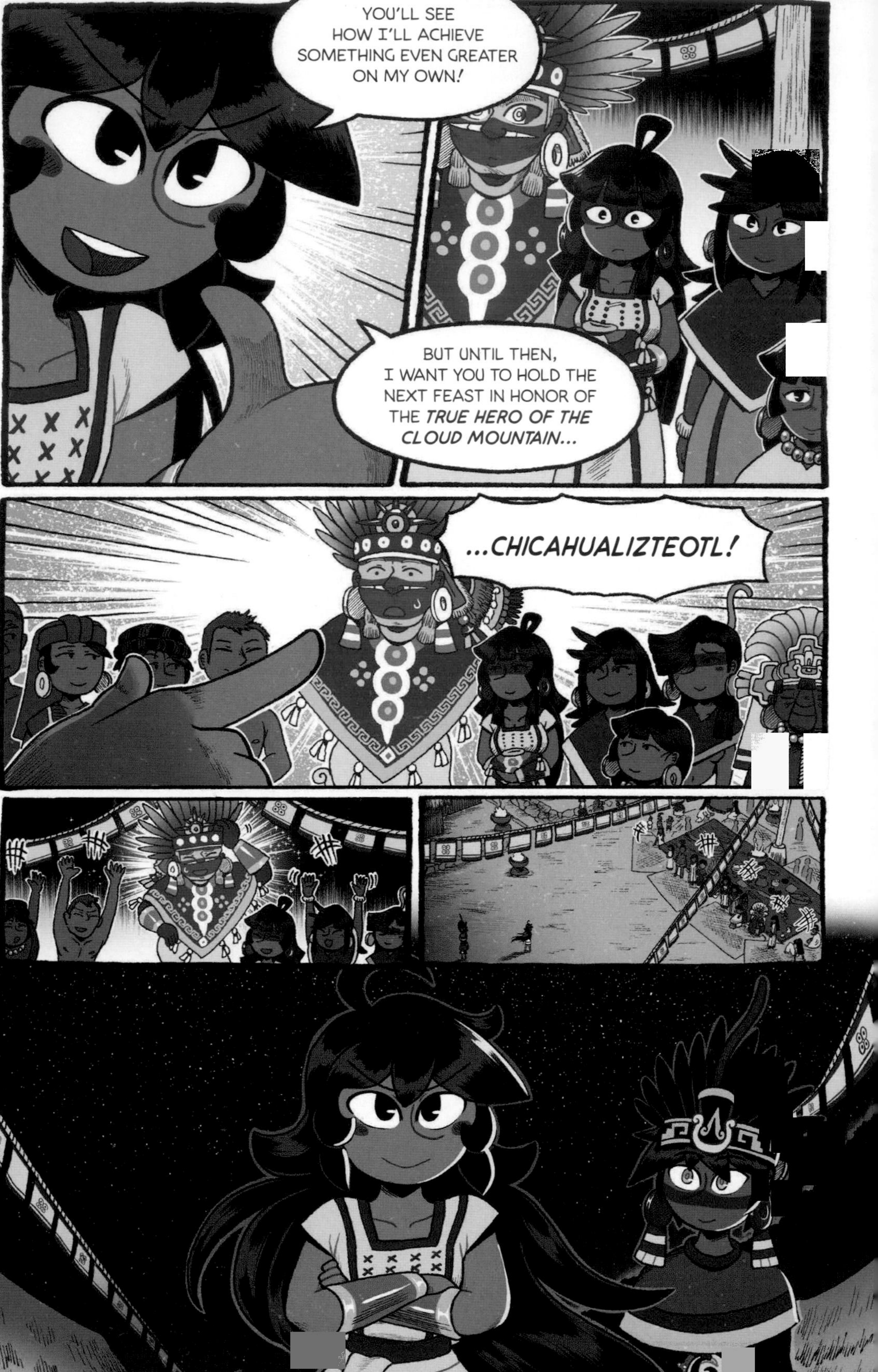
YOU'LL SEE HOW I'LL ACHIEVE SOMETHING EVEN GREATER ON MY OWN!
BUT UNTIL THEN, I WANT YOU TO HOLD THE NEXT FEAST IN HONOR OF THE *TRUE HERO OF THE CLOUD MOUNTAIN...*
...CHICAHUALIZTEOTL!

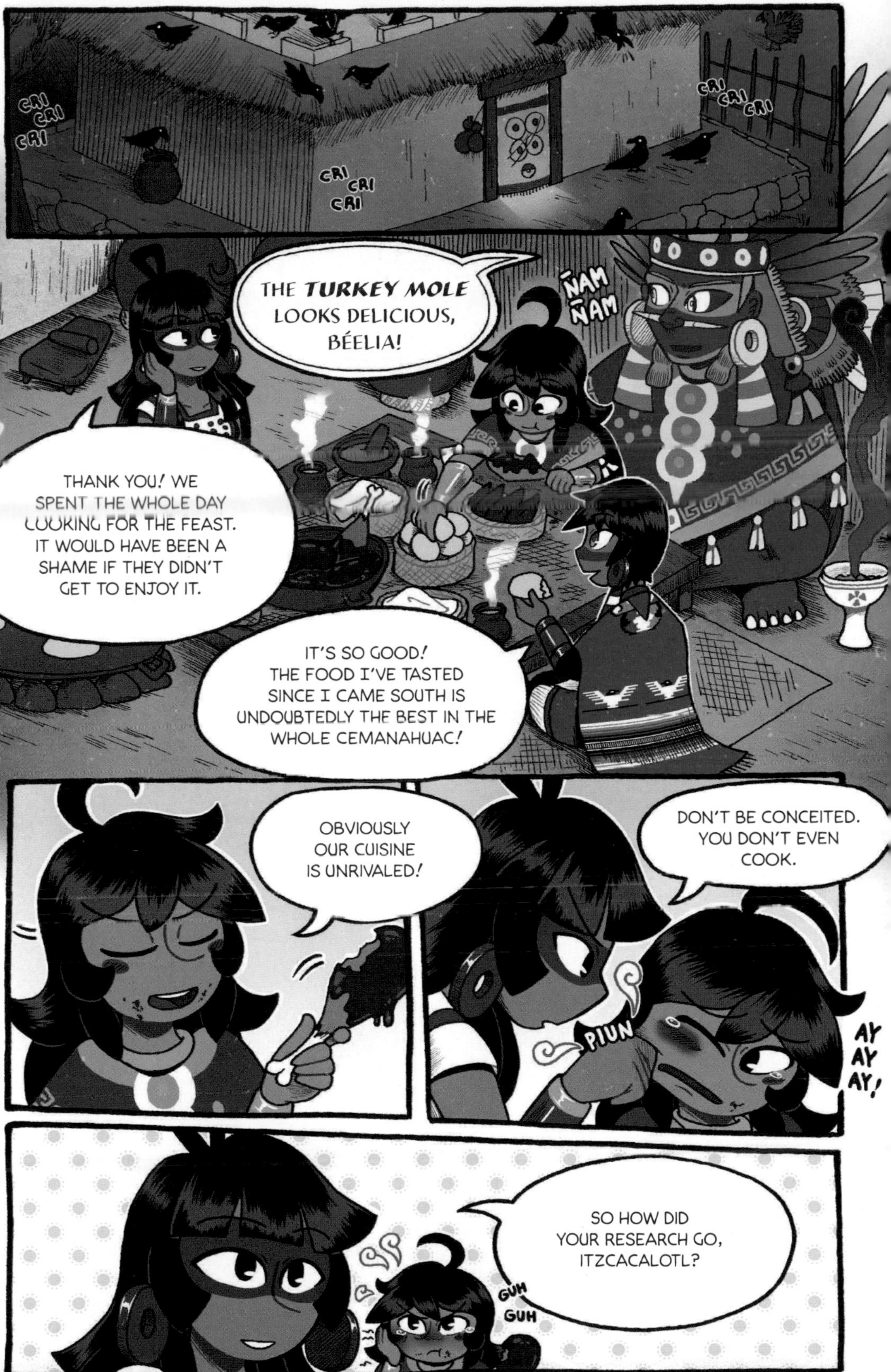

CRI CRI CRI
CRI CRI CRI
CRI CRI CRI
THE *TURKEY MOLE* LOOKS DELICIOUS, BÉELIA!
ÑAM ÑAM
THANK YOU! WE SPENT THE WHOLE DAY COOKING FOR THE FEAST. IT WOULD HAVE BEEN A SHAME IF THEY DIDN'T GET TO ENJOY IT.
IT'S SO GOOD! THE FOOD I'VE TASTED SINCE I CAME SOUTH IS UNDOUBTEDLY THE BEST IN THE WHOLE CEMANAHUAC!
OBVIOUSLY OUR CUISINE IS UNRIVALED!
DON'T BE CONCEITED. YOU DON'T EVEN COOK.
PIUN
AY AY AY!
SO HOW DID YOUR RESEARCH GO, ITZCACALOTL?
GUH GUH

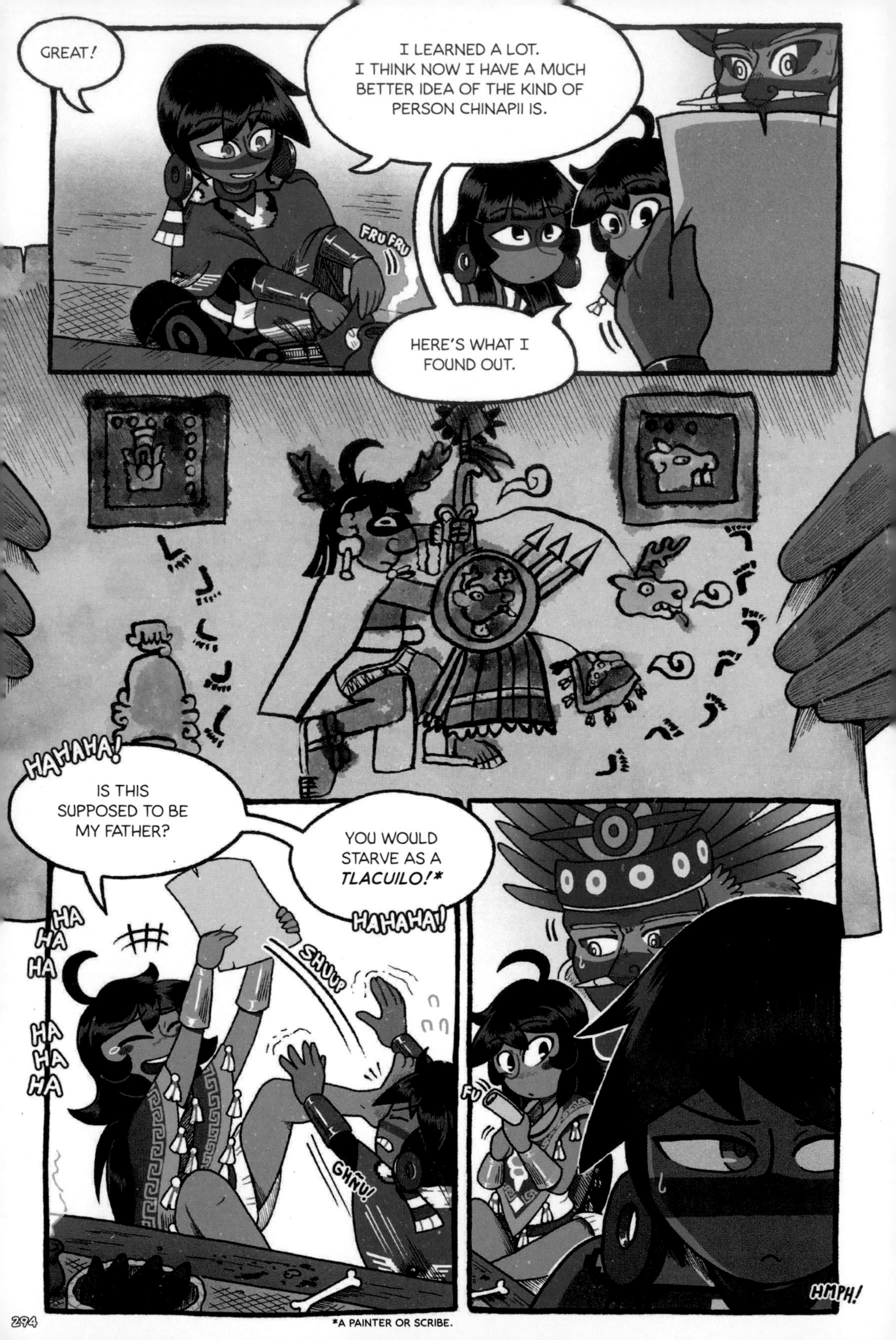
GREAT!
I LEARNED A LOT. I THINK NOW I HAVE A MUCH BETTER IDEA OF THE KIND OF PERSON CHINAPII IS.
FRU FRU
HERE'S WHAT I FOUND OUT.
HAHAHA!
IS THIS SUPPOSED TO BE MY FATHER?
YOU WOULD STARVE AS A *TLACUILO!**
HAHAHA!
HA HA HA
HA HA HA
SHUUP
GHÑU!
FU
HMPH!

*A PAINTER OR SCRIBE.

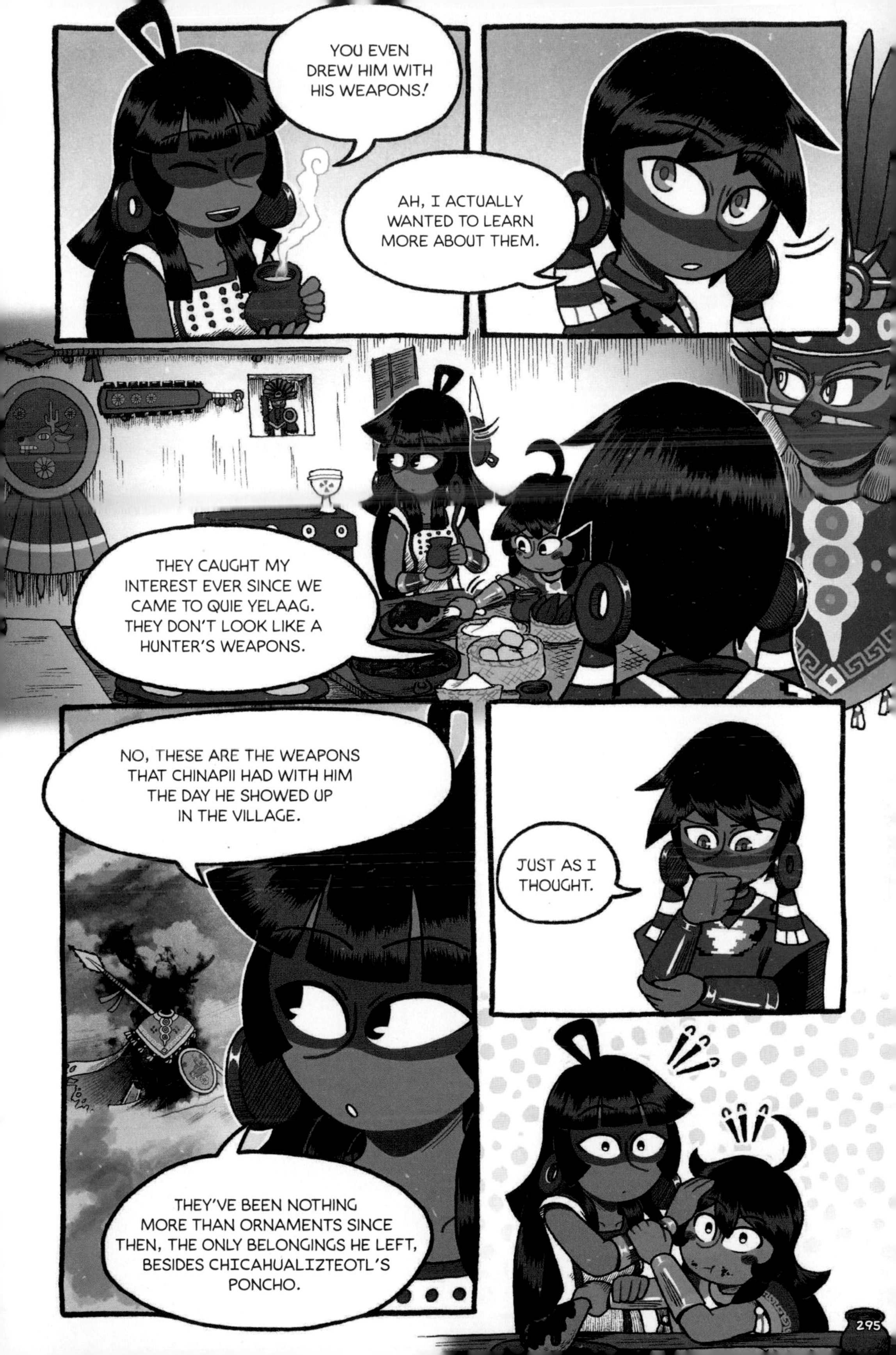
YOU EVEN DREW HIM WITH HIS WEAPONS!
AH, I ACTUALLY WANTED TO LEARN MORE ABOUT THEM.
THEY CAUGHT MY INTEREST EVER SINCE WE CAME TO QUIE YELAAG. THEY DON'T LOOK LIKE A HUNTER'S WEAPONS.
NO, THESE ARE THE WEAPONS THAT CHINAPII HAD WITH HIM THE DAY HE SHOWED UP IN THE VILLAGE.
JUST AS I THOUGHT.
THEY'VE BEEN NOTHING MORE THAN ORNAMENTS SINCE THEN, THE ONLY BELONGINGS HE LEFT, BESIDES CHICAHUALIZTEOTL'S PONCHO.

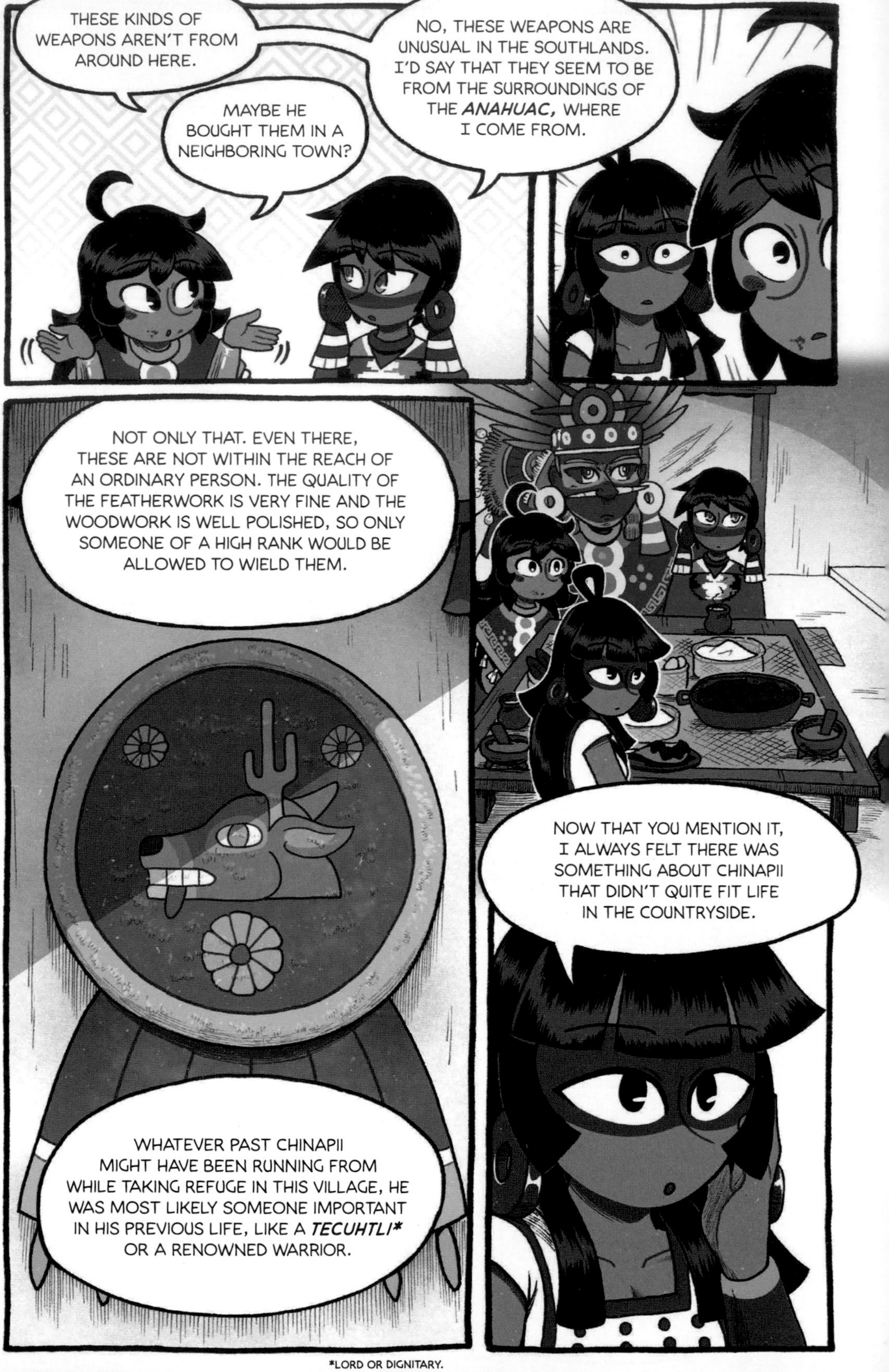
THESE KINDS OF WEAPONS AREN'T FROM AROUND HERE.
MAYBE HE BOUGHT THEM IN A NEIGHBORING TOWN?
NO, THESE WEAPONS ARE UNUSUAL IN THE SOUTHLANDS. I'D SAY THAT THEY SEEM TO BE FROM THE SURROUNDINGS OF THE ***ANAHUAC,*** WHERE I COME FROM.
NOT ONLY THAT. EVEN THERE, THESE ARE NOT WITHIN THE REACH OF AN ORDINARY PERSON. THE QUALITY OF THE FEATHERWORK IS VERY FINE AND THE WOODWORK IS WELL POLISHED, SO ONLY SOMEONE OF A HIGH RANK WOULD BE ALLOWED TO WIELD THEM.
NOW THAT YOU MENTION IT, I ALWAYS FELT THERE WAS SOMETHING ABOUT CHINAPII THAT DIDN'T QUITE FIT LIFE IN THE COUNTRYSIDE.
WHATEVER PAST CHINAPII MIGHT HAVE BEEN RUNNING FROM WHILE TAKING REFUGE IN THIS VILLAGE, HE WAS MOST LIKELY SOMEONE IMPORTANT IN HIS PREVIOUS LIFE, LIKE A ***TECUHTLI**** OR A RENOWNED WARRIOR.

*LORD OR DIGNITARY.

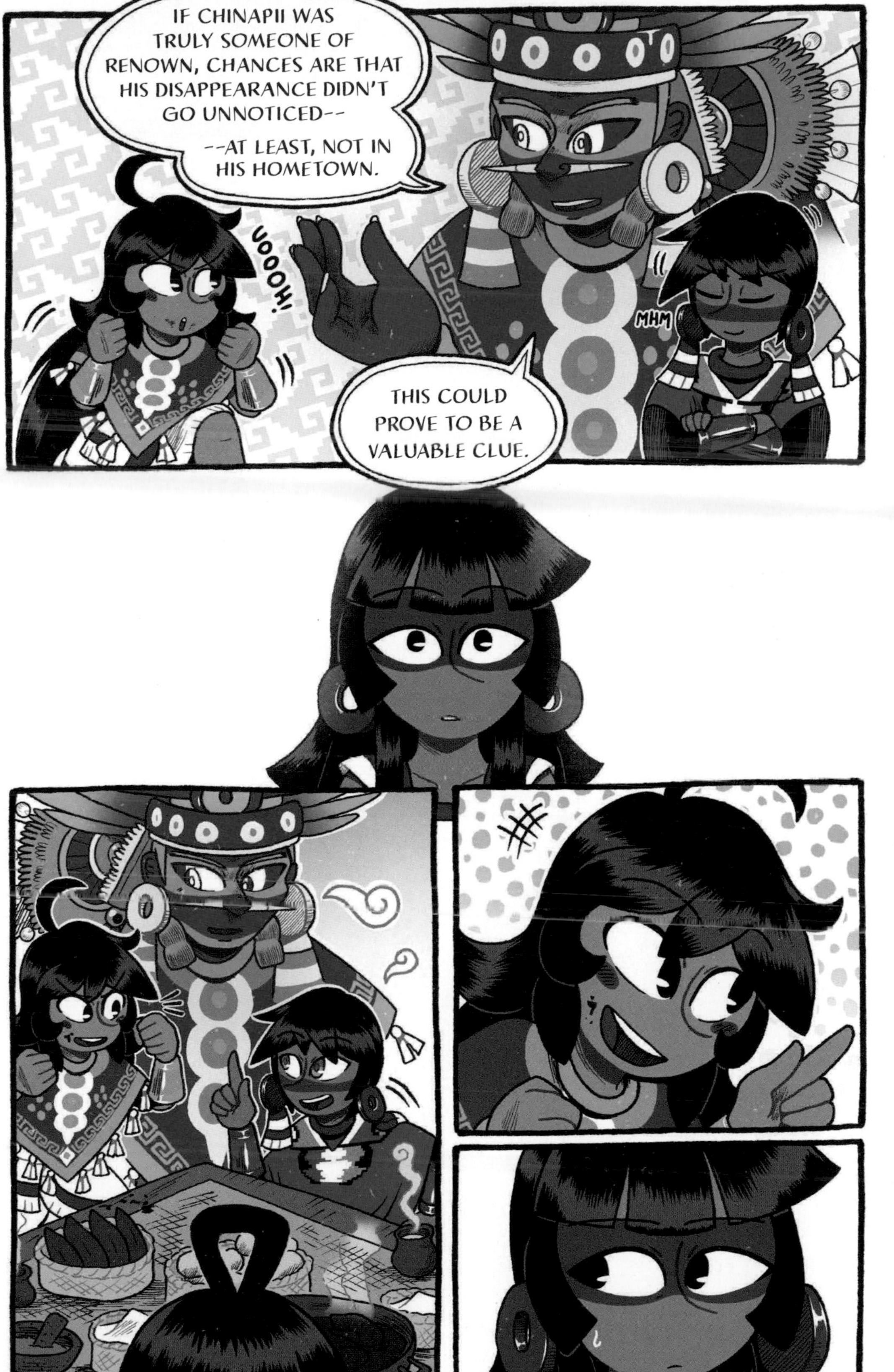
IF CHINAPII WAS TRULY SOMEONE OF RENOWN, CHANCES ARE THAT HIS DISAPPEARANCE DIDN'T GO UNNOTICED--
--AT LEAST, NOT IN HIS HOMETOWN.
OOOOH!
MHM
THIS COULD PROVE TO BE A VALUABLE CLUE.

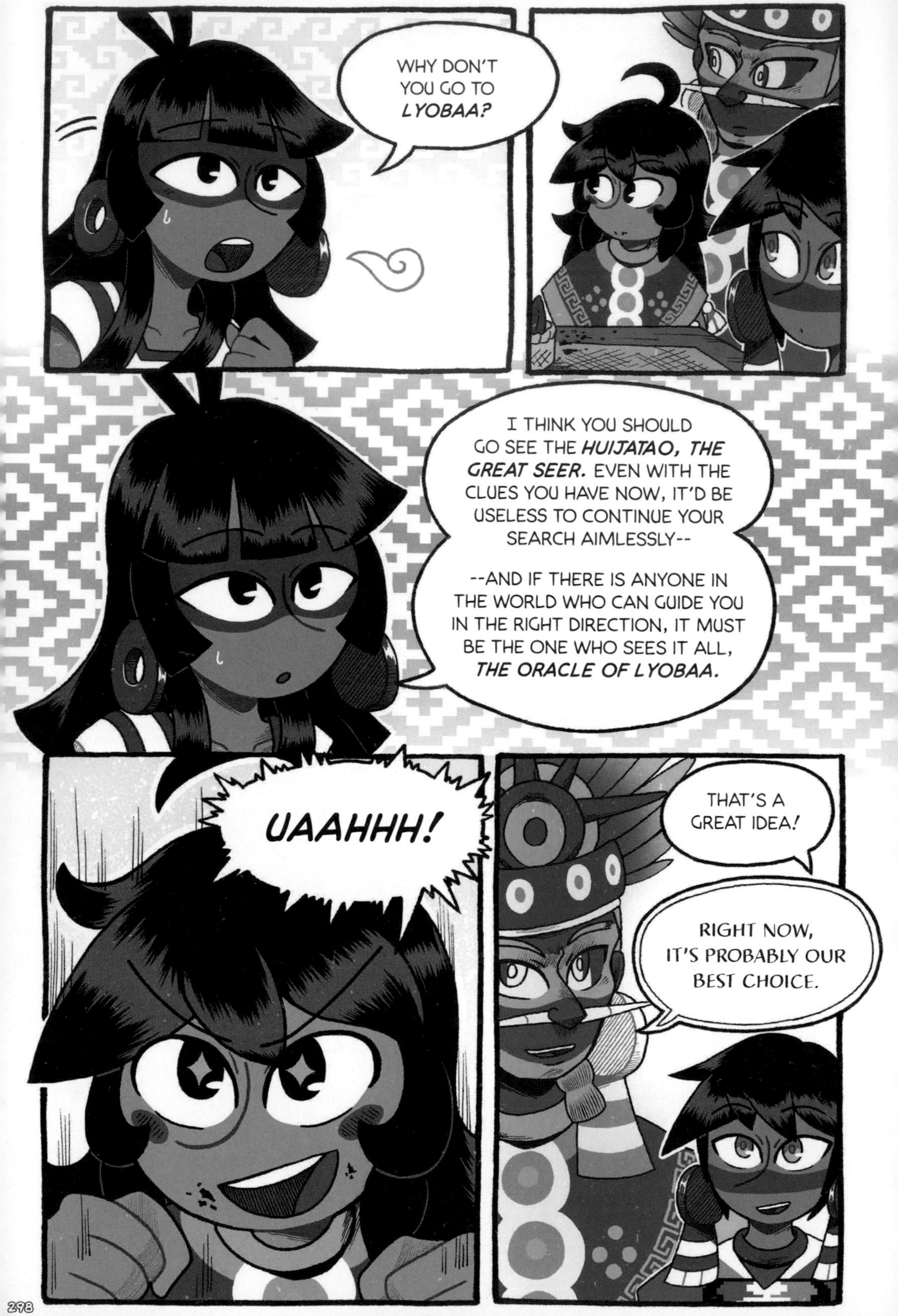
WHY DON'T YOU GO TO LYOBAA?
I THINK YOU SHOULD GO SEE THE HUIJATAO, THE GREAT SEER. EVEN WITH THE CLUES YOU HAVE NOW, IT'D BE USELESS TO CONTINUE YOUR SEARCH AIMLESSLY--
--AND IF THERE IS ANYONE IN THE WORLD WHO CAN GUIDE YOU IN THE RIGHT DIRECTION, IT MUST BE THE ONE WHO SEES IT ALL, THE ORACLE OF LYOBAA.
UAAHHH!
THAT'S A GREAT IDEA!
RIGHT NOW, IT'S PROBABLY OUR BEST CHOICE.

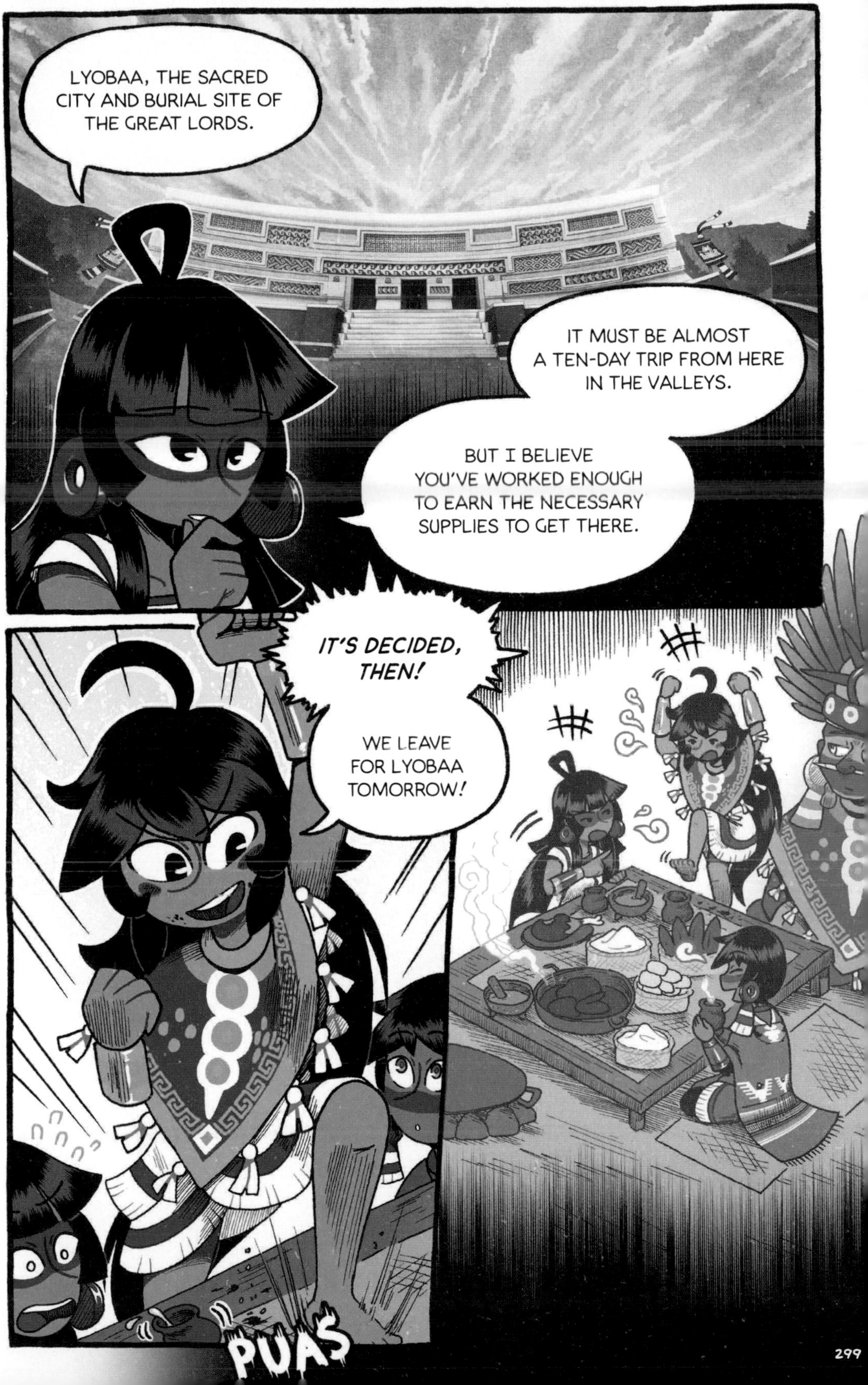
LYOBAA, THE SACRED CITY AND BURIAL SITE OF THE GREAT LORDS.
IT MUST BE ALMOST A TEN-DAY TRIP FROM HERE IN THE VALLEYS.
BUT I BELIEVE YOU'VE WORKED ENOUGH TO EARN THE NECESSARY SUPPLIES TO GET THERE.
IT'S DECIDED, THEN!
WE LEAVE FOR LYOBAA TOMORROW!
PUAS

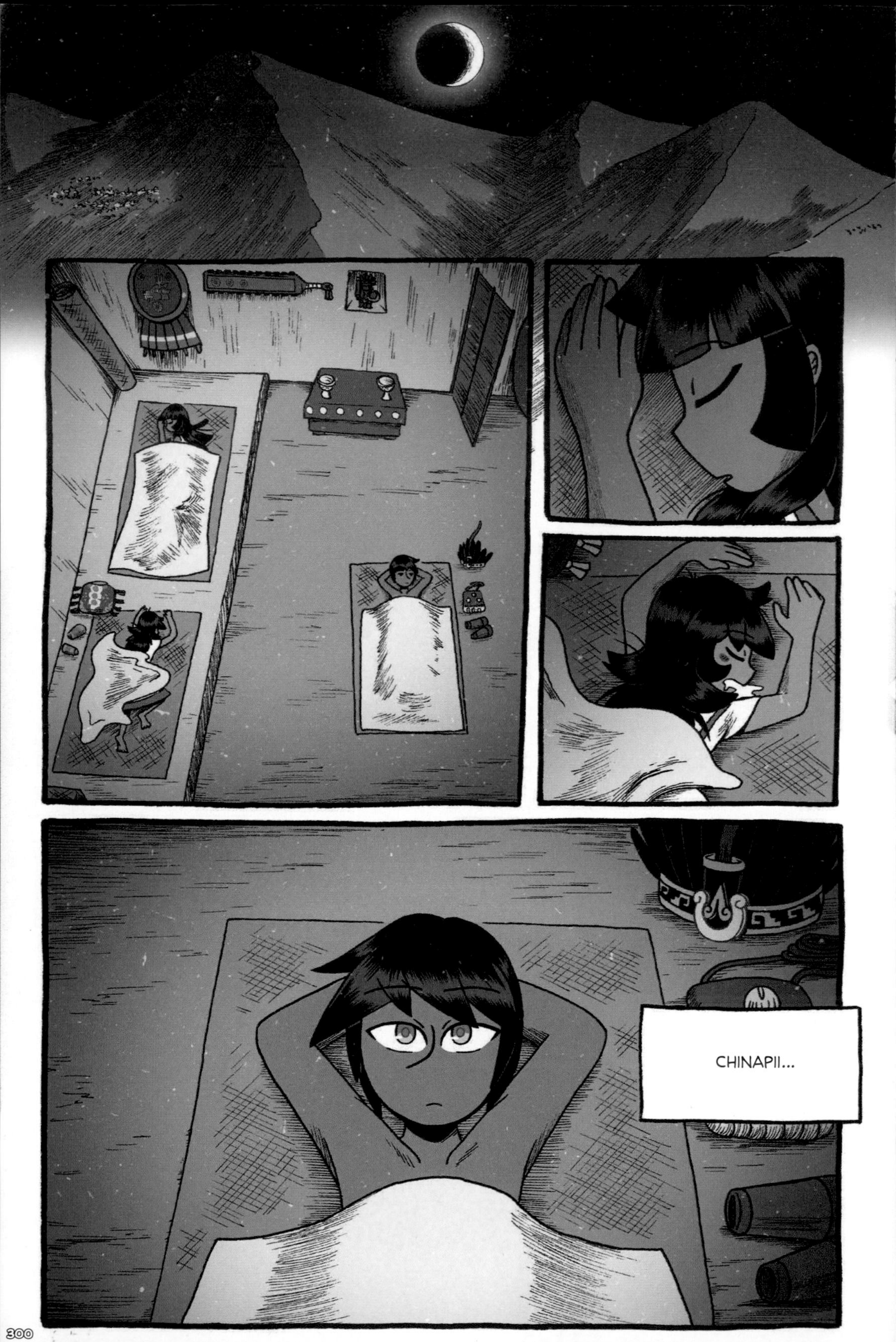
CHINAPII...

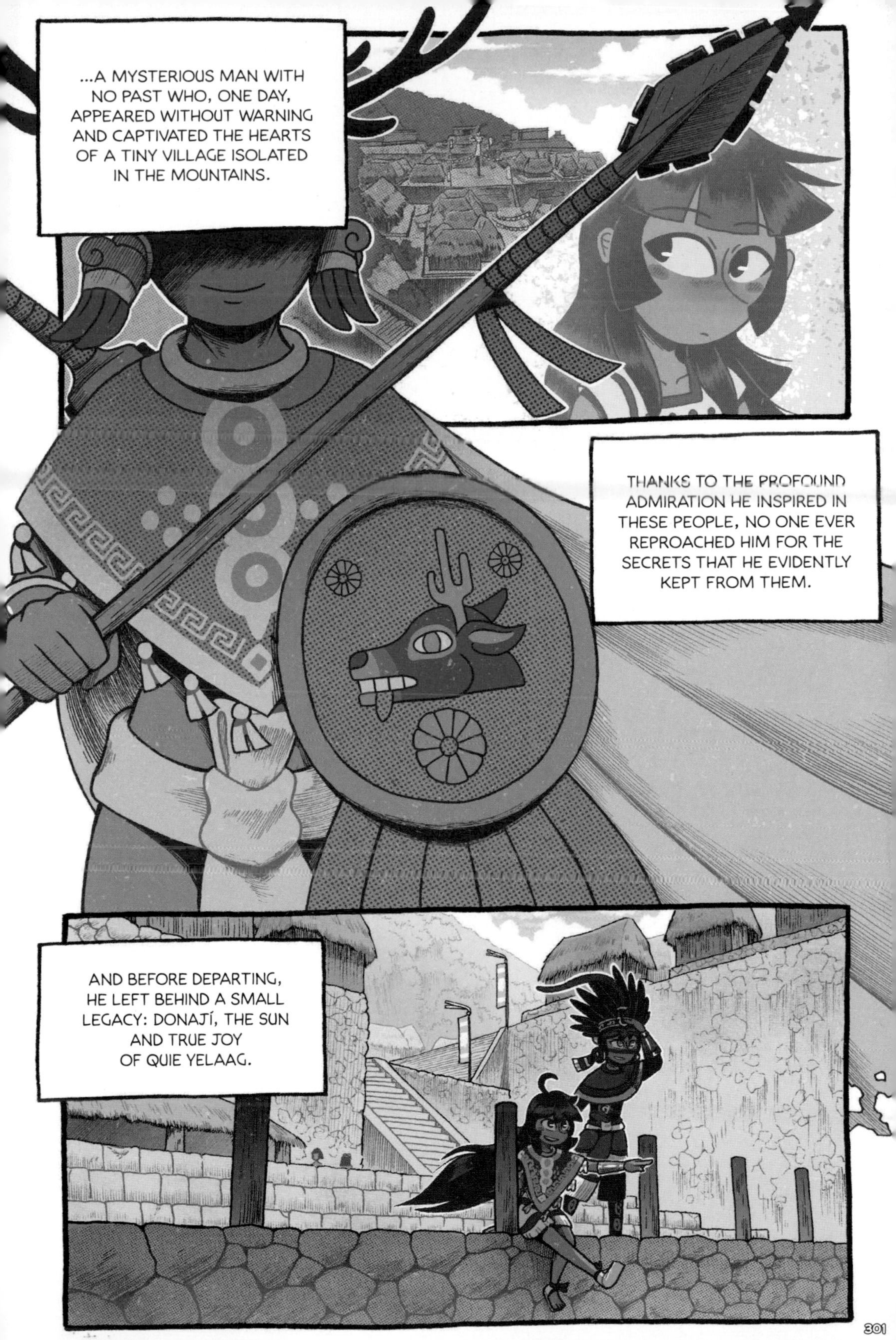
...A MYSTERIOUS MAN WITH NO PAST WHO, ONE DAY, APPEARED WITHOUT WARNING AND CAPTIVATED THE HEARTS OF A TINY VILLAGE ISOLATED IN THE MOUNTAINS.
THANKS TO THE PROFOUND ADMIRATION HE INSPIRED IN THESE PEOPLE, NO ONE EVER REPROACHED HIM FOR THE SECRETS THAT HE EVIDENTLY KEPT FROM THEM.
AND BEFORE DEPARTING, HE LEFT BEHIND A SMALL LEGACY: DONAJÍ, THE SUN AND TRUE JOY OF QUIE YELAAG.

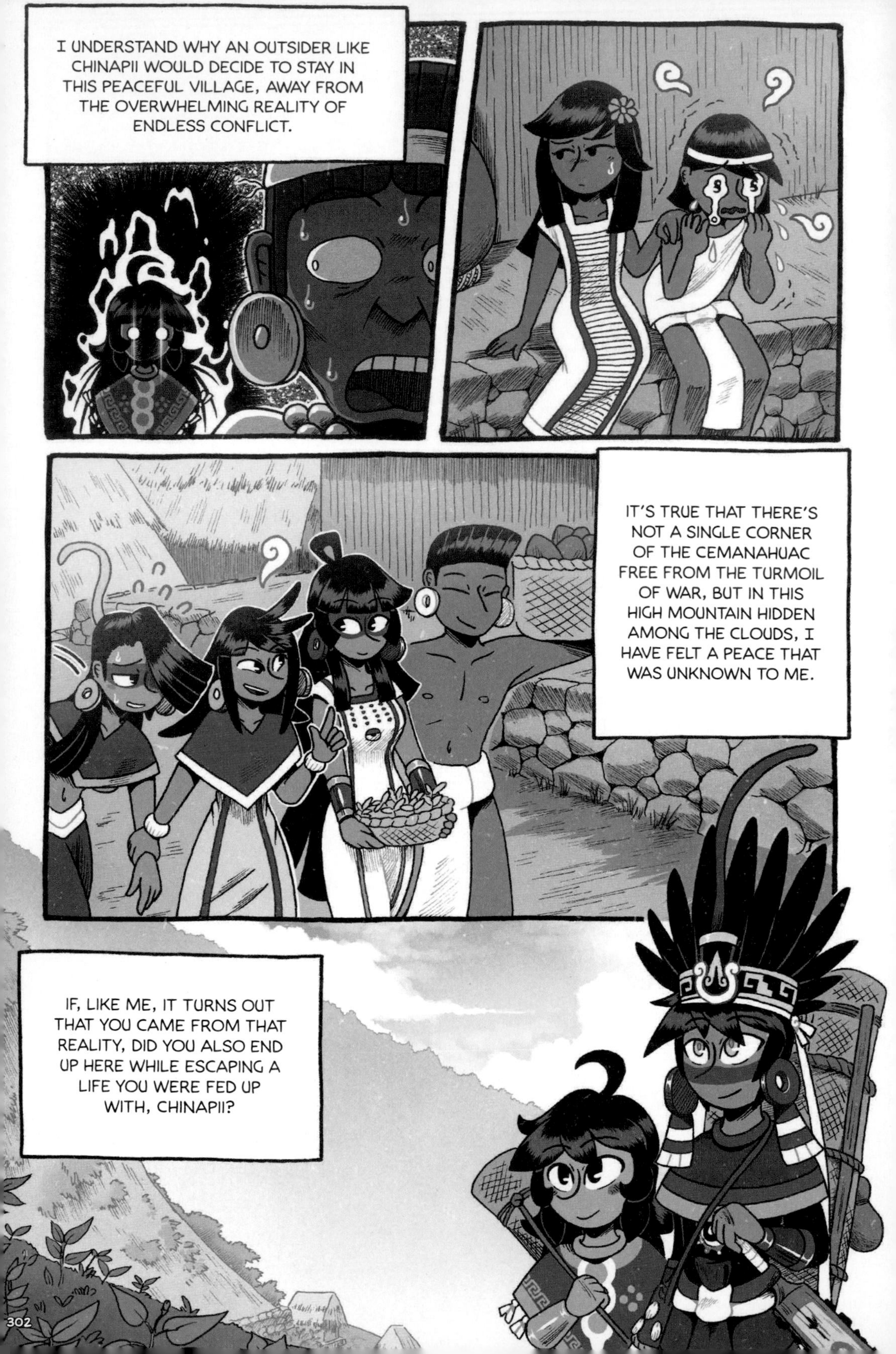
I UNDERSTAND WHY AN OUTSIDER LIKE CHINAPII WOULD DECIDE TO STAY IN THIS PEACEFUL VILLAGE, AWAY FROM THE OVERWHELMING REALITY OF ENDLESS CONFLICT.
IT'S TRUE THAT THERE'S NOT A SINGLE CORNER OF THE CEMANAHUAC FREE FROM THE TURMOIL OF WAR, BUT IN THIS HIGH MOUNTAIN HIDDEN AMONG THE CLOUDS, I HAVE FELT A PEACE THAT WAS UNKNOWN TO ME.
IF, LIKE ME, IT TURNS OUT THAT YOU CAME FROM THAT REALITY, DID YOU ALSO END UP HERE WHILE ESCAPING A LIFE YOU WERE FED UP WITH, CHINAPII?

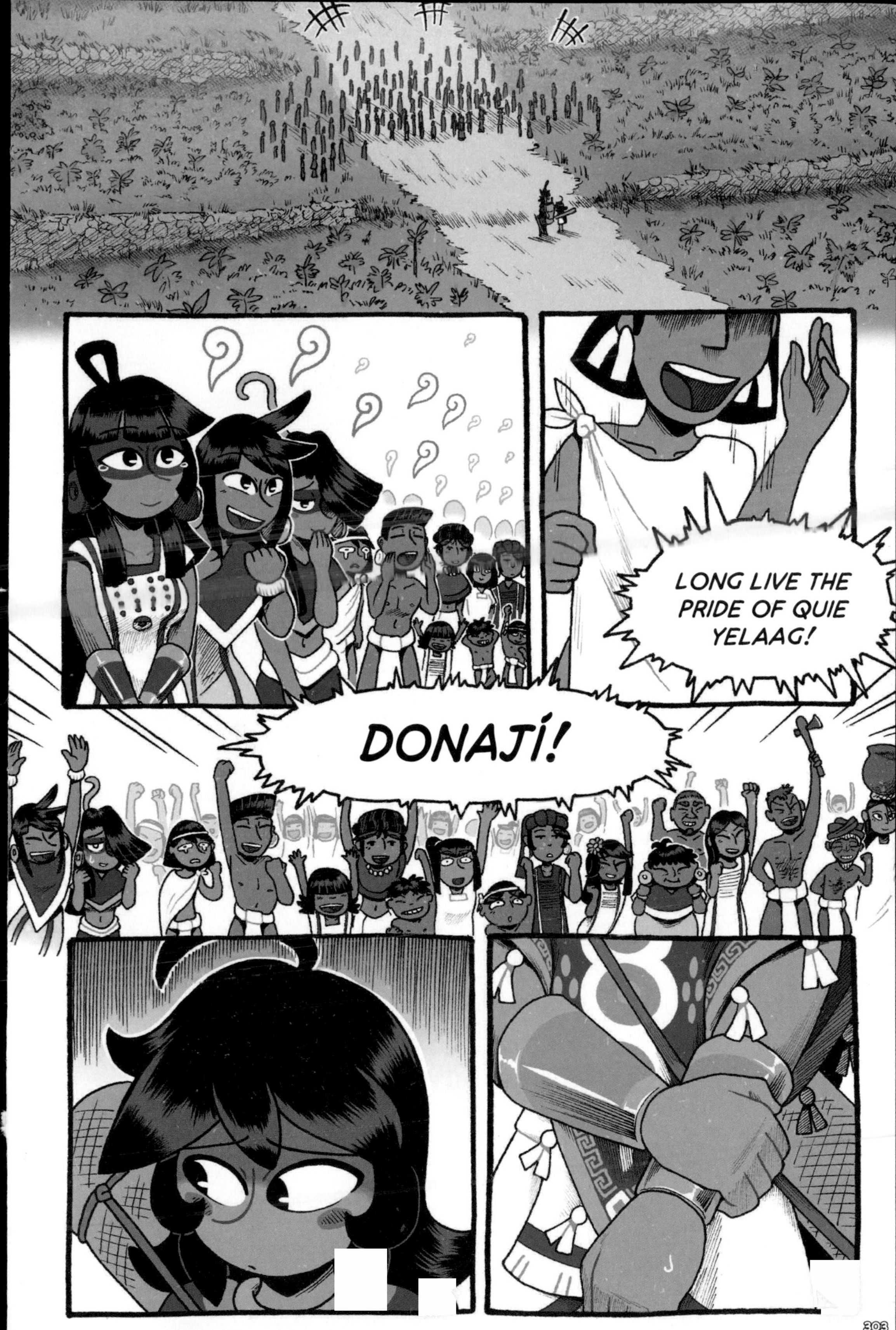
LONG LIVE THE PRIDE OF QUIE YELAAG!
DONAJÍ!

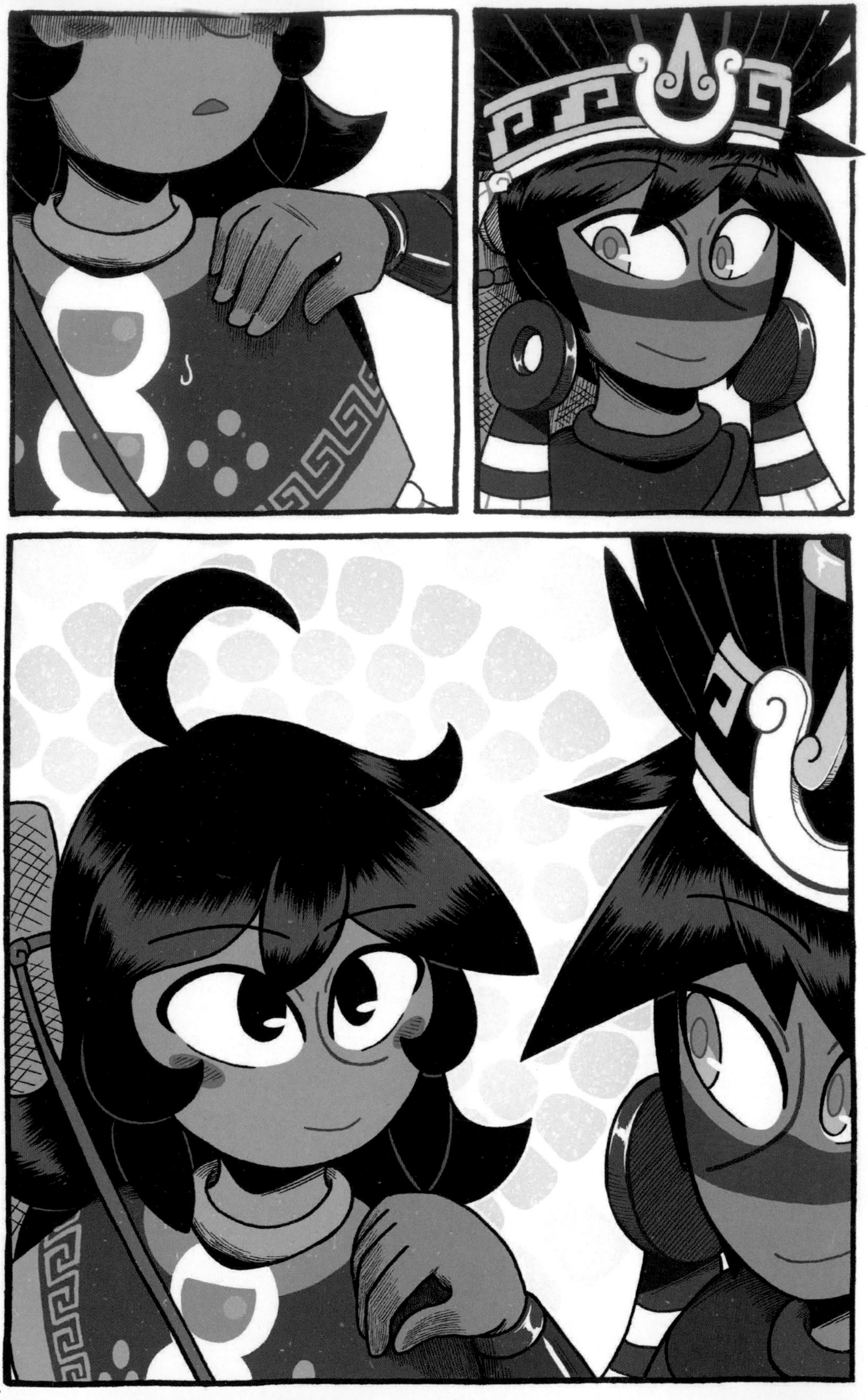

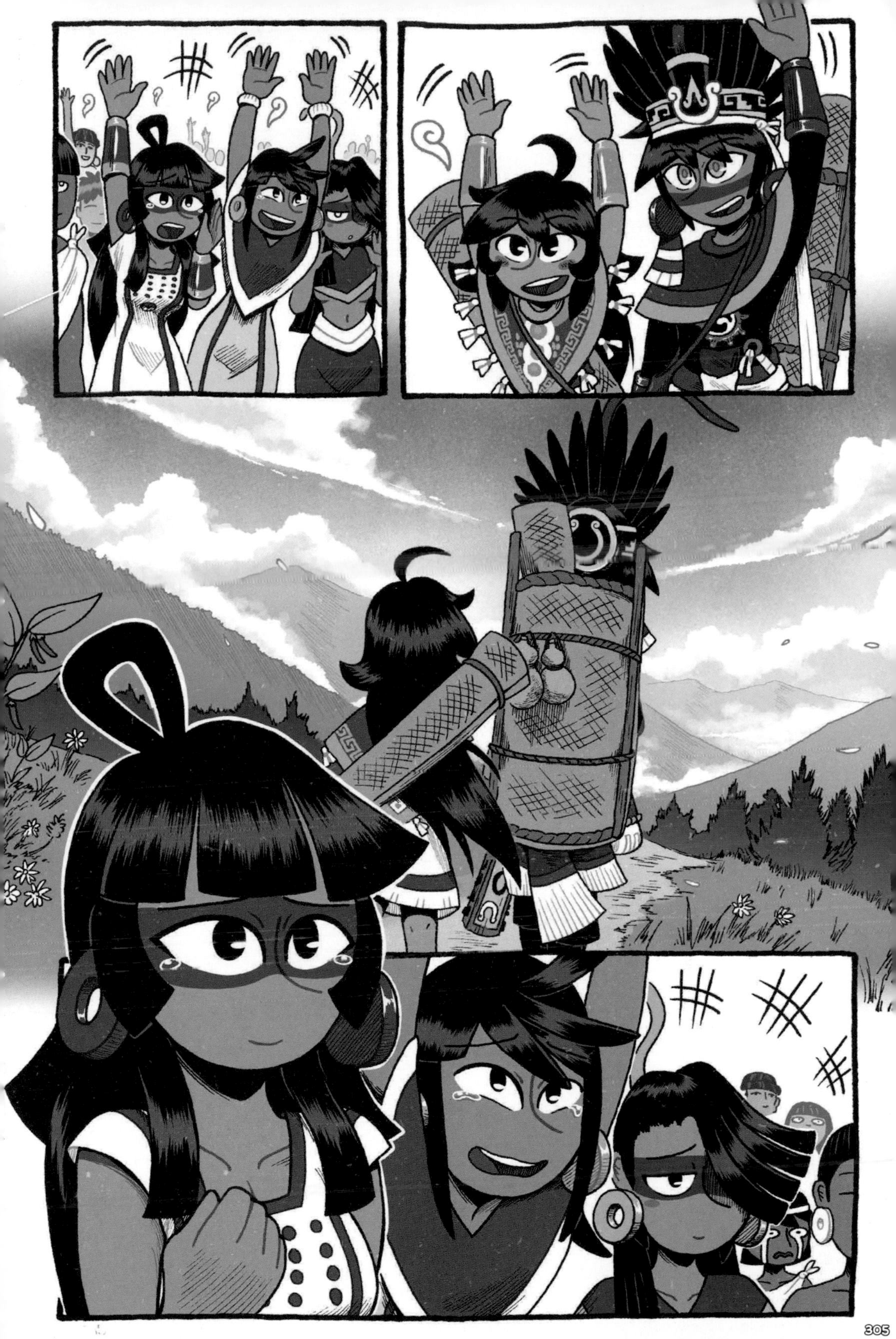

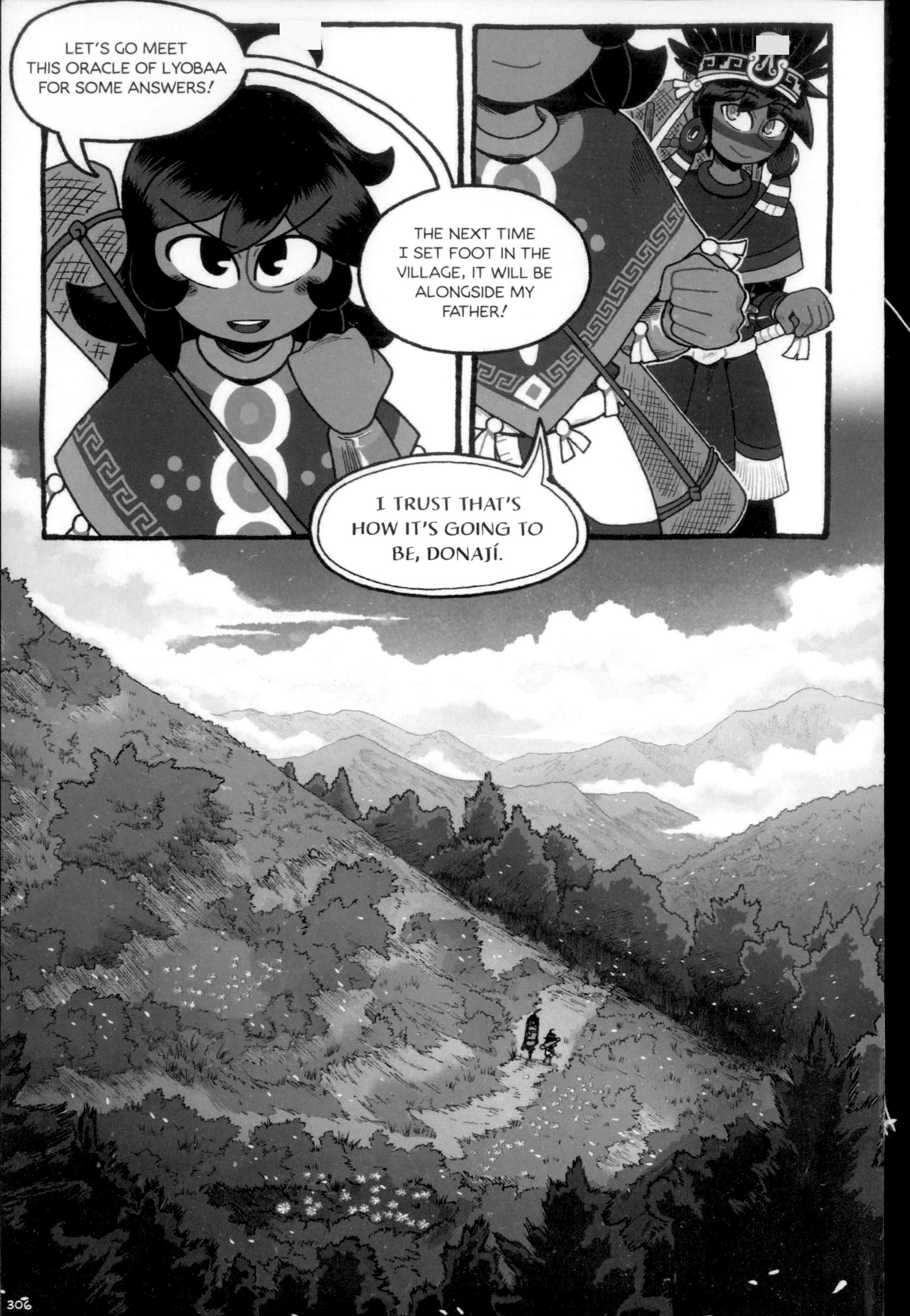
LET'S GO MEET THIS ORACLE OF LYOBAA FOR SOME ANSWERS!
THE NEXT TIME I SET FOOT IN THE VILLAGE, IT WILL BE ALONGSIDE MY FATHER!
I TRUST THAT'S HOW IT'S GOING TO BE, DONAJÍ.

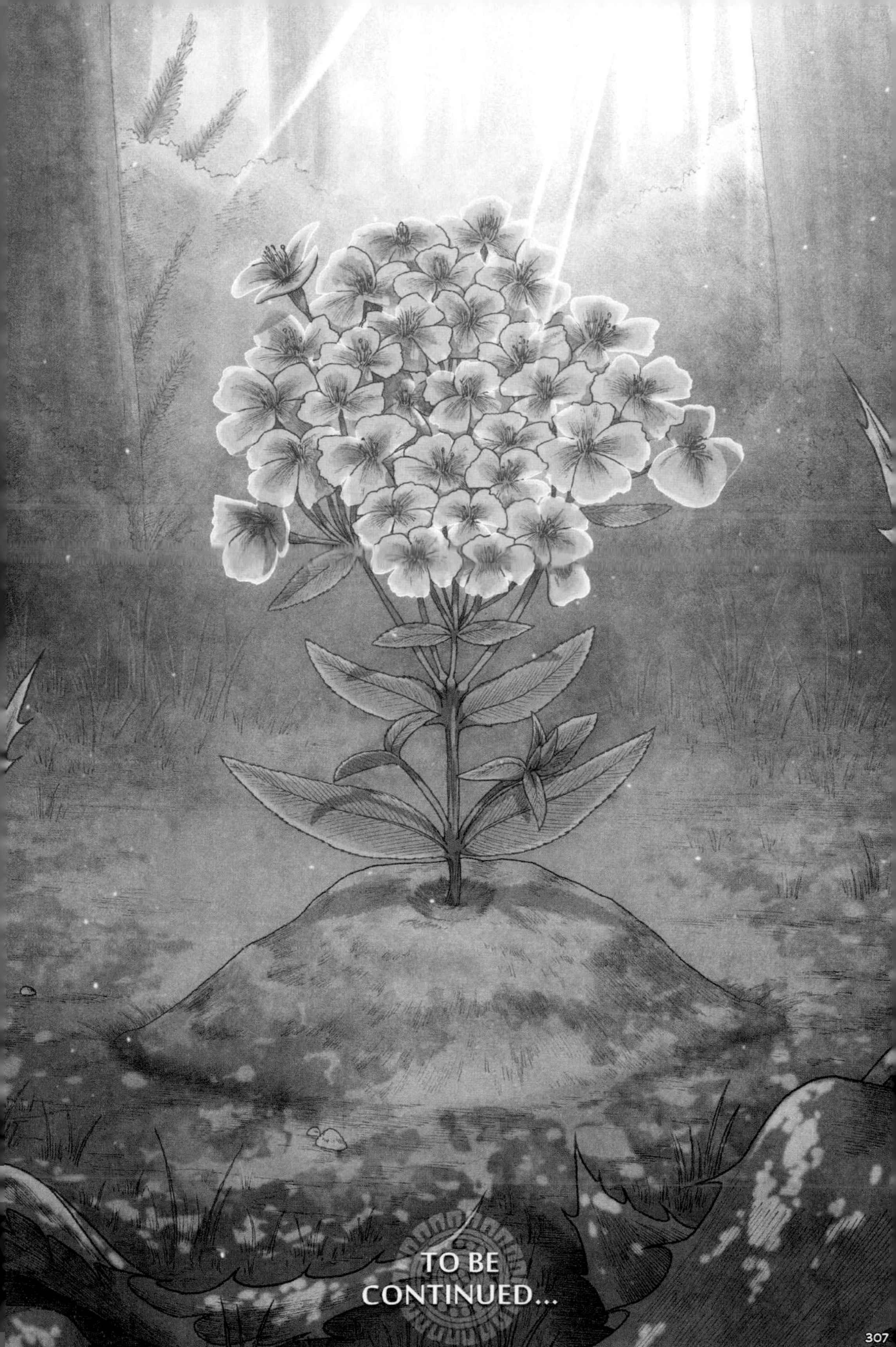
TO BE
CONTINUED...

CAMILO MONCADA LOZANO

Camilo Moncada Lozano (1994) is a Mexican artist based in Mexico City.

Lover of crows, mythology, and Japanese culture. Despite his background as an animator and visual arts graduate, his true passion lies in creating characters and telling their stories.

He has spent most of his life weaving a fictional universe that connects all these stories, one of which is *Codex Black*. The development of an obsession. His friends often can't remember the last time they saw him, some even wonder if he's actually real.

"I like crows."

ANGEL DE SANTIAGO

Angel was born and partly raised in Mexico before migrating to Texas. He is in love with color and the atmospheres, emotions, and moods it can convey. Stories with beautiful landscapes, horror, and the surreal are always guaranteed to be his favorites.

He can't remember a time when he wasn't drawing, but in those rare moments between, he can usually be found napping with his dog.

NAME GLOSSARY

by Camilo Moncada L.

Here's a basic guide of name pronunciations. So far, most character and place names are either in Nahuatl, the language spoken by the Nahua ethnic group, such as Mexica like Itzcacalotl, and Zapotec, spoken by Zapotec people. However, these languages have a wide variety of regional dialects that can sound very different from one another. So this guide does not intend to go in depth into all the particularities of each language, just to be a guide for those struggling with imagining what certain names would even sound like.

Stress syllables are indicated in all caps. Some noteworthy letters/combinations of letters that will show up quite often are x and tl. The x always sounds like the English "sh" sound, but the tl is more complicated. The first t is pronounced normally, but the l is pronounced by letting the air flow through the sides of the tongue, producing a sort of subtle click sound all together.

Also, the letter j, as seen in Donají's name, always sounds like a Spanish j, which is a stronger h as in he, unlike an English j.

MAIN CHARACTERS:

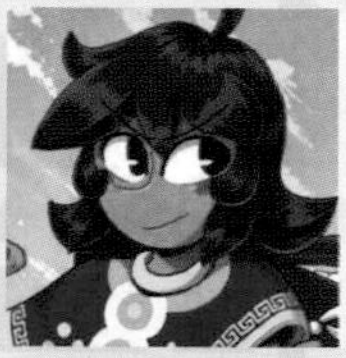

Donají
"Great Soul" [do.na.HEE]. (The last "jí" syllable has a long sound and is pronounced like he in English.)

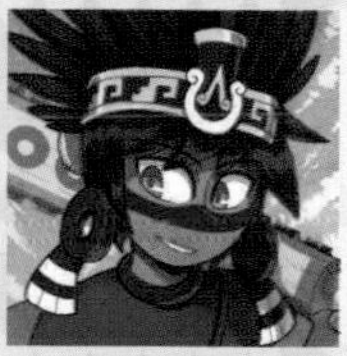

Itzcacalotl
"Obsidian Crow" [its.ka.KA.lo.tl].

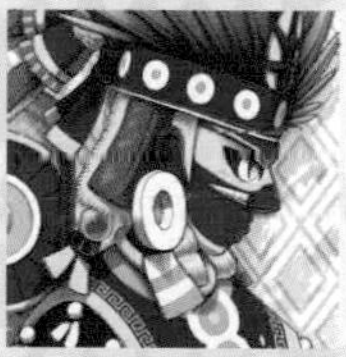

Chicahualizteotl
"Powerful God" [chee.ka.wa.lis.TE.o.tl].

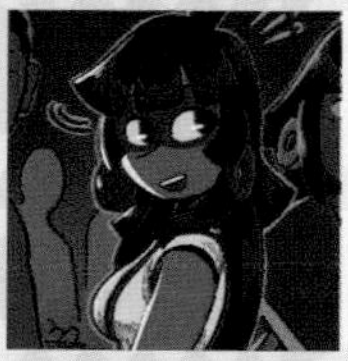

Béelia
"Star" [BE:lia]. (The two e's, as in there, are pronounced separately, producing a long sound, represented by the ":".)

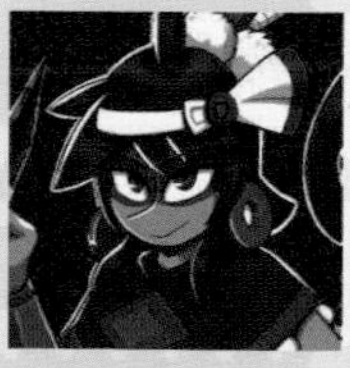

Citlalmina
"Piercer of Stars" [see.tlal.MEE.na].
(The "mi" syllable is pronounced like me in English.)

OTHER CHARACTERS IN ORDER OF APPEARANCE:

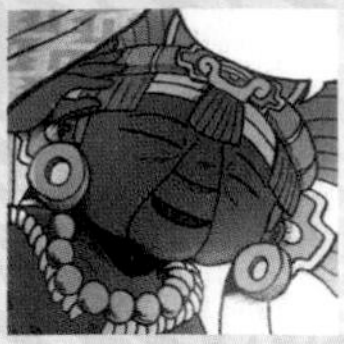

Bitza

"Sun" [BEE.tza]. (In this case the z sounds just as it does in English, as opposed to Nahuatl names where it always sounds like an s.)

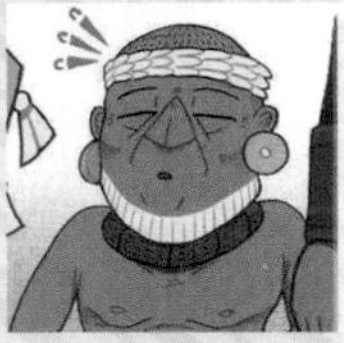

Nirudo'

"The First" [nee.ru.DO']. (The apostrophe marks a "glottal stop," meaning the vowel is "cut" midway, like when saying uh-oh in English.)

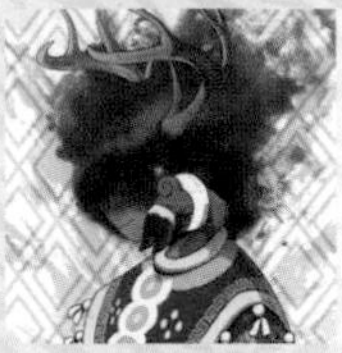

Chinapii

"Wind Deer" [chee.na.PEE]. (The "china" part is not pronounced like the country's name but rather like "cheena." The final "pii" syllable is a long vowel and sounds like pea in English.)

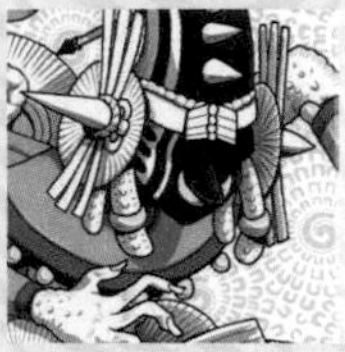

Itztlacoliuhqui

"Twisted Obsidian Knife" [its.tla.ko.LIU'.kee].

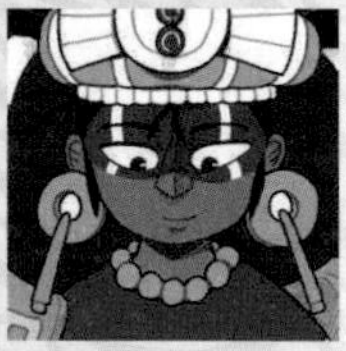

Cosijoeza

"Thunder of Flint" [ko.see.ho.E.sa].

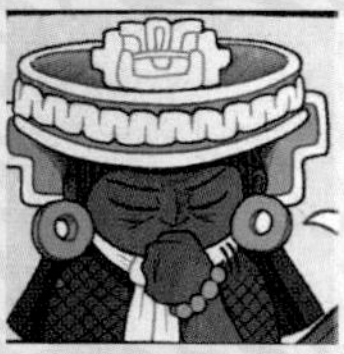

Alarii

[ah.lah.REE].

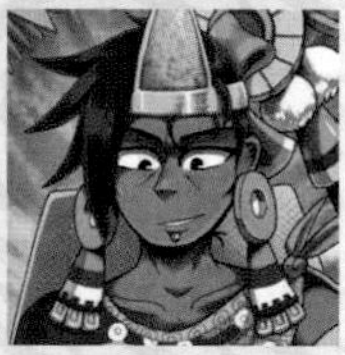

Ahuizotl

"Water Thorny" [a:.WI.tso.tl].

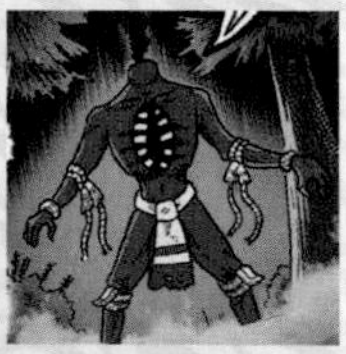

Yohualtepuztli

"Night Axe" [yo.wal.te.POOS.tlee].

PLACES:

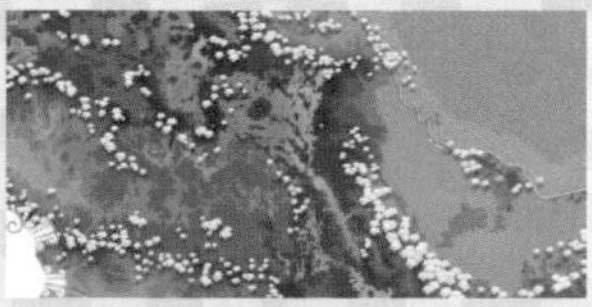

Cemanahuac
"The Known World" [sem.a:.NA.wak].

TRIPLE ALLIANCE MEMBERS:

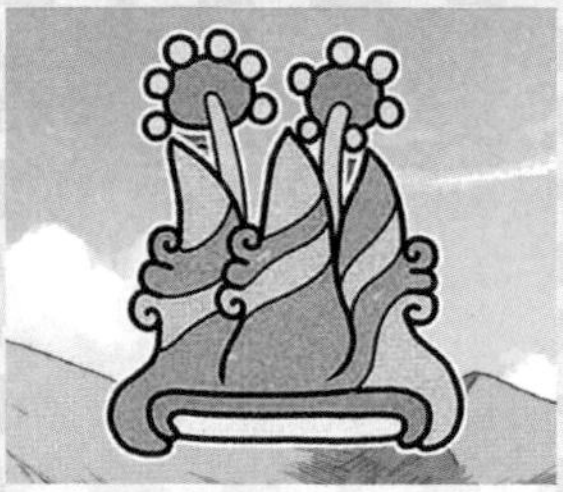

Texcoco
[tets.KO'.ko]. (The original meaning of the name is unknown today; however, in this case, we know the original name was written Tetzcoco, so this x doesn't sound like the English "sh.")

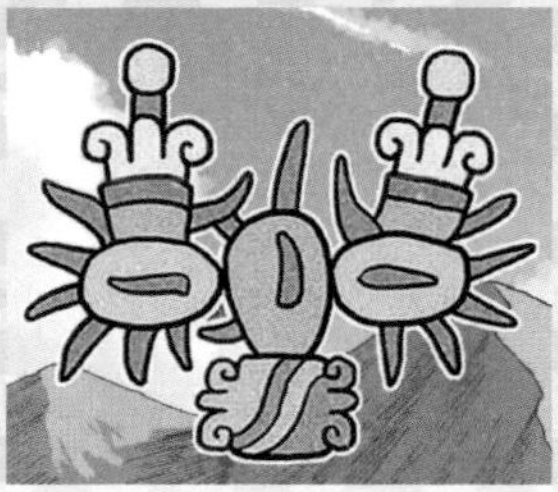

Tenochtitlan
"Among Stone Prickly Pears" [te.noch.TEE.tlan]. (Also called by its full name: Mexico-Tenochtitlan.)

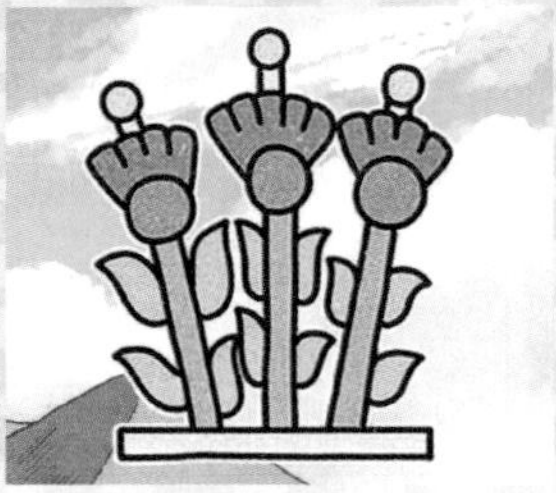

Tlacopan
"Place of Flower Stems" [tla.KO:.pan].

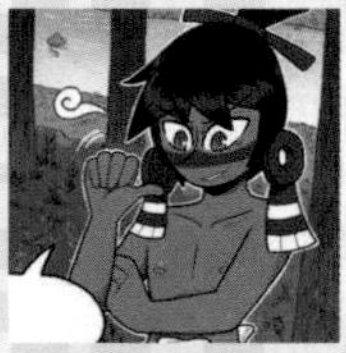

Telpochcalli
"House of the Young" [tel.poch.CAL.lee]. (The school where Mexica warriors like Itzcacalotl were trained. The two L's are pronounced separately.)

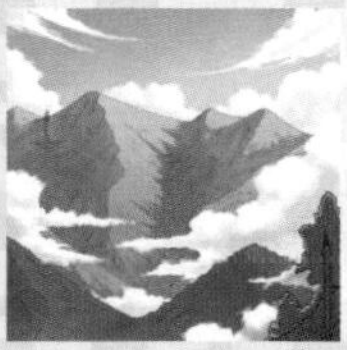

Quie Yelaag
"Cloud Mountain" [ki.E ye.LAAG].

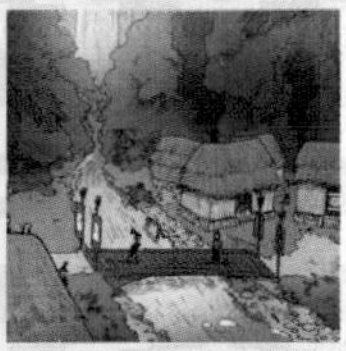

Cacalotepec
"Crow Mountain" [ka.ka.lo.TE.pek].

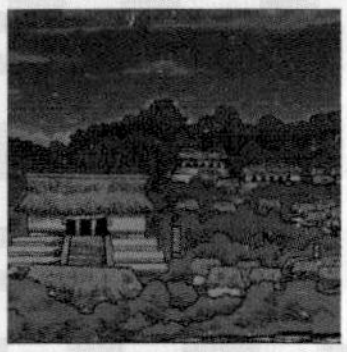

Guizii
"Jaguar Hill" [gui.ZEE]. (The "gui" is pronounced like in guitar and the "zii" sounds like sea but with an English z instead of s.)

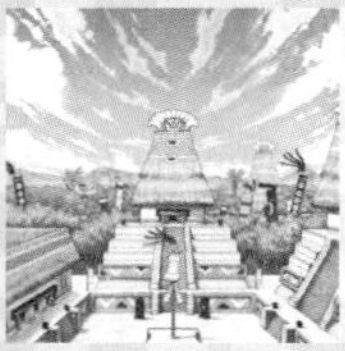

Guidxiguie'
"Place Among Flowers" [gui.dji.GUIE']. (The "dxi" syllable in Zapotec sounds similar to the "gi" in digital. Both "gui" parts sound like that of guitar but the last one adds an e as in there with a glottal stop.)

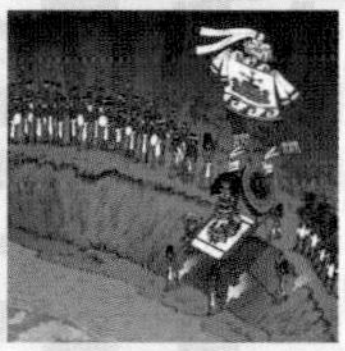

Zaachila
[ZAA.chee.la]. (Some translate this name as "The First Earth's Daughter," while others claim it was named for the first kings who ruled the city. But the truth is that its true meaning is uncertain. It may be related to zaa, which means cloud in Zapotec.)

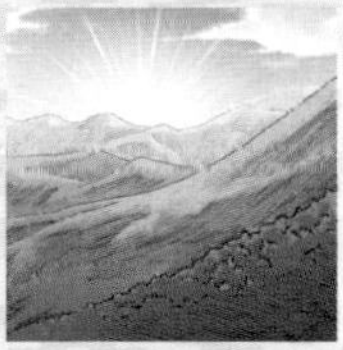

Quiaabeche
"Jaguar Hill" [kiaa.BE.che].

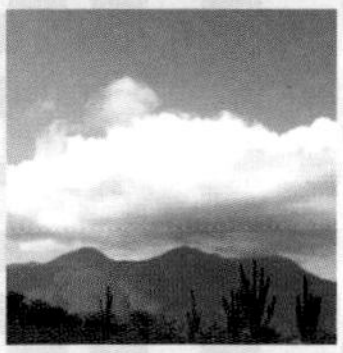

Guiengola
"Ancient Mountain" [guien.GO.la].

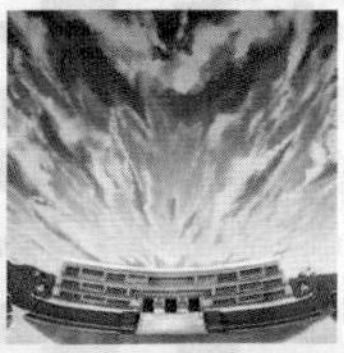

Lyobaa
"Place of Rest" [lyo.BAA]. (The two a's at the end are pronounced separately to produce a long sound.)

HISTORICAL CONTEXT

by Camilo Moncada L.

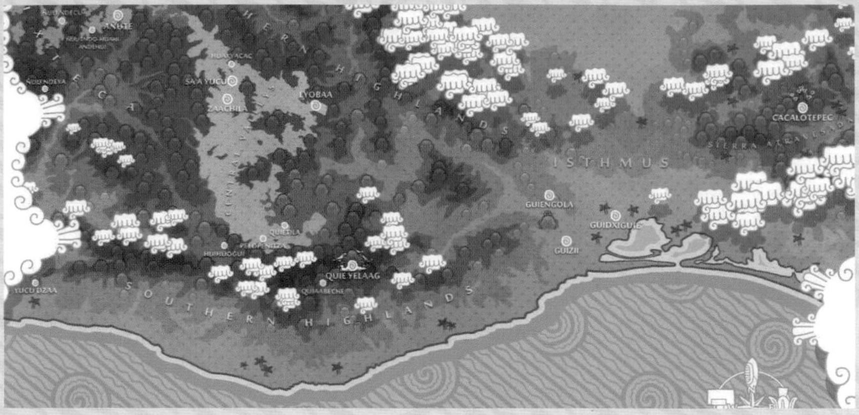

ANUTE
NDENDEYA
SA'A YUCU
ZAACHILA
LYOBAA
CACALOTEPEC
ISTHMUS
GUIENGOLA
GUIDXIGUIE
GUIZII
QUIETILA
QUIE YELAAG
QUIAABECHE
YUCU DZAA
SOUTHERN HIGHLANDS

Codex Black is, first and foremost, a work of fiction. As such, most of its characters and the events depicted in it are fictional, as well as certain locations where the story takes place, which is the case with Donají's village and the jungle village of Cacalotepec. However, as a historical fantasy, the story is set in a very specific context: the Mesoamerica of the late 15th century.

Donají and Itzcacalotl's adventure begins in the year 1493 of the Common Era, dubbed as the year 1-House in the calendar used at the time. It was a time period marked by conflict and instability all across the Cemanahuac. Most of the territory was divided by scattered constellations of independent city-states, competing against one another for power and survival.

In this context, few great powers expanded their control beyond their own cities' borders, mostly through long-lasting alliances and fierce wars of conquest. Among these, two empires clashed as the biggest entities of the Cemanahuac: the P'urépecha Empire, with its seat in the city of Tzintzuntzan, located in the west, and the Triple Alliance (a.k.a. the "Aztec Empire"), an alliance between the Mexica of Tenochtitlan, the Acolhua of Texcoco, and the Tepaneca of Tlacopan, all of which thrived in the Anáhuac region.

In just about 60 years since its establishment, the Triple Alliance had risen to be the most remarkable power of its time, and under the rule of its emperor—or Great Tlatoani—Ahuizotl, its control was bound to expand to never-imagined frontiers. However, as much as the Alliance had submitted lordships all across the Cemanahuac, in very distant regions and from all kinds of peoples and cultures, the complex and volatile relationships with these nations made it very difficult to maintain a tight grip over them, and rebellions would burst all over the place quite frequently. As such, despite the presence of rising powers like the P'urépecha and the Triple Alliance, there was no such thing as a unified territory or a single dominant lord for that vast land of courageous people.

Not all was war, though, despite the great emphasis that lords put on it. It was also a time of flourishing cultures and intense exchange. The most beautiful art in the form of murals splashed the growing cities with colors, and intricate designed textiles and artisan crafts adorned the palaces and flowed through the bustling markets, which, thanks to the extensive trade routes and commerce, offered merchandise from the vast Cemanahuac, from coast to coast, and even from faraway lands far beyond those that comprised the Mesoamerican area. Cultural exchange was more intense than ever, and artistic expressions and particular styles had transcended cultural boundaries, reaching the many different regions of the Cemanahuac.

This was the reality in which Donají and Itzcacalotl grew up, and is the reality in which their adventures will unfold. Itzcacalotl, as a rookie warrior from Tenochtitlan, the powerful head of the Triple Alliance, saw the warriors come and go into the never-ending campaigns to expand the imperial reach. He and his peers were trained to use war captives for sacrifice so that the Sun would be fed with blood and the world could survive an impending cataclysm that was always looming over their heads. The world in itself was an unstable creation, and warriors had the sacred task of keeping it alive in the name of their patron god, Huitzilopochtli. To the Mexica, among which Itzcacalotl grew up, Tenochtitlan was truly the center of the universe, a cosmopolitan metropolis to which the right to rule this world was given by their god.

Donají, on the other hand, grew up as a peasant in her small Zapotec village deep in the Southern Highlands, almost isolated from the constant wars waged in the more densely populated regions. The Zapotec lordships, along their Mixtec rivals, had been fighting one another for about 600 years since the collapse of the Zapotec empire of Danni Dipaa in order to gain control over the Central Valleys; however, despite the conflicts, a network of traditional alliances, as well as mutually arranged marriages between Zapotec and Mixtec elites, made the political landscape in the Southlands a very complex one, and it became even more complicated once the Triple Alliance broke in and started submitting its lordships around 40 years prior to the story. One might think that as a Zapotec peasant, hearing news of the Mixtec and Triple Alliance's attacks on the Zapotec valleys, Donají would feel resentment toward the invaders, but the truth was that at that time, people's allegiances were community based rather than ethnic based, meaning that Donají and the people of Quie Yelaag felt a much closer bond with their fellow villagers and their closest neighbor—regardless of them being Zapotec, Huave, Chontal, or Chatino—than with other Zapotecs from a distant region like those of the Central Valleys.

Finally, it must be said that despite the never-ending research invested into this work, there's still so much to learn about this time period and the people who lived in it, and that several aspects are still the subject of heated debate among historians and academics. Therefore, there are instances in which I've had to take creative licenses in order to fill the gaps. In the end, the goal of this story is not to be a one-hundred-percent historically accurate narration of the past. Although I do hope to be able to make the most authentic portrayal as possible, in trying to maintain a balance, I will always favor the narrative.

THE SUPERNATURAL

by Camilo Moncada L.

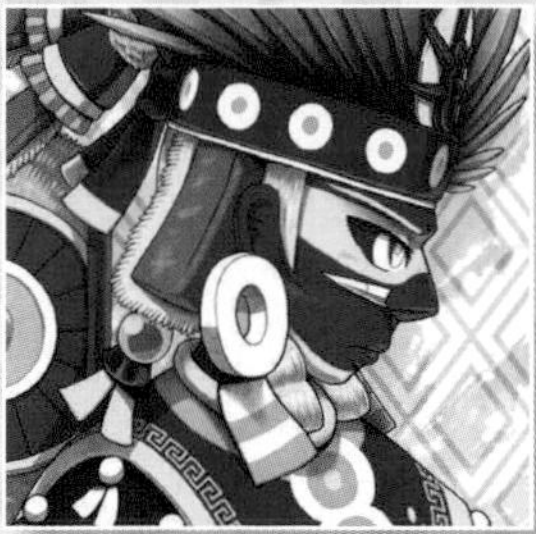
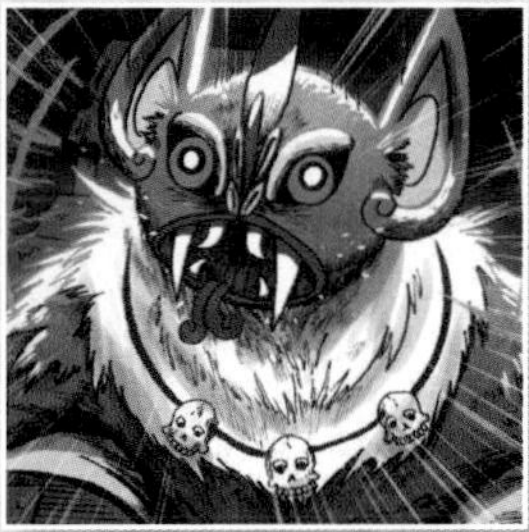
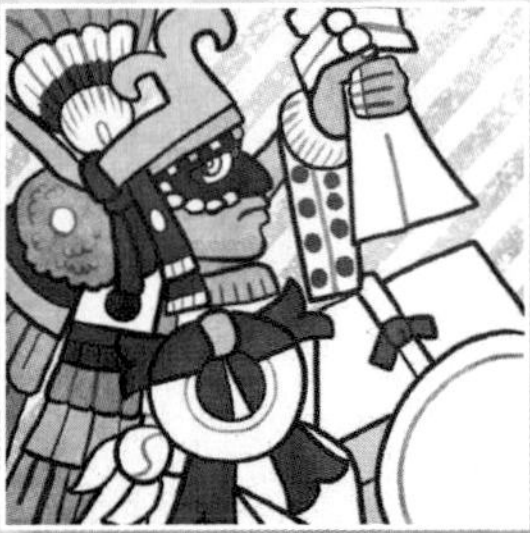

The Cemanahuac's religion is polytheistic, meaning that they believe in multiple deities that govern and intervene in pretty much every aspect of daily life, nature, as well as the supernatural or sacred. Although the specific pantheons vary from group to group, from city to city, several deities and myths have a widespread cult and others have their equivalents in different cultures. In other words, some deities are worshiped by different people under different names, but are in essence the same.

Then, how many deities are there in the "Cemanahuac's pantheon"? Hundreds, if not thousands! Almost every city and town has its own local deities, apart from the most important ones whose cult is shared throughout the entire region.

Truth is that there are a lot of secrets surrounding the true nature of the gods and the divine, which escapes the grasp of human understanding. Also, what has Itzcacalotl become, and how does it relate to the world of the supernatural and the divine? These mysteries may be unveiled as the story progresses—or will they?

Chicahualizteotl, "Powerful God" – The god of fortitude and strength, and by extension a god of health, as fortitude prevents illnesses.

Huey Tzinacantli, "Great Bat" – The huge bat monster upon which Donají and Itzcacalotl stumbled in the jungle near Cacalotepec. Its huge claws can easily decapitate a person in a single sweep. Bats in general are associated with earth and the night, as well as with decapitation and menstruation, the offerings of blood to the earth. This monster's loincloth and the three skulls necklace suggest that it has a certain degree of intelligence and crafting skills. However, a monster that size is something unheard of, so there may be something else at work in the shadows that caused such a fearsome beast to suddenly appear.

Itztlacoliuhqui, "Twisted Obsidian Knife" – God of cold and ice, as well as god of punitive justice. Itztlacoliuhqui in certain myths is associated with transgression, therefore making it fitting that he who knows sin is the one to punish it. He's often represented with a blindfold or with a mask made with agave fiber or the skin of a human thigh, perhaps indicating that the people of the Cemanahuac also believe in a "blind justice." It is said that the dart stuck in his head is a battle scar from a confrontation he had in his association with Venus against the Sun. Itztlacoliuhqui is also often associated with the birth of corn, and is an avatar of Tezcatlipoca.

Yohualtepuztli, "Night Axe" – A specter of the night who appears in the form of a headless man with the chest open and his heart exposed. People know he's close when they hear the sound of an axe chopping trees in the middle of the night, which is the sound of his chest closing and opening like a guillotine. He appeared at solitary roads and challenged people to a test of courage in order to reveal their destiny. Those who succumb to fear and flee or black out upon the apparition will fall ill, be captured by enemy warriors, condemned into forced labor, or even die as a result. Courageous individuals instead have to swiftly pull the specter's heart from his chest before it chops their hand and bury it in the ground. The day after, the heart will have been replaced with certain items that reveal the person's fate: white feathers and thorns announce a bright future, while coal and rags are signs of a grim fate. Some fearless warriors and priests wander around these solitary roads at night, seeking to challenge the specter themselves to put their courage to the test. Yohualtepuztli is also an avatar of Tezcatlipoca.

Tezcatlipoca, "Smoking Mirror" – Perhaps one of the most important, yet most enigmatic gods of the Cemanahuac. God of the night, chaos, and darkness, he protects both kings and slaves, inspires valiant warriors while he's also patron of sorcerers who act in the shadows. Tezcatlipoca is the one who gives fortune, but will also take it back on a whim. Most importantly, Tezcatlipoca is god of fate, revealing it in the most convoluted ways, and as a good trickster, he will laugh at and mock those with a grim future.

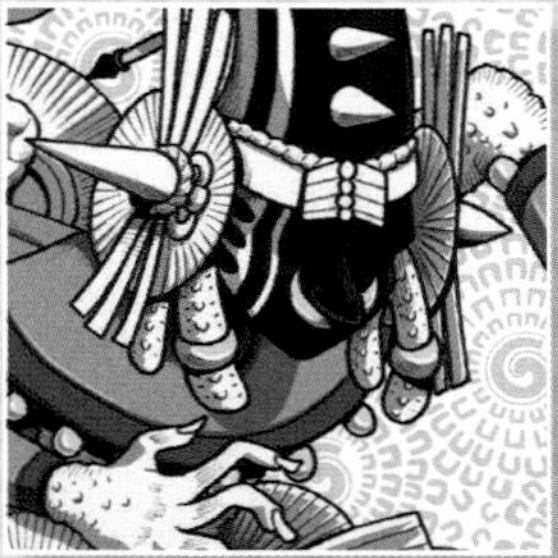
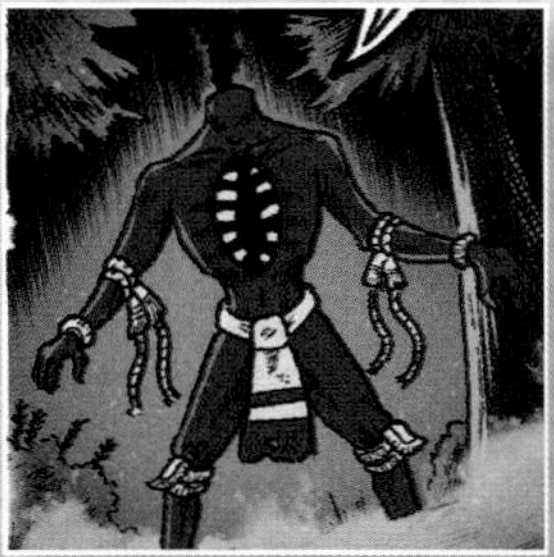
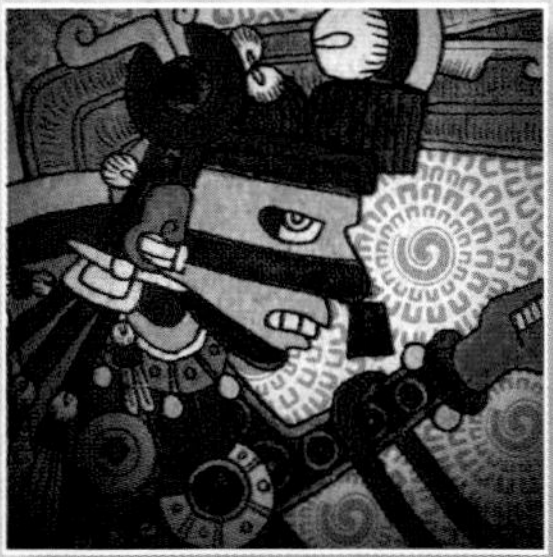

HOW IT ALL STARTED

by Camilo Moncada L.

Codex Black is a love project that originally started as a web comic, until it became a graphic novel. The idea of writing this story began as a crossover between two characters I had created separately.

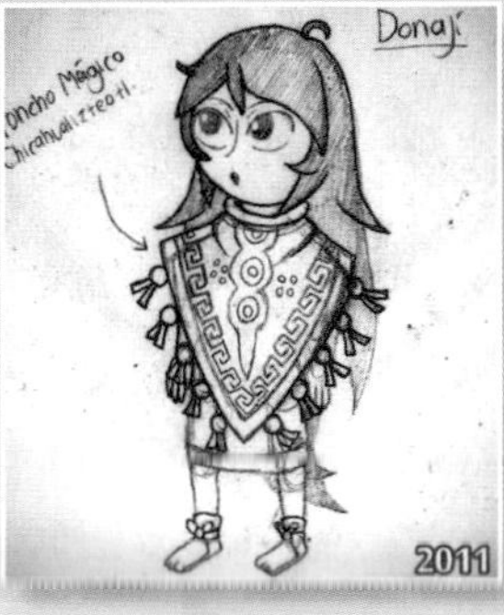
Donají
2011

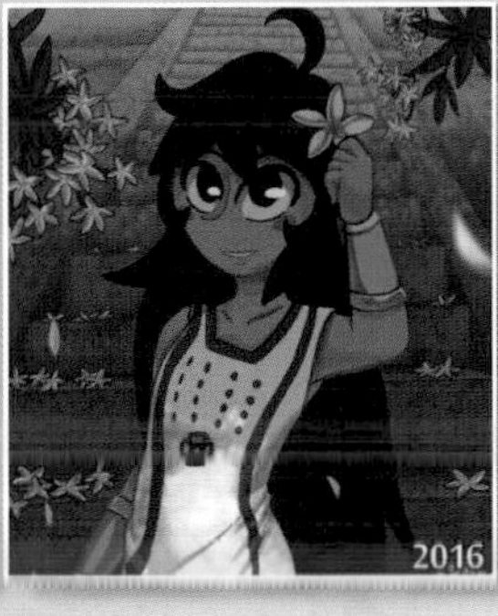
2016

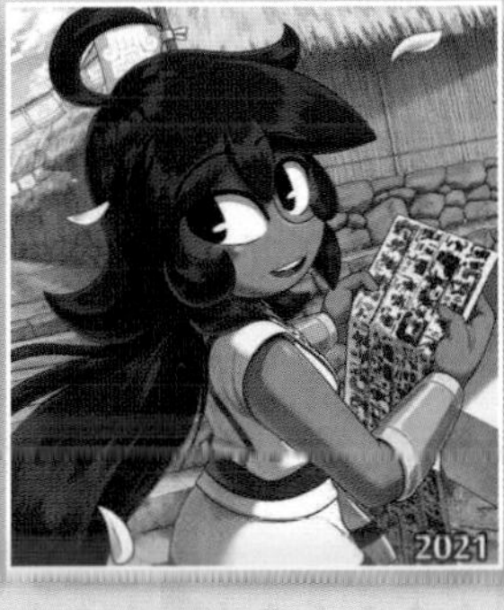
2021

I created Donají in 2011 for an assignment in my last year of high school, for which I wrote the short story "Donají and the Magical Poncho" that I later revisited as an animated interactive story in 2014, and afterward re-adapted and expanded as a short film in 2017. This original story narrates the events in which Donají confronted Itztlacoliuhqui, the god of cold and ice, and introduced other characters like Chicahualizteotl and Béelia.

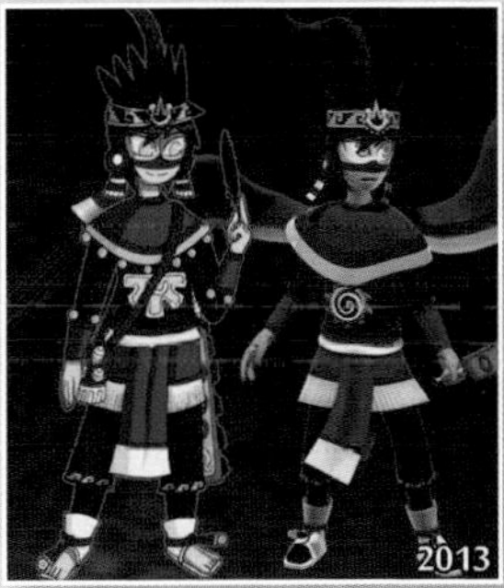
2013

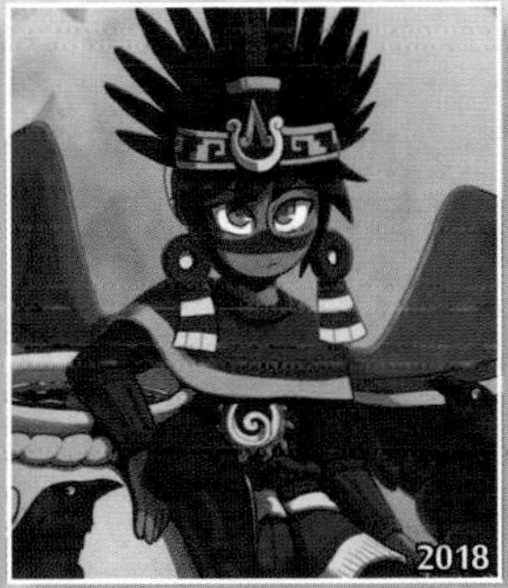
2018

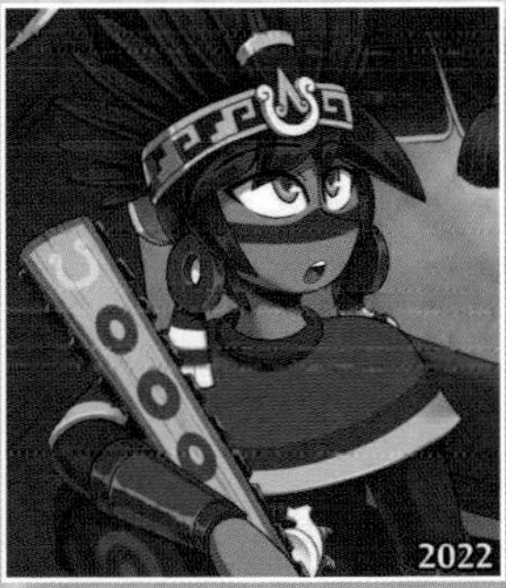
2022

Itzcacalotl was born as a character in 2013 when I went to Vancouver, Canada, studying character animation. There, I created a short film called "Black Feathers," in which Itzcacalotl is trapped in a pit that he only manages to leave by growing wings after eating a bunch of crow feathers—an allegoric quest for freedom. This short story was adapted into the sequence in which Itzcacalotl grows his wings in the first chapter of *Codex Black*.

CODEX BLACK

After I returned to Mexico in 2014, I started playing with the idea of mixing these characters together in a comic series. At first, it was supposed to be a kind of warm-up to test my storytelling skills, my first materialized narrative endeavor, as I had other, more ambitious projects on the back burner. I had planned it to be an episodic comic series with Donají and Itzcacalotl going on adventures all around the Cemanahuac, fighting creatures from Mesoamerican legends, like in the old Santo movies where he fought mummies, vampires, and even invaders from Mars.

However, as more interesting characters whose stories I wanted to explore started to pop up, and as I started defining a plot that allowed both characters to meet and gave a meaning to their journey, I parted from the episodic format. *Codex Black* turned out to be a more ambitious project than originally intended, until it evolved into what it is today. In 2017, once I felt I had a pretty solid story in my hands, I finally started drawing the first pages, and thus, the web comic started in 2018.

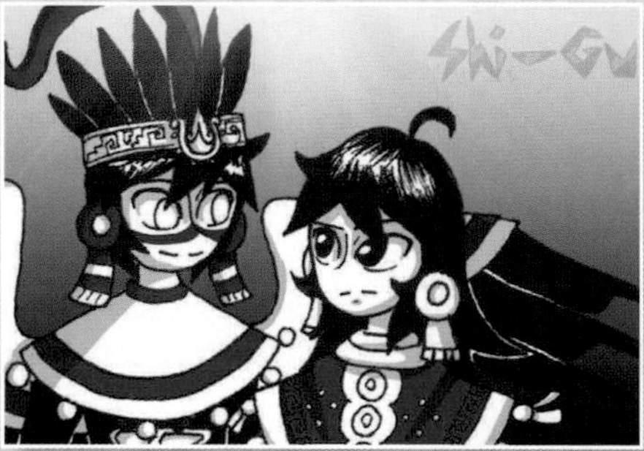
Shi-Gu

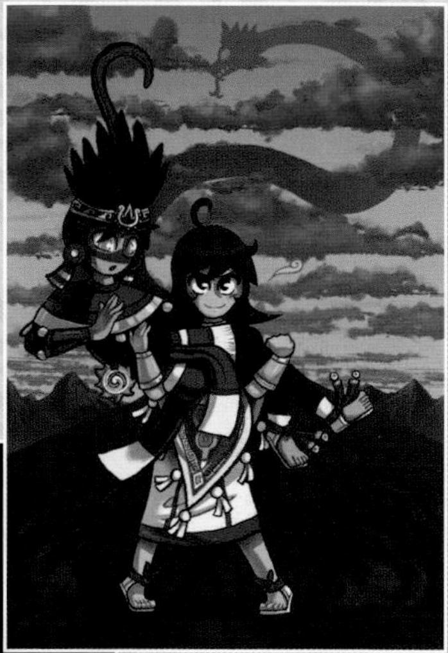

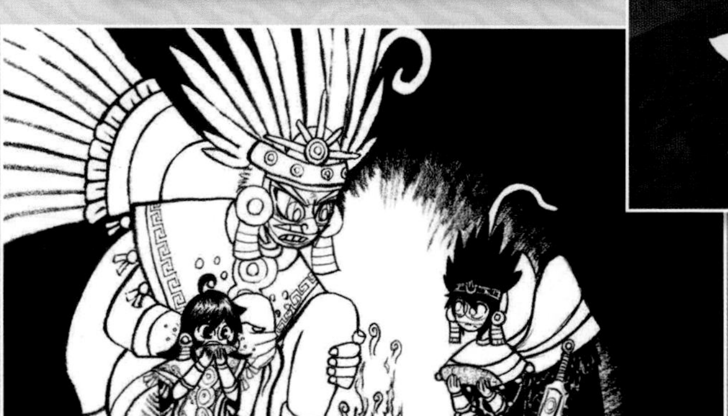

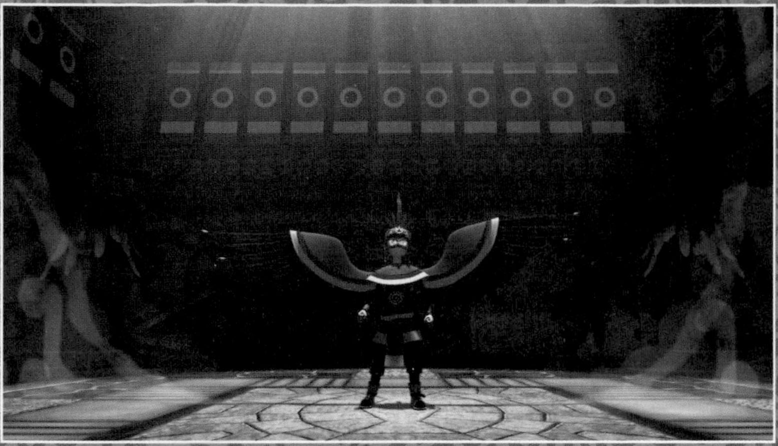

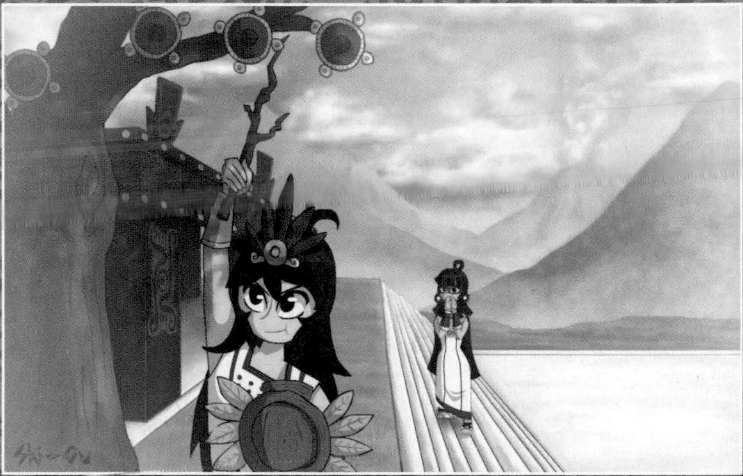

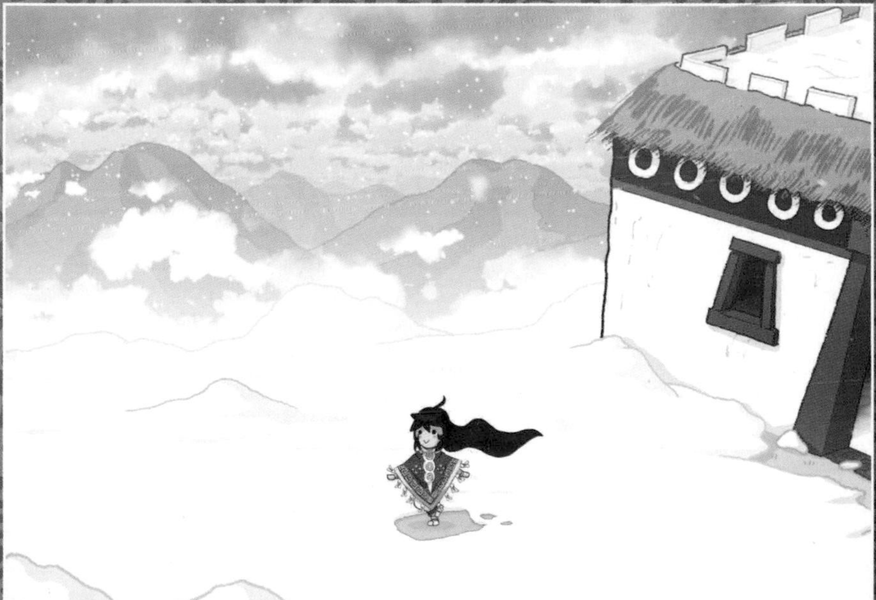

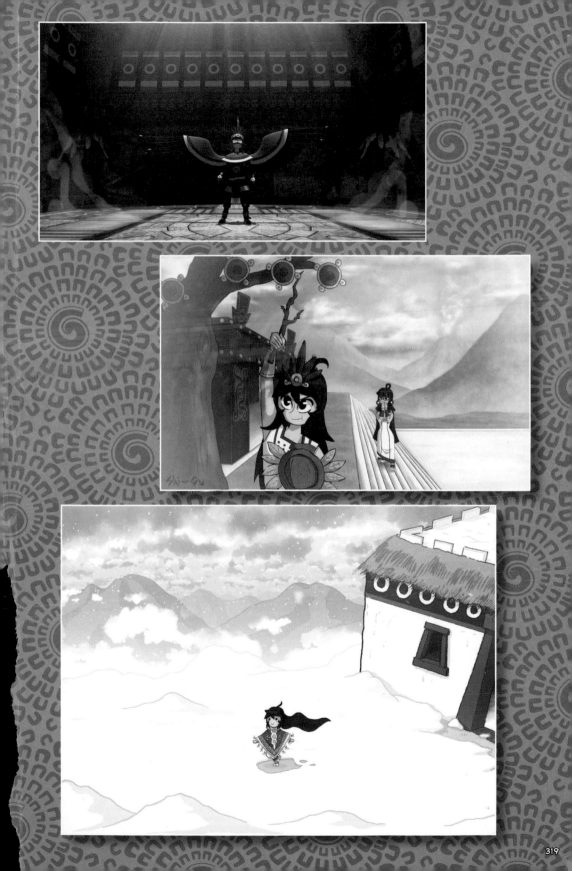

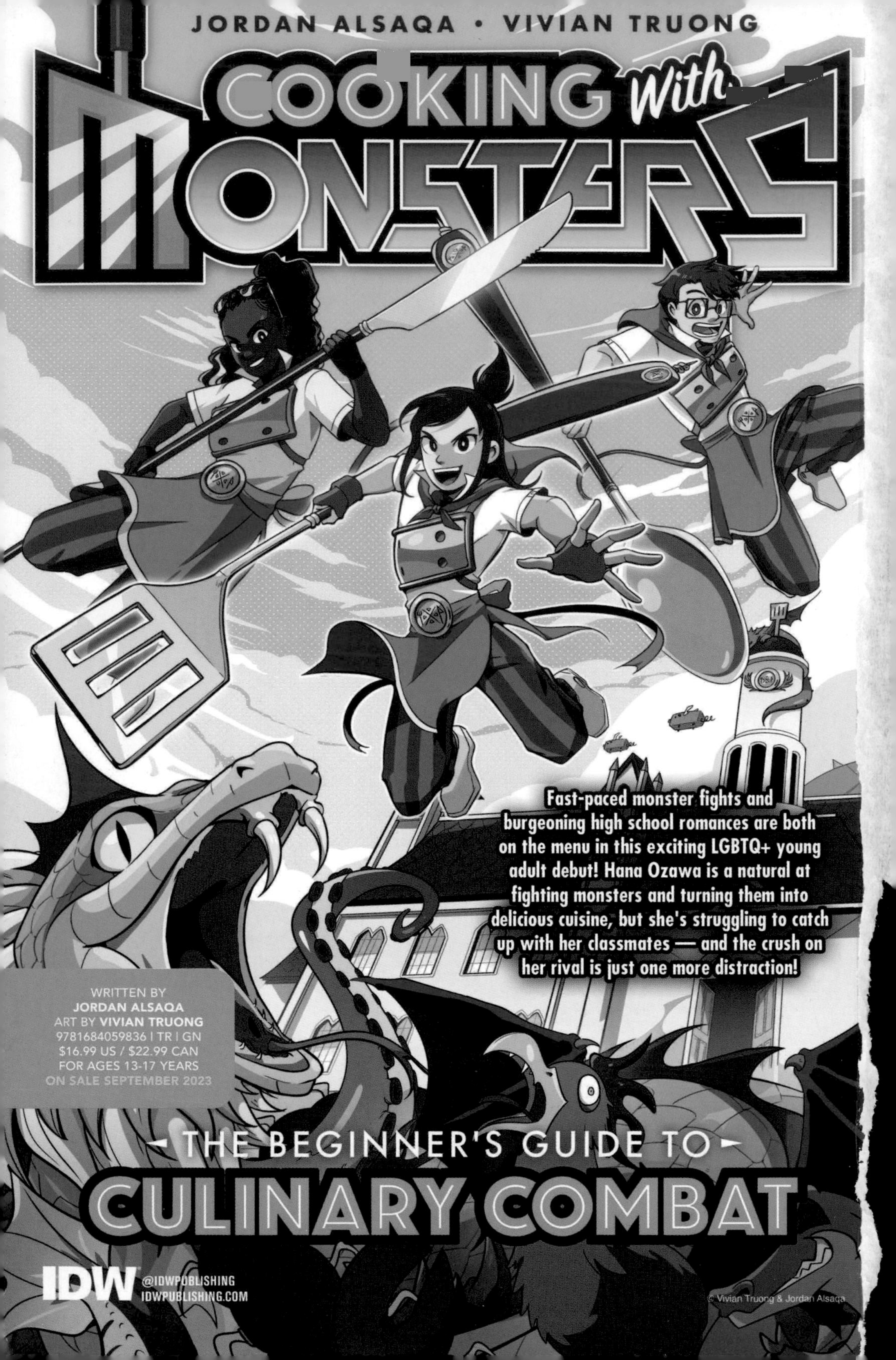

JORDAN ALSAQA • VIVIAN TRUONG
COOKING With MONSTERS
Fast-paced monster fights and burgeoning high school romances are both on the menu in this exciting LGBTQ+ young adult debut! Hana Ozawa is a natural at fighting monsters and turning them into delicious cuisine, but she's struggling to catch up with her classmates — and the crush on her rival is just one more distraction!
WRITTEN BY JORDAN ALSAQA
ART BY VIVIAN TRUONG
9781684059836 I TR I GN
$16.99 US / $22.99 CAN
FOR AGES 13-17 YEARS
ON SALE SEPTEMBER 2023
THE BEGINNER'S GUIDE TO
CULINARY COMBAT
IDW
@IDWPUBLISHING
IDWPUBLISHING.COM
© Vivian Truong & Jordan Alsaqa